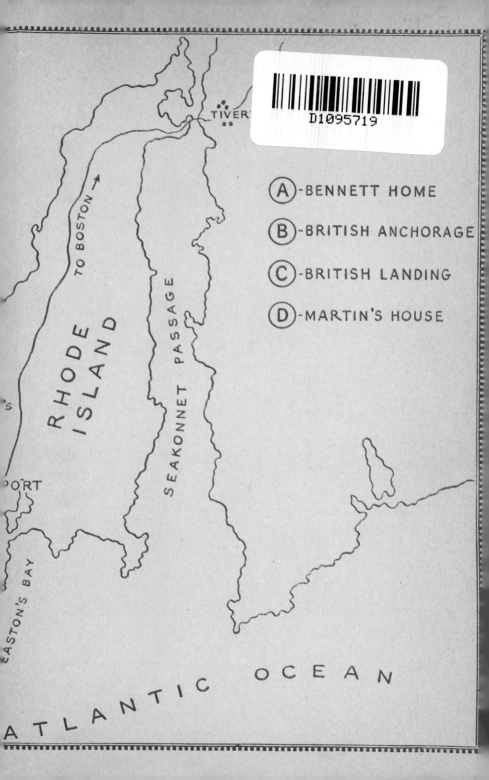

TIVER[T]

A - BENNETT HOME

B - BRITISH ANCHORAGE

C - BRITISH LANDING

D - MARTIN'S HOUSE

RHODE ISLAND

TO BOSTON →

SEAKONNET PASSAGE

S

PORT

EASTON'S BAY

ATLANTIC OCEAN

STARS ON THE SEA

To Andy:

A very Merry Christmas
to our Navy's Finest!

From
Lillian & Ed.

1941.

STARS
ON THE SEA

F. van Wyck Mason

GROSSET & DUNLAP
Publishers   NEW YORK
By arrangement with J. B. Lippincott Company

TO MY SONS,

F. VAN WYCK AND ROBERT ASHTON

AND

TO ALL AMERICANS OF THEIR GENERATION

MAY THEY FIND INSPIRATION IN THE

COURAGE, CLEAR-THINKING AND

UNSELFISHNESS OF THE MEN WHO FOUNDED

THE UNITED STATES NAVY

Author's Foreword

THE further one delves into the history of the American Revolution, the more ample, and, therefore, the more contradictory, the evidence becomes.

At the outset of the struggle, few people bothered to make observations or to record their impressions. Officers were then too inexperienced to realize the vital necessity of preserving the orders they issued and received.

In crossing the boundary from 1775 to 1776, an author's early difficulty in securing any accounts whatsoever, changes to a perplexity over the proper evaluation of too much information.

A writer in this position, therefore, is forced to analyze, and to interpret as accurately as possible, all available material.

In the matter of the Siege of Charleston, for example, it was necessary to study, item by item, eight authentic accounts, all of which varied sharply as to detail.

When an eyewitness describing a battle or an event is proved to have occupied a given position and then calmly tells of happenings which, logically, he could not possibly have seen, one is inclined to question his accuracy—even though the balance of his account may be flawless.

To his critics, the author can only say that his interpretations are based on what seemed, in the light of careful research, to have been the most probable course of events.

Other than patently historical characters, the men and women appearing in STARS ON THE SEA are wholly fictional—the Bennetts, the Percivals, the Proveaux, the Dulacs are imaginary families. They do, however, represent families typical of the time and region.

Incredible as some of the episodes described in Saint-Domingue may seem, they are, nevertheless, based on well-substantiated accounts.

Mr. Robert H. Haynes and certain other members of the staff of the Harvard College Library were extremely patient and helpful in selecting and supplying research material. Miss Mary Moseley of Nassau, Bahama Islands, was very generous in directing the author's research at New Providence.

To the staff of the Charleston Library Association, I am indebted for the privilege of examining some of the rare and unique documents in their possession. Miss Janice Perlstin of that city was of great help in securing certain detailed information.

A great deal of credit is owed Captain Paul A. Curtis for his valuable suggestions concerning research about firearms during the latter part of the eighteenth century.

I am much indebted to Miss Rebekah Johnson of the Congressional Library for her great help in supplying data on the flags of the period.

Much appreciation is due Dorothy L. Mason, who patiently read and criticized the manuscript from start to finish.

To the author it has long been a disappointment that the dramatic first expedition attempted by an American Naval Force has been so seldom and so inadequately recounted. In attempting to correct this situation, it has been the author's purpose to picture America as she was when she lacked a strong Navy, and to show how deeply a blockade can affect every walk of American life.

F. van WYCK MASON

Riderwood, Maryland

Contents

Book One - Blockade

PART I—THE ROXBURY LINES

1	Sergeant Bennett	15
2	Sergeants' Quarters	21
3	At the Congress Inn	27
4	Talk by Firelight	34
5	The Lunar Enlistments	44
6	The Commander-in-Chief	53
7	Mrs. Percival	57
8	Meditation by Firelight	63
9	The Blue Hills	68
10	The Bundling Board	84
11	The Road to Tiverton	90

PART II—CONANICUT ISLAND

1	Homecoming	103
2	Desire Harmony	108
3	Peaceful Haven	114
4	Supply Party	125
5	The House on Bannister Street	132
6	Riot	137
7	Five Came Back	144
8	Mr. Southwick's Book Store	147
9	Bennett & Son	151
10	The Long Rifle	161
11	Reverie	168
12	Ebb Tide	169

13   Isaac Percival   171
14   Flood Tide   176
15   The Lean-to   184
16   December 10, 1775   189
17   Raid   196
18   The Orchard Fight   202
19   The Barn   206
20   The Refugees   209
21   The Ferry Road   211
22   The Ruts   218
23   Ashes   221
24   Plunder   230
25   Ruins   235
26   At the Pitt's Head   240
27   The Merchants   245
28   Man from Congress   248
29   The Oystering Skiff   259
30   Providence   262
31   Mrs. Norton   266
32   The Munitions Vendors   273
33   The Privateersmen   278
34   Nadir   286
35   Ships Southward   306
36   The Watchmen   311
37   The Sabin Inn   313
38   The Rhode Island Cruiser *Katy*   327
39   Empty Port   329

Book Two - Southern Waters

PART I—THE FLEET OF THE UNITED COLONIES

1   The New Flag   335
2   Liberty Island   342
3   Cape Henlopen   347
4   The Storm   355

5 Grand Abacco 358
6 The First Prizes 361
7 Surprise Attack 365
8 Fort Montague—I 370
9 Fort Montague—II 378
10 New Providence, March 4, 1776—I 381
11 New Providence—II 384
12 Spoils 390
13 John Petty, Esq. 393
14 Adelina 404
15 Departure 409
16 Vendue 413
17 The *Live Oak,* Brigantine 419

PART II—CHARLESTON

1 Ferguson's Swamp 424
2 Exit 439
3 The Proveauxs 442
4 Market Day 448
5 Second Company Dismissed 453
6 Kincora Hall 457
7 Charleston, June 1, 1776 468
8 Sails Off Rebellion Row 473
9 The Siege Begins 482
10 The Master of Hobgoblin Hall 487
11 The Wateree Company 491
12 Charleston Bar 500
13 Earthworks 506
14 Enemy Landing 511
15 The Yankee 515
16 Dawn, June 28, 1776 519
17 The First Line 526
18 Broadsides 531
19 The Second Line 534
20 The Maneuvers of a Major-General 535
21 Gunpowder 542
22 The Georgian 547

23 Three Frigates 550
24 Flight 553
25 The Dirk 559
26 The Ebb Tide 564

Book Three - Letter-of-Marque

PART I—SAINT-DOMINGUE

1 Mademoiselle Dulac 571
2 Cap François 581
3 The Bribe 589
4 Les Délices 600
5 M. de Cockburn's Ninepins 611
6 Night-blooming Cereus 614
7 Prices 623
8 The Private-armed Brig Narragansett 626
9 Farewells 633
10 Off Turks' Island 636
11 H. M. S. Growler 640
12 The Chevalier de Cohars 644
13 Privateersmen 649

PART II—KENTUCKY: 1777

1 Rockcastle Creek 659
2 The War Bag 667
3 Skanawati 679
4 The Stone Jug 686

PART III—STARS ON THE SEA

1 The Sempstress 694
2 The Seaman 702
3 At the Crooked Billet 708
4 The New Flag 713

BOOK 1

☆ ☆ ☆

BLOCKADE

PART I—THE ROXBURY LINES: 1775

I

SERGEANT BENNETT

THE clouds darkening Boston Harbor looked so low and ghost-like Sergeant Timothy Bennett guessed snow would soon begin falling. In fact, the jumbled dark roofs and church spires of distant Cambridge were already graying out of sight. He would welcome the snow. The cantonments around Roxbury were becoming mighty foul and unsightly, so the fall of a few inches of snow would be like spreading a clean cloth over a table marked by wet glasses. A snow storm would please Lucy, too. Somehow the sight of falling flakes exhilarated, animated her.

The sergeant's red, useful-looking hands tightened about his musket. He would have welcomed a pair of mittens, knitted loose, the way Desire Harmony worked them. Good thing his sister had been a handy knitter ever since she'd been big enough to hold a set of needles. At the sting of his chapped fingers, Bennett grimaced. Should have dosed them with bear's grease before reporting for guard duty. Lucy surely couldn't find much to admire in such rough hunks of redness.

Crimanently! To think that, in a short while now, he'd have his arms about Lucy again. A lapse of seven months was hard on a fellow who loved a girl the way he did Lucy. Deeper color stained the sergeant's high cheek bones. Recollection of those warm lights in Lucy's blue eyes helped him put up with the draughty cheerless quarters, wretched food, and the prevailing indiscipline of the Provincial Armies.

Lucy must have changed some since last May. He had. As junior sophister of Rhode Island College the cut of a waistcoat, the gait of a saddle horse, had seemed confounded important; but now, to be a judge of flints, a soldier who knew enough to sleep warm on the

15

smoky side of a fire was what counted. He had even learned enough to thump stock fish with a musket butt before trying to stew it. Would Lucy be useful around a kitchen? Odd, he had no idea.

Shouldering Abner Hull's musket, he set off down the fire platform towards an eighteen-pound cannon marking the further limit of Post Number Six. Halting, he once again painstakingly studied the vast gray and white panorama below the Heights of Roxbury. In a field beyond a system of bastions protecting the British position on Boston Neck, some crows briskly explored the snow between rows of tattered cornstalks.

The thin parallels of smoke rising above Boston were few. Must be running short of fuel down there. Matt Allen, after using his prospect glass, had reported the disappearance of every last fence in the beleaguered town. Pretty soon the Redcoats would begin to use Patriot houses and barns for wood yards.

In succession, the crows arose and, cawing, flapped heavily off in the direction of Charlestown. The sergeant's wide-set gray eyes narrowed. An enemy detail was relieving sentries shivering in a pair of *flêches* the British engineers had erected in advance of their main defenses on the Neck. For all their high bearskin hats and gray greatcoats, the enemy grenadiers looked small and insignificant from the summit of Roxbury Hill.

Timothy Bennett rested the firelock against a timber bracing the parapet, began to flail his arms. Damn! His home-made sergeant's epaulet of red worsted was fetching loose again.

The British were right in allotting so many washerwomen to each regiment. A pity the preachers, swarming about every cantonment in Cambridge and Roxbury, wouldn't hear of following such a sensible precedent. Even a few washerwomen could have accomplished miracles with the health and morale of the Second Rhode Island Regiment.

Crimanently! Tonight the wind had teeth like a ferret. It must be a real blizzard blowing up, his wounded leg was aching so. Still, he mustn't show it. Not many fellows of twenty-two were sergeants.

The crows, he noticed, still beat into the wind over a pair of floating batteries which had been caught by a cold snap and frozen into the ice of Back Bay. Now vicious flurries were powdering that redoubt on Breed's Hill which, last summer, had cost Lord Howe a thousand and more good men in winning.

On Plowed Hill the snow was covering Hezekiah's shallow grave. Among thousands of men who had marched last August 26th, why should God have selected his brother to be one of the four men killed? Zeke, of course, hadn't entertained the vaguest notion of what was going to happen. Boys of nineteen didn't think along such lines.

Shivering, Sergeant Bennett shouldered Abner Hull's heavy old St. Malo musket and tried to dwell on New Year's day. Then the New Army would come into being. He hoped Nathanael Greene wasn't going to forget his promise. Imagine being a lieutenant, a commissioned officer! Bennett guessed now he would have to spend some money for real regimentals—a blue tunic with white waistcoat and breeches.

General Washington was said to encourage the several colonies and provinces to show their traditional color on cuffs, collars, and revers. Turkey red for Virginia, white for Maryland, brown for Pennsylvania, and so on. Rhode Island, most everybody figured, would elect pale blue.

If this were so, he would be in luck. Pale blue was Lucy's favorite color, maybe because her soft, honey-colored hair never looked prettier than when she wore a cap with blue ribbons.

"Lieut'nt. T. Bennett & Wife," should look mighty impressive written across a tavern's register book. His thoughts raced on. Suppose this war lasted a while. Why wouldn't he soon be writing "Cap't. T. Bennett & Wife"? The right sort of an officer might climb high. Wasn't Nathanael Greene, only just turned thirty-four, Brigadier-General over the entire Rhode Island Army?

The gale tugged harder at Tim's three-cornered hat. Now he could hear snow singing high up in the darkening sky. In Boston and in the King's Castle down harbor, pin points of light were blinking into existence. Aboard the great fleet of enemy vessels swinging to its anchors off Hudson's Point and Long Wharf, lanterns commenced to glow. By this half light the enemy's frigates and ships-of-the-line appeared unusually sombre and ominous. Even the lesser men-o'-war, sloops, bomb ketches, and transports, looked menacing.

Blong-g! A church clock in Roxbury added its chime to a straggling, brazen chorus rising in the besieged town. Half-past four. On this, of all evenings, his relief was half an hour late.

"You are a bloody fool to be out here," he informed himself. "Sergeants ain't required to freeze their butts." But he knew Abner Hull was still terribly weak of the flux for all that a staff surgeon had declared him fit for duty. Such weather would have been very bad for him. Besides, Ab came from Conanicut Island—home.

If he kept thinking about Lucy maybe the time would pass quicker. Could it be possible that he was really going to see her tonight? Lucky, after all, that Lucy's Grandma Warren had come so near to dying up in Concord. Nothing else on earth would have persuaded Mrs. Percival to attempt a mid-winter journey all the way from Newport.

Suddenly, the snow began to fall in small dry crystals that stung. God in the foothills! What could be keeping his relief? He was in savage impatience to get back to his quarters and to begin sprucing up. The job of making himself presentable was not without its problems. He wasn't smelling exactly like a rose nowadays and enough hot water for a real sponge bath wasn't to be found for love nor money. What to do? What to do?

Sergeant Bennett swung sharply at a sound of a muffled cadence. He made out a line of figures advancing from the direction of camp. Heads held low, the relief bucked the gale until they found a measure of shelter in the lee of the firing platform. They had begun stamping their feet when from somewhere up-wind, came a flat, quick report. Bennett sighed in his relief. That had been a rifle, and the British had no rifle companies. He wondered why rifles didn't give off a fine big-bellied *boom!* like a smooth-bore musket.

"Hear that?" asked one of the relief.

"Yep," grunted the Corporal of the Guard. " 'Pears like them goddam rifflers must be drunk again." The corporal had knotted a muffler over his hat and under his chin. It gave him a mumpy appearance.

"Them Pennsylvany Dirty Shirts ain't ever satisfied les'n they are bragging or carving somebody up. Sure act crazy as loons. Fall out, Number Six!"

A tall private numbly began to tighten a rag protecting his musket lock. Wind-driven snow had a nasty trick of spoiling a man's priming.

After descending a ladder, Bennett brought his firelock to "port," and called, "Who goes there?"

"Corporal o' the Guard, an' relief."

"Advance, Corporal of the Guard, and give the watchword."

"'Cooke,'" grunted the man in the muffler, then blew a bulbous nose with his fingers.

"Come on, Corporal, don't you know you are supposed to demand the countersign?"

The Corporal of the Guard protested, "Sure I do. You damned well know *I* know the countersign is 'Hancock.' Great blazes, man, 'tain't sensible to go through such rigamarole every time you post a sentry."

Number Six, a sharp-faced young private with watery eyes and great red ears, clumsily presented arms, started climbing the ladder. As the little column clumped on through the snow, Tim fell in at the tail of it.

Walt Remington, another Conanicut boy, dropped back a number to keep step with Bennett. He wore a rabbit's skin cap pulled low over a broad red face. "Heard tell yer intended's come to town."

Though Tim's nod was curt, the other watched carefully through the great puffs of his breathing, "Yup, got me a letter from the folks." He could restrain himself no longer. "What do you think, Tim? Lucy's Pa has been buying vessels!"

Sergeant Bennett, paying but half attention, hunched his shoulders to keep flakes from falling inside his collar.

"I'd say he was moonstruck."

"So would I, Tim, so would I. But Pa, well, he's always held Mr. Percival was smarter 'n hot mustard. Why should he begin buying vessels, with the blockade setting in tighter than ever?"

With difficulty, Timothy Bennett overcame a resentment surviving from boyhood. Walt Remington had milked his lobster pots all one summer; he was dead sure of it.

"Say that again."

"Ma, she writ Mr. Percival has just bought three vessels up to Providence." The scrawny youth hawked and spat. "Yup, I allow a mort of people would give a eye-tooth to explain such a move. Hell, Tim, what with Royal cruisers along this coast thicker 'n ticks in a sheepskin coat, most ship owners 'round Narragansett Bay are itching to be quit of their craft. I'd like fer to know if old Percival ain't workin' with—"

Tim cut in sharply, "Don't start any loose talk, Walt. Mr. Percival signed the Association."

"I ain't sayin' he didn't." Angered, Walt stared off through the bitter darkness. "But I wisht I knew certain-sure."

So Isaac Percival had suddenly begun to buy ships? If this was so, was Pa doing likewise? Probably. For all Asa Bennett's mild Quaker's manner, he was nobody's fool. His was one of the precious few fortunes 'round Newport or Providence which hadn't got its start through privateering during the old French war of '56. The Russells, Malbones, Wantons, Nightingales, and Clarkes, all had prospered in it.

Even less savory riches had been amassed in the "triangle trade" by Polypus Hammond and Jeremiah Clarke, for instance. Though nobody mentioned it nowadays, Newport knew that Isaac Percival had first appeared as the second mate of a Liverpool slaver.

Tim was proud that Pa had done so excellently as a simple merchant in the West India trade; that his chandlery business with Jamaica and the foreign Sugar Islands had justified his building a fine new rope walk and a fleet of four fit merchantmen.

Why hadn't he heard from Pa? Was the old man poorly? It was two months now since he had written. Well, Lucy would undoubtedly bring him news. Stung by hard-driven particles of snow, the second relief neared a snow-haloed cluster of lights.

2

Sergeants' Quarters

Timothy Bennett and the other sergeants of the Third Company occupied a two-story frame dwelling on the eastern limit of Roxbury. Though the house boasted two chimneys, it was very old; a badly chinked log wall at its rear let in so much cold air that ice formed readily in the buckets. Tonight, however, the billet presented an almost home-like air because golden pencils of light were slanting through tears in a blanket draped over a sashless window. These beams sketched cheery bright splashes on the ground and momentarily tinted the falling flakes.

Shivering, Tim Bennett kicked the snow from his shoes and stepped inside. Fat old Sergeant Bemis was bent over a skillet and busily frying a mess of salt pork and onions.

"Blowin' up, shouldn't wonder," he remarked without looking about. "Expected it."

"Why?" The fragrance raised by the cooking onions started fountains playing in Tim Bennett's mouth.

"Noticed some fowls pickin' and preenin' this morning. Sure sign. Hope our next wood ration ain't so gol-dummed green."

Old Bemis kept right on talking even when Tim started upstairs. The staircase's treads were worn, and had long since lost its balusters to the fireplace. The familiar reeks of wet wool, damp straw and dirty linen grew stronger the higher he climbed. Being a new sergeant, he had to share his quarters with two other men. Room Number Four was a wretched little hutch and extra draughty because its old-fashioned mud plaster was peeling away from laths hand-split nearly a hundred years earlier.

Tim reminded himself he must find better replacements for some of the original floor planks which earlier tenants had ripped up. The present substitutes were much too narrow and permitted the wind to beat up into his bed of loosely piled straw. He took pride in having contrived a kind of frame to keep his bedding together. Around the cantonments of the Army of Observation lumber of any description was scarce as roses in January.

Luckily, MacPherson had eaten early and gone on duty so he now had Number Four to himself. Ah! There would be no delay about supper. Joe Child had left a heel of bread on a chest for him and a copper kettle of stock fish stew was vaporing beside the hearth.

Tim got to thinking so hard about Lucy Percival and of how soon he'd be kissing her that he wolfed his food and got the hiccups. Locking his teeth against the chill, he spilt some hot water into an old soup tureen Joe Child had got in a trade for a bullet mould Mac-Pherson had "found." Off duty, the tureen made a dandy washbasin.

The wind kept howling down the chimney and beat so much acrid blue smoke into the room that his eyes began to smart. A red-nosed sergeant of Thomas Tew's Company poked his head through an old quilt slung to serve as a door.

"Naow, Bennett, mind you go easy with that soap and water. You'll shorely take your death if you wash off all them protective layers of dirt."

Shivering, Tim stripped off his shirt, felt goose pimples breaking out all over his shoulders. "No, no more than two layers—I promise you. Is Ab Hull any better?"

The visitor stepped inside, stood picking gapped teeth with a splinter. "He's poorly. The Captain says if Abner don't soon begin to mend, he'll fetch a woman over from Milton to tend him."

From down the hall somebody called falsetto, "I'm ailin' bad. Please sergeant, dear, git me a woman from Milton, too. God above, it's time out of mind since I've pressed a petticut."

The sergeant from Tew's Company grinned, called over his shoulder, "Wal then, Joel, you must be close to dead."

A harsh voice from another room declared feelingly, "By God, I'm so hard up I'd give five shillings for a time with anything white."

"Sterling or C-continental?" Tim Bennett's teeth had begun chattering.

"Continental, and be damned to you!"

"Christ!" growled the first speaker. "Round this hell-hole of a place a feller can't buy even a grass sandwich for that."

The sergeant from Tew's Company tentatively fingered some sticks of fire wood. "Say, Bennett, kin I borry these? We're running kind o' low and it's getting pretty keen outside."

"Mind you return 'em tomorrow."

Groaning softly at the bite of the air, Tim Bennett for the first time in weeks scrubbed clear down to his waist. What about those wrinkles in his neck? Toweling on an old shirt he glanced in a fragment of mirror, saw a long, square-jawed face dominated by light gray eyes that showed tiny flecks of amber in their irises. His brows, he decided, were too wide and thick to help his appearance. Maybe they're all right after all. They kind of balanced a mouth that stretched a considerable distance across his face. As a final precaution, he dipped a damp corner of the shirt into a salt box he kept handy, and rubbed his teeth, hard.

Two questions kept obtruding themselves. *Why* should Isaac Percival have begun to buy ships? Even more disturbing was Pa's failure to write in such a long time. To start with, Asa Bennett had written at least once a week. Suppose something had gone seriously wrong back on Conanicut? No use worrying, though.

No matter what he did, he knew he stood in desperate need of a friseur. Imagine meeting Lucy with his hair looking like a last year's bird's nest with a hole in its middle. This evening would surely give her devotion a test.

Gone blue-lipped with cold, he donned a fresh shirt and knotted his best stock with care. He dislodged a splattering of dried mud from his heavy, gray-worsted stockings, then lifted his best coat from between a fold of canvas hidden under his straw. The tunic was unmistakably of civilian cut, and of brown Quaker broadcloth though gilt buttons had replaced hooks and eyes, and its collar and cuffs had been recently turned up in light blue serge. A fat epaulet of red worsted was stitched to its right shoulder. When worn over a white waistcoat, he hoped his Quaker coat suggested a military garment, even if his gray duroy breeches never could.

Seized by a sudden inspiration, he explored Ensign Joe Child's haversack. Somewhere in it he kept a flask of the French scent he used whenever he aimed to keep company with one of Deacon Potter's sprightly daughters. Where the devil was it? He finally located the cologne in the toe of a spare boot. Since Joe was a friend, he surely wouldn't object if he rubbed some of the fragrant stuff into his hair and spilt a little inside his shirt. Whew! That was powerful stuff.

Flooded with satisfaction, he stirred the fire to blaze and critically inspected his silhouette cast against a bedroom wall covered with instructively obscene sketches and ribald verses rendered in charcoal. His stock looked straight and his swallow-tailed hair ribbon fluttered almost jauntily at the nape of his neck.

Last thing he did was to pin to his damp tricorne hat the blue-and-white silk cockade Lucy had made and had given him their last evening together. The apple trees had been blossoming then.

Most of the Second Rhode Island's cantonments were miserable; just three tiers of logs laid cabin-fashion and capped by one of the canvas tents which had sheltered the regiment ever since June. Colonel Daniel Hitchcock had ordered the company streets to be laid out in orderly fashion, even if most of his fellow colonels didn't take the bother.

Nearly every day some brand new type of shelter was devised. The Vermonters and New Hampshiremen, for instance, were partial to huts half dug out of the ground, and finished with logs and boughs. The Connecticuters preferred canvas shelters fashioned from old sails removed from merchantmen lying useless and weather-beaten over in Boston. Tim Bennett decided that the Boston Irish of the Massachusetts regiments came off best. The little sod huts they built for themselves were both warm and weatherproof.

Striding down Prospect Hill towards Roxbury village, Bennett noted that many sentries had, of necessity, built watch fires. He figured the blizzard would surely last all night; as fast as it fell, the snow kept blowing off the roofs—an ominous sign.

On the outskirts of the village, Tim Bennett became aware of yells and shouts emanating from beyond a snow-haloed cluster of lights.

A drunken voice began bawling, "Guard! Help! Help! Wheresh them damn' guards?"

Unfortunately, the road led directly toward a blur of men milling about in front of the Red Bull. It was a miserable place, and Joe Child claimed that the liquor served there wasn't fit to rub on a dog's backside. When he saw the frightened way the crowd kept backing away, he began to walk warily. This looked like no ordinary brawl.

A bottle came crashing through a windowpane, disappeared into the snow drift.

Inside the inn a woman was screeching, "He's gone crazy! Stop him. Oh, my Gawd, he'll slay someone! Don't, Sam, don't ye dare! Don't, fer Gawd's sake!"

A weird cry, unearthly and more fear-inspiring than Bennett had ever heard, beat out into the street. There was an animal savagery in its quality that set the hair to twisting and tingling on his neck. Only thing comparable was the cry of a catamount he'd heard screech years ago when visiting Grandpa up in Deerfield, Massachusetts.

Men were calling through the driving snow, "What's up?"

"Ranger's drunk."

Furniture crashed over and the woman screamed shriller than ever when into the bright yellow rectangle of the inn's door swayed a loose-jointed figure. Sleeve and cape fringes a-swing, the rifleman glared about until a Connecticut corporal in a calfskin coat made a grab at him. Tim had never seen anyone move with such amazing speed. All in one motion the rifleman freed a long knife; his arm licked out with the speed of a snake's tongue. Forearm squirting streams of blood over the dirty snow, the corporal staggered back.

Though a few men seemed too astonished to move, most of the crowd broke and ran. So, for the first time, Tim Bennett got a clear impression of that gaunt figure in buckskins. Dark features convulsed, wild mane of black hair flying, the rifleman hesitated. Something like a horse's tail was in his left hand. He was fighting drunk all right. Suddenly he sprang out into the street and, brandishing his broad-bladed knife, he backed a recruit against the inn's wall.

"You got it?"

"G-got w-what, Mister?"

"You stole my skelp, you no-'count piss-ant!"

The boy wriggled, his eyes enormous. "No! No! Don't hurt me. I ain't got it. I ain't seen it." In his eagerness to get away, the recruit fell sprawling in the snow.

"I'm a r'arin', tearin' wolverine!" roared the man in greasy buckskins, "and I c'n lick any ten o' you psalm-shoutin' sons o' smoothbores." He lurched violently sidewise and long rawhide thrums decorating the front of his hunting shirt fell apart, revealing the word "Liberty" printed in white across his chest.

From an upstairs window the innkeeper began yelling, "Guard! Fetch the guard! Oh, my God, why don't somebody shoot that Pennsylvany son of a bitch?"

"Shut up," snarled the ranger. "Some Yankee whoreson has stole one o' my skelps. Had six, all good Tuscarora and Cherokee hair— one's gone."

Lithe as a wolf in a thicket, the rifleman darted forward so fast that, before Tim Bennett could make a move, the knife was glimmering in line with his stomach.

"*You* got it?" A reek of raw Jamaica rum beat through the whirling flakes.

"No. I just got here." As steadily as he could, Bennett looked into the fellow's bloodshot black eyes. "You better take it easy."

"Ye lie! I saw yer in there!" The knife point hovered scant inches away. Tim Bennett felt his stomach pucker up and writhe. "Pass it over."

"Take it easy, friend," he advised, guessed that he would never stand nearer to death. The gleam of that cruelly long blade was taking the starch out of his knees. "I tell you I've just got here."

"Pass over that skelp." The rifleman's shoulders lowered, "Or I'll surely cut yer gizzard loose." He gathered himself.

Men crowding the Red Bull's entrance called warnings, raised breathless cries, but made no move to help.

Tim tried desperately to keep his expression impassive. "You've miscounted. All six scalps are in your hand. I can see them."

"There ain't but five!"

"There are six, I tell you. Are you too drunk to count straight?"

"I ain't drunk—" Though the rifleman kept his skinning knife poised his gaze flickered to the scalps in his left fist.

Bennett struck instantly, as hard as he could. But his blow was short and impacted against the side, not the point, of the rifleman's jaw. Still it jolted this tall fellow enough to make his arms fly wide open and send the hunting knife flying off into the dark.

Afraid to leave matters so, Tim Bennett followed up and put his weight behind a really fine hay-maker. This time his fist reached its target. His fringes wildly a-flutter, the rifleman went over backwards. Half in and half out of the light beating through the inn's door, he lay quite still.

3

AT THE CONGRESS INN

THROUGH a layer of steam and frost dimming the Congress Inn's diapered and leaded window panes, Sergeant Bennett saw that the taproom was jam-packed. After brushing flakes from his bottle-green riding cape, he stepped into an atmosphere rank with beer and tobacco fumes. He felt as if someone in a hot and smoky cloak had flung both arms about him. Voices, pitched to a fourth or fifth drink, rang in his ears.

"Yassah? Tek yo' cape, suh?" Lately the Widow Haskins had given up serving wenches, had bought some little nigger boys. Her wenches, she declared, became pregnant so often she couldn't ever keep her staff full.

Heated faces swung to consider him when he clumped into the candle light and began kicking the snow from his shoes. "Hey! Shut that damn' door!"

Behind the bar glowed the Widow Haskins' winter apple of a face. Right now it might have been freshly varnished, it was so shiny. Her white linen blouse was stained with sweat and splashings.

"Hi, Rhode Island," a nasal voice greeted. "Been over to Breed's Hill yet? Didn't see you there the seventh of June. Where was you?"

The taproom bellowed. All the army knew that on the day of the great battle both Rhode Island regiments had been kept cursing and sweating in idleness on Jamaica Plain.

Bennett's chilled lips formed a stiff grin. He made the stock reply, "We were too busy sleeping with your sister."

Instantly Joe Child, who knew the whole routine, demanded, "Why were they putting out?"

A dozen men answered, "Poor gal wanted to buy shoes for the Connecticuters."

"Why?" a whole chorus wanted to know.

"So the sons of buggers could run faster!"

Everybody enjoyed the back-chat, even the Connecticut man who had hurled the first insult. Glasses and blackjacks banged empty on long trestle tables, clouds of tobacco spiraled up to the low ceiling.

Ensign Joe Child came from the corner table at which he had been solemnly rolling dice, left hand against right. "Hi, Tim. You're so prettied I hardly knew you."

"Lucy here?"

"Yep. Her Ma, too."

Would Joe recognize his own French scent? If Joe caught on, he'd never hear the end of it. The ensign's stub nose, however, was too full of pipe smoke and rum fumes.

"Where is she? How does she look?"

Joe Child removed the churchwarden pipe and looked solemn. "Why, I should say Mrs. Percival looks positively elegant. Wearing a beaver tippet, green bombazine, and that same old be-damned-to-you look. You're the lucky boy, my lad."

"You go to hell, Joe," Bennett snapped. This was no time for jesting. He sought the Widow.

"They are sharing my three shilling room, front." Thrusting out her lower lip, the proprietress blew a drop of sweat from the end of her nose. "Lord's mercy, young man, but that old lady's a tartar. Went on a rare rampage, she did, when I told her she and her daughter would have to share a big bed with the Colonel's lady, Mrs. Hitchcock. As if beds 'round Roxbury weren't skurce as honest niggers."

Tim Bennett perplexedly nursed bruised knuckles. Mrs. Percival in a temper was a fine person to steer clear of. He drew a deep breath, smiled, "Pray inform Miss Percival that Sergeant Bennett is —er—here."

"Inform? Fiddlesticks. Pray tell her yourself." She heaved up a tray of brass-bound leathern mugs. "I'm busier than a cat with its fur afire." By the cider barrel she paused and filled a brace of pewter tankards.

Still gripped by indecision, Tim Bennett watched her jerk a red-hot mulling iron from the hearth. After blowing it free of ashes, she plunged the iron, hissing, into a tankard. Next she made selections from an array of spice boxes which perfumed the taproom with threads of pungent steam. At this sudden hissing a great tabby tom-cat which had been dozing beneath a settle sprang up, bristled its tail; then, perceiving its error, pretended it had really got up to wash its face. Now the Widow's plump, capable hands sprinkled cloves and cinnamon over the liquid. Petticoats a-swing, she bustled off among the tables.

Intuition told Tim Bennett it wouldn't do to knock at Lucy's door like a confounded chambermaid. Behind the bar a small negro was sleepily burnishing pewter with sand and a handful of rushes. He had a bad cold, was snuffling drearily, but, glimpsing a half penny in Bennett's palm, he brightened right up. "Yassuh?"

"Convey Sergeant Bennett's compliments to Mistress Percival—"

Smiling shyly, the slave cocked a bullet head to one side. "Mi'tess who, suh?"

"Mistress Percival. Inform her that I await her—er, below."

"Yassuh!"

At the foot of the stair Bennett cocked a hopeful ear.

"For pity's sake, child," came Mrs. Percival's staccato inflection. "Blow your nose, then tell Mr. Bennett I will be down directly."

Tim Bennett wanted to cuss. Why in blazes did Lucy's Ma forever have to keep butting in? She must have been young and in love once—or had she? Maybe not. Folks claimed old Ike had only married to save himself the salary of a good bookkeeper. If ever two people were adept in coaxing a sixpence into doing a shilling's work, it was Lizzie and Ike Percival.

So Mrs. Percival would be down directly? Choked with disappointment he plunked himself down at Joe Child's table. "Be patient," he advised himself. "Lucy will come down soon." She must know how desperately he awaited the sight of her.

He had really guessed how much Lucy meant to him that day the Second had driven in British outposts on the Neck to burn the George Tavern and poor Jim Brown's house and barn. Those musket balls whining about his head brought home the depth of his love. Suppose, like Zeke, his luck broke? The possibility scared him—four feet under ground he would never taste sweet intimacies.

Joe Child, unusually grave, was saying, "D'you know, Tim, we'll soon be in a pretty pickle? Every day it grows harder to keep the men from deserting."

He forced himself to reply, "Are your men shy of the reenlisting, too?"

The ensign sent a great cloud of smoke towards a row of copper beer pots dangling from pegs let into the ceiling beams.

"Aye. They seem ready to credit a fool rumor that they will be tricked into signing a long enlistment—five or ten years. Many of the boys are growing worried over their home folks."

Seriously, Child went on, "They ask, 'Why should we stay and fight for these blue-nosed Massachusetters?' Everybody knows how our commissaries, from Colonel Phillips down, get robbed hereabouts. Why, yesterday, there was one old weasel came to camp

asking eight shillings for a chicken and the damned fowl favored
a heron more than anything else."

"You'll meet with mean-spirited folks everywhere you go," Bennett
agreed absently. He still went squirmy inside when he thought of
that Pennsylvanian's knife. What a perfect savage of a fellow.
Damnation! This evening wasn't going at all as he had anticipated.
First that rifleman, then the crowded inn, now Mrs. Percival's inter-
ference. The gilt was fast rubbing off of this shining hour.

"You hear what is going on in Sullivan's brigade?"

"No."

"Well, they say the New Hampshire officers ain't rejoining.
Damned hay-shakers figure they stand to get slighted in the New
Army. One of their majors heard he would only rate a captaincy in
the Continental Service so he hiked himself off home. Fact."

"Good riddance," grunted Bennett.

"Maybe," Child agreed, "but he took a whole battalion with him.
They were all from the same county. It's bad. We shouldn't have
so many men from the same district in one regiment."

"But it's only natural, Joe. The gentleman from Virginia will find
it hard to alter that."

The ensign wagged his fair head. "It will have to be changed—
along with short enlistments, different pay rates, and the men's
electing company officers.

"Now take these lunar month enlistments—" Joe Child went on.

"What's wrong with them? My company enlisted lunar month.
Works all right with us."

"Of course. Why should you men cavil at getting paid for twenty-
eight days? New Hampshire, Massachusetts, and the rest of us
Rhode Islanders must serve thirty or thirty-one days for the same
pay. 'Tisn't fair, or sensible."

"You're dead right," a captain of the Massachusetts Line growled
over the rattling of the windowpanes. "Who likes to work two or
three days free for nothing?"

"Kitchen spits are all busy," puffed the Widow Haskins. "Have
to use this fireplace, too." She used a key to wind the clockwork

motivating a big brass roasting jack, then firmly impaled a joint of mutton on an iron hook set below the contrivance. Once she had given the joint a sharp turn, the mechanism set up an oily *cluck-clucking,* commenced monotonously to revolve the meat before the flames. Soon the tom-cat roused, began licking up spots of fat which fell near the edge of the fireplace.

Suddenly Joe Child's foot nudged Tim Bennett's. "Make ready your sword, St. George," he chuckled. "Here comes your dragon."

Her high-bridged nose wrinkled in distaste, Mrs. Percival was advancing into the taproom with the air of a martyr exploring a den of lions.

Bennett jumped up and made the erect, gaunt figure a formal bow—like that of the officers off the Royal ships—but it was an awkward attempt. The Society of Friends did not approve of salutes, bows and curtseys. Expressions of respect, they maintained, must be reserved for the Creator alone.

A mirthless smile briefly disarranged the habitual "prunes, prisms and persimmons" set to Mrs. Percival's mouth. "I trust I find you in good health, Timothy?"

"Yes, Ma'am. I hope—"

"Oh, dear, such a dreadful, common place. Pah! How can a body breathe such air? Just you answer me that, Joe Child, and don't go sneaking off." Her expression relaxed. "I don't bite—often. Believe it or not."

Joe abandoned his furtive retreat, looked more like a school boy than a commissioned officer as he said, "The entire Rhode Island Army regrets, Ma'am, that Roxbury is so small a village. Its comforts are—er—deucedly limited."

Mrs. Percival looked levelly about. "I have seen worse inns. Well, Timothy?"

"I am most sensible of your tarrying here on your journey home, Ma'am." The words came out not at all as Tim Bennett had rehearsed them. Hang it! Lizzie Percival's small blue eyes were appraising him to the last detail. She must be seeing how really dirty he was, for all his pitiful attempts to slick up.

"You look older by two years," she announced. "Thinned out, kind of. You have not been acquiring loose habits, I trust?"

"Er—Lucy? Is she well, Ma'am?"

"Thriving." Mrs. Percival's ruler mark of a mouth relaxed. "At present, my vain child is prettying herself in your honor." Without change of expression, she suddenly demanded, "Are your father's ships safe? Two of them are so long overdue, people in Newport are—well, wondering."

"They must be secure, Ma'am, else I would have heard." Though Tim Bennett spoke easily, he was no little disturbed at Mrs. Percival's manner.

Lucy's mother, he knew, dipped her pointed nose into more people's affairs than any five other females in Newport. But hers was no idle curiosity and she told no tales out of school. Once, in an unparalleled burst of frankness, Lizzie Percival had observed that the people who got furthest ahead were those who learned what was going to happen early, and who kept that knowledge to themselves.

Why hadn't Pa written in so long? The question commenced to gnaw, rat-like, at his peace of mind.

"No news, eh? Well, it seems like a long time, I must say."

Ensign Joe Child tossed a few shillings on the table. "I must go on duty, Ma'am, so pray excuse my departure. Is it true that Mr. Percival has purchased some vessels?"

As if to prove it was possible, Mrs. Percival's spine assumed an even more erect position. "He may and he mayn't—it's no concern of yours, Joe Child."

"Quite true, Ma'am," the ensign grinned. Then, bowing, he caught up a buckled hat and retreated in haste.

Wouldn't it be politer to tell Mrs. Percival his great news about the commission, rather than save it for Lucy? The question bothered him. Women admired uniforms, even the older women.

"The reason I ventured into this bedlam, Timothy, was for a brief word with you," Mrs. Percival briskly informed him over the hum of conversation. "It's my opinion that the sooner you quit this playing at soldier the better. Between the Congress and the King's ministers, anything can happen these days. If a body is to keep his trade, he is wise to be Johnny-on-the-spot."

To Tim Bennett, the atmosphere grew suddenly smothering. "Your enlistment expires December first, don't it?" Mrs. Percival was fixing him with a penetrating look. For all she must be near sixty, her hair was still black as an Indian's.

Falling all over himself mentally, he blurted, "Why, why, no, Ma'am. We all enrolled for eight months; means we must serve 'til the tenth. But I had something I wanted to tell—"

"—Never mind about that," she cut in. "You get back home by the *first week* in December or you'll regret it!" Lizzie Percival's jaw muscles softened a trifle. "Now don't go telling everyone I advised you so. If you and Lucy weren't promised, wild horses wouldn't get me to talk like this."

"But—please. I—had something to tell you—"

"It will keep, I expect." Mrs. Percival turned away. "I am returning to my room. Even the clacking of Mrs. Hitchcock's tongue ain't so bad as this pig pen. By the bye, you had better find a fitter place to receive Lucy. 'Twon't do for my daughter to sit here with this parcel of lustful soldiers staring at her."

4

TALK BY FIRELIGHT

SADLY confused, Tim Bennett went to a window and stood there looking out. It was blowing a real blizzard now and growing colder, no mistake. He surely pitied those poor devils tramping the parapets of Roxbury fort. The out-sentinels posted on the seaward slopes might find something of a lee, though. Every time someone came in or left the inn its windows rattled and the door shut with a nerve-shaking bang. Where the devil could he take Lucy? A pity the Congress was just a common country tavern; until the Siege it had probably never entertained more than ten guests at a time.

He sought the Widow Haskins and confided his problem. "You see, Mrs. Haskins, it's eight months since I've seen Mistress Percival, and now her Ma declares she is not to enter the taproom. What can I do?"

The Widow dabbed a frankly downy chin with the cleanest corner of her apron, stared at him in amazement. "Pity's sake, what do you want me to do? Turn my guests out into the street?"

"No, but isn't there—"

"You two keeping company?"

Tim's instant smile made him look very young and appealing. "Mistress Percival has promised me."

The Widow's heated features relaxed. "You must have leapt mast-high to win such a looker. 'Pears like her folks ought to have money, too—even if her Ma did try to beat me down."

Desperation shone in Tim's eye as he said, "I'm mighty pleased to hear you express such flattering sentiments, Ma'am, yet it's not telling me where I can see her."

Lips pursed, the Widow cocked her head, gray under an untidy mob cap, to one side. "Got any currency?"

"Why, yes."

"How much?"

"Three dollars."

"Continental or Provincial?"

"Massachusetts, Ma'am."

"Good. Me, I don't take stock in this new Continental currency. 'Round Massachusetts Bay we can deal with any thieves who get at the Treasury, but Philadelphy's too far away." She broke off, beckoned vigorously.

"Hey, Sambo!" With a measuring spoon she fetched the child's woolly head a whack. "Pity's sake, can't you do nothing but set by the fire and pick your nose?"

Flipping up her skirt she groped in a pocket let into her red and white striped petticoat top and produced a small brass key. "Go brighten the fire in my room. Pity's sake. Get a move on you,

Sambo. You might meet with a snail but you'd never pass him. Just you hump yourself, boy, when I speak!"

Cheeks glowing like winesap apples by the light of the whale oil lamps, she cocked her head to one side. "I guess you two can set in my room. I don't ever let it out. If 'twas anyone else, I'd ask five dollars, but you can use my room for cost of sea coal you burn. I really relished a bit of spooning when I was young and pretty."

The Widow was appalled at her own generosity. Yet, somehow, this tall young fellow in the Quaker-cut coat and his old-looking eyes moved her no end. Must have been hard for such a man in the Army after he had been brought up in style; he had been, she was sure. Harder for his sort than for the young mechanics, sailors and farmers who had, long ago, learned to absorb life's knocks.

"But is that enough?" Tim protested. "I—"

"You hush up," snapped the Widow Haskins. "Guess I know my prices! At the head of the stairs face about and you'll see a door with a French lock to it. That's my room. I'll send your young lady word where to find you."

She looked at him steadily. "Mind you leave my door open. I won't stand for any hanky-pank in this place."

Near the head of a flight of stairs rising almost perpendicularly beside the chimney, Tim Bennett found a door with a fine French lock and the instant he opened it he knew he was in luck. Warm, clean-smelling air rushed out. On the mantelpiece, a Betty lamp was burning dimly and a broad bed of sea coal glowed in a brass and wrought-iron grate. A great four poster bed with three steps leading up to it, a dresser, and two well-upholstered chairs completed the furnishings.

Crimanently! This *was* a pleasant surprise. The bedroom's walls had been tinted the warm red-brown color which was achieved by steeping rusty nails in vinegar. The library at home was of the same restful hue. It was hard to reconcile this little room's cleanliness with Widow Haskins' uncompromising frowsiness.

Mrs. Percival, he knew, would have six different kinds of cat fits if she ever learned he had arranged to meet Lucy in a bedroom. But of course they would leave the door open—a little.

Before the mirror he paused, gave his clubbed dark brown hair a tentative pat and mechanically straightened its swallow-tailed ribbon of black grosgrain. Though he strained his ears for a footstep, only the sound of wind mourning about the eaves could be heard. Minute snow flakes had begun to sift in through the north window's frame, tracing a black-and-silver fan over the rag rug. Certainly was snug up here.

He was mighty glad now he hadn't gone with any of the painted girls who slunk about the fringes of the Army. Not that it hadn't been next to impossible sometimes to resist their honeyed urgings.

Quite a few of the younger men did listen, though; and some had found cause to be sorry. Everybody thought it was funny as all get out when Luke Abel and Josh France came down with the French itch; everybody except Luke and Josh. They had been sitting around like sick crows ever since and you didn't hear them brag any more about being handy between the sheets.

He suddenly realized that he was very tired. Every morning at five, the drums routed the Second Rhode Island out to man the lines. Then there were drills over a soggy or frozen parade ground. It was considered remarkable that General Greene's troops were ordered to drill every day except Sunday.

Fighting impatience, Tim Bennett seated himself, watched the steam rise from his wet boot soles. Damn it all, what had Mrs. Percival been driving at? Well, it didn't matter; he wasn't going to give up the Army. His men liked him and so did Colonel Hitchcock and the other officers.

In time he was sure to be elected captain—especially if he talked Mark Remington and Ben Elley into reenlisting. To have some home boys serving under him gave an officer standing. In a pinch, a man could almost always rely on men from his own district. Right now he was only sure of Jedediah Franklin and Abner Hull—if Ab got better.

Would Pa lend him enough cash to buy a sword, a camp bed, a brass cook kettle? Except for his sergeant's pay—two pounds, eight shillings the month—he hadn't a stiver.

The door swung noiselessly back and into the firelight glided Lucy Percival. She halted on the threshold and looked at him with her small head tilted a trifle to one side and her eyes half veiled by bluish lids. A yellow shawl rested about her slim shoulders in pleasing contrast to a full-skirted gown of pale blue lute-string.

Their eyes met, she rushed to him arms wide spread.

"Ah—Lucy—Lucy!" he choked. "Thee is lovely as—as—" Only their breathing and the faint crackle of the sea coal sounded as, limb to limb, breast to breast, they blended close. The slender body in his arms seemed as much a part of himself as any of his limbs, and when the cool tip of Lucy's nose nuzzled his ear, Tim quivered, felt a shiver of delight trickle the length of his back.

Each could feel the other's heart pound, could sense the other's nerves thrum. From Lucy's hair, shining and silver-gold, a delicate, nearly-forgotten perfume was rising. It surely made Joe's French scent seem crude, overpowering.

"Ah, my sweet Tim!" she panted under her breath. "Hold me so —forever. Never free me—"

"Never, dearest heart! Never again."

"How could eight months be so—so *endless?*"

The cheerful cleanliness of the room, the warm and fragrant pliancy of Lucy's body after these miserable starved weeks, raised a dizzying shimmering mist before his eyes as his lips found hers again. Why must so exquisite, so tormenting a hunger continue until Lizzie Percival could parade her daughter, like a prize-winning filly, before the curious and envious of Newport?

Why make marriage a sort of county fair? To what profit an elaborate church wedding?

All that really mattered was that now they were alone, healthy, vibrant with life, and in love. Suppose just one of those musket-balls there on Boston Neck had been aimed scant inches lower? He had been very lucky with that rifleman tonight—luck wouldn't hold forever, though. Here was life in his arms. Why not? Soon, perhaps tomorrow, more bullets would fly, maybe lower this time. He shivered in remembering how implacably the unsanitary hutches around Boston were stalked by Disease.

"Lucy—" His eyes felt hot, heavy, as if he had just roused from a profound sleep and he began fumbling at a brooch securing her shawl. A throaty sigh escaped her as its ends fell away and his lips began to caress her throat, the soft flesh trembling above the modesty piece of her bodice.

"Oh, Lucy—" he breathed. "Lucy—dearest—I—I—"

Her large, smoky-blue eyes were bright with a light he would never quite forget as spasmodically, she pressed his head tight, fiercely tight, against her breast.

"Oh, my dear, my dear!" Her voice was rich, vibrant, like the lower notes of a harp. "But you are a soldier, Tim, a fine brave one —and I'm glad, glad of that."

There it was. That possibility of a bullet tomorrow. Suppose tonight they had—well, bad luck?

At length Lucy stopped trembling, gave his cheek a gentle pat and fixed on him a tremulous, uncertain smile. "Now, I vow I love you more than ever."

He straightened, but kept hold of her. "And I—you."

"I declare, Tim, you've grown strong as a bear." Lucy's voice still sounded shaky. "You squeeze me tighter than some awful French stays Mama bought me at the Committee of Safety's confiscation sale last week."

Forgetful of bared shoulders, of the fact that her bosom throbbed, half revealed, she spun lightly away, balanced herself back to the bureau. "No, stay where you are, Tim, I want a good picture of you to treasure in my memory. La, sir, how brown you have become and how broad your shoulders!"

In his home-made uniform, he didn't much resemble the serious young Quaker who had come a-courting her two long years ago. She would have married him then, oh, so gladly, but she had barely turned fifteen. Though many of her friends had married even younger, Mama would not hear of it.

Still breathless, her long-lashed eyes shining, Lucy remained poised, studying him. Wouldn't Tim cut an elegant figure in a flowered waistcoat, velvet coat and gold-headed stick?

Much as her whole body craved caresses, she knew she must stay where she was. Didn't dare to trust herself, yet. Smiling, she permitted him to feast his tired, hungry eyes on the bodice she had purposely stitched tight enough to betray even minor curves and modelings. It didn't seem immodest, only right that he should do so.

At length, he motioned to an arm chair. "Come sit down, Lucy."

After resetting her shawl, she obeyed, sat there primly smoothing her half-dozen skirts and petticoats. At length she looked up and queried timidly, "Do you mind awfully about not being—about not being a Friend any longer?"

He shrugged. "Yes. I did, at first. Chiefly on account of Pa. He was sorely grieved when the Meeting set me aside. You see, he earnestly believes in the Friends' way of life."

Tim came to sit on the arm of her chair. "Lucy—I—I've some monstrous fine news for you—for us."

Small even teeth gleamed. "Oh, Tim, I'm so very glad." Firelight sketched Lucy's round chin, short upper lip, slightly snub nose. "It's that you're coming home, isn't it? Your father needs you, Papa says."

There was Mrs. Percival again. Impatiently, he waved away her suggestion. "No, it's better than that." He drew himself up in mock seriousness. "Ma'am, before you stands a future Hannibal, a Caesar in the mould."

"Oh, Tim, you great silly, what—"

"Come the New Year, your humble admirer will be an officer, a lieutenant, no less, in the Continental Service of the United Colonies. Five pounds, eight shillings a month."

"A lieutenant, so soon? Oh, Tim, you *must* be a fine soldier. You're wonderful! I'm so pleased. Oh—kiss me."

He swooped on her and though she stood five feet four and was firmly built, lifted her easily out of the chair.

His wide-set gray eyes beamed delight. "I knew you'd be pleased, Madam Lieutenant Bennett. You'll make an elegant soldier's wife."

"And why, pray?"

"That time Zeke's catboat tipped over, you didn't scare. The other girls screamed and carried on."

"I'll keep your buttons and gorget ever so bright."

She had twined an arm about his neck and was drawing his head down for a kiss when all at once she straightened, her sparkling mood departed. "Oh dear, I quite forgot, I can't be Madam Lieutenant—"

His previous disquiet returned intensified. "Eh, why not?"

"Because, my lamb, you are returning to Conanicut Island and Newport. You were going to marry a girl down there." She lifted her face. Vivid lips curled into a smile. "Remember me?"

"Let's see—you're Ellen? Betty? Don't tell me—" he chuckled— "I've got it, the name is Lucy. I'm to marry her sometime Christmas week." He kissed her, beamed down at her. "My leave is all arranged for—three weeks."

Lucy's smile became less certain. "That won't do."

"I don't understand, dear."

"Mama—Papa, too," she added hurriedly, "won't hear of my marrying into the Army."

"Won't hear of—" Tim gaped. "But—but—can't they see that we have been fighting up here to protect every merchant's rights and trade? Surely, your father realizes this?"

Lucy's gaze wandered over the bedroom's well-sanded floor. "I don't know, Timothy, but I fear that is the way he feels."

Tim got up, jaw set, stood in front of her. "Well, what else does he say?"

"He declares we couldn't possibly live on an officer's pay." She spread her hands in a little discouraged gesture. "I guess we couldn't either, Tim. Not two of us on five pounds, eight. Every day Mama reminds me that there's no sense in marrying a soldier. He's so likely to get killed or crippled. Besides, how would he know how to earn a living, once the war is done?

"Oh, Tim—there's good sense in what she says!" At the hurt in his expression she held his hand tight against her cheek, kissed it. "Haven't you borne arms, been wounded and promoted? Nobody can ever say you have not done your patriotic duty!"

Tim swallowed hard, with unseeing eyes regarded a tinder pistol on the mantelpiece.

Lucy went on talking softly, urgently. "Everyone feels that this war is as good as over. General Washington has the Ministerial troops cooped up in Boston. They can't get out, so before long they must sail away."

Tim's previous elation escaped like wind through a split sail. "The Lobsterbacks aren't licked," he objected. "They're still full of fight and they're stubborn. Colonel Hitchcock says these Colonies are too rich a property to be let go without a long, hard war. England fought France too long to make sure of us. No, beloved, the British will not let us go, even granting that Howe will be driven out of Boston. Nat Greene and General Washington both say so."

Lucy—or her mother—must have anticipated this argument, because she so promptly said, "In that case, Papa will not object to your joining a new regiment which is being raised for service within Rhode Island. You've no notion how many of the smartest young merchants in town are enrolling in it."

"I'll bet!" Tim agreed bitterly. "That blasted regiment is wrecking our best chance of reenlisting trained men."

Slowly Lucy lifted her face, her gaze steady but troubled. "I wouldn't want you to do anything dishonorable, Tim, not ever. Always remember that I will wait."

"But my commission! What would the boys from Conanicut say? Abner Huil, Walt Remington, Jed Franklin, and the Gardners?"

"What can they say if you join the Provincial Guards?"

"Plenty," he snapped, and his cheek bones began to stand out. "Everyone here knows troops like that are a joke—a bad joke."

"Is that not yet to be proved?"

He shrugged. "Militia is no use. Won't stand and fight once in a 'coon's age."

There was something terrifying about this girl's serene tenacity as gently she reminded, "Then there is your father to consider. He has taken Hezekiah's—er—passing very hard."

"But can't Dee cheer him up?"

"Desire does all she can, but she's only a child—really. It's you he needs when his vessels are so long overdue as they now are."

Tim insisted desperately, "Everything is all right, else I would have been told."

"There is yet another reason, dear," the soft voice persisted. "Papa is most anxious that you return not later than the seventh of December."

"Why by the seventh?" Straight brows merged, he probed the depths of her eyes.

"If I knew, I'd tell you. Why should you stay?"

Perplexedly, he rubbed weather-beaten hands together. "Well, the—my company is just beginning to pull together. We are no longer shaky militia. Now we are becoming real soldiers, useful troops."

Lucy's smile faded. "In other words, Tim, you are dead set on having this commission?"

Without reply, he stalked over to watch the snow hurl itself against the windowpanes. Somewhere guard drums were rolling, summoning another relief.

Come to think of it, there was something fine about fellows who, for the sake of their rights as they saw them, would stand out there in a blizzard. They certainly weren't enduring a night like this for the sake of two shillings, four pence a month.

Lucy began talking again. "Do you know? I have been collecting our furniture. Last week, I found some of the dearest twifflers and sneak cups. Papa's partners are going to give us a garnish of pewter. Then I have been looking for a house—a cottage really. Remember Ames, the Tory, who sailed for the Bahamas last spring? He'd a cottage at the foot of Washington Street, right by the water. Oh, won't it be fun being Mr. and Mrs. Bennett in our own home?"

Petticoats softly hush-hushing, she ran over to him. After he had kissed her gravely, she lingered, following the design of his belt buckle with her forefinger.

A mouse crept from under the bed and, sheltered between a pair of slippers, considered them from tiny pin-point eyes. The taproom door was slamming frequently now and liquor-heated voices called stupid, loud "good-nights."

"You will come back?"

"I don't know, Lucy," he said stonily. "I don't know. If I don't stay, it—it might set a bad example."

Gentle as drifting shadows Lucy's arms crept about his neck.

"My love is yours—for always and always," she murmured, "whatever you decide."

5

THE LUNAR ENLISTMENTS

MATTHEW ALLEN, pudgy but increasingly able Captain-Lieutenant of the Second Company, threw down his goose quill pen. He blew so hard on his fingers that his breath vapor rolled across the office like a miniature fog bank.

"Har-rrumph!" the way he cleared his throat, warned Sergeant Bennett of something unpleasant. Crossing arms over the tarnished buttons on his chest, Captain Allen buried his hands in the warm areas under his armpits.

"Sergeant, men burnt a lot of wood last night. Har-rrumph! Company Commanders report there ain't barely enough fuel to cook today's dinner."

Tim Bennett began to grin. He was handy with his fists and, in his present state of mind, a free fight would be a relief. Some of the Connecticut men were dandy scrappers.

"Har-rrumph! Better hitch up the light sledge and draw from the brigade wood pile. Pick yourself any fifteen men. You seem to relish the assignment?"

Tim's grin widened. "Yes, sir, I do." Fifteen men would be fine; that allowed him five toughs to fight off rival fuel details and ten workers to load the ever-scarcer firewood.

At a dug-out barn sheltering the regimental ox-teams, Tim came across Ensign Child preparing for a similar errand. He, too, had brought along the hardest characters in his company. The men began bragging.

An immense corporal with a broken nose balled his fist, waved it about. "You watch me. I'll swaller them mother-beatin' Connetycut bastards 'thout even greasin' their ears!"

Sharp-faced Mark Remington came out of the barn. "Haw!" Expertly, lightly, he used his goad over a span of big red and white oxen. Obediently the creatures wheeled, halted and waited patiently for their yokes.

As few men, Mark understood these powerful, sweet-smelling beasts and, despite scurrilous remarks, slept between them of a cold night. "Haw!" Snow squeaked beneath the sledge's hardwood runners as the team set off between a long line of huts.

For a while, the oxen made heavy going of it; last night's fall had disguised deep ruts frozen hard as iron. Under a blurring, five-inch blanket of snow, sod houses, timber huts, half-tents and other shelters had achieved a rough uniformity.

"Bet the Lobsterbacks froze their butts off last night," drawled freckle-faced Jed Franklin. "They're near out of wood."

Still graveled by Lucy's arguments, Tim slouched shamelessly. In a detached way he deduced that a wounded man must have gone this way. Every few feet was a small pink splash with a bright red core.

Absently, he tested a lump marking the wound in his left thigh. Good job that bullet hadn't hit the bone or he'd be shy a leg.

Had he, as Lucy insisted, really done his share? She was right about no war lasting forever, of course; but it wouldn't do to pull foot now, no sir.

Joe, clumping along with his pipe in his mouth, was saying, "I've been wondering how soon those Massachusetts snots will get their come-uppance. It's comic, their notion of calling two hundred and fifty men a regiment! Good God, they've more colonels, captains and majors to the square foot than a dog has fleas, and half of them ain't nothing but politicians in fancy regimentals."

Tim glanced over his shoulder. The detail was keeping up in good style. They tramped along with their breath clinging to their black, three-cornered hats. With the right sort of officers they'd make dandy grenadiers and light infantry.

"What does this reorganization amount to?" he inquired of the Ensign.

"The Congress figures on boiling the four Provincial Armies—us, Massachusetts, New Hampshire and Connecticut—down to one. Mr. Washington figures to reduce our forty-odd militia regiments—all of different sizes—to twenty-eight of seven hundred and thirty, even. Call the New Army 23,700 men paid with taxes levied on all Provinces."

"What is the term of enlistment?"

"A year," Child said. "Washington wanted it for longer, but they wouldn't agree—"

Suddenly Jed Franklin hailed from the rear of the little column. "Hey! Take a look over there. Them Connecticuters is acting up!"

A horseman, a general officer by his pink cockade and silk sash of the same color, came cantering through a grove of willows. Because of the deep snow, his horse was having trouble. He made quite a sight in his blue uniform overcoat; the gold lace on his hat glittered.

"Hey, boys, it's Nat Greene!"

"Detail, halt! Ten-shun!" Ensign Child stood very straight and his new gorget flashed when he whipped up a hand in salute.

Everyone stiffened. Of course, one of the oxen would choose this moment to spill its droppings onto the snow.

Barely thirty-four years of age, Nathanael Greene was by far the youngest general officer in either army; his squarish face was heavily lined and his powerful jaw seemed, daily, to grow more rugged. Right now he looked excited, worried, beneath an outward calm.

"Stand at ease!" he ordered in a crisp, deep-chested voice that wasn't a bit pompous.

Reining in, the Rhode Island general looked hard at Tim. "Sergeant, tell off half these men, march them to the Connecticut camp at once. General Charles Lee is to address the troops there." Greene hesitated a moment, then added, "You will note and report what the General says, Sergeant. You will find me at Brigade headquarters all morning."

"Yes, sir." Cold air rushed up Tim's sleeve as he saluted.

Tim Bennett's detail found Spencer's Connecticut regiment drawn up under arms in a loose hollow square on a cow pasture behind its cantonments.

"Say," one of the Gardner boys observed suddenly. " 'Pears to me like these fellers are headed for home."

"What makes you cal'late so?" Jed Franklin wanted to know.

"Use your eyes, you dumblock. Ain't they got their blankets rolled? Ain't their haversacks loaded?"

With a mittened thumb he indicated a file of men marching towards the parade ground. There was no snap to their stride. Though a few of them shouldered muskets, the majority carried only staffs or walking sticks. Tim calculated that about every fifth man in Colonel Spencer's regiment wore a blanket roll over his shoulder and carried a cooking kettle at his belt.

Unobtrusively as possible, Tim moved his detail into a gap between two companies and ordered it to halt. As a rule, the arrival of Rhode Islanders at a Connecticut formation would have resulted in cat-calls, groans and hoots of "Hey! Jamaica Plain!" But not today.

Connecticut officers, swathed in a wide miscellany of greatcoats, stood in front of their men. They were conversing in hurried, angry undertones. Many of them carried their swords unsheathed. To the

Rhode Islanders, their wind-nipped faces seemed drawn and tight.

Always curious, John Gardner wandered over to the nearest Connecticut squad. "Say, what's eatin' you fellers?"

"Our enlistments are up today," explained a sergeant with a red bandanna tying down his rabbit skin hat. "We 'listed lunar, fair and square; but a lot of bigwigs down to Headquarters claims we got to serve calendar. Means ten extry days with no pay, either. I get paid by the moon. If my pay stops, I go home."

"I ain't standing for it," coughed the man next beyond. "Still got my winter's wood to cut. Ain't nobody else fit to do it on the place. I'm going home and don't anyone try to stop me."

One of the Gardner boys grunted, "Maybe so, but if you fellers high-tail, it will leave the rest of us kind of short-handed."

"Hell!" said a man in a deerskin vest. "The Massachusetts people can call up their milishy, can't they? Boston's their town, not ours."

The Connecticut men, Tim recognized, were mad, mad clear through.

"Heard what that Virginia General aims to do with our Fourth Company?" inquired a sergeant while swinging his arms to get warm.

"No."

"He'd set a God-damned New Hampshire lawyer over it. But they ain't going to tolerate it."

By now about three hundred men had collected among the gray glacial boulders on this uneven field. The wind was coming up and caused a wild fluttering among the coats and capes of the men standing in disorderly rows.

Out over the comparatively untrampled snow in the center of the square marched four drummer boys. Because their short legs made hard going in drifted places their drumming was ragged. A moment later, three horsemen in long, wind-tossed cloaks rode out into the cleared space. Immediately, Tim recognized General Sullivan's puffy, purplish features.

"There goes old Spencer," growled a Connecticut sergeant. He was scowling at a gray-haired, flustered-looking individual bun-dled all out of shape in a captured British greatcoat. Probably it had been taken by John Manley in the *Nancy*. That one little cruiser had done a lot to help feed and clothe the army—and at King George's expense. Pity Congress wouldn't supplement the six feeble gunboats General Washington had equipped on his own initiative.

"Stand back, confound you! Out of my way, you comic clowns!" Into the square was galloping a scrawny, sloppily-dressed officer. His thin, bitter-looking mouth was twisted into an angry inverted crescent. A great pointed red beak of a nose jutted out from between small yellowish eyes. No one pretended that Major-General Charles Lee was in the least prepossessing.

"Look out, boys," came a derisive yell. "Old Boiling Water is a-steaming fit to b'ile over. Mind he don't blister ye!"

A rolling shout of amusement made the general's horse shy. Everybody knew Lee's Indian nickname.

More taunts rang in the clear cold air. "Git back to Poland!" "Why ain't you down in Boston with the rest of the Britishers?" "We don't relish no turncoats amongst us!" "Go home to Virginia!"

For all his carelessly buttoned and food-marked regimentals, despite a green cockade canted crazily over his hat brim, General Lee made an imposing figure as he sat his horse with magnificent ease. He quite ignored the taunts, seemed wholly absorbed in the antics of two white woolly dogs which were frolicking about his charger's legs. Tim had never seen any dogs like them; someone said they came from Pomerania, a place in Germany.

Alarmed by a steadily mounting clamor, the company officers faced about, waved their swords, shouted hoarsely for silence. The uproar continued, however, until General Sullivan signaled his drummers to beat a taptoo.

When the drums stopped rolling, Colonel Spencer called his regiment to attention and, none too eloquently, begged his men to take advantage of a lunar month enlistment.

"I adjure you, by all you hold honorable, to remain until the tenth of December and to reenlist."

"No reenlistment!" "Go chase yourself, Spencer!" "Our enlistment's up!"

Going gray in the face, Colonel Spencer waved his arms. "Each reenlisting soldier will be granted a furlough, a preferred post in the new army—I'll try to get you a bounty! Now isn't that fair enough?"

He looked about expectantly. All the responses he earned were groans and catcalls; but some of the men began to look uncertain.

"Well, then, we will talk of reenlistment later." Unwisely, Colonel Spencer hesitated before continuing, "Now how many of you brave boys will stay 'til the tenth of December when we can muster some militia to take your places in the lines? Remember, all I'm asking is ten days' further service. Those patriotic-minded will take two steps backward."

He was smart, Tim figured, to word his command as he had. The disaffected soldiers would thus be left standing in plain view of such men as intended to remain. It came as a severe shock when less than a third of the regiment stepped backwards. Right along side of him a youth of eighteen was swallowing hard, craning his neck this way and that. He seemed fearful of what his officers might do.

The tumult grew and some companies began to break ranks when General Sullivan tried to make himself heard. It was no use. Tim saw him shrug, turn to Charles Lee, making a helpless gesture with his rabbit's fur gloves.

Against the cold blue of the sky, Lee's face went red as fire and viciously he spurred his charger, a powerful brown stallion with black dappling on its rump. Outraged, the animal reared, lashed out with its hoofs, made its bridle flash and otherwise captured all eyes.

The gaunt figure snatched open his holster covers exposing the brass butts of a pair of heavy horse pistols. But Lee didn't draw his weapons, only stood in his stirrups bellowing.

"Halt, God damn you! Stand still! Don't a rogue among you dare move!"

At the sight of his hand hovering over a pistol butt, the disordered ranks steadied, halted. In a voice that was harsh and penetrating as the sound of a carving knife dragged over steel, Lee shouted,

"Men, I don't know what to call you. You are the worst of all creatures! You are the utter dregs of humanity! What have I done that I am condemned to command such a pack of infernal spiritless scoundrels? By the living God! if I've my way, every last man who quits camp today will be hauled to the halberts, then driven through the gauntlet. I will have his blasted head shaved to mark him for a chicken-hearted poltroon!

"Get back in your places!" The General spurred at the nearest men, almost rode them down but, at the last instant, curbed so sharply that his leopard skin saddle cover flapped and his mount reared again with its hoofs pawing the air over the heads of the troops. Cursing beneath their breath, the men fell back.

Lee's nasal voice was snarling now. "By the splendor of God, if you don't stay I'll order you knaves to charge Bunker's Hill! You wouldn't like that, would you, you rascally mothers' mistakes?"

"Our enlistment's up," bellowed a voice. "We're going, and be damned to you!"

Livid with fury, Lee wheeled, but could not recognize the speaker. "No discharges will be written until the tenth! Try to desert before then and I'll order the rifle companies out to shoot you down. They'd jump at the chance, too."

"That Irishman is ready for murder," Tim thought, but grinned to see such self-satisfied smiles on his Rhode Islanders.

Sharp blue chin a-quiver with fury, Lee jerked his stallion's head about, thundered around the square with his Pomeranians in yapping pursuit.

"Officers!" he roared. "Write down the names of these dogs who won't stay. Now, all brave fellows who choose to remain, two paces backwards, march!"

There was a general backward movement, but still nearly a hundred of the Connecticut men remained where they were, sullenly defiant.

Anxious to redeem their previous ineptitude, captain and lieutenants went among those who still were for going home. They argued awhile, then, amid angry curses, commenced to take down names.

"Everyone staying will get a gill of rum!" Colonel Spencer called. "Rest of you, turn in your muskets."

"Devil take yer rum and you, too," rasped a big sergeant. "Come along, boys, let's go. We ain't eatin' any more of that damned Irishman's sass!"

There was something truly devilish about Charles Lee's fury. He kicked forward his horse and, reaching down from the saddle, grabbed the malcontent's musket by its barrel. Jerking it free, he brought the weapon swinging down hard on the sergeant's head. Shuddering, the fellow collapsed onto the snow as the two Pomeranians ran up barking.

"Anyone who tries to persuade a man to leave will get these." Charles Lee jerked forth his pistols, brandished them in the air. "When that poltroon comes to, put him under arrest!"

Wheeling, the Major-General rode off at breakneck speed.

Tim's detail met Ensign Child and the wood party heading back for camp. Under a heavy load of birch logs the sledge's runners creaked and snow crackled cheerily beneath the weight. Tim was pleased the boys had found birch. If a chimney place was faulty birch smoke was much the best to have in one's nose.

For all General Lee's ranting small parties of men were beginning to quit the Connecticut camp. Sometimes an officer or sergeant would walk along with them a distance, arguing.

"Lee is dead right," Ensign Child opined. "Any man who'd quit with the Army fixed as it is now, ought to be hanged."

"Suppose their families really need them?"

Joe Child's blunt red face hardened. "After all this time, ten days more can't matter so much. The next ten days here are the most critical. Suppose Billy Howe in Boston learns we are trying to reorganize from top to bottom? Why, even he will attack; and if he does, God help us all!"

6

THE COMMANDER-IN-CHIEF

IN compliance with his brigadier's instructions, Tim Bennett dismissed his men and set off for Headquarters. Nat Greene would be interested to hear about Spencer's request. Besides, he didn't want any slip-up over the leave Matt Allen had promised him. Come hell or high water he intended to reach the Congress Inn as soon as possible. At one o'clock Lucy and her mother would resume their trip southwards.

Mrs. Percival was not one to wait on laggards.

Tim hurried so hard he began sweating. Maybe he could get in to see the Brigadier right away. He *must* have another talk with Lucy. He was still all hair-hung and breeze-shaken over their interview of the night before and as yet hadn't the faintest notion of what he was going to do.

It was only a quarter past ten when he reached a low, white-painted dwelling doing duty as headquarters for "the Rhode Island Army of Observation." He stepped by two privates on guard at the entrance. They made a smart appearance, thanks to new blue and white uniforms. For a miracle they had bayonets fixed to their King's Arm muskets.

"Sergeant Bennett, sir, reporting to General Greene."

The adjutant, a yellow-complexioned, solemn young fellow with a bad squint, inclined his head slightly. "General Greene is occupied; take a seat."

"Will I have to wait long, sir? You see—I—"

"How in blazes would I know?" snapped the adjutant. "Am I a mind reader?"

A single colorless drop clung to the end of this officer's nose, Tim observed. Every time he signed a document the drop trembled and threatened to fall. But it never did.

As if to sharpen Tim's impatience, a clock ticked steadily above the adjutant's desk. Streaming perspiration, he watched its hands descend, start upwards. The minute hand, he noticed presently, was not the original. It was an imitation carved out of wood.

At ten minutes past eleven a door was opened upstairs and a colonel, wearing the green silk sash of a staff officer, came clumping down.

"Damn' cold day." He nodded, secured the loops of a gray watch-cloak about him and strode out.

"Throw a stick on the fire before you go up," the adjutant requested, without looking up from his paper work. "They'll send an orderly down to fetch you."

Here it was almost half-after eleven. Damn all generals! Why couldn't Greene see a man straight off? Even now he still could make it to the Congress Inn, but he'd have no time to wash.

He was waiting for Greene's orderly when, outside, the sentries' hands went *slap! slap!* on their firelocks. That extra loud click of their heels argued someone of rank.

From the head of the stairs an orderly called, "The General will see Sergeant Bennett."

Tim felt better. His report shouldn't require five minutes to deliver. Now he was sure of seeing Lucy and if he described what had happened in the Connecticut camp, she ought to understand why he couldn't possibly come home now.

He had started upstairs when the adjutant got up so quickly, he overset his chair. "Atten-shun, there!"

Something in his voice immobilized Tim and he stood to rigid attention beside the newel post. A blinding glare off the snow flooded the hall. Feet stamped and spurs jingled, then a square-shouldered figure in a wide cloak entered. Tim noted he was so tall he had to incline his head to avoid knocking a blue and buff cockade against the lintel.

He was the Commander-in-Chief of all the Provincial Armies. To the last detail General Washington's uniform appeared faultless. Every last button glittered and the smother of French lace at his throat and wrists fairly sparkled.

There was no doubt that General Washington was chilled through. His lips, tight drawn over ill-fitting false teeth, were of a purplish blue and his clear gray-blue eyes were watering so hard that a succession of tears traced bright channels over the vivid pink of his cheeks.

He smiled stiffly, said to the adjutant, "Pray present my compliments to General Greene. Will he devote to me a moment of his time?"

The adjutant fairly bounded upstairs.

"Beastly cold," the General remarked to his staff officers, then sought the fireplace. As he stood warming himself, his heavy riding cape fell open, revealed a light blue ribbon of watered silk slanting across his waistcoat.

Tim remained at attention though the General's aides began pulling off gloves and blowing on their fingers.

After a bit Washington called, "Pray stand at ease. One forgets on occasion that you Rhode Islanders are so well disciplined."

Tim Bennett covertly surveyed the Southerner. Crimanently! There was something mighty impressive about the C. in C.—even if he was a Virginian.

Frantic activity was ensuing upstairs; chairs scraped back and forth, feet raced about. General Washington's eyes flickered upwards and a smile tugged briefly at the corners of his mouth.

"It would appear that General Greene is not expecting company," he remarked, drawing his thick cloak further back. Tim now saw broad lapels of pale buff secured by golden buttons and the guard of the French dress sword. It was of gold and handsomely jeweled. Flecks of mud, however, dappled the General's boots clear up to his knees.

Looking at Tim he slowly rubbed the back of one hand against the palm of the other. "Are your men warm, Sergeant?"

"Yes, sir, tolerably."

"They receive sufficient rations?"

"More than enough, sir."

The General's voice was grave and even and without a trace of the pompousness or ill-temper you generally got from a general officer. "You will reenlist, I presume?"

"Why—why, yes, sir. I expect to."

"Capital! The New Army stands in great need of experienced men. Young ones endure a hard campaign better than oldsters."

The General's aides crossed to the window and stood looking down a row of gray beeches edging the drive. The General turned back to the fire, wiped his cheeks on the back of his hand. "You have served since when, Sergeant?"

"Since last May, sir."

"Then you must have fought at Breed's Hill?"

"No, sir. We were ordered—to Jamaica Plain."

"Well, then, you men still have an opportunity to demonstrate your mettle. Perhaps it is just as well." He sighed, "Quite a few of the gentry who fought there seem inclined to rest forever on their laurels. But you were at Lechmere's Point?"

"Yes, sir." Under the General's reserved friendliness, Tim felt less ill at ease.

"Your regiment was little hurt?"

"Yes, sir. We had only one wounded."

"Who was he?"

"I, sir."

The General's smile widened and Tim noted that, sure enough, his teeth were not his own. "My compliments, Sergeant. Most men would long since have been describing their wound."

Greene's adjutant reappeared, hurried downstairs. At his heels was the sturdy, squarish figure of the Rhode Island Brigadier. Tim guessed that Greene and the Commander-in-Chief understood one another, despite the fact that one was a Virginia aristocrat and the other had begun life as a Quaker blacksmith.

"Good morning, sir. Rhode Island is unduly honored," Greene declared. Both were above average height; the Northerner broader across the shoulders and shorter in the leg. Greene had a slight limp. Even though it didn't hamper the Brigadier it had kept him out of the militia a long while. "I was contemplating a ride to Cambridge even as you rode up."

General Washington's smile faded. "I have heard of this trouble among Colonel Spencer's men. I am most eager to gain your impressions." As a delicate hint, the General's level gaze wandered over to the staircase.

"Shall we repair to my office?"

"With pleasure, sir," General Washington replied, making a courteous suggestion of a bow.

Before they reappeared the clock stood at a quarter past two.

7

MRS. PERCIVAL

DRIFTING snow had erected a series of smothering barricades across the turnpike. In consequence, Mrs. Isaac Percival's two horse pung made painfully slow progress towards Dedham. When, at last, lights glimmered in the distance, Lucy's mother reached over a leather apron and prodded her stableman's hunched shoulders.

"Whip up, Enoch! We will bide the night in the village."

The driver said "Yes'm" from the depths of an immense red woolen shawl, then "Gup!" to the team. Tired from many battles with the drifts they paid no attention until the stableman untwined his whip. The pung's red-painted runners raised billows of powdery snow as the bays took up a lumbering trot.

For a miracle, a private room was available at the White Hind. Dutifully, Lucy aided her mother out of her traveling capes. Little conversation had passed between them since midday. For Lucy it was a shock to learn that enlisted men were not their own masters like officers. Poor Tim must have been prodigiously disappointed to find her gone. What could have delayed him? For a miracle, Mama had waited a full half hour after the scheduled hour of departure.

A pity this had happened. Up 'til now everything had been such fun. She had never been so far away from home before. To travel in the dead of winter was a feat few girls could boast of. Come to think of it, this trip was a real joke on Mama. Cousin Tom's letter had described Grandma Warren as half through Death's door. Mama certainly had been justified in voyaging from Newport to Concord. No sooner had they arrived than, quite perversely, Grandma had taken a turn for the better. Now the frail, black-clad sparrow was up, spry as ever.

"Lizzie, I believe I could whip my weight in wolverines!" the old lady had chuckled. "I fear the Bristol land and my gold and onyx earbobs will not be yours this year."

Grandma must know that Papa was tighter than the bark on a tree, even with her granddaughter. She didn't disapprove, didn't hold with spoiling young folks. But Grandma must have suspected that she, Lucy, had a mind of her own else why had she given two pounds *sub rosa*.

The taproom of the White Hind turned out to be crowded with soldiers—Connecticut men—on their way home; she and Mama dined in their room. When, very innocently, Mrs. Percival ordered up a pot of boiling water, the chambermaid had looked at her askance. Mama, however, only gazed into space. Various Committees of Safety to the contrary, if Mama wanted a cup of tea, she got it.

Lucy was nervous, though. Suppose the wench got suspicious? Back in Newport people had been proscribed, even jailed, because someone had found tea leaves in the swill. Ever since the Boston Tea Party the use of tea had been considered unpatriotic.

After the maid shuffled out, Mrs. Percival said, "Lucy, hang your cloak over the keyhole. That nosy-Parker will be losing an eye if you don't."

A traveling kit marked "medicine" having yielded a small package of Bohea, Mrs. Percival brewed herself a fragrant cup of tea, sweetened it with rock sugar.

It annoyed Lucy that Mama didn't offer her even a taste and here she was still chilly. A fire of damp wood hissed, didn't heat the bedroom much.

When she had finished, Mrs. Percival took care to spill her tea leaves into the flames. No use taking chances. Some people were too crazy patriotic for any earthly use.

By the dull red-yellow light of a tallow dip taper, Mrs. Percival surveyed their cheerless quarters, passed fingers over the dresser and wrinkled her nose triumphantly when their tips showed gray. Next she examined the sheets of the lumpy-looking bed, even inspected its cords and coverlets with care. As her mother pulled a trundle bed out from under the four-poster, Lucy trembled lest Mama bid her sleep on it among icy draughts near the floor.

But Mrs. Percival shoved it back out of sight, announcing, "May as well go to bed; we'll take our deaths, else."

"Yes, Mama." Lucy hurried to shovel coals and hot ashes into a battered brass warming pan. Still wondering what could have kept Tim, she thrust the pan under the blankets and circulated it slowly lest the bed clothes scorch. Mrs. Percival, meanwhile, draped cloaks before the bedroom's two small windows. The wind was fairly whistling through shamefully loose frames.

Glory! Lucy didn't anticipate undressing. Right now the cold struck through her worsted stockings like nettles; it would require long hours with honey and milk of almonds to get her cheeks and wrists back to the genteel, pallid hues approved by Mama.

"Make haste, child. It is going on eight, and we must arise early." Mrs. Percival placed a screen before the fire, then blew down a storm glass protecting the taper. To permit any ray of light to illuminate a chamber in which she and her daughter disrobed would be highly immodest.

Because of the dark and the fact that her fingers were numb, Lucy made slow progress in letting down her hair and plaiting its pale strands into a rough queue.

Lifting her dress over her head she thought, "Oh dear, why did Mama have to cut off the fire with that screen? She must have seen me undressed hundreds of times."

The process of unknotting the tie strings of her six petticoats required a frigid eternity. The business of unhooking stays stiffened with whalebones and hickory splints was like wading slowly out into ever-deepening ice water.

For an agonizing instant Lucy stood nude, her skin graveled and small, pointed nipples tingling, then with a triumphant sweep she sent the cold flannel nightshift swirling over her head. All in one movement she slid into bed and hardly raised the comforter at all.

Luxuriating in warmth generated by the warming pan, she heard Mama's teeth clicking like a spinning wheel. When she pulled off her shoes she groaned. Her corns must have been hurting.

Lucy tried to feel sympathetic with poor Mama but she couldn't. After all, she *had* blocked off the fire.

Once the two lay with the odor of warm wood ashes ascending the valley between their bodies, Lucy began to feel less depressed. But only a little. Why hadn't Tim come to the Congress Inn? His failure to do so had been a disappointment as novel as it was sharp.

Of course, it couldn't have been Tim's fault. Probably an officer had ordered him away on an errand. Tim, dear, earnest Tim, still floundering about what to do with his life.

She slipped her lower lip over her upper one. M-m. The skin was still tender from the crushing of his mouth, and her chin had been chafed by the little bristles on his cheek. Lying there, watching the play of flames on the ceiling and thinking of the lean handsomeness of him, her whole body began to glow.

If only it could be Tim here beside her. As always, Mama smelt of castile soap. What did people, married people, do in bed? She wondered if someday Mama would tell her. For some strange reason, none of the girls had ever confided. Once Clorinda, the kitchen slave, had begun a really interesting vein, but unluckily Papa had overheard; the whipping Clorinda received sealed her lips as effectively as a needle and waxed thread.

"Lucy?"

"Yes, Mama." She recognized a peculiar clear quality in her mother's voice, dreaded it.

"You have not yet informed me as to when Timothy is returning home."

Lucy's fingers curled. Oh dear, what *could* she say?

"I am waiting, Lucy."

"Well, Mama, he didn't say he wouldn't."

"We had it distinctly understood, did we not, that he is to return?"

"But, Mama, you don't understand. Tim is a soldier, a good one. They are going to promo—"

"—I suspected as much last night," Mrs. Percival coldly informed her. "They want to make him an officer; of course, Timothy is flattered and dazzled. Nevertheless, there is no real profit in soldiering."

Below her night bonnet Mrs. Percival's long, sharp profile showed in silhouette. Her expression was a queer blend of weariness and impatience. "Young people should make their own way in the world. We did."

"Yes, Mama."

"Plague take it, child, stop saying, 'Yes, Mama' and 'No, Mama.' Is Timothy returning before December the seventh?"

"I—I don't know," Lucy confessed miserably. "He was going to tell me this morning. Last night he felt it his patriotic duty to remain with the Army, and—"

"—And to strut around in fancy regimentals." Mrs. Percival sniffed, whether because of the cold or from contempt, Lucy couldn't tell. "Well—it is perfectly clear that his duty to you calls him home. You must never permit your husband—er—Timothy to forget that his first duty is to his wife—and family," she added belatedly.

"But for me, Mr. Percival would have gone traipsing up to Louisburg." Sniff. "Look at poor Uncle Benjamin! The Army

spoiled him." Sniff. "Hasn't amounted to a pinch of ashes since."
Sniff. "All he does is to shoot, fish, and sponge on his brother."
Sniff.

"But Uncle Ben seems happy, Mama."

"His is the false happiness of indolence." Sniff.

Lucy resented that. Of all Papa's numerous, tight-lipped family,
there was only Uncle Ben she could really like. He was gentle, almost
shy. It was he who described for her France, the Low Countries, the
Cape Colony, and mysterious, teeming India. Yes. Uncle Ben could
make her see, could make her live in lands far beyond the horizon.
If a local rajah's cannon ball hadn't taken off Uncle Ben's foot in a
silly little skirmish near Pondicherry, she guessed he would still be
drifting about the globe.

Mrs. Percival recommenced talking. She sounded not so severe as
she re-tied the strings of her night bonnet. "My dear, it is *greatly* to
Timothy's interest that he return before the seventh."

"Why the seventh, Mama?"

"Matter of Business." Mrs. Percival's thin jaws shut with a soft
click. "You would not understand, child. But this you can understand: if Timothy does not return," sniff, "Mr. Percival and I will not
consent to your marriage."

Lucy felt colder than when she had been standing nude. "Oh,
Mama, you *couldn't* do such a terrible thing!"

"My dear, it is sometimes necessary to be cruel in order to be kind,"
Mrs. Percival said with her eyes shut. "You might think of—well, of
Ira Thaxter. His father, we understand, is well off, and Ira seems a
practical young man."

Mrs. Percival sighed, turned over, presenting a bony back.

8

MEDITATION BY FIRELIGHT

THOUGH it was barely half-after eight, the rooms upstairs were dark. From his seat in the kitchen, Sergeant Timothy Bennett could hear a regular chorus of snores, grunts, and sighs. If he hadn't been so worried, he'd have laughed at such a magnificent symphony. He shifted restlessly on a musket chest that did duty as table, bench and food locker. Glowing ashes in the kitchen hearth revealed gray-haired Supply-Sergeant Woodford to be snoozing peacefully. Every now and then the old duffer would get off a particularly lusty snore. It sounded like somebody slowly ripping a linen sheet.

It was growing chilly so Tim laid a birch log on the fire. Soon yellow flames began licking oilily upwards. When they grew bright, Tim smoothed on his knee the first of two letters a postrider had brought in at sundown.

One note was so brief he already knew it by heart. Lucy had written it only the night before.

> Friday, December the First
> Dedham
> Most Dearly Belov'd:
> To your poor Lucy it was a cruel, cruel Dissapointment that you did not come to the Congress Inn. What chanc'd to prevent it?
> Sweeting, you will come home? I pray you will decide Wisely. Papa is quite Determin'd we shall not Marry this Yeare if you doant. I surmize Papa hath Affairs in Mind which will be greatly to your advantage. My dearest Darling, I begin to fear Mama is right. Though you adopt the Army for a space yet are you not a Merchant at heart?

He paused. Was he? Or was he a soldier by instinct? Look how well he had come along—why he had even won a commission, fairly too, in less than a year. A merchant at heart? He went on reading:

In the name of our LOVE I implore you to leave the Army. God willing, this will be the first and last test to which I shall ever be constrain'd to put our mutuel DEVOTION.

Thy tenderly Adoring,
Lucy.

At the foot of the letter was scrawled a triple row of circles. Impulsively, Tim pressed the paper to his lips. Then for a long time he sat, elbows on knees, looked into the heart of the dancing flames.

At length he took out another letter. Its envelope was addressed in Asa Bennett's fine Italian script. As he broke the flying seal and unfolded the single page he guessed that Pa's sight certainly must be failing. Here and there he had run words into each other, and the written lines wavered uncertainly across the page.

Conanicut Island
15th Day of 11th Month,
1775

My Son:

Greetings. I pray this Finds Thee well & Clean in the Sight of God. Greatly has been my affliction at having received no word from Thee since mid Tenth Month.

Alas that my News is indeed so Heavy. Keep it to thyself, else we are compleatly Undone.

We? Tim was startled. In the past Asa Bennett had always referred to his possessions as *my* business, *my* vessels, *my* ropewalk.

The *Patience* & the *Prudence* are so many Weeks overdue out of Curacoa I do feare them lost because of this ruinous blockade. The *Hope* rots Useless at the wharfe here on Conanicut. I do not dare send her to sea. So many Vessels of this port have either been Burnt or condemn'd at His Majesty's Court of Vice Admiralty in New York.

Yestereve Friend Robinson's fine new *Peace & Plenty* was made a prize to the *Rose* frigate. With Fayal & Canary wines fetching 3/4 the bottle As Thee well knows, such a price is truly Amazing. A sore tryal to Friend Robinson this must be.

"As Thee well knows." Tim's forefingers rubbed his chin. He didn't know. Pa was becoming forgetful. Hezekiah was the one who so easily kept current prices at his finger tips. What could an ex-sophister of Rhode Island College know of such matters?

Well, all possibility of becoming a gentleman was now over and done. He couldn't feel sorry about it. He had always felt more comfortable around ships and wharves than in the dim study halls of New University Hall.

From the start, Pa had been dead-set on having a scholar and a gentleman head the Bennett family once he himself was laid to rest in the Friends' burying ground.

I have deemed it best to order the *Narragansett* held in the French Sugar Islands until such Time as we may, with God's consent, see better days.

Alas! My chief Clerk, Wheelock, has been press'd into the H. M. S. *Bolton,* bomb ketch. With exception of a single young Clerk, I am alone in the Management of Bennett & Company. Therefore, I adjure Thee, my Son, to return, with all speed.

Here, there is no man to whom I can entrust my affairs. The times are parlous and a loose tongue can spell Ruin. I am like a captain at sea, bereft of a first mate. Thee is the only one to whome I may turn.

Tim raised his eyes. How old was Pa? Nearing seventy, but 'til now he had given no sign of his years. Poor Pa! His wife gone. Zeke gone. His business failing, his ships unreported. And he had toiled so unsparingly of self for his dependents.

There exists a very privy & urgent Reason for thy swift return but the matter is so Secret I durst not set it in Writing.

If I have done aught to afford Thee the Advantages of a good & Godly education, I trust Thee will obediently hasten back to Newport before the seventh day of Twelfth Month.

May God keep Thee safe, my son & I hope Thee has not forgot continually to Praise and Magnify His Name.

Thy father.

The seventh again! What the devil was afoot down in Newport? Pa had never been one to exaggerate—quite the contrary. Running fingers again and again through his strong brown hair, Tim tried to see the rights of the problem.

Perhaps he had already discharged his duty to the Colony? Hadn't he taken a heavy wound? To look at it from Pa's and the Percivals' point of view, he really had nothing to show for his eight months of soldiering but empty pockets and a sore leg.

The British did seem as good as licked anyhow. Hadn't shown even a spark of fight since Breed's Hill. Yet he found himself remembering how discouragedly General Thomas, commanding at Roxbury, had said to Greene, "—more than powder, we stand in desperate need of experienced men—young men."

Plunging hands in pockets, Tim got up, paced up and down, kicked a greasy soup bone out of the way. Sergeant Woodford across the room kept right on puffing and snoring.

"Is there any logical reason why the Army can't get on without me? No. Does Pa need me more than the Army? Yes, it seems so. Aren't I aiming to become a family man? Well, rather! Of course, we couldn't live on even a captain's pay. Is it not intelligent to plan now, for the peace that must come eventually? Yes. Pa has always said a successful man saw what was coming before anybody else, and took steps accordingly. This seventh of December business suggests an example of such foresight. A wrong move at this time can warp my whole life. Let's figure this theory out.

"Since '74 a lot of the old business houses must have failed it stands to reason that soon some men nobody has ever heard of will be riding about in coaches. I am not a coward. Nor am I afraid to gamble with my life to carry our trade wherever Pa says."

He paused in his pacing and the sound of a rat gnawing somewhere in the wall was distinctly audible. Enroll in the home service regiment he would not—no more militia for Timothy Bennett! Why wouldn't it be possible to go on trading and get in some licks at the Lobsterbacks *at the same time?*

Then he saw some objections. Congress would grant no letters-of-marque, had been opposed to the practice from the start. Again, Pa was a Friend. Imagine such a thorough-going Quaker permitting cannon to be mounted on any vessel of his! Still, Tim figured he might form a syndicate, arm a vessel, and wait for the Congress to change their minds. He figured they must change them—the greed and necessity of the shipowners were growing greater every month.

Suppose he decided to go home? He couldn't. His enlistment

wasn't up until December fifteenth. Pure bad luck it carried eight days over that date, which in Newport, appeared to be of such considerable significance.

He re-seated himself on the musket chest, drummed fingers on its greasy lid. The Connecticut men must be well on their way home. For all that Lee had said about them, they had been perfectly within their rights. It had required the courage of their convictions to march off. Pa certainly did need him; there was no getting around that.

He tried not to let Lucy enter into the problem. She had said she would wait, hadn't she? Suppose he went home just long enough to help Pa through this affair of December seventh? Yes, that was what he'd do. He could return in time to re-join and to take up his commission. He would!

He frowned. But his enlistment wasn't up 'til the fifteenth. Tim commenced to scratch as lice, warmed by his rising body heat, went to work. All at once, he saw an answer and almost ran over to select a sheet of foolscap. With a pocket knife he repointed a quill, then opened the company clerk's leaden ink bottle. By the light of a handful of birch bark tossed on the fire, he commenced to write.

When he had finished, Tim figured he had fully explained his intentions to Captain Matthew Allen. So long as he intended to come back, nobody could object much if he took advantage of the lunar month clause in his enlistment agreement. Now could they? Men who were rejoining were granted leave anyway. It didn't occur to him that these men had been required to sign the reenlistment papers before going on leave.

"There isn't a doubt but my enlistment is up," he thought. "Just to make sure— 'Thirty days hath September, April, June and November.' Thirty-one days in May gives a three days' credit. In June I get two more, July and August six more days. Why, right now I've exceeded my enlistment, served thirteen extra days with no pay. Um.

"All I'm asking is the use of eight of these days—and I'm coming back, too. No one can reasonably find fault. Nobody can say I ain't patriotic."

He sanded, sealed the letter with candle grease, then stuffed it into

Captain Allen's pigeonhole.

The light of a splinter of candlewood showed his room-mates sound asleep, drew a flash from the burnished metal of Joe Child's gorget hanging there to a nail driven into the window frame. He would be wearing one soon.

Raw-boned Bill McPherson, lying on his sack of smelly straw, talked softly in his sleep. Mac was one of the best. At Lechmere's Point, it was he who had tied a tourniquet above the bullet hole, had lugged him to a dressing station and stood off the sawbones who had wanted to amputate. He really wished he could say goodbye to Mac. He'd write Mac, to Joe Child, too. Wouldn't do to have them mis-understand his "going lunar."

How was Abner Hull getting on? Abner had been very low all day. He wished he knew. His mother would be sure to ask about him.

Deliberately Tim collected a marching kit. It was hard, mighty hard, to leave behind that grenadier's shako he'd brought off after the skirmish on Boston Neck. It would have made a fine trophy to show, but with the big brass plate on the front of it, it weighed a lot.

He needed a pair of spare shoes much more. Wet shoes caused sores and chilblains. He'd have to hurry, too, what with this bitter weather and the roads blocked. Into his haversack he thrust a horn of bear's grease, a spare shirt, some stockings, and all the scraps of food he could find in the kitchen.

When he closed the kitchen door on the supply sergeant's snufflings, the stars were very bright; it was so cold the snow creaked under his feet. For a staff he selected a tall stick from the fuel supply.

Light-heartedly Tim Bennett struck off along the icy road to Dedham.

9

THE BLUE HILLS

SAM HIGSBY, late private in Thompson's Pennsylvania Rangers, felt elegant at being shut of civilization. Being cooped up, living on fat rations tied a man's bowels up, his spirit, too. In the woods like this, a feller felt more like a man, less like some damned herded sheep.

By force of habit his jet, faintly oblique eyes explored a line of dark green firs crowning the next ridge. He laughed silently. As if there was an Injun worth worrying over within a hundred miles.

What a crowded gawd-forsaken land! Why, since sun-up, he hadn't noticed more than fifteen or twenty deer and a bear or two. 'Round these parts the wild things had grown almighty 'cute. Must have been hunted hard for a long time. Wouldn't be any elk or buffalo in these woods, he reckoned. Plenty of foxes, though, and bob-cats. There were tracks all over the place.

For reasons sufficient unto himself, Higsby was traveling a series of rocky ridges running parallel to, and above, the stage road winding down from Boston to Providence, in Rhode Island. For one thing, the snow didn't drift on ridge tops. Of course, there weren't any Indians about. In Western Pennsylvania or Kentucky no ranger in his right mind would have walked a ridge top—not if he wanted to wear his hair for a while. Yesterday's blizzard had left the tree-trunks white on the west side.

Higsby's eyes, black and narrow and bright in his long, flat countenance, traveled in restless semi-circles. They noted even minor details without effort. It was growing so cold he reckoned pretty soon tree branches would start cracking. Yonder a buck had stropped his horns against a gray beech. Further away lay the remains of some rabbit an owl had got to. The approach of sundown put an edge to the wind. Higsby's brown complexion was turning coppery under it. Rhythmically, his hastily-contrived snowshoes *whiss-whissed* along the powdery slopes.

Sam Higsby was thinking—and, as he often did on a long trip, he began to talk to himself.

"Ain't nobody goin' make me salute any snot-nosed lawyer who happens to wear a gorget. I didn't promise, either, I'd freeze my butt in a hole in the ground 'thout naught to shoot at. Never swore to do that. Not on the Bible, leastways.

" 'Come along, boys,' says the recruiting feller. 'Ye'll get yer bellies

full o' fighting. We'll set up a row of live, red-coated targets fer ye
to fire at every day, an' twice on Sundays.' 'Twas lies, all damned,
dirty lies. Ain't had me one shot at a live target in near on three
months."

Even though the shortest line home was by the Springfield road,
Higsby reckoned it would be smart to cut a trail closer to the sea.
We're fewer provost patrols posted in this direction.

In ducking under a fir bough he touched it, loosing a cascade of
fine snow, but his outer cape of oiled leather was drawn hood-like
over his head and kept him dry.

Soon the sun swung low over a nearby hill and he began walking
on the bluish shadows of the trees. Better figger on finding shelter
soon. Of course, he could fell a cedar and make himself a den, but
it wouldn't do if this cold didn't ease up. Again, he hadn't been able
to hook a blessed morsel to put in the brass cook pot slatting over his
right buttock.

"Shore is colder 'n a old maid's bed," he grunted, as hairs on the inside of his nostrils began to congeal. He shifted his Leman—one of
the two long rifles he was lugging—to the crook of his left arm. At
the same time he eased the thong to which he slung the extra weapon.
It was a fine piece built by Adam Foulke of Allentown. Most folks
would have claimed it was better than his Leman. But he knew his
old rifle's balance, and Bella had a fine steady trigger pull.

Right now he figgered on selling the Foulke for the price of a ship
passage to Baltimore or to Philadelphia or some other place not too
far from home. The Foulke had belonged to Phil Dougherty of
Crescap's company. The damned fool was forever bragging of how
strong his belly muscles were, inviting strangers to punch him.
Shouldn't have tried stopping what he reckoned was a spent cannon
ball with his belly. It was that ball which had broke his back for
him. Dying, Phil had given him the Foulke because they'd served as
scouts together for Lord Dunmore against Chief Cornstalk.

The shadows were lengthening fast now, all purple-blue across the
snow. Higsby whirled, cat-quick, when a grouse, surprised at his

noiseless approach, thundered off through a clump of junipers. He came on a trail leading down a narrow valley and decided to follow it.

Better make tracks and come to a settlement before dark. The badly gapped fringes on his leggings whipped faster through the under-brush and a buck's tail fastened to his deerskin cap rose and fell more rapidly, steadily to his stride.

"Oughter be a road somewheres down yonder," he reasoned. "Country falls that way."

Sure enough in about twenty minutes, the trail debouched on a traveled but unplowed road. He didn't know where it might lead but he knew which direction to take.

About half a mile along he came across the charred ruins of a big log house. With half an eye he could tell it had been burned only recently. The building looked to have been a tavern; its half-consumed stable was away too big for an ordinary farmer.

"King's people, maybe," he muttered.

The sun had dropped out of sight, swiftly pulling the golden blanket from the whole rocky slope to his left.

Pretty soon he gained the crest of a rise and saw a column of gray-blue smoke climbing into the bitter air above a sea of spruce tops. A single column? Good. A detachment of troops would have kindled a dozen or more fires.

Despite frozen ruts hidden under the snow, Higsby made such good time that a haversack containing his bullet mould, powder gauge and pig lead began to pound his hip. A track branched off to the left, and since the smoke appeared to be rising in that direction, he left the main road. Um. His caution grew. Quite a few people had passed this way; ox and horse droppings darkly marred the snow.

In the center of a sizable clearing stood a large dwelling house. Because its second floor projected over the entrance, Higsby reckoned it must have been built when there were still Indians in the country.

The smoke which had attracted his attention was curling up from one of the largest brick chimneys he had ever seen. This place sure did look mighty homely with a bar of lamplight beating towards him across the snow. A down-puff of smoke brought him odors of onions and frying meat. Goddam! Springs of saliva rushed in his mouth.

After his long day's march he was hungry enough to eat a polecat, hide, hair and all. Everything looked all right; still it wouldn't do to rush in. If he got captured and brought back to Cambridge he knew what to expect. A deserter must expect a Moses law flogging at the very least. An educated feller from Boston said it wasn't the Moses law, but something called the Mosaic law. But forty cane strokes, less one, on a feller's bare back felt the same, no matter what you called 'em!

His snowshoes leaving an oval pattern the Pennsylvanian circled house, barns, corn crib and privy so stealthily that not even the farmer's dogs noted him. No soldiers were in the barn, just six or eight tired nags champing hay in the dark.

Under the branches of a towering pine Higsby stiffly cast loose his crude bear-paw snowshoes, laid them across some low branches. It might come on to snow, and he didn't want to take them into the house, either. If a feller had to quit a place in a hurry, the less he had to lug, the better.

After shaking a dusting of snow from his leggings, he eased the blue wool muffler Effie Shindler had knit him and hiked his belt straight. If them there folks expected money, he'd have to think fast; but maybe they would stand him to a free meal and lodging. Flipping open the pan of his rifle, he made sure the priming hadn't sifted out.

Mechanically he lifted his war hatchet free of its sling, then knocked on the door and jerked its latch string almost simultaneously. No use letting people get set if they aimed to make trouble. Rifle held careless-like, yet ready, he stepped inside. A flurry of wind-driven snow swept by his feet onto the flooring of the rough boards ahead of him.

All the people sitting at a trestle table jumped up; an old sharp-nosed woman working before the big open fireplace screamed, "My Jesus, it's a Injun!"

"Howdy, folks." Slipping a hand from its rabbit skin mitten Higsby raised it palm outwards. "Cold, ain't it?" Listening for noises upstairs, he stood quietly in the light of a bullseye lantern and two or three tallow dips. So there were only three able-bodied men in the place? He could handle them all right.

A barrel-chested fellow in patched leather breeches and a heavy gray flannel shirt started forward.

"Hey, what you mean by breaking in? Fer tuppence I'd—"

Framed in the doorway the man in buckskins looked pretty tough, bigger than he really was. Higsby made no immediate reply. To make a stranger wait was to set him wondering what you might be going to say; it gave you standing. Old Crippled Wolf of the Shawnees had told him that. You could learn a heap from the Injuns if you'd a mind to.

"For pity's sake shut that door," called the old woman's nasal voice. "Don't stand like a ninnyhammer letting in all outdoors."

Higsby closed the door then swept off his fur cap, gave its buck's tail a special flourish as he bowed a trifle.

"Servant, Ma'am." He tried to say it like the tidewater planters. "I was wonderin' whether you folks could obleege me with a meal of vittles? 'Pears like that ordinary up on the highroad has kind of gone out o' business."

Goddam! A couple of wenches were coming out of a shadow. One of them was pretty as a young fawn and her color was high from the heat of the roaring fireplace. The other was well built, but plain as a sod house.

The men at the table still said nothing. Beside the farmer who had come forward, there was a fellow wearing a homespun suit and a leather jerkin. The third man was dressed almost dandy in his black suit and lace jabot. Right off, Higsby set him down as a foreigner.

Without invitation the rifleman stood his two rifles near the door and everyone watched him unsling first his haversack, then powder horn and camp kettle. He kept his war hatchet and skinning knife to his belt, though. Grinning amiably, he swung over towards the fireplace and stood there toasting his hands.

"Well, folks, reckon I could lean into a platter o' that there ham an' chitterlings mighty easy. An' some of them elegant-looking turnips."

Then came the question Higsby had been dreading. The farmer still glowered, was slowly opening and closing big red hands as he asked, "Kin you pay?"

"Sho'," the ranger lied easily. "Just been discharged. Got most o' my pay."

"Ye'd better not be lying," the farmer rumbled. "Else I'll beat the tarnal tripes out of ye." He was big enough to do it, too.

The rifleman took no offense, declared affably, "I only lie to Injuns."

Before he had speared a second chunk of meat with his skinning knife, Higsby had covertly sized up the company as a farmer, his wife, and two daughters. The other two he took to be merchants who, like himself, had found themselves stranded among the Blue Hills.

The man in black had tied his napkin about his neck and was, with little finger extended, delicately employing a pearl-handled knife and fork from a pocket set. This lean, yellow-faced individual's powdered periwig had been carefully curled and his stock was of fine black silk. When his coat fell open, some mighty fetching perfume beat across the table. Such weather must bite sharp through his silk stockings and thin, silver-buckled slippers.

Higsby reckoned such a spandy-dandy would insist on getting a bed all to himself.

The two girls, giggling, bright-eyed and patently unfamiliar with rangers and their ways, watched him eat and brought him more as soon as his wooden trencher was empty.

Mrs. Anderson complained, " 'Pears like you ain't et in a month o' Sundays," and grudgingly placed before him a slab of pumpkin pie. "Hope you got enough currency to pay for all this."

She was a messy creature whose greasy gray hair dangled lank over a sweat-stained collar. Her few remaining teeth, as purple-yellow stumps, made her breath smell like the battlefield at Yellow Creek after two days.

Always she kept nagging querulously at the two girls and com-

plaining. She kept her house well, though, and her husband couldn't
have been poor. From the rafters dangled strings of onions and ears
of popping corn. Threaded on strings, pieces of dusty-looking dried
apples hung in festoons between chunks of dried summer squash and
vegetables.

Higsby sighed, let out his belt, and slowed down his eating. Now,
he felt more inclined to look about.

The daughter called Betty, a bold, pretty piece nearing eighteen,
was sly for her age. Whenever she passed, she always brushed his
shoulder with her thigh. Once when she backed against him, he
slipped a hand up among her petticoats. Goddam! the girl only wriggled. Had on three petticoats near as he could tell—all of common
cotton.

Aggie, the elder sister, had a really fine figure, but the smallpox
hadn't helped her looks any. At first he reckoned she was shy but
soon it seemed to him that, for all Betty's tricks, Aggie looked more
like a going concern. When she bent over to pop a popper of corn, he
thought he saw a strip of lawn beneath her striped, show petticoat.
Um! Lawn? Now that was right interesting.

He topped off his meal with popcorn soaked in beef gravy. It certainly filled out a man's stomach.

All along, farmer Anderson and the traveler in gray kept pulling
at a jug of hard cider. They were getting a little thick in their talk.

Whew! He was fit to roast. The Pennsylvanian loosened the lacings
of his outer knee-length hunting shirt and settled back on his three-
legged stool. Aggie's eye lit and Betty openly admired his inner doeskin shirt. It was sumac-dyed but its full fringes were of bright green.
Winking, Higsby pushed his jet hair back over the collar and wiped
his mouth on his sleeve.

Anderson belched, turned a fire-red face and stared hard at Higsby.
"Say, stranger, you ever fit any Injuns? Or you only dress like that?"

"Only last spring, me an' the Shain boys an' a couple of Tomkinses
raided old Oconostota's village at Keowee all by ourselves."

"Kill any?" demanded the man in gray from the depths of his
cider noggin.

"I got me half a dozen skelps."

Anderson started, narrowed his bloodshot eyes beneath dense brows.

"Six? You sure are a plain and fancy liar."

Higsby started to rouse his dander, but Betty was smiling at him from the shadows so he only stalked over to his haversack.

"Am I?"

He flung six snake-like lengths of braided black hair among the dishes. At the thick end of each was a ragged circle of what looked like a piece of dry calfskin.

"Oh my!" Betty's blue eyes flew wide open and Agatha gasped over the spiced cider she was mulling.

"Mon Dieu!" For the first time the man in black seemed aware of Higsby's presence. "Those are scalps from human heads?"

Higsby's teeth flashed in his dark face. "They ain't horse tails." Highly enjoying the moment, he shoved aside the table-ware and arranged his trophies in a row. He held a scalp to the light, loosened the lock near the big end.

"Lookey here, Mounseer. Kin you see how these hairs sort of swing around in a circle—like a little whirlpool?"

The Frenchman's intense eyes narrowed. "But yes."

"That's the poll piece. Nuthin' else don't really count, 'cause there's only one poll to each head. Hair don't grow like that nowheres else."

Anderson belched, fumbled thick fingers at one of the scalps.

"Suppose yer Injun's bald?" he guffawed.

"Well, then, you've got to take what you kin get—like this here one. That ain't a prime skelp. See fer yerself, Miss."

Betty gave a mouse-like squeak when he tossed a braid into her lap.

Mrs. Anderson swelled like an angry hen, made a pass at the scalp with her splinter broom. "Just you put them nasty things away in a hurry," she shrilled. "I'll warrant they're crawling with varmints."

Higsby laughed and returned them to his hunting pouch.

"How many you got—altogether?" Agatha inquired, her eyes softly admiring.

"Ma'am, I've took over twenty since I turned fifteen," Higsby replied, considering her with care. "Only brought six along to this war, though. Got into a turrible rumpus t'other night 'cause I figgered somebody had rooked me of one, an' 'twas in this here bag the hull time."

The man in gray remarked, "I was wonderin' where you got that mouse over your eye. Who done it?"

The rifleman laughed shortly and his jaw muscles tightened. "Wisht I knew. I was in likker. If ever I come acrost him, I'll shorely cut his lights out. I claim 'tain't sportin' to hit a man when he's in likker."

Mrs. Anderson sniffed, looked down her sharp nose. "So you was drunk?"

"I ain't often, Ma'am." Higsby produced a frayed twist of tobacco from his shirt bosom, bit off a piece. "But when Sam Higsby likkers up, the Mingoes, an' Cherokees, an' Shawnees washes off their war paint; the catamounts light out for tall timber; the ol' he b'ars settles down to sleep 'til he sobers up."

Higsby, looking very tall in the center of the low-ceilinged room, bowed to the farmer's wife. "Ma'am, I kin say with all modesty that Higsby in likker is a r'arin', tearin' whirlwind of destruction."

"*Je crois bien,*" murmured the foreigner, fingering a wine glass from which he took an occasional sip. "Tell me, *mon ami,* the siege of Boston, how does he progress?"

Higsby pursed thin lips, became cautious. "We-e-ell, suh, things is dead. Deader 'n ditch water. Most o' the home boys are right disgusted." The Pennsylvanian's voice deepened, filled the whole firelit room. "Ain't no sense to this war, anyway. What'd we march North fer? To fight the Britainers, o' course. What do we do most of the time? We just set around wearin' out the seats of our britches waitin' for orders, havin' to turn out an' salute a lot of snots who don't know a deer trace from a hog track."

Ostentatiously, the old woman blew out the bullseye lantern and snuffed one of the candles.

Conscious of the Frenchman's bright-eyed interest, Higsby went on. "Yes suh, them Yankee sons of bitches tried to make us, the fightin'est men in America, stand out in the wet when even a bug-tit would know there wouldn't be a hostile for miles around.

"Will them Britainers come out and give a feller a target? Hell an' destruction, no!" The Pennsylvanian squirted a long parabola of brown juice into the fireplace, watched it sizzle on the end of a log. "Will these psalm-shouting Massachusetters attack an' make 'em fight? Hell no! Me, I'm headin' somewheres where a feller kin keep his fightin' eye in."

Interrupting the deft manipulations of a gold and quill toothpick, the foreigner suggested, "It is not yet time, perhaps? Is it not possible that these Provincial generals lack supplies—bayonets and gunpowder for example?"

Higsby shook his head. "They've plenty; 'sides this is a hell of a war!"

The Frenchman's lean lips creased into a mechanical smile, and he regarded the ceiling. "There is no need to inquiet yourself, my friend. Soon there will be combat—many hard combats."

Anderson kicked a gaunt cur which was sniffing at a bone dropped beneath the table. "Fighting? Where?"

"On the sea," came the prompt reply. "I, François Pliarne, will hazard my word on it. Why should I not? I have already hazarded my fortune," he added grimly.

Higsby and the others stared at the prim, lean figure.

Anderson knit his bushy brows. "Why do you think that, Mounseer Plee-arn?"

The foreigner's shoulders raised in the most delicate and deferential of shrugs. "Since you express interest, Monsieur, one may point out that soon or late you Americans will have to fight on the sea."

He leaned forward, talking to Higsby rather than Anderson. "So long as the navy of the King of England rules your coast, you can have no commerce. With no commerce with which to pay for supplies, you will quickly be ruined.

"One would not like to be an American if the Parliament wins, *ma foi non!* However—" he glanced quickly about, like a bird just perched on a limb—"unless one has greatly misjudged the temper of these Colonies, one is convinced that to enjoy free—free—*comment le dire?*—you will fight to the ultimate for your trades and business enterprises."

The merchant nodded excitedly. "You're dead right there! Me and Abner Lawson owning four of the soundest craft as ever plied the triangle trade, ain't turned a penny of profit since the Boston Port Act. We're gettin' despirit, we are."

Higsby picked up a piece of kindling, began absently to whittle at it. Of the merchant he inquired, "—An' what do you folks aim to do about it?" He wasn't particularly interested but he always enjoyed argument.

The man in gray snorted. "Do? Hell's roarin' bells, we'll go privateering, that's what! Us and a lot o' others will get their change back out o' English shipping; bide your time and see! Once we begin to prize their vessels, the British ship owners 'll raise an almighty holler to Parliament and make 'em call off this numbskull war."

He blew out his lips and stared belligerently at the somber Frenchman's figure. "I say we only need a few privateers to fix them Britishers!"

M. Pliarne finished his wine and set down his glass with deliberation. "It is as you wish, *mon ami;* but still one cannot believe that any number of American privateers and letters-of-marque can drive the English away."

"Say!" Anderson set down his cider jack with such a bang it slopped all over his lap. "I don' like your talk, Mounseer. Damn' if I do. Us Massachusetts fellers are dandy fighters—proved it at Louisburg, as you Mounseers might recall. Aggie! Fetch me some hot cider and get a wiggle on that lazy backside of yours."

Betty came over and stood so close alongside Higsby he made sure that, though her thigh was smooth and soft, her petticoats were undoubtedly of cotton.

The merchant's semi-bald head wagged. "Don' tell me New England privateers can't whip the British," he belched. "Back in '56 I took six prizes off you Frog-eaters my own self."

M. Pliarne inquired quite unruffled, "And among them, how many were ships of war?"

The merchant blinked suspiciously.

"The Mounseers didn't have none cruising this coast; we'd have tooken them along o' the rest, I expect."

"One is always entitled to one's opinion." M. Pliarne's parchment-hued features remained calm as his thin and somewhat grimy fingers explored a tortoise shell snuff box. They brought out a pinch of the brownish powder.

"Might one observe that *nos amis, les anglais,* have not yet quite recovered from the rude shock of that combat at Charlestown? Their armies for the moment remain insensible, paralyzed in a measure."

"—That makes sense," Higsby drawled. He finished a noggin of cider Betty had sneaked him. Wow! That was powerful liquor. Must be what the Yankees called applejack, not cider at all. Hard cider frozen, drained off and then distilled.

Better fight shy of any more else he'd be raising a ruckus worse than night before last. He flushed from the neckband of his dull red shirt clear to his high and prominent cheek bones. It was a damned rare day anybody could knock Sam Higsby off his pins, and before a bunch of blue-nosed, penny-pinching New Englanders, too. That had been the worst of it.

If he ever came across the feller who'd hit him, they would have it out for keeps. If the feller had his share of guts, they'd fight an Injun duel. They'd each take the corner of a neckerchief 'twixt their teeth, back off as far as the cloth would allow, then lash out with hunting knives 'til one or the other let go.

Anderson was getting fuddled. He kept swilling at the applejack jug though his wife screamed abuse. Shrill as any squaw, she exasperatedly boxed Aggie's ears for nothing. When her sister slunk aside, snuffling, Betty giggled, held Higsby's bright black eye.

The merchant, his sweaty face scarlet in the firelight, still wanted to argue about privateers. "Say, Mounseer, what makes you so sure a big private-armed vessel couldn't whip a man-o'-war?"

The Frenchman set the snuff to his slightly humped nose and inhaled gratefully.

"Long ago the ancient Romans learned that only a navy can defeat a navy," M. Pliarne replied with so deferential an air that he might have been addressing an ambassador.

"To hell with a navy!" the merchant rumbled. "People of Massachusetts don't want one."

"And why?" The Frenchman flicked snuff grains from his jabot and bent forward, patently interested.

"Look wha' happened—Cromwell's Revolution."

"One is deplorably uninformed, Monsieur."

"Well, our Army declared for Cromwell and the common people; but the goddam Navy stuck by ol' King Charles. That's why it's called the *Royal* Navy—even if Army's called British Army."

The man in gray hiccoughed, scowled in an attempt to recover dignity. "Suppose we don't always hold with what the Congress does? We don't want a lot of gold-laced whoresons of navy officers threatening us plain folks. Nossir!"

"Hear! Hear!" Anderson rumbled. "Folk round here is dead set agin a navy. Too dear."

Ma Anderson grabbed the dog by the ear, hauled him yelping to the door and shoved him out into the star-lit cold. Whew! The draught that came beating in was like the blade of a sword laid across one's face.

"A navy is most assuredly costly," the Frenchman admitted. "Yet consider the costly destruction of your seaport towns."

Higsby reluctantly took his eyes off Betty. Screeching catamounts, she was scouring a pot, and a fine pair of rising beauties were jiggling tantalizingly to the circular movements of her scraper.

"Reckon yer mistaken, Mounseer," said he. "The Britishers won't burn helpless towns. That's the Injun way o' fightin'."

A twinkle shone in M. Pliarne's pale gray eyes. "Ah? It appears that Monsieur has not yet learned what has occurred at Bristol in the colony of Rhode Island? Nor of what has more recently been done at Falmouth in the Maine District? The one port was bombarded; the other burned to the ground—quite destructed. My point, if you will permit, is that a single American man-of-war might well have driven off the English and so have preserved both towns."

Then the merchant got up mumbling, "Privateers is good enough for us. When a war's done, a privateersman can go back to peaceful tradin'. Don't have to be fed by us taxpayers 'til some more trouble starts. Well—good night, all—"

"You are right, it grows late—" M. Pliarne collected his ivory-handled fork and spoon and tucked them in a wooden case. Next he collected his wine bottle and glass. He bowed formally to Mrs. Anderson who only sniffed, "Breakfast's at six sharp. I don't wait on nobody."

"I wish my bed warmed." For the first time the Frenchman spoke sharply.

"Just you keep your wig on. I can't do everything at once." Snuffling dismally, Mrs. Anderson gathered her shawl, filled a copper warming pan with coals and vanished in M. Pliarne's wake.

Yawning cavernously, Anderson stumbled over to the front door and when he lingered just outside, Betty giggled.

"He makes Ma awful sore when he does that." Agatha grinned and, in bending over the slowly seething pot, showed quite a lot of that lawn petticoat. It must be a really fine one, the firelight beat through it so effectively. A shame her face was so cruelly pitted and scarred.

Still buttoning greasy leather breeches, Anderson reappeared and shuffled off. They heard him tripping over the furniture upstairs and cursing the feeble light of his tallow dip.

Once Higsby and the two girls were left in the kitchen, the sisters suddenly acted shy, but kept stealing glances at that virile figure standing so rangy, so easy-like, before the chimney place.

Betty rolled her eyes at the sleek blackness of the hair tumbling about the fringed cape of his sumac-colored shirt. Mercy, it shone like a crow's wing. There was a sort of freshness about this gaunt stranger and he smelt of wood smoke rather than of food fumes. That word "Liberty" across the chest of his outer shirt was impressive, even if the white paint was faded and the lettering all cater-wampus. Betty wondered what had caused those gaps in the long fringes down his legs. The buckskin had had hard use; thorn scratches, snags and patches showed and the skin was glazed and greasy at elbow and knee.

Mrs. Anderson came thumping downstairs, a pellucid drop trembling on the end of her sharp red nose.

"Waal, young man, and where you figger to sleep?"

"Why, Ma'am, since you ain't said nothin', I don't rightly know."

The old woman blinked suspiciously in the candle's smoky red light. "You sure you've plenty of money?"

"Yes, Ma'am."

"Hard money?"

Higsby laughed easily, slapped his pocket as if it contained more than a couple of walnuts and a curb chain.

"Sho'. Plenty an' to spare."

"You got—" Mrs. Anderson hesitated, licked her lips—"six shilling?"

Higsby got cooney. "Sho', Ma'am, but not fer a single night's lodgin'."

She looked relieved. "Three, then?"

"Sho' 'nuff."

"I don't know wheres I could bed you unless I let you bundle with one of the girls."

The sharp way she looked at him set Higsby to thinking. "That would be mighty handsome of you, Ma'am."

"Well, which one you want to bundle with? Aggie or Betty?"

Immediately Higsby drawled, "Why it don't greatly matter, Ma'am, does it? But since you ask, I reckon Miss Aggie an' I might get along."

He could catch the amazed click of Betty's jaw. She turned scarlet. The idee! Passing her up for poor plain Aggie. Why, everyone held Betty Anderson one of the prettiest girls in Suffolk County. Pity's sake, this ranger fellow must be clean out of his senses.

Mrs. Anderson was so surprised she came dangerously near smiling as she beckoned Higsby towards the staircase.

"Guess you mean all right, young feller. Betty, you go get the trundle out from under our bed. You can bed with Pa and keep my side o' the bed warm."

Still red with anger, Betty tossed her head, lit a Phoebe lamp with a splinter from the fire, then with a disdainful flounce of her cotton petticoats, disappeared up the hollowly-resounding stairs.

10

THE BUNDLING BOARD

SAMUEL HIGSBY and Aggie waited until he had finished his applejack. Aggie kept smiling, pleased as a cat in a creamery.

"Will you tend the fire, Mr. Higsby? I—I guess I'm pretty tired."

"Sho' will."

When she figured the rifleman was busy banking the kitchen fire, Aggie swiftly, silently, snatched up a noggin the merchant had left half full, and drained it. The applejack, she hoped, would send the blood pouring into her cheeks; she would look a little less plain.

She wished she hadn't skinned her hair back so tight. Anyhow, her figure was trimmer than Betty's. She had longer legs, narrower hips, and full, firm breasts. If only those cursed pits weren't in her cheeks.

She still couldn't credit that this big, strange-looking brown-faced fellow had preferred her over Betty. Why had he? She really didn't care why, though; she felt all sort of warm and happy. Only beaux she had ever had were Betty's cast-offs. La! Betty's expression had been something to frame.

"You plan to bide long 'round here, Mister?" she inquired softly.

"No, Ma'am. Reckon I'm moseyin' down the coast."

"Why don't you stay? Pa needs a man. Gordon, my brother, he adopted the Army last summer. A fortnight ago our bound boy run off. Pa was awful mad."

Flushing, she indicated the stairs. "I guess Ma will be ready by now."

"You go ahead," Higsby told her. "I'll be up in two shakes of a buck's tail." He reckoned it would be wiser to go outside now and 'tend to his business. In the morning it would be colder than Canada with the lid nailed down.

When he reached a small room built right under the eaves, Aggie was already between the covers. According to custom, she had, with the exception of her shoes, kept on all her clothes. Mrs. Anderson was just finishing stitching the out edges of the blankets.

"What's that thing, Ma'am? A deadfall?"

Higsby grinned at a narrow hickory plank fixed edgewise the length of the bed. One end fitted into a groove nailed like an inverted U onto the headboard of the bed. A staple and a hasp at the other end made it possible for Mrs. Anderson to secure the barrier to the footboard, thus dividing the bed into uncompromisingly separate units.

"For all you chose Aggie, I don't trust any man further'n I can throw a bull by the tail," Mrs. Anderson snuffled. "You get under the covers now, young man."

When he had done so, she stooped over the fire and began heating a stick of red sealing wax.

"Some women would be fools enough just to stitch a center seam," she remarked. "I ain't."

"Now, Ma," Aggie whined. "You ain't no call to talk like that."

"Hush your stupid mouth. I ain't forgot the way you carried on with Bob Burdsall's hired hand. Nor the whacking your backside got either, I guess."

Witch-like in the firelight, she appeared over the footboard. "I notice you hold yourself to be a pretty smart young man. If you can get this board up without my being able to know it, you ain't wrong!"

Slowly, because her fingers were cold, Mrs. Anderson passed a red and white thread through the hasp and secured its end to the footboard with sealing wax. From her petticoat pocket she fished a coin, spat on it, then used it as a seal. She held it up.

"That's a pine tree shilling and there ain't three more this side o' Boston. If I find yonder seal so much as cracked in the morning, Mr. Anderson will surely beat the lights out o' you afore we turn you over to the law. Whoring," she glanced first at Aggie, then at Higsby, "ain't laughed at in these parts."

Without a word of good night, she stamped off down the stairs taking the candle with her.

Agatha had her eyes tight shut, Higsby noticed it when the fire flared. Goddam! If that old woman wasn't cute as a vixen with a den full of cubs. She sho' hadn't left much room for six feet of bone and muscle between the board and the stitched-down covers. Even to turn over would be difficult.

Because the fire wasn't much more than an excuse, it was getting cold as sin in the bedroom. He reckoned water in the wooden bucket would be frozen solid before morning. Why hadn't he drunk more of that applejack?

Who would ever have guessed the girl would go to bed with all her clothes on? That was one thing he hadn't figured on. She might at least have shed a couple of petticoats. That fine lawn one for instance. Hell's bells an' panther tracks! This wasn't the way he'd reckoned things would go at all, at all.

Diminishing firelight beat against the rafters, revealed some gear hung to them. He recognized a horse-poke, a cheese press folla, a withered old bridle and some ears of feed corn. There were lots of mud wasp nests and pale places where earlier nests had been broken off.

By turning his head a little, he could glimpse Aggie's profile. Why, she'd a pert, well-shaped nose, a prettily curved chin, and her teeth weren't bad. Her eyes opened suddenly and she whispered, "You makin' out all right, Mister Higsby?"

"Can't say 'yep' or 'nope' to that, Ma'am. Mighty cold, ain't it?"

"Yes, terrible. Been cold all week. Gets so I hate getting up and I hate going to bed. The bed's so awful cold and Ma won't grant me a warming pan. I'm—" she heaved a slow sigh, and a gray plume of breath vapor went swirling up. "I—I'm still kind of cold."

For a while they lay so silent that he could hear small embers snapping in the fireplace. He could hear Aggie's breathing, too, sort of irregular. Who-o-o! This chill was striking through to his leggings.

She pulled a hand out from beneath the cover, laid it on the board and smiled. "I'm cold, still." Her eyes half closed; she thought, "By Joe, he is something to look at; so full of life and cussedness. Can't be over twenty-seven, either. Bet his body's hard as a board."

She guessed Mr. Higsby was very different from the Burdsall's hired hand. That one had acted scared and so sheepish she had wanted to slap him. Different, too, from Tom, the road master, who had reeked of horses and stale sweat.

Imagine this handsome stranger having preferred her over Betty! Why was he so quiet? Right now he was staring hard at the ceiling as if he was doing some tall thinking. Why was he so slow? A local boy would have been at her bodice laces by now.

All at once he gave a little sigh and took her hand. She wished it wasn't so hard and chapped.

Maybe a good way to get him interested would be to ask what Indian women were like.

"Most of 'em ain't much," he explained in his deep, leisurely accents. "Their skin's tough an' leather-like—what with the b'ar's grease an' other stuff they put on their hair, they stink somethin' fierce. Once in the Creek nation I bought me a winter wife, an' she wasn't bad. Toyota was plump, an' paler than most."

"Why, Mister Higsby! You *bought* her."

"Sho'. Cost me a cross fox an' ten prime beaver. I built us a cabin an' she kept house for me a hull winter. We had so much fun I spent too little time trappin'. Lost money that season. Yep, Toyota was—"

"Never mind about her." By now Aggie knew she'd made a mistake. "You—do you like me?"

Higsby sighed again. Hell's bells, was there no other way? "Sho' do, Miss Aggie. Wish this board wasn't here."

"So do I," Aggie whispered. "Guess we'd both be more comfortable if only that old board wasn't there."

"I wisht there was some way to out-smart that there sealing wax. Too bad. Reckon you don't get much fun."

Aggie said breathlessly, "Not a lot, but more'n you might think." Her head strained over the board towards him. "Mr. Higsby?"

He got a lot of cold air down his back before he was able to kiss her. To his surprise, her teeth closed on his lower lip and, gently but firmly, held him. The kiss lasted; became one he wasn't going to forget in a coon's age. Goddam! Who'd have suspected hot blood so far north?

They had to settle back. The air was too insufferably icy.

All at once Aggie began to snicker softly. "La, Mr. Higsby, ain't you the biggest stupid?"

"Reckon so—" he smiled in the dark. All right to let her think so; just like in Injun trading.

"I know a way; the clerk of the Court up to Dedham showed me—"

"I'll bet—"

"No, it's about the sealing wax. You got your knife along?"

"Yep. Why?"

"Then you kin get the seal off easy. Go get it."

Out of bed he felt like he'd fallen through the ice on the Allegheny again, but he got his knife.

"Go on, heat the blade in the embers," Aggie's voice directed.

"Spoil its temper," he objected.

"You only have to warm it." Her voice was muffled because she'd ducked under the blankets. "Just push the hot edge of the knife gently under that seal. It should come off easy—but for God's sake be careful. Ma will skin me alive if it's disturbed."

Guiding his knife's point with his left thumb, Higsby urged it under the seal. Sure enough, the wax came away with ridiculous ease, hung dangling at the thread's end.

His feet were growing numb by the time he had slipped the seal through the hasp and had gingerly leaned the board against the wall. To keep the tiny fire going, he threw a couple of sticks on. Later, he reckoned, he would need the flames again.

Aggie snuggled up to him like a kitten. "More comfortable with that old board gone, ain't it?"

"A heap sight." He drew a deep breath, prepared to make the big gamble. "But it'd be a sight pleasanter if you'd shed just a couple o' them petticuts. It's like bein' in bed with a draper's store."

Without a word Aggie wriggled out of bed and untied her blue and white striped outer petticoat and the lawn one, which left her one and her shift.

God, but she was a fine armful, and her breath was sweet. On the march up from Pennsylvania, he'd had fun and to spare, but nothing like this.

Aggie kept calling him "darling," not "honey" like the gals further south. It wasn't long before he learned that Aggie Anderson could teach those other gals quite a few tricks.

When Sam Higsby waked himself, it was colder than ever. Off in the woods he could hear branches snapping like pistol shots. Far away a fox was barking. By stopping his breath and lying right still, Higsby could hear variously pitched snores from other parts of the house. Out in the barn a restless horse was stirring in its stall.

Aggie lay fast asleep, her face pressed against his shoulder. Instinctively he knew it must be going on five. Damn. Time to get moving. It was so fine and warm here in bed. He loathed the thought of going. Very gingerly he removed his hand from her breast; but when he edged away she did not even stir. Only wrinkled her nose and made a little noise deep in her throat.

The fire had nearly died, so, shivering, he fed pine splinters to the few remaining embers. The resultant flame was like a single hot spike driven into the iciness of the room, but it served to re-heat his knife blade. When he reaffixed the seal, he inspected his work by the light of a pine splinter. It was a pretty job.

While he warmed his moccasins and knee-length hunting shirt, Aggie snored softly—like the spindle of a hard-driven spinning wheel. It was half past four, he reckoned, when he went over to the far side of the bed and fumbled until he came across the petticoats. He had it. It hadn't been an easy prize, but he had it.

It was a real treat to feel such fine lawn between his fingers. That petticut should make the jim-dandiest rifle patches. A lawn patch burnt off clean, didn't leave behind smoldering shreds that would ignite a charge poured too hurriedly down one's rifle barrel.

Quiet as an owl ranging a forest, Higsby descended to the kitchen. There he paused long enough to tuck some bread and the heel of a ham into his shirt front. As an afterthought he stuffed a couple of cold sweet potatoes into his mouth.

It would have been easy to skin out leaving the Andersons to whistle—he'd intended to do that all along—but Aggie had been so friendly, he just couldn't. Pulling out his scalps he selected one. It wasn't prime, but still it was a genuine scalp. Using a piece of charcoal, he wrote painfully on the hurdle table:

Fur room & bord. This hair Wth. 20 dolars anywears in Pa.

The stars were casting a blanket of jewels over long reaches of snow when, after slinging the two long rifles over his shoulder, Higsby's snowshoes raised little powdery spurts of snow. Settling his chin into the stained old muffler, he struck off with a long, bent-kneed stride which carried him along at a good four miles to the hour.

Brr! He hoped it wasn't going to be a long way to the seacoast. Curiously enough, what that Mounseer had said stuck in his mind. For all he was an ignorant foreigner, he'd sounded as if he knew what he was talking about.

II

THE ROAD TO TIVERTON

EVEN if the Fall River was gray and all clabbered with ice, ex-Sergeant Timothy Bennett found it gratifying to be back in Rhode Island. The four days he'd spent in traveling down from Roxbury had been tiring, but tonight, if nothing happened, he would sleep in his own room.

He experienced a sudden craving for the deep peace of Pa's white clapboard farm house on Conanicut Island.

Peaceful Haven was well named. Of course, Asa Bennett could have afforded a handsome brick or stone house in the English style just as well as Mr. John Bannister on Pelham Street, or Captain Maudsley on Spring Street. The Society of Friends, however, were dead-set against ostentation or show of any sort, so he had built a plain, square house. Its only distinction were pairs of well-proportioned Doric pillars rising to either side of the entrance.

Three miles an hour was the best Tim had been able to average. Few roadmasters had got out snow plows. This was probably because Commissioners from the armies surrounding Boston had bought up all the sound ox teams they could locate and not many spans were left in private hands. The War had upset everything.

Barring a short lift given him by a passing mail sledge, Tim had legged it every inch of the way and he felt proud of not having developed a single blister. Each night he would alternate his two pair of socks and rub their interiors with soap or candle grease.

Since morning, the Boston road had become more traveled. Every so often he met a freighter's train jingling along. The big horses wore bright blue or red collars brave with bearskin housings and scarlet fringes. Ever since boyhood, Tim had admired them. Sometimes a farmer's sledge, drawn by four steaming horses, would come straining over a hilltop into sight. Oxen were used to the heft of the freighting, though. He guessed no stage coaches would start running until the township roadmasters routed out enough men and boys and oxen to dig out the worst drifts.

Presently the road crawled down into a small valley lying between two bare and rolling hills. A Y-shaped intersection lay ahead. Following the other arm was another lone traveler. Eager for companionship, Tim lengthened his stride and reached the fork a moment before the other.

Not wishing to seem over-forward in striking up an acquaintance, he stared hard at some irregularly-lettered finger signs. One of them, streaked with droppings of long departed summer birds, read: "To New Port 8½ Miles." Another, "To Fall River, 10 Miles." The largest and newest sign stated that Tiverton lay but two miles ahead.

"Howdy, friend," the other traveler hailed cheerfully enough. "Cold enough fer you?"

When Tim looked up, his breath stopped short in his throat. Crimanently! Swinging toward him was the very rifleman he had dotted on the chin back in Roxbury! Or was he mistaken? There was a general resemblance among many of the insubordinate, lanky, long-legged rascals who followed Morgan and Thompson.

When the other drew nearer, his last doubt faded. There was the word "Liberty" scrawled across his hunting shirt; and, sure enough, the rifleman still bore traces of a black eye. Tim gathered himself. He wasn't afraid to fight, even if the other had been drunk the last time they'd met. The Pennsylvanian hadn't been an unsteady drunk —wide-open and easy to hit—but wild, crazy-fighting, like a wolverine.

"Hello," he greeted in that flat voice a schoolboy uses when he decides to stand up to the class bully.

The man in buckskins looked at him hard, suddenly diverted his gaze towards the distant river, then looked at him again.

Drawled he, "Back a piece folks said there's a town called Nooport somewheres along this road. That correct?" The buck's tail on his cap stirred to a damp wind beating in from the ocean.

Wondering why the ranger should be carrying two rifles and so little traveling gear, Tim relaxed. Also why was he traveling *away* from the siege?

"Yes, that's true."

"Is it likely a feller kin take ship there an' get back to God's country?"

"You're in God's country right here," Tim smiled. "We've the best land in America in Rhode Island."

The other's wind-reddened face remained so devoid of expression,

Tim couldn't guess whether he'd been recognized or not. "Not fer huntin'. What about ships?"

"Depends on how the British are running their blockade. There used to be a-plenty clearing for New York, Philadelphia, and Charleston. I take it you are headed that way?" Tim added casually, and his wide-set gray eyes swung to meet the stranger's narrow black ones.

The rifleman hesitated, looked hard, narrowing his lids. The moment seemed eternal, then he said slowly, "Yep. I aim fer Pennsylvany, but a vessel fer Virginny or Maryland would do."

Suddenly he extended his hand. "My name's Higsby, Sam Higsby. How's fer keepin' together a piece?"

"Glad to." Tim gave Higsby his name. Then the other had been too drunk to recognize him. Or was he wrong? The rifleman's eye was lingering suspiciously long on the worsted epaulet which remained stitched to his right shoulder.

"You been up to Boston?"

Tim nodded. "My 'listment ran out." And it had. There was no doubt of it.

"So did mine." Higsby grinned like a winter wolf, wiped a drop from his nose on his cuff. "By my ratin', that was the hell of a poor war. Where's the profit just settin' 'round freezin' in ditches, killin' nobody? Why, you ain't allowed to take a skelp. By God, up there a feller has to get leave to visit the backhouse!"

Tim resettled his brown overcoat and shifted the shoulder strap of an all but empty haversack. "This isn't buttering any parsnips, as we say 'round here," Tim suggested. "Let's make tracks."

Higsby nodded. "Goin' far?"

"To Newport—it's still a good piece ahead."

Higsby was puzzled by this square-built, husky young feller. Seemed familiar somehow. Why? That was another trouble with General Washington's army. It was a heap too big. Every time a feller turned 'round there was a new face at his elbow. It wasn't a bit like the comfortable little armies of two or three hundred men that had fought along the frontier since time out of mind. You got so's you knew most everyone by sight, at least.

"Hungry?" he asked.

"I think I could eat an ox—horn, hide, and tallow. Haven't a farthing—" Tim explained.

"Then we will fill our bellies drum-tight in the next village," the rifleman promised.

"That's elegant. When we reach Newport I'll pay you back. Pa's a merchant near there." Tim remained Quaker enough not to describe Asa Bennett as "one of the biggest merchants." Boasting and bragging still ran against his grain, and it was surprising how often he almost reverted to the "simple language."

"You were mighty lucky to get paid off. Lots of men weren't."

"Shucks, friend, I ain't got a penny."

A flush mounted Tim's broad cheeks. He hated to be made a fool of like this. "Then how in blazes are we going to eat?"

Higsby's flat features remained impassive. "We'll eat a-plenty *if* you've got enough guts."

"Your scheme works?"

"All the way from Eaton's Station to Boston. You'll see."

On the outskirts of Tiverton, Higsby looked Tim bang in the eye. "Friend, I figger I kin trust you with my spare rifle. Take care of her 'cause she was built by Adam Foulke of Allentown. Next to Bella, my Leman-made, I reckon she's the shootin'est weepon you will find this side of Pennsylvany."

A small but persistent doubt nagged at Tim's peace of mind. For the life of him he couldn't decide whether the ranger had recognized him. The boys in the regiment allowed that a frontiersman didn't forgive an injury any quicker than an Indian.

Tiverton's rutted and muddy main street was busy, filled with a noonday crowd. From the Bower Anchor's chimney poured greasy billows of smoke; the delectable odor of a stewing fowl perfumed the air. Outside the inn waited half a dozen ox spans; standing close by, a post rider's nag gnawed at a hitching post while his master tried to collect fees from the inn-keeper.

Tim wondered why they didn't find a better system. If people didn't happen to come looking for mail, letters sometimes lay in a basket on the bar for days at a time. It wasn't up to the post deputy —otherwise the tavern owner—to see whether the mail reached its ultimate destination or not. Why should he? Didn't he draw pay by the number of letters arriving? Most of the post riders were crooked, Tim had heard. They were prone to carry letters privately, undercutting the Government rate. They had to be pretty 'cute about it so they concealed illegal letters in packages made up of straw, leaves, or chips.

"Well," Higsby grunted, "here goes for a mess of vittles." Drawing out his war hatchet he tilted back his head and sent winging down the street that same eerie, terrifying screech Tim had heard in Roxbury. People froze in their tracks. Some horses shied, others tried to run away.

"E-e-e-e! Yah-yah! O-o-n-a-h! Oo-nah!" Twice more Higsby raised his scalp yell, then commenced a furious whirling dance which gradually brought him to the main crossroads in the village. The ranger threatened the sky with his war hatchet, whirled, and bent over; then, fringes fluttering, brandished his long rifle at arm's length. All the while he screeched an unintelligible chant. Tim saw muscles along the ranger's throat standing out rigid.

Within twenty seconds most of the windows fronting the street were banging back, became crowded. From the foot paths, villagers gazed open-mouthed on Higsby's long black hair flying beneath the buck's tail, at the thrums whirling madly across his chest, at the gleam of brass on the long rifle's now well-filled patch pocket.

Children squalled, scattered in terror when, as a grand finale, the rifleman raised a terrific yell and flung his war hatchet across the street. Spinning, it passed between a couple of townsmen and lodged quivering in the Bower Anchor's door frame.

When a pair of serving wenches who had run out to see what was amiss, uttered squeals and ducked back inside, Higsby burst into panting shouts of laughter.

"Heyo, friends! Come one, come all, an' I'll l'arn ye how us timber-beasts shoots along the Clinch River. Yonder, it's a mighty pore day a man don't get to cure a half dozen fresh skelps." He beat himself on the chest, dropped into the Indian mode of brag.

"Brothers attend! Brothers attend! I kin shoot the eye out'n a gnat, the leg off'n a louse, the head off'n a pin! Brothers attend! In my lodge hang twenty-six skelps—all warrior hair.

"When I comes a-r'arin' down the trail, great sachems trot out wampum, their nixiest squaws, an' their sweetest terbaccer! Brothers attend! Last year, I whipped a big brown b'ar with my bare hands."

Higsby paused, panting a little, looked about, then beckoned a bulky man who, in a leather apron, stood scowling before a smithy door.

"Come on out, friend," he invited. "I don't aim to eat you. If you kin shoot, trot your gun out."

Bare-headed, the smith stepped out. "I ain't afeared of a screechin', braggin' furriner. Tall talk don't rate tuppence in Tiverton."

Higsby's dark features broke into a smile as, bunching his shoulder muscles, he wrenched free his hatchet. "You're right there, friend. Braggin' never did lift the hair off even a hen cottontail."

A woman called to the blacksmith, "You teach him how to shoot, not talk, Abner."

"Abner pretty good?" Higsby inquired amiably.

The post rider, mail bags slung over shoulder, stepped forward. "Abner Tilt ain't only champeen over the milishy of this county, but he's the dandiest shot *I* ever see on any route I ever rid."

"Well, then, maybe our friend Tilt ain't opposed to fixin' up a friendly shootin'?"

The blacksmith began to untie a scorched leather apron. "What'll we shoot for?" Red hair bright in the sun, Abner Tilt came out of his shop lugging a trim French musket. Tim judged its barrel length as five foot six.

By twos and threes patrons of the inn appeared, pulling on various garments as they chewed last bites of their food. Because of the long rifle he carried, people also began eyeing Tim with curiosity. More inhabitants gathered, including a lot of women, girls and old people.

Small boys were racing about shouting,

"Mr. Tilt is goin' to fight a Injun! Run like ever'thin' an' tell ever'body."

Tim felt absurd and ill at ease amid all this noisy nonsense, but he did like the feel of that long rifle. The Foulke was so light and its bore was so small it seemed more like a toy than a deadly weapon. Why, it couldn't possibly fire a ball weighing over an ounce.

The weapon certainly had been finished with a wonderful attention to detail. Even the least important metal parts had been built with the precision of watch parts: butt plate, lock, trigger guard, muzzle band, tumbler hooks—all were of brass. The stock and barrel guard were of bird's-eye maple and felt like satin under his fingers.

In the center of a straggling, ever-augmenting procession and convoyed by excited curs the two marksmen entered a side street, to the discomfiture of a flock of geese which were happily splashing about a thawing mud hole. Pretty soon the contestants reached a stump lot and everybody paused, stood about expectantly.

"What will we shoot for?" The blacksmith protruded a jaw sandyred with stubble. "No point wasting expensive powder and lead just for the fun of it."

"I reckon no Yankee would think so," Higsby observed, pushing the hair back over his ears. "All right, friend, I'll risk this here rifle agin a square meal for my friend an' me—an' lief to pass a hat— that I hit *every* mark you put up, an' that you don't hit *any* of the marks I put up. How's that?"

"Fair enough!" called a bookish individual wearing a clerk's wig.

The crowd gathered back of a line drawn by the post rider. It was lucky the day was warm. Most of them had been too interested to go home and put on top clothes. Right at Higsby's elbow stood a baker, floured up to his elbows. A shoemaker was still carrying his broad-headed hammer. There were plenty of girls, too. Something about Higsby attracted them as honey drew flies.

"You set your mark first, Mr. Tilt," the Pennsylvanian invited, and without a word the blacksmith measured fifty paces over the snow. Then, to a murmur of astonishment, stepped off ten yards more.

Tim blinked. Sixty yards? That was extra long range for accurate shooting. Most of the men in his company wouldn't have dared try to hit anything over forty.

From a sheaf of shingles the post rider had brought along, Tilt selected a fair white piece and on it drew a charcoal circle. To the rangy figure waiting between a pair of stumps which marked the firing line, he called, "Go ahead, Mister, just you try an' hit *that!*"

Higsby looked uncomfortable. "You don't expect me to hit that?"

"You'd better. You talked mighty big."

From the way the Tiverton man spoke, Tim guessed he was eager to win the ranger's rifle.

"I ain't used to shootin' at such a mark," mournfully protested the rifleman.

"That's my mark. Shoot at it or surrender that gun."

Higsby lifted his weapon's frizzen, glanced into the pan, then snapped it shut. Curiosity silenced the onlookers as the Pennsylvanian cocked; the Leman's mechanism gave off a soft *click! cluck!* Higsby was still raising the long rifle when it went off.

"Shucks!" he rasped. "Damn' thing went off 'fore I was set."

The crowd jeered. "No excuses! You can't credit a Southron. You missed!"

"Shouldn't marvel," mourned Higsby, slowly withdrawing his ramrod from its channel. "I wasn't rightly ready. But since I stand to lose my rifle, maybe one of you boys had better run out an' take a look. You might just find a worm hole 'round six o'clock."

An apprentice raced away, stooped and yelled something before he bounded back. "Talk about bull luck!" he yelled, waving the shingle.

"He missed?" Tilt asked tensely.

"Naw. The dad-blamed furriner has nicked the bottom of the bull."

Higsby, reaching into his kit bag, drew forth a circular patch of fine lawn. He grinned at Tim. "Here's one gal's petticut that's sho' seein' action again."

The Tiverton man grunted, then, stepping to the line, leveled his musket and sighted with care; his thickset figure braced itself against the expected kick. The blacksmith's red head lowered over the musket stock. *Bom-m-m!* A swirl of dense, dark-gray smoke momentarily obscured the marksman. A breathless yell went up. Split cleanly into two parts, the shingle was lying on the snow.

"How's that, Mister?" The blacksmith's grin revealed teeth gapped by decay. When the mark was held together everyone could see a big, black-rimmed hole at the top of the bull's-eye and a smaller aperture piercing its lower edge.

"That's right pretty shootin'," Higsby admitted with genuine admiration. "My turn to rig a target, ain't it?"

"Yep," the smith said, pouring powder down the still smoking muzzle of his piece.

Having seated a bullet with slow, steady pressure on his horn-tipped ramrod, the Pennsylvanian selected a fresh shingle, strode out among the stumps. At the same range as before, he planted the slab of pine with its edge towards the shooting line.

"Hey!" Tilt objected, "you've got that mark set wrong."

"Nope, I ain't," Higsby contradicted solemnly. "Sho'ly you don't mind riskin' a shot at it?"

"You're addled. Nobody can hit a sliver at sixty paces."

Unconcernedly Higsby went over and stood by Tim, adjusting the set-screw securing his flint. "Maybe not."

A low rumble of astonishment arose; small boys hugged themselves in a delirium of excitement; the women talked sixty to the minute. Most of them had wrapped their arms in their aprons. One or two dispatched unwilling children to fetch shawls.

"Go ahead an' shoot, Mr. Yankee," Higsby invited. "Didn't I fire at your mark?"

The Tiverton man started to raise his musket, but put his weapon down again. Said he angrily, "You can't make a fool out of me! Set up a mark a body can sight on."

"I have, Mister."

Higsby's rifle barrel rose, sank smoothly, steadily, to the horizontal; because his bucktail began whipping about his neck, he relaxed, threw fur cap onto the ground.

Tim heard the ranger's breath draw in. When he had half exhaled, Higsby's fore-finger slipped under the triggered guard and its tip just came to rest on the wood on the far side. Gradually, the rifleman's whole hand tightened until the hammer fell and a spit of smoke spurted vertically from the lock. A staccato report caromed against a grove of trees on a distant hillside, came rattling back.

"The Lord preserve us!" Amid incredulous shouts, the apprentice ran out, brought back two pieces of wood. Neatly as a knife, Higsby's ball had cut the slab of pine across.

The Pennsylvanian never batted an eye, but Tim caught a strange tight expression at his mouth corners.

"Maybe yer eyesight ain't good, friend. We won't count that one there. Let's try another kind o' mark. Your turn."

The Tiverton man, deadly serious now, nodded grimly.

"Willie, trot down by the crick and cut me a willer branch thick as yer thumb."

A square of paper three inches on a side was set into a split in the willow. In turn the twig was driven into the snow, offering a white mark against a white field.

Tilt deserved his reputation, Tim decided. The blacksmith's ball carried away one-half of the patch; but before the apprentice could replace the square, Higsby's ball shot away the remaining section.

Unconcernedly, the ranger blew grains of expended powder from the Leman's pan, then squinted into the channel leading to its chamber. Using a horn measuring cup which fitted over one end of his powder horn, Higsby poured in a fresh charge. Lightly he passed a patch over the deer's grease contained in the "patch pocket" in a hinged brass compartment let into the stock.

Next he placed the greased lawn over the muzzle, spat out a ball from a supply he held in his cheek, and drove it home with his hickory rod.

"Your turn," the musket man invited seriously.

Higsby sketched a four inch circle on a shingle. Features barren of expression, he beckoned his opponent. "Just you hold this 'twixt yer knees while I shoot at it."

"Eh?"

"I said, just you hold this shingle 'twixt yer knees while I take a shot at it. If I don't put my ball plumb in the center o' that circle, I'll hold it fer you an' that goddam cattle gun."

Tilt flung aside the shingle. "Not me. It's too risky."

"Scared, eh?"

"I may be crazy, but I ain't no fool."

Higsby's smile was easy. "Why, there ain't a thing to be wary of. Just to prove it, my friend will hold the mark."

Suddenly, Tim saw what Higsby had been leading up to all along. Crimanently! The ranger had worked him 'way out on a limb. He could make a cripple of him and everybody would believe it was an accident!

He was mad clear through to have been out-foxed like this. At the same time, he knew he wouldn't let himself be backed down by any spindle-shanked dirty shirt from Pennsylvania. In silence, he handed the Foulke rifle to the clerk and walked over to Higsby who was waiting there, easy-like, with a meaningless smile on his lips.

Tim muttered, "I'll hold thy damned mark, but don't thee dare make a mistake, or I'll knock hell out of thee *again!*"

Higsby suppressed a start. Hell's bells and panther tracks, this was the feller—the one who'd slapped his jaws outside the Red Bull back in Roxbury! Must have been drunk as a skunk not to have recognized him. Bennett was a great fool to give himself away like this. Punch a feller in his likker, would he?

Arteries throbbing painfully, Tim watched Higsby stalk back to the shooting line. Of course, the ranger wouldn't dare kill him, yet he could plausibly enough break a leg or an arm without getting prosecuted. His heart sank when he saw how far away the rifleman looked.

To hide his dread, he tried to think on other matters. What would Desire Harmony be like—must have grown up a lot since he went away. Why all this urgency over the seventh of December?

"Get set!" Higsby warned, and Tim took up the shingle. His knees were shaking when he bent over and placed it between them. Suppose by accident or design Higsby fired just a little high? That would be bad. Lucky the nearest onlookers were a good twenty yards distant. He guessed he was growing pale.

"Oh Lord, watch over Thy servant," he breathed. "And watch hard!"

In an instant the other would shoot. Setting his teeth, Tim realized that the whole pasture was black with people. Some were standing on stumps. Beyond them, a church thrust its white-painted spire high above the comfortable, weather-beaten roofs of the village. A flock of pigeons was scurrying about the sky.

Memories of the numb impact of that bullet he had stopped at Lechmere returned in all vividness. Numbness, giving way in turn to a dull burning—to an almost unbearable, searing pain.

His mouth went dry as a bone. A split second before the rifle's report, something fetched the shingle between his knees a sharp tap. Looking down he saw in the yellow surface a small round hole with grayish edges. It had appeared a shade to the left of the bull's-eye.

Higsby came gliding forward, his eyes a brighter black than usual. Gravely he offered his hand. "Friend, I reckon we eat. You got yer share of guts."

PART II—CONANICUT ISLAND

I

HOMECOMING

A FISHERMAN, mighty glad of a sixpence, rowed them over to Conanicut Island from Coddington Point. He had to work, though, because an ebb tide kept pushing pieces of floe ice across their course.

"Yonder is Conanicut—straight ahead." Tim, seated beside Higsby in the stern, indicated a long narrow island.

The Pennsylvanian saw that it was subdivided into pastures by rough stone fences, and dominated by three softly rounded hills. Beyond low places between these rises, they glimpsed the further, or Western, passage of Narragansett Bay. Though a few clumps of fine tall trees remained, a greater part of the virgin stand had long ago been timbered away.

Hunched over, and uneasily eyeing the slate-gray current, the rifleman shielded his gun lock from flying spray and made no comment. Tim noticed he didn't talk much except for a reason—or when a likely wench hove into sight.

The nearer to home he got, the more he began wondering what he would find there. Why in blazes had *both* Pa and Mr. Percival been set on his hurrying back to Newport in such an all-fired hurry? Pretty soon he ought to have the answer. Peaceful Haven was, of course, still invisible, being concealed by the range of hillocks rising behind Taylor's Point. Over his left shoulder he could see Newport downstream, sprawling down its hillside to the harbor.

The town looked very familiar. The windmills on the bluff back of town still swung their arms: one above the burying ground; one behind Jew Street; finally, Mr. Young's fine new mill.

To think of Lucy being barely a mile distant. Lucy, sweet, sweet Lucy!

His eye, trained to look for such things, quickly picked up the glacis of a battery thrown up just beyond the upstream end of town. Fort George on Goat Island seemed to have been enlarged. In the old days the Fort had been a favorite place for picnic parties.

When one looked carefully, one saw other signs of the times. All the way from Rome's to Overing's wharf the waterfront was cram-jammed with idle shipping. Half a dozen of the ships Ike Percival used to send on the triangular run lay under bare yards at his wharf. More slavers, coasters and a whole huddle of West Indiamen lay beyond them, their topmasts sent down. All in all, the waterfront presented an unfamiliar and deeply disconcerting panorama.

Mechanically, Tim's gaze sought Redwood's wharf. When the Bennett vessels didn't go straight to Pa's big warehouse over on Conanicut, they usually tied up there. None of the vessels moored at Redwood's looked familiar.

There was some sort of flag flying from the lookout of the Court House, but what its design might mean he couldn't guess.

Today so many strange flags were flying over the United Provinces. One heard of pine trees, of anchors, of rattlesnakes and grid-irons. They inspired wit and plenty of confusion, too.

As the heavy rowboat swung further out in the stream, Higsby said wonderingly, "Now ain't that quite a town? Must be nigh as big as Williamsburg, I'd venture. What's them big buildings fer?"

"Nearest is the Redwood Library and the red brick thing is the Town Hall."

Higsby's gaze took in row on row of neat and shining shingle roofs. Here and there clumps of leafless trees spurted up between the house tops like jets of water from between the boards of a landing stage built too low to the water. A bluish-pall of kitchen smoke hung over Newport.

In the harbor, more ships swung to their moorings: pinks, snows, stumpy bluff-bowed whalers, tiny fishermen, broad-beamed coasters, and any quantity of river boats. Tim pointed them all out.

"What's them long thin sheds up under the hill—look like Iroquois long houses?"

"Ropewalks. When we get home you'll see one close to." He forgot his Quaker precepts. "Pa has one of the biggest in Rhode Island."

The fisherman, momentarily relieved by a favorable current, flicked the sweat from his face. "Should have been hereabouts last month. That goddam Captain Wallace turned ugly, brought the *Rose* frigate, a bomb brig and a couple of armed schooners upstream and bombarded the b'Jesus out o' Bristol."

"Why did he do it?"

"Dunno, lest 'twas to scare the folks up there into feeding his crews."

"Didn't they fight back?"

"Couldn't. Was only a little battery there. Both our cruisers was up the Bay to Providence."

"Cruisers?"

"Yep. Didn't ye know? We got a couple of them. They're the Rhode Island Navy: the *Washington* an' the *Katy*. Old Abe Whipple commands the *Katy*. He sailed her clean down to Bermuda last summer."

"What for?"

Expertly the fisherman fended off a jagged ice cake and kept his eyes on the stream as he said, " 'Pears someone warned Governor Cooke the British had a powder magazine there."

"Whipple got the powder?" Tim demanded.

The fisherman resumed the oars and took up his characteristically choppy stroke. "Naw, a vessel out of Philadelphy, and 'nother from one of them there Southern Colonies beat him to it. A marine commissioner from the Congress last week spread the news."

"What's a marine commissioner doing 'round here?" Tim demanded. "Can't we run as small a place as Rhode Island without advice from those perjured lawyers in Philadelphia?"

In the Army before Boston everybody, from its generals down to privates, damned Congress at every turn. It was the fashion.

"Some says one thing, some says another. Folks our way figger he's come to stop the Newporters from renewing their treaty with Bloodybones Wallace."

"Who is this Wallace?"

A hard look came over the fisherman's lumpy features as, viciously, he spat through the blackened stumps of his front teeth. "James Wallace—and I'd admire fine to spit in his eye—is captain over the *Rose* frigate and commander of the British pirates infesting these here waters.

"I'd admire a chance to get *my* change out of him. His ratted tender confiscated my pinky last September. His boat parties is always raiding for cattle and wood.

"Any minute now you'll sight the *Rose*. 'Sides her, he's got the *Swan* frigate, the *Bolton* bomb brig, the *Glasgow* armed transport, a tender, some armed schooners, and sloops. Oh, they're strong enough to blow Newport all to hell. There they are—see their tops over the Island?"

Goat Island, in falling astern, gradually unmasked the enemy ships. All of them flew the familiar White Ensign.

As Higsby stared at those British flags, the outline of his cheekbones grew gradually more pronounced; he began to grin at the oarsman and said hoarsely, "Say, friend, take us over. I reckon I could pick me plenty of Britainers off them sticks—like squirrels outer a tree—only easier."

The fisherman's crusted red eyelids flew wide open. "Mister, you must be plumb addled! Inside a hour them Britishers would bombard Newport off the charts."

Higsby's shoulders sagged under his cape fringes. "Now may God damn me if I kin make head or tail outer you Yankees. 'Round my neck of the woods when a man sets out on the warpath he goes after his enemy 'til one of 'em is cold turkey."

When a fife and drum began sounding on a brown and yellow painted man-of-war, the fisherman spat again. "In a day or so the Lobsterbacks will be coming ashore to draw their treaty rations. Shouldn't wonder but there'd be trouble this time. Folks here hev just learned about Falmouth."

"Eh?" Higsby grunted. "What's Falmouth?"

"Falmouth is a port up in the Maine district. Britisher named Henry Mowat—just tie to that name, Mister, 'cause he's broke his parole—took a man-o'-war, the *Canceaux,* into Falmouth. First he cannonaded the port, open and defenseless as it was, then landed men —just like a common pirate—and burnt the hull town flat.

" 'Twarn't nothin' to him that a hundred wimmen and children was left t' starve 'thout a roof to their heads. Ain't no back settlements up in Maine, there, you know. Back o' the seacoast, there's only wolves, woods an' Injuns. Yessir, we figger this Cap'n Mowat fer a fine humane gentleman."

Newport having always been a favored port for His Majesty's men-of-war, it seemed quite natural to Tim that a British squadron should be anchored in the harbor. But it was a shock to note gun ports triced up, cannon trained on the town. His misgivings increased. Under such conditions it wouldn't take much of a spark, Tim figured, to touch off a fight.

By God! Here was the siege of Boston all over again. The enemy within reach and nothing being done. Still, he *could* see the sense in Newport's understanding with Captain Wallace. Even a brief bombardment could erase the results of a hundred years' arduous trading, slaving and privateering.

As for Higsby, he was remembering what that yellow-faced Mounseer had said about keeping an enemy offshore. Looked like he was right about that, too.

When the boat neared Conanicut, a big flock of shelldrake rose from the beach on which they had been resting and went winging off to join a great raft of sea coots and eider ducks that were diving and raising their eerie laughter offshore.

Presently the keel grated on seaweed-covered rocks. Timothy Bennett was home again.

2

DESIRE HARMONY

SAM HIGSBY remarked suddenly, "Right old-lookin' 'round these parts. Folks must have dwelled here since the Year One."

"Well, it's near on a hundred and fifty years, anyway." Tim smiled. "Folks claim this end of Rhode Island was settled 'round 1639."

As they swung along over the muddy road, the Foulke slanted ever so comfortably over his shoulder. For one thing, the long rifle was lighter than the ten-and-a-half-pound Brown Bess he'd left in Roxbury—maybe by three pounds.

Could he borrow some money from Pa without having to explain what he wanted it for? If Pa ever caught on, the old Quaker would, of course, lend him not a penny. It made him feel like an irresponsible boy to find his thoughts running like this.

When Higsby had suggested seven pounds, Tim knew the Foulke must be worth easy twice as much. Shrewdly, he guessed the ranger was making amends for that business back in Tiverton.

"I reckon I've as many faults as there's fleas on a dog," he had said when Tim demurred at the price, "but goin' back on my pledged word—except to Injuns—ain't one of 'em."

On breasting a gentle hill they could at last get a clear view of the West Passage.

"You'll stay the night, Sam?" Tim guessed Desire Harmony would be fascinated no end. Certainly she could never have beheld anyone remotely resembling this picturesque, soft-spoken foreigner. Even as a little girl that had always cottoned to a well-built man, she had always admired a fine set of teeth. When not stained with tobacco juice, the ranger's were strong and white as if hewn out of marble. He explained their condition by saying that every day he rubbed them and their gums with a chewed twig dipped in salt, a trick he'd learned from the Creeks.

When they were about abreast of the Elley place, a tow-headed kid in a blue shawl ran out on the porch crying, "Land's sakes, there's Mr. Tim back from the war!"

A minute later a whole brood of little Elleys came tumbling out of the house like puppies out of a kennel; but when they spied Higsby's fur cap, fringes and bucktail, they stopped short and stood staring, round-eyed. A couple of leggy little girls even scurried back indoors.

"Where's Joe? Where's Ben?" Mrs. Elley came shuffling out of the house, a shawl draped over head and shoulders. "My boys all right?"

Tim tipped his faded tricorne to her. "Ma'am, last I saw them five days back, they were in fine shape."

"Where are they?"

Blood climbed into Tim's cheeks as he called back very easily, "They'll be home any day now—provided they don't reenlist."

Mrs. Elley, a plain plump woman with shrewd gray eyes blinking behind square-cut spectacles, came halfway down the walk with a half a dozen hens hopefully trailing her.

She hesitated, looked puzzled. "Ain't you back a mite soon, Timothy? We sort of figgered all you boys would come home together around the fifteenth."

"No, Ma'am," Tim said, forcing a laugh, "my enlistment was up, so I came home."

Mrs. Elley smiled, shook her head. "I declare I can't keep anything straight these days. I could have vowed Benjy wrote our regiments was to stay in Massachusetts 'til the tenth."

"The boys will be back before you know it." Tim waved genially but lengthened his stride nevertheless.

"Rich country," Higsby opined as they tramped past a plain, unpainted house and the well-filled barn behind it. A yard was crowded with fat brown and white cows. "Enough to make a Tuscarora's or a Cherokee's mouth water."

From the crest of a hillock, they could see into Fox Hill Cove. A grateful warmth flooded Tim's being at the sight of the familiar farm houses, orchards and pastures. Why he could even recognize Billy, Mark Remington's hunchbacked brother, working at his ferry landing.

He pointed out Joseph Clarke's fine house and the little sea-meadow beyond it. Further up shore, though, Gardner's tanyard seemed quite deserted.

The Widow Franklin's yellow painted house with a tall elm growing at each corner of it looked wonderfully serene and comfortable.

"That's our place." Tim tried hard to suppress his pride.

Higsby saw a big, white square house set under fine tall trees. Beyond it a barn also white with a big cupola, proudly dominating a cluster of lesser structures—henhouses, pigstys, corncribs, carriage sheds and privies.

"Say! ain't *that* sumpin'?" The ranger was definitely impressed.

"Further over are Pa's wharf and warehouse, and that's the ropewalk." He indicated a long shed which, for a hundred yards, paralleled the gray sand beach of a small cove.

"Thank God!" Tim sighed and a big load dropped from his shoulders when he saw lying to the wharf a three-masted schooner of about ninety tons' burden.

After a second look he lost some of his elation. The vessel was dismantled, forlorn looking. Though it was only mid-afternoon there was no sign of activity around the warehouse save for a negro mending lobster pots on the sunny side of the wharf. On top of the usually busy warehouse a row of gray and white harbor gulls was basking.

In keeping with Quaker tenets, the exterior of Peaceful Haven boasted no graceful pilasters, no elaborate cornices. Yet the house possessed distinction, the dignity of handsome proportions and good taste divorced from ostentation.

Ivy, brought from England by Asa Bennett's captains, had so prospered that the vines muffled the entire southern and western walls of the house. Here and there points of a low picket fence enclosing the yard showed above the snow. Occupying the center of the front lawn was a worn-out, but neatly-painted dory which, in summertime, bore an argosy of flaming nasturtiums.

By the back door a very thin old negress, Mamba, made a hatchet twinkle in the pale winter sunshine as she split kindling. About her graying head was knotted a yellow kerchief of the sort imported from Santiago in the Captaincy-General of Cuba. Preoccupied, she failed to notice the two figures descending the lane, vanished indoors leaving a flock of absurdly fat white ducks to inspect the chips she had made.

"Suppose I raise a war whoop to let the folks know you're home?" Higsby suggested amiably.

"Heavens, no! Pa's a Friend. You mustn't ever forget it, either."

Behind the white barn—the only painted one for miles—Tim made hurried explanations concerning his prospective purchase of the Foulke. "Killing and war are dead contrary to Pa's principles. I'll have to play carefully to get that money."

"That's yore funeral," the rifleman conceded slowly, "but goddam me if I kin understand folks who claim it's sinful to fight. Fightin' is a natural state. Didn't God give a b'ar claws, a wolf teeth and us guns to fight with?"

Through the open barn door, they glimpsed a shaggy plow team drowsing placidly in their stalls, but the instant their shadows fell inside, a large brown and white mongrel jumped up and bared his teeth. Another disappointment. Mamba hadn't seen him and now his dog didn't recognize him. Was *anything* as it had been?

The instant he clapped his hand against his thigh in a curiously boyish gesture and called, "Don't you know me, Snapper, old boy? Want to go after rabbits?" the dog cocked an ear and scurried forward, thumping an ecstatic tattoo on the loose straw. Next he scared the ducks into fits by barking and racing about the barn yard while Tim concealed the Foulke in the oat bin.

At length, Mamba thrust a grizzled head out of the kitchen door. "Git long wid you, you addled bone-destroyer. Whut fo' you so foolish? You got dem fowls all a-twitter. Ah sho'ly—

"Heabben's glory! Mister Tim! Mister Tim! Thank Gawd my sweet l'il boy is safe back. Praise Jesus, praise de good Jesus!"

The old negress flung both arms about Tim and kissed him.

Right queer people, these Quakers, thought Higsby. Imagine letting a nigger act so familiar!

Cuffy, fat moon of a face all soapy, came running down the steps as fast as he could waddle and pumped hands. "My, my, Mister Tim, you certain has fined out some."

Higsby saw that these darkies surely set a heap by young Bennett. Why, that old hen nigger was looking at him just the way the dog had.

"Fined up!" Mamba snorted. " 'Pears mo' lak the po' chile ain't et a real meal o' vittles since he went away."

"Any apple pie around? Been bragging to Mr. Higsby about it."

"Ah sho' has." For the first time the servants noticed that gaunt figure in buckskins. They remembered manners, jerked curtsey and bow. This done, Mamba rattled on, " 'Deed I has pie an' chitterlin's, too. All dis gen'man kin eat."

Where was Pa? In the setting room. Miss Desire was upstairs.

"Well, Mamba, you fix us a snack, we'll lean into it pretty soon. Come along, Sam."

As they circled around to the front door, he turned an anxious face. "Try and remember, won't you? No cussing, no talk about war, scalps, or killing 'less Pa asks."

"Sho', sho'," Higsby agreed easily. But what was a feller to say if he wasn't to talk about war, shooting or fights? He reckoned he had best clear out as fast as he could.

A handsomely carved fanlight lent the main entrance distinction. Tim was reaching for a knob of silvered glass when the door swung open revealing Asa Bennett.

Maybe because of the sudden glare of sunshine on the snow the old Quaker stood there uncertain, blinking hard. In a glance Tim saw that this was no longer the hale and placid old man he had left behind in May. He was terribly aged.

"Pa!" Tim's throat closed spasmodically.

"My son, my son!" For all it was contrary to Quaker teaching to betray undue emotion, the old man flung open his arms and his big, blue-veined hands quivered as they patted Tim's shoulder blades.

Asa Bennett then kissed his son on the forehead in the biblical fashion, raised faded blue eyes to the sky. "I praise the Lord, I praise the Lord my God that He hath brought safe home my son." His square, strangely unlined face quivered.

"Oh, Timothy, Timothy, how worried we have been, thy sister and I." He broke off, controlled himself with an effort. "Pray, who is this? A friend of thine?"

No sharper contrast could have been presented than the old Quaker in a long-skirted, buttonless brown coat, long vest, gray thread stockings, and the ranger in fur cap, butternut-tinted hunting shirt, fringed leggings and war-like gear.

Higsby leaned his rifle against one of the porch pillars, whipped off his cap, said shyly in his soft voice, "My name's Sam Higsby, an' I'm proud, all-fired proud, to shake hands with Tim's Pa. Him an' me are friends."

If Asa Bennett felt any misgivings over the long rifle leaning against his front porch, he concealed them. "Friend Higsby, thee is welcome to our poor home. Are thee a-hungered?"

"Thanky, suh. Reckon me an' Tim *could* pack away a meal."

Tim stood aside to let the Pennsylvanian pass by. Higsby entered, took two steps, then halted suddenly. Tim bumped into him.

A young girl was descending a flight of stairs so lightly that she seemed to float. She was dressed, Quaker fashion, in dove gray. The strings of a fresh white apron deftly emphasized the slenderness of her waist, much as starched cuffs did for her wrists. Though the dress had been cut on severely simple lines, yet the maker had endowed this semi-uniform with a subtle individuality. Primly it hinted the existence of high and full young breasts, long legs and arms.

Yet all that Higsby noticed was this girl's eyes. It seemed he had never before beheld such merry, sensitive, lovely brown eyes, nor such very long lashes. There were small splinters of golden light in them—Tim had such splinters, too, but the brother's eyes were gray and smaller.

So this was Desire Harmony. Goddam, she was pretty as a speckled pup! In a second glance he realized that her face was broad across the brows, but narrowed down towards the chin. Her nose was short and straight, and her nostrils took a little upward lift which pleased him strangely.

From beneath a small gray cap edged in white, some curls escaped. Sunlight beating in the front door made her hair shine like good, but unpolished copper.

The rifleman all at once became aware of the intensity of the look Tim's sister was fixing on him. Goddam, she was lovely! All fresh and clean and bright. Like an October hillside at sun-up.

Suddenly her lids fluttered and, running down the last few steps, she sped by him.

"Oh, Tim, Tim, praise the Lord thee has been spared!" Her surprisingly deep voice trembled. "If only I had laurels with which to deck thy brow. Oh, Tim, thee looks—looks like Achilles home from battle!"

The old Quaker coughed, interrupted mildly, "My dear, pray restrain thy language. Friend Higsby, this is my daughter, Desire Harmony."

Desire Harmony smiled, dropped a demure curtsey and turned those disturbing golden-brown eyes on the dazzled Pennsylvanian.

3

PEACEFUL HAVEN

To TIM, full of supper and sprawled in a great wing chair before the living room fire, it seemed as if his ears never could have ached from the spiteful snarling of musketry, could never have been deafened by the crash of a battery going into action. Had he ever felt his skin grow clammy at the whine of a close-passing musket ball? Surely, it could not have been he who for two mortal hours lay cursing and gasping and bleeding on a shutter? Had Tim Bennett ever bitten through a leather gag to suppress screams when a surgeon began probing at a ragged, purplish hole in his leg? Surely, any moment, Zeke must come bursting in, his grave young face all bright with winter.

Looking very like an Indian save for his too well-filled leggings, straight nose and paler complexion, Sam Higsby sat in a far corner of the room. He kept his deep-set black eyes mostly on the wavering flames, but every now and then his gaze would flicker, quick as a bee, over to Desire Harmony, then come away. All on her account, he had suffered the agony of combing his tangled blue-black hair, had scraped away a scanty beard.

The usual hour of testifying had come to an end and now, with a few passages read from the Book, the simple service would end.

Asa Bennett began, his voice falling and rising like wavelets on some quiet lake:

> —"And if I have *the gift* of prophecy and under-
> stand all mysteries, and all knowledge; and
> though I have all faith so that I could remove
> mountains, and have not charity, I am nothing.
> And though I bestow all my goods to feed the
> poor and though I give my body to be burned—"

He cast a longing look at Timothy—

> "—but have not charity, it profiteth me nothing."

Tim reached down to pat Snapper who had stretched out on the hearth beside him. The dog had been spreading his toes to the deep glow of the oak logs, but now he had begun to whimper softly because he was very hot and much too lazy to move.

Soon Mamba would shuffle in to fill a whole battery of warming pans with hot ashes. Neither she nor Cuffy were slaves. Long since the Society of Friends had proscribed that evil.

Though the logs snapped cozily, a disturbing thought crossed his mind. The boys up on Roxbury Hill couldn't be near so comfortable. They would have four more days of it since today was December sixth or, as a good Quaker would put it, the sixth day of Twelve-month. Joe Child must have been pretty surprised to find him gone.

He would have given a lot to be sure that Abner Hull had bettered his flux.

Among the sparks and swirling smoke Lucy Percival's face materialized. Lucy was near, in her father's fine red brick mansion on Bannister Street. His hands tightened slowly on the chair arms.

Oh Lucy, my own darling, how deeply I adore you. To have you I'd swim an ocean of red-hot coals. When I think of you, I feel all torn inside. Come hell or high water, we will marry Christmas week. I'm a full man now and I won't be denied any longer.

Snapper heaved himself up reluctantly and stalked out into the hall to cool off.

Across the room, Desire Harmony's knitting needles clicked primly. Bolt upright on her rush-bottomed chair she kept her eyes on a gray worsted stocking taking shape beneath her fingers.

How much she had matured in seven short months. Maybe the troubled times were responsible? All trace of a previous awkward immaturity had been lost. Suddenly he looked at her very intently. She wasn't listening to a word of Pa's reading, either, and a private little half smile curved the brightness of her mouth.

Snapper re-entered the room, went over to sniff at the rifleman who gently pulled his ears and murmured something in an Indian lingo. It concerned her, Desire thought; somehow she was dead sure of it.

He was handsome, not comparable to John of course, nobody else could be so beautiful, so wise—so—so god-like! Queer that he should be a foreigner, too. Though this dark stranger hailed from the South he wasn't a bit like the Rutledges, the Proveauxs, the Pinckneys, or the Hugers who, every spring, traveled to Newport to escape the heat and that deadly summer fever which, from May until October, ravaged the environs of Charleston.

Summer fever must be awful; 'Toinette Proveaux had said one of her brothers and a sister had been carried off, that hardly a family along the Tidewater had escaped its ravages. Curiously enough, the disease seldom troubled the slaves who had brought it over from Africa.

Sam Higsby? A lively name. For all his quiet ways and soft gentle speech she guessed he was a killer and a devil with women. He reminded her of a bobcat Zeke and Tim had brought up from a kitten—one minute it was all soft fur and winning ways, then zingo! the kitten got its claws out and became a spitting fury.

Mr. Higsby must have seen a deal of the world. When opportunity offered, she must coax him into a conversation. There was so much she wanted to learn about. Such a nuisance being all of sixteen and having Pa still treat her like a silly precocious child.

Covertly watching the play of muscles under the ranger's dull red doeskin shirt and under the stained leather of his fringed, tight fitting leggings she felt a little breathlessness. Queer, how exciting the woodsy smell of his hunting shirt was to her. He had painted "Liberty" across the leather and the world could take it or leave it. She admired him for that. He must be monstrous formidable in battle—a modern Horatius.

Desire visualized him at the door of a blockhouse, smiting down one painted brave after another. Somebody should write a play for him—Mr. Farquhar—or possibly Mr. Cibber. She would play the pioneer maiden, terrified yet dauntless, too.

Hurriedly Desire switched her thoughts. This isn't being loyal to John. Dear adorable John. Oh the gay, gentle, elegant manners of him. None of Mr. Richard Brinsley Sheridan's heroes possessed a prettier command of language.

She started, guiltily aware that Papa had closed the Book and was rising.

The old man went over to Higsby and said, "Good night, Friend Higsby. For so long as thee is so inclined, pray make thyself free of this poor house. Thee will abide a few days?"

Uneasily, Higsby ran fingers through his hair. "Well, suh, I—had figgered on moseyin' South, but maybe I'll tarry a day or so, if tomorrow you don't mind my riggin' a lean-to in a holler I seen."

"But surely, Friend, thee would be more comfortable indoors?" the old Quaker protested mildly.

Teeth briefly a-glint, Higsby shook his head. "My body sho' would be, Mr. Bennett, but I'd be oneasy in my mind. Reckon I been 'round people too much lately. By nature, I ain't a herd-bound critter.

"It will serve me fine to cut loose an' traipse around by myself. I ain't rigged a twitch-up for a rabbit in the longest time." He looked embarrassed. His long hands made small explanatory gestures. " 'Tain't that I don't admire your askin' me, suh; I do. But—well, when I get off alone for a spell I get to feel easier inside."

A gentle smile spread over the old man's pink and shining features. "Friend Higsby, I do indeed understand. A need for thoughtful meditation dwells within every man of sense. It is truly said that solitude restoreth the soul."

He pushed the steel-rimmed spectacles up on his forehead. "Daughter?"

Desire stood before him, eyes dropped.

"Thee will attend the Women's Weekday Meeting on the morrow?"

"Yes, Papa."

In the candle light Asa Bennett's shoulder-length gray hair gleamed. "It is a gratification to me, Daughter, that thee is taking this greater interest in studying the Word of God."

Tim was surprised. Of the entire family, Desire had always been the most reluctant to attend meeting. Well, maybe this was an indication that she had grown up—was getting sense.

Or hadn't she changed so much? Maybe he was just more noticing of women? In the Army you began right away to appraise every girl you came across. Joe Child used to brag that inside of five minutes he could tell whether the girl would go to bed or not.

Old Bennett was saying, "I will have thee carried over in the gig, Daughter."

Tim said quickly, "That's fine because I must go over to Newport too."

"Eh?" The old man blinked. "No, thee is needed here. In the morning we will talk of the world's business—Friend Loammi Freebody, thee, and I."

Time Pa learned his son was off lead strings—for good. Great God, hadn't he had the feeding, disciplining and leadership of sixty grown men? Hadn't he led a charge on a British outpost?

"You will have to excuse me, Pa. Our business will have to wait 'til the afternoon."

Asa Bennett's eyes widened, and he looked bewildered. To Tim's surprise, he said hastily, "Very well, my son. I shall keep Friend Loammi for supper. Good night. God grant thee rest. Thee must be weary."

Higsby decided that Tim most likely would want to talk to his sister so he presently swung off upstairs, carefully shielding his candle flame.

Snapper scratched warningly at the door; Tim let him out. The fresh air felt fine. It was like old times to hear wild geese gabbling and complaining down in Fox Hill Cove. There was no moon but starlight on the snow made it possible to see dark woods crowning the far shore of the West Passage. When he went back inside he was surprised to find Desire still standing straight and supple before the fireplace.

She began to talk rapidly. "Tim, I have decided there's no sense in our 'theeing' and 'thying' each other in private. The simple language may suit Pa and his Friends, but—well, it makes me feel silly." Her eyes narrowed, faintly defiant. "How can anyone be sure that 'you' is an improper word? It appears to me that, by this talk, we set ourselves above people, and a true Friend doesn't encourage that."

"I have pondered just that question, too, Dee. Pa would say it is not for us to question. But be careful. It would hurt Pa terribly if you became one of the world's people. Zeke and I—well, we *had* to."

"Why, why—I'll try not to, Tim," Desire promised earnestly. "I love Papa, but I am no longer a child. You can understand that, even if he can't, can't thee?"

He took her hand, for the first time noted the soft clearness of its skin. "I expect so. Ever since I saw you on the stairs I've known it. But it's kind of a surprise to find you a grown-up, I suppose."

She smiled. "Thank thee—er—you, Tim. I believe the hour is at hand when every man—and woman, too," she added a little breathlessly, "must stand up—make sacrifices for what he or she truly believes in."

"Dear little backslider." He flung an arm about his sister's slim shoulders. "You talk mighty big and fierce, but don't risk swimming too far out from shore." He couldn't help coloring as he asked, "Have you seen Lucy?"

"Why, yes," Desire replied, a mischievous quirk to her mouth. "Yesterday with Ira Thaxter—again."

"Not with that pot-bellied pen-pusher!" The yellow splinters in his eyes glowed suddenly. "By God, I'll—"

"La, sir, thee had best put a check to thy temper," Desire broke in. "The Army didn't curb it for you, did it? Thee *is* mad about her, isn't thee?" She laughed until her shoulders quivered.

Tim glared suspiciously. "If thee has been funning me, I'll turn up thy petticoats and paddle thee."

Desire nodded. "Of course, I have, my poor, fond lover—"

She backed away holding hands over the threatened area. "She has been seen with Ira only twice or thrice all winter."

Deftly she diverted the conversation into safer channels. "They do say Ira and his Pa are coining money."

"How come? Thought trade 'round Newport was deader than Pontius Pilate."

Desire came so close he could smell the lavender which she always kept in her clothes press.

"Dr. Senter and Judge Taggart say they are discounting British bills."

"What do you mean? British bills?"

She looked quite mature, capable, as she replied, "Now, as always, the King's government pays naval officers of the America station in drafts drawn on merchants and bankers in Boston, Newport, and other places.

"The Committee of Safety, of course, has ordered our people not to honor their drafts. The poor British officers, therefore, hold only worthless pieces of paper—unless someone cashes them.

"Confessed Tories like Dr. Halliburton and Rowland Robinson have been doing so from the start. When the Committee of Safety caught Mr. George Rowe at it he had to run for refuge aboard the *Rose*. But it's a profitable risk; they say the Thaxters and some others charge discount at seventeen per centum."

Tim listened, deeply interested. "You say it isn't only out-and-out Loyalists who discount enemy bills?"

His sister nodded brightly.

"So?" Tim gazed into the flames. "Here's another thing. Why was Pa so dead-set to get me home by the seventh?"

Desire was genuinely astonished. "What did he say?"

"Only that," Tim replied. "I was wondering. As usual the old man will tell me when he gets God damned—er—er, thy pardon, Dee—when he gets good and ready."

His sister giggled, suggested hopefully, "You must have had plenty of fun at the Siege."

He frowned, then grinned. "Not so much as you'd think, still there were moments—"

He checked himself. "By the bye, Mistress Bennett, what lies back of this folderol?"

"What folderol?"

"Your attending the Women's Weekday Meetings in addition to First Day Meeting? You act like a newly convinced candidate undergoing preparation."

"Well, so I do attend." Desire's reply was prim.

"Thee can't fool me," Tim said. "I know that sweet 'carry-me-off-to-Heaven' look. Thee is up to some deviltry."

"I am not! Thee is a nasty pig!" Desire snapped and her heavy lashes dropped down as if to repress a surge of blood to her cheeks.

Ever since childhood a natural pigmentation had sketched faint brownish shadows beneath Desire's eyes. Now they had an oddly stimulating effect. Tim sighed. It was reassuring to recall that the Arbitrators and Solid Friends were able in dealing with problems of the flesh.

Who might be interesting his sister? Young Tom Hazard, Geoffrey Watson, or maybe Bob Knowles? Knowles, of course! For a Quaker, Bob Knowles was lively, continually being "overcome." That was who it was. He suggested so.

"I am not in love, Mr. Noseybody, with Bob Knowles, even if he does testify as if he believes life ain't something to be lived in books."

All in the same breath she hurried on, "What is our army like? Are the officers very brutal with their men? When they're displeased do they have their soldiers tied to cannons and flogged?"

"Why, no. Where ever—?"

In the firelight, Desire's naturally high color glowed brighter still. She spoke eagerly, as if avid for information. "Do the American officers game? I hope not. Last week a leftenant in the *Swan* lost a whole year's pay at pharo—"

"—And just how did you learn all this?" Tim inquired sharply.

Desire slipped a walnut between teeth no less white and sparkling than Sam Higsby's.

"With trade gone and done for, what else is there left to do in Newport but to gossip?" she queried easily. "Tell me, did you actually kill anybody?"

"Guess I tried plenty hard, but I ain't sure," Tim admitted. "Most all our firing was by volleys."

"Tim," Desire inquired slowly, "why can't this trouble be mended? It would be so nice if there were no more fighting and we could still have our King."

"The King's refusal to accept our petition has made this impossible, Dee. I mean the one Mr. Dickson sent," Tim explained soberly. "His Majesty's attitude has made the Congress feel entirely hopeless; it has made them feel that we must stand on our own feet."

"You mean the Army is for—" she hesitated as if awed to utter the words—"for independence?"

Tim replied, "Independence is the only way out. Now what could have been softer than that last petition? Good Lord, Dee, old Dickson fairly groveled, just about licked the King's boots for the mere privilege of addressing His Majesty. What happened? His Majesty flatly refused to even hear the petition, though every Englishman is supposed to have the right of petition to the Throne."

"But what else can we do? We haven't a single frigate or a sloop of war, let alone a ship-of-the-line."

Her brother's voice deepened. "If we drive the British from our shores, then their ships will *have* to starve."

"I know, Tim, but I wonder if any of us know how very powerful the British are? They say the Parliament is mustering a great new army just to suppress this rebellion. Part of it is to invade the Southern Colonies."

Tim wanted to go off and think about Lucy so he yawned and got to his feet. "Good Lord! When I came home I guessed I could forget about this damned war awhile."

"Don't go," Desire pleaded. "We haven't talked in ever so long. Tell me, what are Boston girls like?"

"We didn't get to see many. The British are holding them in town."

"Are—are there many—do many of the American officers have—"

"Eh?"

"Well, do the American officers take fancy women along on campaign? The British do—some of them. The colonels, that is, and generals and titled officers."

Tim regarded his sister steadily. "Where have you been hearing such stuff?"

"Oh, nowhere." The firm outline of Desire's chin rose a trifle. "I just overheard some soldiers talking."

There would be small profit in trying to quiz her now. An odd piece, Desire Harmony. At times she would refuse advice from the Twelve Apostles.

"Why don't our generals have 'ammunition wives'?" she persisted. "To be really genteel they would have to, wouldn't they?"

"That will do!" Tim used his parade ground voice. "Thee ought to be ashamed—thee ought to condemn thyself in Meeting."

"You and Papa and the Friends believe that ignorance is best for

—for women," Desire announced succinctly. "I do not."

Tomorrow it might be instructive to see where his sister passed on her way to and from the Meeting House back of Farewell Street.

Desire said suddenly, "You must be dreadfully tired—suppose we go up to bed?"

"Lord, yes. It's late—almost nine."

As of yore, Snapper preceded him to his room. Provided it didn't interfere with Pa's mysterious plans, Tim hoped he might get away soon and kill some ducks. All at once he thought of something and laughed softly.

You couldn't often shoot black ducks except at dawn or twilight; and sharpshooter though the Pennsylvanian undoubtedly was, he doubted whether Higsby could bring down a black duck flying against the moon. He could himself, had done it lots of times.

The familiar odors of burnt birch bark and oiled leather greeted him in his room. Perhaps as a hint, Mamba had left a big brass pot of hot water beside his fireplace. So, weary as he was, Tim washed until the water was best not looked at; then, comfortable, he pulled on a flannel nightshirt, tied the strings of a nightcap beneath his chin, and relaxed. Heigh-ho!—A damned big improvement over that pile of stinking straw—or was it?

All in an instant Sam Higsby came wide awake, swung his legs out of bed and groped for the haft of his war hatchet. Yes, by God, careful footfalls *were* descending the hall. He listened. What had waked him wasn't just a board expanding.

Shivering in the chill gloom, he listened intently. Though the prowler had no light, he or she was moving quickly, surely, towards the staircase. Who could it be? Tim, Mr. Bennett, Miss Desire—one of the servants?

For sure it couldn't be a Britainer—they invariably made a heap of noise—so it was none of his fry who was out there.

Replacing his tomahawk under the pillow he listened to the footfalls descend the stairs; pretty soon a door latch clicked. Whoever was quitting the Bennett house surely didn't aim to advertise the fact. His curiosity deepened when his ear caught the distant and snow-muffled thud of hoofs that drew nearer and finally stopped somewhere near the barn. The rider, he calculated, was heading for the West Ferry.

Funny about them enemy vessels in the harbor. It wasn't noways reasonable to tolerate them. Why it was like a feller's sharing his cabin with a hungry wolf.

He had just decided to go back to sleep when a second series of footsteps, heavier than the first, passed his door. They also descended the stairs and went outside. What the devil was going on?

Pretty soon he thought he detected a subdued commotion down near the water. At the cost of thrusting his head out of the window and letting a blast of freezing wind into his shirt, he learned the dull noise came from a warehouse occupying the landward end of Mr. Bennett's wharf.

By straining his ears, he recognized the creaking of a pulley, the dull rumble of wheels over a wooden floor. What the devil could old Mr. Bennett be up to at this hour of night? What about the first set of steps?

He fled back to bed and found it cold. Goddam! He wished Aggie had been keeping the sheets warm, or maybe that yellow-haired girl out in Winchester. Both their petticoats had made fine patches —burnt off clean as a whistle.

4

SUPPLY PARTY

PHIL, the Widow Hull's gangling, sad-eyed youngest boy, sailed a fine straight course from Conanicut over to Bannister's wharf in Newport. The sailing skiff cruised past the British men-of-war so close that Tim saw details of the smartly-kept rigging, of the fancy gilt scroll work on their sterns.

Right now there were four ships in port: *Glasgow,* armed transport, twenty guns; *Rose,* frigate of twenty; *Swan,* a sixteen. Smaller, less graceful, was the *Bolton,* a bomb brig. In addition to her great brass mortar, Phil counted six guns mounted amidships.

"Pretty, ain't they?" he grinned. "Wisht I'd a chance to draw them like that, with the sun on them—"

"—Pretty? May the doorsteps av hell be their tombstones!" snarled Shamus McCool who, glad of a passage, crouched on the floor boards. Three years back he had come to homestead on Conanicut Point, the northern end of the Island and already could boast of four children and a flourishing little farm.

"Why so bitter?" Tim wanted to know.

"Last month thim brass-bound Sassenachs yonder lifted me foine young bull, butchered him, and left me his hoofs and head for thanks. May his beef choke all av thim!"

Phil Hull turned a grave face that was peppered with smallpox pits. "Some of Captain Wallace's men hewed down Ma's maple grove for fire wood. It was the finest sugar grove on the island. Someday, I'm going to get even."

Desire Harmony had not been listening. She turned a face fetchingly pink under the hood of a gray cloak and indicated the *Rose.* "Oh, Tim, isn't she lovely?"

Though he hated to admit it, he had to agree. The frigate with her well-trimmed yards, taut rigging, yellow streak and dark blue sides made a brave display. He judged the insides of her must be painted red because the under edge of her raised gun port lids were painted that color. They sketched ten deadly scarlet patches along the frigate's yellow streak.

Because the breeze was off-shore, those in the skiff heard a bell tolling in Newport.

"Must be somebody dead?" Phil suggested.

"Faith no. 'Tis the bell on the jail," corrected McCool, spitting towards the men-of-war. "Haul yer mains'l, Phil. We'll maybe reach town in time for the execution," he added hopefully.

Presently Tim spotted the look-out set on top of Isaac Percival's house. Until now it had been masked by the Congregational Meeting House's square tower.

Too bad Sam Higsby had refused to come along. He would have been mightily impressed by Newport, third port in America. He should see the number of its wharves, warehouses, and the big brick market in which prize court commissioners auctioned captured vessels and cargoes.

All during breakfast the Pennsylvanian's black eyes had kept swinging over to Desire, like a compass needle attracted by a magnet. He hadn't said much.

In making for the inner basin, Phil Hull sailed close by three big slavers tied up at Lopez' Wharf. Though they must have been decommissioned since nearly a year, a nauseating reek clung to them. No gaudy blue, red, or yellow stripes decorated their sides. Their entire hulls were painted jet as the miserable cargo they transported from the Gulf of Guinea into Barbados, Jamaica and Charleston in South Carolina.

Like the other laid-up vessels, the slavers were bereft of top masts and yards. When he glanced along the curving waterfront, Tim was reminded of a dry, weatherbeaten and long-drowned forest.

Once the skiff had passed under a small drawbridge into the Basin, that change which had come over Newport was more poignantly to be appreciated. Everywhere dejected throngs of unemployed riggers, stevedores, seamen and officers wandered aimlessly. The usually bustling sail lofts and chandlers' stores crowding Thames Street were silent as so many churchyards.

Tim handed his sister onto a public landing stage that was all slippery with ooze and refuse.

Once they reached the street, signs of stagnation became even more inescapable. The windows of Bolton, the candlemaker, were thick with dirt—his door nailed shut. With little or no whale oil finding its way in, no one could manufacture spermaceti candles. A tin mold dangling as a sign above Bolton's door was rusting through.

"What's up?" McCool hailed the loafers.

"Some thief's to be whipped," a man in striped jersey told him.

"Oh gee, Mr. Bennett, a robber!" Phil Hull lost a little color.

"Wonder what it was he stole," Desire demanded.

"Bill Kenyon didn't steal nothin'," a passerby corrected. "He's just a blasted Tory, an infernal British-lover."

"What did he do?"

"Rowed out and sold six sacks of turnips to the *Glasgow*," explained the man angrily. "But a Committee man caught him at it."

Suddenly Desire's fingers closed on her brother's arm. Tim, following her look, watched four longboats pull clear of the British flagship. In a leisurely rhythm, oar blades winked and blinked. At the bow and stern of each boat were patches of scarlet.

"The devil take 'em." The only thought in Tim's mind was of finding Lucy.

Arm in arm the Bennetts followed Thames Street toward a triangle formed by Queen, Bull and Anne Streets. On this was located the Court House in addition to the school, and some of the handsomest residences in town.

The crowd grew denser every yard they traveled and, once the jail bell stopped its dolorous clangor, all the people began to hurry towards Church Street. As every urchin in Newport knew, a criminal flogged at the cart's tail was started from the Court House and led down Spring Street as far as Beech. There the cart turned right and kept on until it reached the waterfront. If the punished wretch hadn't fainted by then, the cart turned right once more and rumbled back up to the Court House. This afforded almost everyone a glimpse of the spectacle.

When, in the distance, a pair of drums began rattling and banging, startled flocks of pigeons rose, went winging over the house tops, wheeled higher and higher into the sky.

"Well, God bless my soul! Welcome home, Friend Timothy." An old family friend touched him on the shoulder. He was elderly, with gray hair framing his features. Squinting short-sightedly, he halted. "Thee is on Christmas furlough, I presume? Thy father must be overjoyed that the Lord has spared thee from the fate of those who live by the sword."

Because he had been an Elder who had voted for setting Tim aside, he looked a little uneasy.

As he moved on Desire asked in surprise, "Why didn't you tell him your enlistment has expired?"

Before Tim could find a reply a pair of drummers in blue uniforms, coats sizes too big for them, appeared down Church Street. Next came the sheriff in sash and sword, stumping impassively along. Every few yards he held up a warrant of execution so that everybody could see it.

In his wake rumbled a big two-wheeled cart pulled by a shaggy gray horse. The ancient creature's head drooped forlornly and its lower lip swung slack, a shiny pink crescent. A loose-kneed youth in a dirty green coat guided the horse by its bridle. He kept slipping on the muddy cobbles because he was continually turning to watch the prisoner.

Shouts arose. "Tory!" "Skin the damned English-lover alive!" "Traitor!"

Desire drew closer to Tim. He was amazed to feel the violence of her trembling.

"I'm sorry," he muttered. "I had expected we could get by in time."

She caught her breath, and felt her cheeks go hot. To see a man weeping, wincing under a rope's end, evoked queer, inexplicable emotions. When the cart came closer and she could see details, she felt a stirring in her breasts, and a strange buzzing began in her finger tips.

"Oh, it's monstrous," she cried, but didn't look away.

Deliberately a black-bearded seaman stooped, gathered a handful of gutter mire. The cart's iron tires rang louder, also the inexorable *clip-clop* of the nag's big splay hoofs. Though Desire could not get a clear view of the prisoner, yet she heard him uttering a series of squealing cries.

A shifting in the crowd suddenly revealed the condemned wretch. His long pale face looked greasy with sweat and his mouth was blood-smeared from the spasmodic biting he was giving his lips. Both Kenyon's hands were lashed tightly to an iron ring let into the cart's tail and every time the lash fell his head would snap jerkily skywards.

The blood roared loud as a cataract in Desire's ears. She felt sick but she didn't dare let go of Tim.

"String him up!" "Hang the son of a bitch!" "Peel his hide off and sell it to old Wallace!"

"Oh, the poor friendless soul!" A woman in Quaker gray turned away blindly.

Tim wasn't shocked. In the camps around Boston, men were always being triced up and flogged much worse than this. To make his regulations respected, General Washington firmly advocated flogging. Why, that rope's end wasn't a patch on an army cane, let alone a navy cat-o'-nine tails. Even so, its knots had torn the skin on the fellow's shoulder blades and were marking his whole back with lumpy purplish bruises. What really astonished Tim was the hatred of the populace for the British. He hadn't realized that there was all this feeling.

Pebbles, handfuls of horse dung, snowballs, continually struck the condemned man who neither could hasten nor retard his pace.

"Hey!" A rotten fish had caught the jailer on his shoulder. "Hey, mind yer aim, or quit it!"

The sailor walked out into the street and flung his handful of muck so accurately that it not only blacked one whole side of Kenyon's face, but ran in jet rivulets over his gaunt ribs and spattered the fish-belly pallor of his stomach.

The crowd voiced savage delight. Desire, sickened, covered her eyes, but an inner force dragged them open again. The drums went banging past Ben Peabody's carpenter shop.

Like a drunkard, the prisoner lurched around the corner into Thames Street. In a ribald procession apprentices, slaves and town riffraff followed.

"Committee needn't have been so hard on Bill," a man in a decent gray suit said. "His folks were nigh to starving. It ain't right. There are plenty of high-and-mighty folks in this town who sell the British a damned sight more than a few sacks of turnips."

"—Like Ira Thaxter?" someone sang out.

The black-bearded sailor grabbed the man in gray, whirled him about. "Say, Mister, more Tory lies like that and you'll join Kenyon!"

The man in gray, not in the least cowed, spoke in such a low voice that the crowd had to quiet to hear him.

"You know about Rowland Robinson's stock and grain boats, don't you?"

"Yes, but it ain't against the law to ship to Connecticut," the sailor growled.

"It *is* legal. However—" the speaker's voice rang out, filling the whole street—"I would like to know why a British tender *always* captures Mr. Robinson's vessels and their supplies? Why said vessels are never burnt, but sold so he can buy them back for a song?"

The throng was quiet, listening hard, now.

"You can't explain that, eh? Well then, perhaps you can tell me why, despite these seizures, Mr. Robinson has been able to buy three new sloops during the past six months?

"If we must punish those who deal with the British, should we not punish great and small impartially?" He looked at the sailor. "Well, and what have you to say now?"

The black-bearded fellow mumbled something inaudible, turned away.

What was Desire making of this?

"Well, I'm jiggered!" She had disappeared. No matter. She must be at the Women's Meeting within a few minutes.

5

THE HOUSE ON BANNISTER STREET

THROAT ready to burst, Tim followed Isaac Percival's walk of slate slabs. Having had no opportunity to buy new clothes, he wore an old suit of Quaker brown that was a little big because he'd lost weight in the Army.

Would Lucy like him out of uniform? Too bad he'd had to come home now; officers of Continental Line Regiments were to wear blue tunics, buff waistcoats and white breeches and plenty of gold buttons and lace. Lucy always had fancied color. His stride lengthened. Lucy! Lucy! Everything blurred except that glittering silver name plate and a knocker on the door.

Clorinda, the Percivals' mulatto serving wench, opened the door about as soon as he had knocked. She was fairly wriggling with excitement. "Come right in, Mist' Bennett. Come right in! Us has been expecting you some time."

"Tim! Tim, darling! I *knew* you'd return!"

Small features eloquent of an inexpressible happiness, Lucy dissolved into his hungry grasp. "You came back! Oh, how I prayed and—"

Pressing her tight to him, he swam in the heady delight of Lucy's nearness. Couldn't find a thing to say —could only dwell in the radiant aura of overwhelming love.

The wench giggled and fled, leaving an orange-colored angora cat to watch the proceedings with aloof interest.

"Darling—I—I—can't believe you're back. I didn't dare to believe you would give up your commission. I—I—almost wish you hadn't. It must have meant so much to you."

"Sweetheart—"

"Oh, you *are* unselfish and kind—too kind, I fear." Passionately, Lucy pressed her face against his. "I will try so hard never to make you sorry of your choice. Please believe that." Her long-lashed eyes swung upwards. "And you gave it up for *my* sake—"

"Yes—" he whispered and, for the moment, he honestly thought he had. "Let's look at you, dearest. I need another portrait in my private gallery."

"La, sir, what nonsense is this?"

"During the Siege I used to look at memory pictures of you—ever so often. I have one of you in the peach orchard. Remember? And another when you wore a green and a yellow chip hat." The intensity of her gaze betrayed her rapturous interest. "Then, at Captain Whipple's ball you wore gray silk and a red—"

"—Claret, dear."

"—Claret shawl, and God knows how many petticoats. And you had an ivory and silk fan."

"Oh, Timothy. To think of you remembering all that! You shall have your new picture—"

Lucy retreated, slowly spreading wide a skirt of pale blue challis. A fichu of Valenciennes rushed, like a sea foaming over a reef, from her shoulders to cross over her breast. As an added bit of jauntiness she had fixed a pair of blue-dyed everlastings in her hair. The blue enamel and silver brooch he had given her secured her collar.

Superbly bored, the cat yawned, cocked an ear backwards.

"Lucy!" He wanted to kiss her, but she whirled aside on tiny heelless slippers and the scarlet circle of her lips blew him a kiss.

"Mama," she whispered.

Between Mrs. Percival's present manner and that of the preceding week there was a world of difference. A genuine warmth softened her worn features as she came forward.

"Welcome home, Timothy." She pecked him on the forehead. "Mr. Percival *will* be surprised! But I—well, I always vowed you had your Pa's fine commonsense. Mr. Percival declared you would rather stay at Boston and butcher the poor British than attend to business."

"Butcher the British"? That was a new way of putting it! Since the eighteenth of June very little killing had been done except by camp fever, the flux, smallpox, and lung fever.

Only a handful of fanatics had ever cried out for a slaughter of the Ministerial troops. To most men, the British Army simply constituted a barrier to New England's commerce which must be removed, as cheaply and painlessly as possible.

"Shall we seek the withdrawing room?" Mrs. Percival tucked a gaunt, black-clad arm through one of Tim's. Lucy took the other. Mama *would* call it a withdrawing room. Most folks around Newport referred to their best room as the "Sunday room" or the "parlor."

Quakers called such a place their First Day room since they didn't hold with regulating Christian lives with days named after pagan gods. Felt the same way about the months, too. Why, January was named for a heathen Roman god called Janus, March for their brutal god of War. Even now, when he was tired or excited, Tim found himself referring to "the seventh day of Twelfthmonth!" just as he would "Thee" and "Thy" his sister more often than not.

He was mightily relieved to find Mrs. Percival in so agreeable a mood. At Roxbury she'd appeared forbidding, ready to spoil his plans—and Lucy's.

That his call had been anticipated was proved by a fire crackling in the 'drawing room grate. A stagnant chill in the air argued that the dim elegance of this chamber was reserved for special occasions. Yes, this must be "an occasion" since Mrs. Percival ordered in sherry and biscuits and even allowed Lucy a glass. She drank it gaily and hoped for more, but in vain.

The straight-backed woman in black went to a window and, peering down the street, complained, "I can't imagine what can be keeping Mr. Percival. He was to have been home an hour ago. It had to do with the matter I spoke of in Roxbury. You recall?"

"Yes, Ma'am. Today is the seventh, I believe."

"Possibly Mr. Percival has decided to converse with you at the warehouse later." Lizzie Percival made no effort to conceal an obvious annoyance. "I can't imagine what can be keeping him. He was up to Providence yesterday purchasing barrel staves."

Barrel staves? Tim wondered. What would a Newport merchant

want of barrel staves in times such as these?

Demurely, Lucy smoothed her skirt. "Mama, just before you came in we were talking—"

"Indeed?" A spark of amusement lit the older woman's somber eyes. "I must be growing deaf, I didn't hear any conversation."

Lucy looked hard at Tim, silently urged him to speak. But the way her lashes curled sent his blood surging in such a succession of stupefying billows that it required a full minute to grasp her intent.

"Mrs. Percival, Ma'am, up to Boston Lucy and I—"

Precisely, Mrs. Percival's dark head inclined. "Mr. Percival and I have decided that you will wed come the twenty-eighth of this month. The first reading of banns will be on Sunday next. This is a good time of year. A holiday season inclines people to generosity."

"Oh, Mama!" Lucy went crimson, burst out, "How can—"

Lucy's mother laughed. "Your wedding gifts will probably be a heap of unwanted Christmas presents, but half a loaf is better than none in these hard times."

The twenty-eighth! And this was the seventh! Only twenty-one days, three weeks, then Lucy would be his—the long, dreary waiting at an end. He had been smart to come home, by God!

Suddenly Mrs. Percival looked up as if she had overlooked something and was annoyed with herself about it. "Er—what news of your father's ships?"

Tim smiled. "The *Hope* is safe at Conanicut."

"Yes, we know that. But what of the rest? The *Prudence,* the *Narragansett,* and where is the *Patience?*"

"Pa says he has ordered the *Narragansett* held at Cap François in the French Sugar Islands. The schooners are expected daily."

Mrs. Percival pursed thin lips of very pale pink, her jet earrings quivered. "We will feel vastly relieved when they make port. Only yesterday, Mr. Percival was saying—"

She broke off short. From the direction of the harbor a dull tumult was rising. It reminded Tim of that time General Washington's provost guard had arrested Gamble, leader of those riflemen who had mutinied rather than do drill or stand guard.

For a while, it had been touch and go. Half the rifle regiments were drunk, swearing they would rescue Gamble and scalp anyone who tried to stay them. The Commander-in-Chief, however, was the kind of general who somehow always had plenty of his men on hand when such outbursts took place.

"You must bring Desire in to see us very soon," Mrs. Percival said as the outcry dwindled. "It is edifying to observe a child of her age so very taken with religion."

Something about the way Mrs. Percival spoke roweled Tim. But what the devil? He and Lucy were together again.

Lucy was bubbling with excitement. "Mama says tomorrow we may look at a house. It lies beyond the end of Thames Street—almost to Brenton's Cove. Oh, Timothy, won't it be fun being all by ourselves with such a lovely view of the harbor? Mama says—"

Downtown the bell on the jail began to clang, not as it had for the flogging, but wildly, breathlessly.

Though Tim jumped up and sought the window, he couldn't see anything. Across the street two men had stopped and were facing the harbor.

Down at the cross street someone was yelling, "Turn out! Turn out! Out!" The two men hurried, began to run. Two or three youths, accompanied by dogs, tore past carrying clubs in their hands.

"What is this disturbance, Timothy?" Mrs. Percival's voice was metallic.

"I can't tell, Ma'am. I will go down and find out." Pretty quickly Tim found the alarm giver, a wild-looking fellow with a big bleeding bruise on his forehead.

"Come on!" he yelled at Tim. "Britishers are sacking the town!"

Tim ran back into the hall and grabbed his hat and coat. Lucy clung to his arm.

"Oh, Tim. Don't go! Please don't."

"I must. Be right back, dearest. Can't let the Lobster-backs run riot—"

6

Riot

"Come on! you cursed Bloody-backs," roared a printer's devil, "or do you always wait for night before you steal our pigs and burn our barns?"

By the time Timothy Bennett crossed Spring Street, he realized that the British were not plundering Newport—not yet, at any rate. The trouble, he gathered, was taking place at the waterfront.

By climbing a stoop Tim glimpsed, over the shifting heads of the mob, some twenty-five or thirty Royal Marines lined up under a weatherbeaten sign reading "Moses Lopez & Brother. Hides, Wines, & Salt Fish." In the door of the warehouse at their backs lay huge heaps of sacked potatoes, turnips, hams, sides of beef and great brown bunches of smoked salmon.

The lieutenant in command was young, with a sensitive, classically-handsome profile and a wiry, erect figure. Breeding showed in the last detail of his bearing. Right now, he was with no great success, attempting to appear unconcerned by the savage temper of the crowd. He gripped an ivory hilted sword just a little too tight to be quite convincing. It was a silly sort of sword to carry on duty, Tim thought; all that fine carving on the guard would be useless in stopping a cudgel.

Everywhere the townsfolk called questions, milled about with apparent aimlessness. A majority carried weapons: a poker, a cudgel, an axe, or even a hanger left over from privateering days. Very few firearms were visible.

"Go home, you damned pirates!" shrieked an old woman.

"Figger to burn us out, like Falmouth, don't you? Well, just you try!"

"Leftenant St. Clair, sir!" Red-faced, a sergeant strode over to the slim young officer and fiercely urged some step, but the lieutenant shook his head so sharply that his scarlet and black cockade fluttered.

Inside Lopez' warehouse more marines in scarlet, black, and white, guarded a party of ill-dressed and bare-footed seamen who were sullenly lowering supplies into the *Rose's* longboats. These marines had to keep a sharp look-out lest the seamen run into the crowd and so desert.

When Tim drew near, less than fifteen feet of muddied cobbles separated the marines from the mob. Imperceptibly, this distance was decreasing. Pretty soon those in front began pushing backwards because the Britishers were closing up, eyes hard and jaws set. Any minute now their bright bayonets might swing low. Some of the shore party, particularly the younger privates, were pale beneath the big pewter plates decorating the front of their red and white caps.

"Starve the pirates out!" a man deep in the crowd began to yell. "Seize their food and they'll have to leave!"

More voices added to the clamor. "Come on, boys! Don't let good Yankee food stuff British gullets!" "Let's get it back—treaty expires today!"

The Marine Lieutenant took a turn across the landing stage. His manner was so calm, so infuriatingly contemptuous, Tim felt a sneaking admiration. Why, he was acting as if this swarm of angry Provincials were no more than so many yapping puppies.

He was ill-advised, though, Tim knew. Too many of these people held a real grievance: a son impressed into the Royal Navy; a handsome wood lot hacked down; a drove of sheep or a herd of beef oxen driven off without a by-your-leave, let alone a penny in payment.

The crowd began to back up as if gathering for a rush. Someone grabbed at Tim's arm. It was Lucy, great-eyed, vigilant and anxious.

Exasperation flooded him. "You should have stayed at home. You're apt to get hurt."

"So are you," she retorted. "If anyone's going to hurt you, I— well, I want to get at him."

She wasn't talking for effect, either, didn't seem frightened of this cursing, elbowing mob. The way her eyes danced and the eagerness with which she peered this way and that gave him a new insight into Lucy Percival. She had even caught her breath as if to yell something at the British.

Away down Thames Street bayonets appeared swinging, flashing in the sun. Apparently, another detachment of the troops, sent to draw rations under Captain Wallace's treaty with the town, had visited the inner harbor and were having a hard time. Tim could see missiles raining on the Redcoats.

Better get out of this. God! If anybody got crazy enough to fire a shot. In Boston they still talked of "the Massacre" which, as he saw it, had been no massacre at all, but troops shooting in self-defense.

Lucy's grip tightened on his wrist as a window opened just above and a well-dressed man called out, "Let us have no violence—not until our treaty with Wallace is honorably expired!"

A cobblestone smashed a pane above the speaker's head and he ducked hurriedly out of sight. Some people laughed, but others shouted, "No renewal! No more treaties with the Bloody-backs!"

The man at Tim's left growled, "Why should Newport nourish Wallace so's he'll be able to raid elsewhere?"

Once young Lieutenant St. Clair saw what threatened, he called in a clear voice, "Sergeant Hallam, fall in two squads and proceed to Mr. Monkton's assistance. Mark this well, Sergeant: no firing unless fired upon!

"If this rabble gets too cheeky, you may use your butts, then your bayonets—"

Allowing his sword to dangle from the knot of silver braid attaching it to his wrist, the youth produced a snuff box, and coolly measured a pinch. In amazed silence, everybody heard its lid close with a little click.

"No, you don't! Bide where ye are," the crowd began to shout. But sixteen men composing Sergeant Hallam's detail started off, silver-fronted caps winking. The crowd stiffened and gave back so slowly that the sergeant, red under his tanned skin, sang out, "Nah then, myke room, ye bleedin' beggars. Stand aside!"

In thus dividing his forces, the British lieutenant had made a serious error. His guard before Lopez' wharf was reduced to but fifteen men. Facing them were over a hundred townsfolk, all of them mad as hops.

"Ye hear that? He called us beggars!" bellowed a tall man, pulling off a threadbare sea coat. "Aye! They'll beggar us—*if we let 'em!* Who'll help me get back that food?"

From the crowd burst a hoarse, incoherent sound and immediately a rain of stones, sticks and other missiles fell on the handful of marines.

Lucy's fingers dug into Tim's sleeve like claws when a marine's musket clattered onto the cobbles. He was clutching a gash on his chin.

"Go!" Tim rasped. "I've got to see this through—"

Lucy gave him a tremulous smile, grasped realities and was sensible enough to begin a retreat. She used her elbows liberally.

Tim resolved to keep his head even if it did make him mad to think of the enemy marching around Newport as if it were a captured town. Such a situation was as grotesque as it was intolerable.

"Kill the lousy town-burners!" "Stop 'em!" "Cut 'em off!"

Sergeant Hallam's men became hemmed in, hesitated. Once they lost their stride, a crush of men and boys immediately rushed out of Mary's Lane. Swinging clubs, broken oars, fish spears, net-handles, they charged the relief party so rapidly that their foremost were able to knock up the marines' muskets before the men in scarlet could use their bayonets.

Commands, curses, and the furious trampling of feet reverberated among the tall warehouses lining Thames Street. A second shower of stones was hurled at Lieutenant St. Clair's men.

"Want vittles do they? All right, let's feed 'em—cold iron and hot lead!"

A shriveled little man to Tim's left suddenly jerked a boarding pistol out of his coattail pocket.

Tim's arteries froze. He was soldier enough to foresee the deadly effect of a volley in this packed street. Worse still, the instant that damned idiot snapped his shot, the squadron out yonder would commence a bombardment. Swinging his fists, ignoring angry shouts, he lurched after the little man.

"Poise firelocks!" The Marine Lieutenant's voice was taut and penetrating. He had lost his languid look, was using the ivory-hilted sword to dress his handful of men into a thin double rank barring the warehouse entrance.

"Cock firelocks!" A half brick sailed through the air, struck a corporal squarely on the metal plate of his cap which spun away. Panting obscenities the N.C.O. dashed threads of blood from his eyebrows and shook his fist at the hot faces halfway across the street.

Out on the wharf, work stopped. Two seamen suddenly dove into the icy water and disappeared.

"Stand fast!" The guards leveled their weapons. The rest of the seamen cringed, stood shivering. The shower of missiles continued. Another marine was hit with a brick and sank to the ground groaning loudly.

"Take aim!" called Lieutenant St. Clair. A line of twinkling muzzles swung in line with the rioters' eyes. The officer's sharply-etched features were tense as those of a boxer waiting to deliver a killing blow.

As the young lieutenant caught his next breath, Tim prepared to throw himself flat. Still the Marine Lieutenant gave no command to fire, only called out, "Stand fast, Provincials. There will be no firing unless you shoot!"

It was amazing how rapidly that fellow with the pistol could slip through the crowd.

"Stop him," Tim shouted. "Don't let that fool shoot!"

At his cry dozens of sweaty red faces turned, some beneath blue jersey stocking caps, some beneath varnished leather hats and others under greasy woolen caps.

"Stand aside!" Furiously, the little man was brandishing his pistol. The rioters before him shrank away. Like a man in the throes of a nightmare, Tim saw the weapon's brass mountings gleam.

In his gay, white-lapeled regimentals the young lieutenant presented an un-missable mark. Tim gave a desperate, surging spring and managed to jam his palm between the pistol's flint and the frizzen. The hammer falling, pinched him like hell, but the flint couldn't touch the steel.

When he wrenched the pistol away the little man turned in amazed fury.

"You spoiled my shot, you bloody Tory," he snarled. "I could have killed that sneering whoreson over there. I'll see you suffer for this."

He was weeping with the resentment of a small man who has been robbed of an opportunity to make a wide impression. When he tried to sink his teeth in Tim's wrist, he got a slap which knocked him spinning.

Meanwhile, Sergeant Hallam's party had had to turn back; the weight of men was too great against them. Savagely they used their iron-shod musket butts, slashed with their bayonets to clear a path back to the warehouse. A couple of marines, having had their muskets wrenched away, were reduced to fighting with bare fists.

Sergeant Hallam's white crossbelts were splattered with manure, and muck stained the white cuffs of his red tunic. Quite alone he assailed a knot of stevedores.

Because the mob had stopped throwing stones, the lieutenant's men had lowered their pieces to the "handle arms" position. They were obviously eager to join in the mêlée, but their officer rasped:

"Stand fast, curse you! I say, Sergeant, fetch me a brace of prisoners!"

The crowd suddenly fell back leaving two civilians in the grip of the sergeant's men.

"Good," the lieutenant remarked. "We will keep them to replace those seamen who got away."

Tim was sucking at his injured hand and figuring that the worst of this sorry mess was over when he heard the thin whimpering of a boy:

"Help, friends!—Going to 'press me! Oh God! Please, *somebody* save me!"

Though the cry was shrill with terror, the voice sounded familiar.

Turning, Tim saw black-gaitered legs braced hard. Two burly privates were tugging the Widow Hull's boy towards the warehouse.

Tim reached the edge of the crowd in an instant, yelled, "Let him go, damn you! He's only a child!"

The sergeant turned. "Yus? Wanter tyke 'is plyce?"

As Tim dashed in, Hallam aimed a swing which would have jolted an ox, but Tim stooped, immediately straightened, driving an upper-cut which, inexplicably, failed to land true.

"Come, lads," bellowed the sergeant, "we'll tyke this un along an' cool 'is 'ot 'ead at the foretop!"

Immediately a corporal rushed in from behind and dealt Tim a blow that made his teeth rattle.

Risking an uppercut, he ducked blindly and gained an instant's respite. The sergeant's hot red face, bloodshot blue eyes, flattened twist of nose, appeared. Tim drove hard with his left but only grazed him. Got his balance back, anyway. Must hit men holding Phil Hull. Sergeant and corporal were behind—couldn't hurt him for a sec-ond— His right smashed into a tall marine's middle just above his belt buckle and the fellow's breath went out in a sibilant *whoosh!*

The Hull boy was striking out futilely, bent-armed. Though the other marine tried to hang onto the lad Tim now had room enough for a real punch. Phil was free, ran like a hare.

Crowd must be keeping the sergeant busy, Tim judged. A marine, however, ran up and drove his musket butt smack into Tim's side. Immediately the only colors Tim's optic nerves now registered were white and red. A queer, singing sound began in his head. Strange, he felt a little like this sometimes—when he was kissing Lucy hard. He let fly, wildly, felt his knuckles crackle against someone.

"Here come the others. Git!"

"Take that man. Capture him!" the officer yelled.

Tim shook his head, cleared away the red mist before it got too thick. Crimanently! He hadn't felt so fine since leaving Roxbury.

A marine, hatless, his crossbelts twisted out of position, made a dive at him. Tim side-stepped and got in such a hard punch that the lieutenant called:

"Good blow! My compliments, sir. You are very handy with your dukes."

Tim whirled and got back into the crowd just as a third volley of sticks and stones fell among the British. Tim guessed they would shoot this time. But still they didn't. Crimanently! That was discipline!

The officer's incisive voice bit through the tumult. "You will be *made pay for this!* Never fear."

7

FIVE CAME BACK

THAT he had taken no ordinary beating Tim realized on turning up a quiet side street. He'd a bruise on his cheek, he had skinned the knuckles on both hands and his mouth was swelling fast from an extra hard punch. Worse still, his coat was split down the back.

Good girl, Lucy, though. Plenty of loyalty, wit and nerve. They would get on fine together.

"Heyo, Sergeant! How's the folks?" Even before he turned Tim recognized Mark Remington's nasal drawl. Still wearing his home-made uniform, Mark swaggered as if he were a jim-dandy scrapper instead of a slow-footed and slower-witted military teamster.

With him were his brother, Jed Franklin, and the two Gardner boys, Walter and John. All were considerably liquored up. As if to remind Tim that he was no longer a superior, Walt grinned boldly, but the others didn't seem quite sure of what attitude to take. Judging by their blanket rolls, haversacks and walking sticks, they must have just reached town. John Gardner looked mighty peaked, all tuckered out.

"Why, hello, fellows, what are you doing here?" Tim asked, though he had long since guessed. The explanation gave him a sinking feeling.

Walt Gardner showed big yellow teeth in a still more impudent grin. "Being as how we always held you were a pretty smart feller, Tim, we figgered we better do what you done—go home."

Mark Remington blew his nose with his fingers, gaped foolishly up at some bare elms arching above the street.

"Pa, he wrote there's a bull calf to be altered," he remarked. "Figgered I'd better get back. Ain't nobody on Conanicut c'n nick out a bull's parts slicker'n me."

Sadly, Tim looked at them. The departure of five able men would make quite a hole in any company. Impulsively he said, "Wish to God you fellows had stayed."

Truculently, Jed Franklin squared his shoulders and his pocked face got red. "Say, who the hell are you to lecture us? Wasn't you the first one of all to clear out?"

"Yup," Walt sneered. "And if the Captain or Joe Child ever comes up with you, they've promised to beat the 'tarnation stuffings out of you."

"Heard tell the Colonel is preferring charges—desertion—against you." John Gardner sniffed, leaned hard on his stick.

A trickle of acid sweat stung Tim's eyes but he never noticed it. How? Why? Whoever would have thought?

Walt spat resoundingly, eased a pack strap. "I wouldn't take on, though, Tim; we all had the right to go and we're grateful. But fer you pulling foot, none of us would have had guts enough to use our lunar enlistments."

A numbness gripped Tim's brain. He felt suddenly weary, inexpressibly bewildered. "You—you say Matt—Captain Allen was—was displeased? Why, I told him I was coming back!"

"Displeased?" Jed laughed. "Oh, my sweet Jesus! He was r'arin', tearin', rampagin'."

Jed Franklin tilted his battered cocked hat to a more rakish angle and leered at a pair of pretty girls across the street. Mark Remington fingered his walking staff as he said:

"Yessir. Colonel Hitchcock read your name out in front of all the Rhode Island regiments. Kept quite a few fellers from going home, shouldn't wonder."

Tim felt so weak he reached out and grabbed hold of a fence picket.

John Gardner asked hesitantly, "Say, Sergeant, I—well, I'm pretty footsore, you maybe could take us over home in your skiff?"

"Guess so," Tim replied heavily. "Inner harbor, one o'clock— Say—" he looked up suddenly—"how is Abner Hull? Better?"

"Naw. Ab, he died. Some fool told him what the Colonel said about you—"

Mechanically, Tim nodded then his legs took him on. Great God! It was hard to see how he could have reasoned so wrong. Imagine Sergeant Bennett held up to scorn and shame before all the Rhode Island troops.

What hurt worst of all was that neither Matt Allen, nor Joe Child, nor the Colonel had given him the least benefit of a doubt. When he thought about Abner Hull's death he wished he could vomit.

In a semi-daze, he walked along Mary's Lane towards Spring Street until, all at once, he realized that Ira Thaxter was waving, friendly as pie.

"Welcome home from the wars, Timothy." His round, well-fed face was creased in a smirk. "All Newport is proud of your distinguished service under Colonel Hitchcock. Father hears you have been nominated for a commission..If that is so, pray accept my heartfelt congratulations."

"Keep them," Tim snapped. Why in blazes did that jelly-bellied fool have to talk like that, right now? It was like having a wound probed.

He stood on the muddied sidewalk and tried to straighten his stock.

Ira looked surprised, but still amiable. "Why, Tim, I really meant it. You've done fine. Father had it from General Greene himself."

"Stow it. I—I've left the Army." He stared belligerently at this plump, smooth-faced fellow. Ira was wearing at least four heavy gold seals to his watch fob and his vest was embroidered and stitched like any London macaroni's.

Ira blushed, moved to warm his back in the sunlight. "Well, well then, I take it you will engage in er—commercial enterprise—business with your father?"

"You might."

Ira Thaxter winked elaborately. "Smart of you to serve first. The Committee of Safety will grant you favors that they'll never do for me—nor anybody who ain't enlisted. Yes, Tim, I'd say you are real smart." His eyes brightened, grew more intent. "Say, you've got some sheep on the Island, haven't you?"

"Some few, I expect."

"Well, I'd like to buy them. Give you top price, five dollars apiece."

"Why?" Tim started. "It's against the law to ship mutton out of the Province."

"Not to a sister Province," Ira corrected blandly. "Between you and me, mutton is fetching good money down on Long Island."

"At how much?" He kept on talking so as to keep from thinking.

"Why—er—I haven't the latest quotation."

"I'll think on it," Tim promised.

8

Mr. Southwick's Book Store

DIRECTLY after the closing prayer of the Women's Weekday Meeting, Desire Harmony had hurried away. At Mr. Southwick's book store there were only two customers and these gazed at her incuriously.

The proprietor smiled. "You are earlier than usual, Mistress Bennett."

She followed him to a back corner of the shop, her prim Quaker's dress rustling softly. "Yes, we are returning to the Island early. You have my—my Sheridan ready?"

"Yes. But would you not prefer poetry today? 'The Stratagem' is just in from the Continent, by a Mr. Cartwright. They speak very well of him in London."

"I will try it. I am not in the mood for Sherry." It lent her a sense of importance to use the abbreviation—as John did. Where a tall bookcase hid her from casual customers she settled on a set of steps and began reading.

The other people left and it became so quiet she could hear the loud ticking of Mr. Southwick's clock. When she came to a dramatic line, she would gaze into space and try to give it life. Softly, she read aloud:

> "There are two births; the one when light
> first strikes, the new awaken'd sense; the
> other, when two souls unite. And we must
> count our life from thence: when you love me
> and I love you, then both of us were born anew."

How very beautiful, how perfectly it described John and herself. " 'We must count our life from thence—Then both of us were born anew.' "

Someone came in her direction.

"To be a poet, or to tread the stage must be monstrous fine, Mr. Southwick," she said lightly. "When the life can be so gay, so varied, what boots an existence so dull as mine?" She sighed, fingered a stack of plays beside her. "Yes, Mr. Southwick, I vow I could serve Mimos with distinction—nay, to a turn!"

"Pa's cane will serve thy backside to a turn," Tim's voice sounded angrier than she had ever heard it. As she jumped up, he glanced contemptuously at the books. " 'High Life below Stairs,' 'The Busybody,' 'The Fair Penitent.' How dares thee read such worldly bilge?"

"Why—why, I meant no harm."

"Thee knows very well the reading of poetry and plays is against the rules of the Society," Tim burst out. "Thee is a shameless baggage and shall condemn thyself before the Meeting!"

In a fine, defiant flourish his sister's head went back, and she struck a pose which made her seem taller than her scant five feet three. "Don't thee dare talk Quaker at me! Thee has no right! I shall read whatever pleases me and neither you nor Papa, nor anybody else, shall gainsay me!"

His growing sense of confusion deepened. Was the whole world topsy-turvy? "But, Dee, why? Why must thee read such trash?"

"It's not trash!" she burst out passionately. "From plays one learns about—about people. One acquires knowledge. I would not be one bit surprised if, a hundred years from now, people were still reading 'She Stoops to Conquer.' "

Though her voice gained in volume, it remained harmonious, low-pitched. "Mr. Goldsmith shows a body why people living in this very town talk and act as they do. Why, 'Mrs. Malaprop' is your precious Mrs. Percival to the life."

Tim remained unimpressed. "I'll wager it was one of those vain, feather-headed summer visitors from Charleston who put you on to this. That Proveaux girl, most likely! They are forever talking of their theater, the St. Cecilia Society and such giddy nonsense. Come. We leave for home at once."

Desire turned scarlet, faltered. "But—but—my Meeting has a—has a preparation class. The—the Lightbody girl has professed truth. Really, Tim, I *must* attend."

"After reading such lewd and worldly books?" Tim was really shocked. "Thee, I mean you, will not attend any meeting! You are coming with me."

"I will not!"

"Thee will!" Tim took her by the arm.

"Unhand me, sir!" Desire ordered with lofty dignity. Not even Mrs. Norris could have issued the command more eloquently, she thought. Little Mr. Southwick, who had come poking around a bookcase like a mouse in steel-rimmed spectacles, flinched back.

Desire stood rubbing her arm, dark eyes intent. "And pray, fine sir, what sets thee in such a monstrous hurry to leave town?"

"No concern of thine," Timothy snapped. "Come, else I'll tell Pa about thy reading plays."

Else? So there was a doubt about his tattling? 'Til now she had thought there was none. Apparently, she'd struck on something. Tim wanted something, so he'd keep quiet. She thought she saw it. He'd been fighting—that was plain enough—didn't want Papa to know. What with his quick temper, Tim was always getting into scrapes.

"If I give up my Meeting, thee—thee will not tell?"

He hesitated, looked sullenly away. "No."

She smiled bewitchingly, patted his cheek. "Very well, dearest brother, we shall make a covenant between us. Meantime, you had best remove that fearsome scowl. It doesn't improve the aspect of thy bumps and bruises. Pray wait while I settle with Mr. Southwick for this foolscap."

Grandly, she swept off among the dusty tables of books with Mr. Southwick pottering along behind her vigorous strides.

In the dealer's office she caught up a lead stick, wrote hurriedly:

Dearly Beloved of my Heart:
    Alas! the Fates play us False. I cannot meet you this Afternoon. Fly to my arms at our usual Meeting Place Sunday night. Sweeting, your Desire dwells in darkness most noisome until that delicious Moment.
                                        Thy ever adoring
                                                    D.

Hurriedly, she sketched a whole platoon of circles and kissed them.

"Here is the money," she said a trifle too loudly; then, in an undertone, "You will give it him when he comes in?"

"Thank'y. Your tuppence, Mistress," gabbled old Southwick and winking, tucked the note into his waistcoat pocket.

They were descending Queen Street towards Long Wharf when the blow fell. A dreadfully clear voice among a group of men inquired,

"Say, ain't that young Bennett, the feller who quit Matt Allen's company?"

"Who deserted, you mean."

Desire flinched. "Oh, Tim—you *didn't!*"

"No, I didn't desert," he insisted, lengthening his stride.

"Then, tell them so!"

He shook his head. "It will do no good. There was a misunderstanding."

"Oh." Desire's voice sounded small, infinitely astonished.

Phil Hull, his clothes ripped, and still white under his freckles, came out of hiding near the skiff. In the waist were crouched five other men from Conanicut.

They weren't looking any too happy, either.

9

BENNETT & SON

ASA BENNETT's counting room could only be reached by a set of steps built against the exterior of the warehouse.

Tim had removed the marks of battle as efficaciously as possible, but he was afraid Pa might notice the faint bruise on his cheek. He began climbing.

As never before the big warehouse looked desolate and disused. Only a narrow path had been shoveled through the drifts down to the shore. Snow, for some reason, had been removed from the wharf and the vicinity of the *Hope,* a chunky little brig of ninety tons.

As Tim's tread clumped up the steps, a trio of gulls arose from the roof, went flapping out over fields of drift ice clogging the West Passage.

One thing was surprising. Although the *Hope* appeared woefully weatherbeaten and forlorn, no snow mantled her decks, and a thin tendril of wood smoke was curling up from her galley's chimney. He hadn't imagined that anybody could be living aboard. Laommi Freebody, the *Hope's* master, and her two mates had homes in Newport.

In the faint warmth of the counting room, he found Captain Freebody and his father in close consultation. Loammi Freebody, lean and tall with eyes the color of granite, had a heavily veined nose. With it, his cheekbones formed a right triangle of scarlet.

Although plenty of Quaker sea captains were available, Asa Bennett, for reasons known only to himself, had never given a Friend command over any vessel of his.

Sunlight, slanting in, touched Asa Bennett's silvery hair, clearly revealed his features. Suddenly, Tim felt a lot better. That unfamiliar, puzzled look he had noticed the night before was gone from Pa's face.

"Close the door, Timothy, and sit down." Asa Bennett spoke briskly.

"Thee remembers Captain Freebody?"

"Yes, Pa. How are you, Captain?"

"Can't complain." The master of the *Hope* hitched up his trousers and the buckle of his broad leather belt gleamed like a fiery eye in the pleasant gloom. Minute reflections wavered over the accountant's desk, briefly revealed rows of neat ledgers and letter books.

Enduring a covert scrutiny by Freebody, Tim took a chair. They sat silent. Finally the old Quaker loosened some hooks on his coat and began to speak.

"My son, from today onward I have determined that Bennett & Company shall be known as Asa Bennett & Son." When his shrewd eyes looked for and found an eager uprush of response in Tim's more of the weary lines faded.

"But, Pa, would I not be useless? I know little or nothing of the affairs of this concern." He had to be—wanted to be—honest about it. If ever Pa were to be convinced that a few cannon aboard the Bennett fleet would not mean sure damnation, he must labor to win the old man's respect and confidence.

The announcement had come as a surprise. A big surprise. Could Pa, the kindly, prescient Power of his boyhood, be preparing to admit that his day was drawing to a close? That was about what "Bennett & Son" amounted to.

Queer that he should be the "& Son." It should have been Hezekiah. But Hezekiah's body lay freezing, rotting, on Plowed Hill.

"Aye, for a while thee will be of small use. Nevertheless, I have been given to understand—ahem—by friends, that thee understands the handling of men; that, in a small way, thee possesses the quality of leadership."

Captain Freebody spat into the fireplace. It irked him that the owner hadn't seen fit to confide what all this was about until now. Irritably, he thrust blunt, heavy-soled shoes towards the heat.

"Young sir, we must all scratch hard to make even moderate bread," he observed. "Takes a smart man to stay in trade spite of Parliament, Congress and God Almighty's ways with His ocean."

Gravely, Asa Bennett joined thick-knuckled fingers over his stomach. "No doubt, my son, thee has wondered why I was so insistent that thee return by this, the seventh of this month?"

Tim's brown head inclined. "All the way down from Boston, Pa."

Old Bennett bent, pitched a faggot onto the fire, then commenced to talk briskly, just like his old self. "Through the kind offices of a friend, a delegate to the Continental Congress, I have learned of the passage of an Act which affects this whole Province—and us. Son, a rare opportunity presents itself. It lies before us to win a fortune, an honest fortune, stained by the blood of no man."

What the devil was the owner driving at? Captain Freebody bent forward, squirted tobacco juice. Most of it cleared the hearth but some few drops landed on the firedog and dribbled down, sizzling furiously.

Asa Bennett continued, gaze riveted on his son's strong brown features. "This intelligence is, I believe, known to but two or three other merchants of this port."

Isaac Percival, of course, was one.

With each word, the old man's shoulders lost more of their weary sag. His voice gathered strength as he almost shouted, "Son, the Congress *is lifting the embargo on trade* with the West Indies!"

"Eh?" Freebody stiffened as if he'd sat on a sailor's needle. "We can trade again? Well, now by Jiminy, that *is* good news!"

"Yes. Thee will keep mum, Friend Loammi?"

"I can keep my mouth shut 'thout it's sealed up with wax."

Tim was trying to digest, to see what such a repeal would mean. Pa went on talking. "The gentlemen in Philadelphia have decided that a revived commerce with the West Indies can do our cause small harm."

Freebody smiled faintly. "You mean they stand in desperate need of hard money."

Old Mr. Bennett didn't seem to notice. "Tomorrow, Committees of Safety all over New England will receive orders directing them to clear vessels for Saint-Domingue, Martinique, Jamaica, Barbados— all the islands."

Asa Bennett's cheeks grew pink. "Because the Parliament neglects and ignores them, there is desperate hunger, want and despair on many of the British Islands. The Congress hopes that, by succoring them at this time, we shall—er—gain the sympathy and affection of our fellow colonists."

"Um." Freebody began to chuckle again. "The Congress must want currency, arms and ammunition a sight worse than most people guessed."

So trade was to be reopened? Capital! But British cruisers swarmed the seas. What of them?

"I urged thy return, son, so thee might sail in the *Hope*. With Friend Loammi's guidance, thee shall learn the ways of navigation."

"I am eager to begin, Pa," Tim burst out. Crimanently! If ever he had wanted to leave Newport. In time, the rights about his leaving the regiment would come out. People must remember his good record, his wound, how often he'd done guard duty for poor devils like Abner —Abner! Another call pulled him to this voyage. Ever since he could remember, men had described the blue skies, bluer seas, great shadowy plantation houses drowsing beneath a lashing sun. Wouldn't it be something to see Port Royal, St. Kitts, the Grenadines?

Suddenly, he understood what Desire Harmony had meant. She must be cast in the same mould as himself. Live life—and not only in books. How were bulls fought? What kind of forests yielded mahogany, log and dye-wood? He was especially eager to see the sugar mills which manufactured that molasses from which rum was made. Rum had built, and was building, many a stately New England mansion. He wanted to see vultures rocking in the sky.

At first he failed to digest his father's next words. "Stands to reason, first vessels south will win the highest prices." Pa began to chuckle.

"Friend Loammi and I have secretly provisioned and refitted the *Hope*—all by night. Little remains save to sling her yards, step her topmasts and to bend on her sails." The old man slapped his thigh. "Hee! Hee! No more than a single night's work."

"That was mighty shrewd." Tim demanded eagerly, "Pa, when does the brig set sail?"

"Tomorrow night, son! Thee will learn plenty this trip, and Freebody will— Eh? What's wrong?"

"Tomorrow!" Tim got up. "But, Pa, I can't go tomorrow."

"Can't!" Asa Bennett got up too, and his jaw muscles stood out. "What kind of talk is this?"

Helplessly, Tim looked about. He got no help from Captain Freebody who seemed utterly absorbed in the shape of his fingernails. "But, Pa, my wedding—it's all settled. Mrs. Percival has set it for the twenty-eighth."

"Jehoshaphat's blood and bones!" That was the nearest Asa ever came to cursing. "Thee's a confounded ungrateful puppy! This Percival girl must wait! This is trade, son, trade!

"Old Ike must bide his time. And, mark my words, he'll respect thee vastly more if thee returns to Newport with a pretty black figure to show on thy balance sheet!" Grimly he added, "I know Ike Percival better than thee. Show and gold are his idols. I say thee will sail."

Tim stood straight as at an inspection by General Nat Greene. He would not sail. He would not leave Ira Thaxter near Lucy, smiling his cat-cream grin and coining money.

Pa was only too right—if he could see it from another angle— old Percival was all for the main chance. "I beg thy pardon, Pa, but for me it is more important to stay till Lucy and I are wedded."

"A pox on what thee thinks!" The old man's breath came faster and his white hair seemed to snap. *"I am head of this family! I say thee shall sail!"*

"No, Pa, I will go back to the Army, first."

The same stubborn quality was in them both, thought Loammi Freebody, though he had never seen his owner stand on one toe and lay down the law like this.

Said he, "Hold on a minute. Don't get all het up, you two. Maybe ye can both have yer way."

"Eh? Tell us how, Friend Loammi, and I will be in thy debt forever." Asa Bennett was looking dumfounded. He sensed that Timothy would really go back to the Army, and he didn't want that.

"Either the *Prudence* or the *Patience* must make port soon," observed the lanky figure in sea serge. "Why don't you ship yer son in one of them? Ain't that I wouldn't admire to have him aboard but he'll do better on his first Indies cruise as a married man."

Loammi hoped they would listen. He didn't propose to wet-nurse a green super-cargo. Not these days! Any mistakes this voyage would count extry costly. He needed his share of the venture. So did Hepzibah and the six children.

"Friend Loammi, thee is right," the old Quaker admitted after a long pause. The starch had gone out of his owner, though, Freebody felt. "It is natural for young people to marry, even in haste."

He turned uncertainly to Tim. "It would grieve me less were thee not joining with the World's People. But thee truly loves the lass and she thee. The Lord willing, thy issue should be well blessed with this world's goods."

Tim felt better now that Pa's practical side was back to work. Pa knew as well as he did that Lucy was the only heir to that imposing home on Bannister Street. Again, no less than World's People, was Pa aware that maids were slippery as an icy footwalk.

He beamed on Freebody. Well pleased with himself, the sea captain spat into the fire and let well enough alone.

A sly look twisted Asa Bennett's mouth. "As I have confided, for the past ten days we have been loading the *Hope* at night. Aye, salt fish, salted beef, corn meal, cordage, pine wood and especially slave cloths, will seem as pearls of great price to planters in the Sugar Islands. Truly, son, there seems small gain in forewarning our competitors."

And folks claimed old Ike Percival was smart! Pride filled Tim. In his quiet way Pa was even smarter. Had Ike Percival a vessel so nearly ready? Hardly. Come what might, it looked as if the *Hope* and at least one of the schooners should reap a golden reward for being among the first vessels to reach the Indies in nearly sixteen months.

He supposed he didn't guess how jolted Pa was over being stood up to. The old man kept looking at his son as if this solid and well-built young fellow were a stranger whose eyes were years older than his face.

Seldom encouraged to visit the counting room in the past, Tim was viewing a new and most interesting facet of his father's character. This

brisk, shrewdly-scheming merchant little resembled that benign figure which presided over the Quarterly Meetings at the Friends'
House on the hill above Farewell and Marlborough Streets.

Presently all three men descended to the great chilly store room and
set to work rounding out the *Hope's* cargo.

"I cal'late some pig iron would come in handy." Dubiously, Captain
Freebody explored the scanty hair under his leather cap. "Always did
fetch a spanking price in Georgetown."

"No doubt, Friend Loammi," Asa Bennett agreed. "But slaves cannot subsist on iron. My—er—*our,*" he glanced at Tim, "correspondents
declare that most slaves in Jamaica and Barbados have been on half
rations for months. Also they go ragged. Food and slave cloths will
form the heft of our cargo."

"And they are?"

"Osnaburg, Penninston checks, ticklenburg, seersucker. Down to
Charleston in Carolina the only legal slave cloths are duffle, kersey,
blue and check linen and coarse calicoes. Yes, son, food and cloths. It
is merciful to relieve the poor suffering blacks—"

"—And enjoy top prices," Freebody informed the world at large.

The late afternoon sunlight beat in over canvas baffles rigged high
enough to ward off curious eyes. The old Quaker had never encouraged curiosity, least of all nowadays when his warehouse was stocked
with choice West India merchandise.

Let a loose tongue wag and, like as not, a raiding party would turn
up. The British squadron was always short of supplies, thanks to the
presence of so many cheese-paring rascals in the Admiralty.

At one end were stacked tall coils of yellow-gold cable, manufactured in the Bennett's own rope walk, churns of cheese, chest on chest
of bacon, soap and hardware.

Gaps in a lofty barricade of flour barrels showed that a considerable
supply had already been stowed aboard the brig. There was still plenty,
though. White splashed barrels stood stacked right up to the roof.
Sacks of corn, barley and oats reinforced this peaceful bastion along
one wall of the big dim room.

In the air, the odors of hides, vinegar and molasses predominated; but strangest of all was the peculiarly erotic smell of the salt fish which swung in great sheaves from roof joists.

"These," Asa Bennett indicated a row of chests, "contain striped Hollands, fustian, baize and callimancoes. I figure the planters in the French Islands—note that, Friend Loammi—will be mighty glad of some cloth. Food to Jamaica, cloth and general cargo to the foreign islands."

"Yep." Captain Freebody spat accurately through a rat hole. "Lucky they've such merciful law down in Saint-Domingue."

"What's that?" Tim inquired curiously.

"French King says every owner must furnish each slave a complete set of clothes, twice each year. Yes, Asa, with good luck and good management, the *Hope* should earn her price twice over this voyage."

"You'll touch at Kingston?" Tim asked.

"No. I favor Montego Bay. A safer side o' the island. There ain't no navy depot like Port Royal handy. Kingston side, you always got the fear of meeting some cockerel new in command of a sloop who maybe figgers 'twouldn't be nowise a bad idee to seize a helpless vessel and take her into Cuba and sell her."

"Thee is entirely right there," old Bennett agreed quickly. "I am thinking that thee had better touch at Charleston. There is yet room for five or six hundred weight of rice."

The shipmaster cocked his long, horse-like head to one side. "December rice?"

"Nay. Nothing so dear. Just middlings, slave food. Thee should be able to purchase all thee wants at fifty shillings the barrel."

"Shucks, Asa," Freebody grunted, " 'tain't been that low since time out o' mind."

Asa Bennett said innocently, "Nonetheless Henry Laurens complains to the Congress that all the warehouses in Charleston are fit to burst with it."

"What do those chests of bacon sell for?" Tim inquired. He thought he would catch on pretty quickly. He'd a memory above the average. Why, inside of a week, he had been able to name every man of the Second Rhode Island Regiment. He had tried to be a good soldier and, no matter who said what, he *had* been one, too.

Pa was saying, "A chest of bacon costing twelve shillings usually is calculated to fetch seventeen." Gazing through a cobwebby window, he studied a low tidal marsh extending from the brown and white shore far out into the slate-colored current.

"In these times, however, a Jamaica planter should be glad to pay twenty-three, maybe twenty-four."

"Don't go gittin' too optimistic," Freebody cut in acidly. "I ain't no miracle man."

"Twenty-three or twenty-four—at *least!*" old Bennett repeated.

Tim grinned.

"This," the merchant nodded to a pile of lumber, "is prime oak and pine planking, but we'll not venture any this voyage. We must think of the poor hungry blacks in bondage. Lowly though they are, they are yet God's creatures. Truly to deal in human souls is sin, a very deadly sin."

Tim nodded, though he didn't quite agree. Ike Percival had got his start in the Guinea trade, and Abishai Thaxter. Up in Providence, Nicholas Brown and his brothers could thank the triangular trade— rum to Africa, slaves to the Indies, sugar to New England—for their comfortable way of living.

A brown rat sped from a pile of hides to a hole beneath a row of soap chests. "Thee had best lock Snapper in here tonight."

"—And what will Captain Freebody bring back?"

The master of the *Hope* replied, "Why, young sir, if I have luck and don't get took, I'll bring back sugar, fine muscovado molasses and, if I can lay my hands on any, coffee from the Blue Mountains in Jamaica. Then I aim to take on pimentos, turtles—"

"—Turtles?"

"Aye. There's good profit in them." Freebody nodded. "Pay six shillin's for each critter down there, sell 'round here for thirty-six. Sea cooks and owners are mighty partial to a green turtle."

"Why is that?"

"If ever you go to sea, you'll learn why," Freebody said humorlessly. "It's the only fresh meat that'll stay healthy fer weeks and weeks."

"Don't turtles ever die?"

"Oh, yes. They'll be hale and hearty so long's they lie at the bottom of the cask, and whimper and complain when they come to breathe. But when the critters flop 'round, stay up on the surface, you'd best dish 'em up in a hurry. Yes, sirree."

At length the old man said, "Son, it grows chilly and thee has learned enough for today. Directly the *Hope* clears, we will study drygoods. There is need of haste, too. The *Prudence* and the *Patience* must make port any hour now."

They were sister ships and three masted schooners. Aunt Abigail had named them at a double launching. Poor Aunt Abbie, dead three years now. Only recently had Tim come to realize what a poor, if well-intentioned, substitute she had made for a mother.

Too bad Harmony Bennett hadn't ever been right after giving birth to Desire. In spite of everything Dr. Moffat tried, Ma had died the following year. That was why the Bennett children numbered only three in a generation when nearly everyone else reckoned eight or ten offspring just an average family.

"What about the British cruisers?" Tim asked as the three of them trudged up a rise towards the warm lights of Peaceful Haven.

Captain Freebody looked grave. "It's fear of the Committee, not of the blockade, that has kept most of us idle. Aye, 'tis a sad story if, after you've dodged the bulldogs, the Sons of Liberty condemn your vessel, auction your cargo, blacklist you. Plague take all red-hot patriots! I don't expect any trouble from the British tomorrow morning. Given half a chance, I figger I can out-sail 'em in the *Hope*."

"Why not?"

" 'Cause old Wallace has come to rely on the Committee to enforce the blockade—from the other side of the bulwarks, as it were. Your Pa has it all figgered out. If you're blessed with half his wits, Mr. Timothy, you'll sail into a fortune with stuns'ils set."

10

THE LONG RIFLE

As QUIETLY as he might, Tim followed the trail over to the Hollow. He'd surprise Sam Higsby, then they'd drink a little rum and swap lies before the camp fire. It would be something like being back in the Army.

He needed further to forget that clear voice asking, "Ain't that young Bennett who deserted Allen's Company?"

At the lip of the hollow he paused, studying a faint flicker of firelight. Striking between the tree trunks, the glow was sketching an orange and black striped pattern. He wondered how Sam was making out.

Mamba, in great wonderment, had described how the Injun-feller had insisted on paying for the blankets, flour, peas, beans and pork Miss Desire had wanted to give him. Towards dusk, he had heard the Pennsylvanian's rifle crack down near Beavertail Point.

Quietly, he descended the ravine. He hoped Higsby had brought the spare rifle down from the barn. He could pay for it now. Another sign Pa had changed was the way he had handed over the seven pounds without question.

He was not fifteen yards from the camp now and grinned to think that Higsby hadn't noticed him. He could see that the ranger had built himself a comfortable lean-to with a log threshold across its front. He must be in its depths.

Tim emitted a little startled yelp as the rifleman's war hatchet went *tchunk!* into a pine trunk just above his head. He whirled about but the slope behind him was empty. Even as he wavered, a streak of silver grazed his elbow and Higsby's long knife sank quivering into another tree in line with his chest.

Deep-throated laughter rose from a laurel thicket. "Friend, I couldn't help it. You sneakin' down so careful an' quiet—like a herd of bison. Oh, my Jesus, if you could've seen yer face just now."

"Keep your parlor tricks for folks with tough nerves," Tim grinned. "How you making out?"

Higsby strode up. "Fine as silk. What's that in yer coat tail?"

"Demerara rum. Watch out for it. Even a Gloucester fisherman will admit it raises blisters on a doorknob!" He produced a pair of whittled wooden cups, and the figure in buckskins watched interestedly as Tim tilted out some syrupy black stuff.

"Never seen stuff like that—lemme try just one swaller as is."

Higsby swallowed, immediately exploded into a series of strangled coughs. Eyes watering, he groped for his water bucket.

"Holy jumpin' Jesus!" he gasped. "Feel like I swallered a red-hot ramrod."

Tim's teeth gleamed in the firelight. " 'Round here we generally lace Demerara about half and half, then grab a good holt of something before we drink. Uncle Ben always claimed 'twas Demerara really raised Lazarus."

"I credit that." Wiping his eyes on the heel of his hand, Higsby dropped an armful of logs on the fire. "Out 'round Wautauga I wouldn't dast build a bonfire like this," he remarked. "It's kind of cheery."

"See you've been busy."

"Shore. It's fine not havin' some gnat-headed officer spoutin' orders." He looked sadly at the flames. "If only a feller could find some fightin' round here. My God, it seems like a real fight in these parts is skurcer 'n virgins 'round Philadelphy."

Higsby flung himself down on a bed of spruce tips. "Ain't them recruiting fellers the awfullest liars? Why one o' them unprincipled dawgs promised us dozens of British skelps a week. Reckon the fellers who stayed home tally a heap higher'n me now."

"How many scalps do you—er—tally?" Tim was amazed that anyone could speak so casually of so ghastly a custom.

"Twenty-three."

"Then you've killed twenty-three Indians!"

"I didn't say no such thing. I said I tally twenty-three skelps. A feller cain't always lay hold of the hair," the ranger declared. "Reckon I've killed near twice that number, mostly Shawnees an' Wyandots an' a fair sprinklin' of Cherokees. Got me a nice Tuscarora sub-chief, once."

Tim felt relieved. "Then you've only killed Indians?"

Higsby sat up straight, dark eyes vicious. "Say, you fixin' to rile me? I'll have you know, I've took three French skelps an' a couple o' rennygades!"

At such pure ferocity, Tim was revolted and must have showed it for the Pennsylvanian burst into shouts of laughter, rolled on the bed hugging his sides.

"Sweet Jesus, you *are* green!" He sat up still chuckling. "Naw! I ain't killed over a dozen men since I've been growed—an' that ain't a puny tally, either. The only skelps I've took was the ones—" he sobered a trifle, "—you saw in Roxbury.

"Remember this, don't ever credit half of anythin' a dirty-shirt tells you. Riflers are the most gifted liars in nature."

Higsby, tall and gaunt in the firelight, reached among the boughs forming his lean-to's roof. "Here's yer rifle. Been cleanin' her up. Had reckoned on tryin' a few shots with her myself but I needed to get this wickie-up finished.

"From the way the birds are actin', it's goin' to turn cold.

"Mister, you are purchasin' a fine piece—prettiest job *I* seen in a 'coon's age. Look at that cherry stock and that fancy patch box!"

When the Pennsylvanian tapped a stud let into the heel of the stock, a long brass panel flew open revealing a cavity filled with a greasy substance.

"B'ar's grease," Higsby explained. "Show you how this patch business works." Contempt entered his tone. "Blunderbusses an' smoothbores don't require none."

From a channel beneath the octagonal barrel, Higsby drew a ramrod. It was nearly four feet in length, wooden and tipped with a little cup of horn.

"Why is it of wood?" Tim queried. "Our iron ramrods come in mighty handy for cooking food."

Higsby sniffed. "See these here lands?" He swung the rifle about, indicated grooves spiraling down into the depths of the bore. "That's what makes yer ball fly straight. Pitch in this one here's about one turn in three feet I judge. Now them there lands is soft iron, an' a metal ramrod would nick or dull 'em. Hickory won't." He clucked deep in his throat.

"Friend, you'll seldom find a finer piece o' steel than is in this frizzen, an' look at the way the silver's been let into the jaws of the cock! My, my, she shore is a pretty piece.

"I'd sell you mine, only I know where to hold my Bella. Takes findin' out. Some rifles shoot high, some low or to either side. Feller's got to find out, an' hold accordin'. I judge this Foulke ain't been re-bored but once. Don't forget you got to get these here rifles rebored every eight or nine hundred shots."

Lank hair falling over his forehead, Higsby bent above the piece. "This bar'l will be about three foot six, full octagon. Muzzle to butt she'll measure four foot eleven—a handy length. Longer bar'l gives you more accuracy, but a six foot piece is unhandy in thick goin', an' it makes loadin' hard."

"What kind of a sight do you call this?"

"A notch behind an' a triangle before is a 'barleycorn.' Take notice of this vent. See? It's lined with gold. Makes a mighty pretty effect, don't it? Easy to clear, too. 'Twon't foul like an iron vent."

Higsby loosened the metal jaws gripping the flint. "This here white flint ain't much good. Wouldn't last but thirty or forty shots with the best of chippin'. Best flints is all Britain an' come from a place called Kent. Knappers over there shore know their trade. Britain troops don't seem to get 'em, though. Their issue flints is turrible."

Higsby raised the Foulke, bent his head briefly over it, tested the trigger. "Mmm! Phil Dougherty favored a heavier pull than most. No real marksman would tolerate more'n a half-pound."

Cross-legged Tim watched and listened.

"Somewheres you'll have to collect you a warbag like this here," from the stump of a branch, Higsby removed first his deerskin haversack, then a large powder horn and finally a very small one. He spilled the haversack's contents onto his blanket.

Tim recognized a bullet mould but was puzzled by an object resembling one of those tinder pistols with which some folks started their fires.

"The Mounseers calls this a 'prouvette'—in plain English, it's a powder-tester. If you're expectin' to do real shootin', you've got to have one."

"Why is that?"

"It's so damned seldom you buy powders of the same strength an' age. Once I lost me a fine suit o' clothes at a shoot near Baltimore— all through not provin' a horn of new powder."

From the tip of the small horn, the rifleman dislodged a small cup of the same material, used it to measure powder into the pan of the prouvette. He cocked the device and glanced up. "See this here numbered dial an' the little arm here? When you fire, a spring pushes the arm around an' you kin tell how strong the powder is by the number she shows."

"I see. But why carry two horns?"

"Big one's ordinary charge powder: FFG or FFFG—if you kin get any. It's right scarce these days."

A raised brow showed Tim's lack of comprehension.

"Suppose you already know it, but gunpowder comes in four grades. FG means fine grain; but it's so coarse you hadn't ought to use it in a rifle—only in cannons an' smoothbores. FFG, fine, fine grain you kin use, but it fouls up a bore somethin' fierce. Fine, fine, fine grain is what you should load with." He picked up the little horn. "This four F powder is only for primin'. So much fer powder an' flints."

Higsby, reaching into the bag, produced a handful of silvery new rifle balls, dropped one onto Tim's palm. "How much do you reckon this weighs?"

"Couldn't judge. It's mighty light. An ounce, maybe?"

The Pennsylvanian shook his head. "Not over half a ounce. Now here"—grinning, he fished out some circular pieces of cloth perhaps an inch and a half across, "—are some rifle patches. Fine lawn, see?"

He winked solemnly. "Friend, if you don't yet know how to get a fine petticut from a gal, why it's fine fun learnin'. I near to froze my feet gettin' this here one." Tim laughed. "Got to be fine linen, though, else it won't burn clean an' leaves a coal at the bottom of yer bore. Then when you go to reload, you might get a couple o' fingers blowed off."

Deftly removing the cap of the large horn, the rifleman tapped out a measure of coarse black powder and poured it into the bore. Next he selected a patch and passed it over the grease, just heavily enough to darken the material. Placing the greasy side down over the muzzle, Higsby made a little impression with his forefinger and in it deposited a ball.

"Now if you was in a hot fight, you'd store yer balls in yer cheek. Watch careful, now."

Setting the rammer's concave horn tip over the bullet, he exerted pressure, whereupon patch and bullet vanished smoothly, evenly, down the barrel. Finally he gave the charge two or three strong taps.

"That, Friend, is called seatin' yer bullet. No call for wads."

"Why? Won't the bullet roll out if you tilt the barrel down?"

"Hell, no. My patch not only greases the lands, but it holds the ball an' the powder in place."

"Crimanently!" Tim exclaimed, "that surely is slick!"

"You bet it's slick," Higsby agreed as he opened the Foulke's pan cover, and primed it. "The Britainers will learn so if us riflers is ever granted a whack at 'em."

"But how can a fellow tell just how much powder he needs?" Tim inquired. "After a rifle's been rebored, I mean?"

"I'm comin' to that." Higsby handed him the rifle, then stirred the fire into a bright blaze. "Remember, you don't *pull* the trigger, squeeze with your hull hand. If you pull, you'll most generally undershoot. Many's the lad who'd still be wearin' his hair if he'd remembered that.

Now aim at that stump. It don't matter whether you hit it. No, hold yer bar'l over that clean patch of snow."

The Foulke's report rang out over the river, and one hill after another echoed the sound, like school children answering a teacher's query. A great flock of geese in Fox Hill Cove took alarm and, yelping, tumbled high into the clear, cold sky.

"Don't move," Higsby cautioned. "Now look at the ground beyond the end of yer bar'l. What do you see?"

"A black streak on the snow."

"Black marks is unburnt powder. When there ain't no more ammunition in miles, a feller can't afford to waste powder."

Tim was deeply interested. "Suppose this was in summertime?"

"Spread sheets. What would you do?"

Tim laughed. "I guess I'd spread sheets, too."

"You hold yer piece good," Higsby conceded. "Maybe you'll make a marksman for all you're a onery, slab-sided Yankee. Now one last thing an' we're done. If you've call to use a strange gun an' ain't got a prouvette, this is a rough an' ready way to judge yer load."

Higsby placed a rifle ball on a square of birch bark and from the big horn allowed a fine cascade of powder grains to trickle over it. Once the bright little ball was completely hidden, Higsby stopped pouring.

"That'll be just about right. Now pour this powder in yer measurin' cup an' mark the inside." He relaxed his serious manner. "Remember all that, an' you'll be a r'arin', tearin' wonder."

Tim felt pretty green and callow. To restore his self-respect he asked, "Can you shoot a duck out of the air?"

"*Flyin'?*"

"Sure, flying."

"What fer? You'd kill a lot more if they was settin'."

"Wouldn't shooting a big bull's-eye give you more hits with your rifle?" Tim suggested.

The other glanced up, surprised. "Kin you really kill a flyin' duck —or are you funnin' me?"

"Comes a good nor'easter, we'll drop down to Mackerel Cove and see how many dusky ducks you can shoot out of the air."

At Higsby's anxious expression, he began to feel better.

II

Reverie

In the sweet-smelling gloom of her bedroom Desir
nett wound both arms about the pillow and presse
it. Her nightgown felt damp with perspiration as sh

"Alas, cold, senseless object, that you are not my
the warmth of this, my breast, could but meta——m
into response!"

Would a great tragedienne express herself thus? I
she criticized her delivery. Not bad, rather good in
she wasn't play-acting altogether.

A cloak thrown over a chair created a tall and
the wall. La! It reminded her of dear John's back
very straight, yet was graceful. He could look so fi

"John, John," she murmured. "How can I en
longer?" It was some help to remember that in three
two hours they would be reunited.

It was somehow terrifying to be so wildly, over w
People wanted to treat her like a child, yet no mer
so distractedly, so madly.

From under her goose down mattress, she bro
green grosgrain—his—and kissed it until she wa
she laid it across her lips. The silk smelled faintly
tobacco.

"My paladin! Never did the Egyptian queen lo
thony half so much as I adore thee! No one on e
sweeting, can plumb the depths of my passion."

When she grew a little calmer she pushed her
her neck. "Dear John, somehow these three nights
Tenth Day night you will read me the sonnets y
You will wrap me in your cloak again and, by the

The Foulke's report rang out over the river, and one hill after another echoed the sound, like school children answering a teacher's query. A great flock of geese in Fox Hill Cove took alarm and, yelping, tumbled high into the clear, cold sky.

"Don't move," Higsby cautioned. "Now look at the ground beyond the end of yer bar'l. What do you see?"

"A black streak on the snow."

"Black marks is unburnt powder. When there ain't no more ammunition in miles, a feller can't afford to waste powder."

Tim was deeply interested. "Suppose this was in summertime?"

"Spread sheets. What would you do?"

Tim laughed. "I guess I'd spread sheets, too."

"You hold yer piece good," Higsby conceded. "Maybe you'll make a marksman for all you're a onery, slab-sided Yankee. Now one last thing an' we're done. If you've call to use a strange gun an' ain't got a prouvette, this is a rough an' ready way to judge yer load."

Higsby placed a rifle ball on a square of birch bark and from the big horn allowed a fine cascade of powder grains to trickle over it. Once the bright little ball was completely hidden, Higsby stopped pouring.

"That'll be just about right. Now pour this powder in yer measurin' cup an' mark the inside." He relaxed his serious manner. "Remember all that, an' you'll be a r'arin', tearin' wonder."

Tim felt pretty green and callow. To restore his self-respect he asked, "Can you shoot a duck out of the air?"

"Flyin'?"

"Sure, flying."

"What fer? You'd kill a lot more if they was settin'."

"Wouldn't shooting a big bull's-eye give you more hits with your rifle?" Tim suggested.

The other glanced up, surprised. "Kin you really kill a flyin' duck —or are you funnin' me?"

"Comes a good nor'easter, we'll drop down to Mackerel Cove and see how many dusky ducks you can shoot out of the air."

At Higsby's anxious expression, he began to feel better.

II

REVERIE

IN THE sweet-smelling gloom of her bedroom Desire Harmony Bennett wound both arms about the pillow and pressed her face against it. Her nightgown felt damp with perspiration as she whispered:

"Alas, cold, senseless object, that you are not my own true love! If the warmth of this, my breast, could but meta—metamorphose you into response!"

Would a great tragedienne express herself thus? Eyes opened wide, she criticized her delivery. Not bad, rather good in fact; but of course she wasn't play-acting altogether.

A cloak thrown over a chair created a tall and stately shadow on the wall. La! It reminded her of dear John's back. He held himself very straight, yet was graceful. He could look so fierce, too.

"John, John," she murmured. "How can I endure this torture longer?" It was some help to remember that in three days and twenty-two hours they would be reunited.

It was somehow terrifying to be so wildly, overwhelmingly in love. People wanted to treat her like a child, yet no mere child could love so distractedly, so madly.

From under her goose down mattress, she brought a hair tie of green grosgrain—his—and kissed it until she was breathless. Then she laid it across her lips. The silk smelled faintly of pomatum and tobacco.

"My paladin! Never did the Egyptian queen love her Roman Anthony half so much as I adore thee! No one on earth, not even you, sweeting, can plumb the depths of my passion."

When she grew a little calmer she pushed her damp hair free of her neck. "Dear John, somehow these three nights will pass. Then on Tenth Day night you will read me the sonnets you have composed. You will wrap me in your cloak again and, by the magic of our love, charm us away to the Hesperides—to the Isles of the Blest."

Oh, but it was wonderful to be in love. She felt an abysmal sorrow that no one else could taste such ecstasy.

Restlessly she turned over and the movement sent air streaming under the bed clothes. She found the draught coolly refreshing—like John's cheek laid softly against hers.

Ever so clearly she could visualize John as he had been their last time they were together. Straight and supple he'd ridden up to her there on the Ferry Road, his triple-caped cloak blowing free.

Oh, the wonderful rough tenderness of his hands. They'd be happy and live in love for ever and ever though to have each other might cost them dear, both of them. She couldn't see how she was going to stand it until Sunday night.

12

Ebb Tide

It was around midnight when the crew for the *Hope* sailed over from Newport. They came quietly, but not furtively, hoping that enemy patrol boats would take them for fishermen going out to haul nets at the turn of the tide.

Captain Freebody's men were hand-picked and knew their work so well the topmasts and yards were sent up in jig-time. Urged by a keen westerly breeze, all hands bent on the sails more by sense of touch than anything else.

Half an hour short of dawn the brig was ready for sea, which was well because the tide was ebbing so fast. Tim could hear the current gurgling about the pilings.

In a great coat with its collar turned up about his ears, Asa Bennett stumped about deck and wharf making sure of a dozen small matters. Snapping orders in penetrating undertones, Captain Freebody and his mates checked every detail of running gear.

To Tim, the preparations were surprisingly reminiscent of throwing up a new breastwork or redan with which to surprise the enemy.

Captain Freebody came ashore, sought Tim. "You've got the Committee of Safety's clearance?"

"Yes. All the papers." He passed over the manifest, bill of lading, a copy of the Articles, and the owner's orders. Into the captain's charge, he also gave letters addressed to Henry Laurens & Company of Charleston; to Messrs. Campbell, Galbraith at Montego Bay, Jamaica; John Petty at New Providence in the Bahamas; and lastly a bill of exchange on Hortalez & Cie. of Cap François, in Saint-Domingue, at the eastward end of Hispaniola.

"Try to get across Jamaica by land and reach Kingston, Friend Loammi," the old Quaker urged. "If thee can secure some hard money owing me from Hibbert, Parrier & Horton, I will grant thee a bonus."

Tim listened, memorized the names as he blew on his fingers. Crimanently! It was raw here on the wharf.

"Will they honor your draft?"

"Mr. Parrier and I have transacted business many years. He will make good the £2,345 his firm owes on my last shipment of livestock."

"Do my best—"

"Then, Friend Loammi, there is nothing more to say. Farewell, and God keep thee and the vessel safe."

"Farewell, Asa, we'll do our damndest. Sorry I won't be here to dance to yer wedding, Mr. Timothy, 'cause I can cut a smart caper when I'm so minded. I'll bring yer bride something purty from the Indies," he added.

The winter stars were paling and by the early dawn the two Bennetts were able to discern the dim loom of South Ferry on the Narragansett shore.

The boatswain called, "All clear, sir!"

Captain Freebody cupped his hands and yelled, "H'ist the stays'l and break out the fore tops'l."

The tide was running faster still. As Tim cast off the lines, chunks of drift ice went *bump!* along the brig's water line. A sturdy craft, this, of good New England oak and pine. Laid down with some evidence of imagination, she was fast without being racy, sturdy without being clumsy. Sort of like Pa himself.

He saw Pa had taken off his hat, was bowing his head. In a deep and earnest voice, Asa Bennett prayed; "O Lord, do Thou prosper this our venture and preserve its captain and crew. O Lord, do Thou bring them back safe. World without end. Amen."

Softly the weatherbeaten canvas stirred, but an ungreased block screeched like a fiend in torment.

"Set the jibs!" Freebody's voice already sounded fainter as the silhouette of the *Hope* slipped away from the wharf and aimed her bowsprit for mid-stream.

Presently the fore course was set and its fullness billowed out over the inky channel. Faster, faster still, the brig slipped through the water, heading for the faint glow of Beaver Point Light.

The old man sighed. "There she goes, son, mayhap the last vessel I shall ever send to sea."

"Oh, no. You—we will send dozens yet."

"I trust so; yet the ways of the Lord are indeed inscrutable."

"Come on up to the house. You are tired, Pa. I told Mamba to fix hot chowder and pie for you."

The old man smiled. "In thy way, thee is indeed a good son. If only thee could be less violent, more heedful of God's word."

13

ISAAC PERCIVAL

ON FRIDAY afternoon Lucy and her father came over to pay a visit. To sort of settle things, Tim figured happily.

In the Quaker's living room the two merchants took each other's measure with respect tinged by suspicion. Ike Percival clapped the old Quaker on his shoulder, went into roars of laughter.

"When I heard how quiet and smart you'd got the *Hope* to sea, I like to split my waistcoat laughing. My *Jolly Beggar* didn't get off 'til noonday. Guess we kind of showed up the rest of the boys, didn't we?"

Asa Bennett chuckled, pulled his long waistcoat down as he always did when he was tickled over something.

"Thee has heard of any other Rhode Island vessels getting clear?"

"Only John and Nicholas Brown's *Triton* and the *Joseph* out of Providence," Percival replied, covertly appraising the living room furniture. Plain as a post, most of it. "Guess that proves us Rhode Islanders know how to keep our traps shut, don't it?"

He seated himself in front of the fire, extended skinny legs to the heat. He was wearing real silk hose.

"Yes, sir, I was mighty glad to hear your brig got away safe. I'll be gladder yet when one or both of your schooners make port. Me, I'm getting worried over my *Juno*. She's a week overdue out of Martinico. I expect to make a pretty penny with her rum and sugar. Prices are high as a cat's back."

Percival was full of good spirits, even discussed the marriage date. The twenty-eighth was a Thursday. A good day. Trade would be slack then. He would see that everyone had cause to remember the wedding supper. The Mrs. had even ordered Lucy's nuptial dress.

In the study Lucy was effectively making Tim forget he'd ever entertained a doubt or a worry. Never had she seemed so loving, so gay, so bewilderingly beautiful.

"We were so glad about the *Hope*." She smiled. "The day of the riot Mama was itching to tell you about the Congress' plan to raise the West Indies embargo. But Papa had changed his mind. He says he has something else to confide to you—something still more profitable!"

Had he? It would be like Mr. Percival to withhold information until the last moment, thus placing a new son-in-law under obligation.

They had grand fun talking and planning. Tim told Lucy that, when the schooners made port, Pa had promised him some shares in one of them, for a wedding gift. He didn't say anything about having to sail as supercargo. Time enough once they were married.

"I've got our table linen all hemmed," Lucy murmured, her pale head bright on his shoulder, "and Mama is going to make us a compliment of that silver service our *Juno* captured in the old French war. Wine glasses, too. And Papa is being very generous. He says he will furnish a little setting room. Grandma Warren—it was she we went up to see at Concord—is going to send bed linen and a pair of elegant patchwork quilts she made all herself!"

Tim said, "Let me know if anybody gives us kitchen coppers. I'm counting on making you a Christmas gift of some."

Lucy hugged his arm, wrinkled her nose at him. "Aren't we the big stupids to go marrying right after Christmas? I guess plenty of people will combine their Christmas and wedding gifts. Ain't *I* the greedy little pig?"

"*Oink!*" he grunted, and kissed her soundly.

"Tell you a secret," Lucy said, looking a little scared. "This time I know what Papa intends telling you. I overheard him talking to a Commissioner from Philadelphia. The sooner you know about it the greater chance you—I mean *we*—stand of profiting."

He looked at her with suspicion. "Are you serious?"

"As ever in my life, dear." She put her mouth so close to his ear that it tickled. He forgot about that when he heard her next words:

"Does your father know that the Congress intends *to build a navy?*"

"A what?"

Her blue eyes very round, Lucy nodded. "Yes, I heard Stephen Hopkins telling Papa. And two of the warships are to be built and outfitted in Rhode Island!"

Outfitted! Bennett & Son were ship chandlers, among other things. She began to talk in a rapid undertone.

"Next week Pa is going to meet the commissioners. Mr. Hopkins said some merchantmen will be armed as a stop-gap until we can build real men-o'-war."

"That's right. We couldn't start work for a good while. Not until spring."

"Mr. Hopkins told Papa some ships have already been bought in Baltimore, in Maryland. One has been purchased here, and two in New York."

"Naval building means good profits for the shipyards," Tim said, thinking aloud.

"We had better take our profit while we can." Lucy was very like her mother now. "Papa fears the merchants of America will be taxed blue in the face to keep this Navy afloat. Personally, he stands for fortifying our harbors. Forts would keep the enemy off, wouldn't they?"

"I guess so," Tim agreed absently. "It would be fine to see the *Rose,* the *Glasgow,* and the rest driven away."

"Amen," Lucy sighed. "They do say the British commander is livid over the riot of the other day. He has been trying to find out who you are."

"Did he?"

She hesitated, laid a hand on his arm. "I don't think so, darling."

Eyes half closed, she held out her arms and they kissed. In the living room the grave elder voices droned on.

"Darling?" She looked up at him.

"Yes?"

"When I repeat 'for better or for worse' I—I will mean just that."

He believed her. How could he help it?

With a flash of annoyance Tim realized that Desire, head tipped to one side and fingers laced before her, was in the doorway and survey-ing them almost critically.

"Such devotion, such felicity," she murmured in her rich low tones. "How kindly the Fates have used you both."

Lucy flamed scarlet but went over to kiss her. "Desire, how are you, dear child?"

"Dearest Lucy, today you look simply ravishing. I do protest I've never beheld anybody look half so exquisite."

Desire was yielding to a perverse impulse. Why was it right for Tim and Lucy to fondle and kiss whenever they pleased? Yet she and John must rendezvous furtively, dodging timorously about like

—like settlers in hostile Indian country? It wasn't fair. Ah, well, just two more nights now. Beneath the gray poplin her breasts rose.

She entered the study; her heels, Tim noticed, had not lost a distinctive little flutter which since childhood had marked her walk. Oh, damn the brat and her la-de-dah airs! Where in time had she picked up this London manner? From her reading, no doubt.

"Your candle-dipping can't be done." Tim was gruff.

"Finished." Desire laughed provokingly, held out a hand marked with a large red blister. "But I shouldn't wonder there's enough grease left to fill a small mould. It would be a rare pleasure to instruct dearest Lucy in the art. It may come in useful once you are married."

Lucy, though sweetness itself, knew a dart when she felt one. "Dear child, 'tis most considerate of you, I vow, but I have promised Aaron Lopez our candle trade. In these days Papa says one must keep trade going—it helps to buy whenever one can."

Desire inquired demurely, "Even British officers' notes, I presume?"

"And pray," Lucy returned, "what new books is Mr. Southwick offering these days? I heard of a simply delicious novel—'The Indiscreet Miss'—I'm sure you would find it amusing—and instructive."

Desire's cheeks flamed and the provocative shadows under her eyes deepened. How much did Lucy *know*? Oh, damn her for being so sure of herself! Better shift her tactics.

"Oh dear Lucy, where *did* you discover such a perfectly ravishing material?" It made her mad clean through. Here was Lucy Percival gotten up in fine blue striped challis and lace, and wearing such a dashing little bonnet. But Quaker gray and a maiden's cap for hat for mousy Desire Harmony Bennett. She would have given a finger to own a Lincoln green cape with a scarlet lining.

"I am so pleased you like my dress, Desire." Lucy smiled, the essence of good nature. She *would* be nice to this chit.

"Oh, I do. But is—isn't it daring?" A wicked twist crept over Desire's lips.

"Daring?" Lucy inquired incautiously.

"Those stripes. They resemble the material Papa sends to Jamaica. I'm told the planters garb their slaves in such stripes."

Sisters are the devil! Tim thought. Why should Dee plague Lucy? Lucy had never been anything but sweet with her.

The taller girl smiled very charmingly. "It may be, Desire dear. I, too, am a slave—to fashion."

The retort came so pat that Desire's ears burned. Suddenly she was sorry. She hadn't wanted to quarrel with Lucy. Lucy was really very kind. What drove her to say such things?

14

FLOOD TIDE

AFTER such a discouraging delay it seemed too good to be true that the *Patience* was safe at last. Yet undoubtedly she was tacking in towards the landing. Tim, hurriedly cramming the tails of his night-shirt into his breeches, wondered why she should be *descending* the West Passage. Ships making port from the sea usually ascended the channel.

Obviously, Polypus Hammond must have learned somewhere that food convention between Captain Wallace and Newport was at an end. Shrewdly, he must have entered Narragansett Bay at night and, instead of following the obvious route up the West Channel, have navigated up the Seakonnet Passage, only to double back between Hog and Prudence Islands to Conanicut.

"Praise de Lawd, praise de Lawd!" Mamba was softly chanting downstairs. "De gold'n ship done come back from de Indies! Gwine have us sugah, gwine have us cawfee, gwine have us turtles an' pimentos agin!"

In the hall Tim heard Desire's wail of "Tim, Tim, wait for me! I'll be into these plagued petticoats in a minute."

Buttoning up, he could hear Pa turning out in a hurry. He called, "Hasten, Timothy! Hasten! Someone must catch their lines."

When he appeared in the hallway, the old man was more excited than Tim had ever seen him. All a-tremble, Pa was cramming a broad-brimmed beaver hat over his tasseled nightcap.

This morning it was so cold that ice had formed across an inlet below Sam Higsby's hollow.

"Which is she?" Desire yelled through her half-open door. "Which do you take her for, Pa?"

" 'Tis the *Patience*," her father cackled. "Friend Polypus shall have an extra share for bringing her in safe. Ah, son, truly there is power in prayer. Thee can have no idea how worried I have been."

All three Bennetts pelted down to the shore. Their feet clumped loudly on the wharf as, helped by a strong flood tide, the *Patience* came edging in.

As he was throwing a clove-hitch over a bollard with the schooner's bow line, Tim noticed a crudely-repaired hole in her port quarter. Then he noted that her topmast had been sent down. It was pretty dark, but he could tell that the schooner had suffered some rough handling from the seas on her voyage North. In a December passage, that wasn't unexpected.

Asa Bennett also was peering into gloom. "Friend Polypus seems a mite short-handed. Where can—" He left the sentence uncompleted when the schooner's bowsprit came nosing over the wharf. Presently she fetched up with an awkward bump. Blocks whirred, and the *Patience's* jibs and mainsail fluttered down.

"Ahoy." Pa's voice sounded thin. "Thee is there, Friend Polypus?"

"Aye, sir. Most of me." Now the stern line landed thudding on the wharf. Tim hauled it in hand-over-hand.

"But the men—where are the rest of thy crew?"

A figure came limping to the rail. "—Dead, Asa, dead; or in prison—" came the doleful reply.

"The Lord's will be done!" The old Quaker bowed his head a moment.

Desire ran forward, helped Tim to make fast the stern line. "Oh, dear—Papa was fearing something like this."

"What is amiss?" Tim shouted.

"Tell you better after we've et and drunk," croaked the schooner's master. "None of us hev had more'n starvation rations come two weeks. It's perishing cold out on the Atlantic."

Old Bennett asked, "What ails thy head, friend Polypus?"

"It's shy an ear," grunted the captain of the *Patience,* climbing over the rail. Almost as broad as he was long, Captain Polypus Hammond was normally a plump, good-natured fellow. Now by the light of Tim's lantern, his haggard features were shadowed by a ragged two weeks' beard. His every motion suggested that he had not slept in days.

"Leave be, lads," he called to the three men who were listlessly hauling the mainsail inboard. "We'll go and thaw out."

William Elley, Tim recognized, Paul Clarke and a one-eyed fellow who hailed from up near Portsmouth. From below appeared a big, gangling negro he had never seen before.

Asa Bennett felt his heart stop. Where were Lucius Hull, Jethro Greene and the others?

"Is that all?"

"Aye—all."

"Come," Desire said. "If the vessel is safe enough."

Asa Bennett noticed what his son did not; that the *Patience* was riding high, ominously high in the water.

While they were drinking cups of scalding "Liberty tea," a concoction of dried raspberry leaves, Asa Bennett shook his head. "'Tis a poor drink. I should have requested thee to fetch up coffee and a measure of sugar from the vessel."

Captain Polypus Hammond rubbed eyes hollow from sleeplessness, emitted a barking laugh. "Coffee? Sugar? Hell's roaring bells, Asa, did you hear me say we've been on starvation rations, or didn't you?"

Desire asked in a small, scared voice, "Then—then the cargo was lost?"

"Every speck," Hammond replied over the noise of the men swilling steaming bowls of chowder. They weren't talking, just shoveling the creamy stew into their unshaven faces.

He turned to the owner, forgot there was anyone else in the room. " 'Cordin' to your orders, Asa, me in the *Patience* and Hazard in the *Prudence* cleared Martinico three months back—tenth of September —gunnel-deep with sugar, molasses, coffee and a chest of specie each."

Bloodshot eyes flickered up from the food. "You was right, Asa, about mules being wanted at Tabago; cleared the outward v'yage expenses out o' them alone."

The schooner captain poured tea into a saucer, blew on it noisily, and swallowed the scalding stuff in long gulps. He sighed. The three Bennetts watched, waited in silence. Pa was looking very old and frail there by the fireplace. His jaw was set like when he had something unpleasant to do, such as pay taxes, or order a sick animal to be destroyed.

The four men of the crew were settled back in their chairs half asleep already, too tired to talk.

"Half a day to the north'ard o' Dominica," Captain Hammond continued, "we fell in with a big British letter-of-marque, sixteen guns. He gave chase, but me and Lot Hazard outfooted him to wind'ard, once we started our water casks."

Asa Bennett listened, arms crossed over chest and fine blue eyes fixed on his master's deeply lined features.

"Only place we dast go to re-water was Tiburon."

Desire asked of Tim in a breathless tone, "Where is Tiburon?"

"On the Island of Hispaniola, Miss. Westernmost end is Spanish, east end is French and called Saint-Domingue." Hammond's bloodshot eyes blinked and irritably he tested the grimy rag about his head.

"Got our water all right and we felt pretty good over shaking that Britisher the way we did. Well, me and Lot figured our best chance was to run the Windward Passage, past Turk's, then cruise North along the 70th longitude. That would keep us clear of British cruisers off the coast."

"Thy reasoning was good," Asa Bennett remarked. "But all the same a British man-o'-war overtook thee?"

"No!" Rage welled into the unshaven mariner's voice. " 'Twas a damned piratical, a Spanish privateer, the *Nuestra Señora de Carmen,* twenty guns, out o' the Captaincy-General o' Cuba. She sailed to wind'ard faster than a scared cat once we raised her accursed tops'ls off Great Inagua in the Bahamas. He fired a gun, bade us heave to."

"But," Tim broke in hotly, "there is no war with the Spaniards!"

" 'Course not." Hammond snorted. "But that didn't hold back Mr. Garaycockeo, not him! Blast his bloody bones!

"Soon's we saw what the privateer was up to, Lot and me split courses and ran for it. But was too late. The Don had the weather gauge."

Captain Hammond belched. "Ain't used to so much food, Miss. Well, Lot got took first and was fool enough to put up a fight. Never did learn whether Lot or any of his people was spared. If the breeze had held, I might have won free; but it petered out and we was deep with cargo. The goddam pirate came up in his boats."

"You got taken without a fight?" Tim inquired in such amazement that Hammond stared sullenly in his direction.

"To what purpose, young man? We hadn't more than half a dozen muskets aboard, just what we use for slaughtering wild cattle in the Spanish Islands, and nary a cannon, of course. They sent three long-boats against us chock-a-block with mustees, Spanishers, and some Frenchies."

The Captain's tone became dreary. His gestures were so lifeless that anyone with half an eye could see that he had been living a long nightmare. Below his wounded ear showed the end of a cut; it still was an angry red, pulpy-looking. Though Desire was eager to dress that rag-bound ear she didn't dare say so.

Without raising his eyes from his plate Captain Hammond mumbled, "The cursed picaroons swarmed aboard and, for no reason save they was the nearest, threw Lucius Hull and Jethro Greene down on the deck and cut their throats—my God, just like they was sticking hogs! I won't ever forget how they begged and hollered."

"Laws," whimpered Mamba from among the shadows. "Ain't dat *gashly?*"

"We 'lowed we hadn't harmed them but they cuffed us all about, even threatened to run us up to the rigging by our private parts."

The one-eyed seaman looked mournful, like a hound that has been kicked for no good reason. " 'More talk out of ye and I'll have yer tongue out,' says he."

"They drove my crew into the fo'c's'le and began to plunder—" Hammond said, swinging dull red-lidded eyes. "When I raised a holler, this Garaycockeo feller spat in my face.

"Sez he, contemptuous-like—he was a Spanisher, but he knew our lingo—'You say you ain't Englishmen no more?' 'True enough,' sez I. 'Then what is your nationality? Where is your flag? Bah! You are Rebels. Pirates! Like so many treacherous Cubanos. Were you English we might think twice before—er—visiting you. Perhaps three times—if there was an English cruiser in the Windward Passage.'

"I cussed plenty and declared he'd be made to pay, but he only laughed in a nasty way and said he was skeered stiff of all the American men-o'-war that were cruising the Caribbean.

"My God! Mr. Bennett, why ain't we got no men-o'-war to protect our shipping down there?" Hammond inquired hoarsely. "Why ain't there a navy to make fellers, like this picaroon, respect our rights?"

Silence fell in the kitchen; everybody could hear Snapper scratching at the door and whining to be let in.

"I don't know," Tim's father replied in slow, bemused accents. "Many people oppose a navy."

"Then," the one-eyed seaman croaked from the shadows, "I ain't never going to sea again 'lest it's under a British flag!"

"He's right," Will Elley agreed heavily. "It's plain and simple sooeyside to cruise the Indies when any crotch-blistered picaroon or buccaneer feels free to pick us off like berries from a bush. By God, if we'd armed vessels, the Spanish would sing sweet and humble."

"They took my cargo?" the old Quaker demanded. "All of it?"

"Aye. When a breeze came, the Don layed his damned, stinking privateer alongside and stripped us to the bone."

Tim felt all choked up. Imagine cutting a helpless man's throat! "Then what?" he asked in a hard, flat tone.

"Mr. Garaycockeo slapped a prize crew of four aboard us under a measly cross-eyed French lieutenant, and ordered us into San'-Ja-Gow in Cuba. Once the *Nuestra Señora* went off with the *Prudence* following, that goddam Frenchman—" Hammond's eyes flashed—"nailed me to the mainmast by the ear so's to keep his crew in spirits."

Only now did Asa Bennett remember the presence of his daughter. "Desire, thee had best retire."

She left the kitchen, but Tim heard her stop half way up the stairs.

"I don't recommend having yer ear nailed to a mast 'specially when a vessel's rolling."

Tim exclaimed, "By God! Somebody ought to walk such brutes up to a main yard."

"Sure somebody ought; but who?" rasped the one-eyed man, wiping his mouth on his sleeve. "Why ain't one o' these great an' prosperous colonies got even a smitch of a sea-going cruiser?"

"Don't get all foamed up," Will Elley advised. "Soon we'll put privateers to sea and plenty of 'em."

"Privateers won't tackle pirates if they can avoid it—never heard of one that would," Hammond insisted. "What we need is a navy!"

"I pray not," Asa Bennett said heavily. "Violence is against the word of God."

Polypus Hammond's haggard features reddened. "What they done to me and my crew and to the poor souls aboard the *Prudence* was against the word of God, too. Mrs. Hull, she's a widder and Loosh was her pride and joy. Now she's got only Abner and little Phil."

"Abner died of the camp fever," Tim told him, "last week."

"The more I pity her, poor woman." The sea captain's heavily-freckled fist came thumping down. "I tell you, as I'll tell all Newport, them furriners won't have the least respect for folks who can't stand up to 'em! Didn't anybody dare sass us when we was under the British flag—not in peace times."

"How'd you recapture the vessel?" Tim wanted to know.

"Will Elley was told to steer second night out, so we got him to dim the binnacle light. Then, when me and Paul Clarke was called on deck to help shorten canvas durin' a squall, I carried a pump bolt in my boot.

"I got a chance to pass behind that Frenchman and I stove his head in. Clarke, here, bare-handed, broke the picaroon quartermaster's dirty yellow neck for him."

"And what of the other three Spaniards?"

For the first time a ghost of a smile relaxed the captain's rigid jaw. "Why, they took the queerest notion to go swimming. Must have been mighty fond of the water 'cause it was above forty mile to the nearest land."

In drying, the seamen's clothes raised a reek of unclean wool reminiscent of the barracks before Boston.

Yawning, Captain Hammond heaved himself to his feet.

Asa Bennett announced, eyes sweeping over the ragged quartet of sailors. "Thee shall not wait for thy pay—and perhaps a bonus for bringing the vessel home. Maybe we can even contrive to succor the Widow Hull. Her last boy is very young."

The old Quaker suddenly squared his shoulders "Friend Polypus, how soon can thee find a crew? I would lade the schooner and put her to sea as soon as maybe. We must work hard to compensate this loss."

"Why, in a week's time, say. Her spars and rigging need overhauling—bad," Hammond added. He did seem surprised. "But mark my words, Asa, I ain't taking the *Patience* out unless her first port o' call is Hispaniola, there to pick up carriage guns, an' swivels, an' powder, an' shot! I hev had a bellyful of this!" With a jerk he undid the bandage about his head.

"Oh, mah Gawd!" Mamba squeaked.

Of the sea captain's right ear nothing remained save two dull red shreds hanging loose, like a dog's after losing a fight.

15

THE LEAN-TO

WHEN it was a quarter past four, Desire Harmony settled her shawl, then tied on a cloak equipped with a hood. In the twilight quiet of the woods she would feel that John was nearer. Weeks ago they had agreed to think very hard of each other at precisely half-past four of each afternoon. Surely, the intensity of their love must create vibrations that could span the space between them.

Walking lightly, heels twinkling as usual, she hurried off through a grove of young birches growing beyond the barn.

Oh, dear Lord, why have you ordained that I must live in such troublous times? Young people *ought* to have a good time. We are young for so short a time.

Not that she, a Quakeress, could ever attend so worldly an affair as a ball. Still, it was something to hear about them from luckier girls. Now the Committees had forbidden shows, anything gay or frivolous. Oh dear, was it two, three years, since the Mr. Hallam's American Company of Players had come up from Charleston to perform on the upper floor of the Court House?

From the edge of the birch grove she glimpsed a figure so long and supple that it must be Mr. Higsby, working at something out near the tip of Fox Hill Point. Her boredom vanished. With cloak whipping about her legs, Desire guessed she must look quite dramatic—perhaps like poor Mary, luckless Queen of Scots, reviewing her troops?

Provokingly, the Pennsylvanian continued working over some basket-like arrangement. She had such good eyes she could see his ammunition pouch and powder horns laid on a flat boulder; against it his long-barreled rifle was handy, too.

What odd, inexplicable creatures men were! All her sixteen years she had lived in a house full of men and was only now beginning to understand them. What in the world could Tim find in a nice-Nancy

like Lucy Percival? Why, her Ma could make Lucy jump through
hoops with a snap of her fingers. She would like to see anybody make
Desire Harmony spring through a hoop—unless she'd a mind to.

What could have prompted Mr. Higsby to desert a comfortable
room at Peaceful Haven—and her own presence—to shiver in a rough
little camp? Why had he looked so hard at her the first night? Desire
guessed he had been taken with her; most men were. Yet he had
gone away; hadn't spoken to her since. Lack of an explanation kept
bothering her.

She skirted some leafless alders on the edge of the woods, and descended a slope leading towards the hollow. How very smooth and
bright the snow looked! In the underbrush some chickadees were
squabbling, quite oblivious of a jay which, spying her, began raising
an absurd rumpus.

Ja-a-ay! Ja-a-ay!

Once among the fir trees she was quick to discern an unfamiliar
outline. Beside a huge spruce just above the floor of the ravine a triangular structure sloped back to a long point. This must be the lean-to
Tim had mentioned.

Naturally observant, Desire wondered why there were no cut
branches or axe marks on any of the nearby trees. When the local
boys went camping, you couldn't miss the place for blazes and hacked
limbs. Plenty of times when she had been a little girl she had been
able to crawl up close without any of the boys suspecting her presence.

It was once when the Gardner boys made ready to go swimming
that she learned that boys were constructed differently.

How would a timber-beast, as he called himself, arrange his quarters? She half fancied that he might be given to worshiping strange
graven idols—like an Indian.

A small pile of firewood stood beside the lean-to. A breathless
temptation to inspect his quarters presented itself. Why not? Mr.
Higsby was way down on Fox Hill Point and this all came under
the head of learning about people. An actress must understand a wide
variety of characters, if she were to become famous.

Timidly, Desire descended into the hollow and paused briefly to inspect a fireplace cleverly contrived of smooth glacial boulders. A slightly charred lug-pole of green elm canted over the ashes and blackened stick ends. A small, scrupulously clean brass kettle lay to one side; the frozen carcasses of three rabbits dangled pathetically from a branch. Stretched on hoops, the pelts of a big raccoon and three red foxes were drying.

Surprisingly enough, not a bit of refuse was visible. She approved. Men were usually so hopelessly untidy. Of course, John wasn't. His training would have precluded such a possibility.

Oh, rats! It 'must be long after half-past four now and here she'd forgotten all about sending John his message.

Heart hammering, Desire thrust her head past an old cowhide doing duty as a door. Um-m. It was dark in the lean-to and the air was fragrant with spruce. She also recognized the smell of tobacco and an odor pungent, yet not unpleasant. It resembled that of a clean dog.

Hanging from a peg was the shirt that had been dyed with sumac. Its rich red-brown hue delighted her. Why in the world had the Friends long since decided that anything colorful was necessarily evil? What with Mr. Higsby's soft voice, black hair, and such a red shirt she stood ready to wager he could catch the eye of almost any girl. She stepped inside.

A dull sheen attracted her attention.

"Well, I never!" she burst out when she realized that it was a petticoat—a fine lawn one. Now why in the world would a good third of it have been so carefully trimmed away? This must mean that Mr. Higsby *was* what John called a lady killer! Funny part of it was, she'd guessed this was so all along. She giggled.

Curiosity mounting, Desire inspected his bed, even sat on it and jounced once or twice. Most surprisingly, it was almost as soft as her own. On a rough shelf lay a razor, a little bag of salt and a twist of tobacco bearing tooth marks.

If only it were possible to meet John in so cosy a hideaway. They both felt it monstrous humiliating to slink about, to meet in the barn or in that dusty recess behind Mr. Southwick's book cases. Love shouldn't be furtive. Love should be brave and straightforward! It

afforded her considerable consolation to know that, in another fortnight, she and John could face the world unafraid, unashamed.

When Desire put down her hand to straighten herself from the
bed her fingers encountered a hard object among the spruce tips.
Why, it was a rifle's lock! What in Heaven's name could Mr. Higsby
want with two guns? Or was it just a pistol? Cautiously, she began to
burrow.

"Oh-h!" Someone fetched her a resounding cut across the bottom.
Another, impartially to the other buttock. In a mixture of terror and
outrage, she whirled about.

Lean of jaw and very forbidding of expression, Higsby was squatting in the doorway, a long willow switch in his hand.

"Well, Miss Curiosity, if you've done rummagin' my affairs, you
kin come out."

"He aims to whip me!" was Desire's panic-stricken thought. He'd a
perfect right, too. Why, oh why, had she ever forgot herself enough
to go prying about a stranger's private effects?

"Come on—"

If she didn't want a further taste of that switch, she guessed she
had better begin to cry. The simpler a man was, the better tears
worked, usually. Accordingly she shrank as far back as she could in
the lean-to, screwed up her face and managed such a pathetic burst
of sobs that she was really quite pleased with herself.

"Oh, please, Mr. Higsby—don't—I—I—I—di-didn't mean any
h-harm—"

The ranger reached in at her, but hesitated, settled back on one
knee. Obviously suspicious, he watched a long minute, then said
anxiously, "Don't carry on that way, Miss Desire. I didn't aim to
strike so hard, only you hadn't no business in my affairs."

More wails and sobs. "Oh, dear, I know you—you're g-going to—
to—whip me—"

"—Not if you hush that fuss."

"Y-you won't tell P-Papa?" Great dark eyes swimming, she peeped
over the crook of her elbow.

"Come out here an'—an' we'll talk about it." Pity she was Tim's sister. Them light brown shadows under her eyes shore warmed a man.

It was only when Desire had emerged that he noticed her cheeks were not even damp.

"Well, I'm damned!" he growled. Fancy getting took in like this. "You're smarter'n a she-fox with pups! You shore took me in."

"Did I, Mr. Higsby?" Desire began to smile, a bit breathlessly. "Did I sound as if I was really crying?"

"Sounded like you was bein' skinned alive." He kept sober with an effort. "You'd ought to be ashamed messin' 'round a man's kit."

Contriteness incarnate, Desire moved nearer him. "Oh, Mr. Higsby, I am so very ashamed. Only the other night Tim said—"

"Tim said what?"

Wide-eyed she looked up at him, then quickly away. She'd been thinking fast how to get on his good side.

"Tim told me what a wonderful Indian fighter you are. I—oh—dear, I did *so* want to see a scalp, to really touch one."

He stared. For the first time a girl was proving one too many for him. Great guns! What a way she had with her. When she got older, he bet she'd set the boys a pretty pace. "You wouldn't really want to see a skelp?"

"Oh, please, Mr. Higsby—" Her face was right at his shoulder, trustful, eager. "—If I'm not over-bold."

A quarter of an hour later she was still hearing just how he'd killed the Tuscarora sub-chief. Higsby, squatting comfortably on his heels, was drawing designs on the ground with a stick. Here was where he had first cut the Tuscarora's trail. Now this was the way he had circled to head him off.

"How prodigiously clever of you." She smiled. "Were you ever in love, Mr. Higsby?"

He was so taken aback he almost cussed. "Shucks! You ain't even been listenin'. An' it's lots harder to lift a Injun's skelp than it is to roll—er—court a gal."

"—Some girls," Desire corrected primly.

"Reckon you're right," he admitted, and narrowed jet eyes. "Why'd you ask that?"

"Just wondered. Maybe, if you were, you would—" She faltered, lost her nerve.

"Would what?"

"Oh, nothing." Another time she'd see if the lean-to could be borrowed.

Higsby grinned. It was nice talking to a pretty gal—this one in particular. Those compelling shadows beneath her eyes were something to think on. Back in Keowee the boys would have called them "bedroom shadows." Of course, that explanation was crazy. Desire Harmony was just a kid, and a nice kid.

She arose, carefully brushed spruce needles and bits of bark from her cloak.

"This has been such fun, Mr. Higsby, really it has," she announced in her rich, low-pitched voice. "And I *was* listening about the scalps. I think you are wonderfully brave. How tall did you say that Tusca— Tuscarora stood?"

"When I laid him out afterwards, Miss, I hope to boil in oil if that Iroquois didn't measure nigh on six foot from toe to skelp lock. That's about as big as they grow. Most of 'em don't run over five foot six or seven."

She let him talk another ten minutes then, sedately, departed for home.

16

DECEMBER 10, 1775

WHEN he heard the night wind commence to moan and whine in from the sea, Tim knew there would be fine ducking tomorrow. A stiff nor'easter made it uncomfortable, if not impossible, for great flocks of dusky ducks to lie out on the Bay. In fine weather it was the provoking custom of this species only to fly inshore for feed and water at dawn and dusk.

Wind, beating down the living room fireplace, blew a dusting of ashes out over the turkey-red carpet. Tim grinned. Maybe Sam

Higsby had never before tasted humble-pie, but come tomorrow he would.

He mustn't put on airs, though. Up to Tiverton Sam hadn't got cocky over his marksmanship. Lifting his six foot fowling piece, Tim squinted down its bore. It shone like glass. A good, if unimaginative weapon, this, and made by Jeremiah Smith of Lime Rock.

"Feel's if might snow any minute," Desire remarked absently. "Isn't that a shame?"

"A shame, why?" Tim glanced across at her. His sister's lips looked dark red and shiny, like ox-blood cherries. She seemed tonight to have taken special care with her hair, too. What the devil was getting into the kid? Sometimes these days she sat merely smiling into space, acting as if her mind were half the world away.

"Oh, nothing," Desire replied with a secret half-smile. It was hard not to show how radiantly happy she felt.

Tim settled back, began to ream out the shotgun's vent. Well aware that an expedition loomed in the offing, Snapper watched happily from the floor.

The brown and white mongrel made a fine retriever. His hair was long and thick and he was a powerful swimmer. Mamba complained about Snapper's coat being oilier than a mackerel.

Tim planned to let the ranger down easy. For the sake of the larder they would first off take a flock shot or two. That should bag easily fifteen birds, maybe twenty, if Snapper fetched in the cripples fast enough. Then he would invite Sam to try some wing shots. He guessed some pretty fancy cussing would follow.

Umm! Mamba had prepared such a whacking big supper that sleep was dragging at his eyelids. Tomorrow the household would feast on dusky ducks or, if it really stormed, maybe a goose. Geese were all right, but if there was any victual in the world Tim Bennett was partial to, it was a big red-leg, stuffed with onions and apples and cooked to a delicate brown.

"Think I'll go to bed," he announced to his sister. "Tell Mamba to leave some pie and chowder by the back of the chimney piece. New bread ready?"

"No, it's rising. We bake tomorrow."

His sister heard Tim call Snapper, then take a candle in a hurricane glass and wait for him on the front stoop. He must be studying the sky, probably figuring where he and Mr. Higsby had best lay next morning. Soon he clumped off to bed. Papa had long since retired.

Desire's fingers flew over her embroidery frame. The work was neat even if the cross stitches weren't as small as they might have been.

> Thee'll mend thy Life tomorrow still Thee cry
> In what Far Country doth tomorrow Lie?
> It stays so long, is fetch'd so far, I fear
> 'Twill prove both very Old, and very Dear.

Embroidery came easier than quilting, even though she could turn out some really elegant designs such as "Fan Mill," "Job's Trouble," and "World's Rose."

Oh, bother! The grandmother clock on the landing was chiming half after eight. Better pretend to go to bed else Mamba would notice. The old colored woman had monstrous sharp ears and a curiosity to match.

The treads beneath her feet felt as if made of wool. La! In a very little time now John's dear arms would be close about her and banish all things save love. Would he wear his new wig? The one with the tight little curls over his ears? John had lovely small ears which lay crisp and flat against his skull.

Without undressing she got into bed, and lay there listening to wind rattling the privy door. There would be a moon later if the clouds didn't hide it. Nine o'clock. Only an hour more!

She would coax him to recite poetry. John really had a prodigious fine speaking voice, like warm honey spread on a hot biscuit.

"Had to walk over,—worth it, though." John St. Clair's slim outline materialized among a grove of apple trees standing in silhouette back of the barn.

"Darling!" Desire rushed to him, felt a gloved hand at the back of her head. It pressed her face tight, almost cruelly tight, against his.

"Ah, sweeting—so many eternities." His boat cloak whipping about them, they clung to each other a timeless interval. At last she took his hand.

"Come, out here we will soon freeze."

"Quite right—it *is* a bit airy!"

The Right Honourable John St. Clair, Sub-Lieutenant in His Britannic Majesty's Regiment of Marine Light Infantry, followed her into the comparative warmth of the barn. He sighed. How deliciously sweet and homely it was here; forcefully reminiscent of those mews behind the great Norman castle which had sheltered the St. Clairs since Rufus the Red had ruled.

Desire, all breathless, cried, "John. Pray stand against that wall. Stand quite still, it's for only a moment."

In a half-light thrown back from moon-dusted snow, John St. Clair moved before a white-washed partition. Her heart lifted. Oh, but he was beautiful in his boat cloak, in his cocked hat that was bound in silver braid and bore a white cockade at a jaunty angle.

Alas that it was too dark to recognize the exciting scarlet of his tunic—it looked black in this light. She could see his silvered buttons and the white revers of his cuffs and lapels glimmer faintly.

The Honourable John was trying his best to look old and soldierly, but remained a nice-looking boy of nineteen with honest eyes, a high-bridged nose and a sensitive mouth.

"You, I take it, constitute a firing squad of one?"

"Of course, my captive."

He began to chuckle. "You are a sweet silly, then. How can a man be slain when he has no heart at which to aim? Mine I lost long months ago."

"Prettily put!" Desire cried. "But please don't move, yet. I—I want to remember you, so."

Obediently, Lieutenant the Right Honourable John St. Clair remained with chin up, feet together. Abruptly his hand flickered to his sword. A slim blade hissed free, flashed up and he held an ivory guard carved in the shape of a mermaid in line with his lips.

"Salute! Tender Commander of my destiny."

Desire's ears glowed and her lungs filled so deep she felt her stay strings ready to burst. La, had there ever been so gallant, so devoted a lover in all the World's long history?

"John—John, I can't bear loving you so much. I—I vow—I'll swoon!" The smooth surface of the silvered gorget about his throat chilled her chin; but his lips were hot.

Said he softly, returning his sword, "The dog?"

"Snapper is indoors," she whispered, clinging close. "My brother is going shooting in the morning. There is nothing to fear. Nothing at all."

She guided him past the three cows solemnly chewing their cuds in their stalls, past a pair of broad-sterned farm horses.

"This way one ascends again to Heaven," he murmured. "Pray lead the way."

Although he couldn't see a thing, the Honourable John nimbly scaled a ladder leading to the loft and found it easier than climbing a ship's side in a sea-way. After the biting wind beating up the East Passage and along the Ferry Road, it felt deliciously warm in the loft.

He had never thought it possible to tumble head-over-heels in love like this. But, pox take it, he had. He was simply mad for this adorable little Quaker. Come what might, he would have her to wife. By Gad! She would make a lovelier bride than had either Reginald's or Barry's.

The Honourable John hurried to unhook his cloak. He spread it on the hay then eased Desire to a seat beside him. Just enough light seeped through the dusty panes of a small window to create outlines.

"At last, my Thetis, at last!" John swept her into his arms, kissed her again and again.

"My darling, what a cruel long eternity this has been," he murmured passing gentle finger tips along her brows. "When old Southwick passed me your note last Thursday I felt as if the sun had gone out. How does Sir John Suckling put it?

"When dearest I but think of thee,
Methinks all things that lovely be
Are present, and my soul delighted

> For beauties that from within arise
> Are like the grace of deities,
> Still present with us, though unsighted."

"Say it again," she begged. "That was truly lovely."

When he had done, John said, "I have news, sweeting, news which must mark the turning of a tide in our lives."

"A battle?" Desire shivered as if she had been plunged naked into a snow bank.

"No, my sweet. The *Swan* has been ordered to Halifax."

She couldn't help a soft wail. "But thee can't go. I vow I will die if thee sails away! I shall!"

His arm slipped about her shoulder, drew her closer still. "No need to take alarm, little Quaker," he soothed. "I have thought it all out, yes, down to every least possibility. Papa and my uncle—the one in the Admiralty—have bought me a full lieutenancy and I have been monstrous lucky at écarté of late. We can be married!"

"Married?" The word shivered, rang in her brain like a note drawn from a tuning fork.

"Aye, sweetest angel. *Married!*" He tried to sound grave and considered, but couldn't.

"Oh—when?"

"In Halifax—perhaps aboard the *Swan.*"

"John—John!"

"Why shouldn't you sail with me? In Nova Scotia we will be among friends. We can let a house up there until this absurd rebellion is ended, and then we shall go home. Some day I shall come into the title. I fancy 'twill do us little harm to be poor a while."

"I will adore cooking and sewing for you, John. I can do both well."

He nodded and the cold braid of his single epaulet scraped her cheek. " 'Twill be only for a little while, my queen. Your hands are far too lovely for servant's work.

"Ah, queen of my heart, how proud will be the day on which I shall present my marchioness at Court. Your coronet, goddess, will be of golden strawberry leaves. It is, I think, set with four great pearls and and a great many yellow diamonds."

"*My* coronet?" Merciful Heavens, could life really be offering such wondrous prospects?

"It belongs to the family," he told her gravely. "And, Dee, in due course it shall be yours.

"I like to think of you as the Lady Desire, Marchioness of Felton-dale."

Odors of shaving soap and pomatum titillated her senses. "John, darling!"

"Two days hence we will be aboard ship."

His lips were so close she could feel their vibrations when he talked. Suddenly, a violent internal trembling seized her legs. The arteries in her throat began pounding so hard she couldn't hear John's voice. Fierce, warm currents invaded her cheeks, her breasts, her thighs. An inexorable force began to bend her over backwards, backwards onto the cloak.

Her hands, groping for support, met only his face and slipped hungrily about his neck. Darkness, fragrant of a thousand dried blossoms. Hundreds of tiny comets, flashing and spinning.

"John—dearest John," she gasped, "you—I—"

"Dee, this can't—this won't—"

His lips brushed the lids of her tight-closed eyes. She shivered. When his hands entered her bodice they were cold and rough, yet so welcome.

"Dee—?"

"What difference?" she heard her own voice ask of the dark. "There is no reason—John—in two days more. Can't bear waiting—for fulfilment—ah, gently, adored lover."

He sounded breathless as a spent runner. "Dee,—my sweet wife." His hands fumbled further, deliciously eager and awkward. "And you *are* my wife—have been in soul—these three months! Soul is what really counts. Rest—stupid formality."

A torrid whirlwind began to blow through the loft. It beat through the folds of the cloak, penetrated the cloth covering their bodies, bared them, fused them.

The whole world began to spin—faster—faster.

17

RAID

WHEN he heard a voice below his window, Tim guessed Higsby had routed himself out early, really too early, and was waiting to go wild fowling. Snapper was growling, though, and raising his hackles. Self-deception ended at once. It could not be just the rifleman. Below sounded not one, but many voices.

Some neighborhood crisis must be afoot—a house afire, a sudden sickness? He recalled that people had come like this the night old Haskins and his wife were murdered by a person, or persons, still unknown. Or maybe a vessel was in distress? That could be, with such a wild gale blowing.

Downstairs, a series of resounding blows beat at the front door panels. Snapper began to snarl louder and ran over to face the bedroom door.

"Open! Open!" a muffled voice was calling.

From his window, Tim was startled to see the lane, barnyard and the front lawn swarming with dark figures. They showed up remarkably clearly against the snow.

Crimanently, this couldn't be just neighbors, too many of them were carrying muskets. In a winding black stream still more men were descending the road from the direction of the East Ferry.

Suddenly he saw it. This was a sudden lightning attack to be aimed against the British in Newport harbor! Under cover of darkness, the Provincials would throw up a battery, mount cannon, and in the morning compel the British to shift anchorage. Around Boston this had been a favored maneuver.

A shattering thud as of an axe being driven hard into the front door dispelled this explanation as well. Voices were bellowing, "Open up! Open up! Get out, or fry in your own juice!"

In the rear of the house Mamba began to raise peal on peal of terror-stricken screams. Snapper set up a frenzied barking.

British raiders! The sickening realization hit Tim. Looked like a mixed landing party. Seamen, marines, and a handful of soldiers. Most numerous were the sailors in their distinctive petticoat breeches and a ragged miscellany of coats and jerkins. They wore big, brass-hilted Navy hangers, and had boarding pistols jammed into wide leather belts.

He made out quite a few negroes milling about in striped jerseys. These carried axes and candle lanterns. Drawn up in the front yard waited a file of Royal Marines.

Defense seemed as impossible as escape. His only chance lay in trying to talk the British Commander out of confiscating too much. As Tim unlatched his door the noise of wood ripped forcibly apart met his ear. Roaring defiance, Snapper bounded past his legs. The front door was sagging, splintered from its hinges.

"Turn out! In the King's name!" The voice was incisive, particularly ominous because of its lack of excitement. "Turn out, you confounded rebels!"

Tim encountered his father at the head of the stairs. Pa was blinking short-sightedly, making small, aimless motions. His long night cap dangled over thin shoulders.

"Timothy," he quavered, "what can this mean? What offense have we committed? The Committee cannot call us to account."

"Pa, it's not the Sons of Liberty. It's the British."

Good God, Pa was old! Why couldn't Pa decide what must be done, as he always had? But he couldn't—he just stood muttering:

"Thee said 'the British'?"

His words were lost in a crash of breaking glass. The noise suggested that musket barrels were smashing every windowpane within reach.

"That will do!" rasped an officer below. "Stop that racket, or I'll have a colt to your mangy backs!"

At the foot of the stairs a red-coated figure was flashing a whale oil lantern. He saw the two Bennetts standing there in their nightshirts.

"In just three minutes," he called, "my men will fire this house. You had better make haste."

"Fiah?" Mamba screamed more wildly than ever.

Cuffy kept calling, "Wheah is yo', Misto Bennett? Wheah *is* yo'?"

Fire? Set fire to Peaceful Haven? The fellow down there must be crazy. Blood surged into Tim's head.

"Clear out of here, you damned Ministerial thieves! Get out! Or we'll—we'll—"

The officer at the foot of the stairs uttered a barking, humorless laugh. "You will what, you poor deluded ass?"

There was the devil of it. What could he do? What help could he expect? There were no troops on the Island, no American men-o'-war in existence. And in all Peaceful Haven there wasn't so much as a pocket pistol.

Oh God, what could he do? He couldn't just stand there and watch the enemy burn down his home.

Do something, you fool. You charged the Redcoats at Lechemere's Point; made 'em run. You can't suffer this outrage like some patient, spiritless clod of a negro.

A ruddy glare began beating through a fall of fine snow. Seamen suddenly appeared from the rear of the house. They were waving torches, and yelling at the top of their lungs. They didn't seem especially savage, just enjoying an orgy of destruction which was more of a lark than anything else.

Some negro raiders, on the other hand, began plundering with a predatory, barbaric enjoyment. The squad of Royal Marines drawn up before the front door stood looking on as if disgusted with the whole affair.

Coughing in the smoke of the pine-knot torches, Tim calculated that that distant glare must be the Widow Hull's house afire—or was it Ben Elley's place?

"Come down, both of you, or I shall not be responsible." The officer saw Tim's scarlet, twitching face and immediately leveled a big brass-mounted pistol. Said he evenly, "One bit of resistance, my lad, and I will shoot you dead."

In the dining room sounded the clink of silver, the heavy crash of a cabinet overturned.

"Gimme dat!"

"Like hell I will—that's mine!"

Asa Bennett shuffled forward. He looked as if someone had just hit him on the head.

"But, Friend, thee must not allow this. This is not lawful. We have done no harm to anyone."

"Rebels forfeit protection," roared the officer, a bony-faced lieutenant with a great brown wen on the point of his jaw. "Get outside!"

But he wasn't too rough in conducting the old Quaker out onto the porch. "Some of you men search the house for arms and powder. Collins, fetch this old fool a blanket."

"Hi-yah! Look! Has Ah got me some fine cutlery or has Ah not?" A skinny negro seaman came surging by. In one hand he waved a butcher's cleaver, and he carried Mamba's favorite brass clock-jack in the other. In the torchlight, his eyeballs shone orange.

Hatless, a ragged seaman burst out of the dining room lugging a window curtain draped over one shoulder and waving Mrs. Bennett's most-prized wedding gift, a real silver teapot.

When he saw that, Tim uttered a strangled grunt and, vaulting over the stair rail, smashed the fellow flat. Berserk, he flailed at the looters who, hampered by their plunder, gave way. He felt the nose bones of a gap-toothed black crush under his blow. The swine was lugging a whole armful of Desire's dresses!

"Restrain that madman," the officer directed hurriedly.

A trio of marines leaped forward and one of them brought a blunderbuss barrel smacking down on Tim's head. His knees buckled and, desperately, he clung to the stair rail, a torrent of hot blood pouring from his lacerated scalp.

That blow did a strange thing to Tim. He was able to tell what was going on, but, for the life of him, he could not command his limbs.

Any ability to move of his own volition had left him. He could do nothing to the pair of marines who frog-marched him out into the front yard.

Everything floated crazily before his eyes. As in a fever, nothing held reality. Mamba's shrill whimpers still filled the night. Cuffy was howling lest he be murdered on the spot.

Asa Bennett winced at the crash some pillagers made in sweeping china from the once-orderly pantry shelves. Furniture was being furiously kicked aside.

Hooligans, gutter-dregs impressed into the fleet, found vast amusement in plunging their cutlasses again and again into upholstery. His own chair, the one in which he sat to read Scripture, was spewing horsehair through a dozen slashes.

So, just inside his front gate, the old Quaker stood watching helplessly through the falling snow an end come to the world he had toiled so hard to fashion. Volleys of curses, shouts and yells assaulted his benumbed ears.

"Thy will be done, O Lord," he kept whispering. "Thy inscrutable will be done." He shivered. Someone was waving a torch behind the shattered windows. How careless, he might touch off a window curtain.

The marines and officers took no part in the looting, only stood apart under the naked elms, talking in clipped undertones.

All at once the bewildered old man, standing helpless amid a stream of seamen carrying pillowcases and sheets lumpy with plunder, remembered what he had been trying to recall.

"My daughter! Kind Friends, have any of thee seen my daughter? In Heaven's pity find her! Keep her safe. She is young and—and—"

"—Don't take on, Gramper." A burly sergeant had spied the thin-shanked old man standing barefoot in the drifting snow. "Collins, spare me a couple o' them bloody blankets.

"Here, sir." He flung them over the Quaker's shoulders, muttered, " 'Opes as 'ow you'll forgive me, sir. This business ain't none of my choosing."

The bony-faced lieutenant in command came tramping out of the front door. "Sergeant, see if there's a wench upstairs. They'll be setting fires any instant."

Tim suffered acute torture whenever he tried to move. His body might have been a stranger's. Subconsciously, he realized that the blood from his head felt cold by the time it reached his ankles and dribbled onto the snow.

The Widow Hull's flaming home lit Peaceful Haven, showed it white, deceptively serene.

Suddenly another hill spouted fountains of fire. The raiders, Tim realized, were visiting John Gardner's, too.

The sergeant called from an upper window, "Ain't no one upstairs, sir."

"Very well," the lieutenant barked. "You may set the fires."

"No, no! That is sinful, wasteful!" In the grip of a pair of marines, Asa Bennett fluttered like a thin old fowl but a squad clanked inside and lit pine splinters at the living room fireplace.

Carrying a halbert in one hand, a big scarlet-clad N.C.O. touched his splinter to a window curtain—to another.

As flames began soaring in all directions, Asa Bennett hid an ashen face in his hands.

"Come along, bully boy, or you'll get scorched." Tim's guards hauled him stumbling, blood-stained and speechless over to join Cuffy and Mamba who were clinging to the skirts of Pa's nightshirt.

"Oh, son, son! Praise the Lord thee is safe." Grimly, he added, "Doubt not that the Lord will visit His awful wrath upon these Philistines!"

Tim tried to articulate some words but it was hard work. "Where—De—Desire?"

"She must have fled," Pa explained.

Cuffy whimpered louder than ever when long banderoles of flame began flying from the parlor windows. They went licking up at the second story. By their light the marine uniforms glowed as though cast of molten iron.

Sparks rained down and little brands fell hissing onto the wet ground. Steadily, the roar of the conflagration mounted until it sounded like some infernal waterfall.

Down by the beach there was great activity. Asa Bennett guessed that other raiders were trundling a long succession of bundles and bales out of his warehouse and tossing them aboard the *Patience*.

When the heat of the burning house began to melt the snow at his feet, the horse-faced lieutenant gave over watching the destruction and said:

"Sergeant, tell off a detail and drive the stock from the barn. Since these bloody rebels refuse to renew the convention, we'll help ourselves to fresh meat."

A rabble of negroes and seamen dashed into the barn and promptly hens began to set up a fearful squawking. A terrified gray rooster came rushing out into the yellow-red glare and a marine lunged at it with his bayonet. Howling with laughter, he heaved the spitted fowl on high, but this motion was so violent that the rooster slipped off his point and landed on the far side of the barnyard near the privies. It lay there dying, panting, its yellow eyes wide.

"Oh—oh, dey just cain't take mah milkers," wailed Cuffy. Nevertheless, the three cows, Daisy, Minerva, and Bluebell, were goaded off down the lane. A party of strange-looking negroes, at the points of their pikes, drove away the gray-blue boar and the two sows.

The big sergeant said, "Corporal, get the horses out of there."

"—Devil take the horses," the corporal grunted, the minute his superior went off. "Can't eat 'em."

The lieutenant formed his men. Said he, "Now for the Remington place. Look lively. They say it lies in a hollow."

18

The Orchard Fight

Sam Higsby awoke at the very first impact of a musket butt against Asa Bennett's door. Despite the wind, he could hear hammering continue in the distance. From the summit of the ravine, he saw lights weaving crazy patterns about the Bennett place. Faint shouts.

By Jesus, if this wasn't New England, he'd say this disturbance had all the signs of a Injun attack. But what the hell? In these parts there weren't no savages worth mentioning.

He hesitated until, back of the road, a dull glow began to show. Sifting through the trees, he saw the glare of several other fires. Their light began to tint the tops of the spruces all about. Running back to his camp, he got busy. By the time he had slung his equipment and had regained the ridge, its whole crest was penciled in a bright pink which steadily deepened to a throbbing orange-red. He could see terrified stock galloping about in the fields nearest the houses. He recognized such firelight.

No doubt now that the Britainers were pulling off a raid. Great screeching catamounts! Farms were blazing all along the Ferry Road. This promised to develop into a real interesting skirmish. His heart lifted and softly he began to hum a Cherokee chant old Standing Turkey had taught him. After tightening his laces, the Pennsylvanian started off towards the northeast. He halted almost at once. Somewhere to the left six, eight, ten shots were fired.

They formed no part of a volley, just a scattered, irregular popping. Survivors putting up a fight would fire like that. He began to grin.

He lingered just an instant studying over that little valley which, bisecting Conanicut Island, sheltered the Ferry Road. From the East Ferry on the Newport side of Conanicut to the West Ferry on the Narragansett side was less than a mile, but it was still a good long way to retreat if folks were shooting at you.

As the ranger broke into a run, he bit off a chew of tobacco, then fed rifle balls into his cheeks until they bulged like a squirrel's in acorn time.

Higsby's grin faded the minute he saw fire spurting from old Mr. Bennett's fine house. One of the plow horses dashed out of the barn and, in blind terror, charged straight across the meadow, tail up, mane flying. When it reached some boulders edging a little creek, the great, clumsy beast fell heavily and floundered about but could not regain its feet. Higsby reckoned the critter must have broken a leg.

Hitching his big powder horn around where it would be easier to get at, the rifleman advanced, ghosting forward among rows of twisted trunks in the apple orchard. Quite unnoticed, he reached a stone wall just below the barn. Though he waited quite a spell for a crack at an officer, he couldn't see one. In the firelit barnyard was only a tangle of red coats, white crossbelts and a swarm of niggers and sailors. The bastards! They were fixin' to touch off the barn, too.

At last, he glimpsed a sergeant—a big fellow carrying a sort of light spear, the kind the Indians had made copies of near Fort Ninety-Six. The Britainer was only forty yards off but with this blizzard blowing he offered no easy mark. Stomach tightening with pleasure, he leveled the Leman over a row of snowy stones.

He took aim for the sergeant's heart but, since he was raiding Tim's Pa's place, he sent the ball through the Britainer's belly, instead.

As Higsby had calculated, the fellow's shrieks of agony diverted attention from the stone wall and the puff of gray smoke drifting above it. Before anybody spotted him, he had more than half reloaded.

"There he is! Down behind the wall. Come on. Kill the bleeding swine!"

Checking their priming as they ran, a trio of marines started down towards him, their bayonets a-gleam in flames that were lighting the whole countryside.

Deliberately, Higsby permitted them to come within thirty yards, then threw his sights on the second man in line. Between the eyes. When he fired, the marine's arms flew violently apart and, dropping his musket, he collapsed in a regular belly-whopper that sent the snow flying far out from under him.

The leader was only ten yards off and yelling his head off in triumph. He knew his enemy couldn't possibly have time to reload. Higsby began to run back among the apple trees.

"Nah, then, yer bleedin' skulker!" The marine halted and deliberately leveled his musket but, before he could pull the trigger, a bright object skimmed at him and his head snapped back so hard it might have been kicked by a mule.

Heavily, he fell.

The third private slowed, halted his advance, seemed disconcerted because Higsby, instead of continuing his retreat, was running forward. Setting one foot to his latest victim's shoulders, the rifleman began jerking to free his war hatchet from the marine's skull.

When it wouldn't come loose, Higsby raised a scalp yell so terrifyingly fierce that the third man never even fired his musket but began to run away. He was foolish. Higsby snatched up the musket of the Englishman he had just killed and took a snap shot.

The clumsy Brown Bess's recoil made the rifleman's teeth rattle, and he cursed in disappointment because the last of his enemies only screamed, dropped his musket and ran on, clutching a shattered arm.

Higsby's flat features lit as he reloaded his rifle. Knocking over three hostiles in five minutes wasn't bad; it made him feel finer than silk.

Aware that the enemy were in hurried retreat from the Bennett place and in no mood further to molest him, he went over to his second victim. Gripping the corpse by its hair, he lifted the dead man's face out of the snow. By the light of the burning buildings, he could see snow adhering to the fellow's eyelashes.

A small black hole showed, a shade to the right of a center shot, 'twixt the eyes. Drops of blood fell slowly from between the dead man's teeth.

Mechanically, the ranger freed his knife and poised its blade to make the initial incision above the Britainer's left ear, but he checked himself. God damn it, people in these parts didn't hold with skelping.

Oh, hell's roaring bells! Without his having proof, the fellers back in Keowee would never credit his having done for three Redcoats inside as many minutes. He had to have proof of some kind, so he cut away the pewter plate from the front of the marine's cap and slipped it into his warbag. As evidence the plate wasn't up to hair, yet it was something.

19

THE BARN

RELUCTANTLY, Lieutenant the Right Honourable John St. Clair roused from blissful semi-consciousness. Somewhere something was causing a rhythmic clinking noise. Couldn't be anything important.

He turned, tried to see Desire's face amid the fragrant gloom. Exhausted, apparently asleep, she was nestled so close beside him that he could feel her breath fanning the rumpled lace of his shirt front. This was his wife, The Lady Desire. Between them they certainly should get a goodly number of strong and handsome children.

What a sweetly passionate little darling Dee was, all burning tenderness despite her fear and pain. He smiled at a pleasurable realization. Since they were respectively nineteen and sixteen years of age and three score years and ten were their allotted span, they'd enjoy a long blissfully happy life together. How very fortunate they were. Precious few people met the "right person" so quickly—if ever they did.

When his arm tightened about Desire her mouth came groping over the white serge of his lapel, blindly, like a little kitten's. She didn't wholly awake even when he kissed her.

Lieutenant St. Clair's eyes flew wide open. In Mr. Bennett's dwelling a dog had commenced to bark angrily, insistently. Damnation! the silly brute might rouse the household.

Suddenly he heard a voice just outside the barn, and not an unfamiliar one either, snap, "Henderson, tell off six men and go on down to the warehouse. You have your instructions."

"Yes, sir!"

Blood in the Right Honourable John's ears commenced to surge and pound like the surf on the shore. Great God in Heaven! That was George Sneyd out there, commander of H. M. S. *Bolton*. What the deuce had brought him over on Conanicut?

Rallying his perceptions, he sat bolt upright, but Desire, child-like, slept on. To his ears came a host of subtle, significant sounds: the clink of a musket butt against a belt buckle, the soft *zwe-e-ep* of a cutlass sliding out of its sheath.

Many voices were below, dozens of them. Damn! He saw it now. This must be the punitive expedition Captain Wallace had threatened when the Rebels had refused to renew the convention. This raid threatened an object lesson to Newport. Why hadn't he been advised? Then he remembered: I played loo right up 'til I had to dash from the wardroom to the skiff I had hired. Stab me! This business is entirely without humor. Sneyd's such a dirty dog he would tattle if he— I must reason this out. Poor Dee, what shall I do?

A sound of heavy blows penetrated to the warm gloom of the hayloft. A horse awoke below, struggled noisily to its feet and began to snort its alarm.

We must try to get out of this in a hurry. Oh, confound Wallace, Sneyd, and the rest. There will be the very devil to pay when her father and brother can't find her.

Desire awoke, sat up and turned eyes that were concentric rings of white. In a tense whisper, she asked, "What—what is happening?"

His hand slipped none too gently over her mouth. It was shaking. "Quiet, for God's sake. Landing party—our ships," he barely enunciated. Didn't want to call it a raid. Even now he wasn't sure about what was afoot. The Right Honourable John kept telling himself he wasn't frightened. He and Dee would get out of this somehow. Of course they would.

Desire, too, seemed calm and collected until she realized what would happen if they were found—if anybody even suspected that she and a British officer had been up in the loft together. Her good name— Cuffy was calling, yelling for her.

"Mist'ess Dee-sire! Mist'ess! Wheah is you, wheah *is* you?"

She could hear Snapper snarling; then he began to yipe. Somebody must have kicked the courage out of him. She could tell that from the way his barking ended on a high, piercing note. She heard him scurry, whimpering, to the woodshed. Snapper always made for the woodshed when he got whipped.

Desperately, the Honourable John sat staring into the dark, trying to find some encouragement in the situation. He must present a ridiculous figure with his wig full of hay, his uniform dusty, and his stock twisted around under one ear. The heat of their love was still upon him and his cambric shirt was damp beneath his tunic.

"What's that?" A rising glare beat through cracks in the wall.

"Bad business," he breathed. "Must keep our heads, dear. Any other way out of this loft?"

"Only down the ladder." Her hand closed confidently on his. "I— I'm not afraid, John."

He couldn't help tightening an arm about her. This was a girl worth having; plenty of head, plenty of nerve.

When the big barn door slid open with a bang, they flinched back onto the hay. Breathless, they watched a tall sergeant come tramping in. He carried a halbert in one hand, a hurricane lantern in the other.

A swirl of seamen, rough, shaggy fellows, followed him. They went into the cow stalls, kicked the beasts into wakefulness. Chickens commenced to cackle.

"Yon's gradely cattle," declared a broad Yorkshire voice. "Reckon they'd give near ten quart a day." The speaker sighed. "Would to God th' owd man had 'em. Pity to bootcher such champion beasts."

"Hold tha' tongue! Art daft, man? Loose their yokes. Leftenant'll be raising bloudy hell an we don't move our arses."

They drove the cows out amid despairing squawks from the hen house. Desire began to get mad. Daisy was *her* cow! They had no right to steal her like this. She had bought Daisy as a calf out of her butter money. Feeling guilty, sore, and frightened she groped at her petticoats, trying to straighten them and her dress by sense of touch.

John sat rigid, listening, trying to guess what was going on at the house.

Suddenly everyone in the yard began yelling. Smoke drifted in the open door of the barn, stung her eyes. A bright glare began to beat in the dusty window beside them.

"Oh, John, they're burning my home. Stop them! They mustn't.

Papa has never harmed the British—or anyone. He wouldn't even pay war taxes. Quakers don't fight!"

"I can't—daren't show myself—" he whispered savagely. "This is a blunder. A stupid blunder. I can promise you there will be the devil to pay when news of this reaches home. We have influence in Parliament, strong influence." His unsheathed sword lay like a silver ruler mark across the hay.

"What must we do?"

"Wait. That's all. If Sneyd doesn't burn the barn we will be safe."

20

THE REFUGEES

OLD John Gardner and his three boys did not linger to watch the fire consume their tanyard. Alarmed by flames soaring near the East Ferry, the Gardners had had more warning than their neighbors. Now they were carrying a few valuables to a shack down the shore a piece. Summertime it was used to store nets in.

Ma Gardner and the girls, though they were so scared they were blubbering out loud, were lugging food. What with the piercing wind, the drifts, and the necessity of carrying blind, bedridden old Granny on a mattress, the family made slow progress.

"Guess this is what we get for quitting the Army," John complained. "Told you it would bring ill luck."

Walt didn't reply. He was too out of breath from staggering along under a blanket full of kitchenware, clothes and food. The youngest sister, aged four, was whimpering, "Cold. Me cold." She had lost her slippers, so old John picked her up.

There was only one redeeming feature to the situation. He and the boys had saved their muskets and powder horns.

Ma Gardner began to cry, she was still feeble from the month old baby Ellen was carrying. "Our home, John, our tanyard! What will become of us now?"

Both the Remington places are afire," Walt remarked. "Yes, by Jesus, Widow Hull's, too. Ain't sparin' nobody. And—look—*look* over to Bennetts'!"

Once they reached the beach, the going became easier. Young John had kept his head when the alarm came and had loaded a shovelful of coals into a pot. Now he ran ahead through the storm and opened the shack door. There was a fireplace in it because the men needed heat to cure the nets. Things seemed a mite better, when they got a fire going and Grandma's mattress was rigged on planks laid across a pair of sawhorses.

Ellen, the eldest girl, began drying the children's feet. Said she briskly, "Quit your howling. Ain't we all alive? Ain't none of the boys been captured."

"That's right," Ma sighed. "Bad as things is, we have considerable to be thankful for."

Once the fire was safely alight, old man Gardner slung his powder horn over his shoulder and took up a clumsy old French musket. Young John followed suit.

"Come on, Walt," said he quietly. "If we aim to make us some change out of them pirates, we must hurry."

"Git us two apiece," Ellen called after them from the shack door. "But don't git hurt!"

"Eh? Two what?" Granny's thin voice was querulous. "Won't nobody tell a pore blind old body what's happened? Dear, dear, why won't nobody pay attention to me?" Her hearing was none of the best, either.

Old man Gardner took up a dog-trot straight for the West Ferry landing. "We will stop by and pick up Tim."

"To hell with him!" snarled Walt. "If he hadn't have fought the *Rose's* supply party maybe the Lobster-backs wouldn't ever have come."

"Son, your jedgment's out o' whack," said old John, his lips flat and tight as thongs. "Tim ain't responsible. The King's men done just the same thing up to Falmouth."

"I'll kill a million Redcoats for this!" panted Walt.

"Shet your trap, son, and mind you don't waste a grain o' powder when the fun starts," the old man admonished harshly. " 'Twill be a long time before we can afford to buy more."

His tanyard was burning so bright it stained the snow on the Narragansett shore a bright gold. Old John felt all empty inside. For twenty years he'd peddled fish, caulked boats, made nets and done a hundred hard jobs to get that tanyard started. He'd worked—God above knew how hard he had worked—from dawn 'til it was too dark to see. Been glad of the chance, too.

Now it was gone. Why? Why hadn't someone opposed the enemy? Even a sloop of war could have prevented a landing. Gone—*gone*—GONE! Starvation lay ahead. No mistake about that. Take a man's livelihood, would they? He was going to do some killing.

"Pa." Walt was pointing to the West Passage. The raiders evidently had cut out Asa Bennett's schooner. With a prize crew aboard, she was standing down stream.

The dark outlines of three men were cutting across a pasture to intercept them. Ben Elley, Jed Franklin, and Mark Remington.

"The bum-blistered thieves hev stole my oxes." Tears were running freely down Mark's smooth, stupid cheeks. "Let me at 'em! Jove and Jupiter was best span this side o' Noo York."

"Now don't get all foamed-up," the old man advised, "and you'll do more damage.

"Come along, you fellers. We'll get Tim Bennett and take after them Redcoated thieves."

21

THE FERRY ROAD

"WHY t' blazes didst tha not get out tha 'orses?" demanded the Yorkshireman.

"Corporal says, let them be; 'tis hogs and cattle we've come for."

"T' hell with him! I'll not stand by an' see doomb, innocent beasts burnt alive!"

Burnt! Like icy claws the word dug into Desire's consciousness. Soon, she and John would be smoked out, like a pair of 'coons from a basswood. What a precious little fool she had been! She began trembling. Not that it made any difference between John and her, but Papa, Tim! She knew she would die of shame. Worse still, Tim would undoubtedly kill John—or try to.

"Fall in! Fall in!" voices kept repeating in various keys.

There must be some way, but what? Why couldn't she find some answer? Because the big double doors had been left open and the house was burning so brightly she could see John for the first time, was dismayed to see how very young he looked in his indecision. Spears of hay clung to his wig and he had his lower lip caught between his teeth. His handsome blue eyes were flickering from side to side, desperately.

Just below, the snorting and trampling of the terrified plow team rang loud.

"Damn 'e f'r stubborn beasts—yer like t' bloody Yankees." The Yorkshireman, a sergeant, began cursing. Presently, he lost his temper and pricked one of the horses with his pike. The animal snorted, reared, then left the barn with a ponderous rush. His mate followed.

"Coom, Dickon, there's nowt more alive in here."

The Right Honourable John heaved a great sigh, wiped a heavy beading of sweat from his forehead.

"We're safe. Sneyd's falling in his men. They will be gone soon."

Someone ran in bringing bright patches of light. It was a negro carrying a blazing brand.

"Hya! Hya!" he chuckled and disappeared. Almost at once swift spirals of fire began to lick up at the far end of the loft where the grain chutes were. Billows of smoke filled the barn. Outside sounded a single staccato shot and just beyond the door, the Yorkshireman clutched his belly and collapsed. He began to scream, to writhe and jerk. Men ran to bend him over. Others ran about.

"Kill that bleedin' skulker!" The screams diminished to dreadful, poignant groans.

The raiders had barely quitted the barnyard than a second report came from beyond the veil of drifting snow. Desire figured it sounded from the orchard. Presently, a third shot. Provincial Militia? The Right Honourable John fumbled for his sword.

Burning hay flung sheets of flame towards clusters of feed corn tied to the rafters and infernally hot waves of smoke beat at the two in the loft. Coughing, they figured to hold out a while longer.

"They've gone. Come." His fingers closed over her wrist, but she thought that someone might still be out there in the firelight and flinched back.

"You sure?" she choked. "What would people say?"

"Jolly well say we're dead if—don't leave. Come." As he ran over to the ladder Desire saw that John had done up his waistcoat buttons all wrong.

Momentarily outlined against the flames, his slender boyish figure appeared black, gigantic, demonic.

Desire groped for the ladder. A fierce eddy of hot smoke beat into her face and seared her throat, caused racking coughs. She couldn't find the next step, missed—fell to the floor. Crawling blindly towards the door, she was aware of a pain shooting through her left knee.

Just inside the door John picked her up, slid an arm under her armpits. Because the wind was being drawn in to feed the flames, they had got fresh air—a second's respite. Dashing water from his eyes, the Right Honourable John saw the yard empty save for a weird miscellany of abandoned plunder.

"All clear, my chick," said he. "We will round the barn and run parallel to the road. Come. There is nobody about."

Lieutenant St. Clair was wrong. On the far side of the ring of fire-light six men were coming up and out of sight, on the opposite side of the barn, Asa Bennett, Tim and the two servants remained in stunned reaction.

Over from the Widow Hull's appeared young Phil. He sobbed with rage, shouldering an old musketoon his father had captured

at Louisburg. Tim, still half stunned, stood staring helplessly while
the servants gathered abandoned blankets in which to swathe his
father.

Though the heat was becoming intolerable, Desire flinched back.
She heard John Gardner hail some person invisible beyond the conflagration.

"Where's yer gun, Tim? What ails you?"

"He's been hurt—that's what," Mark Remington shouted. "Lookit,
there's blood on his shirt."

"Come on, Tim, pull yourself together," urged old man Gardner.
"We're going to harry them devils and— My God! Look!"

Pursued by clouds of smoke, two people were running out of the
blazing barn. One was a slim, gray-clad girl, the other a man in a
scarlet, white and black uniform. He was carrying a naked sword
in one hand and ran with the easy grace of a young buck.

The Conanicut men were too startled to shoot. Before any of
them came to, the fugitives were lost in the ever-thickening snow.

The line of captured cattle moved so slowly over the frozen ruts
that Lieutenant Sneyd cursed feelingly. Very well the beasts knew
they were leaving comfortable barns behind so kept trying to break
away. Now and then one of the heifers would lift her head and give
a frightened, homesick *"moo!"*

The pigs made even worse going of the Ferry Road and slowed
the straggling column to a halting walk, but the lieutenant swore
that every last porker was needed aboard the ships.

Fowls and ducks and geese, tied by the legs and slung in clusters
to the pikes of the seamen and negroes, had long since given up
fluttering and squawking.

When the head of the retreating column came abreast of a small
frame house set at some distance back from the road, Lieutenant
Sneyd snapped, "Somebody touch that shanty off."

"But, sir," protested a subaltern. "Haven't we done enough damage? The country is rising behind us."

"That will do!" Sneyd said coldly. "Orders were not to leave a
single rebel rat's nest standing."

When a detail began pounding on his door, John Martin opened it at once and looked out.

"In God's pity, kind friends," he quavered. "Don't burn my house." Joining his hands as if at prayer, he said, "I am ailing, very poor, and I have done you no harm."

"Stan' aside, you old goat," ordered a petty officer who carried a demi-john under one arm. "We are going to warm yer shack for yer."

"No! No! This is all I have!"

"Get th' ol' whoreson out of m' way," bellowed the petty officer.

A pair of sailors lumbered forward, tried to wrench John Martin through the door, but the old man's skinny fingers clung to the frame.

"Obstinate bugger, ain't you?"

The petty officer slammed his stone jug hard against the hand nearest him. The crunch of the breaking bones was entirely audible. Martin groaned, but hung on with the other hand, still blocking the entrance to his wretched little house.

Up from the road rang Lieutenant Sneyd's angry voice. "Get on with it."

"Garn!" The petty officer jerked a boarding pistol from his belt, held it in line with John Martin's gaunt stomach. "Ye're delaying the leftenant—"

"No!" sobbed the householder, clutching the broken hand to his chest. "This is my home. It's all I've got. I won't leave it! Oh—don't— *don't!*"

The pistol's report gave a deep boom, momentarily lit John Martin's face with an intense glare. He vanished, reeling backwards into the dark through swirls of gray smoke.

A negro carrying a torch ran up and hurled it through the black rectangle of the doorway. As the raiding party tramped on, tendrils of smoke commenced to eddy out of the depths of John Martin's house door.

"Faster, darling," pleaded the Right Honourable John. "You must run faster if we are to come up with Sneyd."

"Can't—hurt my knee," gasped Desire. Her legs felt all weak and

uncertain, like a new-born foal's, and her lungs appeared to be drawing in no air at all.

"You run—ahead." She halted, began rubbing at her injured leg. "I
—wait—here. You bring back some men."

John St. Clair saw that she really was winded and incapable of
further flight. "Capital idea; wait here beside road. I'll fetch squad
back—five minutes."

Before he turned and ran off up the road he stooped, gave her a
peck of a kiss and an encouraging pat on the shoulder.

Shifting his sword to his left hand, the sub-lieutenant of marines
put on as fine a burst of speed as the frozen ground permitted. At
Westminster they had considered him one of the fastest runners in
the school.

Sneyd's men couldn't be far ahead, he judged, because he soon
passed cow droppings which were still steaming. Once he almost
tripped on a shawl abandoned on the road.

"Curse those bloody fools!" he thought when, up ahead, still another house broke into flames.

When Sam Higsby spotted the Right Honourable John, he halted
in the lee of a haycock. The rifleman had been moving parallel to the
Ferry Road waiting for a skirmish to develop and still hoping to pick
off an officer. Certainly he should get a shot at some straggler. This
was good frontier tactics.

The range he estimated as close on fifty yards and since the fellow
was running fast, Higsby whipped out his ramrod and gave his
charge a couple of extra hard *whams* just to seat his ball tighter.

By God, that Britainer, for all his silly hampering uniform, was
coming on 'most as fast as an Injun. He'd pass, he now judged, near
sixty yards off. Say, wouldn't it be grand if only Miss Desire was
here? For a gal she had exhibited a real interest in rifles and marksmanship.

Yessir, just for the sake of them shadowed eyes of hers, he would
make this one a real sporting shot. He would let the Britainer go by
and take him going away—if he was able. The moon was at this mo-

ment near to breaking through the snow clouds. It illuminated the whole scene with a silvery radiance.

Distinctly, he heard the impact of the runner's feet grow louder. When he passed the haycock, Higsby drew a shallow breath. The long rifle's barrel went out and steadied itself. Sighting at the center of the Britainer's back, he knew he was a fool to have let the fellow go by. In jumping to avoid frozen puddles, the runner made a crazy mark to try to shoot at. Nor did the falling snow make sighting any easier.

Now! He squeezed steadily with his whole hand until a pencil of flame spurted up from the pan. The Leman's cold stock rapped smartly against Higsby's cheek as, seventy yards away, Lieutenant the Right Honourable John St. Clair faltered. The speed of his running made him roll over and over—just like a shot rabbit. He lay sprawled on the road, arms twitching spasmodically.

Reloading as he ran, Higsby pelted over to the road. His face lit. Jesus Christ! What a sweet honey of a shot, and—yes—*he had got him a officer!* When he reached him the Britainer was stone dead and lay on his belly with his thin, handsome face twisted 'way over to one side.

Say, wouldn't Miss Desire be tickled particular pink when she heard of his picking off an officer at near seventy paces?

If he figgered on improving his tally, he knew he had better shake a leg. What could he take for proof? Hell, this officer hadn't no hat. But there was a sword lying a few feet back.

The Pennsylvanian picked it up. Shucks, 'twas much too light to be of any use in a free-for-all. Its ivory grip was pretty, though, carved in a queer shape, half fish and half girl. Placing the blade against the earth, he set a heel on the steel and pulled. The blade broke off just below the guard.

Yessir, this hilt would make a damned fine trophy to give Miss Desire.

22

THE RUTS

THOUGH the snow was lessening, Desire realized it was growing colder. Now that she was losing the warmth gained by running, she began to shiver. Had there ever been another night so dreadful?

Her knees, as well as other parts of her, ached and burned. Why hadn't she the wit to bring along her shawl? It must have got lost in the hay. The only redeeming element to this dreadful business was the way John had acted. How very splendid he had been during the crisis. She would love him more intensely than ever, now.

Good thing they had a refuge aboard the *Swan*. After tonight she could never stay on Conanicut. The Gardners had seen her, of course. The rest, too. By morning the scandal would be all over Newport. What she and John had done hadn't been wrong, she was convinced of that. True love was sacred. When people felt as they did, nothing else mattered. If she wished it, they would be married tomorrow. John had promised so and was just as eager as she.

Homes destroyed earlier had resolved to mounds of embers furiously smoking and glowing in the center of rings of black and trampled earth. In a field opposite, some loose horses had gathered and stood with tails turned to the rising wind. Up the road someone fired a shot.

What could be delaying John? She got very worried because now a straggling string of reports marked the beginning of a skirmish of some sort.

"May as well walk to meet him," Desire told herself, and began to limp towards the East Ferry. Though she wanted to turn, the fear suddenly came that she, too, might be transformed into a pillar of salt, like the wife of Lot, the Sodomite. She didn't dare look back to see what was left of her home.

To steady her thoughts she listed items of plunder littering the road.

A strap, a bloodied cleaver, a broken jar, a tea caddy. When she came across a ragged old shawl, she gathered it eagerly about her shoulders. It helped.

Onwards. Where *was* John? Surely he must have started back for her? A clock, a pair of woman's stays, a brass candlestick and the droppings of stolen cattle marked the new snow.

At a sound of hurrying feet, her heart quickened. John and the squad! But then she was aware that these men were coming up from behind. From where she stood on the summit she could see eight or nine of them coming along at a slow trot—British stragglers.

Desire quickened her walk. Ah! The snow lessened briefly and she could make out a dark mass of raiders on the road up ahead. Mercy, they were even burning poor Mr. John Martin's house! That was particularly senseless and cruel. Mr. Martin would walk around an ant's nest rather than kill one.

A snow squall cut off all distant objects.

Something big and dark lay in the road some distance ahead. At first she thought that somebody must have lost his coat but a few more strides told her that it was a man who lay across the frozen ruts. This was strange. The British were conscientious about bringing off their dead and wounded.

A prickling began in her scalp. For all the drifting snow, she could tell now that a dead body lay ahead. Her breath came with a gulp. In all her life she had never seen but one dead person; Uncle Reuben who had died over at Little Compton. How very crumpled and flat-looking the corpse was.

Heavens! That shooting she'd heard! John's party must have been attacked and driven back. The dead man *was a marine*—his black-gaitered legs and the white lining of his tunic left no room for doubt.

All at once Desire became appallingly convinced that she would never become Lady St. Clair. A few more faltering steps told her that never again in this life would John's arms go about her. The intoxicating pressure of his lips would be forever lost. Never! Never! Incredulously, she regarded the slender, clean-limbed body at her feet.

Somewhere, millions of miles away, an owl began hooting.

Mechanically, she stripped off the shawl, folded it and placed it under the dead boy's head. John's head must not rest on mud—not even on frozen mud. No need of a winding sheet; the flying snow would soon spread a clean white pall.

Like an icicle of steel, the broken blade of John's sword lay beside him. What could have happened to its hilt? Somewhere she had read that a dead officer must be buried with hands clasped on his sword. The blade would have to do.

Trying not to see that soggy little hole between John's shoulders Desire Harmony tugged his body onto its back and straightened the disordered buttons. She couldn't help noticing how John's blood went creeping off down a wagon rut, sketching an erratic black course.

Dimly she became aware of men calling in the distance. She only knew that John was looking up at her, with lips slightly parted. There was only a drop or two of blood on them, which she hurriedly wiped away.

"Who's that?" a voice shouted.

Aye, who? Certainly not Desire Harmony Bennett. That girl had died with John St. Clair.

"Well, I'm damned! It's Dee Bennett," exclaimed Jed Franklin. Then angrily, "Say, what you doin' with this God-damned Lobster-back?"

Looking up she saw a dark ring of faces gathered above her. The neighbors were carrying muskets and were breathing hard.

"He is dead," she told them dully. "John has been killed."

"Good riddance," young John Gardner snarled. "Come along, fellers, we must be gettin' close to 'em, now."

Old John Gardner hesitated. "Walt, maybe you had better take Miss Bennett down to Ma at our boat shed. She will freeze to death out here."

"Let her freeze!" Walt snapped. "I'll have no Lobster-back's fancy girl mingling with my sisters." He had always hated the Bennetts, had envied their superior way of life. "I'm going. Coming along?"

Fancy girl! Desire winced and her fingers sought John's hand. It was so chilly it failed to lend her the strength she had hoped for.

"You oughter get whipped through town," Mark Remington growled. He didn't really think so, but he was still mad about losing those fine oxen.

Jed Franklin shouldered his musket. "Aw, let her be. She can peddle her arse through the hull British Navy for all I care."

"Judge not lest ye, too, be judged," warned old John. "I am sorry for the child! Go to our boat shed, Miss Bennett; we have a fire there."

The neighbors went on, all nine of them, leaning into the wind. Little Phil Hull, she noticed, was crying. The musketoon looked much too big for him. Soon the snow blotted out all sight of the Conanicut men.

For the last time Desire Harmony and John were alone together.

23

ASHES

MR. ISAAC PERCIVAL chipped away the top of his egg, sniffed it suspiciously as he always did. Mrs. Percival, ramrod straight at her end of the table, watched him narrowly. So far she hadn't tasted a morsel. Since that glare of fires had begun to glow across the East Passage, she had been up and about.

"Well, Mr. Percival, what do you hear about Captain Wallace's doings on Conanicut?"

Isaac Percival employed a horn egg spoon with deliberation, swallowed a mouthful. "A wretched business, my dear—wretched, for *some*." He regarded his wife expectantly. "You follow my meaning?"

"—Of course, I'm no numskull." Across a white expanse of table-cloth their eyes met. Though they had never loved, they enjoyed a community of understanding. "You mean such a—a brutal deed will benefit us?"

Ike Percival made a clucking noise in the back of his throat. "How can it fail to? The Provincial Legislature will—must, in retaliation—authorize an outfitting of letters-of-marque and privateers. The Continental Congress—ahem—may follow suit."

"Shouldn't wonder."

"In that case, my dear, I shall sell our chandler's stores at a neat profit. Yes, a *very* neat profit."

Lizzie Percival cocked her head to one side and her jet earrings flashed. "It would help me to understand the precise definition of a letter-of-marque."

Mr. Percival's thin arm prolonged itself in the direction of the honey pot. He was careful, however, to keep his wrist lace free of the butter.

"A letter-of-marque, Mrs. P., is an armed merchantman. Her chief function is—ahem—to transport merchandise. She is armed essentially to preserve her from attack. Of course, should she chance to fall in with a weak vessel belonging to the enemy—ahem—a letter-of-marque's commission entitles her to attack and capture such a craft."

"—And a privateer?" Lizzie Percival knew perfectly well, but equally well she was aware that it flattered Isaac to appear wise at the breakfast table. Desperately, she wanted him in a good humor on this of all mornings.

"A privateer, my dear, is either built as a vessel-of-war, or is converted to the purpose from a fast merchantman. Ahem. She signs a crew twice to three times as large as an ordinary merchantman and a double complement of officers." His sparse gray brows knit themselves. "Expensive, my dear, very expensive—especially those extra officers."

"And her purpose?"

"—Is to cruise, not trade. She sails to seize as many enemy vessels as she may—ahem—with the least possible risk to herself.

"In the last war, Abraham Whipple took twenty-three French ships; earned his owners close on a millions pounds. Good man, Whipple. The Malbones, the Hazards, Bannisters, all laid their fortune privateering. John and Nicholas Brown's *Oliver Cromwell* made them a mint."

"Such fortunes are to be expected?"

Mr. Percival's gaze sought the window. Out on the street knots of men had gathered, were talking angrily. By consequence of the descent on Conanicut quite a few of them had brought muskets and powder horns but handled their weapons as if they were not sure what to do with them.

"By no means. In the old French war, Robert Rodman lost his *King of Prussia* on her very first cruise. 'Twas off Madeira. Tom Childs had his *Mayflower* captured right after taking three fat prizes. Privateering, my dear, is a chancy business. Ahem! Not for sober merchants like me."

A sound of movement came from upstairs. That would be Lucy. Poor child, she had been crying ever since the news got around that Captain Wallace had ordered an attack on Conanicut Island.

Absently, Lizzie Percival heard her husband holding forth across the table.

"The solid, if less spectacular, profit lies in equipping these privateers and letters-of-marque. An owner anxious to get his ship to sea in a hurry will seldom quibble over the spending of a few pence more here and there. Why in '62, I sold cable as high as three shillings the running foot. Not the first quality, either."

Mrs. Percival's teaspoon made a tiny ringing noise in her cup.

"Mr. Percival?" When Lizzie used that tone of voice, Isaac knew she'd something on her mind.

"What will happen to the Bennetts?"

There it was! He had hoped Lizzie would say nothing until he had gleaned further. Sighing, he wiped his mouth, leaving a yellow crescent on the napkin.

"I have been pondering that question, my dear, with due attention."

"They are ruined?" Shrewd black eyes met sly gray ones.

"Inevitably, Elizabeth, inevitably. Asa Bennett is—er—beggared. Must be."

"Why?"

"Polypus Hammond, Bennett's captain, admitted the *Prudence* was taken by Spanish picaroons and Wallace's rascals cut out the *Patience* last night. She lies among the British ships at this moment."

How in time had Isaac learned about the loss of the *Prudence?* His plain, almost stupid appearance was eternally deceptive. Certainly Isaac had evolved a most efficient method of gathering intelligence.

"Even so, that still leaves Asa two ships."

Percival frowned. Why should Lizzie sail this tack? Why couldn't she see that the Bennetts were losing out? All this talk about Tim's having deserted was dead against popular sentiment.

"Maybe, maybe not. They say the *Narragansett* is somewhere in the French Sugar Islands. As for the *Hope*—" He smiled a bleak, private smile which again set Mrs. Percival to thinking that her husband knew something she did not.

"Under the circumstances, ahem, well—wouldn't it seem advisable to—er-r—?"

"—To postpone the nuptials?"

He beamed at her because, curiously enough, he had expected stiff opposition on that point. "You put the very words in my mouth. You are a very clever woman, Elizabeth."

His wife looked hard at her plate. Her mouth thinned. Isaac had stolen a march on her. She disliked that.

The merchant spread honey thickly over a crumpet. "You are entirely right. For some time to come, I fear, Timothy will be in no state to assume—ahem—additional responsibilities."

Mrs. Percival looked her spouse squarely in the eye. "But what of Lucy? She dotes on Timothy."

"As always," came the bland reply, "Lucy will do as we tell her. I am entirely confident on the point."

Mrs. Percival sat quite still.

He glanced up, surprised. "Do you imply that our child will not obey?"

Mrs. Percival pursed lips of the palest pink. "I have brought her up so well I presume she likely will. But—"

"—But?"

"Young people in love—well—sometimes they don't see the commonsense of things."

"Love? Rubbish! Silly twaddle."

Mrs. Percival's wax-hued features softened and, as her color rose, she became almost handsome.

"Love? What do you know of love, Isaac? What do I, for that matter? We know nothing about it. Guess we—well, we hadn't time for love. That has been our loss."

Isaac Percival drew breath to protest, but stopped. What Lizzie said was too true to deny. They hadn't had time for love. She had been the eldest of nine children and the Warrens had been poor, poverty poor. He himself had come out from Liverpool on a slaver. He'd starved, had suffered African fever, had been kicked about ever since an orphanage had sent him to sea. Lizzie was right but—

"Nonsense," he snapped. "Pray recall the adage—'When Poverty enters the door, Love flies out of the window.' Come, come, Elizabeth. Whatever has got you so addled?"

Mrs. Percival stared at her plate. For once she wasn't priding herself on its being real china.

"Can't rightly say. It's that—well, maybe I'd like for Lucy to enjoy some of the things I missed—and you missed, Mr. Percival."

Beneath the surface of her words she thought how wonderful it would be to find in Isaac's eyes such a light as some of her friends found in their husbands'. And many of them had been married for years and years.

Percival shrugged. "Come, come, my dear. You are distraught." He used the word as if it were a big concession.

Mrs. Percival paid little attention. She was listening to water splash into a slop jar. That meant Lucy would be down any minute now.

On witnessing her daughter's terrible grief and apprehension, she had taken fresh stock of the situation. Well, no matter what, she must guide Isaac's policy.

When Lucy appeared she had stopped crying but her eyes were

bloodshot and her nose pink and swollen.

"Well, child, and how is my favorite daughter this morning?"

Eyes brimming suddenly, she wailed, "Oh, Papa, it's so awful not knowing. Tim may be hurt, even dead!"

Mr. Percival cleared his throat and his pale eyes sought the window. He hated a display of emotion.

"We trust not. Shortly, we will become informed as to just what has taken place. Ahem, Benson has been up since dawn. I gave him instructions to question anyone arriving from the Island."

Lucy nodded mechanically. "Thank you, Papa."

She didn't immediately seat herself at the table but wandered over to a window and stood looking blankly out onto the garden. By the sickly light of this dark winter's morning the summer house looked tremendously forlorn. Withered flower stems and fallen branches poked cheerlessly up through the snow.

It was terrifying not to know right away whether Tim was safe, especially when she felt so sure that something had gone wrong with him. She was certain of it as if somebody had already told her so.

No matter what Papa or Mama said, she was going to find Tim, and at the very first opportunity. Though Papa was what people called "near" with his money, she was not quite penniless. Up in Concord, Grandma Warren had winked and given her two pounds.

"Want you to have this," she'd said. "Isaac Percival is closer than the bark on a birch and always will be. Keep this. You may need it some day."

Dear Grandma Warren. For all her razor-edged tongue, that old dried apple of a woman, like so many New Englanders, was generous and kindly beneath a forbidding exterior. Foreigners were different. Patsy Pringle from Charleston was all smiles outside, but inside— well, you never knew where you stood with her.

Her mother's voice recalled her to realities.

"Lucy, pray take your place. A young woman must feed her strength else she will fall victim to vapors and megrims."

The girl slipped her napkin from its ring, dropped heavily onto her chair. "But what is known to have chanced?"

Her father shook his head dolefully. "Only that Captain Wallace's men ravaged the Island—ahem—with fire and sword." He liked the sound of that. Fire and sword was a fine, round phrase.

"But, why, *why?*"

"As an object lesson, my dear, as an object lesson. Captain Wallace intends, ahem, to force us into supplying the King's ships. First Conanicut, then Newport, if the food treaty is not renewed. If we continue to supply his ships, he will spare this port."

Mr. Percival broke off because the back door had banged. Lucy heard boot soles being dragged over a scraper. Clorinda shuffled in. "It's Mr. Benson, suh."

"Show him in, you idiot!" Isaac Percival was as near to excitement as an iron self-control and an impassive nature permitted.

The news at last! Lucy's hands stiffened, slowly gathering the table-cloth fabric beneath their fingernails. Her breast felt cramped, as if some invisible fiend were drawing her stay strings tight, insufferably tighter.

As footsteps shuffled nearer along the back hall Mrs. Percival's hand came to rest on her daughter's. Big brown freckles dotted its back. It was a plain, strong hand, unornamented save for a narrow wedding band.

"Whatever chances," she whispered, "you *must* believe that I act in the interests of your eventual happiness."

Lizzie Percival was surprised at herself. 'Til this moment she hadn't realized that she cared tuppence about what went on inside Lucy's honey-blonde head.

A furtive, round-shouldered little man in a dingy scratch wig shuffled in. His blunt nose was purple and moist from the cold.

He bowed hurriedly to his employers. "Sarvice, sir; sarvice, Ma'am, Miss."

Ike Percival sat straight, glared, as he always did at his employees. The rascals never understood kindness.

"Well? Speak up! Speak up, man!"

"Yes, Mr. Percival, sir." Nervously, Benson began revolving a battered fur cap. "It were an awful thing, that raid. 'Pears that near midnight Cap'n Wallace's people drove the Conanicut folks right out of their houses into the snow. 'Twas a monstrous thing—"

A gesture from Isaac Percival cut him short. "Dispense with dramatics, Benson. Tell me what was done with Mr. Bennett's property."

Lucy's hands gripped the sides of her chair fit to snap its arms off. She guessed she knew now how an accused person felt when he stood up to hear the verdict. Wasn't Benson ever going to speak? Oh, curse him! Why did he have to stand there, stupidly crumpling his cap?

"For pity's sake, speak!" she blurted out. "Answer Mr. Percival."

As from a long distance she heard Benson reply, "Pardon, Miss, I— I hates to say it, but they—well, they burned down Mr. Bennett's house and barn. They cut out a schooner he had laying to the wharf; then they fired the warehouse—"

"Did they burn his ropewalk, too?" Mrs. Percival demanded.

"Yes, Ma'am. Mr. Bennett ain't got nothink left, not a stiver! It's cruel hard on one so old."

Nothing left? It seemed as if hard, blunt fingers were being jammed into Lucy's ears.

"But the family?" she managed to ask. "Mr. Bennett and his family are safe?"

Benson misunderstood. "The old gent' took a chill, but they've brought him, and the wounded, safe to Mr. Warner's."

"Then there *was* fighting?" Percival interjected.

"Yessir, five or six of the Bloody-backs was slain. One was a officer. And quite a parcel of them wounded."

"Don't be stupid," Mrs. Percival interrupted. "Is Mr. Timothy— old Mr. Bennett's son—safe?"

Benson forgot himself, scratched under a wig on which inky goose quills had created a smudge. "Why, Ma'am, somebody said he got himself hurted bad."

"Badly! How badly?" Lucy felt the table, the whole room, sway before her.

Benson jumped, curled his cap brim into a desperately tight roll. "Why, Mistress, some says one thing, some says another."

"Damn it, man, why don't you know?" Ike Percival shouted. "Why did I send you down to the harbor?"

So young Bennett was wounded, maybe incapacitated for weeks. Um. Should be easy as rolling off a log to snap up Bennett's old customers.

"They say he got hit in the head, was kind of stunned."

Lucy got up, chin quivering. "I must go to Tim—"

"You will not! Lucy, sit down!"

Trying to smooth things over, Mrs. Percival said, "I trust Mistress Bennett suffered no harm?"

"Why, Ma'am, I guess she is all right." Benson shuffled. Embarrassed, his eyes sought the floor.

"What does that mean?"

"Please, Ma'am, if I may make so bold—I—well, I ain't given to tale-bearing."

"Go on, man, speak up," Isaac Percival roared. "What in blazes holds you gawping there?"

The clerk looked helplessly at Lucy but, aware of Mr. Percival's baleful stare, stuttered, "When the Englishmen set fire to Mr. Bennett's b-barn, Mistress B-Bennett came running out."

"Well, what of that, you idiot?"

"A B-Br-British officer was with her!"

A faint, acid smile flitted over Isaac Percival's narrow mouth and he spoke softly, to himself it seemed.

"So Mistress Desire hides a scarlet letter beneath her Quaker's gray? What a pity. The Bennetts used to be a fine, respectable family. I pity Asa, one of his children a deserter, the other a trollop!"

Lucy turned, round-eyed, on her mother. "But, Mama, what could Desire have been doing in a barn at midnight?"

"You are too young to know," Mrs. Percival replied promptly. "You may go, Benson. Clorinda will give you some soup. You must be cold."

"Why, why, thank you, Ma'am."

Benson was fair taken aback. The world certainly had gone crazy when the Percivals considered an employee.

24

PLUNDER

AT FIRST Desire had an idea she had better take refuge in the hollow. Sam Higsby, though fierce and primitive in many ways, didn't seem cruel. Though he wasn't a neighbor—she somehow felt he'd be kind and understanding, maybe because he was close to wild things. Wild things felt intensely, without artificial rules.

Nobody with a voice like his could be brutal, at least not to women. On Conanicut she knew she would be judged harshly. What the Gardners had said was indication enough. Right now abuse, contempt, would kill her. Less tolerable still would be pity.

When she awoke around eight of the morning, Desire couldn't for the life of her think where she was. This wasn't her room with light yellow walls. Though she listened, she couldn't hear Mamba grumbling, rattling pots and pans downstairs. Where in the world?

Last thing she recalled was closing John's stiffening fingers over his sword blade. This undoubtedly was a woodshed, and she was terribly cold. Whose? Oh, yes—she half-remembered creeping up to warm herself at the ashes of John Martin's house.

Lying there in the straw, unrelated things came back, fitted themselves into a pattern. Exquisitely beautiful promises made in a hayloft. A painful, rapturous, sublime interlude. Fear. Terror. A shot in the frozen distance.

Oh, no! John wasn't dead! This was an illusion, horribly vivid. One couldn't love anybody so much and have it end like this. No force was powerful enough to remove John from her scheme of things.

Her awakening faculties fought against the awful suspicion that her recollections were realities.

Standing in the door she dug dirty knuckles into eyes which ached in the snow and sunlight. The ashes of half a dozen homes sent smoke climbing sullenly into a low and threatening sky. Right now the sun was shining through a mere porthole puncturing slate-gray clouds.

Desire knew she must find something to eat otherwise she would never be strong enough to look for John's body. Despite the heavy fall of snow, she guessed she could locate it.

A lot of people were collected down by the East Ferry; must be waiting to go over to Newport. Beyond, the King's men-of-war kept cannon trained on Newport. When she recognized H. M. S. *Swan's* brown and yellow topsides, her sight blurred and she held onto the door frame.

Mr. Martin's house had not burned entirely because a tabby stone wall had separated his kitchen from sort of a walled back porch. In this she discovered a sheaf of smoked salmon hanging from a roof beam. Also some frozen potatoes and onions in a little bin. This encouraged her to forget the snow in her shoes, her wet stockings and numb fingers.

A further search yielded a wooden noggin and a pewter plate containing a nondescript sticky mess. This she scrubbed as clean as possible.

Desire lowered the well sweep and drew a half bucket of icy water. After taking a long drink, she bathed her face. The water did clear her mind a bit and she perked up enough to tie a torn horse blanket about her.

In pulling the hair back from her eyes her fingers encountered a wisp of hay. She almost broke down at that. Never in her life would she see hay but that she would remember the dawn of December 11, 1775.

Lord, how sore she was. Every step hurt. Though a hot bath and a change of underclothes were what she needed, such luxuries were out of the question.

When she went to the front of the ruins she was amazed to see a lot of ox carts and wagons down on the road. The drivers appeared to be collecting booty deserted by the raiders.

Oh, dear, they must have come across John's body! Of course they wouldn't leave him lying there—even if he was an enemy. The thought of his body dumped into a farm cart was awful. She hated herself for having wasted unforgiving moments in sleeping and eating. Now there was nothing she could do to protect her husband's body from the wrath of a vengeful people.

At her utter helplessness, tears slipped down her cheeks. Still, Conanicut people were decent. They wouldn't maltreat a corpse. It wasn't in them, no matter what they said or did to the living.

All at once she thought she recognized Cuffy and Mamba walking beside a hay cart. In it lay an old man under blankets. Papa!

Desire darted behind the mound of blackened stones and didn't move a muscle till the group was well by. After last night she couldn't ever face Papa again; nor anybody she had known. They would say, or at least think, horrible things.

Oh dear! The Committee might arrest her for—for having to do with a British officer. Plenty of people got sent to a prison for less than that. Phil Hull had said British sympathizers were being imprisoned in an old mine at Simsbury, Connecticut. Did they send women Tories there, too?

Provided she could hunt up some more blankets somewhere, Desire figured she might make out in the deep straw of Mr. Martin's woodshed for a while, but the smell of wet, charred wood and burnt plaster would remain forever in her memory. Her next move required deep and careful consideration. Here she ought to remain unmolested for a while. John Martin had no relatives and was known to be very poor.

By noon, travel along the Ferry Road had thinned to a straggle. This whole end of Conanicut had become deserted—a blighted, uninhabited area—and so it would undoubtedly remain until Spring. Desire wondered whether anything had been done to the farms above Cranston's Cove and James Town Crossroads.

One fact was unmistakable. The sooner Desire Harmony Bennett left Conanicut and Newport, the better.

Of course, the Society of Friends would promptly condemn her and set her aside. She could imagine certain prissy old maids and timid, nice-Nellies of the Week Day Meeting licking sanctimonious chops and appearing ever so scandalized. To hear the beautiful thing that had happened to her called ugly names would be intolerable. She must go away. But how? She'd no clothes, and never a penny to bless herself with.

Seated on the chopping block in John Martin's backyard, Desire pondered. Dared she appeal to Tim? He had been away and should have grown broad-minded. Maybe he was, in general, but with his own sister?

Probably Tim would get mad and unreasonable because she had fallen in love with an Englishman. He could forgive her having been in the barn with John more easily than their having destroyed Peaceful Haven. After all, the Parliamentary Troops had wounded him pretty sore so it was to be expected that he would be blazing hot against the British.

Still, Desire wasn't frightened at her predicament. She had always prided herself on being more self-sufficient than the Franklin, Gardner and Elley girls.

An exploration of the wreckage augmented her supplies by a crock of pickled eggs, a skillet and a couple of forks which, though they'd had their handles burnt off, were still serviceable. Another bit of luck was finding a rusty old kitchen knife stuck into a beam in the woodshed. The hens were coming back, one by one, from the woods.

When the sun slanted low over the Narragansett shore, Desire decided it was safe to reconnoiter. Nothing moved on the road now, save crows picking at some refuse. John St. Clair's body had been removed, but at the spot where he had lain a claret-colored stain marked the trampled snow. A cold, empty feeling invaded her with the realization that their married life had begun and ended within the span of one hundred and twenty minutes.

The half-blanket about her shoulders, she hurried past the ruins of the Remingtons' and the Widow Hull's houses. Down by the river, Gardner's tanyard was still giving off smoke. Very likely the piles of bark there would smoulder for days.

Of Peaceful Haven nothing remained save the big chimney and four elms which would never leaf again. For yards about, the snow was black with burnt-out brands. Down in the pasture beyond the apple orchard one of the plow team lay dead. The poor beast's legs poked queerly up out of the snow.

By the white near hind hoof she knew it was Bob. Why had Captain Wallace felt it necessary to kill Bob? For the first time she commenced to cry. Of the world she had once known, nothing remained, nothing at all. Like black, jagged teeth the pilings of the warehouse, once Pa's pride, rose above the ice-choked tide.

So might Andromache, her lover dead, have gazed on the ruins of Troy Town! The thought rallied her. Now was no time to play the fainting, sighing maid. No weeping for a dead life. She would be tragic but courageous, like poor Mary of Scots.

She found that the snow had been helpful in burying no end of useful objects: two blankets, a bundle of her own clothes containing a blouse, three petticoats, a shawl, three pairs of stockings—one pair silk—and a pair of shoes with heavy sterling silver buckles. Luckily they were solidly sewn and Boston cobbled. Her search also yielded the big silver spoon with which Papa had always ladled gravy and, best of all, a comb.

Her patient search brought her at last to the orchard. There she stopped, horrified at the sudden discovery of a corpse. A British marine was lying slumped in a corner of the orchard wall. Though there were dog tracks all about, the body apparently hadn't been noticed by humans; probably because of a row of snow-laden bushes screening it from the barnyard.

Because a bluish hole marked the center of his forehead this broad-faced Englishman looked as if he were considering the evening sky from three eyes.

Conquering an impulse to be sick, Desire remained still, trying to think what she might find on him that would prove useful. His musket? It was gone. So was his powder horn. Too bad, she could knock over a rabbit as easy as Phil Hull.

Hesitantly, she approached the corpse. It was curious to see only half of one black-gaitered leg. Snow had blown over his feet and had quite hidden his hands. The mouth was half open, exposing yellow and brown teeth between dry-looking, purplish lips.

By using the whip of logic on herself, Desire forced herself to crouch above the scarlet-clad body. This man was an enemy. He had helped to burn her home. Anything she could find was rightfully hers, especially hard cash.

There wasn't much in the dead Marine's pocket—only three silver shillings and her mother's silver thimble. His coat felt invitingly thick and warm but her fingers were too stiff to slip the buttons through their holes. His leggings, she figured, would keep the cold from her legs when she waded about in the snow. It was dark before she finished undoing the marine's gaiters.

Utterly fantastic, incredible, all this. Yesterday at this time she had had a comfortable home, servants, plenty of food and a bed to sleep in.

And John.

25

Ruins

Two days went by before Tim Bennett could even raise his head without feeling all the world go spinning about. His split scalp itched and burned so he fell into a feverish doze which endured for interminable hours.

Somehow Sam Higsby had found him, had taken him away from Cuffy. To accommodate his guest the ranger must have widened and lengthened his lean-to, besides raising a log front to it. Now it resembled a rough, triangular cabin. Sometimes Higsby went out and would be gone hours at a time. Where he went was of no interest to the patient.

Often he failed to hear the Pennsylvanian leave or arrive. It seemed incredible that anyone could move so softly.

From practically every absence he returned carrying a shirt, a blanket, or a soft cloth with which to dress his friend's raw and angry scalp.

"You sho' have a powerful thick skull," Higsby drawled. "That Britainer fetched you a mighty mean lick."

Not before the thirteenth of December did a measure of Tim's strength return. He felt better, able to do a bit of thinking. Previously, when he attempted to collect even two or three ideas they would whirl apart—like a card house.

From the length of bluish shadows streaking the hillside opposite, he judged it must be late afternoon.

"Let's see," he muttered. "Damned British raided Sunday night and Sam says this is Wednesday. Sam says Desire Harmony and Pa were taken over to Newport the next day. Probably they would stay with the Malbones a while."

A half-formed recollection came to haunt him. Something, he knew, had gone wrong about his sister but, for the life of him, he couldn't remember what that was.

Chiefly from what the ranger hadn't said he deduced Pa's property had suffered serious damage. How bad was it? Why couldn't he remember anything after attacking those thieves in the hallway? Queer, he had been walking, too.

Tomorrow he had better get up and find Pa. Pa would undoubtedly be developing a plan of action, retrenching, just as he had when he'd faced heavy reverses in the past. Like back in '66 when the *Covenant* went down off Hatteras with all hands and £10,000 worth of goods.

He must ask Pa further details about the four Bennett ships. The *Narragansett's* orders, for instance. She was the fastest and handiest of them all. Was she to be held indefinitely at Cap François?

A jay began screeching up the hollow. Further off, a second jay taunted in reply.

Did Lucy know of the calamity? Dear Lucy, if only she could be here now. His bandage wanted changing and, despite the best of intentions, Sam was anything but gentle about the task.

Feeling mighty thirsty, he edged himself to a sitting position and drank from a birch bark cup set beside the wooden water bucket. He was still drinking when the jay squawked again just outside and Sam Higsby's flat brown face darkened the door. He pitched a limp turkey gobbler onto the floor and slipped in. He had a parcel tucked under one arm.

He grinned. "Heyo. So you figger to sit up an' take notice?"

"Feel some better. Head don't whirl so bad anymore. Where did you find that turkey?" Tim knew a wild one hadn't been seen on the Island in years.

Higsby looked very innocent. "Well, I was driftin' through that patch o' woods above the main road when I see this bird feedin' in a field. Sez I to myself, 'Sam, that pore critter looks God-awful cold an' lonesome out there. Wouldn't he look better all browned on a sassafras stick?'"

Admiringly, he extended a bronze-tinted wing. "Purty, ain't he? An' fatter'n a squaw in the family way."

Higsby was trying to act casual and cheerful-like because Tim was in for some very bad news and the poor feller didn't look fit to endure it.

Tim asked, settling back on his blankets, "Have you been over to town yet?"

"Nope. Don't figger it's safe yet. Fisherman told me Gen'r'l Washin'ton's all of a lather over desertions. Said every deserter took is given thirty-nine lashes, no pay an' double duty."

Sinking on to his heels the ranger commenced vigorously to pluck the turkey onto an old blanket. "Now I wouldn't mind a lickin' an' I'd head back fer Boston right now, if I only was certain to see some fightin'."

He grinned over his shoulder. "That there little brush with the Redcoats t'other night pleasured me more than a kag of Mr. Booze's best whiskey. Wish't folks in this neck o' the woods wasn't so pernickety. I picked me off a officer an' under his wig he'd the softest skelp lock *I* ever laid a hand to."

At last Tim asked, "There's not much left of Pa's place?"

"Nope."

"Warehouse burnt?"

"Yep."

"Rope-walk, too?"

"Uh-huh." On the bed of spruce tips, Tim's face looked ghostly.

Sam frowned. He had done picking the turkey's back and was starting in on a leg. "Fine fowls, ain't they? These tame critters is different colored from the wild ones. They're redder an' smaller. Injuns, Conestogas 'specially, favor turkey-cock feathers in their headdress."

Tim wasn't to be diverted. "Sam, did you learn where my sister has gone? She came through safe, of course?"

"Heard tell so." Higsby studied to keep his voice steady. "Folks saw her after the fire was over."

She was a cute piece, all right. Her wide, little-girl eyes sure had fooled him. Imagine Miss Deshe gittin' flushed out of a loft, an' with a goddam Britainer!

Yep. He was a fool not to have tumbled her when she came pesterin' about his camp the way she had. Of course those shadows under her eyes should have told him, but who would have figgered what she really wanted? He guessed he'd still plenty to learn about gals an' their 'cute little ways.

Tim sighed, turned sidewise to support his weight on an elbow. He was wearing somebody's blue coat. It had pewter buttons which dug into him sometimes. And he still had on his bloodstained nightshirt. It smelt fierce, but such details didn't bother Higsby so long as the bandage was changed regularly.

"Fisherman say where Pa is?"

Higsby stopped plucking and his gaze wandered out of the doorway. Damn! He reckoned he'd have to spit it out after all.

"Yer Pa was stayin' with a feller, name of Redwood, a elder in yer church."

"*Was?* Where is he now?"

Higsby's hand, all fluffy with small feathers, came to rest on Tim's shoulder. "Tim, I—I'd ruther be skun alive than tell you—but, well—I guess I got to. Yer Pa is dead. He died day after the raid."

A succession of icy tides swept up Tim's back and the lean-to commenced to spin about his head again. Pa dead? Why, that wasn't possible! For all his age, Pa was strong and tough—as enduring as the sun and the seasons.

Since he couldn't think of anything further to say, Higsby went on plucking the turkey. Little feathers drifted about, settled on Tim's bandage and unshaven cheeks.

At last he asked in a strained voice, "They—they wounded him?"

"Nope. Yer Pa got took off with the lung fever. Doctor claimed 'twas caused by standin' 'round in the weather so long. A woman named Hull died o' the same ailment." He plucked faster. "They planted yer Pa this mornin'. I'm—I'm right sorry, Tim. Yer Pa was a fine old feller, mighty fine—even if he didn't hold with fightin'."

Next day Tim was set on going over to Newport. Though Higsby wouldn't let out a word, he sensed that something was wrong about Desire Harmony.

It was a bitter surprise to have had no word from Lucy. Wasn't it strange she had made no effort to find him? Then came the reassuring suspicion that the British had forbidden all traffic in the harbor.

Tim broke the news to Higsby by saying, "I'm going over to town and collect some debts that were owed Pa."

"You'd better," the rifleman agreed. "Some folks hev a short memory. Here, see if you can get into these."

From a canvas sack, he dragged out a blue woolen jersey, some linsey-woolsey stockings, shoes and a pair of brown duroy breeches. All the clothes were in pretty good condition save the jersey. It had a small hole under its left arm; not a worn hole, either.

"Where did you get these things?"

Higsby spat tobacco juice at the fire. "Off'n a sailor."

"What did they cost? I want to pay you back."

"Nawthin'."

"Nothing?"

"Nope. He'd no use for 'em."

Tim gazed at the clothes. "You killed him?"

Higsby held up the jersey and, running his finger through the hole, wiggled it gently. "Naw, a bee stung him."

26

AT THE PITT'S HEAD

TIM decided that his bandaged head, sunken eyes and unshaven features were to thank for the absence of comment which attended his slow progress up Mill Street. Every few rods he had to stop, panting, to rest.

He knew he should stop in at a friseur's and have his week-old beard removed. But he was in too great a hurry to find Lucy. Of course, she could not have been told about what really had been done at Peaceful Haven.

The Percivals, through mistaken kindness, probably had given her false hopes and reassurances. Both of them imagined their daughter to be much more fragile and high-strung than she actually was. Lizzie Percival was forever insisting, "Lucy is so sensitive! The slightest excitement sends her into the vapors."

The snow was melting from nearby roofs, especially near the chimneys. Times must be hard when some shopkeepers dared offer such cheap and miserable Christmas gifts. Their stock was nothing but battered, unsaleable, left-over merchandise. To whip up trade, Messrs. Hinchley & Bell had posted inviting broadsides offering "A fine piece of Barley sugar with every Purchase amounting to 1/6 or more."

Each stride was taking him closer to Lucy of the smoky-blue eyes and the white-blonde hair. Never had he realized she lived so far out on the edge of town. Damn this weakness!

When he saw the big brick and clapboard Percival house beyond the Congregational Meeting House he wanted to run but his legs felt heavy as lead. Little bright points of fire began wavering before his eyes.

To Tim's vast surprise, Mrs. Percival herself, brown taffeta skirts rustling primly, answered the door.

She made no gesture to kiss him, only gave him a look of deep compassion. "Pray enter, Timothy, and accept my heart-felt sympathy."

Once they had seated themselves in the study, Mrs. Percival spoke at length, reviewed in surprising detail Asa Bennett's fine character and many kindly deeds.

When she discovered that Tim was in complete ignorance of how his father's last hours had been passed, she related everything of importance.

There was little to tell. The old Quaker's chill had progressed swiftly into lung fever and very quickly he had become delirious and had died without uttering a coherent phrase.

Since tokens of mourning and pomp of any sort were abhorred by the Society of Friends there had been no black, no wailing music, not even a choir. Nevertheless, the burial service had been impressive. Great quantities of people, Quakers and the World's People alike, had attended. Folks had come all the way from Tiverton, Narragansett and Little Compton.

Nearly every merchant and shipmaster in Newport had been among the multitude which gathered on the bleak hillside burying ground to hear "solid" Friends testify before the Lord that seldom had a more godly and generous man "traveled in the service of truth."

Now Asa Bennett was resting in an unmarked grave. The Friends did not hold with elaborate monuments. Of late, though, it had been conceded to those who yearned to mark a last resting place that they might, in propriety, raise an "unmarked stone no greater than eight by fourteen inches."

Tim listened heavily. It still seemed impossible that Pa would never again read from the Book in his deep, memorable voice. Presently he blurted out, "Where is Lucy? I—I need to see her."

Mrs. Percival's mouth tightened. She had been steeling herself for this. "Timothy, she is away—on a visit."

"Away!" The misery in the young fellow's bloodshot eyes gave Lizzie Percival a twinge. "She went away—now?"

"Don't you dare to misjudge her," Mrs. Percival warned sharply. "My daughter has only adopted a course which we all deem wise under the circumstances."

Had a mortar shell exploded at his feet, Tim could not have been more stunned. The only thing that had held together his courage, his reason, had been the prospect of curing his hurts with Lucy. How easily her gentle nature could have smoothed his anguish.

And now Lucy wasn't there with the expected encouragement and confidence. She had run away! "What we *all* deem wise—" that was what Mrs. Percival had said. *"All."*

Mrs. Percival put forth a hand. "You, a man of the world, surely understand how unwise, how impossible, it is for you two to be wedded under the circumstances? Especially—"

"—Especially what?"

"There is the matter of your—I hesitate to mention the matter, Timothy, but it seems that I must—the matter of your having—er —come home early. People are saying hard things of you—quite un- justly, of course. Yet it will be now extra hard for you to undertake a fresh beginning."

"But Lucy, what does she say?"

"Your answer is that Lucy has gone away."

"Where is she?"

Mrs. Percival merely looked aside.

Angry color began to creep up along his bearded cheeks. "You bet- ter tell me where she is!"

The ruler-backed figure stiffened and the black eyes flickered back to him. "Timothy, pray don't make the situation more difficult than necessary. Anger will mend nothing."

She half held out a hand. "Believe me, I reasoned with Mr. Percival as long and hard as I dared; the most I was able to persuade him to grant was this: he will not oppose your wedding, if, *within a year,* he feels assured you can properly provide for Lucy. After all, Tim- othy, a year will pass—"

"A year?" A truculent twist hardened his wide mouth. "Aye, what's a year to people like you and old Ike? What's a year to a pair of dead, dried-up trees?"

"Timothy! How dare you!"

"I won't believe she has gone. She wouldn't leave me like this!

"Lucy!" his voice grew hoarse as he called, "Lucy? Are you here? For God's sake answer—tell me you haven't gone away—I need you, Lucy!"

All the reply he got was a startled clatter of dishes in the pantry.

Ignoring Mrs. Percival's outraged protests, he climbed the stairs, wrenched open a door, "Lucy, where are you?" Another door. "Lucy! Come out. I can't stand this."

When he came at last to her room and he felt how cold it was, the truth sank in. The fireplace could not have been lit in some days.

It made matters no better that, stuck into a red, heart-shaped cushion, he recognized a silver and coral pin he had bought in Cambridge for her. He had posted it that September day when first he had been able to limp along without a stick.

"Ah, this can't be so—can't be—" His voice trailed miserably away.

But it was.

He didn't even see Lizzie Percival when she put a hand on his shoulder and guided him back downstairs. She was silent. It was so bitterly true, what he'd said about dead, dried-up trees. That had hurt. She felt desperately sorry for this big, bewildered young fellow.

"Don't take on so, Timothy. Life is really not so brief as it must appear to a soldier."

To hell with her false sympathy! It wasn't as if she and old Ike hadn't enough idle money to help half a dozen daughters through the first difficult years of marriage. Ike could help, if he would, and he knew that Tim Bennett was no idler, that he came of sound merchant stock.

In desperation he pleaded for a loan, for a modest measure of co-operation in getting Bennett & Son back on its feet. That now he was sailing a wrong tack he guessed by the way Mrs. Percival's face froze.

"There is only one sound way for a young couple to get ahead."

She switched her petticoats. "They must make their own way, asking favors of no one. We did. Can't say I admire this carrying on, Timothy. Mightn't it be more profitable if you made some provision for your precious, innocent little sister?"

He looked at her sharply. "Why do you talk like that?"

Lizzie Percival scanned him. "You want me to believe you don't know?"

"Know what? Take care. She's my sister."

"You needn't speak so tart," Mrs. Percival snapped, "and I shall say what I choose in my own home. I will only repeat what was reported by several of your neighbors who chanced by your Pa's place when it was burning."

Tim caught his breath. Had this to do with Sam Higsby's reluctance to talk about Desire? "Well, what did they say?"

"When fire was set to your father's barn near midnight," her acid tones emphasized the hour, "your sister got smoked out of it—in company with a British officer!"

The accusation was too enormous to have been unfounded. Tim could only gape.

"The Englishman got shot during the retreat, they say. God's swift judgment against lust, no doubt!"

Desire. How could she—his own sister—have been in the hay—like that? Bringing disgrace on a name which had been honored since Rhode Island was settled. What had happened to the world? First Lucy, then Desire. He would never trust another woman—never!

Mrs. Percival's voice impinged on his misery. "And now, young man, you can march yourself right out of here. Though I have tried to be kind and civil, it has got me nowhere."

Gone all cold in his insides, Tim halted, gray-faced, at the door and said slowly and distinctly, "You are wrong. Thank you for reminding me that there never was a Percival worth a Bennett's little finger. Not Ike, your ex-slaver of a husband, nor your precious, faithless daughter! And by the great Jehovah *I'll prove it!*"

The front door slammed.

27

The Merchants

Jacob Rodriguez' second clerk was so polite to Tim as to be offensive. Mr. Rodriguez offered his most humble service, but he was engaged in a transaction with two French gentlemen, a most important transaction. Could Mr. Bennett come next week, perhaps?

Solomon Southwick, printer and publisher of the "Mercury," appeared, inky apron and all, to state that he would have no dealings with a deserter. He looked Tim right in his hollow, stubborn eyes.

"Your Pa was a whole man. I'd have given him the shoes off my feet, but you—you'd better get out, you damn' moon-watcher!"

Tim held out an appealing hand. "But, Mr. Southwick—"

"You deserted! Colonel Hitchcock has sent me a list o' you heroes who ran out ahead o' turn. I'm going to publish it, and I defy you to stop me."

Tim didn't even flinch. "That's a damned lie! I didn't desert. I can prove it. And I'll sue you if you publish that list. Now I want the twenty pounds you owed Pa—"

"Suppose you try to collect it?" Southwick sneered. "Your English-loving sister, either!"

He went back to his press.

When, feverish and on the verge of collapse, Tim reached Captain John Lawton's tavern, he had made no progress. Even the bar wench at the Bull House measured out his beer in silence and wouldn't meet his gaze; an attempted joke fell flat.

Though there wasn't a farthing in his breeches, he had figured it would be all right. Often he'd invited Captain Lawton over to dine at Peaceful Haven. The Captain was an extra fine wing shot and had given him many a useful pointer.

When the barmaid asked for the money, Tim went over to Captain Lawton. The other regarded him as if he were a stranger, then said:

"There is no charge, Bennett, but I don't desire your patronage in the future. I wish you good day."

"But damn it, John, I *ain't* a deserter! Listen." Tim, in careful detail, explained all about his lunar enlistments.

Lawton turned away, shrugging. "That's as may be. Anyhow, what you did looked cowardly and set a bad example. The Committee disapproves."

He wiped his hands on the tail of his apron and stood barring the entrance to the dining room. "If you don't get taken up by a provost's patrol, you'll be luckier than you deserve."

As he stalked out into the street, something young and fine shriveled and died inside of Tim.

There remained only one debt he knew all about. Benjamin Peabody's. Peabody did a furniture trade with Surinam and had made a note of hand to Pa for £97—3—6. The indebtedness was on file at the Court House.

Oblivious of contempt, he browbeat a clerk at the Court House into making a copy. When he presented the bill to Peabody that red-faced individual declared that he'd be blessed and blistered before he would pay a single penny. Unwisely he added, "especially to a family which runs to whores and deserters."

Heedless of consequences, Tim smashed in Peabody's front teeth, then helped himself to what currency he found in the till drawer. Lastly, he warned the bloody-faced importer that if any trouble ensued he would return and give him a real trimming.

On his way to the waterfront, Tim Bennett stopped long enough at the Bull House to slam a shilling onto the counter and invite Lawton and his guests, collectively or individually, to go sample the climate of Hades.

Walking down Queen Street, he tried to consolidate a few solid ideas. He supposed the *Narragansett* under Captain Griffin must still be awaiting orders at Cap François. Of that he was reasonably certain. The *Hope* had, in all probability, evaded enemy cruisers off this coast. If she had been taken, she would have been brought in by now.

Heeding nothing of his surroundings he entered into Thames Street. To hell with Newport. If Pa, hampered by rules laid down by George Fox, had made the World give him what he wanted, it shouldn't be any harder for a fellow who believed in fighting for what he wanted.

What if Desire Harmony had made a mistake? Could a girl of six-teen be expected to know what to do under every circumstance? He guessed she needed a lot of kind words and comforting right now. Just as soon as he located his sister, the two of them would start again elsewhere.

Why the devil had she played the fool, and with a British officer of all people! Usually Desire Harmony showed good sense, for all her poetical flights of nonsense.

A year ago, he guessed he would have felt different about her having done what she had, but in the Army you learned that a thing wrong for one person was understandable, and not necessarily wicked, in another.

He felt more sorry and worried than angry. Desire Harmony was probably safe because she had a mind of her own and plenty of backbone. Where in Tunket could she have betaken herself? If he understood her nature, she'd never seek refuge with an old friend. Even as a small girl, Desire Harmony had possessed a stubborn pride.

Consequently, he canvassed the cheap inns and lodging houses huddled beyond Shipwright Street but met with no success. A round of the posting stations revealed that no one had seen or heard any-thing significant.

The few acquaintances he made bold to address informed him curtly that they neither knew nor cared what had become of a British officer's mistress. He came to understand that the British were really being hated now—not merely mistrusted or feared. The town was deeply outraged over Lieutenant Sneyd's raid on Conanicut.

Unfortunately, Captain Wallace's brutal "object-lesson" had

achieved its desired effect. Despite furious remonstrances by a determined group, the Town Council had voted to renew, for an indefinite period, their Food Convention with the British squadron.

Strange, how disasters struck in clumps. Perhaps it was better so. If you were taking a bad beating, you didn't feel individual blows quite so hard.

Starting back to the landing stage, Tim began for the first time, consciously, to appreciate his sister's sparkling good nature, quick wit and warm understanding.

Gradually he became convinced that if Desire Harmony had played the fool with that young officer, it must have been for a good reason. There was nothing cheap or shallow in her nature. He'd find her. Of course he would. Tomorrow he would search the Narragansett shore. By a miracle she might have got across the Westward Passage.

A knuckle was still bleeding, Tim realized. Would Peabody have the law on him? If so there would be one jim-dandy fight before the bailiffs clapped him in jail.

28

MAN FROM CONGRESS

SUCH a big crowd had gathered before the old Town Hall Tim figured at first that another ration drawing party from the fleet must be preparing to land. But a seaman said, "Naw. It's some fellers from Congress speechifying. Say, ain't you young Mr. Bennett?"

Tim recognized the speaker as the one-eyed man who had come with Polypus Hammond in the *Patience*. "Captain Hammond about?"

The one-eyed man nodded. "Yessir, you'll find him in the crowd somewheres. He's so hopping mad at being done out of his command, I shouldn't wonder a bit if he did some speechifying on his own hook."

"How come the British turned you loose when they seized our schooner?"

The fellow grinned, pointed to the cataract in his right eye. "Wallace ain't taking one-eyed hands, not yet; but they kept Will Elley and Paul Clarke. Paul fought like a stack of wild cats but they pressed him into the *Bolton* just the same. Will is in the *Rose,* so they say.

"Mr. Bennett?" The fellow hung by his side. "If—if you goes privateering, why I can lay a gun better than most. Served as gun captain in the liner *Experiment* a year; jumped her in Port Royal. Yessir, I was a prime gun captain. I can—"

"When the *Hope* returns, look me up." Tim nodded, joined a slow current of men eddying towards a big brick market house at the corner of Thames and Queen where, in the old days, rum and slaves used to be auctioned.

Four men were standing on a rude platform made of planks laid across some barrel heads. At first glance Tim recognized General Charles Lee as one of them. The adventurer's stock was as carelessly tied as ever, his tunic as wrinkled and the purple sash across his chest discolored with food spots.

Narrow jaw thrust far out, Lee was glaring at the crowd, evidently concluding a burst of oratory which had attracted people from all directions.

"—And I say to you lily-livered merchants, 'put your house in order!' Shame on you for making a treaty with that flatulent old fool aboard the *Rose!* God's bloody bones! Had I been here your Council would never permitted his emissary even to land!"

Lee's voice was shrill with passion and his untidy wig curls fluttered. "What species of patriotism is it to spare yourselves at the expense of your suffering brethren in Connecticut, Massachusetts, and New Hampshire? Shame! Purge yourselves of all faint-hearts, Tories and traitors! Turn out the rascals in your high places! Make them swear the awful oath I forced on the doubtful in Providence. See to it that this disgraceful private covenant with the enemy is expunged by the fierce, hot flame of patriotism!"

The crowd stirred; tricornes, varnished leather hats, knitted caps turned uneasily. That Lee's tongue-lashing raised doubts was patent.

"You Rhode Islanders did well to start with, and can do well again, I'll be bound! The next speaker will tell you of plans the Congress is preparing for your protection."

"Hurrah!" bellowed the crowd. "Hurrah for Charley Lee!" "That's talking!" "What does the Congress want?" "Round up the Tories!" "Hang the traitors!"

When Lee descended grandly from the platform, the crowd cheered like mad. Behind him he left a civilian and a pair of officers in uniform. Tim had no trouble in recognizing these last as two of the most famous privateer captains in New England: Esek Hopkins and Captain Tom Hazard.

The latter wore an odd attempt at a uniform. Gold braid had been stitched to the shoulders of an ordinary master's pea-jacket and someone had sewn a lavish supply of brass buttons to his bright yellow waistcoat. In addition, he wore old leather breeches and homespun stockings. One of his shoes lacked its buckle. There was nothing unbusinesslike, however, about the navy cutlass he drew in an effort to gain silence. In the winter sun its heavy blade glittered bright as quicksilver.

Puzzled, Tim asked what the uniform purported to represent.

"It's naval, I guess. Tom's commander over the *Katy*—"

"*Katy?*"

"Sure," the fellow said through a thick fog of rum fumes. "She's the biggest of our Rhode Island vessels, b'God. The other is the *Washington* and Ben Whipple commands her. A wonder Ben ain't here, too."

In short, badly-mumbled sentences, Captain Hazard proudly reviewed the efforts of the tiny Rhode Island navy. It had captured the *Rose* frigate's tender; better still, the two Provincial men-o'-war recaptured a dozen or more prizes from the British. Why, on the night of June thirteenth alone, it had rescued three Rhode Island merchantmen.

"Bully f'r you, Tom!" roared a drunken voice. "Hurray for the

Rhode Island navy! More ships, lads! Le's drive ol' Wallace out to sea!"

Tom Hazard shook his head, waved his cutlass. "Reckon we might, friends, if we weren't too poor to build big enough vessels."

"The hell with big ships!" It was Polypus Hammond yelling from a stoop across the street. "Give me enough men and I'll guarantee to carry the *Rose* by boarding."

Captain Tom Hazard shook a shrewd, somewhat brutal-appearing head. "Like hell you could, Polypus. No, friends, the only thing will help these colonies are stout, fast ships that were built to fight: sloops, frigates and, maybe sometime, ships-of-the-line!"

Everybody stared at Tom Hazard. It was absurd even to dream of weak little Province building a three-decker. Why, to construct a single such vessel would cost more than to equip three regiments of troops.

Polypus Hammond sang out angrily, "Aw, quit raving, Tom. Tell the Congress to grant us privateer commissions and we'll wind up the King's clock in a hurry!"

A great resounding shout beat up the street.

Hazard's face went red. "No!" he shouted. "What we need are men-of-war. If there had been some Continental cruisers hereabouts the folks on Conanicut wouldn't be living on charity this minute! Can't you see that, you blamed, stubborn old mule?"

An angry cry rang against the weatherbeaten houses, rolled out to the British vessels across the lead-hued water. The *Glasgow* was no longer there, but the *Rose,* the *Bolton* and the *Swan* still swung to their cables with guns trained on four captured merchantmen. One was the *Patience.*

A young seaman clambered up on one of a row of stone posts set to keep carts from scraping warehouse walls.

"Granting what you say is gospel, Cap'n, but war vessels cost money. Shucks! We hear this Colony is hard put to supply even the *Katy* and the *Washington.* Where will we find money?"

"Now, I wanted someone to ask just that." Captain Hazard placed a broad tattooed hand on the shoulder of the civilian at his left.

"Friends, this here is Cap'n Steve Farish of Boston, delegated by the Marine Committee of the Congress to bring us some important news. I can promise you he won't talk tootle."

"Hurray for the Congress!" "Bully for Steve Hopkins and the Marine Committee!"

A small individual wearing a sea captain's worn blue serge coat stepped forward. A tougher-looking little man Tim had never seen. Like an old-style mariner, he wore a tiny gold ring in his left ear. While he waited for the crowd to quiet he fished out a red bandanna and began to mop an utterly hairless head. He had a strong face burnt brown by the sun of many an ocean, and fierce gray eyes set beneath hairless lids.

Because the delegate was so short, men began rising on tiptoes, stretching their necks to get a good look at him.

A roar of laughter followed when someone in the heart of the crowd hollered, "Hey, Mister, will yer stand up so's we kin get a look at you?"

"Hell! He's already standing up."

Tim had become jammed in the depths of a crowd of anxious, hard-sailing captains, mates and the decent merchant sailors. The odors of rum, wet wool and damp leather were strong in the air.

For a man of his inches, Captain Farish owned the biggest voice Tim had ever heard. The effect was ludicrous—like a canary bird singing bass. But when the delegate from the Congress commenced to talk, they forgot all about that.

"Feller seamen," he began, plunging hands deep in his pants pockets, "if you'll favor me, I want to tell you a thing or two 'bout myself just so we'll set sail on the right tack. I ain't going to spout book-learning but I've had fair-to-middling experience.

"Back in '74 my own vessel was took by the British; next I got impressed off Canso and served in a bulldog for two months. Down to Norfolk in Virginia, I got a command but she, too, was made a prize of. I got clapped in the Stone Jail in Boston and played 'hull-gull, how many?' with rats and roaches all that winter. I dare say some of you know what that's like?"

A surprising number of men sang out that they did.

Captain Farish took a few quick steps along the platform until the crowd quieted.

"Now, we fellers hold conviction we're good fighters, don't we?"

"We'll stand up to them lousy Lobster-backs any time."

Captain Farish cocked his hairless head and studied a weather-vane above the market. "Suppose I tell you the British ain't so convinced? Queer, but they ain't."

"Proved it at Bunker Hill, didn't we?"

The little delegate in threadbare serge had his answer pat. " 'Pears we were lucky in the British generals. We lost the hill, too, if you'll rec'lect.

"Now here's something you may not know— The English never have cottoned to their Army like they do to their Navy. No, fellers, we'll never convince the English us Americans amount to a pinch of ashes 'til we've fought 'em, ship to ship, gun for gun, on deep salt water *and trounced 'em!* Your true-blue Britisher fancies that on the sea he's God's own gift to creation!"

Farish's voice boomed on, "Just an' right, right an' just, say you. But where do us Americans come across the ships and guns to fight with?"

The throng was really impatient to hear; it fell quiet.

"Listen, all of you! Listen hard. *The Congress has voted to build a navy.*" Such deafening uproar followed that Esek Hopkins stopped scratching a bulbous red nose and looked solemn.

Echoes came flying from the hill back of the town. The speaker talked faster, thumped his hairy hand against its mate. "I seen the plans the Congress has voted." The small delegate's eyes glistened like the blade of the cutlass Hazard had forgotten to sheathe. "First off, we're going to lay down a fleet of thirteen men-o'-war. One for each of the United Colonies."

"What rig?" Polypus Hammond bellowed through cupped hands.

"Five 32-gun frigates, five 28-gun frigates and three corvettes all of 24-guns, and ship rigged!" Captain Farish bellowed back. " 'Tain't much, but it's a beginning. Now here's some news will please you better still. Two of them vessels are to be built right here in Rhode Island!"

The really deafening cheer which followed finally set alarm drums to rolling and thumping aboard the British squadron. High over the roofs of Newport, startled pigeons darted in ragged formations.

"Sure, Cappen, but me, I'm a shipwright," someone sang out. "I know to build ships—men-o'-war in partickler—takes time. What will this port do in the meantime? We'll all be starved dead come a year."

Like a gamecock surveying the field of battle, Captain Farish swung to face the question. "While them thirteen vessels I spoke of is a-building, a temporary fleet will be equipped and put to sea. It may look queer but, jumping Jehoshaphat, 'twill be a genu-ine navy!

"Now fellers, I'll belay and make way for a gentleman who now ranks equal with the great and respected General Washington— only he's a Yankee and therefore better! Come on now, three cheers for Esek Hopkins, Commander-in-Chief of the Navy of the United Colonies!"

The cheer was given, yet without too much enthusiasm. Washington was an unknown quantity and therefore capable of performing miracles, but almost everybody present knew the Hopkinses— Stephen the Congressman, and Esek the privateer. The family had been around Rhode Island since 1640 when Tom Hopkins first took up land. He would be Esek's great grandpa and had been Town Sergeant. Next came Major William Hopkins, then another William who'd had nine children. Properly, four of them had followed the sea. Another was Colonel Hopkins.

Esek's older brother, Stephen, had been Governor and now sat in the Congress. But it was Esek everybody looked up to. In the old French war he had made such a daring privateer captain.

The new Commander-in-Chief stood up, resplendent in a high-collared blue uniform coat that was nattily turned back in turkey red. His red waistcoat was brave with yellow lace and his breeches were blue.

Esek Hopkins' slightly protruding dark eyes were quick, veined with red, and his big, blunt nose of a companionable hue. At fifty-seven, his stubby figure was solid and his stomach ample. The jaw, blue with close shaving, was fleshy, but that of a fighter. There was something about his voice, too, that commanded and held attention.

"Fellow inhabitants of Rhode Island, under orders from the Marine Committee I sail in three days' time to take command of the new fleet which is to rendezvous at Phillydelphy.

"I ain't here to talk. I'll leave that to politicians and preachers." Loud laughter. "I only want to say, friends, I guess we all of us want this colony to make a extry good showing in this new navy. Wasn't it us Rhode Islanders took and burnt the *Gaspée* back in '72? Ain't we always turned out the handiest seamen in America? Look what they did in the old French war!"

"You're right there, Esek! The best ever."

"—And the best captains?"

"Sure, of course!"

"—And the best fighters?"

"You said it, Admiral!"

"Well, then, let's prove it again. A likely feller who craves a shot at the enemy can come to the Sabin Inn directly this rally is done with. The Articles will be ready for signature!"

"Hey, Commodore," yelled the one-eyed sailor. "What's a seaman's wage?"

"A handsome sum, my lad," Hopkins replied easily. "Sixteen shillings a month—and found."

"—And prize money?" a dozen voices demanded. Everyone listened for the new commander's reply. It was important—it meant everything.

Esek Hopkins hesitated, reached up and scratched a red spot on his chin. "Why, men, you can count on the Congress always being generous with patriotical-minded men."

"Yes, but what's the share rate to be? Stop being cooney and spit it out!"

Hopkins shot an unhappy glance at Hazard, then said, "Why, one half the worth of a captured man-o'-war goes to the crew, other half to the Congress."

So? The crowd sobered. Everyone knew there was small profit and a big risk in tackling a man-o'-war.

"What share on merchantmen?" Polypus Hammond called. "That's where the fat lays!"

"Why, it's a third to the crew—"

Whistles and groans drowned out the rest of Hopkins' words. "Only a third! Plague take such a measly share!" rasped the young sailor's voice.

"Listen to me," Hopkins shouted, his face fiery with the sudden temper for which he was famous. "Listen to me, you goddam bilge rat. It costs the Congress a lot to outfit a man-o'-war. The Marine Committee needs the other two-third shares to build ships with!"

"Balls!" jeered the one-eyed man turning away. "We ain't that gullible. Aboard a privateer, the ship's company goes shares on the whole value!"

"Do you always have to think of shares?" Esek Hopkins demanded, his neck thick over his stock. He was mad clean through. "To join the Navy is a patriotic duty!"

"Sure, it's easy for you and some others to tell us so—you got plenty of privateering money salted away!"

Hammond looked uncertain, then came forward. "Share or no share, I'm for joining Esek. My ear's still sore. I'd give a lot for a cruise against the picaroons of Cuba."

The young sailor whose broken nose had been slewed around to one side of his face came up to the speaker. "There will be fighting—real fighting? We will really go against the English?"

The new Commander-in-Chief laughed raspingly. "You'll get a belly-full of broadsides, honor bright. Any man don't join up right away will be sorry, because there will be quick promotions soon as the new ships are commissioned. There will be fun and to spare in port and you will have money to spend. You will see the world at no expense—the Indies, Europe, Africa, maybe India."

"Catting?"

"There'll be no flogging worth mention," Hopkins beamed; he was away from the most dangerous subject. "Limit is to be twelve strokes! No real mariner would even notice that.

"Down in the Sugar Islands is plenty of grog and brown girls— Creolians, we call 'em—waiting for you."

"By God, he should know," Tom Hazard guffawed. "Ever hear tell of how Esek, Brose Paige, and Nick Cook and me cleaned out that grog shop at Paramaribo?"

Captain Farish frowned, but the crowd chuckled and began to smile once more.

"Yes, boys; join the Navy and you'll see strange sights, better yourselves and have a fine time. And, best of all, you will be a credit to Rhode Island. Your folks will be proud."

Hopkins looked about, began briskly rubbing his hands. "Every man jack who signs today will be given a glass of rum, with my compliments. My quartermaster and an officer are at the Sabin Inn."

A whooping began at the far end of Anne Street. That, and a clatter of hoofs. Heads jerked about when the yelling continued.

"News! Hey! I got great news!" Jim Trumbull, the postrider, astride a blown and lathered nag, came riding up the outer edges of the crowd. He was bursting with a rare self-importance. "Hey, fellers, listen! I just heard the news up to Tiverton."

"Well, don't stand there bellerin' like a bull calf," Farish snapped. "Speak up and get out. You're interfering with the Commodore's speech."

"All right then. Listen, fellers, listen!"

People crowded in around the panting horse.

"Know what? *The Congress is going to allow privateering!*"

"Oh God!" Captain Hazard looked ready to kill the post rider. "Some bloody fool in Phillydelphy has blabbed!"

"—And old Adams promised us a fortnight's start," Hopkins began cursing under his breath.

Farish scowled. "Wager 'twas that slippery-tongued Si Deane— I never did trust a Connecticuter."

Shouts which had risen heretofore were by comparison like the chirping of crickets in a wood pile.

"When?"

"Don't know yet," Jim Trumbull beamed. "But 'twill be soon, they say."

Ten minutes later, John Clarke tacked a sign to his warehouse door. It was so wet he smeared quite a few letters.

WANTED!

Able-bodied recruits for
the Private arm'd brig-of-war,

DEFIANCE

Guaranteed to be ready for sea when
Commissions arrive.

FULL PRIZE MONEY!   LIBERAL SHARES!
HIGH WAGES

Men had begun fighting to get near Clarke's warehouse when, down the street, Abner Coffin began calling through a leather speaking trumpet.

"Hi, fellers! Come this way! This way! The *Defiance* is only a brig. Sign on for my *Retaliation*. She's a full-rigged ship and will mount eighteen carriage guns. This way, lads! Abner Coffin starts paying wages the minute you sign Articles!"

A swarm of ragged seamen deserted Clarke's, but most of them kept on past Coffin because Ira Thaxter was swinging a big dinner bell and yelling in his thin voice:

"To every man signing up on my vessels *Gamecock* and *Diamond,* I grant a four shilling cash bonus. Hurry on, lads! Offer expires in an. hour. Hurry, for the glory of old Newport!"

They hurried.

29

THE OYSTERING SKIFF

IT WAS lucky for her, Desire Harmony realized, that the weather had remained windless. Even so, at night, it was dreadfully cold in the woodshed. Suppose a hard blizzard came? She guessed she would freeze to death without ever waking up.

When she went out to hunt food among the ruined farms she kilted her petticoats high about her waist and buttoned on the dead marine's spatter-dashes. Though large, the long black gaiters kept her legs fine and warm. She was careful to avoid the vicinity of Higsby's Hollow. Now and then she noticed a column of smoke rising, so surmised he must still be there. Several times in the depths of fear and loneliness, she almost plucked up courage to seek the rifleman. But what about that petticoat she'd seen in the lean-to? He had been very cordial before, but she wasn't just sure how he'd act under these changed circumstances.

Oh, what was a girl in her place to do? She was so terribly in-experienced in the practicalities of life; sometimes she almost hoped she would freeze.

One fact had to be faced: She simply couldn't endure living like a hunted wild creature any longer. It was the being alone that bothered her most. For hours and hours she would just sit thinking of Pa and Tim and most of all about John lying dead across the frozen ruts. She lay awake long hours in her nest of straw. Was it possible to recall every last moment they had spent together? That was what always started her crying as she huddled shivering.

Increasingly, her ingenuity was taxed to scrape together food enough. She hated having to cook; always had. The fires she man-aged to kindle in the woods back of John Martin's place stung her eyes and their flames inevitably seemed either scorching or feeble.

It was during a foraging expedition above the West Ferry that

Desire discovered an oystering skiff. Half full of water and ice, it lay in Great Creek Gut. It had belonged to Paul Clarke who had sailed in the *Patience*. She figured he must have been captured and imprisoned the night of the raid.

By ranging patiently along the shore, she pretty soon discovered Clarke's oars and a sprit-sail in the depths of a juniper thicket. Her breath began to come faster. Tomorrow she would leave Conanicut, would dare a plunge into those blinding fogs concealing the future. Moping over John and her lost family certainly wasn't getting her anywhere.

When she got back to the woodshed, she cried a little. The great world she had talked of so bravely now seemed monstrous formidable. Wiping her eyes, she calmed down and took stock of her resources. They were slim enough: a silver ladle, a silver thimble, a pair of silver shoe buckles and three shillings she had found on the dead marine. If used sparingly, the silver should preserve her from starvation until she found employment.

Staring into the twisting flames of her campfire, she tried to decide on the best place to head for. Narragansett Bay was dotted with villages all the way up to Providence.

Idly she watched feathers of steam rise from the gaiters buttoned about her fine, long legs. Had she ever been clean? Her underthings felt stiff and certainly they were no longer fragrant.

Why not go to Providence—if she could? By sailing at dawn, she calculated she might reach the town before nightfall, provided a favoring wind blew. Somewhere she had heard that Providence by water wasn't much above thirty miles distant. Good thing Pa had kept a chart of Narragansett Bay hung to the counting room wall.

Probably her wisest move would be to set a course up the West Passage until she passed Hope Island. Then she must try to get through the narrow strait separating Patience Island from Providence Point. Once Rum Stick Point was weathered you were in the Providence River.

Having been a tomboy had its advantages, she reflected. Wager there wasn't a single nice-Nancy in Newport who would dream of doing what she planned. She hugged her knees, felt her courage rise. Why, she was just like Hagar—driven off to fend for herself.

Maybe, if things went hard, she would become a female pirate like Mary Rhead. Why not? Society, in robbing her of her husband, had branded her—she faltered over the term—a bad girl. John Gardner's words still burned her ears.

Just exactly how would a girl take up piracy? She arose, swaggered back and forth before the fire a few times, and ended by striking a challenging pose. To complete the picture of a "Notorious Female Buccaneer" she needed a knife between her teeth like Mary Rhead in the engraving. The old kitchen knife filled the bill, but the rust and cold grease on the blade tasted so awful she took it right out.

Crawling into her nest, Desire curled up and, shivering, waited for the body warmth to accumulate. To comfort herself and to make the dark less fearsome, she began talking aloud.

"First thing is to get to Providence, and I guess I can do it. Pa used to say that trade was better there than it is in Newport because Newport lies off the mainland. It's ever so much closer to Boston and the Post Road. Wonder where the Post Road goes? To New London, of course, and maybe to New Haven and so to New York. Tim used to say Providence was an elegant, handsome town. He went to college there, so he ought to know."

She wondered how Tim was making out? How had he and Papa stood the news of her having been with a British naval officer? Whenever she thought of what awful things the neighbors had said there on the Ferry Road, she felt hot clean down to her toes.

In the birches back of the shed, an owl hooted. Presently, she recognized the despairing death shriek of a rabbit.

Br-r-r-r! It was cold, but the harbor water must be colder still. Her eyes stung and filled. When a British sailor died or was killed at sea, the vessel's sailmaker sewed the remains into a hammock with a round shot at the body's feet. John had told her all about it

once. But the fleet lay in port. Had they possibly given the Right
Honourable John St. Clair a shore burial? It was agonizing not to
know.   .

"I mustn't think about you so much, beloved," she murmured.
"I should be thankful our love, while it lasted, was so perfect."

Dear God, how well she remembered the ardency of him; the quivering of his whole clean young body.

Would she ever again feel for a man as she had for John?

30

PROVIDENCE

A GENTLE southeast breeze blew so steadily that, in mid-afternoon,
Desire saw Providence dead ahead. Many rows of buildings were
crawling up a hillside beyond Fox Point. Some of her fright evap-
orated. Though the port looked strange, there was an unexpected and
reassuring familiarity about the distant waterfront. Certainly that
shipping at anchor in the river looked peaceful and un-menacing.

Just as at Newport, wharves, docks and warehouses edged the
waterfront. Behind them rose a barricade of tree tops, roofs and
chimneys. From what Tim had said, that handsome brick building
up on the hill must be New University Hall of Rhode Island College.

Oh, dear. Could someone recognize the skiff and, suspecting robbery, summon the watch? While steering in through the anchored
ships, she had kept all hunched over so nobody would know she was
a girl.

After bringing the skiff to a bumping halt, she caught up her
bundle, darted onto the wharf. Long since, she had written on the
sail in charcoal. "Boat property of P. Clarke, Esq., Conanicut, I.
Kindly return if found."

Someone was coming out on the wharf so, heart thudding, she

crouched behind a pile of yards. Round-eyed, she watched a whiskery old man amble by. Apparently he did not even notice the skiff, but squatted on an empty barrel and studied the harbor.

On tiptoes Desire Bennett threaded her way ashore, skirted a big warehouse and started along Water Street, outwardly as prim and confident as if she had lived in Providence all her life. But she was so scared her teeth clicked together. How did one go about finding cheap food and lodging? Probably the poorer districts, as in Newport, would be along the edges of town.

It was queer to see so many people and not to recognize a single one of them. How rough and unfriendly 'most everybody seemed. Everywhere, she heard men discussing the probable date on which the Congress would grant privateer commissions. Ugh! What an ugly town—this part of it, anyhow. The houses were untidy, jammed all together, and the street ankle-deep in smelly mud.

She passed a group of ill-fed looking seamen in knitted red wool stocking caps. They were arguing furiously over the probable number of British cruisers on blockade duty off Point Judith.

"We'll get out easy," one of them prophesied. "Heard tell they ain't but a single frigate left down to Newport."

Desire felt an impulse to set him right, but that would have been forward. Nice girls didn't speak to strange men. Though terribly hungry, she dared not enter any of the public houses she passed. Food in such places was sure to be expensive.

She knew she must look a fright. Her hands were black with charcoal and dirt that wouldn't come off, no matter how hard she rubbed with plain water. Her hair she guessed looked like a rat's nest, and her clothes—well, under her spare petticoat they were scorched, stained and greasy. Of course, her face must show smudges—she had no mirror to tell her where. Carrying her bundle, she must look like a story-book orphan. No help for it, though.

At last she found a baker's shop which didn't look formidable in any way. A single loaf and a few stale-looking buns were exposed in its window. Most encouraging was the fact that a woman and not a man was inside. Perhaps she might know of a situation suitable for a respectable young widow.

When the door closed the baker's wife stopped trimming the wick of a mutton-fat lamp and squinted over her shoulder.

"Well," she demanded sharply, "what do you want?"

Desire had to force herself to speak.

"I—I—please, how much are those b-buns in the window?"

"A penny apiece. Flour is very dear, nowadays."

"Well, please let me have—t-two." Desire hated herself for stammering, but she hadn't the least notion how to get onto the real purpose of her visit.

Snuffling dismally, the baker's wife plunked the two discouraged-looking buns onto the counter and stared suspiciously at the firm oval of Desire's face. In the large smoky blue eyes, the soft shadows beneath them, and the naturally bright lips, she found grounds for inaudible disapproval. Muttering, she carried Desire's shilling over to the candle-light.

Desire felt a flash of anger.

"My money is all right!"

"A body can't take no chances," she sniffed. "There's too many raggle-taggle girls coming to town nowadays."

"A raggle-taggle girl!" Desire gasped. "You'll not say such things to me! I'm a respectable married woman."

"Indeed? Then where's your ring?"

"When my husband died I had to sell it. We were very poor."

Though she wasn't in fact married, she would always think of herself as John St. Clair's widow.

Desire drew herself up to her full five feet three and lifted her chin. "Madam, I find you needlessly insulting."

The woman blinked, "You needn't give me none of your sauce." She wiped a drop from her nose on the back of her hand. "You're mighty young to be a widder."

"Yet I am, and—and I am in desperate need of employment."

Hands on bulging hips, the baker's wife surveyed her. "Well then, Mistress, I'm sorry for you because there ain't a smitch of honest work to be had in this town. Won't be neither, 'til the private-armed vessels begin sending in prizes."

Desire gasped. This was a shock, all unforeseen. "But—but I had heard the shipyards here are busy?"

"So they are. But this outfitting means scraping the bottom of the till for most of the merchants and ship masters here," she snuffled. "Business in this port is 'down to the last shot in the locker,' as my Pa would say. He was a privateersman," she added. "Captained the *Rover* for Nicholas Brown."

This was too much. Dropping her bundle, Desire buried her face in her hands and wept until her slim shoulders quivered beneath the ragged shawl.

The baker's wife hesitated, but when she saw real tears trickling through Desire's grubby fingers, she sucked in her breath and said softly, "There, there, child. Maybe things ain't quite so hard as I let on. Just you sit by the fire, my pretty, and eat your buns while I fetch you a mug of milk."

When Desire had swallowed the last crumb, she felt a little braver and even mustered an uncertain smile. "Perhaps, Ma'am, you could tell me of a lodging house where a bed wouldn't—wouldn't cost very much?" Then she added brightly, "I shall find work tomorrow, I know."

The baker's wife showed gapped teeth in what was supposed to be a look of encouragement. "Now, I mind me of a woman, name of Norton. She keeps a lodging house up towards north end of town. Number nine, James Street."

Her plump hand patted Desire's shoulder, and she nodded to herself as if enjoying some private satisfaction. "I don't know this Mrs. Norton real well, but I heard tell she lets the rooms real cheap. I figure she might take pity on you."

Desire felt an immeasurable relief. The baker's wife was now friendliness itself.

"Mrs. Norton? Oh, thank you! The Lord bless you," she babbled. People were good and generous after all. She wanted to kiss this untidy, red-nosed creature. "I will go right to her straight off. Please, may I have my change?"

The baker's wife's run-over shoes slap-slapped towards the back of the shop. Presently she returned and counted out some coins. That it was an ha'penny short, Desire timidly pointed out.

"The ha'penny?" the baker's wife demanded icily. "I'll give it you when good rich milk flows down river."

What a low, mean way of making a ha'penny! Desire almost flared up but, well, the woman had acted kindly for a while. In disillusioned silence, she knotted the coppers into a corner of her shawl and caught up her bundle.

"Shut the door tight," the baker's wife sniffed. "It will be perishing cold tonight."

31

MRS. NORTON

EVEN THOUGH Mrs. Norton's dwelling stood on James Street in a neighborhood where grog shops outnumbered private homes by two to one, Number 9 proved to be a neatly-shingled structure with white trim and a certain air of respectability about it.

Picking a course among belated geese and pigs splashing about puddles in the street, Desire was hesitating before Number 9 when across the street a woman appeared and emptied a bucket of swill into the mud. Like a shot hogs appeared from every direction and, grunting and jostling, cleaned up the mess in short order.

Desire had never felt more frightened, more uncertain, nor more determined. It was necessary to remind herself that she was a Bennett, that the Bennetts had always stood on their own feet and asked no favors of anyone. She hoped her Quaker gray dress wouldn't go against her. Many people were dead-set against the Friends because they wouldn't fight. Some Quakers were even refusing to pay taxes levied for the benefit of the Army.

Plucking up courage, Desire knocked timidly at the clean, green-painted door. Sedately, the geese waddled off down the street to resting places in yards and under doorsteps.

Two sailors came reeling up James Street and, spying the girl, tilted hats at a rakish angle and swaggered up.

The taller of the pair nudged his companion. "Ahoy, mate—curse me if yonder ain't a pair o' the trimmest spars I see in a year."

"By Jeesus, ain't she something?"

Fear held Desire rigid when they teetered closer, tarred pigtails waggling over greasy coat collars.

"Hi, sweetheart, how's for a cruise in the goosedown?"

She could only stare, round-eyed. The younger and stouter plucked at Desire's sleeve. "Come along, lass, got m' bounty money, just sign' articles on the *Jupiter*." He tried to put an arm about her waist.

"Oh! No! No!" Desire flattened against the door panels. How dared they! The reek of strong tobacco and stronger rum enveloped her. In desperation, she clung to her bundle, pounded on the green door.

"Li'l spitfire, ain't she?" the taller of the pair snickered. He wore a dirk at his belt and a pair of grimy petticoat breeches which looked as if they might once have belonged to a British man-o'-war's man. "Come down out o' the rigging, my pretty pet, and let's set a course for the One Gun Inn."

Desire grabbed desperately at the door knob and said, "Please go away. Please! I—I'm respectable."

"Say," demanded the shorter one scratching his head. "Is this here Jim Str—"

The door burst open. "Clear out of here, you slimy scum of bilge brothels!"

On the threshold appeared one of the fattest women Desire had ever beheld. The apparition had heavy black brows and a perceptible mustache. Between amber and gold earbobs her face, above a starched white collar, glowed red as any love apple.

"Of course she's respectable! Now clear out of here, you bow-legged mother's mistakes!" The seamen fell back before the big woman's advance.

She shook her fist with such force that a ring of keys hitched to her belt began jingling. "Scat! Away with you or I'll call the watch."

The seamen retreated further, glowered, then muttered something about "officer's ratings" and, arm in arm, see-sawed off down James Street bawling out a fishing song called "Down on the Cape."

The fat woman smiled the jolliest imaginable smile. "Never mind those boozy swine. Poor devils get six bob in their jeans and fancy they're lords o' the earth. Step inside, my dear, you look frightened to fits."

A bull's-eye lantern glowed in a wide hallway and threw a fine strong light. It must cost a pretty penny to fill—with whale oil bringing what it did. In a full-skirted dress of dark green taffety, the black-browed woman seemed completely to fill the hallway as, critically, her penetrating black eyes appraised the trembling girl.

At length she smiled mechanically. "It would appear, my dear, that you told those—those specimens the truth. One would hazard that you are a good girl, good as of habit, at least. What age have you?"

For the first time, Desire noticed an unfamiliar accent to her benefactress' speech. "Sixteen, Ma'am. Close on seventeen."

"Seventeen? That is well," the woman in green nodded emphatically. "And may one inquire what brings you here—to my home?"

Looking small and very scared, Desire launched into an explanation she had evolved during the voyage up from Conanicut. She was a widow, she explained; her husband had been killed in the British raid on Falmouth.

"So young and a widow already! Ah, my poor child, that is very sad. I know very well how it is." She dropped her eyes. "Mr. Norton died many years ago. The life of a widow is not one of the easiest." Mrs. Norton sighed, then cocked her head a little to one side. "You have parents—family, that is to say—living nearby?"

"No one, Ma'am."

"Where is your home?"

Desire had an answer for that, too. Better still, she could mimic to perfection the accent of the summer people who came from South Carolina. She began to talk just like Sally Rutledge.

"My husband," she stated with a soft inflection, "came from the Maine district of Massachusetts. John's mother was a Wright." I must remember that, Desire thought. I must remember everything I tell Mrs. Norton. "I am Mrs. John St. Clair from Falmouth, Maine."

"St. Clair?" Mrs. Norton's mustache widened to her smile. "That name has a French sound. I am sure your husband loved you very much. Your eyes, my dear, are very unusual—*très seduisants*.

"Come, let us seat ourselves. It is more comfortable so." Mrs. Norton waddled into a small sitting room which was tightly shuttered and smelled of verbena and lavender.

Because a faint odor of tobacco lingered in the air, Desire deduced that Mrs. Norton accepted male boarders as well. Paintings of Greek gods and goddesses decorated the walls. They were foreign, Desire judged. Mercy, how easy and natural those people looked, for almost all of them were naked as so many eggs!

Voluminous skirts billowed when Mrs. Norton, puffing slightly, seated herself. She smiled encouragingly. "So. We are more comfortable, no? And now is it not time to tell me why you knocked at my house?"

Having risen at dawn, Desire was dead tired. It had been no easy matter to sail the skiff, either. To make matters worse, she was still terribly hungry.

"I was seeking lodgings but I—I fear, Ma'am, this is too nice a place for my purse." Her dark red lips drew back from her teeth in a slow, rippling motion.

"Why?"

"I am looking for a situation, you see."

"Ah? One perceives your difficulty. Let us consider—"

Mrs. Norton bent her head in thought, thereby adding another chin to her original three. Somewhere in the back of the house—or was it upstairs?—a flute was being played; feet moved back and forth.

"My child, you have come to Providence before an ill wind," Mrs. Norton sighed. "The good God alone knows how the cursed English have stopped our trade. Ah! If only they could be driven away. What is your occupation?"

Desire put up a bold front. She would work at anything, she declared, anything that was respectable.

"That," Mrs. Norton declared comfortably, "is fortunate. Nice, fresh, clean-minded girls are scarce in a seaport. You sew?"

Desire sat very straight on the chair, her bundle on the floor beside her. "Oh yes, Ma'am, I can sew very elegant on silk, on flowered muslin, on catgut. I can do satin-stitch, quince-stitch, tent-stitch, cross-stitch, tambour, and embroidery on curtains or chairs. I—I think I could make flowers and profiles out of wax if anybody would instruct me."

The bland smile widened on Mrs. Norton's florid features. "One perceives that you have been brought up a lady, Mrs.—er—St. Clair. Yours are rare accomplishments. Unfortunately, the housewives of this town have more need of cooks and chambermaids.

"Let me see your ankles—"

Desire flushed, but obediently thrust out a foot. In its damp, clumsy shoe and torn woolen stocking, it didn't make much of a showing.

"Ah, as I thought, small like your hands. You could not do heavy work."

Lord, she mustn't let Mrs. Norton suspect her bundle contained only a comb, old clothes, shoe buckles, two shillings, and a silver spoon. She wasn't counting the thimble of her mother's among her assets.

"You can cook? Bake?"

"Not very well, Mrs. Norton," Desire admitted honestly. Then added, "But I learn quickly, and I can spin yarn better than most."

Mrs. Norton, stooping to pluck a thread from her knee, momentarily exposed a small gold crucifix caught between breasts resembling batter puddings as to size and texture.

Pursing up her lips, she studied the ceiling so hard, Desire guessed she must be reaching a decision. Would there be work? She bit her lips to hide their frightened trembling.

"Genevieve Norton is a fool of the worst sort—a soft-hearted old fool. I should not trust a strange girl for a week's rooming. Definitely not!"

There it was. Desire felt she would burst right out crying. "Oh, Mrs. Norton—please—"

"Do not interrupt me, little one, because I shall be a great, soft-hearted fool and trust you for your lodging. I shall even tell Chloë to give you a fine hot meal! *Mon Dieu,* you look as if you had been pulled through a keyhole."

"Oh, how good you are. Oh, dear Mrs. Norton, thank you, thank you! You will never regret this kindness." Desire couldn't help running over, kissing a very soft red cheek that smelled of verbena. She even cried a little. She couldn't help it. No one had been kind to her in ever so long.

The room to which Mrs. Norton led her was narrow and sparingly furnished, but its bed was surprisingly wide and comfortable-looking; it boasted maple posts. A couple of chairs, a washstand and a tiny chiffonier lurking beneath a huge horizontal mirror, completed the furnishings.

Desire guessed she ought to inquire into the rent but it seemed ungracious, besides she felt just too tired and weary to bargain. Hadn't the baker's wife said Mrs. Norton let rooms very cheap? To-morrow would be time enough.

"This chamber is not large, little one," Mrs. Norton's tiny jet eyes twinkled, "but neither are you. Ha! Ha!"

"This door is convenient," she indicated an entrance at the far end of the room—"it leads into a small lane. Fortunate, no? If your work should get you up early, or keep you out late, you run no risk of rousing my household. I prefer you to use it as a rule."

In the doorway the landlady turned, hesitated, one huge bust swaying to either side of the door frame. "And did you say what your name is?"

"Mrs. St. Clair—John St. Clair."

"But no, my little one, your Saint's—your own name."

"Desire Harmony."

"How pretty!" She tilted her smooth black head to one side. "I am sure your husband, if he was even part French, called you Désirée. I shall call you so. The name is pretty, even intriguing."

Mrs. Norton sniffed like a cat at a mouse hole. "My faith! Where can you have been to smell so of fish, sweat and wood smoke? Chloë will bring you some buckets of water. Name of God, use it well."

The supper Mrs. Norton sent in was a good one: a pair of turkey wings, cornmeal mush, turnips and honey on bread. After a week of scorched potatoes, tasteless salmon, and frozen beets, Desire ate like a little pig. Chloë, a sprightly mulatto, watched her from sympathetic, liquid black eyes.

"Ain't you goin' try some o' that, Mis' St. Clair?" The mulatto indicated a small black bottle on the tray.

Desire smiled, "What is it? I was so hungry I fear I didn't notice."

Chloë giggled, teeth flashing in the candle light. "'At's claret wine, Mistress."

Wine and the devil! Desire flinched, the echoes of a thousand sermons ringing in her ears. "Oh, I couldn't. I really couldn't."

"Don't you be afeared of it, Missy. Claret ain't got much spread to it—nawthin' like brandy or rum. Just a glass don't harm nobody, and it sure downs a heap of misery."

A little later, Desire decided that Chloë knew whereof she spoke.

32

THE MUNITIONS VENDORS

M. PLIARNE employed a large and limber piece of bread thoroughly to mop the last vestige of sauce from his plate. M. Prenet, fingering a slender-stemmed claret glass, watched him with one brow raised.

"Pas mal, eh?"

The older Frenchman sighed, wiped his mouth on the last of the bread, ate it, then gently slapped his violet and yellow brocade waistcoat. "Unusually delicate. Most American food is atrocious; good Norman hogs would turn up their noses at it. One perceives why you insisted on dining at the 'Marquis of Granby.' My compliments to the chef. His turtle stew is to be remembered."

M. Pliarne smiled. "But by chance, the so extraordinary General Lee spoke of this chef—the extraordinary Cuffy Cockroach. The very devil of a name for a sound cook, no?" Anxiously he eyed his companion, "You will agree the stew was notable?"

M. Prenet, a blue-eyed blond Norman and a Huguenot, belched behind delicately raised finger tips. "But yes. With a *soupçon* of saffron added, his *tortue à la Jamaica* would enchant the great Vatel himself. *Bon Dieu,* it is the first meal worthy of the name since we quit Canada! What a beast of a country, this America!"

M. Pliarne smiled into the flames drawing golden flashes from well-polished andirons. "At the risk of introducing a controversial note on a happy occasion, I maintain this is a beautiful country—beautiful but immature." He raised his wine, gazed into its glowing depths. "Like a young girl of Caudebec who will some day become lovely, fruitful and strong."

For a Marseillais, M. Pliarne was unusually thin and quick. He poured cognac for the gaunt man in fashionable bottle green, raised his own glass. "To your health, my partner, and to our continued prosperity."

"*Salut!* In Cambridge, you made progress, my friend?"

· "Not so much as one might desire. This new Commander-in-Chief is not one to be hurried." A diamond flashed as M. Pliarne spread expressive hands. "He says—and it is the truth—he cannot buy, or even contract for the munitions until this absurd Congress of Philadelphia approves. You know how they are!"

M. Prenet frowned, sipped the golden fluid. "And do I not! With their Committee for Military affairs I had a time of the most difficulty. Such selfishness, such jealousy, such pettiness can only be matched in Versailles! But there is hope, François; the situation grows more serious.

"*Grace à Dieu,* that incredible German dolt in Whitehall has refused a legal petition of the most humble. Not even the most chicken-hearted in Philadelphia can find hope." Prenet chuckled, rubbed big hands. "You deduce what follows?"

"Independence, my dear Claude?"

"As always, François, your insight is an inspiration. But yes. What other course is left open?"

"How long before they will throw off the King?"

"In a few weeks, or months. Who shall know?" Prenet shrugged and lifted onto his lap a small gray kitten which, tempted by a morsel of turkey, came wabbling over from a basket by the hearth. "Yes, my adorable *Minet,* even you will perceive that, though the hour of a declaration of independence is uncertain, the necessity for it is not."

He studied his partner carefully. "It is my opinion that these Americans will wait a little while. They must. They are nearly destitute of powder. Eh? In the spring they must find themselves in an even worse case for munitions. So, *mon ami,* before our little feline raises her voice in love, we shall do business, magnificent business."

"—With the Congress?"

"Eventually, François, but first with the privateer owners. They are positively ravenous for cannon."

"The Americans will send for them?"

Pliarne held his feet to the flames. "But of course. They understand that they must take delivery from our *depôts* at Cap François and in Martinique. And with the Army, I have secured orders amounting to 150,000 livres. Tonight, if God agrees and my plans succeed, we shall greatly add to them."

"*Bon!* Newport is the greatest privateering port in America, one hears."

Prenet's smile faded as, absently, he rubbed the kitten's round stomach. "But who will protect these ships *en route?*"

"*Le Bon Dieu* or the devil, until our dear fiddle-foolish M. Beaumarchais makes up his mind. As I pointed out to M. Christopher Gadsden and M. John Adams, to transport munitions of war is their and not our responsibility. Indeed is it not strictly forbidden for French subjects to furnish arms at all?"

Purely through force of habit, M. Pliarne reached out and pinched the thigh of a gangling, freckle-faced girl who brought in sillabubs, tarts and pie.

Said Pliarne's dry, incisive voice, "It will be necessary for *Pliarne, Prenet et Cie.* to move with rapidity. Soon our dear friend, de Bonvouloir, and the Spanish will be in the field.—Hem!—Hem!—Yes, any day *Hortalez y Cia.* will enter competition."

Prenet nodded emphatically. "Yes, we must hasten before the English make bigger their squadrons and strangle this pretty new trade of ours."

Pliarne selected a long and very thin cigar from a silver case. "But will *le bon Roi Georges* strangle this revolt so easily? Would you consider me mad if I hazard that he may not even be able to strangle it at all?"

"I would never think you mad, *mon cher.*" A smear of grease on M. Prenet's chin glistened. "Just an imbecile!"

The two Frenchmen sipped their cognac in silence. The kitten, after playing with M. Prenet's watch fob, drifted into blissful slumber on his lap. They were thinking hard.

Assuredly they had need of consultation, of a comparison of notes if the last sou of profit was to be wrung from 200,000 livres' worth of cannon, muskets, bullet lead, bayonets, cartouch boxes, harnesses, blankets, uniforms, sabres, swords and pistols now groping across the Atlantic.

It had taken time to erase the royal lilies from the breeches of the heavy cannon, but M. Vergennes had insisted upon the precaution. On no account were Messieurs Pliarne et Prenet to embarrass the Government of His Most Christian Majesty, Louis XVI.

M. Pliarne spoke through a nimbus of cigar smoke. "No. An American victory is not wholly impossible. This army that the General from Virginia is making before Boston is not chic, nor well drilled, nor well armed. But in *esprit* they are strong, far stronger than any army one has observed in many campaigns."

"*Esprit* unarmed kills few men."

"True, but reflect, my old." Pliarne leaned forward, talking earnestly. "Have you considered the British supply problem? They must feed and arm their men across three thousand miles of open ocean. Vessels require six weeks to three months to make the Westward crossing."

"I have thought of that," Prenet admitted. "At present, these rebels have no means to cut this flow of supplies—in short, no ships of war."

"Give these Yankees, barbarians though they are, one half of the men-o'-war we lost in the War of Seven Years and they will drive Lord Howe and Admiral Graves back to England!"

Pliarne's voice deepened. "*Mon Dieu,* one cannot comprehend how these people love to fight. If nothing else offers, the marksmen from the middle Colonies will fight among themselves."

"I pray you are right. A long war means long profits."

Silence fell. The kitten awaking, hopefully leaped onto the table, commenced a fruitless inspection of plates speckless as only the scouring of a French gourmet can leave them.

In the street below a watchman sounded his klopper. Clearly they heard his voice, "Eight o' the evening, a fair southwest wind, and all is well."

M. Pliarne roused himself, opened a portfolio and produced sheets of paper covered with very fine writing.

Prenet said, "I am worried about the goods and supplies clearing at Bordeaux and Brest. Will not the British consuls there raise questions?"

His partner's smile was wide. "*Du tout!* How can they object since these supplies are French owned, are consigned to the French West Indies, and carried in French vessels? How can they object?"

Prenet's delicate finger tips massaged his temples. "But so many cannon, so much powder, when we are at peace with England?"

"Do not disquiet thyself. Months must pass before a possible protest will reach Paris, and as many more before action will be taken."

"But what of their men-o'-war? The British will set them to cruising in the Windward Passage."

Pliarne chuckled. "It is for the Yankee supply ships and privateers to find their way. It is for us, *Pliarne, Prenet et Cie.* to offer for sale what they will need." He rubbed heavily ringed fingers together. "We should profit enormously. These privateers will swarm to Saint-Domingue like wasps to a beer pot."

"You encourage me. We may expect a two hundred per centum profit?"

"At least, my dear friend. *Mon Dieu,* and it will afford me no little satisfaction to see these Yankee ships burning and sinking the accursed English."

The kitten, disappointed in its cruise about the table, commenced, with a fragile paw, to play with the lace of Pliarne's stock.

The Norman glanced at the door, then hitched his chair closer and spoke very quietly. "Suppose by—er, by chance, of course, the English learn when some of these Yankee vessels expect to clear Cap François? If an owner loses a vessel, he must fit out another—and *chez Pliarne et Prenet,* let us hope!"

M. Pliarne treated his companion to a slow, impassive look. "My faith, you *have* been associating with politicians!"

He pulled out an enormous watch. "It is time we address the ship owners."

Prenet carried the kitten back to its nest, rubbed its ears momentarily. "Regard, François, this sweet little feline. Now he is so tender, so young; but soon he becomes a ferocious male, eager to make love, to make war, to kill. His future approaches the human, eh?"

After dropping a silver pistole onto the table, the Frenchman donned a black cloak with a triple collar. Over his shoulder he said to his partner, "Pray do not take offense at a word of advice. May I suggest that you do not permit yourself to be deceived by a lack of finesse on the part of the merchants, sea captains and town councillors you will soon meet? They are far from stupid and possess a cunning surpassing even that of the English."

33

THE PRIVATEERSMEN

A FIRE of damp logs smouldered in a small meeting room on the old Town Hall's second floor, but it didn't do more than take an edge off the chill. The body-heat of the thirty-odd men present really did more to dispel it.

Tim, seated in a far corner beside Captain Lawson, recalled Pa's oft-repeated advice to do plenty of listening and precious little talking. It had been a relief to find the town's animosity diminished from active and often abusive contempt, to a passive tolerance. Tim figured that the results of the raid and Pa's sudden death were mostly responsible.

The gathering he saw was thoroughly representative of Newport. Parr Rose, William Ladd, Moses Lopez, Isaac Percival and the Thaxters, father and son, represented the powerful bankers and wealthy merchants. Simple ship owners were there in the persons of John Clarke, Tom Freebody, Loammi's second cousin, William Rhodes and a leavening of Bannisters and Wantons.

Most numerous of all were the bronzed, slow-spoken sea captains who actually navigated the Newport vessels: Robert Rodman, Jeremiah Clarke, Polypus Hammond, Abner Coffin and James Tillinghast.

Yessir, if he kept his ears pricked, he ought to pick up pointers, facts and figures that would be of value in shaping the course he was gradually deciding upon. Sprinkled through the group were members of the town council: big, tough-looking George Irish; clerkish, hard-mouthed William Tweedy; Dan Holloway, though belligerent of appearance, was a really mild sort of man.

Included in the group collected under a pair of dim whale-oil lanterns was doughty little Captain Stephen Farish, the Marine Committee's Delegate, and big weather-beaten Major John Handy.

Esek Hopkins wasn't present, but he had sent his stolid, persevering son, John B. Hopkins. Rumor ran that John B. would Captain a vessel in the new Continental Navy. The Hopkinses were famous for looking out for their kinfolk.

George Irish, the Town Councilman, had the floor and was saying, "I believe we should back up this navy idea. We've damned well got to!"

"Got to?" Ike Percival cut in. "May I inquire why?"

"Because the Army needs such support! How in Hell are they going to whip Lord Howe while he remains free to import all the supplies and men he wants? If we don't put a stop to it, General Washington will get snowed under."

Up jumped Major John Handy, spick and span in his new Continental uniform. He had just that day arrived from Cambridge.

"Gentlemen, I want to say that Mr. Irish is right, dead right! We must cut off Howe from his base in Europe. It can be done. Look at what Manley, Martindale and the others have accomplished in Massachusetts Bay! Not one of their vessels measures seventy foot over all, yet they have captured above fifteen British transports!"

"Then why don't we stick to seventy-footers?" Ira Thaxter's father hurriedly suggested. "They don't run into money like frigates and sloops of war."

Young Major Handy shot him an impatient look. "Because, sir, seventy-footers daren't tackle any vessel mounting armament worth two pins and they can't keep the sea if it blows a gale. To keep from being captured they have to stay in shallow water most of the time."

Abed Thaxter shrugged. "You go ahead; talk all you please, Handy, but I'll still be dead against building a fleet."

"Why?"

"Because a navy tends to create an officer class which will soon begin to lord it over us merchants."

Nicholas Brown of Providence rubbed his bald head. "Wal, there's something to such a notion, but you'll never run such a danger from privateer officers."

He looked challengingly about. "When a war is over, what do the privateersmen do? Why, they go back into sailing merchantmen. Most private-armed vessels can return to trading without much trouble—not like frigates and sloops of war. *I* vote to put every penny into arming and equipping privateers."

Tim watched Solomon Southwick get up into a chair. "Mr. Brown is wrong. Privateers won't ever fight to defend our ports or commerce because patriotism pays no cash shares. So you can't expect 'em to. Never yet heard of a privateer who'd stand up to a bulldog 'less he was cornered. Friends, what we need are *forts!* Forts to protect harbors!"

Handy raised his voice. "My God, man, use your head. How can we build enough forts to defend a seacoast extending from Maine to Georgia? We haven't a tenth enough men, let alone guns."

Farish, who had kept still, sprang up, hairless head nodding emphatically. "You'd do well to listen to what this army feller is telling you! Place to beat the enemy is off-shore, before he can get in to put in his licks. Ten guns afloat on the right kind of ships and served by the right kind of men are worth the whole kit and bi'lin' ashore."

"That's right!" Handy cried. "All an attacking force has to do is to land out of range and take your forts in the rear. What else has Lord Dunmore's squadron been doing in the Chesapeake this fall? Maybe you gentlemen haven't heard about the holy hell this noble lord has been raising among the plantations along the Elizabeth and James Rivers?"

"Maybe so. Maybe so. But we could never dast fight the British Navy," William Tweedy opined. " 'Sides we got no trained officers, no men-o'-war's men."

"Who the hell says we need any?" Abner Coffin was getting riled. "There is plenty of us right in this room who've whipped the picaroons, French and Spaniards."

Nicholas Brown stared at him with approving interest, so did Jeremiah Clarke and all the sea captains. Not one of them relished the prospect of obeying orders. At sea they had always stood on their own feet and decided matters for themselves; they wanted to go on doing it, intended to.

George Irish began hammering on the table with his fists. "Order! Order! This kind o' talk is butterin' no parsnips. How many of you want forts?"

The suggestion brought only a few scattered "Ayes."

"Who is for relying on privateers?"

The reply was a thunderous "Aye!" and Tim yelled loud as the rest. He couldn't see why, if there were enough of them, privateers couldn't so hamstring Great Britain's trade that the Parliament would have to give up.

He got up and, obtaining recognition from Irish, made his point.

"Aye! Bennett is right," Abed Thaxter cried. "Let our privateers bleed Britain's commerce awhile. Once the Jamaica, Liverpool and London nabobs find their profits shrinking and their assurance rates rising, they'll force the Ministry to listen to reason."

Isaac Percival looked the other way. It was clear he was astonished to find Tim Bennett here and so well received.

By now the rank smoke from a dozen churchwarden pipes was clouding the air. The fire blazed higher, revealing half models of many designs of vessels, yellowed tariff schedules secured to the walls. Men began to shed their hats, to unbutton their coats.

"You fellers seem to forget a very important argument against this navy scheme," Ira Thaxter's bleating voice penetrated the hum of discussion. "Us New Englanders would be called on to furnish the bulk of ships, men, and pretty near all the money. The Southern and Middle colonies will derive benefit of our risk free for nothing."

Captain Farish glared across the meeting room. "That's a comical notion, young feller. And why do you presume that might be so?"

"Southerners ain't sea-faring."

"That's right!" someone agreed. "Virginians ship in British bottoms."

"All the more reason for them to favor a Continental Navy," Farish countered. "With no foreign vessels to lug their merchandise, they'll be forced to build their own ships or go under. Stands to reason the Virginians will be anxious to see those new ships protected, don't it?"

Farish walked over to the Thaxters, looked at them steadily. "Meantime, 'pears to me like you Newporters might pick up a pretty penny carrying freight for them!"

Tim wrote the suggestion large on his mental slate. Good thing he'd attended this meeting. He was learning.

George Irish flipped aside his coat-tails in order to warm his legs at the fire and said to Isaac Percival, "What the devil can be delayin' those Frog-eaters?"

"Don't know, but we better watch out. That Pliarne feller talks as slick as butter, and it ain't often you catch a Mounseer climbing out on a limb for the sake of a noble principle."

Irish picked up a leaded inkwell, banged it on the table. "Order! Order! Boys, we been casting our jaw tackle loose long enough. Let's get down to brass tacks. What about this navy?"

"If it's to be a Rhode Island Navy, I'll vote 'aye,'" came John Clarke's hoarse voice. "To a Continental Navy I vote 'nay!' I ain't sending no son o' mine to sea under some sister-selling son of a bitch from Pennsylvania, Massachusetts or New York!"

Solomon Southwick spoke up and everybody listened with the attention due an educated man. Few of those present read anything other than invoices, ship's papers and the Bible.

"Fellow patriots, history has a queer way of repeating itself. Consider another young country which once sought to maintain its freedom against a tyrannical sea power. Friends, I refer to the Roman Republic. Now, the Romans at that time were a united people. It made no difference whether the men hailed from Rome, Naples, Tarentum, Salerno, or Marsala. They were all Roman citizens. By their union they founded a great central power."

Everybody was so quiet feet could be heard climbing the stairs.

"In the second and greatest of the three Punic wars, matters went from bad to worse for the Roman Republic until those Romans built a united fleet which went out and whipped the pants off the Carthaginians—if they had pants, which I doubt.—Anyhow, they cut Hannibal off from his base and he had to git for home. In the end, Rome won!

"We may reckon ourselves smart and handy at sea, but considered separately, these colonies are poor and weak." Looking over his spectacles, he reminded Tim of the old Quaker who had taught him the three R's. "A Navy of the United Colonies can, and should be, strong!

"Gentlemen, I don't see that our situation is one whit different from that of the Roman Republic."

Captain Farish ran over and wrung the printer's hand. "Jumping Jehoshaphat! That's prettily put. I call for a vote. Who's for a Continental Navy?"

He was smart enough to guess that Southwick's talk had made a deep impression. His motion of support was carried but most of the big privateer owners were still in opposition.

Tim didn't vote. Figured he didn't yet understand the rights of the case. After what he'd seen in the Army, it was mighty doubtful if thirteen colonies scattered along two thousand miles of seacoast could ever be brought together.

Some of the men had begun buttoning their coats when the council room door swung back and the two Frenchmen entered. Messrs. Pliarne and Prenet bowed elaborately, declared themselves vastly honored to find themselves in such distinguished company.

George Irish recalled the meeting to order, announced that Mounseer Pliarne and his friend were here on a matter of business.

Familiar now with New Englanders, M. Pliarne wasted no time in flowery preliminaries, merely informed the assemblage that fine new carriage guns—twelves, eighteens, and twenty pounders—were immediately obtainable at Cap François and also in Martinique.

The cannons offered by Messrs. Pliarne, Prenet et Cie. were not old, worn-out Spanish pieces of ordnance, assuredly not! They were beautiful new guns cast in the private foundries of the Most Christian Monarch. If a purchaser cared to examine closely, he might perceive the spot from which the royal fleur-de-lis had been erased.

Everyone listened intently when M. Prenet, in his turn, listed the varieties of shell, roundshot and powder dealt in by his firm. He dwelt on the superb quality of the small arms he and his colleague had imported from Charleville, Maubeuge and Toulon. In addition to out-and-out munitions of war, all manner of ship supplies—food, wines and liquors—would be found at Cap François.

John Clarke smiled. For the past two days he had been at his wit's end to know where to look for the two dozen twelve pounders he intended to divide between his *Mermaid* and his *Defiance*.

Abed Thaxter was silently deciding he would add six stands of muskets and maybe a case of cutlasses to the four twenty-four pound carriage guns he'd been planning on all along.

Shoving in their eagerness, ship owners massed around the Frenchmen. Isaac Percival, among the foremost, figured on playing a different tune from his rivals. He wasn't going to pay these Frog-eaters fancy prices. Not Ike Percival! First thing would be to arrange the transfer of his vessels to a dummy purchaser in France. That would give him the protection of the fleur-de-lis flag.

Next he must discover the identity of the crooked government officials who were supplying Pliarne and Prenet. Um. Mightn't be a bad idee to invite these foreigners to dinner. The partners exchanged a quick glance. M. Pliarne would be charmed to accept, also M. Prenet.

M. Pliarne opened his portfolio and, seating himself at Mr. Tweedy's right, commenced to enter various orders into a letter book. Farish watched the proceedings in open contempt. What a passel of pinch-penny fools! All they'd a mind for was their infernal privateering.

Finally, Tim was able to draw M. Prenet aside. "—For a vessel of one hundred and fifty tons?"

M. Prenet looked grave, communed with himself. "One would suggest, M. Bennett, the purchase of four eighteen-pounders and as many eight-pounders. So small a vessel could not support a heavier battery."

"I imagine not. What about small arms?"

"Two stands of muskets should be sufficient. It is worth much to be safe, no?"

"I intend running no risks. What else?"

"Monsieur will, of course, also require cutlasses, pistols, swivel-guns, round-shot, grape-shot, chain-shot and star-shot. A generous supply of powder is a necessity. Say, eight barrels of F. G., one of F. F. G., half a cask of F. F. F. G.?

"*Bigre!* I nearly forgot shackles for securing prisoners." M. Prenet looked up sharply. "When will your vessel appear, Monsieur?"

"As soon as I can get to Cap François—the *Narragansett* is there now."

"You will pay cash, of course? Lamentably, our firm will be unable to honor bills of exchange."

"Oh, yes. I'll pay cash—" Though he had no idea how he could raise the money, Tim went ahead and countersigned his order.

34

NADIR

SOMEWHERE a church clock was banging its seventh note. Mercy! How could she have overslept so badly?

Because she no longer owned a night shift, Desire slid all naked out of bed. A glimpse of her slender figure in the mirror held her poised, one foot still between the sheets. Never before having seen all of herself at once, she could not help looking. At Peaceful Haven there had been but one tiny looking glass. Such devices were conducive to vanity, the Friends held.

The glass revealed a lithe, slender girl with a riot of brown-bronze tresses falling to the level of breasts that still looked immature and were tipped with small pink nipples. Her waist? She realized that it was uncommonly small—just like that of the nude Greek goddess she had seen pictured in a book at Mr. Southwick's. Her stomach was flat at the top and rounded gracefully down to the hip line. Hips? Not as narrow as she might have wished. She turned slowly, studied her back and small rosy buttocks. Certainly there could be little wrong with her long, slim legs, neat ankles and feet. The girl in the glass smiled at her.

The only heat came from a flicker in the fireplace and her skin went pebbly in the chill air. Humming a roundelay, she ran over to the chimney piece. Oh bother! Her shirt, stockings, and two under petticoats were still damp, but at least they were clean.

Still barefooted, she washed then brushed her hair until once more it glowed like dull copper. La! She felt a new girl this cheery winter's morning.

"Let the world beware!" she laughed.

In the house no one was stirring, but a man was snoring away just overhead, fit to choke. She would hunt employment as a sempstress. Carefully, she secured her shawl with a few stitches, pins were much too dear, then primly let herself out into the lane.

The morning was so warm fog veiled the harbor and lower river, but she could hear hammers, saws, busy in a nearby shipyard. Up James Street, a man was wheeling a barrow. "Fresh fish! Cod, haddock, hake! Cod, haddock, hake!" But elsewhere ruled a penetrating apathy. She bought a bowl of bread and milk for breakfast and listened to two men dispute.

"When ships went a-privateering out o' here before," a weather-beaten old man pointed out to a group of street corner idlers, "we'd the British navy to sweep the seas free o' Frog-eaters and Dons."

"Yes, but ain't we going to have men-o'-war of our own come next month?"

"Men-o'-war? Fiddlesticks! Esek Hopkins ain't no more a fit navy officer than I am. He'll make a damned sight better buccaneer than admiral. Mark my words, him and his hot temper will come to grief before a year's out."

By dinner time, Desire had not yet found a situation; not even the hope of one.

One and all, the town's sempstresses had laughed at her; some angrily, some pityingly. Now that the supply of silks and satins from Europe had been cut off, they had had no work for weeks. They were bitter, were the sisters of the thimble and thread.

"But—" she had stammered, "but people's clothes have to wear out, don't they?"

"Any woman wu'th her salt can cut homespun," one of the kindliest had explained. "That's what every housewife in town is doing. It's silk and satin that is too dear to risk with clumsy fingers."

By five, Desire had grown so weary that she could scarcely set one foot in front of the other. In desperation she approached a candle-maker, but it was hard to force a cheery, confident smile.

"Shore," he cackled. "I'll give you a job the instant you find me enough spermaceti oil to work with!"

"But—but I can make ordinary—tallow candles. Fine straight ones."

."Sure," the chandler nodded. "Don't doubt it one mite. So can most women. It's beeswax and spermaceti candles that calls for skill to make. I am sorry, Mistress."

"My sympathy, Mistress." *"No use, Mistress."* "NO WORK HERE, MISTRESS!"

To take the sharpest edge off her enormous appetite, Desire invested in a bun and a mug of milk. She still felt hollow to her heels when she went out into the dusk again. Merciful heavens! To think she had ever let Mamba carry off her plate half full. Never again would she leave a morsel on her plate.

Back in her narrow room, she lit a beef-drip candle. Though there was no fire the room was warm because a chimney backed into the wall beside her bed, thank heaven! Stiffly she pulled off her stockings, the thick woolen pair. Her feet were so red and hot, she wished she dared wear her silken pair. She stretched out on the bed and wiggled her toes. Her bare feet began to cool.

Through the near door head she heard in succession, the front door-knocker bang, floorboards creaking under Mrs. Norton's ponderous progress, a man's voice, over-jolly, then some girl's high-pitched laughter. Silence for a while, more footsteps hurrying about the kitchen and upstairs. More laughter, music from a stringed instrument of some sort. Gales of laughter. Desire wanted to bid them hush. What right had anyone to laugh and be merry when a fellow human was so weary, so friendless, so desperate?

Tomorrow? Of course, tomorrow would be different and there might be laughter for her. But how could there be when all she could see was John St. Clair with his beautiful head sagging back into a frozen rut? John would never laugh with her again over their own sweet jokes. Mustn't think of that—must try to be content with memories. Their manner of meeting, for instance.

Others on the excursion had begun a silly game of fox-and-geese, so she had wandered off by herself along bluffs above Easton's Bay. Lying among the brown-eyed Susans and watching great white pillars of clouds it was fun to recite Mr. Goldsmith's:

"When lovely woman stoops to folly
And finds too late that men betray,
What charm can soothe her melancholy,
What art can wash her tears away?"

She hadn't heard footsteps. The first hint she'd had of John's presence was a soft "Bravo" followed by applause. Never, never would she forget the charm of his flashing smile, the elegant way he wore that scarlet and white and black uniform.

Smiling a little, she slept.

All the next day, Desire hunted work but there didn't seem to be a shilling in Providence that wasn't being spent to outfit a private-armed vessel of war.

Long since, she saw that the baker's wife had not exaggerated. "Fancy" girls walked in legions about the streets; pathetic creatures beneath their paint, bold glances and flashy gowns. All day, they haunted public houses and stage stations. Some were old, discouraged and hopeless; others young. Everywhere women sought work of any kind. New-made widows abounded. The war and the blockade were responsible, people said.

On the evening of Desire Harmony's fourth day in Providence, disaster met her face to face. Her shoe soles had worn through and there were big raw blisters all over her feet. They hurt her so she limped and had to lock her teeth to keep from crying. Though her last ha'penny had been spent, she was so hungry she was ready to faint.

The long horizontal mirror above her bed warned her of lost weight. Those shadows beneath her eyes which had so intrigued Mr. Higsby—all the men for that matter—had deepened from a soft buff to a dark brown.

As if enough had not already gone wrong, she was now pretty sure of another cause for worry. Somehow her rhapsody with John had upset an otherwise regular routine.

By careful calculation she should have gone under the weather the day she sailed for Providence. Of course the delay might be entirely normal—due to hunger and fatigue. On the other hand could what she and John did have any connection with these circumstances? Strange how details of that heaven-sent experience escaped her.

Oh dear, why hadn't she listened when the Wanton girls began giggling and whispering after school. They had had a newly married sister. Betty Gardner, too, had once implied that she knew what married people did—and how they got babies. Oh, if only Betty weren't 'way down the Bay.

Lord, but she was hungry! At a street corner pump, she had drunk all the water she could hold. It didn't seem to help though, only sloshed unpleasantly about in her stomach.

What was she to do? No work of any sort to be had in Providence. The portly owner of the Stirrup & Spur had pronounced her too frail to be a barmaid unless she was willing to "pass the time of day" with certain patrons. When she guessed his meaning she had scurried off, red to her bodice top.

It was odd Mrs. Norton made no mention of her room rent, even though every evening she would happen by and plunk her massive body onto the bed. About the only cheering element these days was the sympathetic way the Widow would, with ready sympathy, listen to her account of disappointments.

Mrs. Norton must be truly kind or she would have long since demanded her board money. It must be, as she said, her great, foolish heart at work. Probably lots of tenants had taken advantage of her. Here was one who wouldn't. The Bennetts always honored their debts —just ones. She would pay Mrs. Norton every farthing—indeed she would.

Sometimes as she lay waiting for memories to put her to sleep, Desire heard singing. Once she had been astonished to hear panted curses, thudding feet. But it had been very late at night when gentlemen were expected to get drunk.

Following Mrs. Norton's suggestion, she never used the front door. She was glad not to because then she wouldn't smell the cooking odors. Mrs. Norton's cook came from Guadeloupe and made skillful use of garlic, onion, mace and saffron.

Tonight the candle Mrs. Norton had left in her room that first night had burnt out, so it was dark. Desire felt the tears gather in her eyes. Every joint in her body burned and ached. In all her life she had never experienced such grinding fatigue. Not even when she was at John Martin's. Tomorrow, she couldn't wear her shoes.

What should she do? All at once, she sat right up on the bed. For pity's sake! how could she have forgotten about the sterling silver ladle and the other things? Warmth flooded her. So much silver must be worth a fair amount because silver was scarce these days. Papa had said so many times.

First thing she'd buy would be a big bowl of stew. A good meal would grant her strength to hunt work in the morning. Maybe the ladle would bring enough to let her run a notice in the "Providence Gazette & Country Journal." That would give her standing. Something like:

A young Widow in Straitn'd Circumstances desires genteel Employment as Preceptress to Young Females, or as Sempstress.

Her heart sang as she ran over to the chiffonier. In the depths of its top drawer she found a spare petticoat, the dead marine's spatterdashes. The other drawer, of course. When her fingers encountered no hard objects, her heart sailed up in her breast like a deer jumping a pasture fence.

In frantic haste, she emptied both drawers onto the bed. Then sobbing, she searched her room from floor to ceiling. She had been robbed! Like a cold downpour, the fact chilled her.

A thief had taken her silver! *Her* silver. The things couldn't have been misplaced. Very distinctly, she recalled putting the ladle and buckles at the back of the top drawer. Panic-stricken, she wrenched open the inner door. "Help! Help! I've been robbed!"

Almost instantly Chloë appeared. "Hush yo' mouth!" The mulatto glared, her previous deferential air quite vanished. "Mrs. Norton sayin' prayers."

Desire gripped the door frame, panted, "I don't care what she's doing. I must see her at once! I have been robbed! I'll call the law!"

"Hush!" Chloë ran forward, tried to clap a hand over Desire's mouth. "Mis' Margaret's got comp'ny!"

"I don't care," Desire's voice rose in anguish. "My silver spoon and buckles are gone. I want them! Do you understand? I've *got* to have my things back!"

Like a ship-of-the-line sailing into action, Mrs. Norton loomed down the corridor. In one hand she had a crucifix on the end of a string of beads. A stick of kindling wood was in the other. Considering her bulk, the landlady moved with astonishing rapidity.

"Fiche moi le camp!" she hissed at Chloë. The yellow girl cringed, vanished like a wraith, closing the door behind her.

"What is the meaning of this?" The landlady's bright black eyes were menacing. "How dare you stand screaming robbery in my house?"

"But I *have* been robbed! My—my silver! I'll tell the watch—I'll—"

Lights exploded as the piece of kindling flashed down, caught Desire a smack across the cheek. *"Tais-toi, misérable!* How dare you make such accusations?"

The blow stung and burnt like fire, confused everything. Desire wanted to hit back but she was too weak. She could only stagger back until she tripped onto the bed. Pressed against the farther wall she tried to shield her head as, puffing heavily, Mrs. Norton dealt her three or four more stinging blows across thighs and legs.

"Will you ever again dare to call Genevieve Norton a thief?" Deadly as St. Michael's sword, the stick wavered before Desire's terrified gaze.

"Don't! Don't!"

"One word and *I* will have the law on *you!*"

"No, no, please! Don't hurt me—" Desire babbled. The woman meant to kill her, she was sure of it. "Didn't mean that *you* stole my silver. Only I—I—it isn't here. I can't find it and—"

"—Don't lie, you ungrateful species of a worm! You named me, a respectable widow, a thief! You howled it at the top of your lungs."

Mrs. Norton's jet earrings were jiggling madly, her face purplish. She had to pause for breath.

"Pay me my money and leave this instant! No person shall stay in my house and accuse me of such things. My money, where is my rent money? I want it this minute. Give it to me!"

To steady herself, Desire gripped the head board. It seemed as if her stomach were bloated by a black acid which, welling up, up, was poisoning her heart and brain.

"But—I—I can't!"

"Comment? No money? What nonsense!"

"Oh, Mrs. Norton, I haven't been able to find work. I—I've tried, but there isn't any!"

"Of course, there is work to be had. Bah! You are just lazy! If you fancy one can cheat Genevieve Norton, you are in error. Come, I want my money!"

"How—how much do I owe?" Desire quavered, certain that this mountainous creature was about to beat her further. Her cheek stung and the blows on her thigh throbbed. If she hadn't been so empty, she might have risen in self-defense, but she was too weary.

"One pound and ten shillings. It is little enough. I was sorry for you."

One pound ten for less than a week! The whole room swayed before Desire's eyes. In Providence, boarding must come ever so high. One pound ten! So much for such a tiny little room and no real heat.

"I—I haven't got it."

"Nom de Dieu!" Mrs. Norton raised the stick, bent over the bed and grabbed Desire's ankle. She hit her only twice, then paused fluttering in her struggles for breath. "So, miserable one, you plotted to cheat an honest woman? Well, we shall see.

"Now attend! If I am not paid every penny of your debt by to-morrow, you will find yourself in the debtors' prison."

Panting, Desire stared up fearfully. "Prison? Oh no! No, I couldn't stand it." Asa Bennett's daughter in jail! She could never endure such a disgrace, never would.

"Then pay me my money."

"Oh dear, I *can't!* I didn't dream—so expensive." Desire couldn't see things clearly. Her head was ringing like an anvil under a blacksmith's hammer.

Mrs. Norton relaxed a trifle, slipped the rosary into her belt beside the big brass hoop of keys. "Either you are the most unprincipled little liar I have ever seen or you are an utter fool. No girl your age could be so incredibly naïve." Her beady little eyes stabbed like stilettos! "You were never married, of course—just in love and a little indiscreet. This is the right tune, no?" She must have read a confession by the misery in those smoky-blue eyes.

"I am sorry for you, Désirée, but I am not rich. I must have one pound ten shillings tomorrow—or you go to the debtors' prison. It is a question of setting an example lest others attempt to copy your method."

The Widow straightened, smoothed her hair and glanced at herself in the mirror. She seemed her old kindly self as she said, "Now then, it is but half after seven of the evening. No more nonsense. If you care to entertain a friend in your room I shall not disapprove."

She looked hard at the tear-stained girl. "*Au contraire.* If your friend desires food or some wine, you have only to call Chloë. No more naïveté now. It is time to be sensible." Like an autumn gale in a forest, Mrs. Norton rustled back into the house.

When the door closed, it excluded a tantalizing aroma of stewing meat and the sweet scent of chocolate. Desire remained where she was, sniffling, absently rubbing her hurts.

If once Mrs. Norton got her committed to the debtors' prison, she might never be freed. People said women in such a position had to do awful things to get out. Well, it was clear she had to find the money.

Suddenly came a heaven-sent inspiration. Through her recent study of poetry, she could recite verse on verse of it, could declaim long speeches from half a hundred plays. Her voice, she felt, was good even if it had not been trained.

Suppose she prettied herself up and then made a round of the Stirrup & Spur and the other better class ordinaries? She should be able to earn some money singing or giving recitations. She was practical enough, however, to see that she could never earn so much as one pound ten shillings in a single night—not unless she was amazingly lucky.

It was quite a lengthy job to remove so much sticky mud from her shoes, but she did it; then fitted folds of cardboard over the holes in their soles. She stripped, washed carefully and, after bathing her face to reduce the welt raised by Mrs. Norton's stick, she put on her clean under petticoat and a fresh blouse. If only she hadn't spoiled the light and well-built shoes in which, long ages ago, she had gone to meet John.

Surprisingly enough her silk stockings had not been stolen and she found among her things, some unfamiliar lengths of silk ribbon. The sensation of the silk stockings sliding up her legs plucked up her courage. Why, this was an adventure. She was like the poor orphan girl in Mr. Hallam's play.

By the light of a candle Chloë brought, Desire dressed her hair with great care. No Quaker cap now. Had all the disasters which had befallen the Bennetts been due to her back-sliding? Poor Papa. Lucky he was in Newport and couldn't know that she was going to play-act, sing even, in a public house.

Good, the stick mark was fading. Tilting her head back a little, she forced a smile, studied her image. When she lowered her lids, they showed blue near the corners and through no improvement on Nature, either.

"Thus, my poor sweet Desire, do we struggle on," she whispered to her reflection. Mrs. Norton's remark about her name suddenly reoccurred. Désirée did sound prettier, more dashing, more befitting a neophyte in the cult of Mimos.

She became possessed of a curious exhilaration. At least, she wouldn't be lonely any longer. She would again be where there was light and laughter.

Her position became luminously clear. Desire Harmony was about to play her first role—that of Mademoiselle Désirée. Whatever Mlle. Désirée was called upon to say or do must be considered just a part of the rôle in no way affecting the real girl—Desire Harmony St. Clair. Queer that the Fates thus, willy-nilly, had summoned her onto the broad stage of the world.

A conviction came that, ere she was retired, she must play many parts.

For all her determination, her excitement in playing her first part, Désirée's knees trembled when the raw night air nipped at her ankles. Gradually her courage faded until, arriving outside the Stirrup & Spur, she vacillated. Drunken voices were bawling out verse on verse of a lewd ballad. Oh, she couldn't go in! Her kind of songs would draw no applause, only pitying laughter at best. Maybe sober people might listen, though, and toss her some coppers.

Imitating with dreadful skill the gait of the girls she had seen in One Gun Lane, Désirée began sauntering along Wickenden Street.

In a soft soprano, she commenced to sing:

> "Foolish Swallow, what dost thou
> So early, at my window do?
> Cruel bird, thou'st ta'en away
> A dream out from my arms today;
> A dream that ne'er must equal'd be,
> By all but waking eyes—"

Around the first corner loomed a broad-shouldered young fellow in uniform. He was a lieutenant, Désirée judged by his single epaulet. The facings to his blue tunic were a gay turkey red. A nearby fan-light drew brief flashes from the guard of a sword.

Touching his tricorne, he halted in front of her, blocking the foot path but applauding gently at the same time. "May I, a poor soldier, venture the opinion that you enjoy a rare fine voice?"

Mlle. Désirée, aware that her heart was galloping up her throat, twisted her lips into what she hoped resembled a shy little smile. "La, sir, I am charmed that my p-poor accomplishment should p-please you."

"There are more verses?"

"Oh yes, sir." She kept her eyes modestly dropped so didn't see his quizzical, sardonic smile. She knew though that this officer, while not exactly handsome, was yet far from ugly.

"And how many more verses are there, Mistress?"

"F-four or five, sir." Hot impulses bathed her neck and breast but she forced herself to say, "It—it would be pleasant to sing them."

His laugh was soft. *"Est modus in rebus!* You see, Mistress, until now I never knew that Mr. Cowley's 'Swallow' had more than one stanza and I would like to hear them."

"Pray don't be mean," Désirée shrugged, turned aside her head. Then rallied. "It is scarcely gallant to force a lady to confess that she would even invent some verses to please so appreciative an audience."

Not bad, Désirée, not bad. That was almost clever. Could she persuade this solemn young officer to buy her a meal? When he slipped his arm through hers, she felt herself go all trembling inside.

"In est clementia forte. I trust you will deign to cheer a poor Myrmidon's lonesome hours?"

Desire couldn't guess what a Myrmidon might be, but she thought it seemly to hesitate a little.

"But—but, sir, I hardly—"

"—Your wit delights this weary toiler at the forge of Mars. Where do you live?" He came closer, white-lined military cloak a-sway in the sharp wind, and took her chin gently in his hand.

"Look at me. Do I appear formidable, fierce?"

He didn't. Just a sober young fellow with a humorous mouth relieving the general thoughtfulness of his expression. "I should be charmed to see you home. Perchance to enjoy more of your lovely singing. Which way do we turn?"

The only two petticoats she had fit to wear didn't furnish sufficient weight to keep the fabric pressed tight about her legs, thus excluding the cold. The whole lower part of her body felt numb.

"N-not far away," she replied, slowly lifting her eyes. Heavens, he had dark red hair. It was much redder than her own bronze tresses. "In fact, I was on my way to dine."

He must know she was lying, yet he gave no hint of it, only chuckled. "Capital! I also was on my way to supper. What a great and happy coincidence."

Though he had just consumed a thumping big supper at the Harpoon Inn, this slim, dark-eyed creature was enough to refresh anyone's appetite.

In almost no time they had turned into the little lane off James Street and Désirée was fumbling in her stocking for the side door key. Though she exhibited a stimulating length of limb—she felt her role called for such tactics—the officer remained standing among the shadows, admirably restraining any eagerness he might have felt.

With one hand on the latch she hesitated and had to remind herself this night was dedicated to avoiding the debtors' prison. To get out her next words was a struggle, but she managed it.

"Pray, sir, do not misunderstand, but I—I am not wealthy. If you wish wine, I shall—I shall have to send out for it."

"Of course, we must have wine, my dear. And of the best. What poet worthy of the name ever declaimed, what siren ever sang, unblest by Bacchus's gracious gift?" He spoke it lightly; she liked him for that.

"For once, the lack of filthy lucre troubles me not." He brought out a bulging purse. "Of pounds, shillings and pence I have sufficient to finance a few excursions into Elysium. Tonight, an the tender goddess consents, we may find surcease from those 'alarums and excursions' of which Messer Shakespere is so prodigal."

In manners and bearing, this tall auburn-haired fellow was so like John that Désirée felt all shaken. Yet at the same time, this lieutenant was entirely different. At the back of his speech lay a hint of mockery; he seemed to laugh at himself, at her, at the whole wide world.

When she lit the candle, she blushed clear down to her bodice when he smiled at the wet stockings and muddied petticoats she had left lying beside the bed. In hurrying to the door to summon Chloë, she managed to kick them out of sight.

When the mulatto knocked she said, "I find that a fire would be pleasant," just as if she were in the habit of having a fire every night.

"Yes, Ma'am." Chloë's quick eyes appraised the lieutenant. "Right away. It is one cold night."

Five minutes later the serving wench brought in a pair of fine wax tapers and kindled a generous blaze. Meantime the officer shed his cloak and hung his hat on a hook let into the wall. Next he carelessly straightened his hair before the looking glass.

"And what kind of a wine would you fancy, Mr.—?"

"Co—er—Colebourne. Lieutenant Nathaniel Colebourne, at your service, Ma'am." He made her quite an elegant bow, but it was not as graceful as John's. "Perhaps a bottle of Burgundy, and possibly a speck of cognac?" But for all his careless way, Colebourne seemed not entirely at his ease.

"Yes, sir." A striking figure in her yellow skirt and scarlet waist, Chloë actually curtsied. "Will you an' Mistress St. Clair require supper?"

"Oh, yes. Yes." Désirée nearly choked in trying to conceal her terrible eagerness. "What have we?"

Teeth and golden hoop earrings flashed. "Dey's ham and roas' fowl, and dey's maybe roas' beef left."

"Beef for me."

"I would prefer chicken. May I?"

Colebourne smiled, "Of course, chicken. *Sua cuique voluptas.*"

Chloë looked doubtful. "Reckon Amélie don' know dat way cookin' a fowl."

"Ah, my dusky Hebe, I fear you mistake me. What I said was, in effect, 'everyone has his own pleasure.'"

Désirée smiled, said, "Mind you hurry, Chloë."

Once the latch had fallen Nat Colebourne came over, took both her hands, studied her from his grave yet lively brown eyes. "While we wait suppose you sing me that second and third verse of 'The Swallow'?"

Désirée laughed. How strange to be really laughing once more, not just manufacturing a noise.

"After dinner, perhaps, Mr. Colebourne. But in the meanwhile, if you wish, I will recite:

> " 'See with what simplicity
>   This nymph begins her golden days!
> In the green grass she loves to lie,
>   And there, with her fair aspect, tames
> The wilder flowers, and gives them names;
>   But only with the roses plays, and does them tell
> What colour best becomes them, and what smell.' "

"Your delivery is splendid, but your lips were made for—this." He kissed her hard on the mouth then, to her surprise, went over and seated himself beside the fireplace and extended legs towards the blaze. From the saddle marks on his doeskin breeches of white, she deduced he must have reached Providence that same afternoon.

"You are from the army before Boston?"

"Was. You observe an ex-lieutenant—in Colonel Prescott's regiment," he added with a touch of pride.

"Prescott's? Then you fought at Bunker Hill?"

He nodded! "Aye, but it was not a pretty affair for anyone that day. I venture I shortened my age by ten years. War is an exacting profession, my dear. For its pomp and glory we pay a heavy fee in bitterness, discomfort and lost illusions."

Steam began rising from his half-boots and, perceptibly, the familiar and homely odor of horses commenced to invade the room.

The warmth from the fire increased, prompting her to ask, "Would you care to remove your tunic?"

"My humble gratitude." He smiled and, after standing a sturdy leather-scabbarded sword in a corner, stripped off his coat.

Chloë was the embodiment of discretion when she re-appeared. On her tray were two glasses, bright with lemon peel and giving off a steam of cognac spiced with cinnamon and cloves.

"I dedicate this delectable toddy to the future!" Colebourne laughed while undoing the golden buttons of his white waistcoat.

The liquor smelled monstrous strong and she would have hesitated had she not been so dog-tired. Better try it. Certainly, Mlle. Désirée could have accepted a sip or two. The first mouthful sent her into such a spasm of coughing that Mr. Colebourne treated her to a quizzical glance. Presently, she began to feel immeasurably refreshed.

"Pray tell me something of yourself," her guest presently invited. "I—I have never encountered anyone even remotely similar. You puzzle me."

He didn't seem just plain curious, but more like a doctor asking what hurt and where, more like a school teacher trying to interpret a difficult passage from Cicero. Désirée, therefore, found herself repeating the same tale she had unfolded to Mrs. Norton, with well considered embellishments. Soon Chloë re-appeared to spread a cloth.

Strident laughter and a tapping of feet as of someone executing a dance step followed the mulatto from the depths of the house.

The ultimate morsel of fowl consumed, Désirée sipped Burgundy, felt cheerier than she had in a fortnight. Complexion heightened by the candle light, she challenged, "Now that I have unveiled my troublous past, pray sir, will you tell me a trifle concerning yourself?"

Dark against the wall, he raised his glass in her direction. "Your wish is my command, O fairest of the Muses. Were you to come closer, my memory—which is none of the best—might be stimulated."

Désirée, grateful for this companionable moment, settled on his knees with the lightness of a thrush on a willow branch. It wasn't so difficult to obey, somehow.

Gravely, Lieutenant Colebourne informed her that he hailed from Tuckernuck, a wind-swept island in Buzzard's Bay. His father, a fierce uncompromising man, was well-to-do, a Loyalist, and had cast him out "root and branch."

Smiling, he let his finger impale a curl that had fallen over her forehead. "So, gentle lady, you perceive poor Nat cast utterly adrift on the sea of an uncaring world. *Mobilis in mobile,* as it were."

In addition she learned that Nathaniel Colebourne had been a student at Harvard college when the Lexington fight took place.

"For the heinous crime of keeping a fowling piece in my chambers," he explained, "the Honorable President and Fellows of Harvard College doomed me to rustication. I had scarce survived this disgrace than the passing of the Boston Port Act prompted the Overseers to move the college to Concord, lest a brutal and licentious soldiery corrupt the students' tender morals."

There was something really fine, essentially modest, about the careless fashion in which young Mr. Colebourne referred to his soldiering during the early days of the war.

Though she made several attempts, she couldn't inveigle him into describing the battle on Breed's Hill. Every time she led up to the subject, his eyes wandered away. His accounts of camp life, though, were fascinating, amusing and a trifle naughty.

While he talked and chuckled like a man who has suddenly re-called the ability to be merry, his hands wandered. One of them came to rest on her lap; gently, but not at all furtively, he explored a knot securing the ribbon she had used to garter her stocking. Though her first reaction was one of indignation, she recalled she was Mlle. Désirée, not Desire; became rather curious to see what might happen if she didn't push away his hand.

For quite a time, he only sat looking into the fire. He, also, was fatigued, she decided. He closed his eyes once.

When he murmured *"Pax in bello,"* she thought maybe he hadn't been quoting Latin just to make an impression. He must be a real scholar.

In a medium-deep voice, rather like Tim's, he described the stag-nant deadlock the Siege had become; the wretched quarters, and the quarrels between various Provincial armies before Boston. That he could not say enough against the Rifle Companies amazed her.

Her guest declared, quite without heat, that most Provincial troops would liefer be brigaded with wild Indians than with Cresap's and Morgan's rangers. Thompson, their colonel, had less control over his Rifle Companies than a boy had over a herd of unbroken colts in an open field.

Désirée, her head at rest against his shoulder, remembering Sam Higsby's slow speech and quiet ways, protested. "But really, Mr.

Colebourne, they can't be just show-offs. They are prodigious fine
shots and tireless fighters."

She suddenly realized that, all unnoticed, he had contrived to
undo her garter—a discovery at once pleasurable and frightening.

"And why should you rise in their defense, most Desired Lady?"

"Why,—I—I have heard that no one could out-march or outshoot these rangers. Some of them are handsome and gentle towards
ladies."

"I have never met with such, *mirabile dictu*. A spot more wine,
an you please, Desired Lady?"

To fetch the decanter, she had to cross the room. Her stocking
fell. When she pulled it up, she briefly revealed a glimmer of flesh
above the stocking top. As she gave him the wine, she noticed with
warm sympathy how worn, how young-old he looked.

"I regret having missed this paragon," Colebourne drawled.
"Most of the Dirty-Shirts, as we call them, swagger and brag as if
they'd beaten a British army single-handed.

"Actually, they've not yet fought even a skirmish. Unless one is
an utter ass, he won't credit a word a ranger says. They are the
champion liars in Creation. Quite a few of them have deserted to the
enemy."

He found the other garter knot; slipped it.

"Deserted?" Somehow, after having known Mr. Higsby, she
couldn't believe that any rifleman would do a thing so cowardly.
"La, sir, such a report is hard to credit." His hand on her bare knee
felt rough; the skin there tingled.

"I do not exaggerate. At sharpshooting I'll grant you they have
no equals, but they quarrel, mutiny, kill each other and anybody
else. When in liquor they become beasts! Like wolves and savages
of the frontier, they are doomed once civilization catches up with
them."

It wasn't so hard, playing Désirée to this thoughtful young gentleman. He was so truly gentle, so obviously lonely. What he had
said about his father's having cast him adrift had caught her sympathy. Besides, it was comforting to be talked to kindly, to be

caressed. Almost naturally, her arm slipped over his shoulder.

The warming effect of the wine added to the heat. He blew out one of the candles and loosened his stock, then they sat side by side on the edge of the bed staring into the flames.

"Haec olim meminisse jubabit," he murmured and for once she inquired what he had said.

" 'It will be pleasant to remember these things hereafter!' " His use of Latin still irritated her a little, but a scholar, even in uniform, had her entire respect.

For the first time she understood why the long mirror on the opposite wall was hung as it was. Without moving, she could see her guest and herself perfectly. He was smiling at her. A single reddish curl over his wide-set eyes gleamed coppery. In the candle light, he presently gathered her to him, rested his head against hers.

From outside came the creaking of a loose shutter and the wails of a pair of tomcats daring each other to battle.

"What a devilish futile existence mine has been this past year. Soon must it recommence. So pray sing to me again, Desired Lady—something soft and gentle."

Timidly fingers crept up, brushed his cheek. "—You return to the Siege?"

"No. War is not pleasant, but one can derive from it experience, ideas of lasting worth. I fear that beneath yonder regimentals there remains a scholar, a philosopher in embryo. Having studied the ways of men engaged in slaughtering each other on land, I have sent in my commission."

"Why?"

"I would learn what men think and do when they plan to slay each other on the ocean."

"But you can't like fighting?"

To her surprise he deliberated a considerable time over that. "I must confess that, at times, I derive a certain awful pleasure in the primordial lust of inflicting suffering and death." Hurriedly he added, "As a rule, I would not harm a mouse."

Recalling her own sensations on watching that wretch flogged at the cart's tail, Désirée comprehended his meaning. It was surprising how well she understood this man.

"It is heavenly here, my sweet, so peaceful—" His fingers fumbled, freed the lacing of her bodice, pulled down the shift and bared her breasts.

"You are—are on your—your way to N-Newport? You—you will join this new Navy we hear about?" She stammered in embarrassment.

He drew her face down and kissed her lips before he said, "It is my intention to apply for a sergeancy in one of the two battalions of Continental Marines which have been recently authorized by the Congress. A clever compromise, don't you think?"

"Compromise? I—I vow I cannot follow you, M-Mr. Colebourne."

"You see, I know nothing concerning the management of a vessel of war, yet it would be foolish not to profit by my previous service.

"Marines, my dear, are, in effect, but soldiers afloat. At Tun's Tavern in Philadelphia, we shall learn whether their recruiting officer will accept an ex-sophister of Harvard College and an ex-lieutenant of Colonel Prescott's Massachusetts Regiment. And now, pray, a song for me."

With his head in her lap, his hand on her breast, Désirée sang:

" 'If rightly tuneful bards decide,
      If it be fix'd in Love's decrees,
    That Beauty ought not to be tried
      But by its native power to please,
    Then tell me, youths and lovers, tell—
      What fair can Amoret excel?' "

The fire faded to a ruby glow. It was not impossible or unpleasant to pretend that she was only meeting John again.

Her lips of dark red felt like smooth, fragrant fruit warmed in the sun. He kissed her, long, hungrily, sighed. "It would be uncommon fine to think of you waiting for me to return from sea."

Next morning she cried impulsively, "Oh, Nat, you are so good, so—so understanding. Why must we part? Why can't I go to Philadelphia with you? There is nothing to keep me here—nothing!"

He laughed and sat up, hair all damp and rumpled. "I can just imagine little Désirée aboard a naval transport. No, my sweet, I should be engaged in a dozen duels a day!"

"But why could I not join you there?" She held lips close to his ear. It was terrifying to even contemplate loss of the security he was lending. "Perhaps—maybe a merchantman will sail? Oh, my dear! You found me at a moment when I could not have needed kindness more. I—I don't know what will become of me."

She looked so scared, so very young by the morning light, a thoughtful look aged his brown features.

35

Ships Southward

FOR THE CAROLINAS
Peace & Plenty, Brigantine
Jno. Wentworth, Master
Hath good passenger accommodations.
Ready to sail December the Twenty-seventh.
J. Russell & Co., Agents

From Mr. Russell, Désirée and Lieutenant Colebourne learned that he had decided to risk British cruisers, winter gales and the strange decisions of the Committees of Safety in order to import a cargo of rice.

Mr. Russell scratched the hairy mole on his chin, allowed the commodity would fetch dazzling prices in New England, even if it went begging down South. Yes, he intended his brig to touch at Philadelphia on the way. It was advisable to keep up with the latest whims of the Congress.

Without even inquiring the price, the red-haired lieutenant en-

gaged a passage for his "married sister." He looked so concerned
when he bade Mr. Russell to "look after her with the vastest consideration" that Désirée wondered why.

She wasn't in love with him, at least not yet. But she did very
earnestly enjoy his company, his wit, and profound intelligence.

Yes, she had become monstrous fond of him. If only Nat Colebourne would shake off that bitterness, would give up his attempts
to rationalize this crazy business of war. What he needed to do
was to stop laughing at life in such a detached way, to unbend and to
enjoy it.

On Christmas day they held a small celebration all their own.
Nat made her the compliment of some handsome coral and gold
earbobs and she presented him with a gorgeous red silk sash which
he knew he would never be allowed to wear in uniform.

In the afternoon, they attended church—his church—like a truly
married pair; no one had so much as raised an eyebrow at this
muscular young lieutenant and the soberly clad young woman at
his side.

Above her mantelpiece, Désirée had hung a spray of holly, bright
with berries. They ate a little plum pudding, sipped cognac and
grew merry over it. Désirée sang all the songs she knew and
Nathaniel praised her voice until she blushed.

It was then that he confessed his true family name. All he had
told her about himself was so, except that Nantucket was where his
people lived and his name was Coffin, not Colebourne. Désirée felt
a little hurt but soon got over it.

She wondered what sort of a Christmas Tim and Papa were having.

To watch Nathaniel climb onto the Newport stage next day was
frightening. Désirée knew it meant a return to loneliness. Handing
up his bundles, she figured she had not let slip anything which
might have betrayed her true name—not unless she had talked in
her sleep.

Though her affair with John was nothing to be ashamed of,
Newport must never learn that Desire Harmony Bennett had ever

lain with a man for the sake of money.

When the coachman blew his bugle, Nat Coffin leaned out of the window and kissed the girl, standing there so prim and pretty. Today her hair looked more coppery than usual, her lips a darker, shinier red, and the shadows beneath her eyes more appealing than ever. A truly lovely girl.

"Remember now," he said, "you're to go direct to Smith's City Tavern. It's on Second Street, Désirée."

"Oh, Nathaniel, please call me just plain Desire from now on."

"And why should I, you funny little sweetheart?"

"Please—"

"Very well, Desire it shall be—like it better myself." He looked deep into her eyes, searching, asked a little sadly, "You will be good?"

She didn't take offense, just gave him a quick, strangely moving look. "You have been so very generous, dearest, there is no need to be anything else."

"Hup!" barked the coachman.

Bells jingled as the four horses threw themselves into their collars. Nathaniel swept off his hat and its bright cockade flashed in a wide arc.

"*Vale, vale, et si semper indesemper!* in other words, farewell!"

Suddenly, she took fright, wanted to cry out, "Oh, Nat! Nat, don't go!" but she only stood there in front of the posting station waving her handkerchief until tears blurred the vanishing coach.

Clutching the elegant petit-point pocket Nat had given her for a parting present, she started down the street. At the approach of a couple of roughs she hid the pocket in her dress. One thing she had learned was to keep her money with her.

The very first thing Desire did was to go down to where the *Peace & Plenty* lay at her wharf. Her eyes were still convincingly red as she sadly informed Captain Wentworth that she feared she would be unable to take passage after all.

The captain shifted his quid, asked why.

Last night, Desire sniffed, her brother had had ill luck at cards;

had lost more than he intended. So she must give up her cabin.

The sea captain eyed her with suspicion, but only found she looked young and very pretty. Well, well. So he'd lost, had he? Now weren't soldiers the most terrible gamblers? Reg'lar fools over cards. Sailors were different, they preferred solider pleasures, rum and wom—ahem.

Desire agreed with a forlorn quiver in her voice. It was a crying shame that poor brother Nathaniel only had five pounds left and she had that right here. How unfortunate that the passage had amounted to seven pounds. It *had been* seven, hadn't it?

"Yes, seven."

Desire's head drooped. "Oh, dear, what shall I do? I—I must meet my father in Philadelphia or I shall be quite undone."

Chin trembling, she looked out over the ice-filled harbor. How typical of improvident Nat to have agreed to the master's first price. If he had bothered to inquire around, as she had, he would have learned that the usual passage rate to Philadelphia was six pounds. She hated being put upon; besides, two pounds would cover many pressing needs.

The brigantine's master hesitated a long while, pulled his chin whiskers and swore that he was being ruined but would accept five pounds if she paid on the nail. Desire thanked him prettily and gave him half the fare. Papa had often spoken of rascally masters who would engage their cabin space twice over. By sailing a day early, it was easy to leave one set of passengers—those who had been inexperienced enough to pay in advance—whistling for their transportation.

Oh, but it was fine to have become again Desire Harmony St. Clair. Still she had to admit that the role of Mlle. Désirée had fascinated her and had not required much effort, either. Certainly, she had not performed in vain. Fourteen pounds were in her purse and over in James Street was laid away a wardrobe of plain, decent garments. In addition, she had her gold and coral earbobs and this lovely pocket of real petit-point.

One night after she had made Chloë the compliment of a silk

handkerchief, her mother's thimble mysteriously appeared in the washstand drawer. She felt ever so pleased to have it back—her sole tangible link with the past.

A conviction arose, grew, that no matter what happened to her, she would always come out on top. Lucky, that's what she was— naturally born lucky! Nothing really dreadful would ever hold power over her long. Imagine having a dear, kind person like Nat Coffin turn up, just when he had! Suppose she had been walking just a little faster or slower that night? Why, their paths might never have crossed.

That night, for the first time, a brawl took place in Mrs. Norton's house. Desire awoke to hear strident curses, the crash of overturned furniture, a nerve-shattering jangle of smashing glass and crockery.

"Who's took my wallet?" a man's voice was roaring. "Find it, you thieving slut, else I'll kick the teeth out of your damned painted face!"

Doors slammed, feet pounded on the stairs.

"—I won't be quiet," the man kept yelling. "I been robbed. Goddam it, I tell you my wallet was in my britches pocket not five minutes back. I felt it."

The tumult swelled as masculine voices intermingled with the frightened calling of Mrs. Norton's "female boarders."

Désirée had never addressed any of them because they had kept to themselves. Chloë claimed they were jealous of her luck in straight-away landing anybody so rich and elegant as Lieutenant Colebourne.

Mrs. Norton's shrill accents implored silence, but the angry man kept on yelling, "I've been robbed!" A window was smashed, Mrs. Norton called, "Jean! *Vite! Vite!*"

"I'll have the law on—" the enraged patron's sentence broke off short and Desire, trembling in her bed, distinctly heard the sound of a blow followed by a fall. Then comparative silence ensued, except for undertones within the house. At last Desire heard shutters commence to close on the nearby windows.

Somewhere a voice, the girl's, was blubbering, "Don't let Jean beat me, Ma'am. I swear to Jesus my God he didn't have a wallet. Oh dear, oh dear, I've wasted my whole night, too!"

"*Quelle sottise!*" Mrs. Norton snapped. "Be quiet, baggage! Need you have struck so hard, Jean?"

Gradually the rumpus faded, and Desire went back to sleep after tying her money pocket extra firm to her wrist.

36

THE WATCHMEN

A RESOUNDING kick on the door connecting with the house made Desire pop straight up in bed. Heavens! More brawling? What was going on tonight? Groggily, she became aware of early morning.

"Open up, ye damned doxy! Open in the name o' the law!"

The law! Oh dear! What could they want with her?

Bedclothes clutched to her chin, Desire in frozen terror watched the door panels give and shake under a rain of kicks. Suddenly, the latch split; there bounded into her room a breathless, brutal-looking individual wearing a dull-brown watch cloak. In one hand he was carrying a candle lantern, in the other a length of cord and a cudgel.

The intruder's small, mean eyes fixed her. He tramped towards her favoring what must be a sore foot. "Rouse out of that, and be quick about it."

All eyes, Desire could only gape. "But, sir, I—I have harmed no one."

"Don't yer dast talk back. All you whores are cheats to boot. Never met one who wasn't. Come on, rouse out o' there!"

Too terrified to move a muscle, she merely flinched against the wall. Cursing, the watchman reached under the covers, grabbed her ankle, hauled her kicking out onto the floor with nightshift gathered about her neck.

When, scarlet, she pulled down her nightdress and struggled to her feet, the watchman stood panting, watching, hat cocked over one eye, the loop of greasy cord hanging limp from his red fist. Within Mrs. Norton's house sounded heavy feet, shrieks and rough orders.

The watchman was licking his lips. "Cripes! No wonder old Frenchy does a rushing trade. Pity yer got to cool such a pretty pink bottom in jail."

"Jail? Oh—oh—no!" She had to sail aboard the *Peace & Plenty*. She had to find Nat in Philadelphia. "I can't. I'm going away," Desire choked.

"Yer going away, all right, dearie," the watchman grinned, jerking open a bureau drawer. "Providence is a respectable, law-abiding port; time you fancy-Nancies learned that. No nonsense, now, get into some clothes."

"But, kind sir," Desire raised enormous brown eyes. "I have done nothing dishonest. I swear I haven't."

"So say you," the watchman grunted. "A man was robbed and beaten half to death here this night." Even as he fumbled in the bureau, he kept watching the way her billowy nightshift fell open, exposing breasts.

In the next room Chloë began screaming like a stuck pig. Another girl was shrieking incredibly foul insults. Subconsciously, she heard Mrs. Norton, with desperate politeness, trying to buy off a lantern-jawed official whom the other watchman called "Sheriff."

The watchman nodded at the pocket dangling from her wrist. "What's that thing?"

"My—my purse." Her lips felt so rigid she could barely move them.

"Give us a look, dearie." He snatched it, tore it free. When he lifted the pocket, he shot a glance over his shoulder.

"Damn my eyes," he snarled. "Didn't I tell you to get some clothes on?"

In frozen desperation, Desire sullenly commenced to tie petticoats over her nightshift. Hopelessly, she caught up the first gown that came to hand, tucked her feet into her best slippers, then began buttoning her bodice any which way.

A blonde girl was being dragged, weeping, into the hallway. Beyond the open door there, a grubby little man with a two days' growth of beard began tying the girl's hands behind her. "Stand still, you cursed hussy."

To think that, in another few instants, Asa Bennett's daughter, too, would be trussed, haled through the streets like a common prostitute! Desire almost fainted but remained gasping, staring at that greasy cord in the watchman's grimy paw.

"Hold out yer dukes," he ordered, but when he moved closer he suddenly slipped her purse into his pocket and pointed to the door leading into the lane.

"Say nothin'—an' git!" he muttered.

With the speed of a pursued rabbit racing for the shelter of its burrow, Desire wrenched open the lane door and with the watchman's sudden shout of "Prisoner escaped!" loud in her ears, ran in headlong terror.

37

THE SABIN INN

FOR good and sufficient reasons, Ex-sergeant Timothy Bennett waited 'til the day preceding Commodore Hopkins' intended departure before returning to Newport. What was the use of risking unpleasantness and possible arrest? Besides, he'd reluctantly given up all hope of finding Desire. Once when Tim touched on the matter of the barn, Higsby had shaken his narrow head.

"She must ha' been there all right, but I'll never credit she was—was, well, what they thought she was." Pride wouldn't let him admit that he guessed wrong about Desire that day she had come nosing about his lean-to.

Higsby's remark made Tim ashamed he'd been so ready to credit scandal. Still, his sister was headstrong, romantic and of a passionate disposition. He feared she might have done away with herself until Sam Higsby discovered her pitiful camp in Martin's woodshed.

Tim felt better then. "She must have got away," he argued. "She could sail better than a lot of boys, but I wish to God she'd left word which way she's headed."

Christmas came and went without attention from either of them other than to fix up an extra good meal. On Christmas eve, memories, visions of Lucy tormented Tim with especial persistence.

There she was, just beyond the lean-to door, smiling gaily, just as she had last year when presenting him a Christmas gift. He recalled that it had been a transparency of cut paper. The design had consisted of yellow paper mounted on green and depicted Newport harbor so plain everybody recognized it at first glance. Everyone had admired Lucy's delicate handling of the scissors.

But how lovely she had looked standing so slim and graceful before the mantelpiece. Desire had twined its columns with English ivy and had stuck clusters of flaming poke berries into the tumblers of water. There had been a special Family Meeting at which Pa had done some mighty fine testifying as to the goodness and bounty of the Lord.

Now he recalled how Mamba had presented him with a cocoanut shell drinking cup. She had engraved it with a sailor's needle in fantastic African designs full of leopards, snakes and crosses. She implied that the symbols meant something but when he asked, she only giggled and said, "Laws, Mist' Tim, Ah wouldn't want for to be tellin' you. 'At's hoodoo."

Since dancing was forbidden to the Friends, the young Bennetts had had to go over to the Elleys' for their fun. They'd a grand time because Joe Elley scraped a merry fiddle. Nobody could reel off "Faithful Shepherd," "Free Mason's Jig" and "Pea Straw" any better than Joe.

Asa Bennett had pretended to know nothing of it but, nevertheless, expected that, come next meeting, Tim and Hezekiah would stand up and condemn themselves for their worldliness.

Tim, lying on his spruce bed, smiled in the dark. The Elders generally let them off light and such dancing was well worth it.

On Tuesday, the 26th of December, Tim arose with his mind made up. He guessed he'd viewed his problem from every possible angle. He must reach Cap François by hook or crook and take possession of the *Narragansett* as soon as he could.

Maybe he could come up with the *Hope,* too? Pa had ordered her into Hispaniola for instructions. Another thing. He was sure A. Bennett & Co. was owed quite a tidy sum by Messrs. Hibbert, Parrier & Horton of Kingston in Jamaica. Of course, the Ministry had forbidden the payment of debts owed the rebellious colonies, so collection of the obligation boded to be no easy matter.

Pa had always said that Messrs. Hibbert, Parrier & Horton were honest to their finger tips. Besides, they must stand in serious need of slave food. There were over a quarter of a million of them in the Island now.

When, after breakfast, he commenced to make a blanket roll, Higsby drawled, "Where you headed?"

"Cap François."

"Far?"

" 'Bout 2,000 miles."

"Thought you was broke. How you goin'?"

"Don't rightly know," Tim admitted. "But I'm going to get there somehow."

Presently the ranger tightened the throat lacings of his sumactinted shirt, then pulled on his buckskins that had LIBERTY painted on it.

"You going over to town, too?"

"Reckon I've lonesomed enough. Aim to mosey on South," the other drawled.

"Why don't you adopt the Navy? The way Hopkins talks, anybody who signs on with him is sure to get a bellyful of fighting."

The rifleman looked horrified. "What? Me go aboard a *ship?* Hell's roarin' bells, no! I'd be forever tangled in them strings an' things they tie it together with. No suh, I'd liefer dive into a crick o' boilin' fat."

Tim sighed. All along he'd been hoping that maybe he could get Sam to come along to the Indies. As a marksmanship instructor to the *Narragansett's* crew, he would be invaluable. The brig's crew was to be hand-picked.

Polypus Hammond claimed most privateers he'd sailed in were dangerously weak in the musketry department—a big reason why they so sedulously avoided battle with men-of-war of any description.

They broke camp in silence and put out the fire. When they climbed out the hollow, Tim cast a long last look on the heap of blackened ruins which was all that remained to mark the site of Asa Bennett's fine warehouse. Deep bitterness welled into his being when he saw the great chimney of Peaceful Haven standing lonely, like a sinister tombstone, among the four scorched elms.

During the fortnight just past, Tim had really learned how to handle his rifle but his stride, Higsby complained, was still too straight-legged, too soldierly—not long, supple and bent-kneed.

"Reckon I'll look 'round that there town you mentioned up river," Higsby announced, "and maybe cut Miss Dee-sire's trail."

They didn't talk much, only bent into a stiff nor'easter with the long rifle barrels slanting far back over their shoulders.

Once a ferryman had set them down in Newport, Higsby shouldered his pack, cleared his throat a couple of times before awkwardly offering his hand.

"Thanks, Tim, fer lettin' me range 'round yer place."

"Thanks for nothing! If you hadn't looked after me—"

"—Somebody else would have."

"Maybe, maybe not. Anyhow, I'm grateful," Tim said. He felt mighty sorry to part with the Pennsylvanian. Sam knew just when to talk and when to hold his peace.

"Remember this. Tomorrow, or fifty years from now, you'll al-

ways be given a hearty welcome at Peaceful Haven." He laughed
gratingly. "The property ain't much now; but when this crazy war
is over, I'm going to build it up again, only handsomer. I aim to
bring architects down from Boston, over from England, maybe."

Such a desperate earnestness entered his tone that Higsby stared.
By God, if Tim didn't come through, it would be because he was
dead. He looked kind of like his Pa right now—quite a lot, in fact.

To restore the home was only part of what Tim was setting out
to do. He would make the Percivals' house look like a frontier
shanty. Yessir, he was going to lay for the Percivals. He would
wean away their business just as Ike was grabbing at Pa's accounts
right now.

"Well, keep yer hair on," Higsby grunted when they had done
pumping hands.

Trailed by sharp looks and by curious small boys, the russet
brown figure struck off along the waterfront. Tim felt mighty depressed to see such a fine fellow wander out of his life.

Everywhere ships were being reconditioned. Why even a pair of
old slavers, *The Two Friends* and the *Corsair,* were being pierced
for guns. A foolish procedure, Tim thought. They were all of forty
years old, slower than molasses in February, and must fall prize
to the first man-o'-war or privateersman they encountered.

Over Newport hung the pungent odors of melting tar, of okum
and wet canvas. Bright yellow chips and sawdust littered water and
quays. Down at Wanton's yard hammers thundered, shipwrights
cursed and rigging cranes whined as topmasts were hoisted into
their steps. The length of Thames Street was crowded with carts
and drays freighting marine supplies.

Of the British squadron only the *Swan,* frigate and the *Bolton,*
bomb brig remained at the anchorage. The *Rose,* best hated vessel of
all, had disappeared convoying the *Patience* and a fleet of other
prizes.

He came upon a knot of men gathered before a poster and with
them read:

New-Port, Rhode Island
December 27, 1775

Private armed Sloop *Revenge,* burthen about One Hundred and fifteen Tons, or there-abouts, mounting about Twenty-four Guns large and Small, Captain Benjamin Norton, Commander, being bound on a cruising Voyage against the Royal Pirate; If any Gentlemen Sailors or others have a mind to take a Cruise in said Sloop let them repair on board of said Sloop Now lying at Mr. Albert Taylor's Wharff, where they may see said Articles of Agreement and be kindly received. Said Sloop wants a Doctor at present.

Thaxter & Son

Certainly many privateers must be ready for sea. But the commissions without which no master dared sail for fear of being hanged as a pirate had not yet been issued. Tim figured the owners had been a little precipitate. The Congress was becoming famous for its vacillations, dilly-dallyings. Why weeks, even months, might elapse before any one of these ships dared put out to sea.

Thought of Ira Thaxter's having guaranteed seamen's wages from date of enrolment made him laugh. When the Commissions were granted, he reasoned the richest prizes should be found cruising around Jamaica. Prizes! His arteries quickened.

The beating of a drum attracted his attention. An officer in blue clumped into sight in front of a couple of drummer boys in smart green and white uniforms. He carried a leather speaking trumpet.

Behind the drummers shuffled a slack-shouldered youth in an old blue militia tunic. He was carrying a white flag which, for design, had a green pine tree, or something like that, stitched to its center. Above this arboreal effort the word "Liberty" stood out. Below, "An Appeal to Heaven." One corner of the banner was trailing in the mud.

When he reached the corner of Thames and Anne Streets the officer halted, signaled the drummers to be quiet, and mopped his forehead.

Speaking through the trumpet, he intoned: "Hear ye! All brave, intrepid and able-bodied patriotic seamen, hear ye!" One of the drummer boys began picking his nose; the other made faces at an envious guttersnipe.

"The cruiser *Katy* will sail at the first opportunity. Today is the final chance to enlist. Such spirited fellows who are willing to engage will receive a bounty at the end of the War, besides their laurels—"

"Aw pipe down," yelled a voice from the depths of an alley.

The officer went red but repeated, "—Besides their laurels, and fifty acres of land to which every gallant hero may retire to enjoy the gratitude of his country."

"No shares!" a carpenter shouted from the crosstrees of *The Two Friends*. "Pinch-penny! We want prize money!"

The officer shook his fist, bellowed back, "Shut your ugly trap! You bloody privateers will soon enough come whimpering for our help!"

"How are you fixed for men?" Tim asked.

The recruiting officer spat resoundingly into a mud puddle. "I'm still short sixteen hands and may God damn and blast Newport for a hive of self-seeking pirates." He looked worried. "I'm doing all I can, but old Esek is going to raise holy blue hell if I don't find the men."

Up hill in the direction of Bull Street other drums began rolling. "Listen to that, will you? As if we haven't trouble enough, your local patriots figure it's time to begin beating for a home guard regiment."

"I've heard of it," Tim said. How many ages ago had he listened to Joe Child curse over this very unit? "It's handy for local yellow-bellies who want to sport a uniform and 'tend their business at the same time."

Tim was developing an idea. What about the Gardner boys, the Remingtons, Jed Franklin, and Joe Elley? Unless they had been lucky enough to sign on a privateer paying wages from the start, they must by now be desperate for work. Certainly there wasn't room for such a horde of unemployed. He said, "I'm not promising anything, but I will try to scare up some recruits for you."

The officer beamed, wiped a hot red face, cast curious eyes on the Foulke. "I'll never forget it if you will. Old Hop's a devil when he gets r'iled."

"Is Admiral Hopkins really sailing South in a day or so?"

"Yep. You can send your men to the Sabin Inn. I'll be on the look-out for them. Good luck."

Tim was debating his next move when Captain Lawton, proprietor of the Bull House, came splashing across the street, scattering a flock of geese. He called out, but Tim paid no attention. To hell with such a fair-weather friend.

"Hi, Tim! Wait. Wait a minute!" the tavern keeper kept on calling.

At length Tim halted, swung about so sharply his rifle barrel rapped a cooper's swing sign.

"Where you been? Looked all over for you." Lawton came puffing up to him and thrust a pudgy hand. "Wanted to say I spoke in haste the other day. Offer my apologies. Should have known you wouldn't mean to do anything dishonorable."

Tim ignored the other's hand. "You are damned slow with your regrets, Captain Lawton."

The other colored and his plump features contracted. "You'll live to regret that quick tongue of yours, Tim. I said, I'm here to apologize. I'm truly sorry. The ducks are flying and I—oh hang it, man, we're too old friends to quarrel. Come along to the Bull House and have a drink."

Tim took the inn owner's hand. In the past John Lawton had done him no end of small kindnesses.

Once they were seated over leathern jacks of ale, the tavern keeper said seriously, "Reason I been keen to find you, Tim, was because it so happens I witnessed the sailing instructions your Pa gave to George Griffin. You'll recall Griffin commands the *Narragansett?*"

"Yes." What a fool he'd been to come so near freezing John Lawton's good intentions. "That's capital, John. All Pa's records were lost in the raid."

Lawton took a deep draught of ale and smacked fleshy lips ere he said, "Being the smart old feller he was, your Pa figured a long time back that the King's ministers would do just what they have done—declare all American vessels taken on the high seas as fair prizes. So he instructed Griffin to undertake enough short cruises 'twixt Saint-Domingue and the Dutch Islands to pay the crew and upkeep. If Griffin heard of British cruisers in the neighborhood, he was to stay in Cap François or Curaçao and wasn't to sail for home until so ordered."

Lawton drank more of the foaming bitter fluid, belched comfortably, then pushed forward a plate heaped with crackers and cheese. They were fine thin crackers and stamped with a bull's head, his private mark.

"Here's 'nother item might pay you to remember and *to keep under your hat.*" The inn keeper bent forward. "I've received word, no matter from whom, that the lords of the Admiralty are rigging a great expedition 'gainst the Carolinas in the springtime."

He winked. "If the convoys touch at Jamaica to refit after crossing, a smart privateer might pick off quite a few transports and supply ships."

Never in his life had Tim felt so all-fired impatient to be on his way. It would be rare fun cutting out a parcel of fat troopships! The *Narragansett* was plenty fast enough for such work, too!

"Thank you, John. So it's to be a naval raid?"

"More than that," Lawton said gravely. "There'll be troops along, plenty of them. The Ministry plans a reg'lar campaign. So God help them Carolinians!"

By end of an hour Tim's hopes were bright as Lawton's pewter. He had arranged for the innkeeper to realize what he could from Asa Bennett's credits. Though Lawton wanted to do the job for nothing, Tim insisted he accept ten percent of anything he collected. By now, he had noticed that a man only did his best when he got paid for it.

Lawton, too, would secure letter-of-marque papers for the *Narragansett* in triplicate. By separate routes they would be forwarded to Saint-Domingue and by the fastest possible means.

"The privateer brig, *Narragansett,* Tim? That sounds fine."

"No. Remember, it's a letter-of-marque's papers I want."

Lawton paused in the act of refilling a long clay pipe. "That's right; but why ain't you wanting to privateer, plain and simple?"

Slowly, Tim grinned. "We Bennetts have been traders time out of mind, and the *Narragansett* is primarily a merchant ship."

"Then why plan to mount eight guns?" Lawton inquired with amazement.

"Even if I trade, what's to prevent my snapping up prizes now and then? As a letter-of-marque, I will have two ways of making money. Trading and prize-taking. Your privateersman stands only to gain from his prizes, if any. Figure it out for yourself, John."

With a grubby forefinger Lawton explored a mole on his chin. "Take after your Pa in some ways, don't you?" he grinned. He was silent for a moment. "How d'you figure getting down to Saint-Domingue?"

"I'll sail with Hopkins, as far as Philadelphia anyhow." Solemnly Tim drained the last of his beer. "I need to learn how a man-o'-war is handled."

"But your term of enlistment?" Lawton protested. "You surely don't figure on making the same mistake twice?"

Heat climbed into Tim's face. "No. When I met that recruiting party, I thought of a better way."

Because it suited his purpose, Tim postponed until the last moment his visit to Sabin Inn and to the recruiting officer. He was so very short of cash he found it necessary to devote much time in collecting the contents of a sea bag. Canvas breeches, mittens, a pair of woolen jerseys, oiled leather coat, handkerchiefs, stockings.

In addition he purchased needles and thread, a copy of Turenne's "Memoirs," a knitted woolen cap with a red tassel, and a bezoar stone against hemorrhages. He had the whole consignment sent to the Bull Inn.

He was negotiating for a dirk when, in the distance, sounded that unearthly screech which would always set his teeth on edge.

"Three shillings, then," he conceded and, catching up his purchase, began to run as if the Devil were after him.

Again and again that long drawn "E-e-yah! E-e-yah! O-o-nah!" came from the direction of School Street.

As at Roxbury and again at Tiverton, people tumbled out of doors to see what was amiss. Presently, Tim overtook a pair of watchmen lumbering along with their brass-tipped staves purposefully a-swing.

At the junction of School and Griffin Streets, a tangle of men was eddying about over the cobbles. Discarded hats dotted the footpath and small boys hovered gleefully about the fringes of what must be an Homeric brawl.

It took no ghost from the grave to tell Tim that Sam Higsby, being in possession of funds, had promptly reverted to type. Two men sat on the curb holding their heads; one of them was draining blood from a pulpy-looking nose.

"E-e-e-e-yah-yah! O-o-n-a-h!"

While he covered the last few yards, Tim began casting loose his coat. The ranger was fighting at least four or five men at once. Damn these roughs! No sense of sportsmanship in them. Sam was charging first in one direction, then in the other. He must have left his rifle and other weapons inside the tap house opposite.

"Hang on!" Tim began to think it would do him good to give someone a black eye.

Before he could reach the mêlée, a constable ran in from the opposite side of the ring and, from behind, brought his heavy stave thwacking down on Sam's head. The Pennsylvanian's knees buckled and, still trying to fight, he sagged groggily across the body of the last man he had knocked down. Another, spouting obscenities, was crawling away on hands and knees.

Two more of the watch ran up and belabored the rifleman until Tim wrenched away one of their staves. Red-faced, panting, furious, he drove the constable back a few paces.

"Quit that! Leave him be!"

"Keep out of this!" warned a hard-looking young constable. "Or we'll take you to chokey, too!"

"All right, but don't hit him again—he's helpless." Then Tim asked of the crowd in general, "Who started the trouble?"

"Soldier from the Army—that's him lying by the door," babbled a half-grown youth. "Claimed the rifler was just a iggorant Dirty Shirt ailing from constipation o' the brain an' diarrhea o' the mouth!"

Others recounted how Higsby, growing steadily drunker, had terrified a tavern slut into standing against a door while he practiced knife throwing. Successively his blade had grazed her shoulder, her head. It was when he pinned her skirt to the wall between her knees that she had begun screeching.

When the tavern keeper had objected, the Injun had flung his hatchet—the waitress called it a battle-axe—and had cut a cord suspending the taproom's principal chandelier.

Though Tim tried to mollify him, there was no talking the publican out of his revenge. "I'll see that he rots in jail for this! He's done my place six pounds' wuth o' damage. I'll have the law—"

Tim strode over, eyed the fellow steadily, "You go to hell. The whole of your stinking little grog shop ain't worth half of six pounds. How much will it take to settle the harm?"

Too quickly, the publican burst out, "Two pound ten and a new skirt for Susie."

"Agreed!" Tim called a constable to witness. "You heard that!"

All at once a wonderful idea occurred. It was such a fine, rare inspiration that when the innkeeper demanded his damage money, Tim laughed in his blotched and scabby face.

"Smart feller, eh?" snarled the publican. "All right, then, the watch will throw your chum in jail. He'll stay 'til he pays for every last sasser he's broke."

Still in a daze, but struggling, Sam Higsby was frog-marched off to jail.

"I—come back!" he promised. "Skelp every last one you whoresons! Can't do this! 'M freeborn Englishman. 'Tain't legal!"

The constable cuffed him brutally once, twice, "Stow your gab, ye blasted savage. Or maybe you'd like to dance to a cart's tail?"

The constable bestirred himself, confiscated Higsby's rifle and powder horn. Tim tried to rescue his pack but the innkeeper made such a row over parting with the Virginian's property that the constable let him keep it.

Meantime, Tim trotted ahead and, pursuing his idea, had a talk with Mr. Poor, the jailer. By being very polite, he learned just what he wanted to know, and was on his way down to the Sabin Inn long before Higsby and his perspiring captors even heaved into sight.

Lieutenant Grinnell, the recruiting officer he had met on the street, was contemplating a half-empty noggin of mulled port and looking mighty downcast. Across the room, his clerk was audibly enjoying the contents of a wooden trencher of clam chowder. Like abandoned playing cards, a pile of blank enlistment forms lay across the littered table.

"Evening, sir." Tim stood to attention just as he used to up in Roxbury.

The recruiting officer looked up and stirred his drink. "Oh, it's you," he observed without enthusiasm.

"Yes, sir." Tim tried to keep a straight face. "About those men—"

"I'm still in a hole. Only two showed up. Gardner and Franklin. Then there was a boy named Hull. Where are the rest?"

"Privateering," Tim admitted. "They wouldn't listen to me."

"I'm not surprised. This ratted nest of Loyalists and pirates hasn't yielded us ten men in as many days," complained Lieutenant Grinnell.

"Old Wallace's raid on Conanicut has scared the delirious daylights out of this port!"

Tim waited until he had done, then asked, "Sir, if I were able to find you all the men you need, would you make a private agreement with me?"

Lieutenant Grinnell set down his cup with a bang, snorted, "All the men I need? You must be addled! Why. I'm still eleven hands short. Old Hop will be raging."

Tim bent over the table, gray eyes intent. "Have you some ready cash?"

Grinnell jerked a nod. "Twenty pounds still unspent—'twas meant for bonuses and free grog. What means all this mystery?"

"You'll hear in a minute, sir. You see—"

Grinnell shrugged at the inevitable. He had become familiar with the inborn Yankee passion for qualifying any sort of agreement.

"I am anxious, very anxious, to accompany the Admiral southward—"

Eagerly, the recruiting officer shoved forward a blank, then hesitated as if recalling something. He dropped his eyes. "I am sorry, Bennett, but we are not permitted to accept deserters."

Though scalding color poured into his face, Tim was at pains to speak evenly. "I am not a deserter, and can prove it. However, I have no desire to enroll. I wish to be free to leave the ship whenever I intend. Suppose I sign on as—a—well, kind of civilian super-cargo? Perhaps as a secretary to some officer? I am familiar with ciphering."

The other shook his head flatly. "That is quite impossible."

"Then you don't really need eleven men?"

Grinnell flung himself angrily back in his chair, cursed softly. "You know dashed well I do!" He fastened a couple of tarnished waistcoat buttons.

"I can find you eleven sound men. How about it?"

The recruiting officer gnawed his lips, drummed on the table, blasphemed the Congress, Esek Hopkins and the whole of Rhode Island. He ended by spreading helpless and somewhat dingy hands.

"Since you put it that way, I suppose I must find or create a post of some sort. Accountant of private stores, perhaps? You're sure you are clever at ciphering?"

"Yes. Very." Encouraged, Tim said, "I have a friend who is to sail under the same terms."

"A friend?"

"Yes. A master marksman. I will warrant he will be well worth his salt."

At last the Lieutenant looked up, blew out thin, unshaven cheeks and said, "Very well. As you so delicately remind me, I must produce a full complement or suffer official censure. What you propose is irregular, highly illegal, and must be kept private."

Reaching out he selected a goose quill from a clump set in a glass filled with bird shot.

"Where is this friend?"

Tim smiled faintly. "In jail."

"Jail? Why, you goddam son—!"

"Hold on. You can easily buy his way out. This Higsby owes two pounds and some pence. In jail with him are fifteen or eighteen debtors."

He spoke slowly. "They are not felons, mind you, only small merchants ruined by the Non-intercourse and Repressive Acts. Pay their debts and they're yours. The poor devils *must* accept your offer or rot behind bars all winter long."

Grinnell threw back his head and laughed so violently that his wig slipped askew. "Debtors! Oh, my God, why was I such a dunderhead as not to think of that?"

Jumping up, the recruiting officer gripped Tim's hand an instant, then began to do his buttons. "I'll never forget this. Knowles! Knowles! Get me a sheaf of enrolment papers and stir those lazy stumps of yours."

38

THE RHODE ISLAND CRUISER KATY

IT WAS chiming ten o'clock over in Tiverton when the *Katy's* long boat rowed under her counter. Men at the oars were puffing and sweating after the long pull up from Providence.

Tim realized that the little sloop of war lay in Mount Hope Bay and was protected by a battery of guns mounted on Ferry Point. Another fortification lay veiled by snow drifts just below the Bristol ferry landing on the opposite shore.

Not a star shone and a northwest wind was blowing through one of the blackest nights Tim could remember. Water, whipped up by the oars, froze on the thwarts, flew stinging into the faces of the silent and discouraged recruits.

Young Phil Hull, who'd appeared at the last minute, was trying to muffle a half-grown boy's rending sobs. He sounded so sad, Tim wanted to try to comfort him but the boat was too crowded to permit movement. Sam, too, was aboard but still so ornery fighting drunk they'd had to tie him.

Crimanently, but it was black! Though he could hear the oars bumping thole pins in the next boat behind, he couldn't even detect her outline.

The faint glimmer of a lantern shone above and the longboat's coxswain hailed, "*Katy,* ahoy! Boat party. Stand by to heave us a line."

Over head loomed a dim pattern of yards, shrouds and topsides.

The vessel certainly wasn't very large, Tim perceived. Not more than ninety tons. Um. With so many hands aboard, a voyage clear down to Philadelphia promised to be memorable rather than comfortable.

Light escaped feebly through a series of loose-fitting gun ports. Over the *slap-slap* of waves against the little sloop's counter came a hail. "You new men take care. Rail's icy."

Well, for better or worse, this moment marked a turning point in the life of Timothy Bennett. He fully realized this; it sobered him. There would be fewer mistakes made from now on—no Lucy Percivals, false reasonings, or self-deceptions of the lunar enlistment sort.

Lieutenant Grinnell came out of the darkness, said curtly, "Report aft to Captain Whipple. He wants you to prove his paymaster's account immediately. Thinks he's crooked. He is. Be careful, though; the paymaster is your immediate superior."

At four bells of the middle watch, the ten-gun sloop of war, *Katy,* hove in her anchors, made sail and without lights began to grope down the Seakonnet Passage towards the Atlantic. Everyone aboard knew that the *Swan* was patrolling the entrance.

Homesick, Phil Hull began to blubber and made such small miserable sounds that somebody dealt him a swipe across the mouth.

39
EMPTY PORT

LUCY PERCIVAL felt so stiff she could hardly move as she stood on the edge of Newport, trying to disguise her face with her scarf. If the postrider's beast had been a trifle less phlegmatic, an inch less broad in the beam, and had she loved Tim Bennett one whit less, she would never be standing here.

Three days on the postrider's hard pillion had reduced her tender body to a wincing mass of aches, chilblains and bruises. For all her eagerness to find Tim with all speed, she paused to feel a little proud of herself. It was no mean accomplishment to travel from Plymouth to Newport—forty-five miles—in three days, and in the dead of winter.

The big, not overly bright postrider accepted his pound, touched his hat and, mumbling "Thank ye kindly, Mistress," shuffled into the posting station carrying chafed saddle pouches over his shoulder. A boy led the steaming, puffing horse away.

At the head of Jew Street, Lucy hesitated. For the first time the temerity of her deed achieved its true proportions. Oh dear, Papa would be simply seething mad when he learned how very dexterously she'd given Aunt Tabitha the slip.

Lucy's mouth compressed itself into a straight scarlet ruler mark. She didn't care! Papa could—he could go to the devil! That was what. She and Tim really belonged to each other. She was as sure of that now as she ever would be sure of anything in this life.

Tim must have wondered, must have been monstrous hurt. Oh dear, how could she make him believe how she had prayed, waited and schemed just to be with him? He would understand and forgive. Right now she wasn't going to delay a minute in going to him, she was going over to Conanicut.

Only the sound of Tim's voice, the sight of those little golden splinters in his gray eyes, of a grin on that generous, wide mouth of his would ease the intolerable ache in her breast.

Lucy quickened her walk towards the water. It would be wonderful simply to be near him. What a spineless little fool she'd been to let Papa bundle her, willy-nilly, off to Plymouth. She ought to have guessed that Mama's hint about Tim's being able to follow would come to nothing. Yes. Her parents had properly taken her in. She would never wholly trust either of them again. Never. Only Tim.

Straight and supple in her dark blue cloak and quilted calash, she hurried towards Dyre's Point where the ferry left for Conanicut.

What a nuisance. It was thawing and the streets were ankle-deep with mud in some places. Her shoes were thin and very quickly became sodden, but she didn't care. Only a few miles of gray, ice-choked water now separated her from Tim. Nothing else ever should! Of that she was determined.

If only she could bring Tim a great lot of money to help him rebuild Peaceful Haven.

"Oh, Tim darling," she thought aloud, "we'll work hard and build a fortune of our own. I will keep your accounts as Mama used to for Papa."

By the time she reached the ferry her feet were soaked through and felt like blocks of ice, but her heart had never sung more happily.

Luck was with her. The ferry was just coming in. While a helper was getting out a pair of sweeps, the ferryman doused an often-patched spritsail.

Waiting for the little boat to dock, Lucy strained to see over Rose Island to the Conanicut landing. She should reach the Bennett property before dark, easily. Wouldn't Tim be pleased? She longed to feel his arms crushing the breath out of her, hurting her breasts by holding her so tight.

There was nobody aboard the ferry except old Mr. Gardner, and he failed to recognize her as he paid his fare.

The ferryman looked at the single sixpence, said bitterly to his helper, "Three fares in a hull day. We can thank them goddam Britainers."

He began to stop his sail, so Lucy called out, "Please. Wait! I want to cross."

"Too late, Mistress. Man's got to rest—even a ferryman."

"Would you for a shilling?"

"It's too late, I warn ye. 'Twill be pitch dark 'fore I could get back."

"But I've got to get over. Someone is expecting me. I'll give you two shillings."

The ferryman was secretly a-tremble. In the last two days he hadn't earned half that much. But he kept on fiddling with his sail stops as if he didn't care. "Make it three and I might wait for you."

"I'll give you two and sixpence," Lucy said firmly. "There will be no need for you to wait."

She was so excited she couldn't help asking, "Has Mr. Bennett been over recently?"

"Who, the old man? Why, he's been dead a fortnight. Didn't you know?"

Lucy started, felt her throat close. So? Tim's father had died and she hadn't been there to comfort him! Oh, how awful! Poor sweet Tim, all alone. On top of everything else, too.

"No," she murmured, "I hadn't heard. How did it happen?"

"Asa Bennett got took off by the lung fever. They buried him only two days after the British burnt his place on Conanicut—and spoilt my trade."

"Young Mr. Bennett is—is well?"

But the ferryman had turned away and was beckoning his helper, "Jed, we're going back across."

"Shucks, Pa, do I got to go?"

"Do's I say else I'll tan your backside." He turned a worn whiskery face. "What was that, Miss? Oh, young Bennett. He was hurt, but got better of it."

Struck by a sudden possibility, Lucy asked, "Mr. Tim Bennett isn't in Newport, is he?"

The ferryman pushed back his cap, momentarily explored thin and greasy gray hair. "Well now, Mistress, he was. But I heard tell he's gone to sea."

"Gone!" The cold shot up from Lucy's feet, freezing her heart.

"Yep. Gol-durned idjit enrolled with Admiral Esek Hopkins and hez sailed for Philadelphy. Shake a leg there, Jed, wind's set to back agin."

Lucy sat down heavily on a bench. "You—mean Mr. Bennett has—left—Newport?"

The ferryman regarded her uneasily. "Why yes, Mistress. I guess so. The Congress is getting together a fleet. Being as there's no folks can hold a candle to us on the sea, they been 'listing officers and men all up and down the Bay. Now, Mistress, if you'll shift over to—"

"I—I'm not going." Lucy's voice was a hollow wail, like the cry of a seagull lost in a fog.

Young Jed beamed, flailed his arms. "Never mind, Pa. I 'most can smell Ma's fish cakes already."

BOOK II

☆ ☆ ☆

SOUTHERN WATERS

PART I—THE FLEET OF THE
UNITED COLONIES

I

THE NEW FLAG

THE day was cold and raw. A stiff breeze from the northwest was straightening flags set to staffs over in Philadelphia. Bunting snapped also above six vessels of varying tonnage which, set apart from a disorderly huddle of merchantmen, rode to their moorings. Cakes of ice and dingy fields of drowned snow, moving sluggishly out on the tide bumped and rasped along their sides.

At the foot of Walnut Street sounded cheering and strains of martial music. Unexpectedly, the famous Christ Church chimes commenced to strike a spirited tune. Perceptible to a knot of officers gathered on the quarterdeck of the Continental cruiser, *Alfred,* was a flashing of bayonets beyond the merchantmen tied up along Front Street.

"Um, the Committee seems to have turned out some militia," observed Captain Biddle. "Those horsemen in brown and white will be from the City Troop.

"Best thing they do is to parade," he sniffed. Followed by the uneasy glances of his fellow captains, he took a quick turn down the quarterdeck.

They were suspicious of him, Biddle guessed, because he, alone of the new corps captains, had ever held a commission aboard a regular man-o'-war. Other counts against him were that these New Englanders suspected him as a Philadelphian; that his new uniform really fitted. He thought it well conceived; blue with a stand-up collar, cuffs slashed in red, waistcoat of the same color. His blue breeches were close-cut about the knee. He yearned for more of a calf with which to fill his white silk stockings.

As a battery downstream commenced to fire minute guns in honor of the occasion, Biddle's bright blue eyes carefully appraised his fellow captains. They stood bunched, watching a barge festooned with yellow and blue bunting come rowing out through the floating ice.

"Waal, I'd say it's quite a to-do we're causing." The flat nasal accents of Captain Saltonstall came down wind. "Hearken to those church bells and to the gunpowder them spendthrifts are wasting in salutes. Yessir, quite a to-do, I'd say, and all over nothin'."

Abraham Whipple, commander of the *Columbus,* snorted through an immensely long nose. His round face was always so pink, scrubbed so painfully clean, Biddle figured the old privateersman must rise in the night to polish it. He had immensely thick legs and a round little stomach.

"To-do over nothing?" he chuckled. "You ain't by any chance referring to old Hop?"

"Hope the old boy is fit to walk," Saltonstall grunted and sucked air through big yellowish teeth. "I watched him lower away nine bottles of Oporto last night, with stunsails set."

"He can carry it and then some."

A sound seaman, Whipple, mused the Philadelphian, even if he was a Rhode Islander. Having been Commodore of the Rhode Island Navy, maybe he wouldn't relish taking orders from a rival ex-privateersman like Esek Hopkins?

For all his religious mania—Whipple held divine services twice a day—he was a hard worker. The way he kept drilling his gun crews should have set an example to "Sailor Tom" Hazard and some others.

All they'd say was, "Time for drill is when we get to sea." As if a decent gun crew could be trained in a week or ten days!

Meditatively, Biddle ran an eye over a double file of marines lined up on the windward side of the flagship's quarterdeck. Alone among the newly assembled crews, they seemed to possess some inkling of their duties. Probably because, to a man, they were trained ex-soldiers and hand picked.

Yes sir, in their bright green tunics, white lapels, cuffs and breeches and crossbelts, the marine detail yonder made a pretty showing—even if some of them did slouch shamelessly and furtively chew tobacco. Showed what the Corps might come to be like in time. Right now, these sixteen marines were about the only uniformed enlisted men in the whole Continental Navy.

"Thank God, old Hop's sober," Saltonstall sniffed. "He must have been fearful of what the Marine Committee might say."

Lieutenant Hoysted Hacker turned a pudgy face.

"I've noticed there's nothin' backward about some o' *their* drinking!" He winked ponderously at Whipple then blew his nose with his fingers and wiped them on his coat tail.

A fresh series of gray-white smoke puffs spurted out over the water as the battery on Wind Mill Island joined in the celebration.

Silently, Captain Nicholas Biddle counted the interval between salutes. Um, very ragged fire. Sometimes four seconds, sometimes ten elapsed between shots. Should have been six seconds—no more, no less.

Twenty, twenty-one. By God, the Committee must have granted this old privateersman the salute due a full admiral. How *that* would make the Royal Navy laugh!

Captain Biddle wished he were surer in his mind concerning Esek Hopkins. For all that was said, the Rhode Islander possessed many admirable qualities and he knew all there was to know about seamanship.

That heavy undershot jaw of his bespoke determination, unfortunately tempered with a rare obstinacy. Once Esek Hopkins got his back up over a point it required the efforts of the Twelve Apostles plus the Seven Devils to get it down again.

No one could truthfully say that the new admiral wasn't a capable judge of men—and a worker. Day and night he entreated, bullied and bluffed to secure for his heterogeneous little squadron the best available supplies. To date he appeared to be one of the few men outside of John Adams, Stephen Hopkins, and Christopher Gadsden who intended the United Colonies to have a real navy.

Best of all was the fact that Esek Hopkins exhibited fear of neither man, God, nor the devil. These were the qualities, Biddle silently de-

STARS ON THE SEA

cided, which had caused his appointment. His brother, Stephen Hopkins of the Committee, would certainly see to it that the new admiral
continued to enjoy the Marine Committee's unqualified support.

A particularly icy gust beat over the group of captains. Whipple
and Saltonstall swung their arms briskly in the pale sunshine. Captain Hazard, of the *Providence,* in seeking shelter, tripped over his
sword so awkwardly that Nicholas Biddle, ex-midshipman of His
Britannic Majesty's Navy, winced.

"Stab me if we don't act more like a pack of tailors than naval
officers!" Chilled, he took a turn up the quarterdeck, noting with
sharp disapproval that the flagship's crew had been permitted to loaf
all over the deck and among the guns.

Near the color halyard, he came upon the *Alfred's* first lieutenant.
This curious individual was waiting, holding a square bunting tucked
under one of his preternaturally long arms. As his senior drew near,
short, dark-haired Lieutenant Jones stiffened to attention.

"Well, Mr. Jones," Biddle smiled, "before long our Commodore
will have taken official command."

"Yes, sir."

"Pray stand at ease, Mr. Jones. We shall have to set the others an
example soon enough."

From their first meeting, young Captain Nicholas Biddle and Flag
Lieutenant John Paul Jones had got on. Perhaps it was because they
both were so terribly eager to put to sea, to begin swapping broadsides with the Royal Navy.

Lieutenant Jones' gaunt, lonesome-looking features relaxed. Though
he stood barely five and a half feet tall, he gave the impression of
being much bigger. Perhaps his broad shoulders and powerful build
created the illusion. The *Alfred's* lieutenant's gray eyes were sharp
and his sandy hair was drawn back tight from a high, intelligent
forehead. His face was dominated by a pointed nose. When Jones
spoke it was with a faint Scottish accent.

"And when, sir, may we hope to put to sea?"

"At the end of this week," Biddle told him and kept one eye on
the fast-approaching barge. "Unless Hazard and his sort can manu-

facture fresh arguments for a delay."

Lieutenant John Paul Jones tightened perpetually compressed lips.

"I would to God, sir, the Committee would let the Admiral take the sea with just you, sir, young Hopkins, and me."

It was typical of conditions, Biddle thought, that some of the officers referred to Hopkins as "the Admiral"; some as "General." A majority however called him "Commander" or "Commodore."

Curiously enough Hopkins, himself, could not, or would not, make a ruling on the point.

"Aye, Mr. Jones, I wish your suggestion were feasible." His voice came alive. "We might make prizes of vessels better than these wretched merchantmen we are now condemned to cruise in."

Contemptuously, his gaze sought the *Columbus,* a big tub of a merchantman with a high, old-fashioned poop and bows round and bluff as any barmaid's.

Anchored just beyond her lay the *Andrew Dorea,* his own command. In her day she might have been fast, but she was old now and her mainmast was none too sound. Some sections of her planking were rotted, too. In the least bit of a sea, the treenails securing it, it had a distressing habit of fetching loose.

The *Cabot,* commanded by John B. Hopkins, the Commodore's son, wouldn't have been a bad little brig if only she didn't persist in carrying a starboard helm, no matter what corrections the carpenters attempted. Young Hopkins, however, was fast learning to handle his cranky command.

Was it pure chance that he, aged twenty-five, John Hopkins but little older, and young Mr. Jones here, should all be of nearly the same opinion on so many points? Biddle thought not. The oldsters seemed hopelessly cautious and "sot" in their ways.

Was there anything to a prevalent rumor that, down in Tobago, Jones had killed a seaman in a burst of passion and had had to run to keep from hanging?

"I take it you are going to hoist that flag the Committee sent us?" the Philadelphian inquired.

"Aye, sir, but I don't relish the prospect." Jones cast a contemptuous glance at the bunting he had placed beside the binnacle.

Captain Saltonstall turned a long horse-face over his shoulder and bawled, "Hey, Nick! Better come along. Them barges is getting tolerable close now. Mr. Jones, just you send the fellers to their posts."

Biddle choked. Picture the captain of a British frigate hailing a fellow captain by his nickname, referring to his crew as "the fellers"!

"Fall in. Smartly now!" Captain Nicholas, in command of all the marines in the fleet, appeared. Briskly he strode down the green and white ranks, straightening a lapel here, directing a legging button to be secured there.

When he halted to adjust the black leather stock of one of his men, a shout of raucous laughter rose from the disorderly throng of seamen milling about amidships.

"Hey, boys! Look at that soljer's stock! It ain't linen at all. It's only black leather. Haw! Haw! Look at the purty leather necks!" Captain Saltonstall strode to the break of his quarterdeck and, in thundering tones, ordered all the men to their posts.

His quartermaster raised a signal flag and, raggedly, the *Alfred's* broadside guns were run out amid a deep rumbling of carriage wheels and a rattling of tackle blocks.

Once the barge of honor came grinding alongside, Captain Biddle could recognize several members of the Marine Committee: Silas Deane with his long Yankee face and wintry eyes; old Stephen Hopkins, in his seventies but still full of energy; the Southerners, Christopher Gadsden, Joe Hewes and Lighthorse Harry Lee; John Adams looked sick, anyhow he was blue-lipped with the cold.

Captain Saltonstall reset an old French sword dangling from his well-filled belt, glanced uneasily about. "Well now, I guess we better stand by the gangway, boys."

Once the barge sweeps had been raised to the perpendicular, Captain Saltonstall flapped his hand at a marine trumpeter who began a series of flourishes.

Today, Esek Hopkins, Commander-in-Chief of the Continental Navy, cut a fine figure. His powerful jaws were pink from a recent shave, his large dark eyes were clear and full of life, his uniform brave with flat yellow buttons, and his scarlet waistcoat was neat and well cut.

When the new Commodore gained the head of the ladder, Biddle caught his breath. Would Esek Hopkins remember to salute the quarterdeck? He had taken three full steps before he remembered the custom.

One by one, members of the Marine Committee of the Continental Congress came puffing up from the barge, mostly clad in black. Next to the last to appear was John B. Hopkins, the Commodore's son.

A sibilant gasp rose from amidships. At the head of the gangway was standing a minister, complete with cap, bands and prayer book.

"It's never a bit of luck we'll meet with this cruise!" predicted a hoarse undertone.

No one smiled. Every seafaring man in America knew that, next to having a rabbit or a woman aboard, there was no worse luck than finding a minister on his ship.

"Now this is what I call a real fine turn-out," Hopkins beamed. "Your boys have done well." Then recalling his dignity, he straightened and called out, "Mr. Jones, you may hoist the new flag."

Musket barrels flashed when the marines presented arms. Reluctantly, the crew pulled off their caps. The Marine Committee followed suit and freshly powdered wigs gleamed in the sunlight. The ship captains managed a weird assortment of salutes.

"Hoist away!" Hopkins called. A gun roared—another—another. Bitter-smelling gray smoke whipped across the quarterdeck. The other ships, too, began saluting that ensign climbing to the *Alfred's* signal yard. Biddle saw that it was of a glaring yellow, that on it coiled the lively representation of a rattlesnake bearing thirteen rattles. Unevenly stitched across the ensign was the motto, "Don't tread on me!"

"Gentlemen," John Adams cried in clear carrying tones, "the Marine Committee does now declare these vessels commissioned in the Naval Service of the United Colonies!"

2

LIBERTY ISLAND

AMID cheers and to the great relief of God-fearing folk in Philadelphia, the fleet of the United Colonies on January 17, 1776, dropped down the Delaware and re-anchored off Liberty Island only a few miles downstream. The disappointment of those who had expected that the fleet finally was putting to sea was bitter.

"I warned you so," Higsby snarled at Tim. "These vessels ain't never goin' out an' fight the Britainers. Hell's roaring bells! I'm goin' to desert. Other day a feller told me they's some fine partisan skirmishin' fit to break out in the Carolina back country."

"You're crazy," Tim told him amiably.

"No, I ain't neither. He says the Scotchmen that settled along the frontiers are declarin' for the King." Higsby spat into a box of sand.

"Maybe," Tim sighed. "You can't blame the Commodore for not putting to sea with half his crew rotten with the pox. Surgeon reports that half the *Cabot's* crew are dying."

One big advantage Tim found in serving aboard a flagship was that he learned much of what was in the wind and so could discount at their true value most of the wild rumors in circulation.

For instance, some men claimed that the fleet would soon sail north to harry British transports on their way to Massachusetts Bay; other officers swore just as positively that the squadron would be ordered to strike at the British base at Halifax.

A red-headed sergeant of marines occupying a desk opposite Tim's emitted a brassy snort.

"They are all addled—*ad unguem*—to a nicety, one might say." To Tim's astonishment, the marine spoke in a precise, educated voice. "I'll venture that as soon as we're fit for sea, the Congress will, *dextro tempore,* order us to attack the squadron under the noble-spirited Lord of Dunmore.

"It appears that damned old pirate is not satisfied with burning Norfolk flat. Like the heathen, he rages up and down Chesapeake Bay, and every week no end of fine plantations go up in smoke."

Higsby's long, leather-hued features lit. "You really figger we will git to lock horns with the Britainers?"

The marine sergeant nodded, "*Cadit quaestro,* we must, or the noble lord will treat other towns as he did Norfolk."

Tim studied the sergeant with greater care. He liked the fellow's perpetually amused expression, red hair, cultured voice and thoughtful brown eyes. "You've just come aboard?"

"Transferred from the *Cabot, laus Deo,*" the sergeant said feelingly. "The stink aboard would tempt a polecat to vomit."

Higsby asked, "Say, Mister, what force has this here Lord Dunmore?"

"At last report, only a scratch fleet much resembling this," the sergeant replied. "If we exhibit a modicum of vigor we should take them."

Higsby, standing guard before the wardroom door, grounded his rifle and crossed hands over its muzzle.

"Say, Mister, anything in this yarn 'bout two more war boats joinin' us?"

"They won't amount to much. *Experto credite,* perhaps."

The ranger's straight black brows met. "Say, might that lingo be Iroquois?"

The sergeant chuckled. "Scarcely. Tell me, how does one say 'one learns by experience' in Shawnee?"

"*O gone-owe-shesk,*" came Higsby's prompt translation. He still regarded the N. C. O. with mistrust. "I put you a question which you ain't seen fit to answer yet. Is that Huron you been talkin'?"

Tim laughed. "No, Sam, it's just Latin. Where do you hail from, Sergeant?"

The marine sergeant's smile faded as he said, "Nantucket. You behold Nathaniel Coffin, scapegrace son of a Loyalist family. Late lieutenant in Colonel William Prescott's Regiment of the Massachusetts Line."

Unguardedly Tim said, "I was at the Siege, too. Hitchcock's Rhode Island Regiment."

A wicked spark gleamed in Sergeant Coffin's eye. "And how did you find the fine weather in Roxbury?"

Tim flushed. "Wasn't our fault we didn't get to fight over on Breed's Hill." Hurriedly he asked, "Where did they enlist you marines?"

Nat Coffin's laughter filled the whole cramped, dark wardroom. "At the Tun Tavern on King Street in Philadelphia, *mirabile dictu*. Its owner, Robbie Mullan, is also a captain of this noble Corps. You should see our worthy publican pull a tunic on over his apron and swear in a recruit. Does an elegant job of swearing. He's such an all-wool patriot he stands all recruits to a glass of grog on the house."

The sergeant winked, "There, Mr. Bennett, is what I call a man of parts. How many of we poor wights can make this war both a patriotic, and paying, proposition?"

The sergeant stood up, his red head brushing the deck beams. "You are from Providence, I take it."

"No, from further down—Conanicut. Britishers burned us out middle of last month."

"A sorry business this town-burning. Up in Providence I met the poor devil of a girl whose people got burnt out in Falmouth. Those arrant asses in the Ministry must soon give up the practice," Coffin said seriously. "Only serves to outrage the Colonies into further obstinacy."

He sighed, "The British got off scot-free at Conanicut, I presume?"

"Not quite, Mister, not quite. Here, look at these." Higsby fumbled in his warbag and presently flung three pewter cap plates onto the sergeant's desk. "These here don't touch skelps fer sho proof."

His eyes rested steadily on the sergeant's. "I warn't allowed to lift no hair, so I reckon you'll just have to credit me on these. I ain't lyin', honest."

Sergeant Coffin selected a plate, saw that it was silvered and stamped with a foul anchor and the motto: *Per Terram, Per Mare.*

"Very conclusive evidence, I call it. One suspects that the British give few of these away."

Higsby looked relieved; he sure would have made a swipe at that soljer fellow if he had disbelieved. "This here's my tally fer an officer."

From where he stood, Tim could see the grip and guard of a dress sword. The plate was of heavy gold and delicately engraved in elegant script with the name, "Jno. St. Clair."

"A tidy bit of engraving," observed Coffin, running fingers over the cool ivory of a guard which was carved in the shape of a young mermaid.

"How do you take to the sea, Mr. Higsby?"

Tim laughed, "Ask rather what the sea takes from Sam and you've hit the nail on the head!"

Higsby spat. "Anybody who'd go to sea fer pleasure, sez I, would go to hell fer a pastime."

The smallpox did not diminish, in fact became so rife and virulent that the pestilential fleet was instructed to drop 'way downstream to Reedy Island. There, a sudden freeze imprisoned all six ships in two feet of ice.

The guns lay idle under their canvas housings with snow piled bulwark-high between their carriages. Below decks, the atmosphere was fetid, stifling; outside the wind stung like a knife blade.

Gradually, the perpetual fear of infection, the meager inferior food and biting weather began to tell.

Every night more men crawled out of gun ports and walked ashore over the ice, seldom to be recaptured. When the sick died in alarming numbers, their bodies were pitched overside to lie on the ice, shrouded in snow and nothing else.

The captains squabbled with increasing bitterness over such medicines and supplies as did reach the impotent squadron. Hopkins made heroic efforts, but could accomplish little.

Everybody was glad when a violent, unseasonable thaw rotted the ice and sank the bodies. Great fields of ice began drifting off down the Delaware to the Atlantic.

A dispatch boat dropped down from Philadelphia and a messenger delivered to Esek Hopkins a heavily-sealed envelope. Once he had read its contents, the Commodore ordered his captains to report immediately.

They came, ready with complaints, suspicious and apprehensive. Even when the Commodore told them he had good news, their scowls did not disappear.

"We're going to sea, I allow?" Whipple demanded at length.

The Commodore flourished a fat envelope dotted with scarlet seals. "Aye, that we are. But there's still better intelligence: off Cape Henlopen we will rendezvous with two more Continental men-o'-war."

Hoysted Hacker's flat voice demanded, "Read us the orders, will you, Hop?"

"Don't address Pa like that!" young Hopkins glared.

"I am sorry, Hacker," Hopkins explained. "But these here instructions are confidential."

Captain Biddle drew himself up, trying to overlook the fact that Hopkins had draped an old plaid shawl over his tunic. "Sir, are you at least permitted to inform us whether we sail to engage the enemy?"

Esek Hopkins scratched his head, looked troubled. "Well now, Nick—er, Captain Biddle, I'd tell you if I knew. You see, my final orders must remain sealed 'til we get to sea.

"Now I want you all to get back to your vessels and set your weakest men ashore. Fill your water casks. And say, it's been so confounded damp with this thaw you had better sift your powder. That's all for now."

"Do we cruise North or South?" Saltonstall's nasal accents inquired. "You can at least trust us with that, or won't you?"

Hopkins hesitated, puffed out his cheeks and sent a deep breath floating up the grimy deck beams.

"I shouldn't rightly answer that, but I guess, well, maybe there's no harm in your knowing that we have been ordered southwards."

3

CAPE HENLOPEN

BEYOND the gray-white dunes of Cape Henlopen, the Atlantic raged under the lash of a frigid nor'easter.

Three days after a gale had chased Esek Hopkins' six vessels to shelter behind the Cape, numbed and sea-bitten look-outs in the rigging could discern endless battalions of yeasty combers still racing off to the southward.

At dawn of the second day the *Wasp* and the *Fly,* the additional men-o'-war expected from Baltimore, came beating down Chesapeake Bay to join the salt-streaked squadron out of Philadelphia.

When he saw these vessels, a schooner and a single-masted sloop, break out recognition signals and let go their hooks to windward, Hopkins indulged in a blast of sulphurous profanity. Whipple's pink horse face took on an air of pained resignation.

"So them's your fine big sloops from Maryland?" he growled.

"And the Committee promised me two big brigs!" Hopkins raged, his neck swollen thick with anger. "Look at 'em. Why those god-dammed wherries ain't eighty feet overall. They're just overgrown pilot boats. Takes a Congressman's imagination to name such craft men-o'-war."

Nicholas Biddle was aghast. In the British service such craft would have been designated as tenders.

Tim thought that even to sail in such cockleshells required courage. Nat Coffin laughed, quoted some Latin tag about sending boys to do the work of men.

When Hacker and Alexander beheld their new commands, they turned green as a marine's tunic.

Thus the American squadron sawed at its anchor cables, kept look-outs freezing aloft lest Lord Dunmore's squadron come sweeping down the Chesapeake with guns run out and in firm possession of the weather gauge.

Tim, penning requisitions at Lieutenant Grinnell's elbow, could hear the Commodore's heavy tread as he marched up and down his cabin. He was talking to himself—positive proof that he was perturbed. Pretty soon Hopkins appeared in the door, a paper in his hand.

"Pray step in here a moment, Mr. Bennett."

Once Tim obeyed, Hopkins closed the door. Said he, "Being a civilian clark, you ain't under discipline, and I figger you enjoy a fair share of sense, Mr. Bennett. Therefore, I want you to render me an opinion on what this means."

Hopkins thrust towards him a single sheet of paper.

With the shrieking of the gale through the rigging in his ears, Tim read:

To Esek Hopkins, Esquire,
Commander-in-Chief of the Fleet of the United Colonies.

Sir: The United Colonies directed by principles of just and necessary preservation against the oppressive and cruel system of the British Administration whose violent and hostile proceedings by sea and land against these unoffending colonies, have rendered it an indispensible duty to God, their country, and posterity to prevent by all means in their power the ravage, desolation and ruin that is intended to be fixed on North America.

As a part and a most important part of defence, the Continental Congress have judged it necessary to fit out several armed vessels which they have put under your command having the strongest reliance on your virtuous attachment to the great cause of America, and that by your valour, skill and diligence, seconded by the officers and men under your command our unnatural enemies may meet with all possible distress on the sea.

For that purpose you are instructed with the utmost diligence to proceed with the said fleet to sea and if the winds and weather will possibly admit of it to proceed directly for Chesapeak Bay in Virginia and when nearly arrived there you will send forward a small swift sailing vessel to gain intelligence of the enemies' situation and strength—

"How far have you read?" Hopkins abandoned an abstracted inspection of some pine-covered dunes visible through the great stern ports.

"To where they write, sir, about sending 'a small swift sailing vessel to gain intelligence of the enemies' situation and strength,' sir."

Hopkins blew out fleshy lips. "Mr. Bennett, the thing that perplexes me is how in blazes am I going to send a small, swift vessel dead into the wind to search the whole of Chesapeake Bay?"

"It would be difficult to sail a vessel into this gale, sir."

Hopkins, rocking to his ship's motion, looked pleased. "Go on reading."

—If by such intelligence you find that they are not greatly superior to your own you are immediately to enter the said bay search out and attack, take or destroy all the naval force of our enemies that you may find there.

If you should be so fortunate as to execute this business successfully in Virginia you are then to proceed immediately to the southward and make yourself master of such forces as the enemy may have both in North and South Carolina in such manner as you may think most prudent from the intelligence you shall receive; either by dividing your fleet or keeping it together.

Having compleated your business in the Carolinas you are without delay to proceed northward directly to Rhode Island, and attack, take and destroy all the enemies naval force that you may find there. You are also to seize and make prize of all such transport ships and other vessels as may be found carrying supplies of any kind to or any way aiding or assisting our enemies.

You will dispose of all the men you make prisoners in such manner as you may judge most safe for North America and least retard the service you are upon. If you should take any ships or other vessels that are fit to be armed and manned for the service of the United Colonies, you will make use of every method for procuring them to be thus equipped. You will also appoint proper officers for carrying this matter into execution, and to command said ships as soon as they can be made ready for the sea. For this purpose, you will apply to the several assemblies, Conventions and Committees of Safety and desire them in the name of the Congress to aid and assist you by every way and means in their power for the execution of this whole service.

Notwithstanding these particular orders, which it is hoped you will be able to execute, if bad winds or stormy weather, or any unforseen accident or disaster disable you so to do, you are then to follow such courses as your best judgment shall suggest to you as most useful to the American cause and to distress the enemy by all means in your power.

> January 5, 1776
> Stephen Hopkins
> Christopher Gadsden
> Silas Deane
> Joseph Hewes.

"Take heed of that final paragraph," Hopkins indicated it with a gnarled forefinger. "Read again what they say about 'if bad winds or stormy weather.' What do you judge was their meaning?"

Tim chose his words with care. "Why, sir, I would venture the Committee is leaving you free to decide your course."

Hopkins' big black eyes bored into Tim's face. "Damn it, don't generalize! Explain just what that would mean to you if you stood in my shoes."

"Well, sir, it means if you think you should remain in Chesapeake Bay to hunt for Lord Dunmore, all well and good. If, on the other hand, you have reason to deem such a course unsafe or impractical, why then you are at liberty to follow the course you think best."

A slow sigh, eloquent of satisfaction, escaped the Commodore as he thrust a close-cropped, wigless head out of the door and yelled, "Mr. Grinnell! Order the officer of the deck to h'ist a signal for my captains to come aboard."

Despite the ceaseless groaning of the flagship's timbers and the slosh of water in her bilges, Paymaster Lieutenant Grinnell and Tim Bennett could hear the dispute growing more acrimonious. Captain Biddle must be fast getting his dander up.

"But damn it, sir!" he was barking. "To what purpose was the squadron commissioned? To halt Britishers and Tories from ravaging our ports, or to go pleasure cruising to the Indies?"

Hopkins' voice was thick as he snapped, "Drop that sort of talk. I was sailing and fighting my own privateer whilst you were still yowling for a change of swaddling clothes. Ain't nobody can truthfully say I'm the least bit feared of hot shot or cold steel. Took seventeen prizes in the old French war."

"Naow, I allow that may be so," Whipple's nasal accents cut in. "But did anybody ever tell you, Hop, that I took twenty-six?"

"Nobody had call to, Abe. You brag about them prizes so often," Hazard's husky voice cut in. "Anyhow, where's the profit in arguing? We can't fight the British. Didn't you hear what that feller off the *Wasp* said? Dunmore's got a new frigate in his fleet."

"Frigate? What frigate?" Hacker sounded scared.

"The *Liverpool,* 28 guns."

"Hell's banging bells!" Biddle burst out. "What of it? That frigate is the only honest-to-God man-o'-war in Dunmore's squadron. What is the *Otter?* A little two-by-four brig. What's the *Kingfisher?* Just a small half-arse sloop no bigger than the *Katy—Providence,* I mean. And the *Dunmore?* An old converted merchantman, known to be in worse shape than the *Andrew Dorea.* Of course, we can fight Dunmore. As I've said before, that's what we put to sea to do!"

"Pipe down," Alexander rasped. "You're young and hot-headed. Besides, I don't recall the Commodore having invited your opinion."

"Aye, but Captain Biddle's is a voice that ought to be harked to." For the first time, Flag-Lieutenant Jones' harsh and penetrating accents entered the dispute.

"The men-o'-war in a real navy cruise to engage and destroy the enemy." His voice grew more edged. "Commodore, if ye'll grant me the choice of three vessels, I will undertake tae smash Dunmore."

"But I mind nobody required *your* opinion, either," Hopkins shouted, then hammered on the table. "Listen, all of you! By God, listen to me or I'll declare you insubordinate."

He paused, breathing so hard the two men in the outer cabin could hear him.

"There's two views of this question. First, the Congress has given us a lot of fine ships—"

"Rotten old tubs, you mean," someone corrected.

"—They went to a lot of expense to equip us. What will the Marine

Committee say if we get into a battle and right away get their vessels smashed up? Remember, these are the only men-o'-war the Congress has."

Silence greeted this observation.

"I judge we all can guess what would follow. We'll likely be called to account. We might get off, but we stand a better chance of getting broke if the ships are lost or damaged bad."

The Commodore hacked, blew his nose before he resumed. "Here is another point. We still have the pox aboard, nor have we yet got our gun crews in hand."

"Mine are," Biddle announced firmly.

"So are mine," Whipple cut in. "Trouble with you, Hop, is that you're all for making a big haul without risking much. That was your way of privateering. And I've heard an adage which says some critters never do change their spots."

"Hold your tongue, Abraham," Esek Hopkins' voice quivered. "By God, I am Commander-in-Chief of this fleet, don't any of you ever forget it! Here, listen to this paragraph out of my orders:

" '—Notwithstanding these particular orders, which it is hoped you will be able to execute, if *bad winds or stormy weather—*'

"Do you mark that? 'Stormy weather.' What do you call this?" He stopped talking, permitted them to hear the wind keening through the shrouds, the waves tumbling along the sides, the ice bumping.

"Why if it blows any harder, we mayn't even be able to keep this anchorage. How can we beat up the Bay in the teeth of a nor'easter? Suppose we came across the British? They would almost certainly have the weather gauge of us."

He paused. The officers coughed, scraped their feet, muttered.

"Here's the rest of that instruction.

'You are then *to follow such courses as your best judgment shall suggest* to you as most useful to the American cause.' "

"The old boy's got them there, seems if," Lieutenant Grinnell murmured, then pursed lips into a soundless whistle and stared unseeingly at the skylight.

Hopkins' voice had become metallic, rasping, "Won't do for any of you to imagine that I fear a fight. I don't. But I—I've got to take care. Any mistakes that are made will be blamed on me."

"But, sir," Biddle objected stubbornly, "I still say the Congress expects us to fight."

John Paul Jones' voice bit like caustic into the dispute. "Gentlemen, I ha'e observed more than one British frigate in action. Take my word for it, most o' their gunners couldna' hit a bar-rn if they were locked inside of it! Give me the chance and I'll prove it!"

"Silence!" Hopkins bellowed. "Now here's something I bet none of you has thought of."

A surprised silence ensued.

"We all know how hard put the Congress is to collect the powder, naval supplies and cannons for this new fleet that's a-building."

"That is true enough," Saltonstall admitted. "What of that?"

Hopkins said impressively, "It is my considered opinion that we will best serve the Committee if we cruise to capture such supplies."

"That makes sense," Alexander instantly agreed. "If we prove we can be careful of the government's property, we'll most likely get to command those new honest-to-God warships when they are ready. Can't you see that?"

"All I see, Captain Alexander," came Biddle's cold reply, "is that you stand against attacking Dunmore."

"Not if the Commodore so orders," came the crafty retort. "I'll tackle a stack of bobcats bare-handed, if it's orders."

Hopkins asked, "Well, Abe, what's your notion?"

"I'd fight," Whipple stated bluntly. "Barring the *Liverpool,* old Dunmore ain't to be feared. And—" the ex-privateersman's voice took on a meditative quality—"I figger he will likely have aboard most of the plunder he stole from them rich Virginny plantations."

"Well, now, do tell!" Saltonstall ejaculated. "I hadn't thought of that, maybe we had better look for him."

Whipple said slowly, "I guess it's our duty to go after Dunmore."

Tim heard Hopkins chuckle deep in his throat. "Hold on, I ain't done yet about that cruise south for supplies. We could lay siege to

New Providence in the Bahamas with even chances of success."

"But there's a big fort there," Hacker protested in deep agitation, "and another smaller one. I have seen them. So has Lieutenant Weaver."

"I allow it may mean a stiff fight," Hopkins said steadily, "but we should capture the place. The Congress will be vastly pleased with a rich haul of canvas, cannon, and powder. How many of you favor staying in this bay and hunting for the British?"

Three voices called, "Aye."

Grinnell winked, "Will you take a wager on where we go?"

Before Tim could reply, the Commodore boomed, "Without counting my vote, we are five to three for attack on New Providence. Therefore, gentlemen, so soon as this gale diminishes, we will set a course for the Bahamas. My orders will reach you before sundown, and mind you obey them to the letter! That means you too, Abe Whipple, you're all of an itch to get off by yourself."

Once the captains had gone away, Esek Hopkins summoned Tim.

"I want eight copies of this order made, fast as you can write. One is to be delivered to each captain. Do it yourself and mind you get a receipt! I don't want any of 'em claiming they didn't receive my orders."

Between sips of a Jamaica rum toddy, Esek Hopkins dictated:

"Sir:
You are hereby ordered to keep Company with me if possible, and truly observe the Signals given by the Ship I am in—but in case you should be Separated in a gale of wind or otherwise, you then are to use all possible means to join the Fleet as soon as possible, but if you cannot in four days after you leave the Fleet, you are to make the best of your way to the Southern part of Abacco (one of the Bahama Islands) and there wait for the Fleet fourteen days—if the Fleet does not join you in that time, you are to cruise in such places as you think will most annoy the Enemy and you are to send into Port for Tryal, all British vessels or property or other vessels with any supplies for the Ministerial Forces, who you may make yourself Master of to such places as you may think best within the United Colonies.

In case you are in very great danger of being taken you are to destroy these orders and your signals.

Esek Hopkins
Commr in Chief."

4

THE STORM

Two DAYS out of Cape Henlopen a nor'easter pounced on the straggling squadron with a whoop and a roar. Soon spindrift, whipped from boiling combers, raised a mist denser than fog. In frantic haste sailing masters in the squadron reduced canvas to trysails and storm jibs. The seas made up in terrifying majesty until they rose enough completely to conceal in their troughs the smaller vessels.

Like endless lines of assaulting troops, waves cascaded over the *Alfred's* bow and smothered her fo'c's'l' in a terrific welter of yeasty foam. The guns tugged and strained at their tackles, eager as fierce beasts to be free. Captain Saltonstall knew this phase of the business at least, so none of them broke loose.

Tim, less sickened than most of the ship's company, clung to the main shrouds and anxiously watched the little *Wasp's* painful struggles.

He wondered how Higsby and Nat Coffin were making out on the schooner. Too bad they'd been transferred. Why this sudden shift? The only explanation he found was that Esek Hopkins must be developing a secret plan. It was impossible to guess what this might be because the Commodore had latterly grown chary of conversation.

Just as the gale was rising, Captain William Stone in the *Hornet* had, without the least explanation, ignored all signals from the *Alfred* and gone veering off to the westward. This course he maintained until his topsails vanished over the horizon.

"I'll see that goddam, slab-sided, lobster-potter broke for this!" Hopkins had flown into such a fine fury that nobody dared address him. "I know what he's up to. Figures to pull a brave showing before the Committee by prizing merchantmen in the Florida channel. So help my guts, I'll wring his damned neck once I come up with him."

Yellow-green, and holding closed his oiled leather coat, Grinnell staggered over the streaming deck to Tim. Once he'd relieved himself into the scuppers, the paymaster wiped his face on his sleeve.

"It's just plain hell below decks. Some of those swabs in the crew have got drunk. They're fighting and screaming like lunatics!"

Tim nodded, but kept his attention on the *Wasp*. She seemed to be making no better going of it. The eighty-ton schooner would drive her bowsprit sky high, then falter and fall with a squattering smack to bury her whole bow in the sea.

"Looks bad," Grinnell bellowed, "when they send four men to her tiller. Lay you ten shillings she don't last another hour!"

The flying mist thinned momentarily and her freshly coppered bottom showed dull red whenever she gave an agonized roll.

Poor Higsby! Tim suspected the frontiersman was cursing the day of his birth.

Scattered far and wide, the balance of the squadron was reduced to dark smudges barely visible against this turbulent gray background. The *Alfred* gave such an especially violent plunge that all her yards rattled and swayed against their parrels. A stay parted, with the report of a musket. Its end snapped like the lash of a drover's whip.

When she steadied, Tim looked for the *Wasp* again, was just in time to watch her vanish into the heart of a howling squall. *God!* Where was she? Now, now! His breath stopped. She must reappear. No sign of the little schooner.

No sign! Undoubtedly, the *Wasp* had foundered. Tim felt as if a door had been opened letting this icy blast into his soul. Had he also been ordered into the *Wasp,* there would be no arming of the *Narragansett.*

"This—worse," Grinnell's words came raggedly through the bellowing wind. "None—see—land—again."

Tim was too appalled to answer. It seemed hardly possible that Sam Higsby was gone. Such a vital person should die only in battle. Studious, philosophical young Coffin must be drowned, too.

Swinging and swaying beside bulwarks, he found himself wondering whether this same gale might blow in Newport? If so, it would have carried snow. What was Lucy Percival— No. Mustn't think of Lucy!

But he couldn't help himself.

By rights they should be married now and tasting those ecstasies which, with such difficulty, they had denied themselves. Why should the world have gone so dismally, completely askew?

His personal disaster had, of course, stemmed from the British raid. Maybe he was fortunate, after all. If Lucy just wasn't firm enough to contemplate the uncertainties of life it was well he knew it now.

When he remembered the way Lucy had used to look at him sometimes, so serene, so seemingly steadfast, it would never cease to amaze him that she should have deserted him without even an expression of regret or explanation. Yet, the fact of her failure was inescapable. He would, he vowed, never be so confoundedly wrong again.

The flagship rolled over, over, until her lower tier of gun-ports were buried. Crimanently! If this crank old tub didn't dive for Jones, it would be an Eighth Wonder.

Probably the Percivals would select Ira Thaxter for their spineless darling's husband. Blast Ira's bleating voice, pudgy hands and milk-and-honey ways. The devil take Ira's shrewd business sense and gaudy taste in clothes. Unless he made for the Cape of Good Hope and captured an Indiaman a privateersman could never hope to make as much money as Ira.

No more mistakes for Tim Bennett. He would be a clever privateersman and learn all he could before he put to sea. His crew must be hand-picked, his cannon would be of exactly the right weight; if he could determine what that might be. Must have a gunnery officer who knew his whole business. The *Narragansett* would make a name for herself.

5

Grand Abacco

For all the anchor lay six fathoms down, Phil Hull could see it very distinctly. It rested on a jagged pan of reddish corals. Around an exposed fluke darted a school of little fishes. Land sakes, they were marked bright as the colors on a tavern swing board back home. Other gay fishes whipped in and out of weeds and sponge beds.

It was something to learn that all the sea was not dull gray, that all coasts were not rocky and fringed with gloomy evergreens. My, that sea bottom was so beautiful he could not yet believe his eyes.

During most of his fourteen years, Phil had yearned to become a great painter. He might have, too, if Ma hadn't been left a widow, if Abner hadn't died of the flux up to the Siege of Boston and if Lucius hadn't been killed when the picaroons captured Mr. Bennett's *Patience.*

'Til the Redcoats had come to Conanicut, him and Ma had been able to make out—what with butter from the two cows. Ma was smart about chickens, everybody admitted it. She knew how to mix a feed that would keep her hens laying 'most all winter long. Poor Ma. She hadn't fought that lung-fever much. Phil judged she'd been just too tired and sorrowful.

Maybe when this war was over, he could go to Boston and find some artist who'd give him drawing lessons. Now, more surely than ever, he felt he could become a famous artist—he would, even if he had to study a whole year.

Phil rolled over onto his back, let the sun warm his lean belly.

All the hands aboard the *Columbus* were getting sunburnt, and losing the gaunt look they had brought down with them from the North.

When some seamen stripped to the waist, it was a real treat. Some weird and amazing tattooings came to light. Some ugly scars, too. Across the shoulders of a couple of English prisoners who had volunteered for the cruise ran a peculiar, shiny, criss-cross pattern of weals. The sailing master declared that only a navy "cat" could inflict such.

Phil closed his eyes, sighed luxuriously. This life wasn't so bad after all. No more splitting kindling or churning butter, or whittling cheese presses and butter stamps. No more milking, hoeing and haymaking.

It was the news of Abner's death that had hit Ma all of a heap. Abner had been big and strong and, stones or no stones, could drive a furrow straight as any ruler mark. Not that Ma had grieved openly, she wasn't that sort. But she'd taken to sitting before the fire—just staring into space.

Lying there between the Number One and Two guns of the starboard battery, Phil tried to remember all an old Pequot had taught him about mixing colors. Gall wood or scrub oak bark made black; sumac berries gave you purple; and if you needed green, you boiled goldenrod blossoms. Pokeberry juice yielded a fine rich red and he could get an elegant magenta by stewing lichens. Lucky an artist didn't have to "set" his colors with fresh chamber-pot lye, like the women did when they were dyeing homespun.

When the Lobster-backs had burnt the house and barn and had driven away the stock, the Widow Hull had sort of crumpled up.

He guessed Uncle Joshua might have taken him, but his uncle was what the neighbors called "a hard milker."

Yessirree, with this hot sun on him, he felt a sight better than he had three days back when, one by one, the four largest vessels in the squadron had limped into the shelter of Grand Abacco Island.

Grand Abacco had proved to be the kind of tropic island the seamen talked about when they came home—wide, sandy beaches edged with forests of pitch pine. Yesterday, when it had been his turn to go ashore, he had been taken aback to recognize quite a few familiar plants such as dogwood, ironwood and cedar.

Early morning was the best here; then the air was fresh and full of exciting, unfamiliar perfumes. At sundown, countless thousands of crane-like birds flew by. These strange fowls were of a lovely pink, had blunt, hooked bills and long, trailing legs. Flamingoes, the old hands called them. Apparently these birds nested on a group of low coral islands lying away off to the eastwards.

All day long pelicans and rusty black cormorants fished among the reefs and whenever a gun-crew practiced firing, familiar ducks, such as red-heads, canvas-backs, blue-bills, mallards and teal, roamed about the sky like storm-driven clouds.

It was the fish, though, which utterly fascinated Phil. He liked them all, from the playful porpoises and dolphins frolicking beyond the reefs to the tiny little fellows below. Inside the barrier reefs played schools of a beautiful silvery fish which Lieutenant Weaver of the *Cabot* called bonefish. The lieutenant had often sailed this way so knew the Bahamas from A to Izzard.

"You want to angle for them some day, Bub," he'd smiled. "It's fine fun. The Conches—local niggers, that is—use soldier crabs for bait."

Phil was learning to distinguish between a few of the species. Already he knew red snappers and dog snappers, they were emerald green with yellow bars. Also the grunts of varying color. Some were blue, others gray or yellow.

The prettiest of all was the rainbow parrot fish whose scales reflected light in every shade. The gun fish, which traveled so fast that the eye could hardly follow them, held his interest a long while.

That was a string of clowns swimming just above the anchor and yonder lay some prickly fish and puffers which, when touched, instantly swelled out like inflated balloons.

Yes, sir, Phil guessed he could spend years and years just watching the sea bottom. Trouble was that whenever he got well settled in the forechains, a drum would beat and he, along with the other powder monkeys, must skin below to the lead-lined magazine and fetch wads and buckets of powder for gun drill.

Aboard the *Andrew Dorea*, Captain Biddle began to feel he was making progress. His gun crews could raise gunports, remove tompions, and run out cannon before any of the other men-of-war could so much as cast off their gun covers.

Everybody had heaved a big sigh of relief when first the *Cabot* and then the *Fly* appeared at the rendezvous. This left missing only the *Hornet* and the *Wasp*. Nobody held out much hope that either would come in, though the *Wasp* was bigger than the *Fly*.

Consequently, the excitement became intense when, towards sundown, a schooner was sighted on the horizon. It proved to be the *Wasp*, badly battered and lacking her main topmast. The Commodore was so delighted that he ordered a salute fired when the *Wasp* dropped anchor.

Lieutenant Jones grumbled, " 'Tis a zany business to waste good powder. Unless we're uncommon lucky, the Old Man has warned all the Western Bahamas of our presence."

The *Hornet* never did make an appearance.

6

THE FIRST PRIZES

ONCE his course was determined and he found himself cruising on familiar ground, Commodore Esek Hopkins became metamorphosed. His good nature returned, and with it his initiative. On March first, he wore out three gig crews in pulling from one of his ships to the next.

That evening the squadron lined the bulwarks, speculating as to why the sea-stained *Cabot* and *Providence* should mysteriously up-anchor and vanish swiftly on a south-westerly course.

Next day they reappeared, escorting a brace of captured Bahamian vessels. They were dingy little fishing sloops quite innocent of paint and sailing under canvas that was brown as any dried oak leaf.

More consultations resulted and during most of March second, a regular flotilla of captain's gigs floated astern of the *Alfred* with crews cursing at being kept waiting in the heat. Meanwhile, sick and disabled seamen were brought off from the tents in which they had been luxuriating ashore. Everyone prayed that a fumigation of burnt sulphur and gunpowder would rid the ships of the pox for good and all.

When, with issuance of the evening grog ration, the news went about that all marines had been ordered to prepare for shore duty, a subdued excitement pervaded the sunburnt crew.

A majority of the "leather-necks," as the men persisted in calling them, were ordered into the *Cabot* and the *Providence;* the balance aboard the Bahamian fishing boats.

Tim, smoking a quiet pipe at the break of the *Alfred's* quarter-deck, sensed a gradual sobering on the part of the crew. Apparently they were beginning to give thought as to what might happen when roundshot commenced flying in two directions. Some at the foot of the mizzen were talking loud enough to be overheard.

"Goin' into an attack, shouldn't wonder," opined a boatswain's mate.

"Attack, where?" demanded a hairy fellow with a battered pug nose.

"New Providence, o' course. Ain't no other real port in these latitudes."

"What's the place like?"

"Dunno. Like most West India ports, I guess—niggers, stinks, and drinks."

"Anybody been there?" asked the pug-nosed man.

The coxswain of the Commodore's barge nodded. "I touched there back in '56. 'Twas along of Old Hop, too. We put in to careen and ship water. New Providence was a thriving little port then. I hear it's growed considerable."

"How big?"

"About five thousand people I'd venture and they've a pair of forts defending the place. One's right in town. Don't rightly know where the other lies."

"Guns?"

"Dunno."

A master gunner shoved through the suddenly silent group. "Figure they could hold out against us?"

The coxswain looked worried, "Well, Dick, even then Fort Nassau was considerable of a fortification."

Somebody yelled, "Attention!"

As Captain Saltonstall came clumping down from his quarter-deck, the gabble ceased and slow drinkers hastily gulped the remainder of their rum. In vast, seemingly endless, flocks ducks roared by in such numbers as to dull the brilliance of the sunset.

Captain Saltonstall jerked a nod. "Yew can stand easy." Fingering his long blue chin, he looked the group over before he said, "I want ten volunteers to serve in a landing party. Naow I wunt take advantage of yew so I warn all and sundry 'twill be a risky business. Those minded to go can show a hand."

Nearly all of the group raised an arm. Tim, too, held up his hand. If a prospective privateer captain kept his wits about him, he might learn something on such an expedition which might later be of use.

Saltonstall treated him to a cold stare. "You're just a damned civilian clark."

"I have soldiered at Boston, sir. I was under fire."

"So? Then how come you ain't enrolled?" He turned aside. "No, any man in this fleet who can balance accounts ain't to be risked."

By the light of battle lanterns swung in the rigging activity continued aboard the *Providence* and the *Wasp*, until late at night. Men, wakeful aboard the other men-of-war, could hear the clink of steel, the whine of heavily laden pulleys and much cursing and tramping about.

A rumor circulated that the prizes had reported a big British man-o'-war at anchor in New Providence harbor. Some were certain that the marines, supported by a picked detachment of sailors, would attempt a night attack on the forts. Others were equally positive that the entire squadron would sail into New Providence harbor and batter down the enemy by superior weight of metal.

The chief topic of speculation, however, concerned the number of guns mounted on the enemy fortifications. Were there fifty? Eighty? A hundred? Did British regulars form a part of the garrison? Or was there nothing but militia to worry over? Some wiseacres declared a whole regiment of the line was regularly stationed in Fort Nassau.

That night, Phil Hull thought about Ma and how peacefully the moon sometimes shone on the West Passage. Before he climbed into his hammock, he whispered two or three extra prayers. He wished he dared kneel. But he didn't. The first time that he'd knelt, the crew offered all sorts of obscene suggestions. Too bad he hadn't been shipped in the *Columbus*. Captain Whipple called his ship's company to prayers twice every day and three times on Sunday.

Sam Higsby, supremely happy at being picked for the landing party, whistled cheerily as he repaired to the *Wasp's* lee rail and there tested the powder issued him with his prouvette. Apparently no one was bothered about his irregular status.

It was a shame, thought Sergeant Nathaniel Coffin, that out of the squadron's total of two hundred and twenty marines, only a handful had been fitted with the Corp's undeniably effective green-and-white regimentals.

It was more than a shame, Nat mused, it was an error. When it came to uniforms the British mind was impressionable. As it was, the vast majority of Captain Nicholas' command wore white, blue, yellow, or red shirts under their cross-belts and the breeches in which they had enlisted.

As in the Army, he noted his men were talking big right now.

"Soon's the British are whipped, I'm goin' to catch me a pretty brown girl," announced Walt Remington. "Always did have a hankerin' for one."

His corporal raised a gale of laughter by yelling, "Watch out you don't catch more'n a wench!"

7

SURPRISE ATTACK

JUST AS the bells of the squadron were sounding four notes of the Middle Watch, Captain Nicholas of the First Continental Marine Battalion appeared on deck. In hushed tones he addressed the sergeant on duty.

"Your men ready, Sergeant?"

"Yes, sir." Nat Coffin left off wondering whatever could have kept that unfortunate Desire St. Clair from joining him in Philadelphia and jumped to attention.

The captain of marines ran an eye over his men. Like corpses on a battlefield they lay huddled about the deck, asleep in grotesque attitudes. Some lay propped against the cannon, some had pillowed their heads on coils of cable or on squares of canvas.

When, silent and ghostly as a shadow, one of the captured sloops came scraping alongside, Captain Nicholas turned to Coffin. "Rouse them. We leave in twenty minutes."

By the starlight, Nat made out a buck nigger in a ragged striped jersey standing beside the tiller.

"You make a mistake, Sambo," the Marine Captain was warning, "and you won't live to make another."

Nat soon deduced that Captain Nicholas was in command of this furtive expedition. Weaver, leather-faced lieutenant of the *Cabot*, was his advisor and responsible for the fifty sailors of the expedition. Weaver was reputed to know the Bahamas as the back of his hand.

Once the two fishing boats were well away from the anchorage, the pilots studied the stars for a while then began to sing softly:

"You see me, fader? Oh yes!
Tell 'em fo' me! Oh yes!

I'll ride my hoss on de battlefiel'
I'se gwine to go to Hebben in de mawnin'."

The voices faded and an answering chorus floated aft from the
other captured blacks. Faintly against the stars:

"Ride on Jesus! Ride on Jesus!
Ride on conquerin' Jesus!
I'se gwine to go to Hebben in de mawnin'."

There was barely enough wind to afford the *Wasp* and the *Providence* steerage-way but, propelled by a favoring current, they started
out on the same course as the fishing boats.

To Tim, in fuming idleness aboard the flagship, these small men-
of-war presented an unforgettable picture as smoothly, silently, they,
too, departed to meet the unpredictable fate awaiting them at New
Providence.

They must, he calculated, be leaving a good three hours later than
Captain Nicholas and his men.

Once dawn broke Commodore Hopkins ordered his admiral's
flag—thirteen alternate red and white stripes with a rattlesnake
crawling diagonally across them—run up to the *Alfred's* jack staff.

Boatswain's pipes peeped, drums rattled and voices bawled
commands throughout the squadron. Aboard the flagship, Flag-
Lieutenant Jones, and Lieutenants Seabury, Pitcher, and Maltbie ran
to their stations. John Earle, the sailing master, ordered the head sails
raised.

Wearing his second-best uniform and a weather-beaten cocked
hat, Esek Hopkins walked the windward rail of his quarterdeck.
Tim, detailed to messenger duty, was close enough to get a good
look at the old-fashioned, heavy-guarded cutlass which, in a brass-
tipped leather scabbard, swung to the Commodore's side. The weapon
was nothing at all fancy and must have seen a lot of service.

By the growing light, Tim thought he read apprehension written large across Esek Hopkins' big, mottled features.

Gloomily the commander-in-chief watched the *Cabot,* the *Fly,* the

Andrew Dorea and the *Columbus* make sail. Turning to Captain Saltonstall, he said, "I'd give a lot, Dud, to know how well those stubborn jackasses over yonder will follow my orders."

Saltonstall's threadbare shoulders answered with a shrug.

Breaking out sail after sail, the American squadron began coasting the southern shore of Grand Abacco and, as the first rays of sunlight came beating over the horizon, all five vessels broke out their rattlesnake ensigns. Garishly bright, they fluttered against the deep azure of the heavens.

Lieutenant Jones, his slash of a mouth more like an old wound scar than ever, stalked up to Tim.

"Ye ha'e my sympathy, Mr. Bennett," said he. "Had I had my way, we would both ha'e gone wi' the landing party."

Tim smiled on the acid little man. "If half the rumors one hears are to be credited, there should be action enough to satisfy even you, Mr. Jones. At least enough to baptize our flag with a whiff of gunpowder."

Lieutenant Jones' sharp features contracted as he glowered aloft. "That flag, sir, is an abomination. For my part, I shall never see why a venomous serpent should be the combatant emblem of a brave and honest folk fighting to be free. I abhor the device!"

Turning on his heel, he strode off on past the dully glinting breeches of the port battery, a peppery gamecock of a figure.

As the morning breeze freshened and stretched the squadron's canvas, the faster vessels began to forge ahead. At the end of an hour the *Andrew Dorea* and the *Columbus* had assumed a long lead, the *Cabot* came next, while the clumsy old *Alfred* lumbered far astern of all three. Only the dispatch boat, the *Fly,* crippled by her missing topmast, cruised astern of the flagship.

That Esek Hopkins was desperately uneasy, even the stupidest seaman in his crew could have seen. Now he examined through his glass an endless series of keys and islets. Then he would study the set of the *Alfred's* sails. Every so often he would pull out a big watch, study it a moment, then order the log ship to be heaved.

At length he beckoned Lieutenant Jones.

"Whipple and Biddle proceed at too great speed. Signal them to reduce canvas."

John Paul Jones ran over to the flag locker. He had been in agony these last ten minutes. A fool could have told that if the squadron kept sailing at such a rate it must raise New Providence Island long before the landing party could deliver what was hoped to prove a shattering surprise.

In response to the string of vari-colored flags that climbed the flapship's yard, the *Andrew Dorea* took in her main course, then her fore royal, but with no great eagerness.

Though the brig lost considerable speed, Tim judged she yet sliced the blue sea faster than the heavy old *Alfred*. John B. Hopkins in the *Cabot* rendered lip-service to the extent of taking in his main top-gallant, but his brig still rushed along like a frolicsome colt.

The *Columbus,* however, gave not the slightest heed to the flagship's instructions. Captain Whipple evidently intended to follow his own sweet will. When Hopkins realized that, his thick neck swelled until it bulged over his collar.

"That goddam, thick-snouted pig-head ain't paying a mite of attention."

Saltonstall's face was hard as if hewn from granite. "I reckon Abe Whipple is over-anxious to grab a lion's share of the loot and credit."

The Commodore snatched up a leather speaking trumpet and shouted for a signal musket to be fired. Snarled he, once the musket boomed, "I'll see Whipple broke for this! If that precious son of mine don't take in more sail, I'll relieve him of command.

"Mr. Jones!" he flung over his shoulder, "h'ist *Columbus'* private signal and order that insubordinate ass to heave-to. He'll botch our whole endeavor."

"It appears that not one of all those gentlemen on the *Columbus'* quarterdeck ever looks astern," Flag-Lieutenant Jones commented as the second largest American man-of-war blithely ignored his second string of signals.

Young Hopkins, apparently furious at being out-distanced, began to re-set the main top-gallant he had taken in.

When Esek Hopkins saw this he spouted blasphemies. "Tell Biddle to catch them scoundrels, fire on 'em if he has to, but *make them stop!*"

A cutter in the revenue service of His Britannic Majesty was, that morning, patrolling the western entrance to New Providence Harbor. Her commander, on sighting a big sponger running down from the North, bore over to intercept him.

"Look, will yere? That black bugger has set every rag his boat will carry," remarked the customs officer. "Spread 'is blinkin' shirt, too, if 'e 'ad one, I fancy."

"S'trewth, mate," the cutter's commander agreed. "Yer right, bloody Conch *is* 'oppin' it."

As soon as she sailed within earshot, the sponger's black crew began yelling excitedly.

"Men-o'-war in Stirrup Cay Channel, sar! Five ob dem."

"Don't be bally asses—they're our own."

The negro captain looked all eyes and teeth as he bellowed, "No, sar. Dem wahn't proper British vessels! Flied no jack at dey mast-haids. Jus' a yaller flag."

"Spanish!" Both officers lost their indifferent air.

"No, sar, none ob us couldn' see no red in it."

"Sure they were men-o'-war?"

"Oh yes, sar, and dey was a-steerin' straight dis way."

The cutter's commander delayed not an instant in jamming over his tiller.

Twenty minutes later, a puff of smoke burst from the seaward parapet of Fort Nassau. Another and then another cannon boomed the alarm.

8

Fort Montague—I

Aboard the captured fishing sloops the odors of sweaty negro clothing, insects and stale fish vied for precedence. Sergeant Coffin lay under the half deck of the leading vessel feeling perspiration pour down his back in sticky, tickling rivulets.

There were much pleasanter situations than to find one's self sprawled on a pile of ballast among ninety other marines and their equipment. Captain Nicholas was lucky to be up there on deck.

Wearing a ragged smock over his uniform and a frayed palm-fiber hat in place of his tricorne, Nicholas looked almost cool as he stood swaying beside the black fisherman-pilot. The only other persons lucky enough to be out in the air were the sloop's black crew and three white sailors in stained white ducks and grimy jerseys.

From the shore an observant individual might at most have deduced that the *Carolina* and her companion, the *Pelican,* rode so low in the water because they had made a fortunate haul at the sponge beds.

Nat, in trying to forget his misery, studied the Conch at the tiller. He wasn't big, but he must be strong as an ox. Whenever he made a movement, the muscles of his gleaming body undulated like poured tar. Must have a lick of Arab blood in him, his nose was so narrow, and hawk-shaped.

Captain Nicholas' calm voice impinged upon his contemplation, "We will land directly. Get your gear handy, lads."

"Thank God for that!" gasped a purple-faced marine. "I sure been stewing in my own juice the last two hours."

Sam Higsby, at the far end of the hold, was feeling finer than silk. Now it seemed that nothing could prevent at least a skirmish from taking place. To keep from grinning, he bit off a chaw of tobacco, started to work on it real fast.

Yesterday afternoon, he had cast enough rifle balls to last him for at least three man-sized skirmishes. Maybe today would bring the real scrap he was yearning for. Too bad he was down to the last of those lawn patches.

Lying there, with a marine's cutlass sheath digging into his slats, he couldn't help grinning to think of Aggie shivering back in Massachusetts. He bet Aggie never guessed that her petticut would travel clean down to the Indies.

Captain Nicholas had stood up and was studying the beach with great care. At last he bent and from the stern locker fished out his sword and a brace of big boarding pistols. Lastly he pulled off the smock and put on his cocked hat. He came forward and spoke under the half deck, his silver epaulets bright as a full moon.

"You will line up the instant you reach the beach. Marines in the first platoon, cutlass and pistol men in the second."

On deck the sail whirred down and its gaff made a loud *thump!* as the sponge sloop's keel took the beach. It made soft, rushing noises on digging into the sand.

"Everybody on deck!" the commander snapped. "Lively now!"

Higsby sang out, "Hey, Mister Cap'n, where do I fit?"

"Second line, you're not a marine."

Higsby started to get mad but remembered that his rifle would out-range any musket in the first platoon. The sponge sloop overflowed men. By fives and tens, the landing party splashed ashore, holding muskets and cartridge boxes free of the feeble wash. In the bright, double glare of tropical sun and white sand, everybody acted half blind. The other sponger also was beached and emptying armed men.

"Gonna have some fun now," John Gardner declared with feeling. "Damn Redcoats owe me an' Pa a fine tanyard."

Lieutenant Weaver ran up, eyes snapping, his face redder than a beet with the heat. "You'll take a fist in the jaw if you don't keep quiet. Line up, line up! Every minute counts!"

Hampered by very soft and yielding sand, the shore party scrambled about, formed behind Sergeant Coffin and the uniformed marines.

Long before anybody else, Higsby recognized the two vessels which were running inshore to cover the maneuver. They were the *Providence* and the *Wasp*. Both men-of-war had cannon run out and ready.

Little delay attended the column's getting underway. As soon as it began marching westward beneath a pitiless tropical sun, Higsby's jet eyes commenced to explore a lush, emerald-green fringe of vegetation rising some sixty feet from the water's edge.

The ranger had never seen such trees. Did they lose their leaves? Would they bear fruit or nuts?

Suddenly, the men ahead of him began to laugh. By stretching his neck he could glimpse a cluster of huts further up the beach. Black people up yonder were scampering about like winter deer with a panther loose in their yard.

All the men hollered to see half-dressed bucks and *mammees* trying to round up pigs, chickens and children that were as crazy scared as they. When the head of the column was still a hundred yards away the inhabitants made for the jungle, leaving in their wake bits of furniture and clothing.

"It's de Spanishers!" somebody was yelling from behind one of the huts. "Best run fast, chillen."

A seaman called through tattooed hands. "We ain't Spanishers. We don't aim to harm you."

"Silence!" barked the Marine Captain. "Next man raises a holler will get married to the gunner's daughter!"

Captain Nicholas sounded in earnest and as no one relished a flogging, silence descended. Of Weaver, Nicholas demanded, "What is that village?"

"New Guinea, sir."

"How far from it to Fort Montague?"

"Three-quarters of a mile, sir."

"—And New Providence?"

"Near two miles further on, sir."

As the expedition passed the village, the men couldn't help laughing when a little nigger boy dashed out of a palm-thatched hut naked as the day he was born and yelling bloody murder. Nevertheless, he clung to a gorgeous blue and gold chamber pot.

The column was slogging over the dazzling sand past a litter of piraguas, skiffs, and fishing gear when, from far up the coast, came the reverberating boom of a cannon. It sounded just as if someone had dropped a heavy load of planks.

"Somebody has bungled," Captain Nicholas remarked to his subordinate. "Well, Mr. Weaver, this means if there are British regulars in Fort Montague, we'll be catching particular hell before long."

Sergeant Coffin felt a muscle in his cheek twitch two or three times. The way it had at Breed's Hill. For unsupported troops to charge a fort, the garrison of which lay dozing and unprepared, was one thing. But it was quite another matter to expect half-trained men, such as these, to advance over a strip of cover-less beach in the face of grape shot and musket balls.

Over his shoulder, Nat glimpsed a succession of grim, sunburnt faces, all bright with sweat.

Though nothing was said, the whole column guessed what had happened.

"Ever been under fire?" muttered a hard-faced corporal at Coffin's elbow.

"Yes. At Breed's Hill."

The other blew a drop of sweat from the tip of his nose. "Like hell you were."

"*Mirabile dictu,* I was. Though I don't doubt every other soldier you meet will claim laurels won at that exquisitely stupid struggle."

It was odd, right now, that he should recapture the curious exhilaration he had experienced during that night march from Cambridge.

Why? Where lay an explanation? Must track it down when he got time. What ever had happened to those two Virginians who had escaped from Boston Jail and straightaway had joined Captain Knowlton's Company? There had been a young, laughing one named Johnny—couldn't remember his last name. The other was called Ashton, David Ashton. He was a fine figure of a man—a gallant rascal if ever he'd met one.

Sergeant Coffin felt a nudge. A husky young marine hailing from the Hampshire grants muttered:

"Gee, Sergeant, what's going to happen? How'd they learn we was coming? Wisht we hadn't of heard that cannon." He looked very worried.

Pretty soon Captain Nicholas halted the column, mopped his craggy face, then beckoned Higsby. Together, they disappeared into a line of woods which must mask Fort Montague.

Higsby found it all-fired fine to be moving among trees once more; even unfamiliar, strange-looking trees. Picking a route, he preceded Captain Nicholas and moved so quietly that he utterly surprised a group of refugees squatting in a little glade.

When at last they did see him gliding up, they scattered like a covey of quail—all except a weak old man who hid his face behind wrinkled, slate-colored hands and moaned,

"*Piedad! Piedad!* Please doan' kill a po' ol' man, Señor!"

Higsby slapped him on the shoulder as he passed, said gently, "Keep yer pants dry, gran'pa, and tell yer folks we Amurricans ain't fixin' to hurt none of you."

The old man's rheumy, yellow eyes opened, blinked incredulously. "Yo', yo' ain't Spanishers, sar?"

But already the ranger, his buckskins blending with the background, was reconnoitering a clump of cocoa palms.

On the other side of this point of woods lay a beach identical with that on which the party had landed. But dominating this one was a solid-appearing stone fort.

It wasn't large, nor small either, and a big British jack was set above it. The wind had died out though, and the flag hung limp as a whipped puppy's tail.

Peering around a palm, the Pennsylvanian counted eight embrasures, which probably meant this fort must mount nearly thirty cannons.

Higsby swallowed nothing once or twice. Quite a mouthful! Too bad the *Wasp* and the *Providence* lay such a long way out on the oily-looking sea, becalmed and hopelessly out of range.

Shading his eyes, the Pennsylvanian made a careful survey of the fort's crenellated walls. They were of a curious, yellowish gray stone and were dominated by a low tower.

While he watched, two, three, four men in red and white uniforms left the fort on its far side. Despite the blistering heat they ran off hell-for-leather along the beach. Musket barrels were flashing busily all along the battlements.

When Higsby reported these circumstances, Captain Nicholas merely nodded. In silence they returned to the column. The men complained because they got burnt whenever their musket barrels touched bare flesh.

Standing very straight and stiff, Captain Nicholas said in rapid, close-clipped accents:

"Men, we move immediately to the assault, for if the enemy secures reinforcements from the town, we will stand small chance of success." He pulled out an ivory whistle carved in the shape of a dolphin. "Mr. Weaver, when you hear this, you and your detachment will assault the east wall. It is not too high to be scaled if your men stand on each other's shoulders. And see that you carry it! I will lead the main attack against the south curtain."

Seamen, furiously swinging their cutlasses, hacked a trail through the flowering but very tough creepers and lianas which, in prodigal profusion, hung from the trees, and presently came in view of the box-like fort they were to assault.

There was time, Captain Nicholas decided, for the column to catch its breath before undertaking charge. The men, Sergeant Coffin saw, must run nearly two hundred yards, without cover of any sort, and over the soft white coral sand.

"Hi, Cap'n, look!" Higsby pointed and everyone watched a postern gate gradually swing open.

After a brief delay a figure in a scarlet coat came stalking out of Fort Montague. If one went by the gold braid on his tunic, he must be an officer. An escort of two privates with fixed bayonets followed at a little distance. These also were clad in scarlet but wore white cross-belts and floppy-brimmed straw hats.

The officer advanced, from time to time lifting an espantoon to which a handkerchief had been knotted.

Half way to the woods, the vivid figure halted and, looking very small and lonely, stood staring at the men gathered among the pale green shadows.

" 'Pears like he wants to parley," observed Captain Nicholas hooking up his vivid green tunic. Dark sweat rings marked both his under-arms and sweat had also soaked through at the small of his back.

He crooked a finger at Sergeant Coffin. "Follow me."

To Weaver, he said, "If this fellow attempts treachery, you are to storm the fort at once and secure it. Then, as soon as practicable, you will co-operate with the squadron by attacking New Providence from inland. Capture the Governor's Palace. It tops a hill, commands Fort Nassau."

Side by side, the two figures in green and white moved out of the woods and set off towards the trio in scarlet. The sun glanced off the sand with a glare that nearly blinded Nat Coffin.

The Englishman proved to be a greyhound-faced individual wearing a lieutenant's single epaulet. He gave Nicholas a grudging salute. Then demanded sharply, *"Qué quiere usted?"*

"Do you mind speaking English?" Captain Nicholas summoned a faint smile. "My Spanish, I fear, is inadequate."

The other's blood-shot eyes narrowed. "Stab me! Why, you talk like an Englishman. Who are you? What are you doing in this infernal, misplaced corner of Hades?"

While the Marine Captain explained his identity and mission, the Englishman first looked incredulous, then angry.

"Ah. You are merely a pack of rebels, or should I say 'pirates'?"

"I am not here, sir, to call names," Nicholas tartly informed him. "I am here to take yonder fort."

"Take Fort Montague?" the Englishman's heated features contracted. "Plague take such infernal insolence!"

Then he seemed to recall something. "May I send an express to His Excellency, the Governor? I daresay he would be interested in learning of your—er—intentions."

Sergeant Coffin meantime seized his opportunity to appraise the two privates. Were they regulars? That was all-important. Though they wore regulation scarlet tunics and cross-belts, their nether garments varied from any he had seen at the Siege. They wore trousers of blue and white striped seersucker, not breeches.

Their tunics, on second inspection, were both ill-fitting and food-spotted; their buttons dull. Both men looked sallow. He could feel their yellowish and sunken eyes studying him, when they weren't keeping an uneasy watch on the woods.

The *Providence* and the *Wasp* still lay helpless on the glowing green-blue sea, but their masters had boats out, as if trying to tow. It would be hot work.

Captain Nicholas was saying in his abrupt Down-East accent, "Sir, I am directed by my superior, Commodore Esek Hopkins, Commander-in-Chief of the Continental Naval Service, to demand the immediate and unconditional surrender of all forts, military and naval property on this island."

"Oh, do you really?" The lieutenant, a weary-looking career officer of forty or more, lifted a long upper lip in a sardonic grin. "And there is nothing else you would fancy, my good rebel?"

A hard smile flitted over Captain Nicholas's mouth. "If there is, sir, I fancy we will take it. One thing further: provided he is offered no armed resistance, Commodore Hopkins undertakes to guarantee the lives and the personal property of all inhabitants."

The Englishman blinked, pulled a handkerchief from his cuff and wiped a heavy beading of perspiration from shaggy eyebrows. "How many men have you in position?"

"Over five hundred," replied Nicholas without batting an eye. "By sundown our squadron—a very formidable squadron—will be lying off the town."

For the first time a trace of uncertainty entered the Englishman's manner. He seemed to find something convincing about this long-faced fellow in green regimentals.

He nodded carelessly, "Though I daresay all rebels are braggarts as well, it is my duty to communicate your ever-so-charming demands to Governor Browne."

Nicholas jerked out a watch, the seals of its fob flashing in the sun.

"Very well. Please note that it is now a half after three. If we have received no reply within an hour, or if any attempt is made to reinforce your garrison, we shall attack immediately."

9

Fort Montague—II

At twenty minutes past four o'clock a galloper appeared from the direction of New Providence and rode into Fort Montague. In this afternoon sun, the fort was glowing a deeper yellow. Though it could not have measured over a hundred feet to a side, the fortification looked larger, higher-walled than before.

When the oldish lieutenant reappeared under his improvised white flag, he was sullen and did not salute as he growled:

"His Excellency agrees to—damme, to surrender—" he choked on the word—"this fort, provided the garrison is permitted to retire unharmed."

"Granted," Captain Nicholas replied, "provided you undertake, on your honor, neither to remove or damage any Crown property whatsoever."

The lieutenant made angry little motions, bit his lips, "I fear I have no option in the matter."

He was near weeping with humiliation and stamped his foot as he cried, "Oh, damme, this is shameful, intolerable! What can that pot-valiant poltroon of a Governor be thinking of?"

Captain Nicholas was too vastly relieved to say much. Not that he was yet freed of dangerous responsibilities. Dark would have fallen long before he could even properly secure Fort Montague against possible recapture. One thing he dared not risk was a night attack on a hostile and well-fortified town. There was entirely too much likelihood of his half-disciplined men getting drunk or shooting each other by mistake.

"Very well," he said crisply. He felt sorry for the lieutenant. Poor old fellow! To its loss, the British Service was becoming crowded with such friendless and penniless veterans. Good officers, but too poor to afford the purchase of majorities and colonelships.

"We will take possession immediately."

Still cursing the Governor under his breath, the enemy officer turned on his heel and went plowing back over the sand towards Fort Montague.

Lieutenant Weaver, with a hundred men, was to take actual possession. The balance of the column would remain in the woods, ready for any eventuality.

Once the men heard they wouldn't be asked to storm such a solid-looking battlement, they raised such a cheer that dense flocks of terror-stricken green and gold parakeets rocketed out of the tree tops.

"Hooray for the United Colonies! Hooray for Old Hop! Hooray! Hooray!"

Most of them had lately been doing some mighty serious thinking and the relief was tremendous.

In a column of squads, Lieutenant Weaver's command moved out of the woods, trying to keep step and look soldierly.

It had covered perhaps half the distance to a palisade of mastich wood surrounding the fort as an out-work, when a great blossom of gray-white smoke spurted from embrasures. A split-second later, twelve-pound round crashed into the woods and showered the utterly amazed Americans with a rain of falling twigs and branches. Veterans in the detachment flung themselves flat.

A second cannon thundered, and again a shot screamed by. In the depths of the jungle, it sounded as if some Titan's boy was splitting kindling.

"Down! Lie down!" Sergeant Coffin shouted.

"So I ain't to be cheated after all," Higsby muttered, and with a grunt of satisfaction, cocked his long Leman. But before he could shoulder it, Captain Nicholas rasped:

"Put that damn thing down! You've no order to fire!"

A third twelve-pounder sent its ball tearing harmlessly over the heads of the Americans as Lieutenant Weaver's detachment came floundering back to shelter in a disorderly purple-faced column.

There were no more shots. As the last of the cannon smoke drifted lazily out to sea the fort's flag faltered on its staff, dipped jerkily out of sight.

A furious metallic clanging commenced.

"The honorable gentleman is spiking his guns it seems," Nicholas observed grimly. "Fall in, men." Even as he spoke, the postern gate on the fort's far side swung open and disgorged a column which, in a miscellany of uniforms, set off along the beach at the double-quick. The garrison would not number more than sixty, thought Sergeant Coffin. No wonder they were in such a hurry to get away.

With the eagerness of small boys exploring a recently-abandoned house, the Americans swarmed through Fort Montague. Some ransacked the barracks, others examined the officers' quarters. Everybody admired a cistern which was fed with rainwater by a cleverly designed catchment. The tank must have held at least thirty tons of drinking water. Captain Nicholas at the head of a squad of marines promptly took possession of the magazine.

Of the haste in which the fort had been abandoned, there was abundant evidence. Half-eaten food was collecting flies in the enlisted men's barracks, and in the officers' quarters smouldered a mound of half-burned official documents.

As had been anticipated, all the cannon, eight 18's, three 12's, and six 6 pounders had been spiked. The work, however, had been carelessly done. The spikes were too slender and thus failed effectively to seal the vents. By sunset every one of the seventeen cannon was in serviceable condition.

10

New Providence, March 4, 1776—I

Brown, dark blue and black hulls sharp against a translucent sea, the American squadron swung to its anchors behind Salt Cay, some three leagues west of New Providence harbor.

It was such a fair evening that, from the fighting tops, look-outs could discern the topsails of the *Wasp* and the *Providence*. To leeward of Hog Island, they were dutifully blockading the eastern outlet of New Providence harbor.

In his cabin Commodore Esek Hopkins, unshaven, irritable and red-eyed from lack of sleep, sat dictating to a civilian secretary. He was upset. Well, he'd sure given Abe Whipple a dressing-down. The culprit, however, had merely donned a mulish expression and sworn that the *Alfred's* signal flags had blown in such a way they couldn't possibly be read.

It was a very thin excuse. Abe must have known that. So did the rest of the captains. Jealousy, that was the root of such insubordination. Jealousy, and an old privateersman's ingrained sense of independence. Without admitting it, he understood why Whipple had done what he did. Why it was almost to be expected!

He turned to Tim Bennett, "Here are orders even my precious, near-sighted captains can read. See you enter a clear copy of it in my letter book."

The order was for the *Andrew Dorea* to undertake a blockade to the westward of New Providence. Nicholas Biddle was instructed to stop any and all vessels. He must either seize them or drive them back into the harbor. Hopkins had no intention of having his presence advertised throughout the West Indies. Just suppose a British squadron might be passing on its way to Jamaica?

The Commodore had other worries: not only the *Columbus,* but the *Alfred* and the *Cabot,* too, were again rotten with smallpox.

When the first stars commenced to flicker, the wind died away. The *Andrew Dorea's* sails hung almost slack to their yards, and she made feeble progress in proceeding into her appointed station.

James Josiah, the brig's first lieutenant, fretted, kept peering into the sky. "At this rate, sir, we will not reach our station until after midnight. Possibly, if the canvas were wetted—"

"—That will do, Mr. Josiah," Biddle cut in. "If the Commodore expects I'll assume the responsibility for hurting this cruiser all in order to capture a few miserable spongers, he labors in error."

Nicholas Biddle intended to make a name for himself in the new navy. He was also aware that a captain who lost or injured his vessels was seldom among those selected for rapid promotion.

Accordingly, the fourteen-gun brig groped a leisurely and very cautious passage through the reefs, so it was not until two of the morning that she commenced a patrol off North Cay.

As it was, the *Andrew Dorea* arrived barely in time to sight a small sloop sneaking out among a welter of reefs. All but invisible because her sails had been dyed brown, she ghosted confidently through a series of twisting channels.

"Is it possible to catch her, Mr. Dunn?" Biddle inquired of his sailing master.

"It is, sir, if you will chance striking a reef."

All at once Captain Biddle found himself entertaining a lively suspicion why the Commodore sent him orders to chase *every* vessel he sighted! Surely, so experienced a navigator must have known that to cruise such treacherous waters in the dark was no light matter?

Yes, Biddle thought he understood. Hopkins had put him in this position to discredit him. The obvious explanation offered itself. He, alone of all the officers in the squadron, was able to recognize the Commodore's errors—be they in tactics, etiquette, or gunnery.

Sharply he said, "We will not bother with such fry. Hold the course."

The brown-sailed sloop merged into the night, disappeared and so when dawn broke, the *Mississippi* was under the horizon, well on her way to Florida with one hundred and fifty barrels of the King's powder safe in her hold. Come who might, it never now would be used by an American man-o'-war.

Commodore Hopkins, feeling less sure of himself than ever since 1754, lifted heavy eyes. He must wake up, must digest what this messenger from Captain Nicholas had to tell him. The fellow had sailed from Fort Montague clean around Hog Island.

Had the evacuating troops looked like regulars? No. Captain Nicholas believed that the garrison of Fort Montague had contained only militia. Captain Nicholas figured Fort Nassau was going to prove a very hard nut to crack. The King's fort mounted above forty cannons, some of them heavy 32 pounders.

It was all Tim could do to remain correctly impassive. A dozen questions presented themselves. Could a privateer blockade a port— if it weren't too big? Maybe one could demand ransom of a port.

While digesting Captain Nicholas' report, Esek Hopkins paced his cabin, breathing hard through his shiny, purple-veined nose. Curling fingers locked behind his back, he inquired, "You say the inhabitants don't seem ill-disposed?"

"Aye, aye, sir."

"And Captain Nicholas believes that the bulk of Governor Browne's troops are militia?"

"Aye, aye, sir. That's what the Captain cal'lates."

"That's capital!" A smile relaxed the Commodore's florid features. "Guess militia ain't any better in these parts than they are to home."

He swung about with a gesture so characteristic that Tim reached for a quill. "What's this Governor's first name?"

"Montford, sir, Montford Browne."

"Mr. Bennett, pray draught two copies of a—ahem—a proclamation. Address one to His Excellency; the other to the principal merchants. Find no point in getting the Committee's ships shot up if it can be avoided." Esek Hopkins would always be considerate of government property.

At the Commodore's dictation, Tim wrote:

To the Gentlemen Freemen and Inhabitants of the Island of New Providence.

The reasons of my landing an armed force on the Island is in Order to take possession of the Powder and Warlike stores belonging to the Crown and if I am not opposed in putting my design in Execution the Persons and Property of the inhabitants shall be safe. Neither shall they be suffered to be hurt in Case they make no resistance.

Given under my hand on board the Ship *Alfred,* March 3rd 1776.

Esek Hopkins
Cr. in Chief.

II

New Providence—II

In pursuance of orders received early on the morning of March 4, 1776, Captain Nicholas left behind a garrison strong enough to hold Fort Montague and, at the head of nearly two hundred men, set out for New Providence.

Flanking the reduced column, his boots *shush-shushed* steadily over the soft white sand. So the British were going to surrender without a fight? Captain Nicholas could hardly credit that. Why, properly defended, a stronghold like Fort Nassau might hold out for weeks.

Yet the Commodore had received the garrison's offer of capitulation, had accepted it. The Governor's submission seemed, somehow, a bit too precipitate. Could his Excellency be planning a trick? The sailors might do as they pleased, but William Nicholas and his marines would leave no precaution untaken.

Had Captain Biddle stood in Hopkins' shoes, the squadron would have entered New Providence harbor at the first streak of dawn, but all his life the Commodore had refused to be hurried. Probably he would never change in this respect. Certainly he had not appreciated his good fortune in having won Fort Montague so easily.

To Sam Higsby's way of thinking, New Providence wasn't much. Why, the whole sleepy-looking little port boasted only half a dozen wharfs and perhaps twice as many red-roofed warehouses that were tinted yellow, white and brown.

Still, he wished Mistress Desire Harmony could see him reconnoitre the advance. He was drifting silently from shed to barn, to the house corner, then across the road to the next dwelling, testing every palmetto clump of every grove of lemon trees. She would have enjoyed coming along, he reckoned. There was plenty of heart in that girl.

Sergeant Coffin found that entering a town captured from the British was an oddly exhilarating experience. Had Alexander, Caesar and Hannibal experienced similar sensations? In command of the uniformed contingent he was marching two paces behind Nicholas.

Save for the persistent yapping of many gaunt dogs, it was deathly still in this dusty, sunlit street. Suddenly a donkey began braying lustily. It sounded so much like Captain Saltonstall hailing a look-out that Nat almost laughed out loud.

Clump! Clump! Clump! Now that they were on the edge of town, the men began to swagger, to throw out their feet. Silly fools, they hadn't half earned this triumph. The weary, powder-streaked militia who had been driven from that redoubt on Breed's Hill had had better cause to show off.

Without exception, householders had barricaded their doors and had locked shutters of blue, gray, and green. Merchants had boarded up their shop-fronts as for a siege.

All at once, Captain Nicholas dropped back and, lowering his voice, said, "Sergeant! Must move faster! Boats are putting out from the fleet." The Marine Captain's harsh features lightened. "If we allow it, I fancy they will try to pretend that the Navy took this place."

Across the glassy harbor, a whole flotilla of boats was threading its way through shipping at anchor.

It was when the invaders had entered Bay Street and were climbing a hill on which stood the Governor's Palace, that someone shouted:

"Glad you've come! Hurrah for the American Colonies!"

Shutters commenced to swing open. Then everywhere voices began to call, "Down with the Ministry!" "To hell with their taxes!" "Welcome, Americans!"

As he panted up the slope, Sergeant Coffin saw friendly white, brown, and black faces peering out through the bars with which all downstairs windows were equipped.

"Come on out, gals, we ain't wild men," Jed Franklin invited. Pretty soon the inhabitants felt emboldened to flap kerchiefs, scarfs and cloths through their glass-less ground floor windows.

"You poor men must be thirsty." A white woman came out, offered a pitcher. One of the sailors started to drink but Captain Nicholas ordered him back in ranks.

At each important street intersection, a squad was left behind. These stood in the hot sun fingering cocked and loaded muskets and let their gaze rove from the church spire, to Fort Nassau down by the water's edge, then to the Union Jack waving above the Governor's palace on Mount Fitzwilliam.

When they reached higher ground, the marines realized that New Providence consisted largely of three wide streets which paralleled the water, and not above eight or nine thoroughfares running at right angles to these.

At the entrance to the Governor's Palace, Mrs. Browne confronted the invaders with caustic contempt.

"—And where could you expect to find His Excellency?" she snapped. "At his post in the Fort, of course. He is neither a rebel nor one of these beastly Colonials."

Though the Governor's lady was rude, Captain Nicholas remained at pains to be courteous. He even detailed a squad for Mrs. Browne's protection and, quite incidentally, to see that there was no destruction of Crown records or property.

Once the Palace was secured, Captain Nicholas permitted himself to consider another matter of importance. Of a burly corporal, he demanded, "Where is our flag?"

"Here, sir, got her wrapped around me stomach!"

"Good!" Then to the red-haired sergeant who possessed an uncanny knack of appearing when wanted, he said, "We must hustle, Coffin, else the sailors will beat us."

At a brisk double-quick the uniformed men descended Cumberland Street and in so doing passed a stream of Bahamian militia who were evacuating Fort Nassau.

The street was dusty, full of dogs, goats and militiamen in dingy red and white uniforms. These made no pretense of keeping order but shambled shamelessly. Now and then, a militiaman would disappear into a dwelling, eagerly pulling off cross-belt and tunic.

" 'Pears as if the Lobster-backs mean to play fair this time," the corporal remarked.

Over a silver epaulet, Captain Nicholas called, "Parade order! Stand straight and get the step, damn you! Show these islanders how Continental Marines can march!"

All at once, Sergeant Coffin saw Fort Nassau lying straight ahead its landward curtain and bastions glaring orange-yellow in the noonday sun. It was such a fine big fort that a lot of Provincials must have been sent shouting home to Heaven had the enemy elected to defend it.

How big and deadly those cannon looked up there on the battlements. Two massive salients projected quite a distance into the water. Their bases were green with weeds and clustered with shellfish. Two "swallow's nests," or look-out towers, crowned the apex of the landward salients.

Coming nearer, he noticed how tufts of weeds, even little bushes, sprouted from joints in the masonry. Bright-eyed lizards ran freely over cement work of an odd, dark red color. Nat puzzled over this until someone explained that the natives used turtles' blood instead of water in mixing their cement. It was believed to be more water-proof.

Beyond Fort Nassau, the ships of the American squadron were lying within easy cannon shot. Just as the last elements of the garrison crossed a drawbridge spanning a ditch, the Union Jack was lowered. The ensign fell in a series of jerks, as if unwilling to go earthwards.

"Briskly now," the Captain called. He had noticed Hopkins' boats pulling in to a long rickety wharf.

At this moment he regretted that the uniformed detachment's black gaiters and green tunics were grayed with dust, that their white cross-belts had not been freshly pipeclayed. A rough-looking lot—but these sunburnt men were marching in well-ordered ranks and they set their feet down smartly.

The marines crossed the drawbridge without diminishing their stride in the least, passed under an elaborate keystone engraved with the Royal coat-of-arms. Ahead of them opened a dark and forbidding passageway.

After the glare of the street, Sergeant Coffin found it hard to see. He and the rest stumbled blindly over a wild litter of canteens, bayonets, pikes and pistols abandoned by the garrison. Dozens of Tower muskets stood propped, every which way, against the walls. A blaze of sunshine gleamed ahead. It was a square courtyard set in the exact center of the fort.

Maintaining a steady cadence, the marines re-emerged into hot sunlight. Immediately, Captain Nicholas halted his men. He had just become aware of a solitary figure waiting on the further edge of the court.

This officer's scarlet coat was glittering with so much gold lace Coffin judged he must be at least a colonel. So rigid and unnatural was the lone officer's posture that he suggested a schoolboy's drawing. He carried a ring of brass keys in one hand, the other rested on the hilt of a sword.

Hollowly, Captain Nicholas' footsteps echoed through the courtyard as he advanced.

At a distance of ten feet from that figure so bright against the bluish shadows of a gallery behind, Captain Nicholas halted. He saluted, thinking that never again would he see a human face wear so tragic an expression. Contempt, shame and rage all were expressed.

"I, sir, am Captain Nicholas, First Battalion of Continental Marines, and at your service."

Still the gorgeous figure in scarlet and white made no move. Had not a key turned on his ring and flashed in the sun, he might have been a graven image.

"In compliance with orders from my commanding officer, Commodore Hopkins, I am here to take possession of this fort. Whom do I have the honor of addressing?"

The Englishman narrowed hard blue eyes, obviously steeled himself to speak.

"I am His Majesty's duly commissioned Governor over these Islands." Montford Browne's voice was harsh as the rasp of steel drawn over steel. "I greatly regret that I have lived to—to—surrender my authority to a rabble of disloyal rogues."

The Marine Captain's rangy figure stiffened, but he controlled himself. "Your views, sir, are your property, but I must request the surrender of your keys."

The Governor drew a slow hissing breath and set his jaw before passing over the key ring. It was so still in the drill court everyone heard them jingle.

The Governor said thickly, "Mark my words! Before long, you and your rascally crew shall rue this usurpation of authority!"

Nat Coffin was surprised and pleased, too, that Nicholas made no request for the Governor's ebony-hilted dress sword, only beckoned a corporal and said:

"Pray conduct His Excellency to the guard room. You will keep him under close arrest."

This, then, was the way a real soldier acted in his moment of triumph. He must make note of it in his "Observations."

Meantime, Captain Nicholas started in the direction of a worn stone staircase. After him marched a private carrying an ensign the Marines had brought with them from Philadelphia. Sergeant Coffin, guessing what was up, chuckled silently.

Landing parties from the squadron, mustering on a dusty parade ground paralleling Fort Nassau, watched with deep interest a small bundle climb a flag staff on the watch tower. When it could rise no higher into the aching blue of the March sky, the halyards were given a jerk and into the air sprang a flag such as few present had ever beheld.

Straightening under a strong southerly breeze was a design composed of thirteen alternate red and white stripes with a British Jack in its canton corner.

"Now what in the hell is that thing?" one of the seamen growled.

"It's called the Grand Union," an officer told him.

"But, sir, why ain't our yellow rattlesnake flag up there?"

"By Jesus, I got it!" cried a mahogany-faced gunner. "It's them damned leather-necks. They've beat us to it and raised *the Army flag!*"

12

SPOILS

FOLLOWING the fall of New Providence there was little rest for anyone. Invalids had to be brought ashore, ships must be watered, provisioned and prepared for a thorough overhauling. Local vessels must be manned and assigned to patrol duty. Sprung topmasts and yards needed to be sent down. Sails must be patched, dried and otherwise repaired.

There were, however, a number of agreeable duties. One of these consisted of assembling and making an inventory of property captured from King George the Third.

Timothy Bennett, in company with two other accountants, spent long hours over desks placed in the courtyard of Fort Nassau. Most tedious of all was the task of reconciling reports emanating from various sources.

While waiting for a check on shells supplying a battery of brass mortars, Tim copied yet again a final tally of the stores taken at Fort Montague.

He could almost recite by rote:

> 17 Cannon from 9 to 36 pounders
> 1240 Round shott
> 121 Shells
> 81 Iron Trucks for Carriages
> 22 Copper Hoops
> 2 Copper Powder measures
> 1 Worm 1 Ladle
> Some old Iron Copper & Lead not weighted.

"Say, Bennett," one of the clerks called. "How many fuses does Lieutenant Weaver's return call for?"

"Eight hundred and twelve."

"Captain Nicholas claims there was eight hundred sixteen."

"Somebody's daft."

Tim sighed and with the back of his hand removed a drop of perspiration from his nose. Crimanently! It was hotter than Tophet in this infernal court. Walled in on all sides, never a stray breeze could find its way in.

Those little green lizards were lucky. They were free to seek the shade. Absently, he watched one cling upside-down to an arch of masonry and swell a scarlet pouch on its throat to attract blue-bottle flies.

By dint of patience, the clerks were at length able to present:

> An Inventory of Stores &-c taken at New
> Providence at Fort Nassau, March 4, 1776.

> 71 cannon from 9 to 32 pounders
> 15 Mortars (brass) from 4 to 11 inches
> 5337 Shells
> 9837 round shot & 165 chain & dble Hd. do.
> 140 hand grenades
> 816 Fuzees or false fires
> 99 Spunges Rammers & worms

46 Copper ladles
407 Copper Hoops & 5 Copper powder Measures
220 Iron Trucks for carriages
3 Bells
24 Casks Powder
A quantity of match rope
2 Dble blocks with brass sheaves
1 Scale beam
1 Hammer
3 Tanned Hides
2 Boxes tallow candles
4 Bbls flower, 4 do. bread, 4 do. Beef
Part of a cask of Spirit
1 Sun diall & 1 English flagg"

Tim wondered what would become of the two boxes of tallow candles and to what purpose the sun dial would be dedicated.

Once the work was done, he searched for Paymaster Lieutenant Grinnell, found him more than a little jingled at the Bull & Otter Tavern. He was consuming a sangaree. Tactfully, he sounded Grinnell as to the squadron's next move.

" 'Less I'm way off the course, Hopkins will head for Rhode Island and a hero's triumph, the minute our sick get better." He gave Tim a searching look. "I take it you intend to leave us here and get on to Hispaniola?"

"If the squadron is to proceed no further South."

"It won't." Owlishly Grinnell shook his head. "All we heroes want is to be kissed and praised. Ought to be, too, after this. What's your hurry? Be delighted to stand you to a flip—rum if you prefer."

"Thank you—but my Pa used to have an agent here. I was thinking he may know how to get me to the French Islands."

Grinnell waved a loose hand. "Have it your own way, m'lad. You're a fool not to come home, though, and be made a little brass god of. Might even forget you're a deserter."

"Now, goddam you!" Tim's hand flew to the other's neck cloth. "Apologize, or I'll slap your jaws until you do."

Lieutenant Grinnell went red, but didn't like the look of the fist under his nose.

"All right. I 'pologize—my error." Sullenly he added, "You and that damned savage of a rifleman come to the *Alfred* tomorrow and I will pay you off. Expect you'd sooner live ashore, anyhow."

Pa's agent, Tim thought, was named Petty. A negro said, "Yas-suh. Dey's two genmum dat name. Dey's Misto Will Petty. Him daid. Dey's Misto John Petty. Him owns a wharf. Him home on Charlotte Street."

13

JOHN PETTY, ESQ.

THE inhabitants of New Providence, reassured that they would suffer none of the rapine and looting such as had accompanied the Spanish raids of 1684 and 1704, returned, and by consequence, the port's dusty, unpaved streets teemed with traffic.

By the hundreds sailors and marines swarmed and swaggered about the town. Like mischievous boys, they delighted in pinching the buttocks of the slave women just to see them jump and spill the baskets they carried balanced on their heads. Fights over the matter of the flag raised above Fort Nassau raged at almost every tavern.

It lacked half an hour of sundown when Tim paused before a swing board slung above a wide stone arch leading into an inner court. An enormous tiger cat came out from under it, and began to strop itself against his leg.

Badly sun-cracked and faded, the sign was barely legible:

JNO. PETTY, ESQ.
Dealer in Merch'dise of every Nature
Birmingham & Sheffield Goods
China ware, Musical Instruments & Negros

Through the archway floated the melodious tootling of a flute. For some reason the player would, every once in a while, blow an hysterical-sounding sour note but would immediately resume playing.

Deeply mystified, Tim knocked several times then, when no one appeared, he entered the covered passage. Presently, he found himself in a sun-dappled courtyard the center of which was occupied by a flaming flamboyant tree. Along one side were parked a pair of two-wheeled carts.

The music, he found, was being played by a plump, jovial-appearing individual who, seated in the shade of a short cloister connecting residence and storehouse, for the sake of coolness had slung his wig to the back of his chair.

To the player's left was a rack full of music. He lolled, half reclining in his chair, and was blowing an ebony and ivory flute as solemn as any judge. Sitting with one of the musician's bare feet in his lap was a small and extremely ragged negro boy.

After a bewildered instant, Tim perceived that the boy had hold of the flautist's big toe and was, with the point of a long steel needle, attempting to dislodge something from beneath its nail. The pickaninny braced himself and dug so hard that the musician blew a terrifyingly false note and sitting up, snatched his foot away.

"A pox on your clumsiness, Jupiter!" he roared. "D'you have to take my bloody foot off to get at a parcel o' chiggers?"

"Oh, nossuh," the little negro's eyes became perfect circles of white. "Nossuh. Ah goes just so gentle as Ah kin!"

"Very well. See that you do. You may resume your efforts. Mind you don't overlook any egg bags."

He had settled himself and was preparing to resume his music when he saw Tim standing in the archway. He waved a plump hand, and bowed sitting down.

"Evening, sir! A very good evening. John Petty at your service. You must forgive my not rising, but I must remain thus at Jupiter's mercy until he has removed the last of these confounded pestiferous insects."

But the moment he learned Tim's identity, Mr. Petty jumped up so suddenly he sent the little darkey tumbling backwards across the cloister's bright red tiles.

"Mr. Asa Bennett's son? God bless my body and bones! I am delighted to have lived 'til this happy moment. I am, sir, positively overcome with pleasure."

He gripped Tim's hand with fervor. "Wonderful merchant, your respected father. Vastly intelligent. Never shipped me a wrong piece of merchandise—not so much as a button as wasn't saleable. Never a word of wrong intelligence. Never once! Adelina!"

The Bahamian's deep voice boomed, making the courtyard resound, and a flock of hens scattered in confusion. Almost instantly in a doorway set at the end of Mr. Petty's vine-draped gallery, appeared a woman who moved with the fluid grace of a doe stepping out of a thicket.

She was slight, perhaps thirty years of age and had wound about gleaming blue-black hair a bright yellow handkerchief. Her wine-colored skirt was in subtle harmony with the yellow and black apron on which she was wiping floury hands. As she hurried forward, Tim noted small circlets of gold let into her ears.

The barefooted merchant stood there beaming. "Adelina, my dove, this is Mr. Bennett of Newport in America. Mr. Bennett, this is my very excellent housekeeper."

To Tim, it was a surprise that any housekeeper could exhibit such an excellent taste in her clothing. Mamba had worn any old thing that happened to be clean.

As Adelina dropped him a flowing curtsey, he realized that she was not merely tanned, as he had at first assumed, but that her skin was of soft brown mellowed with a golden hue. Her nose was pretty, being both short and straight, and when she gave him a shy smile, strong and even teeth flashed behind lips as dark a red as Desire Harmony's.

"Arouse yourself, my dear!" Mr. Petty boomed. "We must make Mr. Bennett welcome, mustn't we? Send Quacko and Jupiter down to the market directly. We will need pigeon plums, plantains, conch meat—we'll give our guest a real Bahamian *fou-fou*—star apples, a duck or two and crayfish—young ones, tell them.

"You will dispatch Eros to Mr. Forbes's. Present him my compliments, and will he join us at table tonight? Then on to Mr. Parton's, Mr. Drumgold's, Mr. John Card's, and—oh damme, Adelina, we'll bid the whole lot! After all, this is a rare occasion."

The quadroon had started off on small, quick-treading feet when Petty called after her, "Instruct dear Venus to arrange the guest chamber and light some smudges. I want neither roaches nor mosquitoes flying about tonight. Oh yes, remind her about that rip in the mosquito bar, too."

Tim noted that so far the woman called Adelina had not uttered a word. Her vivid lips merely curved as she made a small curtsey and retired, earrings flashing. He was debating whether Mr. Petty's housekeeper was a mute when he heard a voice which must have been hers repeating Mr. Petty's orders.

Petty clapped him heartily on the shoulder. "Damn my blood and bones, you've no idea how glad I am to have you here, Mr. Bennett! We poor devils out in the Islands are perishing for want of new tales, new faces and fresh intelligence of the world. Our brains' grow fallow with monotony."

"I shall be glad to give you all the news I can remember," Tim smiled. It was fine to meet such a wholly friendly person.

"Yes, sir, we shall have a high old time tonight. My fault if we don't." The Bahamian chuckled until his stomach jiggled beneath a wine-spotted linen waistcoat. "By the bye, how long may I hope to have you as my guest?"

His face fell when Tim explained the necessity of his immediate departure for Cap François.

Mr. Petty leading the way into a dim, high-ceilinged room said over his shoulder, "Don't fret yourself, sir, we will soon find you a passage to Saint-Domingue, or Hispaniola, as some call that accursed island."

The house was unique, exuding as it did a sense of disorderly and bizarre comfort. From its living room walls dangled some fearsome

African masks carved, so Mr. Petty said, of ebony wood. Over a steel engraving was tucked a branch crowded with gay, but badly-stuffed humming birds. Another faintly mildewed wall bore a panoply of spears, gleaming assegais and tulwars.

The furniture was of massive oak and upholstered in musty-smelling zebra hides. There were several deep settees fashioned of wicker and piled high with cushions.

In a far corner a red earthenware olla, slung from a raffia cradle, dripped musically into a wide dish set beneath it. On the window-ledge a pair of orange and black banana birds flitted nervously about a wicker cage.

"D'you prefer rum for the moment, or Madeira?" Mr. Petty queried eagerly. "Maybe a dash of Hollands and bitters? No use our parching while Adelina mixes us a bombo. The dear girl is a trifle deliberate, I fear, but her bombos are fit for the gods in Olympus."

He ended by decanting Madeira into tumblers which, having been fashioned with round ends, must be either drained or held in the hand.

Petty raised his drink towards the fly-clustered ceiling. "Here's luck to our trade together and a blight on His Majesty's advisers! If you prove half the trader your father was, we shall flourish."

"Amen," Tim nodded. Trader? How fine the word sounded!

"Papa! Papa!" Bare feet pattered in the corridor and into the room raced a small and excited girl. "Oh, Papa, Papa! My lovebirds! There's a real egg in their nest, I— Oh!"

Noting Tim, she raced over to hide behind Mr. Petty's waistcoat. "Who that man?"

"There is no cause to fear, my pet. Mr. Bennett is a friend of mine. A good friend."

The merchant's plump shoulders squared themselves and as he gently propelled the child in front of him, he looked very steadily at Tim.

"This is my daughter, Venus. Ahem—Adelina and I are thrice blessed with issue. Very soon Eros and Anacreon shall be presented." Mr. Petty swallowed a deep gulp of wine, laughed easily. "Anacreon, yet in swaddling clothes, barely shows on the inventory."

Desperately, Tim struggled to down an instinctive revulsion. Other places, other ways, of course. Had he not learned that in the army?

"How do you do, Venus?" He thought he sounded quite natural. "I should like to see your lovebirds sometime soon."

The child climbing onto John Petty's knee was very like her mother, pale brown-gold. A lovely, big-eyed little thing, she wore a bright yellow smock—a necklace of silver beads—and, as quickly became evident, nothing else at all.

She would, Tim thought, have held the promise of truly stunning beauty had not her hair been marred by a damning trace of kinkiness, had her lips been a shade thinner.

"You bringed me a present?"

"Of course," Tim laughed. "But it's still aboard ship."

"Oh, Papa, he a Yankee?"

"Yes, but he won't eat you. Not tonight at least!" Petty smacked ruminative lips over a second Madeira. "Not bad, not good either. We'll switch to a swizzle."

He gave the child a gentle smack on her bare bottom. "My pet, pray go tell Mama to send in some limes."

It was to a big, square room dominated by a four-poster bed that Tim had been conducted. At present he reclined in a cord hammock rigged to benefit its occupant from possible cross-breezes between door and windows. Above his bed was rigged a mosquito tent which, by means of a pulley, could be lowered to protect the bed from insects swarming constantly through the unglassed windows.

It was luck, sheer luck that had sent him to look up Pa's Bahamian agent, Tim was thinking. Except for his clerk's miserable pay, he hadn't a penny. What a fine, jolly fellow Mr. Petty was. Were all agents so agreeable, so hospitable?

His only concern for the moment was Sam Higsby's undeniable genius for landing in trouble. Would Mr. Petty object to inviting an additional guest?

When he mentioned the matter, Mr. Petty dealt him a thumping blow on the shoulder. "Mind? Of course not, what's one more mouth? Dinner won't be dished 'til half after nine so you'll have opportunity to bid your friend. Don't come back without him. You go along, Eros. Show Mr. Bennett the way."

Fair-skinned, blond and with blue eyes, the Bahamian's eldest child, a boy of nine, much resembled his father. Only a very pale streak of lemon-tinted skin running the length of his spine betrayed the flaw in his ancestry.

Striding along beside Eros, Tim felt invisible weights dropping from his shoulders. More worries would evaporate when he reached Cap François and found the *Narragansett* safe and sound. It was fine being ashore, away from the smelly ships, the slovenly discipline and the perpetual wrangling of the captains with their commander-in-chief.

Now that the specific intentions of the invaders had been proved, all manner of small craft sometimes laden with produce, but more often out of pure curiosity, came beating in from outlying islands. There were spongers, turtle boats, freighters and fishermen from Eleuthera, Great Bahama, Andros and San Salvador.

Eros pointed to a large shed with greasy-looking stone pillars supporting its roof. "Yonder's the Vendue House, sir."

Under it mounds of sponges, turtle shells and conches lay heaped. Smoking, spitting, gossiping, African women squatted on lean gray-black shanks among them.

By the light of dim and smoky lanterns, a swarm of chattering blacks—most of them branded on hands or cheeks—was working. Some husked cocoanuts while others used dangerous-looking knives to gouge the meat from pink-lipped conch shells. Fires glowed and blinked all along the waterfront. Tim noticed that on a majority of the island boats, cooking fires had been kindled on top of a box of sand.

The almost universal repast of these fisherfolk, Eros explained, was *fou-fou,* a dish of dried conch meat, onions, diced fish, red meal. For desert, they sucked stubs of sugar cane chopped into handy lengths.

Tim found young Phil Hull packing a box of water colors. The

boy indicated a basket of parrot fish over which he had been working. "A pity, sir, is it not, that they must die and lose their colors?
They're so beautiful."

Tim, anxious to locate Higsby, nodded curtly, but Phil went on
eagerly, "If you have not been in the woods here yet, sir, you ought
to go. You may never see such flowers and butterflies again."

Though he hated to cut the young seaman short, Tim inquired for
the rifleman.

"I saw Mr. Higsby about an hour ago." Phil grinned. "He was having the time of his life showing some blacks how to throw a hatchet.
I expect they rate him a bigger officer than the Commodore. He went
out towards the edge of town with some of them."

"Where would they most likely take him?" Tim asked of Eros.

"To the Free Village. You can hear them drumming if you listen
hard, sir."

Sure enough, in the distance sounded a rhythmic thud-thudding.

"Come along, we better find Mr. Higsby in a hurry."

Eros hesitated, looked uneasy. "I don't want to go to the Free
Village."

"Why?"

"All niggers are mean," the child declared solemnly. "Free ones
are the worst. When I get to own slaves, I will whip 'em all the time."
Then he added, "I'll show you the way, though, if you'll protect me!"

Their route took them up Hill Street and by a burying ground at
the end of it. A little further on appeared groups of palm-thatched
huts increasingly crowded together. There was a succession of garden
patches behind incredibly rickety fences. Hurrying from them appeared a stream of blacks—men, women and children. Now that it
was dark, it was hard to see what they looked like.

Eros clung to Tim's hand while explaining, "These are slaves. If
they ain't in their master's home when the ol' church clock rings
seven, they'll be taken up by the patrol and get flogged 'less they show
a pass.

"Of course free niggers don't have curfew. Pa says those black
buggers will cause trouble some day. You see, Mr. Bennett, a nigger

can't be freed, but he gets to thinking he's as good as us."

Here, Tim reflected, was odd talk from the illegitimate son of a mulatto.

The drumming came from beyond a bonfire kindled in the center of a circle of beehive-shaped huts. Dozens and dozens of ragged negroes squatted on ground that was slimy with refuse and the droppings of goats, pigs and chickens. From what Cuffy had told him, this must be very like the villages in Guinea and along the Ivory Coast.

Eros stopped in his tracks, eyes goggling and jaw dropped. He had never beheld anything like the scene before his eyes.

In celebration of finding himself on dry land again Sam Higsby was dancing to the cadences that half a dozen bucks were extracting from an amazing assortment of drums.

The rifleman had on his greasy old hunting shirt, the one that had "Liberty" painted across its chest. Followed by the intent gaze of dozens of the squatting negroes, the Pennsylvanian spun, whirled and leaped in an Indian dance of some sort.

Now he was pounding the earth with his moccasins in a very difficult and complicated rhythm that delighted his audience. He would bend very low, then spring erect and throw his head back so fast that, like a stallion's tail in the wind, his jet hair lashed his face.

"*Ani-kwo-dadu-sto-di, da-tli-de gava,*" he chanted. "*Yum-wi ya tsol-tsi-ski awali ula gisker!*"

"Ah-h-h!" cried the audience when he began to swing his war hatchet in glittering arcs. The dance he had done in Tiverton had been as nothing to this fierce upsurgence of energy.

The fire, blazing up, sketched yellow sweaty highlights on Higsby's cheeks.

"The Councilors will be very angry when they hear of this," the boy muttered. "Even free niggers ain't allowed to drum more than two drums at a time."

"Why not?"

" 'Cause they get to remembering their old ways." Eros seemed quite unaware that his own small body was swaying, his bare feet shuffling. He looked frightened.

"Can't you make your friend stop? The niggers will get excited and there will be trouble." The boy looked fearfully about. "The niggers wouldn't dare do this if your ships hadn't come."

Tim was about to call out when Higsby, emitting an eerie screech, tossed his war axe high into the smoke. When he caught it, he stood still, panting, grinning.

A sinewy negro with teeth filed into dog-like points jumped into the dance space. Higsby clapped his hands, ran out of the firelight yelling:

"Go on and dance, but you can't beat me!" The drummers, dragging their palms across the drumheads, drew thundering noises from their instruments.

Tim started to beckon Higsby but felt Eros squeezing his hand. *Tunk-tunk, tonk-a-tonk!* sang the hand drums.

The dancer pulled on a mask suggesting a leopard's head as a friend tied a length of rope over his lean and muscular buttocks. His costume thus completed, the dancer dropped onto all fours and the drumming quickened as he went bounding around the circle.

"Ee-ya-o! Ee-ya-o!" the watchers chanted. The cry was infinitely mournful, haunting. Old and young rocked their bodies more violently.

Though Higsby was edging towards him, Tim could not tear his gaze from that whirling, bounding figure in the firelight. The black dancer was, with uncanny skill, simulating a leopard on the prowl.

A far cry this, from Peaceful Haven, from the Friends' Meeting House.

B-long-g! From the darkness beyond the burying ground, a bell sounded a single shivering note.

Grins and laughter vanished. Blacks sprang up and raced, gibbering, into the dark.

Only a handful of free negroes remained when the clock's seventh note had tolled.

"Hey-o, Tim!" Higsby greeted. "How you favor my Cherokee Eagle dance?"

Relieved to find Higsby sober and ready to accept Mr. Petty's hospitality, Tim expanded, spoke of continuing the voyage to Cap François.

Higsby remained silent until he had done, then drawled, "You won't take it too hard if I say I ain't goin'?"

"*Not going?* Good Lord, Sam, you can't back out now! Why, what'll I do? From the start I have been planning a berth for you aboard the *Narragansett.*"

The aquiline profile faintly seen in the star light remained un-relaxed.

"Why, Sam, I'll give you a chief gunner's share—a mate's— I'll make you so rich you'll never have to starve or fight or—"

"Uh-huh. That's just what I'm a-fearing. Tim, I set a store by you and I hope we'll stay good friends, but the sea and me is like Hurons and Iroquois," he said simply. "Holy Jesus! I'd liefer have a passel of Wyandot squaws go to work on me than feel like I did sailin' down from Philadelphy."

Eros trotted, fascinated, between them.

"No, Tim, ain't any skirmishing in this kind o' war and that's all the fighting *I* know." The rifleman began talking faster. "Heard tell there will be real warrin' in the Cherokee country this summer. Sure to be if old Draggin' Canoe paints himself black an' red."

He gave Eros a lift over a mud hole. "Again, I don't greatly fancy these foreign countries. Folks here sp'ils their vittles with too much pepper."

He gave an impatient snort. "Goddam it, man, 'twould be different if there was such a thing as a deer anywheres. Bein' as you don't take interest in pressin' petticuts, you won't have noticed that in these parts, yer fun's with black wenches or sailor fashion."

"I suppose that's so," Tim admitted slowly. This was a serious jolt to his scheme. All along he had counted on having Sam with him.

Higsby was saying, "Me, I can't stomach these black gals. Smell kinder queer, sour-like. Now a squaw ain't no bunch o' heliotrope, but she's got a woodsy smell to her—kind o' like a well-tanned pelt."

14
ADELINA

THE dinner was a grand success. Messrs. Parton, Forbes, Drumgold and the rest of the Bahamians proved convivial in a noisy and informal way.

After dinner the party lingered, smoking long clay pipes and swilling horrific draughts of flip beneath the flamboyant tree in the inner court.

Higsby, full of dinner, and at a loss for conversation, made an excuse about "catching" a breath of air—and to Tim's alarm disappeared for good.

Tim sat chewing gently on the mouthpiece of his churchwarden and observing one of his father's primary precepts: he listened and, in listening, deduced that these merchants were a shrewd lot and bothered by none-too-many scruples.

The American war, he gathered, was putting them in a bad way— though their condition was by no means as desperate as that of corresponding merchants in the blockaded colonies.

"Give m' right fist to lay hands on a cargo of onions, flour and Jamaica fish," Parton declared, slapping a mosquito from his third chin. "God above! You can ask what you're minded to in Kingston and Barbados for slave food."

He turned a round little head. "John, what did we used to ask for Jamaica fish?"

"Thirty shillings the hundredweight," came Mr. Petty's prompt response.

"There you are," Parton said. "I got sixty-five shillings last venture. Mess beef, once twenty shillings a cask, will bring you forty-five, maybe more. I don't know."

Tim gasped. Jamaica fish, which was nothing but odd scraps and under-size salt cod, could be purchased at fifteen shillings the hundredweight in any Massachusetts port! He listened so intently his pipe went out. Crimanently! If what this Bahamian said was so, there seemed to be greater profit in trading than in privateering.

Tim ran thoughtful fingers through his hair and at length inquired, "What is needed most in the Indies?"

"Food, lumber, livestock," came Mr. Drumgold's prompt reply. "We suffer from a glut of cloth, ironware and tin from England."

During the next few moments the Rhode Islander gathered that spar and cordage prices would soar because West Indian ship-builders, as well as the Royal Dock Yards, were becoming hard put to spar and mast new vessels. Everybody knew that the best spars in the world came from King's Forest in New Hampshire.

"Once you begin trading—" Petty's voice was growing thick—"I'll undertake to locate some prime mahoganies and dye-woods for you. If you should fancy a cargo of salt, why Phil Leslie here can supply you with the purest that ever was raked on Turk's Island. Then we've pimentoes, cocoanuts and sponges."

"What about turtles?"

Petty laughed. "You will have to talk to Adelina about that. Get her to show you the pen she keeps full of 'em. Knows prices—"

By the time the sangaree bowl was refilled for the fourth time, Tim had learned a good deal.

"To 'ell with food and lumber!" snapped Peter Saur, who was growing cantankerous. "Mr. Bennett, the top profit is in the slave-trade. Always was, always will be."

He glowered about, waved the scarlet glow of his pipe. "Don't any-body try tell me niggers ain't become mighty dear in Georgia, South Carolina and t'other plantation colonies."

"That's right," Petty agreed owlishly. "Can't be too many slavers slipping past our dear King's cruisers."

Saur refilled his glass. "Yessir. If my *Corona* wasn't over in Lisbon, I'd direct her straight to Whydah and pick up a koffle of Gambias!"

John Card roused suddenly from a brief nap. "For once, Saur is right," he grunted. "Gambias are prime favorites in Charleston. Good field hands—don't suicide, or die easy like Eboes.

"Mr. Bennett, I take it you ain't been in the Triangle trade so I'll advise you to write on the tail of your shirt the fact that there's all the difference in world 'twixt kinds of niggers."

He bent forward to stir a smudge fire which was, with indifferent success, attempting to discourage dense clouds of mosquitoes.

"Every market has preferences. Now, down Havana way you can't give Senegals away. Why? 'Cause the Dons are harsh and the Senegals are proud and war-like. They don't suffer a lashing without eternally figuring out how to kill whoever gives it to 'em.

"In most Spanish ports Guineas and Engoes bring the big prices." Mr. Card paused, scratched his ear, then said, "Don't *ever* pay good prices for Gaboons. Like I said, they're frail. You have to watch your Coromantees; they're fighters and hot-tempered. Never offer them in Barbados, St. Kitts or Jamaica."

Saur took a deep gulp of rumbullion, shook his head angrily. "John, you're in error about Gambias being prime in Charleston. I've always found Gullahs bring a better price. They're strong and got some wits to 'em, and they ain't thievish."

He turned on Tim, blotchy features heated with liquor. "Come to my Guinea yard tomorrow, then we'll attend the vendue. John Russell's *Live Oak* made port last week."

By midnight the whole party had become so genteelly and satisfactorily drunk that Drumgold and Card lay sprawled side by side on a settee, bawling out an endless succession of bawdy songs. Parton was on all fours, spewing like grampus, whereas Saur, the slave dealer, had rolled under the sideboard and was snoring magnificently.

As for Tim, who had been sampling a lot of weird concoctions, his head was singing like a teakettle. Feeling very light-footed he plotted a course upstairs.

"Mus' remember manners, always be gen'leman, if not an officer —all thanks to Lucy. No, musn' rip off your shirt. Hot, though."

He was wondering where Mr. Petty could have betaken himself when across the head of the stairs leaped a beam of light. His host appeared. He was swaying and had his wig on crooked.

"So *there* you are. Goo' ol' Tim'thy. You goo' fellow after all. Feared you were jus' a damn' Bible-pounding Quaker. Don' like mosh Quakers. Too holier 'n thou."

Petty clutched the door frame and in the candle light his eyes looked yellow as lemon peel. "Don' trus' people don' drink. Fine chap—Tim—think the worl' of you." His face lit. "Tell you wha', you come in here. Don' tell others."

Tim doubted whether he'd heard aright, but advanced when his host beckoned.

"Pretty Petty! Pretty Petty!" He giggled. "Not Pretty Polly, jus' Pretty Petty!"

Suddenly he saw Adelina standing in there in a nightshift so fragile he could see clear through it. At the sight of her body so subtly revealed, he felt hot currents rise in his brain.

"Oh—I—didn't know!"

Apparently the housekeeper had just entered through another door, had believed herself alone with John Petty. Tim watched her languorous smile vanish and an awful, stricken look supplant it. One of her arms rose in a fending motion when Petty clapped her on the rear and flung an arm about her waist.

Laughing throatily, the Bahamian pushed her forward. "You—Bennett—have some—"

Adelina had never looked so colored as when she rolled her eyes in a look of frantic despair.

"But—but, John, you promised after the last— No, I can't," she gasped struggling in his grip. "I love *you*. Don't force—"

"Silence, woman! Don't you dare talk back!" Petty flew into a towering fury. His jaws worked and his fingers dug like talons into her arm. "When I want slave to do something, it gets done quick!"

"Oh, John," she moaned, "how can—"

"I—I'll teach you!" Quite gone was Mr. Petty's usual good humor. Winding fingers in the housekeeper's hair, he wrenched her savagely to her knees.

"Gimme your belt!" he snarled at Tim. "I'll teach this slut her place!"

Utterly taken aback, Tim could only retreat a step. What did Petty take him for?

"I thank you, Mr. Petty, but I—well, I—*can't.*"

"Can't? Why the blazes not?" Petty swung angrily. "She's good, I tell you, warm stuff— Here, take a look at her. You'll change your mind."

While Adelina remained in an attitude of frozen hopelessness, her owner hooked a finger in the neck of her shift and ripped the material clear down to her knees.

"Right, ain't I?"

He was. The housekeeper's body was slim, exquisitely formed. Yet the anguished curl of the woman's lips was more chilling than a douse of ice water.

"Please try to understand, Mr. Petty," Tim choked. "I—I am to marry a girl at home."

"Ho! ho! ho! My God! If you Yankees—ho! ho! ho!—don't beat the Dutch!" The Bahamian let go his housekeeper, broke into peals of strident laughter. "What difference if maybe you are going to marry —ho! ho! ho!—a girl near two thousand miles away?"

Unsteadily, Tim backed out of the door. He didn't want to admit that Mr. Petty might be right and he wasn't affianced—not any more. What would Lucy make of this scene? He began to laugh himself.

The housekeeper had slipped an arm about Petty's shoulders and softly she murmured, "It is very late, John, Mr. Bennett really wishes to retire. Besides I've thought of—"

Putting lips next his ear, she whispered something which sent the Bahamian off into delighted chuckles.

"Capital! Forgotten that—" Beaming now, he waved at Tim. "Goo' night, young Benne'. Buy you wench for your own tomorrow. Lacroix has a pretty Creolian—get her maybe forty pounds—Lacroix's friend of mine. She does some of the damnedest—" Petty's voice dwindled.

Tim's bed rolled and tossed like the *Alfred* off Cape Hatteras until, half in and half out of the mosquito bar, he fell asleep.

15

DEPARTURE

IN THE street outside of Mr. Petty's, lines of oxcarts bringing still further supplies for the American squadron began creaking by.

Tim didn't like to think of the ships as about to sail. He had made a good many friends in the squadron: dour, impatient Lieutenant Jones, capable and aggressive Captain Biddle and the Commodore himself.

Most of all he would miss Nat Coffin's Latin tags and kindly cynicisms. It was queer about the marine sergeant. When the other N. C. O.'s were getting drunk or ruffling the yellow girls, Sergeant Coffin remained at the Bull & Otter writing in a book what he wryly described as "Observations."

He would never let anyone see what he wrote. "I'll publish it some day and astound everyone with my wisdom," he'd laughed. *"Amicus humani generis."*

One night after the Nantucketer had indulged in an extra glass of Barbados rum, he had spoken tenderly of a girl back in Providence. Shyly, he admitted he hoped to meet her in Philadelphia on the squadron's return. There had been some misunderstanding between them. Oddly enough, when he inquired as to how soon they would marry, Nat had flushed and murmured:

"Docendo discimus. There is a matter of deliberation, my friend. There are reasons, plagued sound reasons, I fear, why such a step should not even be considered. Yet—it ain't reasonable—I can't keep from thoughts of my sweet lass. Yon minx is a veritable paragon— sees me as I am, strong here, weak there, yet loves me, I think."

Plague take it, he would miss Nat, and sorely. Irritable, Tim caught up a copy of the *Bahama's Gazette* and read:

Mold and dip't candles are to be sold by Mr. John Christie. Also Corned Becf and Tongue, Hyson, Soochong and Bahia tea; Lisbon and Teneriffe wines.

Messrs. Leslie & Co. reports recent importation of Gloucester & Cheshire cheeses, single refined Sugar, hide & red herring, small shot and bar lead.

The eternal chittering of the lovebirds briefly broke in on his reading.

TO BE SOLD

On Thursday next at 2 of the Afternoon.

(If not disposed of before that time at Private Sale) Fifteen young, handsome and healthy

NEGROES

From 14 to 23 years of Age. Well seasoned to this climate, accustomed to hard Work and property warranted—among them some Neat, clean serving wenches.

The conditions of this Sale are, ½ of the purchase money to be paid in 4 mo. The remainer in 10 mo. approved security being given before the property is altered. Those willing to purchase by private bargain before the time of public Sale may know the terms by applying to,

John Morris, Vendue Master
John Russell.

A knock at the front door preceded the hurried patter of Venus' feet.

"Yes, sir, just come right in, sir. You'll find Mr. Bennett in 'e sitting room."

For once Sergeant Nathaniel Coffin looked entirely grave as he tossed his cocked hat onto a settee.

"Well, Timothy, I fear this is *Vale, frater, et si semper, indesemper vale.* The fleet sails tomorrow at dawn. The seventeenth an I reckoned correctly?"

He looked earnestly at Tim. "You will not change your mind?"

"No, Nat, for many reasons, I must reach Cap François as soon as possible."

Coffin eased the pewter buttons of his tunic and settled onto a chair. *"Quo animo?* Why such haste? Surely a dash more of naval experience would not be wasted on a budding privateer?"

Slowly Tim's fingers closed, and he said in a slow voice, "Once the commissions are issued I intend to be among the first on the cruising ground."

The Nantucketer leaned forward, gravely considered the gray-eyed, broad-shouldered figure opposite. "Why do you so desperately wish to prove yourself?"

"For two, possibly three, reasons."

"And I venture not the least important of them has to do with the charming sex?" He gave a short laugh. "Plague take it, why are the dear creatures so difficult to live with—yet so indispensable?"

Nat settled back, fixed his gaze on a scarlet hibiscus at the window. "Dear God, why must we so frantically seek learning, power, wealth? Were Socrates, Caesar, or Charlemagne happier than yonder blacks we see singing at their work?

"Are we right, Timothy? Is this civilization we toil to build by battles and brains not some engine which may in the end o'erwhelm us? Shouldn't a man be content with a full belly, a woman and a hut just stout enough to keep out the rain?"

Perplexedly, the marine ran fingers through his crisp, dark red hair. "Why does the white race, the smartest in Nature—if we are to believe ourselves—waste time and priceless energy in killing itself off? Is it in order that we may accumulate more property, more responsibilities? Ah, Tim, Tim, I'm not yet sure, but I doubt whether God designed mankind to bear such burdens."

He jumped up, filled a gourd at the olla. When he turned, the bitterness was gone from his features.

"You must pardon me; sometimes I fear I must have been intended to be a wretched, un-witty *dominie*. Is there by any chance a letter you would like to send? I will see it delivered to a reputable postrider once the squadron makes port."

"And where shall you go when the cruise is done?"

"Eventually, to Philadelphia." Nat lowered his voice. "I hope to find the girl I once mentioned. Somehow I feel she would have joined me but for some mischance. *Quo fata ferunt,* as it were."

"Why can't you marry her?" Tim asked with real interest.

A slow flush stained the Nantucketer's tanned visage. "Well, if you must have it, because though but a tyro, she was following a very ancient profession when I met her."

"Ah—I see. A trollop?"

"For God's sake, don't!" The figure in green and white winced. Nat's black-gaitered legs took him quickly the length of the room.

"She was not a true trollop. Circumstances had driven her, yet she remained tender and entertained lofty ideals. She is, I fear, a rebel against the present order of Society."

Tim frowned, went over to look out of the window into the sunny, lazy street with its dogs, pigs, and naked black children.

"I follow your meaning. I once had a sister who was just that sort of a rebel." He would have gone on, but Nat Coffin's mind was following another track.

"Save for my family, I would marry her straight off." He spread helpless hands. "Dear God, is it right for me to introduce into their placid, well-ordered circle what they could, and with reason, call a 'scarlet hussy'?"

"Take cheer, Nat, your pretty little rebel may never appear to plague you." Tim felt comforted, somehow, to find this companion in adversity. "Probably she will not. It doesn't lie in many women to be constant. Believe me, I know."

"To be so bitter about it you must have cause," Nat observed, doing up his tunic buttons. "Well, if you decide to write letters home, I'll get them from you at the vendue."

Long after Nathaniel Coffin's almost sedate figure had swung out of sight, Tim lingered, hot and wretchedly undecided, in what Mr. Petty euphemistically referred to as his office.

"Why the devil should I write to her?" he inquired of a tiny, very furry little kitten which came wobbling through the door. It gazed up at him with smoky blue eyes. "Why should I? I did my very best, didn't I? But did she? No!"

The kitten seated itself, opened a tiny pink mouth, yawned profoundly. Tim decided that he would be damned, nay double-damned before he would come crawling back—even by letter. A man's self-respect imposed certain limits.

He seized a quill from the shot jar, and wrote:

March 16, 1776

Mistress Lucy:

I remain at loss to understand your cruel Defection of December last. Nevertheless, I cannot credit that you would entirely of your own Will have Deserted me in my Hour of Need. Yet how am I to think otherwise?

Ah, Lucy, what infatuated you to Abandon your poor lover? If my whole faith in Mankind is not to be Broke—if I am not to deem you the most Faithless of Females, you will repair to the City Tavern on Second Street in Philadelphia town a year come this Date.

Whether we shall ever meet once more, God and you must determine.

Farewell,

Timothy.

16

VENDUE

IN THE throng shuffling through a haze of silvery dust toward the Vendue House, Tim for the first time had an opportunity to study planters from out-islands of Cat, Grand Bahama, Andros, and Eleuthera. For the most part sunburnt and convivial, they affected floppy, wide-brimmed hats from Leghorn and an amazing array of wigs and garments out-moded by twenty years. Though few of the local merchants wished, or were able to buy, they attended the vendue to a man.

A vendue, Mr. Petty explained, was near as fine entertainment as horse-racing. On such an occasion a man saw nearly everybody in the Islands, met strangers and transacted more business than even in his own counting house. Augmenting the throng appeared many officers and men from the American squadron. Even Commodore Hopkins put in an appearance. Amid considerable stir, he tucked his sword under one arm and selected a seat facing the auctioneer's rostrum.

John Petty mopped his face. "Take good heed, Mr. Bennett. This afternoon you may learn more concerning the true state of the West

India trade than you will by working a year in a warehouse."

The auctioneer, a cadaverous, big-nosed Scot with a bronze-green complexion and eyes the color of amber ordered a slave to ring a big hand bell.

First he offered at auction the cargo of a Spanish smuggler captured, red-handed, off San Salvador. The Cuban tobacco she carried was in such demand that merchants cursed each other for raising the price—and kept right on bidding themselves.

The variety of currencies mentioned was astounding. Bids were offered in pounds sterling, in Jamaica pounds, in pistoles, in louises, in moi-d'ors, even in Virginia scrip. Tim noted that by far the most common offering was in Spanish dollars.

The speed with which the auctioneer's clerk translated these varied quotations into pounds sterling was amazing. Repeatedly, Mr. Laird, the auctioneer, warned, "Not a stiver o' clipped or sweated coin wull be accepted."

As Mr. Parton had predicted, slave food fetched amazingly high prices. On the other hand, European goods, wines and rum were drugs on an already saturated market.

Some of the American officers began to bid. It was easy to distinguish the ex-merchantmen, the former privateersmen. To a man they knew what salt, rum and good Scotch woolens would likely fetch in America. They spent their pay carefully, made it go far. They sweated, fidgeted, watched each other—just as in the good old days before they had worn uniforms and had had to obey orders.

Mr. Petty chuckled until his fat shoulders shook. "By God, they're still merchantmen under those funny uniforms. Look at that old rascal lick his chops! He should; the idea of picking up fine new hawsers at one and three the running foot!"

Tim saw Abraham Whipple's hands keep opening and shutting under his excitement.

Once, when a parcel of bagged coffee was put up, Saltonstall yelled out a winning bid. Hopkins frowned, growled something, but Saltonstall was distinctly heard to say:

"Naow, Esek, 'tain't in me to pass up such a bargain!"

Once the condemned goods had been disposed of, the throng brightened and the auctioneer referred to a stone jug from which he drank with an earnestness that might have gone far towards explaining his complexion.

More people tried to crowd into the stifling heat of the great ill-lighted structure.

"Russell's slaves are next," Mr. Petty explained. "Mind you watch what happens."

The auctioneer wiped his mouth on the back of his hand, pushed strands of dank sandy hair from his forehead and nodded for his assistant. Briskly, the bell's brazen clangor pealed under the hot eaves.

The throng craned their necks, talked louder as a gang of some fifteen negroes, all fresh from the Grain Coast, were herded in. The grown men were shackled, but the youths among them were so frightened they could not have run. The four females in the lot cowered, eyes rolling, before the rostrum. The clinking of iron links over the stone flooring faded.

A beetle-browed fellow in a handsome but overly tight-fitting suit of gray velvet, waved at the auctioneer.

"There's your stock, Mr. Laird, all of 'em and sound as a sovereign." In the humid half light of the vendue shed, the slaver stood, a brutally handsome fellow in a modish buckled hat that accorded not at all with jaws blue for want of a shave. A lock of greasy black hair fell over his forehead, and a red silk handkerchief knotted about his neck fluttered as he nodded to friends in the throng. Belted about a mulberry-hued waistcoat was a brass-handled dirk.

Two of the wenches, Tim thought, were really pretty. Mr. Petty clambered up on a chair to get a better look.

"Um," he commented. "Only fifteen left. The cream of Russell's cargo must have been bought by private tender."

The auctioneer's bell jangled again and, clearing his throat, he leaned far over the pulpit. "Gentlemen, I ha'e the guid for-r-tune tae offer a verra prime bar-rr-gain. I needna' remind ye that blacks such as these are ower scarce noo that Yankee ships are driven off the seas.

"Frae this time on 'tis on the Dons ye must rely, and 'tis puir, diseased beings they bring!"

Eyes glittering behind square-lensed spectacles, Mr. Laird scanned his listeners. "Gentlemen, 'tis my pleasure and privilege to offer ye a parcel o' braw, buxom bucks and lassies imported by our own friend an' neighbor, honest John Russell."

"Honest? Since when?" somebody sang out from the back of the hall. When a general laugh had subsided, another was raised when the wit continued, "Thought the pirates had all been drove out years ago."

Mr. Russell bowed solemnly. "I thank 'e, Mr. Laird, from the bottom of my heart. You have ever been a reputed truthful man."

"Just to whet your appetites, my friends, we will auction the lassies fir-rrst. Jock—" Over his spectacles, the auctioneer glared at his assistant. "Oo—aye— Let me see. Number one is Quasheba. Fetch me up this Quasheba."

A bandy-legged fellow in a red stocking cap used the butt of a plaited whip to prod to her feet a bushy-haired girl. Save for a kilt of slave cloth, she stood mother-naked. Her chin trembled and there was an indescribable wild animal quality to her fright when she was led to a low platform. Everyone could see her large, pointed breasts and thin shanks a-trembling.

"Quasheba," the auctioneer intoned, "is aged about sixteen years and o' the Coromantee people. She is warranted strong and sound o' wind and limb. Turn her roond, Jock. Ye must show these gentlemen Quasheba's back. See? Is't no' a fine, straight back? Yon sturdy wench should fetch Mr. Russell a pretty penny. What am I bid?"

When she was turned to face the dim, smoky throng, the negress shivered and attempted to hide her face in the crook of her elbow, but the auctioneer's assistant slapped it down with his whip handle.

"I bid five pounds, Jamaica," somebody called.

Everyone laughed and the auctioneer paid not the least attention. "What am I bid for this strapping, handsome young vir-r-gin—"

"Perhaps!" called the wit. "If Johnny Russell has caught the yaws."

"She will break to housework, mark my wor-rrds."

"Sixteen pounds, sterling!"

Again Tim glanced at the naval officers, a blur of red and blue across the hall. Their expressions were intent. Hopkins seemed especially interested. As everybody knew, he had captured and sold many and many a cargo of slaves.

Mr. Petty winked, nudged Tim and spoke in a hoarse whisper, "What would you say?"

"Looks good to me."

"No! Never buy a narrow-hipped wench—for a worker, that is. You stand to lose 'em with their first pickaninny," the Bahamian said. "Best buy a good breeding buck. Get one that's strong but not too smart. Last year had one named Pegasus. He earned me near a hundred pounds in stud fees." Mr. Petty sighed. "My God, Bennett, how that nigger doted on his work!

"Had to sell him though, caught the yaws from one of Robertson's wenches over on Eleuthera. You oughtn't to breed a nigger with yaws; the get is generally born blind or silly."

Quasheba fetched forty pounds.

"More than she's worth by ten pounds," commented Mr. Saur in the next row.

The next offering was a girl of eighteen with a figure straight as an arrow. Though her face was flat and an enormous nose spread halfway across it, she was knocked down for fifty pounds because she was big and promised to be a good breeder.

"That's King, Mrs. Fountain's overseer, who's bought her," Mr. Petty said.

King was about to claim his purchase when, all at once, the negress raised a series of dreadful, ear-piercing screams.

"What ails her?" Tim asked.

"Wench must have learned Mrs. Fountain double brands her slaves."

"'Double brands'?"

"Homely ones get burnt on the cheek besides on the left shoulder; pretty ones, on the palm of one hand. You'll hear her screech in a minute."

"My God!" Tim gasped. "Does everybody do that?"

"Double brand?" The Bahamian smiled apologetically. "No. I'm merciful, I suppose. I only burn them on the shoulder. Lately I've taken to tattooing. Hebe, Juno, Jupiter and the rest. I must be going soft. You can disguise a tattoo, but not a brand."

Presently from outside came such an anguished shriek that the blood roared and pounded in Tim's ears. Feeling suffocated, he arose to leave, but John Petty held his arm.

"Hold on, Bennett, hold on," he said not without sympathy. "Better get used to such things. Trading in the Indies ain't no quilting bee. Felt like you did at the start. We're not really hard in the Bahamas—not like in Barbados or Jamaica."

He looked solemnly at his companion. "Mr. Bennett, you just wouldn't credit some of the sights you'll see in Jamaica. Nightmares are pleasant by comparison."

It was only sensible to heed the Bahamian's well-meant advice so, taking a tight hold on himself, Tim watched the vendue out.

"You've some letters?" It was Sergeant Nat Coffin, just come ashore. "Only one—"

The Nantucketer smiled, tucked it carefully into his tunic. "*Amor vincit omnia.* I fancy she will be very happy."

The sound of a drum drew Tim's attention to a short column marching past the next corner. Fixed bayonets flashed in the sun. "Why, who are the prisoners?"

"The Governor, poor dog, and Thomas Arwin, his lieutenant. Arwin is also Inspector General of Customs for North America."

Both prisoners looked haggard and worried as, hatless, they were conducted to the water's edge.

The Governor, Nat noticed, still wore his official scarlet coat. "Why are they carrying Mr. Browne away?"

"Because Fort Montague fired after being duly surrendered," the marine explained. He winked. "I don't doubt these fellers will prove useful for exchange, too."

Secure among the desolate ruins of a tall look-out reputed to have been built by Will Teache, the famous buccaneer, Phil Hull lay in hiding. Now the last liberty boat was rowing out to the squadron, making a deserter of him.

Little chill ripples of excitement coursed the length of his back clear down to his buttocks. Phil Hull a deserter! It was a sobering realization. Nobody could blame him, though; the way that boatswain had kept after him these last few days wasn't to be endured.

Trying to forget the wild hammering of his heart, he rolled over and lay on the disjointed masonry watching a pair of big green lizards shoot out their tongues at insects. Their tongues looked like licking flames.

Once the ships went away, he should be safe enough. He would stay in the Bahamas if they would let him. Paint every kind of fish there was in the Islands. Gently his fingers touched the hot metal of his paint box. Yessir, so much food was growing wild all over the island, he guessed he would never go hungry—as he had sometimes back in Conanicut. Yessir, he'd hunt odd jobs in order to buy paint, brushes and paper.

Bo-oo-om! The final report of the *Alfred's* recall gun rolled in sultry echoes along the coast.

Escorting the sloop *Enterprise,* a local vessel hired to freight such of the King's property as overflowed the men-o'-war, Esek Hopkins' squadron vanished, topsail by topsail, over the horizon.

Phil's smile broadened.

17

THE LIVE OAK, BRIGANTINE

NEW PROVIDENCE, at once relieved and exhausted by such unaccustomed excitement, settled down to enjoy a brief prosperity engendered by the sale of supplies. Save for the out-and-out Englishmen and Crown employees among them, the Bahamians seemed genuinely regretful over the squadron's departure. The local merchants were, almost to a man, sympathetic with the rebellious Colonies and dead-set against the Ministry's greedy, blundering laws.

Provided this Continental Navy was increased and maintained in respectable force, Drumgold, Parton, Petty and most shipping men were in favor of casting in with the mainland Colonies. There was no doubt that the Islanders had been mightily impressed by Hopkins' pitiful scratch fleet.

Would a similar reaction obtain in Jamaica, Barbados, and the other Sugar Islands? Tim thought so. Already the planters and merchants there were raising a mighty loud wail to Parliament. No wonder; many of them were facing ruin. Slaves were reported to be starving in parts of Jamaica, to be rebellious in others.

One afternoon, a week after the fleet had sailed, Mr. Petty came tramping into the house, moodily fanning away a halo of flies with a frayed palm leaf.

"I hate to see you go, Bennett, but word is out that John Russell's *Live Oak* is to clear for Jamaica. Wants to turn over the slave food he bought at the vendue."

"That's capital," Tim said, but was amazed to find how much of his old enthusiasm was lacking. Here in New Providence everyone was friendly, so generous and so easy-going. A far cry from the restless, grasping, suspicious striving under which he had been brought up.

"You'll pardon me if I venture to hazard that you are making a mistake in leaving us?" Mr. Petty remarked between strokes of his fan. A rattan chair creaked under his weight as he dropped into it and sat looking up into Tim's sun-darkened features.

"Privateering is a gambler's game; for a born merchant like you, it's risky. Risky! Barring this fool war, your Pa would have become one of the richest men in Rhode Island, the way he was going.

"Bennett—Tim, why don't you settle down here? Nobody can deny that we've a fine, comfortable way of life." His manner was almost pleading as he waved a hand about the big, cool room.

"We gamble a little, get drunk once in a while and don't kill ourselves with work; yet we eat well, live well and make money, too.

Come, man, be sensible. I'll admit women like Adelina ain't to be found every day, but why not buy yourself a pleasant mestee?"

Mr. Petty settled back and threw his wig onto a settee. "When it comes to doing things your way, a housekeeper has a wife backed clean off the charts. If you use a mestee right, you gain her love; but she'll never forget that you *own* her, too. She won't dast put on airs —not more than once, if you know your way."

Tim nodded, asked curiously, "You'll forgive me if I wonder whether you are really as happy as you would have me think?"

The Bahamian hesitated, then nodded vigorously. "I *am* happy. I am contented as well as any simple man can be. I work, but not too hard. My children are strong and healthy and I enjoy life a sight more than Parton with his psalm-shouting, vinegar-tongued Scotch wife. For all her piety, she don't serve food fit for a pig."

Mr. Petty went to the sideboard, poured two glasses of Canary and brought them back. His jovial features were strangely serious.

"I trust you will reconsider your course," the merchant pleaded earnestly. "Why weep for the stars, Tim? What more can a man ask of life than a well-warmed bed, a full belly and a prosperous trade?

"The rewards of the next world may be all very well, but me, I like those of this world. I like to sink my teeth in 'em while I can. When I grow old, nothing can take away my memories."

Come to think of it, there was a lot in what Mr. Petty argued. A fellow wouldn't have to tolerate whims from an Adelina. John Petty merely had to tell his housekeeper what he wanted and that was all there was to it. His slightest wish was cheerfully, skillfully respected.

When he remembered how many times Lucy had coquetted, had kept him wriggling on tenter-hooks over some trivial matter, he felt like a callow fool.

A cheerful, whistled rendition of "The World Turned Upside Down" intruded on his indecision. Down the street and by the arched door tramped young Phil Hull! Brown as a nut and still wearing the canvas petticoat breeches he'd been issued aboard the *Alfred*, he was lugging a stem of golden bananas on one shoulder. Crimanently!

The boy must have deserted!

He ran out into the street. "Phil, Phil! Come back. I've got to talk with you!"

The idea of this young idiot's having deserted! Any time one of the squadron might put back, or be driven back to New Providence. If they found him, he would swing to a yardarm in no time at all.

When he had finished with Phil, Tim came back and said soberly, "Thank you, Mr. Petty, for all your kindness. You may be right, but —I, well I'm going on. Please engage me two passages in the *Live Oak*."

Next day Tim packed his scanty possessions into a handsome new sea-chest Mr. Petty insisted on presenting. His monogram had already been done on it in bright, brass-headed nails so Mr. Petty must have foreseen his decision.

Suddenly, silently Adelina appeared. She held out a small linen bag and began to speak in liquid accents.

"I wish this were full of gold, Mr. Bennett." The housekeeper spoke earnestly yet with an indefinable quality of impersonality. Her somber eyes became queerly narrowed. "You are among the most noble and merciful of men." She stood in a patch of sunlight, her skirt and kerchief powder blue, her blouse terra-cotta.

Stepping backwards she cast a rapid glance up and down the hall. "You must not tell Mr. Petty. He would be very angry. But I want to—I must give you this *ouanga*. It is a very powerful fetish—black Obeah. Do not look within the black case. It brought to me—Adelina, a poor quarteroon—much happiness."

"Why, Adelina—" Tim was mystified, more deeply touched than in many months.

"I have prayed to God, to the old gods, too, that you would not leave here," she continued in her smooth voice. "But you are a fighting man—a bold one. Some day you will become a wise one, too— if—if—" she averted her face—"you live.

"Last night my fetish talked—" Firmly, her saffron-tinted fingers pressed the gift into his palm. Anxiety in her vivid great eyes, she murmured, "I pray Damballa that this *ouanga* proves stronger than the evil which Mogreb says lies in your path."

The housekeeper's eyes closed suddenly and her accents sounded faint yet penetratingly clear. A note of dismay, so real it seemed to be born of the past rather than of the future, thinned her voice.

"Fighting man! Fighting man! Whatever you do, wherever your *juju* leads—avoid Saint-Domingue. There live the devils!"

The mulatto's voluminous skirts rustled and in an instant she was hurrying off down the corridor.

Within the linen bag lay a small, purse-like container of black horsehide carefully sewn up with scarlet silk. What matter of object lay within, Tim could not ascertain by feeling. A knuckle bone, probably, a monkey's tooth, or some such worthless trifle.

With Phil Hull crouching deep in her cargo, the *Live Oak* set sail on the evening of March the twenty-second and tacked down the eastern channel by the light of a full moon. She met a string of little spongers heading for town. Soft, sweet voices among their crews floated through the balmy air as they prepared their evening meal.

Cooking fires aboard the sloops and schooners painted the sails above them with a palpitating glare. As bright, vibrant panels seen against darkness the canvas glowed, sometimes ochre, sometimes vermilion, sometimes a glaring blood crimson.

When, off Rose Island, the *Live Oak* pointed her stubby bowsprit southwards and began to rise to a series of long and oily swells, Tim drew a slow breath. Somewhere below yonder horizon the *Narragansett* lay waiting.

In less than a week he should be at Cap François.

PART II—CHARLESTON

I

FERGUSON'S SWAMP

IF ONE counted Indians and blacks, Desire Harmony estimated that over two hundred people had congregated at Congaree Cross Roads. Even after dusk, wagons and pack trains had continued to pull in until whole acres of camp fires glowed among the slash pines back of Mr. Joseph Horry's store.

Raucous voices, the sound of axes cutting firewood filled the night. From a freight train drawn up by the woodside came drunken shouts and a girl's squeal of pain.

It was hot, even for May, and absolutely windless. A row of candle lanterns ranging the edge of the loading platform was attracting thousands of mosquitoes. They sounded big as bumblebees. In a not very distant swamp bullfrogs rumbled and grunted incessantly.

For some reason Desire felt a sharp, constantly rising uneasiness. It had to do with the advanced condition of her pregnancy, of course. As "Mistress Daisy Montaigne" and an experienced actress, she shouldn't have got so upset over Brian's insistence on starting off with Mark Antony's funeral oration.

Languidly dressing her hair, she could hear babies crying, dogs fighting and snarling, and the trampling of horses. Down in the freighter trains voices were growing louder. Mr. Horry's red rum must be flowing more freely than ever.

Thank fortune the teamsters couldn't get any more liquor—at least not while she was using the space back of the counter for a dressing room.

By slinging a couple of blankets between bales of pungent and malodorous deerskins, she had managed to achieve a measure of privacy in which to change from her linsey-woolsey traveling dress into one of her two remaining costumes.

She could only hope she was putting her lip rouge on straight. These flaring candlewood splinters shed such a wretchedly uncertain light. In fording the Pocatico River her mirror somehow had become badly cracked. What disturbed her most were those fierce eyes which considered her unwinkingly through the barred, but glassless, windows.

Maybe she should have dressed in the wagon? No. On her way to the factory she would have had to risk a pawing at the hands of the brutish, savage-acting trappers and teamsters.

Last night she and Brian had had a hard time getting through their performance. Somehow, they hadn't easily won approval of an audience as sallow and gaunt-faced as the people around Congaree.

She wouldn't ever forget that audience with its expressionless, flat black eyes, brutish manner and stupid reaction. For a whole hour of singing and acting, Brian had collected only six shillings, four pence. He had been sulky about it all day.

A shrill, ringing whoop just outside the window made her start so violently that she had to re-paint her under lip. Until she had seen a few frontier roughs, Desire had never even dreamt that humans so utterly vicious, brutal and ignorant could exist.

When she realized that, in a few minutes now, she'd have to go on the stage, she wanted to be sick. Imagine having to go smiling onto a store's loading platform, there to endure a mental undressing and ravishing by hundreds of lascivious eyes.

For the first time in her life she was really fearful. Her proverbial luck must work hard tonight if she were to pass unscathed. If Brian hadn't been drinking, ran her thoughts, he would pull them through. He had a genuine actor's gift for winning a hostile or disinterested audience.

People in tidewater South Carolina might appreciate the classics but she judged that to people up here Julius Caesar and Macbeth were just a couple of kings, like King George III maybe.

If last night had been any indication, these primitives both misunderstood and resented Brian Montaigne's Green Room airs and

London macaroni manner. His Drury Lane "egads," "zounds," and "prithees" stuck in their craw, made them feel more ignorant than they were—if such were possible!

Desire felt sure Brian could charm these semi-savages with some bawdy ballads or, if he insisted on Shakespere, a few of the rougher passages from "Troilus and Cressida." She would work him round to it; "Lady Bumtickles' Revels" had always fetched a laugh at the dusty crossroads south of Williamsburg.

To her annoyance, she began perspiring profusely under her make-up. Her shepherdess costume felt insufferably hot, a veritable shirt of Nessus. If only the baby would lie still.

She tested her abdomen. Um. Though she had laced as tight as she dared, her pregnancy now was hardly to be concealed. Nervously, she inspected the dingy lace hemming her apron. Oh, bother! It needed sewing again.

Feeling utterly exhausted, she looked for a place to lie down. All day the wagon train had creaked and jolted over an endless succession of rock ridges. If only she dared cry a little she would feel better.

" 'Mark where the envious Casca stabbed—' "

"—Devil take all dirty furriners!" a raucous voice interrupted. "Gi's a song or a jig, dearie. Allus thought a popinjay could dance."

Inside the store, Desire clutched the door latch and began to tremble as she pushed the store's front door open a little. Of all nights for Brian to get stubborn drunk! Why wouldn't he give this audience what it wanted?

She saw the four torches flaring at Brian's feet, then row on row of unshaven or bearded faces; men, boys, half-breeds, Indians, and mulattoes. Far in the rear a few negroes looked on eagerly.

A rangy individual in a greasy leather shirt stood up and began shaking a clenched fist. "Jig, damn ye! We want a jig!"

" '—So are they all, all honorable gentlemen.' "

In the front row men in buckskins were passing about a stone jug and talking loudly among themselves. They wore hunting shirts like Sam Higsby's, but the resemblance ended there. There had been nothing bestial or dirty about the Pennsylvanian.

With a sinking heart, she heard Brian's voice grow coldly contemptuous. Sober, he would have humored the crowd, cracked a joke.

"Aw, stow that gab! Sing or dance!" more voices bellowed. "To hell with that fancy lingo. Hey! er you a man or woman?"

"Stab me, he's a gelding." Someone mimicked Brian's finicky pronunciation.

Brian, in his flowing toga, made a lordly gesture as if brushing away a troublesome insect. " 'That was the unkindest cut of all—' "

"Me—e-o—ow!" The cry came from among a semi-circle of dusty freight wagons, canvas tops of which were reflecting the footlights. Others took up the catcall.

Desire's heart began to pump painfully. Why *wouldn't* Brian come to his senses?

More whistling and catcalls. Suddenly Brian Montaigne broke off, coolly surveyed his malodorous and heavily-sweating audience an instant. Then in his loudest, clearest voice, he exclaimed, "Oh, ye gods! What boots it for an artist to cast his finest pearls before swine?"

He turned on his heel and, followed by a gale of whistles, curses and hisses, came stalking back into the store past some casks of pickled pork.

In a towering fury he ripped off the toga, stamped on its pathetic painted embroidery. "What canaille! What pigs! To think that I, Brian Montaigne, darling of a hundred Continental Green Rooms, should live to be catcalled by a parcel of nose-picking, louse-scratching country clowns!"

Turning aside, he buried his face in his hands and wept drunkenly.

In through a side door burst Mr. Horry, his face gray with alarm.

"Do something!" he begged. "Some of the orneriest Brass-ankles in Carolina is out there. Onct they get roused they'll stop at nothing. Skun a nigger alive last week just fer the hell of it! Most of 'em's ugly drunk. Quick, er they'll be in here and wrecking my stock!"

The audience, Desire perceived, was yelling all manner of threats. Worse still, not so much as a penny had been put into a wooden trencher hopefully left at the edge of the impromptu stage.

"Duck the goddam English pimp! Call us pigs, will he?" voices growled. "No, wait, I'll go fetch my lash."

Drawing herself up to full height in order to make her condition less noticeable, Desire forced a smile to her lips and ran out onto the platform into a gale of hostile uproar.

"He's a damn' Britainer!" beat against her ear drums. "Le's string him up. If he won't dance, we know how to make him, eh, boys? Got me a bull whip here that will stir a breakdown outen a corpse."

A big, red-haired drover in a green worsted shirt had one foot on the platform as Desire ran to the edge of the stage. Making a dancing half-turn she neatly spun her petticoats garter-high, then reversing the motion gave her audience another glimpse of her thigh.

Back in Trenton the trick had stood her in good stead.

"Patience, kind friends," she called. Then she pirouetted across the whole front of the platform, slender legs alternately revealed and concealed amid a flurry of deftly managed petticoats. The catcalling ceased and so did the whistling.

Heart hammering, she tried to forget the angry, hostile faces at her feet and began a simple country dance which called for a lot of coy winks and head tossing. She found it steadying to fix her gaze on a row of Indians crouched on a log in the background. From their steady unblinking gaze, she gained confidence.

Encouraged, she recited "The Chambermaid's Love Letter" with a pert winsomeness which would not have discredited Mistress Cheer, queen of all soubrettes.

The audience was quiet now except for a couple of drunken teamsters fighting and gouging at each other somewhere among the wagons. As the betrayed chambermaid, Desire found an excuse to show her legs once more, whereat the crowd voiced frank approval of scarlet garters tied in jaunty bowknots.

She was lamenting her indecision as to which lover to marry when a gap-toothed lout in a hunting shirt sang out:

"Don't you worry, Daisy! I'll lick 'em both an' you kin come home with me!"

Desire blew him a kiss, tried to forget the mosquitoes stinging
her neck and arms.

"Don't you believe him, Ma'am," warned the man with the bull
whip. "He's got a hull passel of wives over in the Creek Nation!"

There was another roar of laughter, and the men sat more easily.
Lord, how they stank! It was all Desire could do to smile as she invited:

"If you'll light your pipes, boys, and chase away some of these
skeeters, I'll sing you a chanty all Philadelphia is singing:

> " 'The South teems with events, convulsing ones;
> The Briton there plays no anemic war,
> With gallant face he moves and gallantly is met
> Brave spirits throng the camp—' "

"That's right!" the man in the hunting shirt yelled. "Most of us
fit at Moore's Creek!"

> " 'And not a clown but from his youth' "

Desire emphasized the next line:

> " 'Is trained to speed the unerring bullet to the mark!
> To climb the steep, to struggle with the stream,
> To toil unshrinking under scorching skies.
> This and that trust in Heaven which animates
> The Patriot breast shall far outweigh the lack
> Of discipline—' "

Wave on wave of hearty applause completely drowned out the
last verse.

Behind her, Brian Montaigne was calling in angry whispers, ordering her to retire, complaining that she was stealing his time. The audience, however, would not let her go and insisted she sing the last
verse again. They would gladly have heard her repeat it still once
more had not Brian snatched at her wrist.

"Come in, you little fool, let the canaille yearn!"

Apparently somewhat sobered, Montaigne then scampered out onto

STARS ON THE SEA

the stage to assume the half-witted postures of the unfortunate Launcelot Gobbo.

By now the audience was in such good humor that they applauded, laughed, continued to laugh. When he had done, however, the crowd demanded Mistress Daisy so she and Brian ran through an end piece entitled "The Beaux's Stratagem."

It was received with moderate enthusiasm.

Brian, after bowing acknowledgment, struck an attitude and announced:

"Ladies and gentlemen, this concludes our humble offerings for the evening. Most earnestly do we thank you for your patronage— and—ahem—trust you will generously not overlook the trencher set at the edge of this platform." He bowed deeply. "Hail, fellow lovers of Mimos, and farewell, a long farewell."

"More! More!"

"—If you would again applaud our modest efforts, pray attend the New Theatre in Queen Street, Charleston. Seats are but four pence in the pit."

"To hell with Charleston. We want Miss Daisy!"

"Alas," Mr. Montaigne shrugged, said loftily, "Mistress Daisy is er —indisposed."

"Indisposed? Haw! Haw! *There's* a fancy word for the family way!"

In the stuffy little store, Desire's cheeks burned beneath the rouge. Fortunately, the roughs had gone into such a good humor that they not only allowed Brian to withdraw but invited him to a drink.

Brian's gracious smile faded as he closed the store door. "Wretched female!" he exploded. "How durst you interrupt my scene?"

"But, dearest, couldn't you see that—"

"—A minute more they would have succumbed to my oratory," said he.

"But you left the stage—"

"I would have returned but you spoiled it when I was on the point of winning them." Hurt and mortified, Brian raged on, "Your miserable jealousy does not deceive me—"

"I am indeed sorry," she cried softly. "But, really, Brian, it seemed only wise to mollify them."

"Quiet!"

From his loading platform, pudgy little Mr. Horry was announcing the approaching auction of some prime Gaboon slaves and half a dozen bales of osnaburgs, kersies, calicoes, and callimancoes—

"All right, all right," the man with the bull whip cut in. "Never mind that. What's news?"

Mr. Horry hesitated, stamped on a spark from one of the dying torches. "Why—well, now—some say the British are fixing to send a fleet against Charleston."

Such a sudden hush fell over the clearing that everyone could hear an owl calling dismally in the depths of the moss-draped swamp.

"And an army, too," Mr. Horry added uncomfortably. "Now that ain't gospel, but it's what Captain MacIntosh told me Monday last.

"He's planning on raising a regiment in these parts if you all mean to fight for the Congress."

"Fight? What for?" a man in a hunting shirt demanded. "What in Christ's sweet name have them dapper-dandy planters ever done for us 'cept cheat us on every fur or deerskin we kin bring in?" He turned. "Come on, Jed, le's git back to camp. Ah didn't come heah to stay sober."

The crowd had largely dispersed, though groups of the more drunken lingered to bicker, boast and belch. Desire had never felt more thoroughly exhausted than when she crawled up a little ladder into the back of the freight wagon, a huge affair dragged by eight gigantic horses.

For a not inconsiderable price, she and Brian had been permitted to contrive beds of a sort among the freight which consisted of harness, spades, and hoes. The train was out of Baltimore and destined for Charleston.

Mercy! It was stifling underneath the canvas cover, but she dared not sit outside because the mosquitoes came out of the swamps in clouds so dense the tormented draft horses, tethered as they were to the wagon tongue, kept up a continual kicking and squealing.

Moving with leaden deliberation, Desire struggled out of her costume and sat panting, half naked in the dark. When she tore her apron hem even wider, her eyes filled and ran over. Come to think of it, though, the rip didn't matter. From now on she just wasn't appearing in public, not after what that Brass-ankle had shouted.

She wondered how much older Brian was than the thirty years he confessed to. Missing teeth and thinning hair suggested that he was forgetting at least a decade of his age.

At the beginning of their association she had never noticed such details. Of course, she wouldn't have; back in Providence Brian had arrived in her life like a rescuing champion.

His opportune appearance was further proof that Desire Harmony St. Clair was born lucky. It was a comforting belief.

She would never forget their first encounter—not if she lived to be a grandmother. It had come the third day after that catastrophic descent on Mrs. Norton's establishment.

Thanks to Nat Coffin's free-spending week at the Stirrup & Spur, its proprietor had granted her the use of a little attic room and, for some days, had fed her without asking any questions.

On the fourth morning he had said, not unkindly:

"Ma'am, you and Mr. Colebourne treated me handsomely and I trust I have demonstrated my gratitude. But I've any God's quantity of children that has got to be fed." He'd tipped her a wink. "If you know what to do, Ma'am, the room is still yours."

That evening when she'd returned from still another futile search for employment, someone was declaiming in the taproom. She had never heard anyone speak so well. Not even Pastor Wellman who was famous for his delivery. It was amazing that any voice could convey such subtle shades of expression.

When the speaker had done, she had run to his side, awestruck and enraptured. It must have been her impulsive and wholly genuine admiration which had so attracted Brian Montaigne.

"You—you are an actor, sir?"

"I am indeed a Thespian, my dear, a devoted slave to Mimos," Brian had admitted. "When I supported Mr. Garrick in London, it was I the populace really came to applaud. Of course, poor Davey would never admit it; couldn't, you perceive."

"Mr. Garrick?" she had gasped in a hushed tone.

"To be sure, O loveliest of Venus's rivals, to be sure. But Davey and I got on well enough until la Catesby came between us. Dashed if he fancied her preferring me to him. I say, my dear, would you care to join me in a jorum of porter?"

Before the evening was done, Brian Montaigne, late of the American Company of Comedians, later still of Douglass & Hallam, had promised to coach her and otherwise prepare her for the stage.

She just hadn't been able to credit her luck.

"'Pon my soul, goddess!" he'd exclaimed, ever-expressive black eyes alight. "I do believe poor Brian has made the find of a positive jewel—yea, of a Wainwright in the bud.

"La! Mistress, you have the voice; the figure, too, and above all, sparkle! Sparkle! There's the rub for many a pretty face. Lack but that one quality and you have nothing—less than nothing!"

In her shabby little bedroom, he had invited her to recite lines learned, oh, ages ago, back of Mr. Southwick's bookcases. Even now she could recall the exquisite thrill she had experienced when Brian applauded her first effort.

He had meant it, had been trembling with excitement.

"You have it! You *have* the divine spark. God's blood, I scarce can credit that you have never trod the boards!"

Calming down, he said later, "Your performance is—call it creditable. Yes, certainly creditable. But training, my dear Daisy—I shall call you that on our bills—is what you need. Provided you persevere, I promise that you will become the brightest female star in Brian Montaigne's Company of Thespians.

"We shall open in the Charleston season next spring and with a proper supporting cast for you, I do protest that the most jaded in the audience will be astounded, nay, electrified! Even now I can hear them shout '*bis, bis,*' '*encore!*' until the very rafters do tremble and shake."

To her charmed and wondering eyes, Brian opened vistas of un-dreamed-of glories.

In Barbados, Port de Paix and Jamaica, the planters would fling heavy purses of golden dollars and louis d'ors onto the stage. He knew it because he had toured the Indies in 1755 and 1756 with Mr. John Moody and the divine Mrs. Beasely—"As a mere child," he added hastily.

Naples, Seville, Paris, London. She would see them for herself. Barons, counts, dukes—nay kings, would worship at the feet of Daisy, the incomparable.

He had declared, "An' you have confidence and follow my bidding, sweet goddess, all the world's treasures shall be thine."

She had gathered, indirectly, that he had but recently made a thrilling escape out of Boston.

"Have been held captive there," he declared lightly, "ever since the Rebels, curse 'em, er—the Americans, invested the place."

Brian, sober, could be vastly instructive, not to mention entertaining. His fund of gossip and anecdotes seemed inexhaustible. Lying there in the hot, humid darkness, she could smile pityingly at herself.

How pleasantly awesome it had been to hear names of the Great falling so carelessly from Brian's beautifully modeled lips: Colley Cibber; "Jockey" Rockingham; Lord Sandwich who was known as "Jemmy Twitcher"; and Lord George Germain—"I always called him 'Pussy,' though," Brian declared.

Their overland voyage down to New York via New London had been great good fun. She had reveled in hearing gawping chambermaids gasp:

"There goes Mistress Daisy Montaigne, the actress." To know that village children were pointing and staring at her!

"I boast a host of friends in New York," Brian had told her all through Connecticut. "Stout fellows, they will back me to their last penny."

At that time Brian had been really in earnest over her having a career. Endlessly painstaking, he would rehearse her in "The Rivals," "She Stoops to Conquer" until she was tired enough to cry. Next day they would study still more sprightly comedies such as "Love and Valour," "A Roman Father."

But Shakespere, Brian insisted, was not to be attempted, not even thought of.

"Years must pass, goddess," he once had drawled while pressing a pair of breeches skillfully patched from within. "Years of toil ere you dare to declaim a single line of the immortal Bard."

Oh! She had fallen in love all right; with Brian's glamor, quick wit and sophistication, rather than with him. She realized that now.

"To live, one must love," he had advised her one radiant spring evening. "A fig for the prudes who rant over banns and golden rings."

At such times, Brian invariably presented his remarkably handsome profile. His chin, she doted on; it was round as that on a Grecian coin.

Recitations and discourses earned them their fare and transportation, but no more. Because it paid to be careful, they always included a patriotic ballad; two, if the crowd acted suspicious.

What had rendered their profession so precarious was an Edict the Congress had passed in 1775. It condemned:

"Every species of Extravagance & Dissipation, especially all Horse-racing & all kinds of Gaming, cock-fighting, Exhibitions of Shews, Plays & other Expensive Diversions & entertainments."

The heaviest blow, perhaps because it was the first, fell in New York. The John Street Theatre had been closed! Worse still, Brian's backers apparently had sailed for foreign parts or were in the debtors' prison.

Once the dreadful truth had become inescapable, Brian Montaigne had devoted the last of their funds to a truly prodigious spree and when she ventured to protest such ruinous self-indulgence, he tried to beat her. In terror she had bit him and he had slapped her so viciously that she recalled seeing close on a thousand stars. In pain and humiliation, she had prayed for the shade of John St. Clair to rise. In vain.

When in liquor, Brian Montaigne became a ranting, roaring bully and it usually became his fancy to play Petruchio, to upbraid her unmercifully. Eventually he would burst into tears and go to sleep.

In the morning he would be so bewildered, so desperately contrite over what he had said and done that generally she forgave him at once. Had she had any money of her own there were occasions when she would have left him.

Familiar conditions had prevailed in New York. There was no trade and consequently no work. Hundreds of homeless, hopeless females haunted the streets, tramping sullenly towards disease, despair and ultimate oblivion.

One thing that held her to Brian was his cheerful gentleness when sober. He possessed the priceless gift of saying those very things a girl was craving to hear at a given moment.

Another and more vital force commanded her loyalty. After a particularly successful evening, he had once murmured:

"You are indeed a sweet flower amid the desert sands of life, my goddess. If there is aught in which your humble slave can be of service, you have but to command him."

Too quickly, and perhaps too honestly, she had spoken of her great anxiety. Brian had earned her eternal gratitude by not staging a scene when, in fear and trembling, she had confessed her pregnancy.

"On Life's confounded tricky stage, dear little goddess," Brian had murmured smiling sadly, "the best of actresses have been known to mis-cue. Any offspring of yours would be very dear to me."

He had even promised to marry her just as soon as the Montaigne Company of Thespians was fairly launched.

Too exhausted to sleep, Desire lay staring up into the hot dark. Poor Brian, he was such a baffling blend of genius and—what else? God only knew!

Down by Mr. Horry's store people must be getting roaring drunk. She could hear yells, and Indians were letting out a screech every now and then. Somebody fired a shot. It outraged the gloomy silence of the swamp with its ringing echoes.

Sitting bolt upright, she tried to calm herself by calculating how much they might have earned tonight. It couldn't have been a great deal judging from the thin clatter the coins had made.

Why worry? In a wagon camp people were always shooting by way of celebration.

Why hadn't she brought a jug of water into the wagon with her? A sudden thirst was overpowering. She was only certain of one thing: when the child no longer encumbered her, she intended to become a great actress. In all modesty she knew she had the makings of a real comedienne. Lately, audiences had been applauding her a lot louder than Brian. Maybe that was why Brian had grown so surly of late?

Oh, why wouldn't Brian come to bed? How stupid it was to stay up so late, drinking and gaming. The freighters always started off at half after five.

Her restless thoughts ran back to Philadelphia. A fine city, Philadelphia. A real metropolis. Brian had really had friends there, but his creditors were even more numerous. She learned that one bleak February night. White to the lips, he had come rushing in, whimpering:

"Hide me! In God's mercy, Désirée, hide me!"

While Brian crawled in between her bed's mattress and the bed cords, she had had wit enough to tear off some of her clothes. Probably the finest acting of her career had been done for the benefit of the pair of bailiffs who presently came clumping upstairs.

"Begone! How dare you thus intrude upon a lady's privacy!" She had queened it, stamped her foot, until they had slunk off.

"Magnificent! Prodigiously convincing, goddess." Brian had been all smiles when he came crawling out from beneath the covers. But with that, the first veneer of gilt was rubbed from her idol.

Shifting restlessly because the insect-tortured horses kept stamping, she wondered how many girls had, at seventeen, tasted so deep, so bitterly of life?

South of the Delaware their journey had become a nightmare. Lord Dunmore was still ravaging Chesapeake Bay, so the voyage had to be made by land. Bitter was the people's disappointment that Esek Hopkins had not run down the Britishers.

"Just a damned Rhode Island yellow-belly—that's Hopkins!" Desire had gone scarlet when a Maryland postrider gave vent to his opinion. "Reckon the damned old grandmother wanted to line his pockets with easy pickings in the Indies."

The coachman had asked, "Well, what in hell d'you expect of a reformed privateersman? Ain't more than high-class pirates—the best of them."

Five long weeks they had spent working south along the King's Road. They had slept in more haycocks than taverns. It was hard to make a shilling through lower Virginia and North Carolina. The original tobacco fields were fast wearing out these days and the crop was moving westward.

Once in Wilmington, North Carolina, the cards had favored Brian and for a whole, glorious week they had lived riotously well.

Even now it was difficult to grasp that Charleston, the Golden, lay but a scant forty miles to the south and east. From Brian's description, Charleston was a populous city teeming with color, wealth, and life. It was, he claimed, more like an European town than any in America.

She turned restlessly on her sweaty blankets. Oh, why wouldn't the baby stop stirring? Suppose Charleston proved a less lucky repetition of Philadelphia?

"My luck will hold in Charleston," she almost feverishly reassured herself. "It will."

A teamster, stumbling along towards his wagon, tripped, fell with a crash then sat up, cursing sulphurously. A year ago, Desire Harmony Bennett would never have suspected that such vile words existed.

Though she stayed awake a long time, Brian still did not return. She heard him once or twice singing down by the store. He must be drunk as a lord—his voice was so thick and off-key. Now, for sure, they wouldn't have a sixpence with which to enter Charleston.

Because of the mosquitoes, Desire pulled Brian's greatcoat up over her head and fell, at last, into a hot, unrestful slumber.

2

Exit

At first Desire thought a drunken Indian was screeching but then, amid a series of agonized screams, she heard her name called,

"Désirée! Help! Don't! Help! Oh-h-h! *Don't!* In God's name don't! Help, Désirée, they kill me!"

Unhandily, because of her swollen figure, Desire scrambled into a shawl and dragged a petticoat up over her nightshift. She didn't even stop to put on her shoes but got down to the ground in a trembling hurry. Even so, those nerve-shaking screams had already diminished to bubbling, whimpering noises like those made by a severely whipped child.

A dying bonfire gilded stalactites of Spanish moss dangling funereally above the crossroads.

"Ya-a-ah! I'm a ol' he-wildcat what likes pretty gals. Come here!" bellowed a drunken trapper and he made a futile grab for her as she sped over the soft, sandy road.

"Désirée," came a weak and breathless cry. "Oh-h—they—they've —hurt me so!"

To her surprise not one of the Cherokees or Choctaws remained in sight. Just four gangling backwoodsmen who, swaying, scowled at her as she ran panting towards the fire. One of them, a gray-haired old villain, was wiping his hands on his breeches.

Said he to a young Brass-ankle who was so drunk he could hardly stand, "Shay, le's take 'at goddam shpy's fancy girl inter the swamp."

Never, thought Desire, had she seen so bestial a human face. It was bloated, had furry brows and snaggle yellow teeth.

"Naw," the other mumbled, trying to slip a skinning knife back into its sheath. "Ah don't want no truck with none o' these stage whores. Sting yer fierce. C'mon, Paw, guess we clipped that goddam macaroni's comb short enough so's he won't want to crow fer a long time."

Laughing dreadfully, the four shaggy fellows staggered off in the direction of Ferguson's Swamp.

Last thing Désirée heard the old man say was, "That'll larn him to talk like he was a dook and us swine under his feet. Time he larned this is Amurica, not England!"

Beside a dying fire, Brian Montaigne lay on the bare ground with a couple of half-dressed wagoners working over him. From quite a distance she could recognize his painful gasps.

The bigger driver saw her and warned, "You stay away, Ma'am. Your husband's hurt. Hurt bad."

Invisible hands tightened about her throat, Desire faltered, groped for support on the loading platform of Mr. Horry's store. In the nearest wagons people were waking, calling to know what was amiss. As draught beasts swung heads in line with the fire, their eyes glowed, purple-gold.

At last! Time and again she had cautioned Brian against lofty airs. Townspeople expected pretentiousness in an actor, but not semi-savages like these. Too bad border rum wasn't more expensive—only two shillings for a gallon of the raw, bowel-searing stuff.

"Désirée! Oh-h-h, dear God, why won't somebody kill me?" His voice, from the center of the group, was very weak. Suddenly regaining control of her legs, Desire dashed through a crowd of people in nightshirts.

A tall German with shirt tails jammed into cowhide boots caught her arm. "*Nein!*" he shook a cropped, pointed head. "Not go, Fräulein. Vot dose *Teuflen* haff done—*aber schrecklich ist!*"

"Let me go! I—I—" She peered wildly about.

From the edge of the woods, a drunken voice invited, "Hey, Mistress Daisy, you come to my wagon and you'll find a *man* in it!"

"*Nein, kommen Sie mit.*" The German tried clumsily to pat her shoulder. He had a round sunburnt face and behind his spectacles, he looked immeasurably horrified.

"Come to me, Désirée." Bewilderment and fright was in Brian's voice.

"I can't," she wailed. "They won't let me."

A measure of strength must have returned to him for his voice sounded stronger but still broken, un-pitched:

"Use me gently, kind friends— I fear there is naught you can do—"

A motion from the depths of the group suggested that Brian had managed to sit up.

Over a muttered consultation among the drivers, his voice rose. "I am dying, Thespis, dying. Oh, ye gods, view this sublime tragedy! Hearken to an artist doomed to tread his last measure in a wilderness unseen, unheard. What an infinite reservoir of Art is drained by a savage blade."

"Let me go! My—my husband is calling me—" Desire struggled, almost broke loose, but the German was quicker than he looked.

"*Nein,*" he rumbled. "I am sorry, but you must not see."

Over his shoulder she glimpsed two men, one a teamster in a broad hat bending over Brian's slowly writhing body. Several blood-darkened rags sketched pale patches on the trampled earth. "Oh, what have you done to him?"

"*Ich und Heinrich? Du lieber Gott!* Ve haff done noddings," the German protested. "It vass dem Brass-ankles."

"Brass-ankles? They are—Indians?"

"*Nein.* Vurser. Much vurser!"

When she realized what they had done, the world tilted on edge, her knees went lax and from a great distance she heard the big German's voice saying,

"You to *mein weibe* must come. Ve take care—"

She rallied, "You must let me go. You really must!"

From a second floor window, Mr. Horry's wife began shrilling, "Get out! Don't you dare let that—that pantomimer die on my doorstep!"

Brian Montaigne again managed to sit up, and in a terrible shaking voice, cried:

"Pantomimer? Peace, vulgar female! I have played to command before Princes of the Blood Royal. I—I have supported David Garrick—used to call him 'Davey,' you know. I—*I am a—a star!*"

Brian's voice faded, was lost amid the monotonous croaking of bullfrogs in Ferguson's Swamp.

The man supporting Desire patted her cheek in rough kindness. "So—so—he *todt* iss. Dead. Better so. A man should not live as he vass.

"*Kommen Sie mit, Liebchen*—please no more crying. Already Louisa iss so frightened of dis fierce and bloody country. So many savages, so many Brass-ankles, so many ruined men."

3

THE PROVEAUXS

FROM Maman's glance of warning, Antoinette Proveaux deduced that Papa had something on his mind. When the head of the house had something on his mind, especially at breakfast, everyone from Mrs. Proveaux down to Pansy, queen of the kitchen, moved with caution.

At best, the temper of Louis Proveaux was of the weathercock variety. Antoinette, slipping as quietly as she might into her seat at the breakfast table, read the danger signals. Maman was fluttery; Papa was wearing his oldest coat—a sure sign he was out of sorts.

Roger, however, looked very gay and martial as an ensign in the Second Rifle Regiment of South Carolina. Roger, of course, was what had upset Papa. The Proveauxs had always been merchants, solid Huguenot bourgeois not reconciled to raising their sons as fertilizers for a battlefield. Papa had said so a thousand times.

Sycamore, the butler, sniffed a pair of boiled eggs which a footman had just fetched up from the kitchen, and shook his head with such a fierce expression that Linden dropped Papa's plate.

Mr. Proveaux jumped like a scalded cat, went purple and beat on the table.

"Where, in the dear God's name, am I to find peace? First, shortages in the accounts; then, bad business and impudence from the country factors; then refusal of English sight drafts; and now, I can't even eat a breakfast without disturbance and—and tumult!"

Mrs. Proveaux's gray ringlets fluttered agitatedly under her lace mob cap. "Pray be patient, Louis, do not upset your digestion. Linden was stupid, clumsy. I—I will correct him."

"*I'll* correct him. I'll send him to the Sheriff." Mr. Proveaux sat back puffing. "Perhaps twenty lashes will serve to steady the rascal's hands!"

Antoinette suppressed a smile. Poor dear Papa sounded so very fierce, yet he would no more have Linden flogged by the Sheriff than he would administer the stripes himself.

"Well, Mam'selle," Papa jerked out a heavy gold watch and glared at her. "Are we at last to have the honor of your company?"

"Yes, Papa."

"You know the hour?"

Antoinette's small dark features took on a contrite expression. "I see it is quarter past six, Papa."

"In my house breakfast is served at six!" He cocked his head, neat in its silvery tie-wig, towards a window opening on the harbor. Somewhere in that direction a bell had begun to ring.

"*Voilà!* The market is declared open and, *nom de Dieu,* where are my housekeepers? Dawdling about the breakfast table! By the time any of you reach the market the choicest fruits will have been sold.

"*My* mother would have been down there waiting, basket on arm, since daylight. Bah, you are all indolent, spoiled and lazy! What are we coming to?"

On Roger, Mr. Proveaux fixed a glance eloquent of disapproval. "At what time may I hope to see *Monsieur le Maréchal* appear to do some honest work?"

Roger nervously stroked the starched purity of his shirt ruffle. His uniform lapels of burnt orange glowed in the fresh morning sunlight, as he said, "With all due respect, Monsieur, I may say that my orders call for a practice march out to Wando's."

"A practice parade, that's what it is! Rubbish! For a merchant's son, a criminal waste of time!"

Roger turned sullen, set a strong blue-black jaw. "Mr. Izard and Dr. Pringle don't speak that way of their sons' service."

The old man jerked the napkin from under his pink double chin. "But certainly they do not! What is time to a planter? Nothing. Pringle, Izard, Lowdnes, Middleton and the rest all are planters. If they need their sons at all, it is only during cropmaking. Bah. Overseers do all the real work."

Antoinette and her mother held their breath. Sycamore's eyes were all whites. Mr. Proveaux seldom worked himself up like this.

"Mark my words. The family which pays strangers to do its hard, unpleasant work cannot long survive!" Louis Proveaux glared into the reddened face of his son. "Now, my fine cockerel, you can tell Major Marion that I will not let you go off again this month. I forbid it! Twice last week, twice the week before. Enough is enough. Do you understand?"

Roger got to his feet and Antoinette braced herself. Her brother was furious with shame.

"Sir," he began stiffly. "Military orders cannot be disobeyed. Especially now that—"

"—Now that what?" Louis Proveaux instantly broke in. "What do you mean? Answer me!"

Roger's eyes wavered and he went scarlet above his lace stock. "I —we—that is, it concerns something we ain't supposed to talk about."

"Tell me."

The wills clashed, then habit won and Roger looked anxiously at his father. "Please, Monsieur, you will not repeat? I—I would be punished."

"By now you should have observed that I am no chatterbox," the old man said grimly.

"Well, sir, an express reports that a fleet—a British squadron—is collecting off Cape Fear."

Antoinette glanced at her brother in some surprise. Roger was not given to keeping news to himself.

"Nonsense!" grunted Louis Proveaux. "If there is any fleet at all, it will be our own. One hears that Admiral Hopkins is expected."

Hands clasped behind back, the elder Proveaux circled the break-fast table. He seemed unaccountably disturbed.

"Hm! Hm! Why did you not tell me of this before?" he barked at Roger. "Fine merchant you will make. I warrant Laurens, Richard-son and the rest have been up all night trimming their sails to this news!"

"I only heard it last night." The young man shrugged. "Please, Monsieur, remember that if you speak of this, I—well, I shall be disciplined."

Buttons gleaming in the fresh morning sunlight, he went over and kissed his mother, patted Antoinette's shoulder and smiling said, "When you go to market, don't pay a *sou* over sixpence a bushel for potatoes. There will be a glut in the market."

"Eh?" Louis Proveaux roused from his abstraction. As Roger well knew, such talk was what he liked to hear. "How are hemp prices?"

"Firm, sir, and expected to rise. Colonel Beale's batteaux have just brought in a cargo of fine, water-rotted fibers. Possibly a cargo could be bought cheap."

The old man shot him a quick look. "No doubt. But you forget there is a blockade. Having bought, how is one to ship it?"

Ensign Roger Proveaux paused in the doorway. "By pettyauger to Savannah, Monsieur, then by a Dutch vessel to Rhode Island. The rope-walks there starve for hemp."

"And where, my son, did you learn this?" Louis Proveaux was al-most beaming.

"From an officer of Continental Marines. He comes from up that way."

"What does a penny-pinching Yankee down here?"

"He is to train marines for that frigate the Marine Committee is to build here." Roger lingered slim and straight in the doorway, one hand negligently posed on the hilt of his sword. Dark, heavily lashed eyes swung to his sister.

"I will bring him home for you to fasten to your chariot wheels, 'Toinette. You have a strange *penchant* for New Englanders, *n'est-ce pas?* I seem to remember that you, Sally Huger and the Laurens girls had an elegant time up in Newport."

Mrs. Proveaux seized the opportunity to get off the dangerous subject. "But yes, ever since those summers in the North, I cannot understand what she sees in such grasping, cold-blooded creatures."

"Strange as it seems, this one is educated and a gentleman."

Antoinette made a pretense of tossing her head. "As if there were no well-bred people in Charleston!"

"But yes, *ma chère*—yet you do enjoy variety in your beaux."

Mrs. Proveaux heaved a delicate little sigh.

"Ah me—this cruel war. I shudder to face another hot summer, Louis. 'Toinette will miss her Quaker Friends."

"She will not see them for many summers to come," came Mr. Proveaux's acid comment. "The condition of our business does not warrant extravagances. We have not had a slave ship in this year and there is no more immigrant traffic either," he snapped, accepting his hat from a valet. "One cannot sell a Virginia bill of exchange, let alone a draft on New England, without paying a discount which would curl the wig of a monkey!"

Roger vanished and presently everyone in the breakfast room could hear the nervous hoof beats of his thoroughbred. Mrs. Proveaux crossed to the window, clasped prideful hands. *Dieu!* How brave the lad looked in that blue riding cape with its yellow lining. His cap of black leather had a jaunty silver crescent attached to its front. It seemed especially designed to set off her son's lively eyes and small, flat ears.

Antoinette started her breakfast hoping Roger would not unduly expose himself up at Wando's. Maman had never been the same since summer fever had carried off Angelique and Pierre. For long intervals Maman would sit staring blankly out over the beige-tinted waters beyond the Battery.

Any day now, the dreaded fever would recommence its ravages. The hot months were one long terror to Antoinette. Last August and September she had been terrified to see so many boys and girls of her own age laid to rest in the churchyards of St. Michael and St. Philip.

Sometimes, in a melancholy mood, she would visit their graves and read their epitaphs. One of them, Jinny Prioleau's, was haunting her this morning.

> "She glanc'd into our World to see
> A sample of our Misery
> Then turn'd away her languid eye
> To drop a tear or two and die."

Louis Proveaux tenderly kissed his wife and daughter and went tramping down stairs with no elasticity in his stride.

On the brick footway of King Street he waited for his coach, dark red with dark green trimmings, to come whirling up. Usually he drew a great satisfaction from the vehicle's glistening hub caps, the jingle of trace chains and the brave flashing of its carefully varnished spokes. But not today. His heart was too heavy.

When a liveried footman jumped down and threw open the door, he merely nodded and stepped out of the already hot sunlight into the cool body of his coach. Sighing, he settled back as the whip cracked and the vehicle went rumbling down King Street, its four horses kicking up a terrific column of dust.

Henry Laurens to the contrary, ran Louis Proveaux's thoughts, Congoes made just as good house servants as Gambias—even better. Too bad there would be few, if any, Congoes imported this year. One could turn a pretty penny in leasing slaves, on credit, to the great planters—they, their overseers, rather, were so easily persuaded, so inexacting as to terms.

Louis Proveaux found himself dreading an hour which he usually contemplated with a particular eagerness—that of interviewing his up-country factors. With the British blockade seizing cargoes right and left, it was nearly impossible to keep the poor rascals stocked with any European goods at all.

His factors had used to ask only two dry, well-dressed deerskins for a yard of calico; now cloth was so dear that they must ask four or five skins for the same quantity.

Not that Proveaux Brothers wanted more deerskins! Their warehouses were already bulging with a vast over-stock which could not be moved for want of transportation.

Mon Dieu—the Proveauxs still thought in French when deeply disturbed—if only some magical power could sweep away the strangling grip of those British men-of-war cruising off the bar! Nowadays it was difficult to believe that the conduct of business had once been easy, pleasant and profitable.

No wonder the hunters and small farmers of the back country were growing daily more truculent, even threatening. One could not blame them with the prices of rum, cloth, gunpowder and salt mounting so steadily. Why could they not be made to understand that the fault was not greediness on the part of the merchant's factors in Charleston?

What to do? Suppose the backwoods people executed their threats of moving westward, far away over the mountains? Then all Proveaux Brothers' painfully captured markets would be lost, their exports ruinously curtailed once peace returned.

Mr. Proveaux had found no solution when, amid a loud clatter of hoofs that sent scavenging buzzards flapping skywards, the coach halted before his counting house door.

4

MARKET DAY

OMINOUS banks of black and silver clouds were continuing to pile up beyond the Cooper River. Antoinette Proveaux decided it must begin to rain any minute now and was relieved to see the red-tiled roof of the public market looming just ahead. A glance over her shoulder made sure that Lily, Ivy, Marigold and a quartet of small negresses were following. Her followers made quite a procession with their empty market baskets balanced on their heads.

Antoinette saw a vessel, bound upstream, pass the foot of Broad Street. She must be going to lie a while in fresh water in order to kill teredos and other salt water growths that were spoiling her bottom.

Twelve miles up river there was quite an important dockyard devoted to "Freshening and Careening." There, shipwrights resheathed damaged vessels with lime and deal overplanking if their owners could not afford copper.

Clearing a path for Antoinette with the liberal use of a staff was Oak, her bodyguard. It amused her to see how the gigantic fellow simply couldn't resist poking at buzzards gulping garbage in a kennel that ran down the center of the cobbled street.

Gradually, varied and distinctive calls of the hucksters became distinguishable. Almost without exception the vendors were slaves, offering produce grown by them in the interest of a master or mistress. Like a hoard spread by some prodigal buccaneer, heaping mounds of oranges, lemons and limes brightened the bluish gloom of the market. Fresh beans, carrots, onions, cauliflowers and cabbages, not to mention yams and other roots, overflowed hundreds of wicker baskets.

As her marketing progressed in leisurely fashion, Antoinette inevitably encountered friends, many in-laws and relations. Always they stopped for a few minutes of gossip.

Presently Lily was sent waddling off, her basket heaped high and trailing a comet's tail of pickaninny satellites. Ivy and Marigold stayed, winking and giggling at some young bucks languidly unloading a line of carts.

Opposite the Fish Market a merry jingling of bells drew Antoinette's attention. Intrigued, as always, by the arrival of a freighter's train, she halted on the footway and watched a succession of great four-wheeled wagons go rumbling by.

There used to be many more of them. Last year, so Papa said, over three thousand carts and wagons had used the ferries into Charleston. This train must have come a good distance. The wagon covers yonder were thick with yellow dust and the horses were caked with dried sweat. The bearded drivers kept grinning, waving and hollering to friends.

Like an advance guard, a pair of huge dogs ran before the lead wagon and snarled challenges to the city curs. Tops swaying and rocking, the four wagons composing the convoy drew nearer. From what Antoinette could see, their freight consisted of deerskin, drums of beeswax, hands of tobacco, potatoes, hemp and smoked meat.

Lanky, leather-faced men in greasy hunting shirts walked alongside with a peculiar bent-kneed stride. Antoinette reckoned two of them must be part Indian to have so much copper showing in their cheeks. The lead wagon, drawn by six powerful horses, turned, went lurching down Tradd Street; probably it was heading for Colonel Beale's wharf.

The collars of the second team were mounted in green wool and trimmed with tufts of yellow worsted which fluttered gaily in the paling sunlight. The driver, she saw, was a big blond man with bright blue eyes and deliberate movements.

Ivy reminded timidly, "Fish ain't boughten yet, Missy, an' it sho' fixin' t' rain."

The slave was right, Antoinette realized, so, picking up her skirts, she crossed behind the last wagons. They reached the shelter of the Fish Market just a stride or two ahead of a lashing down-pour which drove hucksters helter-skelter to cover. The rain, Antoinette noticed, sketched curious eccentric patterns on the wagon tops and on the broad loins of the teams.

Entering the gloomy interior, she saw the usual dripping baskets of clams, crabs and crayfish. They would always hold a strange attraction for her. Some fish had been laid out on beds of bright green moss or wet straw and were still alive; their gills kept opening tediously, futilely.

"Heah yo' is, Mis'tess! Heah is prime pond-chickens, all fat 'n' sassy!"

A shriveled old negro hurried up offering a basket of colossal, goggle-eyed bullfrogs. Because Papa was partial to *grenouille à la Marseillaise* she bought them.

"Buy mah fine pikes?"

"Mawnin', Maum, heah's good rockfish, cheap."

"Dis way, please, Maum. Dis way."

The shower was still drumming on the tiles above so Antoinette, drawing her petticoat skirts close, wandered at will over the market's damp and rather slippery cobbles. A family of blacks crouched in a corner were munching shrimps and pitching the shells out into the rain. They looked like wild negroes and were talking in some unfamiliar dialect. It was Coromantee, most likely. Most of the recent shipments had been secured from that tribe.

In a far corner Antoinette was surprised to discover a lone and very poorly dressed white man crouched behind a counter he had improvised of a plank and two empty kegs.

When she saw his offerings, her eye lit. "My, what elegant snappers! You may wrap me up a dozen."

The fisherman's expression brightened. When he jumped up, she realized he was so thin that his joints looked knobby.

"How much are they?"

"Penny, ha' penny the pound, Mum."

Ivy sniffed. Antoinette's smile thinned "That's a ha' penny more than anyone else is asking."

The vendor's red-rimmed eyes dropped and the eagerness went out of him. "Reckon that's so, Ma'am, but me, I can't sell for a farthin' less, Mum.

"They're nice fish," he pointed out desperately. "Fresh caught, still alive, see? I brought 'em in myself."

Antoinette wavered, but Mrs. Proveaux's schooling decided her. "No doubt. But it would be foolish for me to pay above the market price."

The fellow gulped, "Beg pardon, Mum, but what does a ha' penny the pound mean to your sort? To me, it's the difference between starvation or a living."

"Starve?" Antoinette's brown eyes grew round. "But why?"

"I'm white, worse luck. I have nobody to feed me when I can't fish; I have nobody to doctor me or my family. There's no one to buy my clothes. If I was black, it would be different."

Dull color crept up into his gaunt cheeks. "I came out from England, Mum, for the chance of trading free and equal. They promised us immigrants fair treatment."

He spread big-knuckled hands. "But I don't get it. These slave fishermen undersell me at every turn. And why not? Their owner buys them nets, bait, boats—everything. Their owner don't care how many fish his slaves waste just so's he makes a profit."

He indicated a great glistening buck in a ragged gray jersey. "Mr. Hawkin owns him, and him and him. He keeps twenty blacks fishing the bay and the river. Men like Hawkin floods the market a-purpose so's to keep the price so low a free man can't manage. What chance is there for a pore feller like me?"

"It don't seem fair," Antoinette admitted uncertainly. "But slaves are an investment, you know. They have to show a profit."

As she started to turn away, the fisherman cried piteously, "Please don't go, Mum—please don't tell nobody what I said. I—I'll stand to lose me license. Here, take my snappers at a penny the pound. They'll spoil, else. My children got to eat tonight."

Antoinette remained disturbed long after she had left. Something did seem wrong with the poorer whites. White artisans and mechanics such as the saddlers, shipwrights, smiths, chimney-sweeps, glaziers and painters were emigrating by the hundred, moving into North Carolina or over the mountains into the West.

When she reached the river end of the market, the rain was still falling. She saw that she had guessed correctly; the freighter's train had pulled up in front of Colonel Beale's warehouse.

Idly, she watched a woman scramble awkwardly out of the last wagon and stand there in the downpour, gazing dully about. Finally she tucked a big bundle under one arm and started trudging up away from the waterfront.

The woman, who proved to be only a girl, apparently wasn't noticing the rain, only stumped leadenly along with head bent. She was getting her petticoats all muddy about the hem. When she drew closer, Antoinette tried to see what she was like.

At last she looked up from under a dripping straw hat and stood peering into the fish market. What? Who? It couldn't be! Antoinette looked again, placed the delicate oval of that face, those wide-winged brows and the shadows that lurked beneath them.

She dashed out into the rain, clasped the bedraggled traveler. "Desire! Desire Bennett!"

Ivy, Marigold, everybody, gaped.

" 'Toinette Proveaux—isn't it?"

"What in the world are you doing in Charleston?"

Desire's lips moved stiffly, formed the ghost of a smile. "I don't know. I—I had hoped to find you—someone I knew from—old days. I've had ill fortune and I am so very tired."

5

SECOND COMPANY DISMISSED!

THEIR fortnight of field training at an end, the men of the Second Rifle Company answered final roll call, then joyously broke ranks. In groups and singly, the men scattered to their tents, carrying rifles canted every which way. Soon they commenced to depart for home in canoes, pirogues and a-horseback. Because the Second Company was largely composed of tradesmen, a majority of the privates left on foot.

Lieutenant Nathaniel Coffin of the First Battalion, Continental Marines, heaved a satisfied sigh. In two weeks he had been able to accomplish a lot with these plain fellows—far more than he might have with those quick-tempered scions of the aristocracy who wanted commissions in Colonel Christopher Gadsden's First Regiment of Foot, or in Colonel William Moultrie's Second Regiment.

A mighty large stock of patience was required to keep those young planters both sober and subordinate. They were forever begging excuse from drill merely to greet a friend, or to squire one of those lovely young creatures who kept driving out to watch the troops at their exercises.

It was unfortunate, Nat thought, that the State troops lay encamped but a scant two miles out of Charleston. Every evening the cantonments were invaded by a veritable horde of valets and grooms belonging to young Pinckneys, Middletons, Pringles, Maysons, Hugers and Rutledges.

They would make up their master's beds, bring fresh linen, groom the chargers and polish field equipment. Grinning and highly delighted slaves continually brought out hampers of all kinds of delicacies—liquid and otherwise. The effect of such prodigality, Nat decided, was not good on less splendid townsfolk serving in the ranks.

As soon as he learned that construction of South Carolina's contribution to the new Navy would be temporarily postponed, Nat had taken an interest in some rifle companies just being formed. There was no trouble about his being granted leave to help train them. Colonel Thomson, a brisk and efficient transplanted Pennsylvanian, was delighted.

Nat found that instruction came easily to him; on the drill field one really got to know men. He wanted to learn about those details in which Carolinians differed from the Pennsylvanians and Rhode Islanders. America was so big. If independence were ever to be achieved, a fellow with a broad understanding might be of some use. Not limited like the local patriots who couldn't see beyond their own county.

Take Higsby for example—there was a fine, representative type. Pity he'd lost track of Sam. It was odd how well he and the rifleman had hit it off on the long cruise back to New England. When he pleased, Sam could lie like a thief on the gallows, but never on essentials; and he always stood ready to do his share of any work he felt he was supposed to.

Again, the Pennsylvanian possessed a natural philosophy the depth of which was a continual astonishment. Seldom, Nat mused, had he encountered a person less given to self-deception, less easily deceived as to a stranger's true character. He knew his own limitations, did Sam, and was modest, really. He must have caught that habit of bragging from the Indians.

Stripped to his undershirt, Nat Coffin lazed shamelessly on a pallet drenched by late May sunlight. In the distance a woodpecker was hammering lustily on a hollow tree. What he had seen of Carolina during a month was, on the whole, pleasing. Was this because he was held in respect for having twice been under British fire?

Some of the lady visitors had even called him a hero. Exaggeration, he was coming to think, was a Southern failing. Nathaniel Coffin a hero? He couldn't help grinning up at the panel of mildewed canvas above him.

Eyes half shut, he tried to understand the background of Charleston. This flourishing town suggested *multum in parvo* all right. Why should the descendants of French Huguenots and German Palatines be so much more amenable to discipline than those of straight English stock?

Take young Roger Proveaux, for example. The minute Ensign Proveaux understood what was wanted, he executed an order in the smartest, most practical way even if he asked "why" later on. Unlike the other young bloods, he was neither slack nor careless about details.

Once he was told, Proveaux always made his men test their powder with a prouvette. By consequence, his detachment could outshoot any other unit in either of the city regiments.

Too pestered by flies to enjoy his cot, Nat sought the tent's entrance, moodily watched the Ashley flow by and listened to two of his best riflemen argue over the breeding of a heifer. Yonder a party of terrapin hunters were rowing downstream. In Charleston the gilded cross on St. Philip's spire gleamed like a new sword.

From a field chest he drew out a notebook. His "Observations" was by no means a diary, there wasn't time to make regular entries.

Seating himself, he wet the tip of his pencil and wrote:

The husbandmen in this Province stand unasham'd of manual Toil and view with contempt all soft-handed citizenry. In the Bosom of these plain folk the Flame of LIBERTY burns very bright.

Am yet of two minds whether to make a visit with the Parents of my fiery young Proveaux, or to undertake an Excursion over to a Fort building on Sullivant's Isle. Begun last January, it had been allowed to Languish.

How cleverly doth Man build but to destroy! How patiently doth he Labour to cripple and consume his Kind. Why? Why? To what purpose? Shall I ever understand?

A shadow fell across the tent's floor. It was yellow-haired Charles MacIntosh, a sub-lieutenant in the First Regiment.

"Heyo, Mr. Coffin, we're having a main tonight. Prioleau and Pringle are bringing over their birds. Cocking is dead against the Committee's rulings, but you'll come?"

"Why, I—"

"Oh, come along," the other urged. "You'll have to keep your lips buttoned, though."

Nat wavered, "I had thought of visiting in Charleston."

The young fellow, lithe and supple in his blue and white regimentals, stepped inside. "Plague take Charleston! You will have time and to spare for visiting there. Please come. You will be my guest. Pa's plantation lies just beyond Prioleau's.

"We'll fight a main tonight and, tomorrow—if we're sober enough —we can give some colts a needed work-out."

His enthusiasm was so infectious that Nat's indecision vanished. "Why, I'd greatly admire to, MacIntosh."

He stood up, red head brushing the canvas. Suddenly he looked doubtful. "My regimentals—"

"—Plague take your regimentals. They'll do. We will be in effect, *en bivouac,* none of the fair sex to plague us—lest Tom or Lucius fetches in a parcel of hussies."

He winked elaborately. "Hope you can hold your own at the punch bowl."

Nat smiled gravely. He had no worries on that score. Reputedly, all Coffins were blessed with heads which made a granite cliff seem soft by comparison. Maybe generations of seafaring had developed that ability to hold a deal of liquor?

Suddenly he felt impatient to be off. Why, he hadn't been on a real devil-take-hindermost spree since—since, why, 'way back in Providence last January when Desire—

Some of the sunshine's brilliance faded. Desire. Why couldn't he wholly forget her? She was fading from his memory, yet she would never wholly depart. Perhaps tonight he could get her out of his mind?

It would be interesting to observe how these aristocrats acted in liquor. Would they grow boastful, like politicians? Quarrelsome like Morgan's riflemen? Or would they freeze up and get sour like the Massachusetts men?

He hoped that drinking would render them happy and gay like the French and Spanish munitions salesmen he had seen haunting General Washington's headquarters.

6

KINCORA HALL

By MOONLIGHT, Mr. MacIntosh's party tacked up the Wando into a strange and lovely country where great live oaks shed cascades of silvery Spanish moss onto the river's surface. Towering cypresses reared stately sable columns as if supporting the vast inverted bowl of the sky.

From the heart of reed-choked shallows, bull alligators boomed as the sailing skiff slipped smoothly by. Now and then an Indian in a dug-out canoe, or a negro hunter paddling his clumsy pettyauger, ghosted into sight. Everywhere was the squattering sound made by feeding waterfowl.

From its inception, the party was jolly, probably because young Charlie MacIntosh had sent aboard his father's skiff the most sumptuous supper Nat had beheld in many a blue moon. Grinning broadly, his valet and a pair of assistants unpacked hampers of cold duck, turkey, and chicken. Soup and vegetables had been kept hot in a packing of sawdust. Jams, jellies, cakes and fruits of all kind materialized by the dozen. Of wines and cordials, there was a prodigal variety.

For the first time since Nathaniel Coffin had lain on the breastwork of the redoubt on Breed's Hill, he was able to forget the murderous precision with which he had killed a trio of British grenadiers. Yes, he was really beginning to shake off that chill which ever since had dulled a natural heartiness.

While draining a tall glass of Malaga on this glorious May evening very little seemed wrong with the world. Disease and death had thus far passed him by. He was close to evolving a workable philosophy of life. *Ignotum per ignotius,* as it were. These Carolinians seemed really to like him and, for a miracle, his pockets were bulging with currency.

Of course nobody knew just what Carolina scrip might be worth at present; until Parliament had passed the Repressive Acts, seven pounds Carolina equaled one pound sterling.

"Don't fret yo'self, Nat," young Tom Beale was drawling. "Pa says the Province will start that frigate soon's the rice crop's made."

Nat chuckled, studied the silver and jet pattern of the next reach upstream. "I hope so. Why doesn't one hear of more ships being built around Charleston?"

Beale set down his glass quickly. "Suh, Ah'll have you know ain't nobody in creation builds a finer vessel than our John Rose. You Yankees reckon you're the only smart folks in America, don't you? Well, Ah suggest you moderate yo' tone."

"Taste your own prescription, Tommy," MacIntosh advised and waved a chicken leg for emphasis. "You're both right, I'd say. I reckon we *can* build a frigate down here; but it won't be easy, being as short of skilled labor as we are."

"We jus' got open up the port right soon," put in a somber-eyed young captain, "or Pa declares his warehouses will bu'st what with all that rice and indigo in 'em."

"In Heaven's name," Roger Proveaux burst out. "Let us seek escape from war—and business. Mr. Coffin might think we were all weaned on accountant's ink. Look! There's a sky full of stars, a moon and a river of melted silver."

"I'd rather look at that veal pie, again," Nat laughed.

"I wouldn't, sir, it's on the dry side."

"You fellows should taste that slum-gullion they served on the *Wasp!*"

"When we get ordered out, I aim to take my own cook along," declared young MacIntosh.

"Thought we weren't going to talk war, or business," Beale protested. "What the devil? Ain't we out for fun? Ah am ready for a fight, a footrace or a—"

"Don't rush your jumps, Tommy—mayn't be a petticoat in sight. Juniper, you better strike that sail and lower the mast. Wind's gone."

Lying back on a series of cushions upholstering a wide transom, Nat watched six slave oarsmen in red and white striped jerseys put out oars and begin pulling. As they fought a sluggish current, the white-painted shafts of their oars bowed under their efforts.

Softly at first, then, as tacit permission was granted, the rowers raised a deep, inexpressibly plaintive chorus.

> "Mah fathe', whar you be?
> Mah fathe', whar you be?
> Mah fathe', whar you be?
> When mah good Lawd was dere?"

Teeth glistened, blades splashed softly, rhythmically; tangled banks slipped smoothly by.

> "Oh, de jin-i-wine religion
> In dat day—oh—in dat day.
> Oh, de jin-i-wine religion in dat day.
> Wait on, de trump' soon shall sound."

Towards eight o'clock the black coxswain whooped two or three times then the sailing skiff changed her course, made for a landing. Right away lanterns glowed and pine knots flared before a big, white-pillared house. Like giant fireflies, the torches wavered down towards the river.

"Pa's away," young MacIntosh grinned, "and Mother is visiting kinfolk over on the Ashley; so, lads, the Kincora is ours, and God help it, say I!"

Young Beale, now a trifle unsteady, haughtily refused Roger Proveaux's steadying hand.

Nat was beginning to deem the world a vastly pleasing place. These sparkling fellows in their gay regimentals were like so many drawings from a book. They were handsome—every last one of them—and had amazingly small hands and feet. They were not like himself, over-long in the frame and a bit awkward in his movements.

The instant the party stepped onto a sturdy little wharf a swarm of servants took possession of such scanty luggage as there was aboard and bore it, grinning widely, up to the great house.

Whew! It was impossible not to be impressed. Even the mansions of wealthy Philadelphians failed to approximate the tasteful luxury overflowing Kincora Hall. The furniture was imported, every stick of it—as were the immense crystal chandeliers, sconces and vases. Richly carved hunting boards and sideboards shone under massive silver.

In the halls Nat saw any number of oil paintings which must have been brought from Italy and by the foot of the stairs stood an elegant marble statue. It was of a girl, naked as the day she was born, save for a new moon in her hair.

Charlie MacIntosh said the piece came from Greece—he didn't think much of it because it was lacking an arm.

"Pa bought it in '68, the year of the record rice crop," he explained. "We got that tapestry—the one with the Turk on it—two years back. Pa had two ships in from the Slave Coast the same month. He was monstrous fortunate. His captains didn't lose above two slaves to every hundred on the way out."

Fascinated, Nat wandered about. Curious, all this beauty and luxury really blossomed from the ugly root of slavery. To think that the toil of primitive, ignorant savages fresh from barbarism made all this possible!

The realization didn't greatly upset him. If half of what the slave captains in Newport claimed was true, the average negro in his native surroundings lived no life of easy security. A West Coast negro must expect to die early. Wild beasts, famine, or human enemies would lay him low long before he attained his fortieth year.

Certainly a life of servitude on an American plantation offered few joys; yet was it not preferable to being eaten, to dying in hideous pain, to being sacrificed to some enemy's fetish? Captains plying the Three-cornered Trade had more than once made his juvenile blood run cold by supplying details concerning terrible "customs" or sacrifices, celebrated by the kings of Dahomey and Ashantee in honor of their fetishes.

Back on Nantucket, Captain Hussey once had mentioned a "custom" at which King Moussah had caused the throats of over a thousand men, women and children captives to be cut in order that he might fulfil a boast to float a canoe on the blood of his enemies!

A black butler had barely shown Nat his room than Charles MacIntosh began calling from the foot of the staircase.

"Heyo! Stir your feet up there. Pringle boys are on their way 'cross the river. They're bringing some Geo'gia chickens they're fool enough to bet on." He came half way upstairs and lowered his voice. "Er—have you any money with you? Charmed to lend you any amount."

"I've a month's pay," Nat admitted uncomfortably. In all his twenty-two years he had never wagered so much as a sixpence.

"Come along, then, we're going to give Billy and the rest a welcome."

With some reluctance, Nat prepared to descend. There were so many things he wanted to examine further. For instance, how the fans which dangled from the ceilings were operated; the exact nature of stone jars which, standing in big earthenware saucers, sweated and so kept the drinking water sweet and quite cool.

Such luxury awed him. How would it affect a young man to be reared in such an atmosphere? He guessed tonight he might learn.

A body slave kept hovering in the background. "Wash yo' face fo' you, suh?"

Nat nodded and tried to keep his expression straight. Nobody had washed his face since his mother had given over the job. The footman opened a cupboard, produced a coat of linen and some trousers cut sailor-fashion.

"Best put dese on, suh; might spoil yo' regimentals, suh."

Downstairs somebody fired a shot, Nat ran to the window. "What's wrong?"

"Nawthin', suh," came the equable response. "Mos' likely ain't nawthin' but Misto' Beale shootin' at a 'gator. He most always takes to shootin' when he feel his liquor, suh. Done chased me up a hawthorn tree las' Fall, suh. Hee—hee! Misto' Beale gits mighty playful sometimes."

The air in Mr. MacIntosh's coach house was turning blue-gray; voices were rising. Of the fifteen-odd gentlemen who, bearing sacks of gamecocks and bottles of brandy, had appeared from various establishments, three already lay peacefully snoring on a heap of horse blankets. The others smoked, drank and wagered. A well-stocked sideboard installed at one end of that space in which the carriages were washed enjoyed unstinted patronage.

Aware of a very satisfactory internal glow, Nat allowed himself to be initiated into the fine art of heeling a gamecock. Curtly he was warned to keep a tight grip on a fierce white battler while Roger Proveaux, with the help of a scroll-saw, removed the bird's natural spurs. Once this was accomplished, Proveaux rubbed chalk dust over the stumps in order to check a slight bleeding.

"Easy does it, lads. Now watch this."

Dexterously, Charlie MacIntosh eased one of the gaffs over the stump. This was an artificial spur of slightly curved and needle-sharp steel. It had been secured to a strip of very thin leather. Next, Nat's host employed lengths of waxed linen thread firmly to bind the gaff leather onto his gamecock's legs. It was instructive also to watch Proveaux clip short the bird's flaring ruff, to shorten the wing tips lest they "hang up" an opponent's spurs.

This next bout Nat gathered had been arranged between one of Roger Proveaux's birds and a Georgia cock belonging to the Pringles.

Young Proveaux's bird, Moonbeam, was big, snow-white and descended from a famous Jamaican strain. Pringle's Pluto, on the other hand, was black as faces on the outskirts of the crowd.

Suddenly Moonbeam pecked at Nat's hand and when he involuntarily relaxed his grip, the bird struck out.

"Christ!" MacIntosh yelled, popping a dripping thumb into his mouth. "The little devil gaffed me. Told you to hold him tight."

"Which way you betting, Mac?" Tom Beale wanted to know.

"I fancy Roger's Moonbeam. Saw him fight last Autumn. Made mincemeat out of three of Warren Lee's best Dominics."

"I'm on Pluto," Tony Beale hiccoughed. "Sportin' bet. Five hundred pounds—even money. What say?"

"Done," called a sunburnt young fellow at Nat's elbow. He never even raised his voice as he asked, "Who will take another three hundred?"

Nat stood aghast. God in Heaven! A whaler or a fisherman back home might work many years and not earn the half of such sums.

The guests grouped themselves closer about a pit rigged in the center of the carriage house. Pringle, hot and excited, called out, "I really fancy this bird of mine, Charlie. Tell you what. I'll lay you my boy, Mose, 'gainst your Alexander."

MacIntosh's chalky fingers wandered briefly over his chin. Then he shook his head. "The devil I will. I'm onto you. Alexander is just the right weight for that ugly red stallion of yours."

Pringle grinned. "Maybe so, but there ain't anything wrong with Mose, either. Stand up, Mose. I tell you he's a honey when it comes to handling game chickens and Mose is younger than Alex by ten years, easy," he pointed out.

"My handlers suit me," MacIntosh said easily.

"You've got me, Charlie. I admit it. Do need Alexander to school Warcloud. Isn't as if I were trying to *buy* him, you understand."

Nat glanced at the negro in question. He was a small and wiry fellow. Right now he was casting at his owner glances of desperate entreaty.

"Please doan' bet me, suh, if you please, suh." His voice was trembling. "I'se sho'ly wuth mo' den 'at triflin' Mose. Misto' MacIntosh, 'deed yo' needs me. Dat foal Twinkletoes done drop last month is a mighty likely lookin' piece hawseflesh."

MacIntosh grinned. "Vanity! Vanity! Alexander, you astonish me. So you fancy yourself of greater value than Mose? By how much, for instance?"

" 'Steen-year-old boy to boot, suh," the jockey quavered. "Enny-how."

Everybody laughed. Slave boys of sixteen and up fetched the choicest prices.

The young planter patted his slave's shoulder. "Well, don't worry, Alex, because, strange to say, I agree with you. Come on, Harry, pit your bird."

Negroes were everywhere, Nat realized. They had perched on old and worn-out carriages, on saddle racks. Like giant swallows a whole row of them crowded each roof joist.

Above the pit a row of bull's-eye lanterns created a yellow-red glare. As Roger Proveaux and young Pringle stepped into the tanbark sprinkled pit, a bell began ringing far away down the Wando River.

"Somebody's nigger must have run off," Beale remarked, crossing over to stand beside Nat Coffin.

"Well, suh, am Ah ha'd of hearin', or have Ah not had the pleasure of hearin' you express yo' preference?"

"I haven't bet," Nat explained. "I don't know the first thing about cock fighting."

"Do you imply that Ah would take advantage of yo' ignorance, suh?" Beale swayed a little. His eyes were bloodshot and he had spilt wine on the lace of his jabot.

"No, of course not."

Beale relaxed. "Youah pa'don, suh. Ah—Ah give you youah pick of birds. Take one, Ah will back the other. Fair enough?"

Nat was annoyed, but he saw it would not be polite, or wise, to refuse a bet. Oh, well—when in Rome—

"Why, of course."

Beale's heated features came closer, and, all good nature, he draped an arm over Nat's shoulder.

"Youah pa'don, suh. Most Yankees Ah have met will not wager

that a sun will rise tomorrow. What shall we risk? Fifty? A hundred pounds?"

"Why—why—" Nat had exactly thirty pounds, South Carolina money, in his pocket.

"Suppose I back Mr. Proveaux's rooster—"

Beale flinched. "Please! Please! That is a *cock*, suh! Roosters infest barnyards—"

"My mistake. Suppose I back my friend's cock with twenty pounds —currency?"

"Tw-twenty? And currency! Come, come, Misto' Coffin. We ain't children!"

Roger Proveaux looked up, called sharply, "Let be, Tommy. It's possible Mr. Coffin don't enjoy a rich father."

Beale bowed. "Apologize, suh. Ah really do. We will make it twenty—currency."

Nat drew a deep breath. What would people say if it ever got about Nantucket that he had wagered twenty pounds on a cock fight! He guessed they'd never believe it, anyhow.

Suppose—suppose the white roos—gamecock got licked? His collar felt suddenly very tight and he began to perspire. Subconsciously, he noted a peal of thunder a long way off.

The two handlers sank onto their heels in opposite corners. They were separated by some ten feet of tanbark.

Nat forgot to philosophize. Moonbeam *must* win. He found he was yelling at the top of his voice. Wasn't a whole month's pay at stake?

Pulses throbbing, he watched the Carolinians hold their cocks forward at arm's length and, for some moments, permit them to peck, to nip each other's combs and to pull ruff feathers. Soon both birds began to cackle angrily. Other cocks awaiting their turn in the arena began to crow in futile defiance. They were, for the most part, imprisoned in hemp feed bags and suspended from a row of harness pegs.

"Well, Misto' Coffin. Ah hear Pringle's bird is the heavier by three ounces," Beale was chuckling, "but Ah reckon you have picked the winner. Roger's Moonbeam is as smart as a fox. Watch him after the first fly."

"Lay you ten to one he backs up just enough to tease that Geo'gia chicken off balance. You'll see." Together they leaned as far out over the pit as they could.

"Lawd! Lawd! Look at dat. Ain't dat the fightenest chicken?" Alexander was crooning, "Come awn, li'l Moonbeam! Make pie fix-in's outer dat black bird."

A languid, sallow-faced young man named Lee consented to judge. "Count of ten," he announced. "Three counts makes a winner. Ready, Gentlemen? Ready? Go!"

Roger Proveaux stepped back and, flinging his arms suddenly wide, released his gamecock. Nat saw that he was sweating so profusely that his white uniform waistcoat was all stained. Pringle did the same and at their feet exploded a bombshell of whirling feathers and flying steel.

Nat learned the difference between full-fledged gamecocks and the "stags"—birds in their first year of fighting—which had been pitted heretofore. Shortened ruffs flaring, the gamecocks sprang apart, hesitated, beak aimed at beak.

It was then Nat heard the thunder again. Um. *Boom-m-m!* It didn't sound quite right.

That *wasn't* thunder. By God! It was cannon fire! He wondered what it meant. A celebration in town most likely. He straightened, turned his head. Only he was not wholly intent on a furious mêlée taking place in the pit. Once more that dull rumble in the far distance. One report, then two more, quite close together.

He tried to catch MacIntosh's attention, but his host was far too absorbed. Oh, well—

It was nearly impossible to follow each lightning thrust of the spurs. Oh blazes! Red spots were commencing to stain Moonbeam's plumage. How would he pay his mess bill? His laundress?

Presently the black cock got a spur hung in Moonbeam's wing feathers and the two birds flopped awkwardly about.

"Handle yo' birds," the judge commanded.

Roger immediately snatched up his gamecock, began massaging its legs and smoothing its feathers. The judge commenced to toll off ten seconds. At the end of his count both birds were released and flew at each other with murderous pleasure.

The white bird was badly marked now—his comb bloody. MacIntosh watching Pluto, rather than Proveaux's bird, twice had seen Moonbeam's gaffs deliver what should have been telling blows. He must have been in error, though, for that Georgia chicken was fighting harder than ever. Weight, that was the explanation. In the next flurry, the black bowled Moonbeam clear over on his back.

"All right, Charlie," Pringle called, his face scarlet as any love apple. "Your Alexander 'gainst my Mose *and* a prime 'steen-year-old!"

"Done!" MacIntosh said without looking up.

The groom, Alexander, kneeling by the edge of the pit, beat small fists together, groaned:

"Dig yo' heels in, li'l white bird! Oh Gawd, doan lemme leave Kincora. Mah honey gal is heah, li'l bird, doan want dat ginger boy get her!"

Momentarily, Nat ignored that distant cannonading.

No question but that both cocks were tiring. Imperceptibly, Pluto's left wing drooped. Suddenly the black bird rallied. Rocked Moonbeam off his feet. Jumped on him. Savaged him. The white fowl lay sprawling, panting, glaring futilely at his foe.

Oh God! A month's pay. All gone in less than ten minutes. A fool and his money—

"Count!" Pringle directed tensely.

When, on the count of ten, Moonbeam was seen still lying on the tanbark, the judge helped himself to a pinch of snuff.

"Roger, that's a count fo' the black. Yo' chicken had better hurry and get in some licks," he drawled.

Young Proveaux made no reply, couldn't, because he had popped his gamecock's head in his mouth and was sucking away blood which had been obscuring an eye.

"Breast yo' birds!"

This time Moonbeam did not rise to meet the black but gave a sidewards hop which left Pluto rocking off balance. In a twinkle the white bird turned, got in three savage blows with his gaffs.

Beale said so, loudly.

"Mr. MacIntosh! Where's Mr. MacIntosh?"

Everyone's head whipped about. On the drive sounded a staccato rattle of hoofs.

"Here. What's wrong?"

"Raise the country! Ride fo' Charleston. Committee's orders."

All the white men ran to the carriage house entrance.

"What's wrong?" rasped Prioleau.

"Plenty," came the breathless reply. "A British fleet is anchorin' off Rebellion Row. A great fleet of frigates, ships-o'-the-line and—and transports. Dozens of 'em. Forty or fifty sail at the very least!"

7

CHARLESTON, JUNE 1, 1776

FOR two days Desire Bennett luxuriated in a great four-poster bed that was comfortable to a nearly forgotten degree. She was utterly content just to lie still recruiting her strength, studying with absurd interest a plaster ornament set into the ceiling.

How grand it was to lie once more between linen sheets smelling of lavender! Imagine not having to arise and wonder whether they would have enough money for breakfast. Imagine not having to consider and coddle Brian's mood for the day. Poor, poor Brian!

When Desire shut her eyes, she, for the first time in months, recognized the gentle touch of long lashes on her cheek. It seemed almost odd not to feel a cask digging into her hip; not to feel the canvas top leaking onto her blankets. No search for bed bug bites today. In many an ordinary she had awakened, red-spotted from head to foot.

Twice Mrs. Proveaux and 'Toinette had tiptoed into the room. But each time Desire had feigned sleep. She didn't dare talk until she had perfected a plausible tale, had tested it for every possible flaw or discrepancy.

It would go against her grain to lie to Antoinette's mother, yet if she confessed the whole truth—well—she guessed the Proveauxs would bundle her back onto the street in short order.

Lying there in a soft bed jacket of Toinette's she tried to reassure herself that she had done nothing but what she had been forced to. Her affair with John had been honest and they certainly would have married immediately.

Tears welled into her eyes when she recalled him in his scarlet, silver and black sprawled across the frozen ruts. Who had killed him? One of the Gardners? No, they had come up from behind. Another outraged farmer, then? What irony that John had played no part in that tragic, outrageous raid!

Oh, if only John St. Clair had lived at least long enough to hold this child of his that stirred within her. John St. Clair. She was sure now she could never love like that again. Not the way that she had loved John.

Who in the world would have foreseen that her passage money would be snatched from her? She'd had every intention of meeting young Lieutenant Coffin in Philadelphia. He was great-souled, intelligent and so gentlemanly. She guessed he was really in love with her. He would have made a fine husband. Where was he now?

Nat with his deep private thoughts, his ungainly New England frame, red hair and handsome sensitive face. It was pleasant to recall those tender hours together in Providence; peddler's bells ringing in the street below, wagons and coaches rumbling, gulls crying over the river.

It was a crazy world when a girl hadn't the remotest idea of where one's family and nearest friends might be. She didn't really think she had been a bad girl. She hadn't wanted to do—well, do what she had. Only there hadn't been any work.

Once 'Toinette got her to bed, she had slept through the first twenty-four hours without a break and most of the next day, until the stirring of her baby roused her. The child was so very active, she felt it must be a boy.

Suppose she had reached Philadelphia in time to find Nat? How differently things might have gone.

When she and Brian passed through, she had gone to Smith's City Tavern where they told her that a Mr. Coffin had waited a full week before enrolling himself as a sergeant of marines. None of the hotel employees could tell her the name of the ship he was in. And so Nat had gone sailing out of her life with the Continental Fleet.

Having gained perspective, she could more accurately estimate Brian Montaigne. His charm had lain all on the surface. Maybe it was because he was incapable of truly deep emotion that he had made such a really fine actor.

He had been arrogant without grounds, glib without knowledge, yet tremendously generous and tender-hearted. In many of his ways Brian probably had been more wholly naïve than either John or Nathaniel.

What a futile, utterly ignoble fate it was to die drunken, mutilated, bleeding to death before a wretched crossroads store in the wilderness. She sighed, lay counting the brilliant bars of sunlight which penetrated the jalousies and sketched a golden ladder on the wall beside her.

Well, her proverbial luck again had not failed her. The more she thought of it, the more Desire became convinced that nothing now could ever permanently go wrong.

It was fine to abandon the role of Mistress Daisy Montaigne, to be Desire Harmony once more; to be unaffected and genuine in thought and speech.

With the approach of midday, it grew very hot and so humid that Desire pushed off the bedclothes and pulled off her nightshift. She sighed when the air flowed more freely over her swollen figure, her increasingly plump and ever tenderer breasts. Small John gave an energetic wriggle. She smiled, was prompted to try to probe gently in an effort to decide the infant's probable position.

My, having a baby certainly did make a mess of one's figure! Worth it though. When it was all over she would have this part of John St. Clair to cherish for ever and ever.

Her thoughts reverted to Sam Higsby, the gaunt rifleman from

Pennsylvania who had come down from the Siege with Tim. How nice he'd been that time he had caught her snooping about his lean-to. Most men would have taken advantage. She knew now what he'd had every right to think.

There were no grace-notes, no pretty speeches to Sam and he wasn't given to talkativeness. When he did speak in his soft drawl, there was usually sense in what he said. A girl might tie to a man like Higsby. Where would he be now?

She gave up conjecturing to apply some finishing touches to the tale of her mis-adventures. Suppressing only the fact that she and John had not been legally married, she intended to tell the Proveauxs about the raid and its disastrous consequences to Conanicut. She would even admit John's British partisanship and describe his death. It would be both plausible and easy to invent a wedding performed by the pastor of Dissenting sect.

Of course, the Proveauxs must be led to believe that John had bequeathed next to nothing, barely enough money to pay her way to Charleston. She would make no mention of Nat, of course, nor of Brian. Chances were slim that anyone who knew her as Désirée or Mistress Daisy would get so far south. Not with the river swollen and the post roads still boggy from spring rains.

Best of all, the British had cut off all coastwise traffic except for the smallest coasters. She'd no wedding ring. What about that? It could have been stolen. Where? Well, say in Wilmington, North Carolina. Wilmington, she must remember that.

Once her confinement was over, perhaps Mrs. Proveaux could secure for her a position as tutor? 'Toinette and the Laurens girls had mentioned the existence of several "Dame Schools" in and near Charleston. In the old days advertisements had appeared in the Newport papers for "A Genteel Lady to tutor the daughters of a Planter in the Carolinas."

What would Roger Proveaux be like? 'Toinette's brother had never summered in Newport, but she gathered he was fiery, proud and very handsome.

Suddenly possessed of restlessness she got up and, peeping through the jalousie, saw 'Toinette puttering about in a small flower bed. She almost called out but decided that she had better get another night's rest. A few more hours in which to rid herself of the vision of Brian's profile all bright with sweat and contorted under the torch light.

From where Desire stood she could see what appeared to be the confluence of two rivers. Over to her left was a tangle of masts and rigging and canvas, yellow in the sun. Those gulls soaring above the topmasts seemed ever so home-like.

A clatter of hoofs sounded at the far end of the street and came closer. My, they certainly were in a tearing hurry. Peeping downward, she saw a short column of cavalrymen in gay blue and white regimentals gallop by.

They were standing in their stirrups and urging their beasts to even greater speed. Negroes in the street ducked fearfully into doorways and behind fences as the column dashed by and remained there until the heavy yellow dust had settled.

When Desire awoke it was pitch dark. A dull flash briefly silhouetted her window's frames on the ceiling. A thunder storm. No, it couldn't be. Those claps of thunder were sounding at regular intervals: one, then two almost together. Cannon! *Bo-o-o-mm!* A battery, nearer than the rest, let go, made a loose windowpane rattle, caused a series of crashing reverberations among the houses.

Outside Desire's door began agitated noises. Mrs. Proveaux's voice calling, "Louis! Louis! *Mon Dieu!* What can be wrong?"

"Cursed if I know," came the merchant's breathless accents. "No call to fear anything yet, my dear. Those are only alarm guns. Roger? Roger! Where the devil is Roger?"

"He isn't here. He is visiting at Charles MacIntosh's."

"The devil!" rasped Mr. Proveaux. "Why can he never be on hand when I want him?"

A church bell began to clang, then another, not decorously as for prayer, nor mournfully as for a funeral. Their wild, brazen pealing set up a tingle at the roots of Desire's hair.

8

SAILS OFF REBELLION ROW

BECAUSE Louis Proveaux set an example, there was no racing about and wailing as if the end of the world were about to descend on the house in King Street. Louis Proveaux remained stonily calm until his household was thoroughly reassured. Only then did he slip a pistol into his pocket and disappear down a street splashed with torches and lanterns.

Desire had long since appeared with 'Toinette and now was seated in a corner. Even in so short a time she could tell that Aunt Lobelia was a pettish, selfish, complaining old woman, that Aunt Sophie, Mr. Proveaux's sister, was her complete antithesis.

To pass the time Desire, at Mrs. Proveaux's request, gave them a vivid description of Lieutenant Sneyd's descent on Conanicut. For these ladies in peignoirs and boudoir caps, she pictured the maddening glare of the fires, the resounding blows of axes, the shouts and curses of the enemy. Poignantly, she relived her heartbreak at watching the destruction of the only home she had ever known. They wept with her over her account of finding John, so young and handsome— dead on a frozen road.

Out in the hall the slaves were listening, too.

Antoinette, round-eyed, inquired, "Do you—do you reckon the British will treat Charleston like that?"

"Of co'se not," Aunt Sophie put in promptly. "Charleston is much too valuable. Burn Charleston and what is there left in America for King George?"

"How can you say that, Sophie?" objected Aunt Lobelia from the most comfortable chair in the room. "Ain't Mrs. St. Clair just been tellin' us how the Ministerial troops have burnt No'folk, Falmouth and other towns up No'th?"

When Louis Proveaux returned, very grave of expression, it was to encounter Grandmère. Ash and Oak were carrying her downstairs on a chair.

"*C'est indigne!*" the old lady sputtered. "Why would they leave me alone with a siege starting? *I* who endured the siege of Dettingen! *Dépêchez-vous!* Get me down, you lazy rascals."

"Yas, Maum. Yas, Maum."

Grandmère began to chuckle when she saw her son below. "*Quelle drôlerie!* Fancy, Louis, I shall hear shells burst again!"

"*Mais, Maman*—" Mr. Proveaux protested. "You should not come down. The night air—"

"—*Va t'en, petit.*" At the foot of the stairs the slaves eased Mme. Proveaux to her tiny feet. Quite bent under some ninety years, she remained, nonetheless, a solid, bright-eyed little woman. Resting on her cane and disdaining her son's hand, she clicked along into the living room. Everybody ran for chairs and shawls.

Mrs. Proveaux's expression was tense, "Well, Louis?"

"Though there is no immediate danger," Mr. Proveaux assured her, "the situation is indeed grave. Very serious. One learns that the King's Ministers have sent against us not only a formidable squadron, but also an army!"

"Oh dear, oh dear!" Aunt Lobelia wrung plump hands. "We shall all be bayoneted and—and ravished!"

"Vain hopes, 'Belia," Aunt Sophie snapped. "Well, Louis, what is to be done?"

Desire somehow felt immensely self-possessed. She knew already what it was to find an enemy close at hand. 'Toinette was regarding her calm with something like awe.

"Well, go on, go on!" Grandmère urged, thoroughly pleased to have evicted Aunt Lobelia from the comfortable chair. "What has happened?"

Louis Proveaux gulped a tot of cognac and rubbed his chin, deliberating.

"As yet no one seems certain about the number of ships which have anchored off the Bar. But by all accounts, they cannot number less than thirty transports and men-o'-war."

"Thirty?" Grandmère sniffed. "Probably aren't over ten. In a war believe nothing of what you hear and only half of what you see. *Mon Dieu! I* know something of war."

For the first time she seemed aware of Desire. "Eh, who is this young lady? Why has she not been presented to me?"

"Mrs. St. Clair is an old friend of 'Toinette's—from Rhode Island," Mrs. Proveaux explained hurriedly. "Mrs. St. Clair is a widow. Her husband was killed in a battle near Newport."

"Not a battle," Aunt Lobelia testily corrected. " 'Twasn't a real battle, Charlotte. 'Twas a raid. Mrs. St. Clair said so herself."

"Papa! Where do you suppose Roger is now? They must have heard the alarm." Desire could tell that, all at once, 'Toinette was beginning to perceive that war might mean more than parades and handsome regimentals.

In Mrs. Proveaux's eyes, too, was a look she recognized. It had lurked in the expressions of Mrs. Franklin, the Widow Hull, and Mrs. Gardner when folks discussed the Siege of Boston.

"A siege of our own! Imagine a real battle," 'Toinette cried. "Won't it be exciting?"

Mr. Proveaux considered his daughter with irritation. "You will not be here to witness it."

"Oh dear, oh dear." Aunt Lobelia kept wetting her lips. "We shall have to flee or be killed. But where can we go? Who will shelter us, Louis?"

Louis Proveaux ignored his sister-in-law, spoke to his mother who was sitting as straight as she might and taking in everything with amused calmness.

"As soon as day breaks, the Committee will dispatch some expresses to arouse the up-country. Militia and country regiments will be ordered to muster in marching order."

On short fingers, the merchant commenced to enumerate preparations for a defense. "New earth works will be raised, a number of merchant ships will be armed. An emergency meeting of the Assembly will, no doubt, decide our future course."

"Then—Charleston will be defended?" Desire asked breathlessly.

Mr. Proveaux cast her an inquiring look. "I fear so. There will be much damage to property, much suffering among the mechanics and poor."

Gradually, the window frames assumed outlines as the early June dawn began to break.

From the parlor window Desire and Antoinette could see what seemed to be an endless succession of horsemen galloping up King Street. Gradually, the brick footways became crowded with fearful and excited colored people.

Aunt Sophie rose, deliberately smoothed her gray taffeta skirt, said to Antoinette's mother:

"Charlotte, shall I see that the slaves do not begin to entertain foolish fears? I reckon we need a good breakfast this morning more than usual."

"Bon!" Grandmère nodded vigorous approval. "I have found that men, especially those with French blood in their veins, campaign better on full stomachs. That was so at Minden and before Namur."

She smiled at Desire. "Ah, my child, you should have seen 'Toinette's great grandfather in the white of *le Regiment de la Reine*. There, *ma petite,* was a *guerrier* in the grand manner. A colonel who really fought, cursed, loved like a colonel."

"Now when the siege began—let me see, how was it?" Grandmère pursed thin, violet-pink lips. "Ah, yes—first we ladies were requested to bake as much bread as possible, to sacrifice—hee! hee!—all spare petticoats and shifts for bandages. Eh? Who can that be?"

A loud knocking had commenced. Antoinette, glancing out of the window, saw standing on the stoop her father's brother, Marcel. He was spare and, as always, dapper and dandy. At this historic hour he wore a coat of moire, a bottle-green—which was the fashionable color —and a waistcoat of canary yellow brocade. His rather thin and colorful nose seemed designed by Nature to support those gold-rimmed spectacles without which he was blind as any bat.

At his elbow fidgeted the third partner in Proveaux Brothers & Company. Joseph Proveaux was fat as a pig ready for market. It

amused Antoinette to watch his vast stomach undulate under a green
and yellow striped waistcoat when he climbed the winding stone
stairs.

Puffing, Joseph Proveaux waddled into the hall.

"*Voilà!* Observe what this silly, lunatic defiance of Gadsden, Rutledge and the rest has brought on us!" He gurgled like an angry
pigeon, mopped his heavy jaws. "Our trade will be ruined. Aye,
ruined beyond repair.

"Some imbeciles would try to defend this port? No. It must not be!
Mon Dieu, our warehouse! our ships! What would become of them?
Marcel, Louis!" He turned an anguished countenance on his brothers.
"How can you be so infernally calm? Will you take no thought for
your wives, your children?"

Marcel laughed and crossed to kiss his mother's blue-veined fingers.
"There is no call to worry on that score, old fellow. We have all
proved good sires—haven't we? No matter what chances, there will
always be enough of our get to carry on the strain."

Even Aunt Lobelia managed a short laugh because Joseph could
boast of eleven legitimate children.

Oak was about to secure the front door when a tall, solidly built
officer came tramping in unannounced.

"My service, Madame." He made a leg to Grandmère, then clanked
over to kiss Mrs. Proveaux's cheek. It was mottled with a tiny thread-
work of scarlet veins.

This, Desire deduced, was a Major Barnard Elliott, Mrs. Proveaux's
first cousin. He looked reassuringly martial in his artillery uniform
of blue turned up in red.

"Quite a family affair I've stumbled on, eh, Charlotte?"

"This is no time for pleasantries," Joseph grumbled.

"Maybe it ain't," the big man admitted as he pulled off gauntlets
very redolent of the stable. "It would appear that our loving Monarch
has sent troops to call. Well, Louis, what do you aim to do?"

Mrs. Proveaux caught at the big man's arm, asked in a subdued
voice, "Barnard, can you tell us where Roger is likely to be sent?"

"He will be kept safe, my dear. Main reason I stopped by was to tell you that he's turned up at Headquarters with young MacIntosh, Tom Beale and a Yankee friend of theirs. They were still half-seas-over. Young rascals must have been fighting a main."

"But where will he be ordered?"

"To Fort Johnson with the First Regiment," the big man answered carelessly.

Suddenly he saw Desire. "Heyo! So 'Toinette has a Yankee friend, too?"

"Well, I declare, Uncle Barnard!" Antoinette appeared deeply mystified. "How could you tell Miss—er—Mrs. St. Clair is a Yankee? She ain't said a word since you came in!"

"She didn't have to." He winked a bright blue eye. "Just look at the color in her cheeks! None of you local belles have anything to match that. Hers don't come out of a paint pot."

When Louis Proveaux was able to catch the major's gallant eye, he led all the men into a semi-circular library. Here neat rows of volumes in calfskin bindings rose to the ceiling and a flyblown plaster bust of Themistocles glared down from blank eye sockets.

Simultaneously the butler appeared bearing a tray of coffee and a decanter of cognac.

Joseph and Louis declined the brandy but Marcel and Major Elliott poured themselves a long measure.

"Maybe the last for a time," the latter sighed. "Been on the move ever since the alarm came in from Christ Church Parish. Incidentally, we can all thank God our British friends have delayed their attack until now."

Marcel Proveaux squinted shortsightedly over his spectacles. "Why?"

"The roads have mostly dried. In June the hauling of artillery and supplies is not so difficult."

"Then Charleston really is to be defended?" Joseph demanded fearfully.

Barnard Elliott considered the fat man with no great approval. "To the bitter end, my friend. *Ad extremis* or something like that."

Louis Proveaux shrugged, fetched a sibilant sigh, "While it is possible to admire the courage of the Assembly, one cannot say the same of its intelligence. Come, Barnard, why will they not face the facts? What serious opposition can this Province offer?"

He turned to look out of the window at the distant spars in the Cooper River. "You yourself know we have only five or six undisciplined and badly-armed regiments of Provincial troops and militia.

"Have we cavalry worthy of mention? No. We have hardly a piece of field artillery and only an odd assortment of ship cannon to mount on the fortifications. Is that not so, Cousin?"

"I fear so," admitted the artilleryman. He shrugged. "Still, if the Yankees were able to beat off regulars from behind breastworks—"

"This is not stupid old Gage we must fight; besides the enemy will have learned."

"Let us hope not," Marcel exclaimed. "I might feel less discouraged if the levies from the back country were to be depended on. As it is, Louis and I know only too well how they envy and hate Charleston and its merchants and planters. I venture those savages might welcome an opportunity of stabbing the Tidewater counties in the back."

Joseph Proveaux fiddled still more nervously with his watch fob. "And will the Creeks, Choctaws and Cherokees not rise the moment we strip the frontiers of men? My factors and patroons tell me the tribes have been very restless ever since the Tories and Scotch rose under MacDonald."

"They are always restless," Barnard Elliott pointed out. "But Moore's Creek taught 'em who held the upper hand. Right now I fancy the chiefs do feel aggrieved because we have not been able to deliver the gunpowder due them by treaty."

"Why not send it at once?" Marcel suggested.

"How the hell can we? Don't you know there ain't enough gunpowder in the whole Province to fight one major battle?"

"Resistance is madness, if for only one reason," Marcel Proveaux observed in his deliberate, precise way. "There always remains our usual and most deadly peril. Picture the great estates, the villages quite stripped of militia?"

A penetrating silence fell. There was no need for Marcel Proveaux to clarify his meaning. They all knew that, in defiance of a law specifying that a planter must employ one white to every ten slaves, a majority of owners paid no bit of attention. On many and many an estate, the ratio of the black over white was twenty-five or thirty to one.

What made the situation still more perilous was the very high percentage of wild negroes now owned in the Province. Less than a year ago many a big field-hand had been handling his sword, bow and spears on the Ivory Coast.

As Louis Proveaux very well knew, the boom years of 1773–1774 had seen a great wave of slave trading. In those days one could sell anything in a black skin so many fighting negroes—Coromantees, Ashantees and Senegals—were among the recent importation. He had seen them toiling like vicious, cornered beasts ready to rend and destroy at the first opportunity.

Already there had been minor uprisings. In one case a planter and his whole family had been horribly tortured before the revolting slaves killed them and fled into the vastnesses of Georgia to seek an easier form of slavery under the Creeks and Cherokees.

Major Elliott stood up suddenly, gulped the last of his brandy. "When it comes to that, gentlemen, I reckon we are all in God's hands."

He glanced at Louis. "What course do you intend for your family?"

"I will bundle them off as quickly as may be."

"That's the ticket!" Major Elliott continued. "We don't want the town cluttered up with non-combatants. Why don't Charlotte make a visit with Amy to our place on the Santee? We've plenty of room, you know."

Louis Proveaux looked his gratitude. "Magnolia Hill has always been our favorite visiting place."

"You will go also?"

Marcel and Louis Proveaux shook their heads in unison. The former said, "If anybody thinks I intend to abandon our warehouses to a parcel of British, he is in error."

"You will stay, Joseph?"

Joseph Proveaux goggled. He loathed such unnecessary and un-profitable activity.

"Even before this disturbance began, Emma and I were planning to visit my plantation at Dorchester. You reckon it will be safe to remove my stock there?"

The big man in red and blue guffawed. "Safe? Hell no! Once the British capture Charleston, they will head for Dorchester next. Now if I were you, Joe, I—well, I'd not pause short of Camden."

"Camden!" Joe sputtered. "Impossible. Transportation there is not to be had. Dear God in Heaven, you may laugh, Elliott, but you ain't got a row of warehouses full of indigo, rice, and hides."

He twisted moist hands, said sullenly, "Why in God's name did you confounded saber-clanking patriots have to bring down ruin upon us?"

Major Elliott's hard blue eyes considered the youngest of the Proveaux brothers with manifest distaste.

"Think what you will in private but I advise you not to voice that opinion in public, or you'll find yourself proscribed. Such pusillanimous sentiments will benefit neither you nor your family."

"Neither will a siege," the unhappy man insisted. "Did we merchants ask for this war? No. We all were making out right well under the old government. The King's Ministers weren't a bit worse than your damned tyrannical Congresses and Committees!"

Louis suddenly roused himself, spoke sharply, "Be quiet! I will not tolerate such talk in my house."

He was remembering the fate of Lazarus Eden, the way his business had withered once he appeared in the Committee of Safety's black books.

Major Elliott's angry color faded. Buttoning up his red waistcoat he drawled, "Well, Marcel, not being married, I expect you intend to stay in town?"

"But yes," Marcel laughed. "I, too, have what might be called responsibilities."

All Charleston knew of the three lively mestees he maintained in various quarters of town and Barnard Elliott figured the near-sighted old dandy had sired more children than all the rest of his family put together.

9

The Siege Begins

President Rutledge lost no time in publishing the new Government's intention of defending Charleston. He did this in the last copy of the "South Carolina Gazette" Peter Timothy printed before packing his presses for removal to the back country.

There was much amusement over this, some wags maintaining that the legislators could never function without a record being made of their oratory.

All morning the inhabitants of Charleston remained at upper windows and through gazing glasses fearfully watched new sails appear and maneuver into that formidable array assembling off the long streak of white water which marked Charleston Bar.

With the aid of an old-fashioned spy-glass Desire could even distinguish varying classes of men-of-war among the clumsier transports and supply vessels. She and Antoinette had a fine view of the harbor from the second story balcony on which women of the family maintained look-out for Proveaux vessels overdue from Europe or the West Indies.

"Mercy! There's an awful heap of 'em," Antoinette exclaimed in scared accents. "How many do you make it?"

"Thirty-four," Desire replied abstractedly. Sight of those White Ensigns flying out there was conjuring bitter-sweet memories: His Majesty's ships *Rose, Swan, Glasgow* and the little *Bolton* lying off Newport; John being rowed ashore, straight and gallant in a flowing boat cloak.

"I make it thirty-six," Antoinette announced. "I think I see two more transports lying behind Dewees Island. Am I right?"

When at length they sought the cool of Antoinette's room, Desire inquired into the Proveaux family's immediate plans.

"Grandmère, Maman and the rest will leave for Magnolia Hill tomorrow."

"—And you?"

Antoinette interrupted the packing of a wicker chest and her small dark head flashed back. "Why, honey, I'm going to stay— At least as long as that insufferable Suzanna Elliott. I ride quite as well as Sue, and I vow I'm a far better housekeeper."

She sighed. "Reckon Papa and I can get along with Ash, Pansy and only five or six house people. I really don't mind discomfort."

Eight servants! And that was considered getting along! Though some of them were children, Desire had so far counted eighteen domestics employed at the Proveaux residence.

"Do you wish to go with Maman, Dee?"

"Oh no, no!" came the instant reply. "With everything so upset, maybe I can find employment—"

Truth was, Desire wouldn't for the world have missed witnessing at least the beginning of a siege. She would be in no danger from bursting shells. Her infallible luck would shield her.

"Mama says you must be our guest, at least until after—well, you know." 'Toinette blushed furiously and hurriedly packed a pair of elegant French stays.

Again a generous nod from Fortune. Desire wasn't sure what having a baby was like, but she suspected from odds and ends picked up at Mrs. Norton's, that it was nothing extra pleasurable—especially the first time.

"You are all very, very kind and generous, 'Toinette. I vow I will never forget it." She smiled. "I want to stay here and help you take care of Mr. Proveaux and Roger, too, I hope. It will be exciting being in Charleston and really great fun, won't it?"

Antoinette's lively eyes sparkled. "Of course. We shall make Roger invite his handsomest officer friends to dinner. Of course," she flushed, and her gaze, dropping, brushed Desire's swollen figure, "you mustn't expect them to beau—a—a—new widow."

"That is entirely as it should be," Desire said sweetly.

Hurriedly, Antoinette continued, "Of course, we shall keep up their spirits by playing cards and charades with them. And I will play the harp for the ones I like."

Desire intended to try for a conquest or two. Lately her color had heightened and those faint shadows under her eyes looked less brown, more bluish. Maybe if she remained seated she'd get her share of attention, baby or no baby—but she had better not be too successful, 'Toinette had a little tendency towards jealousy.

Impatient, bathed in sweat, Lieutenant Nat Coffin continued to supervise the business of measuring the town's supply of gunpowder. Hell, he felt certain, could be no hotter than this small, ill-ventilated magazine.

The inhabitants were moving out with an altogether unnecessary haste. Unless British generals and admirals had changed their ways, everybody had plenty of time to do what was to be done. His Majesty's forces, so far in this war, had moved with stately deliberation. Of course, no immediate attack would be made. My Lords of the Admiralty didn't proceed like hostile Indians or marauding French and Spanish expeditions.

It was so stifling in this tiny octagonal structure that Nat went over to catch a breath of air at the door. Um. Still another line of refugee oxcarts was creaking by, each vehicle loaded to the limit with bedsteads, wardrobes, desks and great, shapeless bundles of cloth. Here and there somebody's portrait stared from amid a tangle of furniture. Trampling hoofs and steel-bound wheels ground the yellow street dust ever thicker and deeper.

Like the blackened and sweat-streaked men under his command, Nat Coffin went barefoot and he had secured his breeches by a length of cord. In a powder magazine, one wasn't inclined to risk a spark struck from an iron belt buckle or a shoe nail. In the magazine itself the hinges, window catches, measuring cups, powder sifters and airing ladles were either of bronze, copper or lead.

"Hey, Mr. Coffin, take a look," invited a sentry posted in the shade of a tall magnolia. "Yonder goes Mrs. Sumter."

The soldier pointed to a huge coach with a shiny blue body and bright yellow wheels. It had been so heavily laden that its body was pressed snug against springs of steel and leather. The vehicle rolled up Church Street at a snail's pace, looming above an assortment of wheelbarrows, wagons and two-wheeled carts.

In the wake of this splendid affair straggled a long line of house slaves. Even the smallest pickaninny carried a burden of some sort; for once, there was not a bit of laughter or foolishness in the blacks. They looked scared half to death.

Several wild negroes with chains connecting their ankles brought up the tail of the column and marched under the supervision of a hard-faced man who balanced a blunderbuss across his pommel.

"That there is Cicero Ball," remarked the sentry. "Ain't nothin' meaner 'n a mestee who's been granted the whip-hand."

"A mestee? Just what is a mestee?" Nat asked, watching the man in question ride by. Handsome in a coarse, brutal sort of way, the rider's blond hair seemed only just a little crinkly. "You have so many terms for mixed bloods. I can't keep them straight."

Glad of an excuse to relax, the soldier ran a yellow bound cuff across his brows, blotting away a row of pellucid sweat drops. " 'Round Charleston, we-uns rate niggers like this: Straight black; then mulatto, which means one-half white; next comes the sambo, he's two-thirds white; then, you've your quarteroon who is only a quarter colored, and you don't often find pretty colored gals with less white blood.

"A lot of mestees look white 'cause they got only an eighth part colored blood. Last of all come browns, which are even whiter than the mestees."

Nat listened intently. Must remember that. Black, mulatto, sambo, quarteroon, mestee, and brown—but all of them black as black in the eyes of the law.

At shouts of "Runaway! Runaway!" everybody scampered to the sides of the street and flattened against door stoops or dusty clapboards in a trice. Only a slow two-wheeled ox wagon remained like an island in the middle of Church Street.

Nostrils wide and scarlet, tail and mane flying, a bay came tearing along with its saddle turned under its belly. The terrified animal trod on a puppy and staggered off-stride but recovered and pounded on. The puppy writhed feebly in the dust. One of Mrs. Sumter's pickaninnies scuttled back and, finding its pet dying, raised shrill howls of grief.

Lieutenant Coffin worked a little longer then sought the tent in which he had left his clothes. All along he had suspected that there could be nowhere near so much powder in the magazine as a Royal Ordnance Officer's return had indicated. So serious a shortage, he judged, should be reported to Colonel Gadsden with all speed.

When twilight deepened over the beleaguered town, disorderly lines of refugees were yet choking roads that led to the various ferries. Many families kindled fires by the roadside and cooked a hurried meal while their babies squalled and their dogs fought.

A few alert merchants, perceiving a golden opportunity, ordered their patroons—local shallow-water skippers—to offer for charter their trunk boats, barges and shallops. The patroons, however, charged such stiff rates that only a few wealthy fugitives chose to avail themselves of this opportunity.

Once darkness fell, the militia officers posted detachments of guards at all important street intersections, and otherwise patrolled the town. Any negro found on the street was liable to arrest. If he did not immediately halt when challenged, he would be shot down.

By consequence, Charleston at night was unearthly still. In a great majority of homes there were no lights at all. Some inhabitants had secured their ground floor doors and windows by nailing heavy planks across them.

Meantime, express riders galloped until they broke down blooded mounts in raising the country as far as Ninety Six, Wynnsboro, Rougele's Mills, Georgetown and Orangeburg.

Rumors grew wilder, more numerous, with each passing hour but everyone reckoned that at least three, maybe four days must pass before the up-country companies could appear in any appreciable strength. Soldier and civilian alike speculated on when the first elements of Colonel Thomson's Third Regiment of Infantry, of Lieutenant-Colonel Clark's Rangers and of the Raccoon Company of Riflemen would come in. Would the British Armada attack before they mustered in strength?

With these and other disturbing questions gnawing at their peace of mind, the remnants of Charleston's population slept ill.

10

The Master of Hobgoblin Hall

THANKS to Major Barnard Elliott's presence at Headquarters, the Proveauxs had not been stampeded into quitting Charleston at once. Weather conditions, Elliott assured them, would prevent for at least forty-eight hours any attempt of the British to cross Charleston Bar. Even under ideal conditions, passage of the Bar was a dangerous undertaking.

It was a shining wonder, the big major claimed, that the enemy Admiral had not long since sent over some small transports and light men-o'-war to capture the fort standing, less than half completed, on Sullivan's Island. To seize it would be like taking jam off a pantry shelf.

A Yankee serving on Colonel Moultrie's staff, however, had not been so astonished at General Clinton's leisureliness. He maintained that, so far, British generals had executed their strategy with a truly majestic deliberation.

Comfortably, Major Elliott deduced that no onslaught would be made until the enemy could remove the guns from their ships-of-the-line and run the three-deckers over the Bar.

"How big are they?" Desire queried.

"Fourth raters, Ma'am."

"Then they will mount around fifty cannons, will they not?"

Major Elliott's bright blue eyes widened and he made a leg in her direction.

"Well, I'll be da—blessed! I say, Louis, have you ever heard of a Miss who knew a brig from a scow? My compliments, Ma'am." A shadow sobered his expression. "We hear that six more transports have arrived and are at anchor."

Desire knew this. She and Antoinette had spent most of the afternoon on the look-out.

By sunset they had counted nearly forty vessels of various sizes riding the Atlantic long rollers off Dewees Island.

Next day, on the afternoon of June second, Mrs. Proveaux, Grand-mère and the two aunts left for safety. They went in style, too, because at the last minute Roger cantered up bringing an escort of troopers in dashing, horsehair-crested helmets. This greatly pleased Louis Proveaux. There were ugly rumors current concerning raids by the Brass-ankle bands on parties of rich and defenseless fugitives.

Late that afternoon, when it had grown cooler, Antoinette suggested suddenly, "Let us take a promenade before Papa says we can't."

"But I—well, I look terrible—", Desire protested.

"Pooh! There's nobody left in town to notice," the dark-haired girl reminded. "No one that counts, honey. Ash and Linden can take their staves."

"Very well, I'm all of a twitter to learn what all that hammering is about." She really welcomed this opportunity to see Charleston. With a population of fourteen thousand souls—white and black—it must be quite a place.

Twenty minutes of easy walking brought them to the Exchange, to St. Michael's and old St. Philip's. On Broad Street they saw, too, a pretty little ivy-grown stone building. It was the magazine, 'Toinette explained.

The gardens, Desire found wonderfully well kept and brilliant. What surprised her most was the fact that so many of the fine houses had been built end-on to the street, not facing it, as back in New England.

So many broken bits of furniture littered the footways they had to pick their way with care. The streets, too, were eloquent of the terror-stricken flight. Here lay a broken carriage lamp, there a worn-out trace. Crushed boxes, rags, rotten fruit, even abandoned toys littered the dust.

"This is the New Theatre," Antoinette stated not without pride. " 'Til two years ago, some very elegant pieces were presented here."

So this was the Queen Street Theatre? How often had Mistress Daisy Montaigne visualized its boxes bright with jewels, brocades and laces; herself queening it in the Green Room?

The structure's red double doors were streaked with layers of dirt and to a board was tacked a yellowed notice: "Closed by Order of ye Committee of Safety." Attached to it was an extract from the Act against "shews, plays and pantomimes."

At the intersection of Queen and Church Streets a crowd was gathering. It was composed largely of soldiers and unemployed seamen.

"You trot on ahead, Ash, and find out whom they cheer," Antoinette directed. "It must be the up-country troops arriving. Let's go watch 'em. You don't mind, do you, honey?"

When the slave returned he bowed obsequiously low.

"Hit's a great Gen'l comin'. 'E Congress done sent him down frum de Nawth."

Down the street sounded a lot of drumming and fifes began squealing like so many pigs caught under a gate.

By standing on a mounting block, Desire was able to witness the approach of a group of horsemen. There was so much gold and lace work glittered among them, they must be very important.

"There's Colonel Christopher Gadsden," Antoinette cried. "My, ain't he distinguished! And look, honey, that big man with the red face is Colonel Moultrie. Roger says he commands the fort on Sullivan's Island. There's Cousin Colonel Isaac Huger. I think the gentleman beyond is Captain Grimball of the Charleston Company of Artillery. I just dote on the artillery regimentals, don't you?"

"There's the new General." "Hooray fer Gen'ral Charles Lee!"

"Here he comes!" excited voices shouted.

Into Queen Street rode a gangling, hatchet-faced officer astride one of the biggest horses Desire had ever beheld. From Tim's description, Desire recognized Lee instantly.

Blue tunic a-glitter with gold, white breeches gleaming, Major-General Charles Lee rode at least three horses' lengths in advance of his staff. To Antoinette his bearing was surprising; it suggested that of a conqueror entering a captured city.

A sardonic smile fixed on his lips, the new Continental Commander lifted his cocked hat and saluted with it a few times. Haughtily, he beckoned an aide wearing Virginian regimentals and whispered something in his ear. He must have said something very amusing for the aide laughed so hard he shook a couple of bone hair pins out of his wig.

"Three cheers fer Lee! He'll whip the Britishers!"

The new Commander rode by, his leopard-skin saddle housing flashing golden in the sunset. The queer, long-haired dogs Tim had mentioned, trotted warily at the tall charger's heels.

As they were descending from the mounting block, Antoinette remarked, "I'm right glad I ain't a man—a soldier, I mean. What a sour, sneering look he had! I vow I'm sorry he's to command our troops."

"He ain't going to, Ma'am," corrected a uniformed figure. "Not unless President Rutledge grants him leave."

"But why?"

"This gen'ral was commissioned an' appointed by the Continental Congress—not by this Province. 'Til our troops is sworn into the Continental Service, Gen'ral Lee can't give them any orders at all. I'm glad o' that. I don't cotton to no stiff scarecrow like him."

Down by the North Bay huge bonfires had been kindled for the benefit of slave gangs desperately working to load barges with the contents of a long row of storehouses facing the water. In eye-stinging waves, smoke came drifting back over the town.

Everywhere, men stood on street corners staring at ships which,

laid up for months, were now being either warped or towed off up
the Cooper River. Some of them might get as far as thirty miles
upstream, but the larger ones would have to chance Fate some fourteen miles away.

II

THE WATEREE COMPANY

ALISTAIR BRYSON gave the last cow a gentle slap on her rump and
lugged the pail of milk down to a spring house. Like everything
Gordon Bryson had built, it was neatly fashioned of enduring stone.

To Alistair, it was a relief to have reached a decision. He would
have to enroll if the family wasn't to suffer from the same kind of
stupid suspicion which had ruined so many Highlanders in North
Carolina. The conviction had come soon after that sore-bottomed
express rider had ridden on towards the Wylie and Campbell hold-
ings.

Ever since Flora MacDonald—who apparently would never learn
to back a winner—and her handsome young son had raised the North
Carolina Scots for Governor Martin and King George III, a spirit of
unrest had been prevalent in the Wateree country. Every day the line
between Tory and Patriot was becoming more sharply drawn. He
must go. There was no doubt of it.

Feyther would make out all right what with young Jock and
Angus getting to be such big braw lads. Besides there was Jeanie;
she was as strong and useful as a boy.

Alistair halted and absently regarded the cows which, having been
milked, were wandering off down the hillside making a comfortable
tonk-tonking with their bells. All last night he had had no peace
of mind.

Nae doot, 'twas all very well for Feyther to bide his wee and pro-
claim himself unalterably neutral. Feyther had had his share of adventure on the wild field of Culloden and afterwards in the drain

where, for two days, he had shivered while the Duke's orange-coated Tangier Regiment of dragoons hanged and looted in all directions.

Long since, Feyther had slain his Ferguson and had mourned kin murdered from ambush in that feud which, since time out of mind, had smouldered among the misty crags of Sunderland. For all the migration to America he, too, might kill his Ferguson. Plenty of that accursed clan were reported to have come over, too. Hadn't the Mac-Kays and Campbells successfully transported their feud to these newer mountains?

It was only a month gone since Feyther had come home looking very grim, to report that a family of Fergusons from the slopes of Ben Mohr had begun homesteading close by Rougeles Mills. How Feyther's harsh, high-cheeked features had tightened! Mither had not yet lost a haunted, worried expression.

Provided this bicker down by the seacoast came to nothing, he'd borrow one of Charlie Campbell's fine Pennsylvanian rifles and once the hay was in he and Jock would go over to Rougeles Mills and exterminate these Fergusons.

From where he stood under the shoulder of the hill, he saw Angus hoeing corn. Losh, but grain grew with a fine, lavish speed in America. This year he and Feyther had planted six acres in oats against four last year.

Like most of his neighbors, Gordon Bryson had toiled mightily and prospered. It was thought odd that Alistair at twenty-six years of age was not yet married. Of all the children, only he was barely able to remember the Old Country.

Loudly his wooden-pegged, home-made boots clumped across into a kitchen complete to the least detail with spits, jacks, hobs, and trammels. Mither was busy baking thick, round loaves of ship's bread which would be bartered next week with Eli Kershaw & Co. for European and West Indian goods. Of tea and salt in particular, the family stood in serious need. Very little cash circulated in this up-country.

Alistair felt a peculiar and unfamiliar thrill at seeing hanging above the chimney place the targe and claymore Feyther had carried for the Young Pretender.

It was so bright today, he could see the deep notch a dragoon's saber had hacked through the former's tough, brass-mounted leather.

"Why, Alistair!" Mrs. Bryson, surprised, turned a heated face over her shoulder. "What can ye be wanting i' the hoose at this hour? Ye'd best no' let yer feyther catch ye idle."

Seriously, Alistair shook a dark, narrow head. "I have done wi' farming for the now. I've taken a notion to see what a war may be like."

"Oh, lad." Mither's features crumpled. "You canna, mustna—"

"Nay, I must," said he soberly. "Is it no' the part o' gude sense tae have a member of the family on either side o' the fence? Should the Hanoverian usurper's men prevail, I can always go West and it's no great loss. Should the low country people win, then Feyther will have only to say, 'And did we no' send our eldest son to fight against the Crown?'"

"Oh, lad! Lad!" Agitatedly Mrs. Bryson began wiping floury hands on her apron. "Dinna try to be so logical. Feyther knows best. He fought the King and lost every groat to his name!"

"But 'tis not the same this time. I am going anyway."

Mrs. Bryson's eyes, red-rimmed from the smoke of the fireplace, wavered. At last she saw there was no moving him so she straightened and went over to the foot of the stair.

"Jeanie!" she called. "Fetch down Alistair's best breeks an' the fine new stockings ye knitted him the last winter."

Heavily, she turned to him. "You'd best break this news to your feyther, lad."

Alistair found the sturdy old man splitting rails which would eventually enclose a fine, new pasture. When he saw his son coming up Gordon Bryson drove his axe-blade deep into a log, then ran the back of a knotty hand across his cheek. His bushy brows merged.

"An' why are ye no' plowing the north field like ye were bid?"

Alistair's heart began to thump. Never before, in all his twenty-six years, had he dared take direct issue with his father.

"Tomorrow, the Wateree Company is mustering at Pine Tree Hill —or Camden as they begin to call it. I am for the war."

Though Feyther was wearing a kilt, he stood naked to the waist and Alistair could see the stringy muscles mapping his chest and arms. Tugging at his ragged gray beard, he demanded ominously, "Ye ken what I think o' this war-r?"

"Aye, Feyther, I ken it verra well." Alistair's gray eyes clung desperately to his father's blue ones.

"You ken naught of war as it really is," the elder Bryson reminded. "The horror, sickness, pain it brings. Maire often than no', ye'll meet with hunger and despair. I ha'e tasted all these things and I would spare my son them."

"I thank you, Feyther, but aiblins the rebels will win. Suppose one o' the Fergusons fought against the Hanoverians and none o' us had?"

The old man's beard flickered as he shook his head. "Come Autumn, we will attend to yon Fergusons by Rougeles."

An uncomfortable silence ruled. They heard the axe blows of Jock girdling trees in the next valley. By Autumn still another field would be ready for clearing.

"I—I would leave wi' yer blessing, Feyther."

"Ye go against my will so I'll no' grant ye that," the old man rumbled. "But ye shall carry the auld claymore." His voice thickened a little. " 'Tis a good blade and it saw me through my years o' trouble."

"Farewell, Feyther."

"Alistair—"

"Yes?" Alistair's heart lightened as he turned back.

"—Ye'll always recognize a Ferguson o' Ben Mohr in this manner. They're verra dark complected, ha'e beetling brows that meet o'er their noses, narrow jaws, and they're most of them are warty aboot the face.

"No matter what he says, ne'er trust a Ferguson so far as ye can heave a bull by the tail. Ye ken their tartan—so be watchfu'."

Having thus delivered himself, Gordon Bryson deliberately turned his back, dropped the wedge into a crack, stepped back. The old man's axe whirled up, descended with a ringing impact. The rail log crackled, opened a yellow crack its whole length.

In silence, Alistair descended the hillside. For a long time he could remember how the sun was flashing that afternoon on Fishing Creek. How blue the heat lay in the rich bottom lands of the Wateree valley. Some day, if he came across a stout lass wi' no idle Low-Country notions, he intended to homestead over there.

In the straggling village of Camden, as at Bacon Ridge, Monck's Corner, Granby and Jacksonburg, an unprecedented activity filled the air with oaths, boasts and clouds of orange-colored dust. Every few moments a horseman in homespun or doeskin would rein in before Messrs. Ancrum, Lance & Loocock's log store.

More often than not the dusty new arrival would dismount and after unslinging his equipment turn his animal, usually a furry plow horse, over to some small relative who had ridden in behind him.

"Mind you ride easy on the way back," was the usual parting in-junction.

Down by the river quite a few pettigues, dugouts and skiffs were coming in to the landing. Others lay drawn up on the bank like a row of basking alligators.

When the brass sun pins driven into Mr. Loocock's window sill showed noon, Captain John Chesnut caused an Indian drum to be beaten and was mighty pleased that nearly forty men had answered his call to arms. Yessir, this was a fine turnout for so thinly settled a community.

Warmed by a pannikin of good red Jamaica, Captain Chesnut felt inspired to address the volunteers.

"Like Cincinnatus, you have deserted yo' plowshares to defend Freedom and Honor from tyranny, most foul, on the part of the King's ministers," he informed the astonished woodsmen. "Men, you are like avenging angels!

"You are the knights of old who rode fo'th to protect the weak and infirm from the fury of a base oppression! Us up-country wild-cats will sho'ly demonstrate to the Tidewater people what real fighting is!"

Captain Chesnut got so carried away by his oratory that, amid shouts of laughter, he fell off the whiskey barrel on which he had clambered.

Alistair Bryson, leaning on his claymore in the shade of a big basswood, listened attentively though he didn't take stock in such flowery talk. Neither did his neighbors, Jamie and Lewis, the six-foot Campbell twins.

Now he was glad he had heeded Mither's plea to don an old kilt of Bryson plaid—dark red with darker edging, light blue and yellow crossings. The village girls kept looking at the group of kilted Scots and whispering amongst themselves. Now and then they would giggle like anything.

Chewing solemnly on a spear of grass, Alistair kept one eye peeled for the first flash of a Ferguson tartan—green, blue, yellow.

Unlike his neighbors he had been able to bring no rifle to the muster, not even an old musket. Feyther's old long-bladed claymore with its basket guard of bright brass made a brave showing at his hip, though. His baldric, too, was of good leather, broad and liberally decorated with big brass studs.

There were other claymores among the recruits, other tartans. Some were familiar: the Campbells' light green, crossed with darker green, narrow yellow edging; the MacKenzies' blue-green with darker edges and cross lines of red and white. There even was a Munro in red with a broad green stripe, black and yellow checks, and a Cameron and Graeme or two.

Forming another group were the generally fair-haired and brawny sons of settlers from the Palatinate. These spoke German among themselves, and were deliberate in their movements. Probably because the fur trade with Charleston was at a stand-still, a surprising number of silent and lantern-jawed trappers enrolled.

Of course, a majority of Scots had killed two birds with one stone by bringing along some produce which might be sold before they marched away.

When their names had been set down, the Palatines gravitated, *en masse,* to an ordinary run by one Hugo Schmaltz. In honor of the occasion the publican had mounted a barrel of his excellent ale just inside the door and was standing treat to each and every recruit. As for the trappers and Scots, they clubbed together to buy a keg of rum.

"And when ar-re we to depart doon river?" Jamie Campbell inquired of a patroon in charge of three river boats by the landing.

"The minute yonder trunk boat is freighted." He winked. "You ain't thinkin' Morley & Co. are transporting you out o' patriotism, are you?"

Captain Chesnut came up, emitted a snorting laugh. "I should say not! 'Patriotism' is a word none of you crotch-blistered merchants ever heard of."

Morley took it in good spirit. "All right, Cappen, you go right ahead and talk big now. When them British regulars start twistin' your tail you'll sing sweet and low."

"Ah, go soak your head," called a trapper. "We'll swaller them Lobster-backs 'thout even butterin' their ears."

The river captain spat into the greenish-yellow current. "That's a big mouthful, friend. I hear say there's ten thousand troops in them transports."

There was a little silence over this.

"Of dem, ve are not afraid," one of the Germans grinned. "Last spring I, mit mein blunderbuss, two bears mit vun shot killed."

One of the trappers queried with studied innocence, "Tell me, Dutchie, which o' them b'ars shot at you first?"

Alistair had begun to think that the company would never start downstream when, around four of the afternoon, Tom Yadkin, patroon of the largest river boat, came up from the landing and nodded to Captain Chesnut.

"All loaded," he announced.

"Fall in! That means, form in line."

The militia captain bore down on Alistair who was busily munching bread and cheese.

"Bryson, you seem to have a modicum of intelligence. Suppose you act as sergeant over the rest of you Scotch."

"'Scots,' sir," Alistair corrected gravely. "Nae such a thing as a Scotchman exists."

"Call yourselves anything you like." Chesnut grinned. "But for God's sake get lined up."

Aside from his Highlanders, there were around a dozen Germans in broad hats. They were shouldering a weird assortment of muskets, fowling pieces, and blunderbusses.

There must be easily twice as many trappers. In their fringed, neutral-tinted hunting shirts and deerskin hats, they achieved a uniformity of appearance. Invariably they carried a long-barreled rifle and most of them had a war hatchet or a skinning knife swinging at their belts. These "Butternuts," as they generally called themselves, were by far the most profane.

He had no drummer, so Captain Chesnut hammered on an empty molasses keg until finally everybody stood quietly under a row of pines fringing the road.

The captain pulled out a paper and placed a pair of spectacles on his badly sunburnt nose. "Take off yo' hats, boys, raise yo' right hand, and I'll swear you into the service of the Sovereign Province of South Carolina."

A private was to draw two shillings, sixpence a month and was bound to serve for thirty days, or until all danger of a British invasion was at an end. Men lacking firearms could expect to be issued muskets when the Wateree Company reached Fort Watson.

Under a patched and faded militia uniform, Captain Chesnut's stocky figure drew itself up. His eye flickered down the long single rank. "Slope, *arms!*"

The men got their firearms shouldered amid grunts of, "Goddam it, don't you dint my bar'l!" and "Hey, how much room you need?" "Get the damn' scatter-gun outer my face, Dutchie, and fer Christ's sake, take your fat finger off the trigger."

"Silence! Silence!"

It pleased Alistair that the least noisy recruits were his Scots, but on the way to the landing even they cut up a bit. Jamie Campbell solemnly invited the tow-headed barmaid from Schmaltz's ordinary to see what he wore under his kilts.

Giggling, the wench came forward and stooped over. For all he was supposed to set an example, Alistair couldn't help yelling with laughter at the bright red her face went when her curiosity was satisfied.

Making no attempt to keep step, the Wateree Company filed down towards the river. In the largest trunk boat, half a dozen red and white cows were fearfully contemplating the slow, snag-dotted current.

Alistair selected a seat near the support of a collapsible mast which was hinged and otherwise designed to be easily lowered when a bridge or low branches barred the channel.

A boy waded out knee-deep in the river and cupping his hands shrilled, "Hey, Paw, mind ye bring me a Britisher's skelp and not his wig!"

Slave watermen braced poles and sweeps against the bank and sluggishly, the three river boats began to move away.

A man wearing the MacIntosh tartan draped one arm about a cask of beeswax, the other about a stone jug of whiskey and, throwing back his head, sang:

> " 'They said I had neither cow nor calf,
> Nor dribbles o' drink rins thro' the draff,
> Nor pickles o' meal rins thro' the mill-e'e-
> And werena my heart's licht, I wad dee.
>
> His titty she was baith wylie and slee;
> She spied me as I cam owre the lea;
> And then she ran in and made a loud din—
> Believe your ain e'en, an ye trow not me.' "

12
CHARLESTON BAR

BECAUSE a party of wood cutters had not yet returned with a fresh supply of palmetto logs, engineer officers at work on the eastern curtain of the new fort sought the shade and there lit their pipes. In glum silence, they watched the lackadaisical spade work of a slave gang lent by a group of Charleston patriots.

Begun in January, Fort Sullivan should have been completed long, long since. Now everyone in town demanded to know why only the southern curtain—it commanded that channel along which a hostile fleet must pass—had been completed. Frantic efforts were now being made to nullify this negligence.

Like most of the coast in that region, both Sullivan's Island and Long Island, just to the seaward of it, were merely long, overgrown sand dunes densely covered with myrtle, palmetto and other underbrush.

Of big trees, only a few discouraged-looking live oaks and some cedars had taken root. On the landward side of Sullivan, a series of wide salt meadows degenerated eventually into marshes. These, cut into intricate patterns by meandering tidal creeks, extended for miles between island and mainland. At low tide vast expanses of mud were exposed to raise a dreadful sour reek to the heavens and afford a breeding ground for countless millions of insects.

Lieutenant Nat Coffin, recalling the speedy appearance of mile on mile of entrenchments in and around Boston, felt astounded that so small and simple an earthwork should not have been long since completed. After all, Fort Sullivan was only a simple rectangle strengthened by bold salients at each of its corners.

Resting on the seaward bastion, Nat felt he had found an explanation. At Breed's Hill there had been mighty few officers who couldn't drive a straight furrow or shingle a roof. It now seemed impressive to recall that, *in one night,* a single small company of Connecticut infantry had raised a breastwork longer than one whole side of this fort.

Black labor, he observed, was miserably inefficient. Why, to accomplish the simplest of tasks, an officer had to be in constant supervision. This, he reasoned, was the essential difference between free and slave labor.

Another difficulty was the serious shortage of skilled mechanics. Very few of the so-called sappers were even half-way handy with a pod auger or a broad-axe.

Moving along the south wall, he could easily take in details of construction. On each side the engineers were raising a double wall of palmetto logs some sixteen feet apart. These walls were secured and anchored to each other by means of timbers, dove-tailed and bolted at intervals.

Into the space between these walls slaves were dumping baskets and baskets of sand. Behind the western wall a party of Irish stonemasons were laying bricks, constructing supports for platforms which, everyone was praying, would be finished in time to support a battery.

A number of eighteen pounders had that morning been brought over from Charleston in barges. At present they lay on the beach just above the high water mark. Curiously enough, the carriages on which they were to be mounted had not yet appeared.

There was not a single piece of field artillery in the fort. And, so far as Nat could tell, very little roundshot to fit the nines, eighteens and twenty-six pounders. A fine state of affairs.

He would never understand why Sir Henry Clinton didn't simply land a regiment or two and pull down this shapeless tangle of timbers before it got into shape—certainly the weather was fair enough to permit a boat attack.

He was dog-tired, Nat realized, and he opened his shirt to the breeze which, an hour ago, had begun to beat in from the ocean.

It seemed impossible to credit that already a week had skimmed by since that unforgettable night at Kincora Hall. Sometimes he found himself wondering how he would have felt if the cock fight had continued to the finish. Whew! He must have been tighter than a new pair of boots ever to have wagered a whole month's pay.

Suddenly a look-out began to yell, "They're coming! Fire the alarm! By God, the Britishers are headed for the Bar!"

Nat, shading his eyes, was aware of a sharp tingling at the base of his spine. The British commanders then weren't so inept as he'd thought. They would be into Fort Sullivan long before dark, and no doubt about it. All this work was wasted. But that was war.

Stony-eyed, the Nantucketer watched ten, eleven, thirteen crowded transports take advantage of the flood tide, of the ever-freshening southeast breeze. In a straggling line, they set off one by one and steered steadily for the wild white smother marking Charleston Bar.

By the dozen, soldiers, workmen and civilian engineers came running and scrambled up to posts of vantage on the dunes. The slave gangs, welcoming a respite, stared sullenly, incuriously, at those clumps of white canvas moving slowly shorewards.

Everyone looked pretty solemn when a stout twenty-eight gun frigate took the lead position. She was advancing cautiously under royals and topsails and jibs that glowed lemon-yellow in the suddenly sickly sunlight. It was clear that she was following a line of buoys placed during the preceding week by boats from the fleet.

"That's a mean slant of wind for such work," remarked a bald-headed individual just below Nat. "I'd hate to be piloting her."

"Like hell!" objected a gunner. "They got a wind dead astern."

" 'Twon't be when they bear starboard in a minute. I used to be a pilot and I reckon I ought to know."

"Are they setting the right course?" Nat inquired of the ex-pilot.

He raised a weather-beaten, horribly pock-marked face. "Yessir, more's the pity! Wish to God 'twas me steering yonder bulldog. I'd surely pile him up on Hognose Bar."

"Oh, fer Christ's sake, don't talk tootle! Whoever heard of Hognose Bar?" rasped the gunner. "I sailed this harbor a lot, couple of years ago."

"Don't try to teach yore Grandpa to suck eggs," advised the pilot with disdain. "Hognose only formed up again last winter."

The leading frigate bore steadily for the Bar which lay less than a mile away. Everyone could see that she was towing her boats. All of these were heavily loaded in order to decrease the man-of-war's draught. The boats reminded Nat of ducklings following their mother.

The ex-pilot's gaze became critical as he followed her advance. "Britishers ought to have lightened her still more. If they try to get them big barns of three-deckers across, you'll see somethin' to remember."

"Why?"

"On the Bar they ain't over sixteen foot at high water; most of them ships-o'-the-line draws from eighteen to twenty in commission trim."

Steadily the wind rose, whipped stinging grains of sand up from the beach and into the faces of the watchers on Sullivan's Island. Officers began ordering reluctant men away to secure tents and shelters.

"That vessel in the lead is the *Syren*," announced an officer at the telescope. "Next in line looks like the *Sphinx*, frigate. Carries around twenty guns, anyhow."

The Bar was now boiling right under the leading frigate's bow. White water surged up, up until it hid the man-of-war's dolphin striker. Smothered cries, yells of satisfaction broke from the men when they saw the *Syren* reel amid that conflict of eddies which perpetually raced over the sand bar. Red copper sheathing gleamed briefly then, all at once, the wild swinging of the *Syren's* topmasts diminished.

"Over!" the pilot said, thrusting his head far out. "Now we'll know where we fit—if that bulldog bears port, she only intends to anchor off Five Fathom Hole. If she keeps straight on we'd better get our tails off this sand bank in a hell of a big hurry.

He cast a grim look up to Nat. "Say your prayers, Mister."

A second frigate, skillfully duplicating the maneuvers of the first, also passed safe over the Bar.

Both of them *steered to port*, headed for an anchorage off Five Fathom Hole.

It was hard to talk now because the wind was fairly singing, driving up squadrons of clouds to darken the afternoon sky. In an irregular line, a whole covey of transports—mostly large merchantmen—came tumbling along, eager to get over the bar before the wind could rise any higher. In groups of two, three and four, clumsy brigs and brigantines charged for the barrier under bowing masts and straining canvas.

"Sweet Jesus!" the pilot exulted. "Will you look at them clubfooted swabs crowd each other?" He slapped his thigh. "Lay you a shilling, Mister, won't all of that bunch get to the other side in one piece."

Bunched by differing speed and handling, seven merchantmen and a lone sloop-of-war were all rushing down on the Bar together.

"Bet there's some inspired cussing going on out there," the gunner said. "I thank God *I* ain't aboard that vessel furthest to starboard."

Everyone, ashore and afloat, noticed a furious squall beating in from the ocean. In frantic haste the squadron's sailing masters either shortened sail or increased it in hopes of diminishing that concentration of vessels dashing for the narrow passage across the Bar.

"Look at 'em," a civilian engineer cried. "Look at 'em! They're all crowded together like sheep in a lane."

Nat watched a tall ship, an East Indiaman by her round bows and high sides, shoulder aside a pair of little brigs; she sent them staggering off to port so quickly that they collided. Instantly, their yards locked and, helpless, they reeled 'way over.

A big transport running in their wake had not time to veer aside and smashed into the gilded and elaborately carved stern of the East Indiaman. Under the impact, the Indiaman's mizzen snapped and tumbled—a furious tangle of spars, cordage and canvas—into the water. Hampered, the big, old-fashioned ship swung violently to starboard, began drifting for the breakers spouting along the Bar.

The pilot caught his breath with a sharp click. "Watch! Goddam it, watch!"

The words had scarcely escaped his lips than the big transport which had lost her headsails, reared out of the water like a swimmer reaching a landing and hit the Bar with such terrific force that her main and foremasts went crashing by the board.

The two little brigs were the next to strike. As their decks flooded, the crews and troops swarmed into the rigging but were lost as both vessels gradually rolled over on their beams' end.

Other transports found time to come about and begin clawing their way back to join the balance of the fleet in the lee of Dewees Island. As for the vessels which had crossed the Bar, they anchored in a hurry and sent out rescue boats.

Through the failing light, Nat watched a whole flotilla of small boats work courageously to leeward of the Bar. Some of them, by dint of terrific efforts, were able to row up under the lee of the big transport. She was now in a very bad case. Every time a comber rushed over her, fewer black dots remained clinging to her shrouds.

"That Indiaman is pounding bad," the ex-pilot observed. "Inside of an hour she'll open up like an old market basket and we'll have a lot fewer Lobster-backs to worry over."

Standing there on the raw earthworks of Fort Sullivan, Nat Coffin found it strange that these men should have come half across the world just to perish in the boiling water and sand of Charleston Bar.

"Back to your work!" Major de Brahm looked mad. So did Colonel Moultrie, stumping along beside him. The storm must be hurting his gouty leg. Moultrie's second in command, Lieutenant-Colonel Isaac Motte, and the ever-graceful and debonnair Major Francis Marion were taking notes.

The fact that the enemy were attempting to cross the Bar brought home, as nothing else, the dire weakness, the helpless condition of Fort Sullivan. Everyone, even the slaves, began working like mad. When it grew dark lanterns were lit and now that it was cooler even the officers volunteered to work with axe, shovel, and pulley.

13

Earthworks

Wrote Henry Laurens:

Every day leads us in this part of America deeper and deeper, into war-like Preparations, the houses in Charles Town which had been Emptied of their owners and their furniture, and now made use of as Barracks for the Country Rifle-men & other militia.

Sulivant's Island, Hadrell's Point, Fort Johnson, a formidable & Excellent Battery near the latter are all in good order well mounted about Sixty pieces from 9 to 24 pounders but chiefly night Defence.

Threats of Burning & Destroying this fine town are lost upon a People who are ready to Put the torch with their own hands in Preference to Submission & who are Determined the houses in that Fine Town shall never prove Shelters for a cruel Enemy—

When, escorted by the stalwart Ash, Antoinette Proveaux ventured out on the morning of June seventh, she sensed tension in the threatened town was augmenting rather than diminishing. For five days enemy ships continued to cross the Bar until a really awe-inspiring fleet lay, plainly visible, off Five Fathom Hole.

"As soon as their line-of-battleships, *Experiment* and *Bristol* get across," Cousin Barnard Elliott had predicted, "we must expect trouble."

Heart in mouth, Antoinette started along Tradd Street. She was curious to see what the earthworks were like that had been built the day before. On Gibbes' Point she found a great crew of slaves, freshly arrived from some inland plantations, hard at work.

She slowed her stride. Glory be! What business could a squad of troopers be wanting of Mr. John Wragge? She halted when a brawny ensign began to pound on the lawyer's front door.

Nobody opened so the officer made a curt gesture and joyfully, his men began to drive their musket butts against the door panels. When the door splintered and gave, the ensign and his men ran into the big, handsome house.

Antoinette's heart began to pound. Mr. Wragge held the pew next theirs in St. Michael's.

"Oh-h!"

The troopers reappeared dragging Mr. Wragge along by his arms. Antoinette gaped. The lawyer was unshaven and his shirt tails were flapping loose above the waistband of his breeches. She heard the ensign say:

"Whatever your opinions, sir, you would have been wise to send your tools when the Committee asked for them. As it is, you must come with us. Your British friends might drop a shell into your house and kill you, and that would be most lamentable."

Imagine the sedate Mr. Wragge being arrested like this! As he was haled down the street, the lawyer continued protesting but made no impression. Imperturbably, his captors added him to a miserable group of Loyalists who stood under guard at the cross street.

She had started on when the rest of the ensign's men came out of Wragge's house carrying nothing more exciting than a supply of shovels, axes, picks, wicker baskets.

Soon Antoinette perceived that more, and still more, entrenchments were being thrown up along the river's edge. Why, they extended all the way from Halsey's Millpond on the Ashley to Colonel Gadsden's wharf on the Cooper. All this raw earth looked very strange and out of place amid the familiar houses and cobbled streets.

Down by a battery on South Bay, Antoinette got the biggest surprise of her life. All those big solid warehouses which had once stood at the far end of the merchants' wharves had vanished!

Good Heavens. Sunburnt men in parts of uniforms were pulling down the last of Colonel Gadsden's fine counting house! Yonder Mr. Laurens' offices had dissolved into a tumbled heap of bricks.

Where was Papa's counting house? She wanted to break out in tears when she realized that only its foundations remained. Her legs trembled so she had to rest on the nearest doorstep.

As nothing else, this served to bring home the gravity of Charleston's peril.

She went closer. That just couldn't be!—but it was dapper-dandy Uncle Marcel. Minus wig and coat he was working with a shovel right alongside a big, shiny buck negro. So was old Mr. Pinckney.

As in the popular ditty, the world certainly had been "turned upside down." She could scarcely believe her eyes as she recognized other leading merchants doing slave's work. Why there was Mr. Manigault, Mr. Motte, and yonder was Mr. Middleton! Fearful lest she cause them embarrassment, Antoinette raised her fan and hurried away so fast that Ash had hard work keeping up with her.

Wherever an enemy landing might be effected, dwellings, storehouses, factories, warehouses, everything, were being ruthlessly leveled to permit an unrestricted field of fire for batteries.

Citizens had even deemed it practical to mount cannon on the end of piers. A breastwork was a-building on Mr. Laurens' wharf. She could recognize one of his brigs lying alongside. Men were hoisting the guns out of her and trundling some pitiful little nine pounders towards a series of embrasures.

It meant something to be one of the few gentlewomen remaining in Charleston. Lots of people were commenting on how brave she and Suzanna Smith Elliott were. To tell the truth, she wouldn't have missed the excitement for anything.

Desire wasn't so eager now to wander about. The young widow preferred to remain on the look-out 'most all day. She studied the enemy ships with such close attention, one might have thought she had a friend out there.

From the depths of a trench a muddied figure addressed her.

"Fine mornin', ain't it, Miss 'Toinette?"

She had trouble recognizing Charles MacIntosh until he scrambled up, made her an elaborate bow. "I protest your presence here is more welcome than a mint-julep."

"Really, Charles, how you do exaggerate!"

He grinned. "Well, a cooling breeze, anyhow."

"Then I would remain here to refresh Charleston's heroes," she

smiled. Dark and petite, she gathered her petticoats and seated herself on a mound of fresh earth. "We are worried, Charles. We have
not seen Roger in two days."

"No need. He and Tommy Beale have been ordered with Gadsden's First Regiment out to Fort Johnson." He jerked a blistered,
earth-stained thumb toward the northern tip of James Island. "By
the by, first chance I get, I want to present an odd and very amusing
Yankee; he's a friend of Roger's. May I?"

"Of course. To you, Charles, I will confess I die of curiosity about
him. So does my house guest. She is a Yankee, too."

When Antoinette reached home she found it in a turmoil. Pansy
and Linden were blocking the doorway, trying to keep out a big
Scot in a red and green kilt. Obviously, he must be from one of the
up-country regiments.

He was saying gruffly, "Dinna greet, ye blackamoors. If we can
leave our farms i' the planting season, yer Master can weel spare a
leaden gutter and a pewter bowl or two."

Linden's eyes were rolling in despair. "Please, Misto Soljerman,
please jus' wait a speck. Miss 'Toinette gwine be back *di*reckly!"

"We canna' tarry," the sergeant stated and seizing her butler by
the collar, lifted him bodily out of the doorway.

Antoinette donned her most devastating smile, called from the
foot of the walk. "That's quite all right, Linden, you may let the
officer in."

When the dark-faced Scot saw her standing so small and trim behind him he turned poppy-red and hurriedly removed the queer little
bonnet he wore at a jaunty angle. It sported what looked like a
hawk's feather.

"Yer par-rdon, Mistress," he gulped. "I hope ye'll no' mistake my
pur-rpose." Losh, 'til now he had never beheld a female so elegant
or genteel.

In a small leghorn hat and with a cashmere shawl caught about her
slim shoulders, Antoinette Proveaux presented an amazing contrast
to the hearty, broad-hipped maids of the Wateree Country.

For her part, Antoinette was little less intrigued with this broad-shouldered fellow who wore a huge brass-hilted sword slung to a leather baldric. From the top of his stocking she noticed projecting what looked like the handle of a dirk.

Ever so often she had heard Papa speak of the fierce Highlanders who, during the past fifteen years, had been settling in the up-country. Papa paid unwilling tribute to Scottish perseverance and frugality, while deprecating their intolerance and senseless, sanguinary feuds.

Merciful heavens, this gaunt, bronzed young man dominating her front steps would easily make two of Roger or any of her friends.

Said she, "Pray permit me, sir, to make you welcome. Will you not come in?"

Three other militiamen in kilts grinned and winked when she sailed serenely indoors calling, "Pansy! Fetch these gentlemen a jug of milk and some of your best raisin cookies."

Alistair Bryson, red to the roots of his black hair, entered gingerly. "Aye, 'tis a fine grand hoose, ye ha'e here, Mistress. Maire is the pity Captain Chesnut has bade us tae take up any and a' lead the citizens can spare."

"I quite understand," Antoinette reassured him. "Yesterday the gutters were removed from Mr. Mazyck's house. Alas, that we already dispatched our old pewter over to the camp at Lynch's Pasture."

Alistair noticed this delicate, vivid-lipped young girl made the statement simply, without attempt to dramatize the sacrifice. Though stripped of most of their habitual ornaments, the rooms were a revelation to him. As he stood there with bare knees mirrored in the sheen of the drawing room floor, Alistair could sense the other Scots whispering and staring at the gilt.mirrors, the crystal girandoles, the tapestried walls.

Antoinette considered prettily. "Lead? Where can some be? Let me see. Ah! I have it. The window weights. Will window weights serve?"

Losh, this girl was pretty as a butterfly on a sunflower. Uncomfortably he began, " 'Tis a pity to mar so sonsie a hoose,—"

"It is nothing," she murmured. And so it was when she remembered Uncle Marcel sweating over a pick handle; Papa tearing down a warehouse that had cost a good two thousand pounds.

At the end of an hour the detail had collected a large wheel-barrow full of pure lead weights.

"You ha'e been verra kind," the Sergeant declared, his lean features coloring slowly. "I fear ye take us for savages and I wouldna have it so."

She gave him a dazzling smile of reassurance. "I do not think you rude or savage, Sergeant—"

"—Sergeant Bryson, Mistress." He fumbled with his bonnet and looked very young all at once for all his heavy sword and brass-studded baldric. "I trust ye'll forgi'e me if I observe I hadna thought any Lowland lass could be so bonny. If—if ye find aught in which we can be o' service to ye, Mistress Proveaux, ye've only to send word tae the Third Regiment. We camp for the nonce at Lynch's Pasture."

Antoinette's faintly olive-tinted features dimpled. She smiled, in-creasingly fascinated by the extraordinary clearness and penetration of the Scot's eyes.

"Perhaps, Mr. Bryson, when Pansy next bakes raisin cookies, I might chance by Lynch's Pasture."

Yes, he resembled some warrior prophet; was more like a dark, avenging deity than an up-country farmer.

When he swung down the front steps after his men, she noticed that he left behind a faint but remarkably stimulating aura of burnt pine, leather and cows.

14

ENEMY LANDING

INTELLIGENCE that enemy regiments were effecting landing on Long Island produced a tremendous excitement in Charleston. Apparently the almost incredible leisureliness of the British Commanders was near an end for, at six o'clock of the morning of June eighth, trans-ports began to discharge supplies of baggage, munitions and hundreds upon hundreds of scarlet- and white-clad regulars.

In endless relays small boats from the fleet rowed across the glassy harbor, then returned.

Once he ascertained that Brigadier-General Vaughan and Major-General Lord Cornwallis had, unopposed, landed some 2,800 crack troops, General Charles Lee flew into a towering fury. Sulphurously, he cursed the inexplicable non-arrival of some fine Virginia and North Carolina Continental regiments. Where were they? No one seemed to know.

Why the this and that was Fort Sullivan *still* less than half completed? Why, Lee roared, hadn't the Carolina Assembly found him at least one decent military engineer? Why were there no capable sappers in all this fever-ridden, hell-hole of a Province?

Caustic, openly contemptuous, he ordered a review of the up-country regiments. When these raw levies returned to their cantonments, the adventurer's despair became dramatic. He wrung his hands and groaned, asked to know how he had offended Heaven that he should be condemned to command "the very canaille of soldiery."

Nonetheless, this ex-English General prepared for a stubborn defense of the city and made an admittedly sound disposition of his troops. He even injected a semblance of order and discipline into his camp at Haddrell's Point and worked himself and his staff until they were red-eyed with fatigue.

One sultry afternoon, he had himself rowed over to Fort Sullivan and inspected the defense with expert attention. His reaction was not one of satisfaction.

"This silly affair more resembles a slaughter pen than a fortification," he succinctly informed Major de Brahm. "Why in God's patience have you designed so flat a slope to the talus? Any cadet in Germany, sir, could see that enemy cannon balls will merely ricochet over the top and plunge into the rear wall."

Easy-going Billy Moultrie got reprimanded because he let his sentries smoke or chew on duty, that his soldiers slouched about and often forgot to salute.

Angrily, the Continental General ordered the construction of a pair of epaulements which would, in a measure, serve to protect the unfinished east and west walls. As a feeble substitute for the still nonexistent north or rear wall a breastwork was to be dug at once.

"If Harry Clinton learned anything at all at Breed's Hill," Lee predicted to the red-faced and furious Carolinians, "he will cross from Long Island and assail this comic fort of yours from the rear. It must fall in short order and you will lose every cannon, every man in this place."

On June tenth, Major-General Sir Henry Clinton sent in a flag of truce and was properly outraged because some yokel of a sentinel, failing to appreciate the niceties of war, fired upon his truce boat.

Mollified, however, by a handsome apology from the Americans, the British General delivered his proclamation. In it Sir Henry deplored the existence of "a most unprovok'd and wicked Rebellion" in the fair Province of South Carolina and the succession of crimes committed by certain unprincipled habitants. He denounced the tyranny of the Carolina Congress and Committees and vastly regretted the necessity of "proceeding against an Infatuated and misguided Multitude."

In all humanity, he warned the people of South Carolina that he, Major-General Sir Henry Clinton, was empowered to offer, "in His Majesty's name, free pardon to all as should lay down their Arms and submit to the Laws, excepting Robert Howe and Henry Laurens."

Amused attention was all the proclamation procured, but it proved effective in whipping up enlistments. Longer and stormier grew the debates between waspish Major-General Charles Lee and President Rutledge of the Assembly. A climax was reached when the former protested over sending so many troops to Fort Sullivan.

"They're feckless there, Mr. Rutledge, quite thrown away!" he snarled. "Such a ramshackle affair will not hold out half an hour under bombardment. The garrison will be annihilated, my word on that. You will suffer a modern Cannae."

"And why, pray?"

"Because these engineering geniuses of yours have provided not a single avenue of retreat!"

Colonel Moultrie was reported to have rubbed his jolly red nose while murmuring that when the time came to retreat, they would worry over that.

With reason, the Continental General contended that the enemy's strategy was obvious. Men-of-war would bombard the fort while the enemy land forces would, at low tide, ford the narrow, very shallow channel separating Long from Sullivan's Island. A determined attack would be made on the absolutely unfinished rear of the American fort.

When deserters from the fleet confirmed Lee's predictions almost to the letter, his prestige and self-esteem rose to empyrean heights.

It was further ascertained that Admiral Peter Parker and Sir Henry were on the coldest of terms; practically at daggers drawn. This was only to be expected, or so the deserters maintained, because an Admiral, as representative of the Senior Service, would inevitably chafe at finding himself under the orders of a mere Army officer.

In open contempt of Sir Henry Clinton, Lord Cornwallis, and all their works, Admiral Parker had caused a mock battery to be erected on Long Island, well away from the military camp. There he was drilling his crews and marines until they became letter-perfect in the art of storming gun emplacements.

Deserters reported that when General Vaughan had requested that soundings be taken of the ford between Long and Sullivan, Admiral Parker had demurred, had finally dispatched a boat's crew with the very worst of grace. General Vaughan, however, forgot his pique when the sounding party reported that, at dead low tide, less than three feet of water separated the two islands.

Fortunately for the Carolinians, the task of passing the great three-deckers *Experiment* and *Bristol* over the Bar again postponed an attack.

"Give us till the thirtieth and we'll have this job done," Moultrie assured the celebrated privateersman, Captain Lemprière. Along the south curtain now frowned nineteen cannon ranging in size from slim nine-pounders to substantial twenty-eight pound broadside guns.

Doubtfully, Captain Lemprière fingered a bluish chin. "You've a neat piece of work here, Colonel, but—" Significantly, his gaze wandered out to the heavy concentration of men-of-war.

"We shall beat them handily," came Moultrie's easy assurance. "If only Lee will let us alone."

The privateersman shook his head sharply. "Don't deceive yourself, Billy. Two broadsides from yonder fleet will knock your fort to splinters."

"In that case," Moultrie laughed, "I reckon we shall have to lie behind the ruins and try to prevent a landing."

He didn't laugh, though, over the peremptory way Charles Lee depleted his garrison to reinforce Colonel Thomson at the opposite end of Sullivan's. Worst of it was, Moultrie couldn't contend that the force posted to block Clinton's crossing from Long Island had no need of support. It did, and badly. So far, Thomson commanded only the Third Carolina and a detachment from the Sixth, in addition to two very small pieces of artillery.

15

THE YANKEE

ALL the men-of-war now were over the Bar; Clinton's troops had regained their land legs, though they could not be having too pleasant a time on the insect-infested flats of treeless, sandy Long Island. Roger, Cousin Barnard Elliott, Mr. Laurens and everybody reckoned that the British would attack on the first of August.

Many respected citizens were looking gloomy. A pity this General Lee had to be so utterly tactless. His arrogant and unbounded egotism was alienating everybody. Again, friction was developing between the city and country regiments. Every morning an increasing number of shooting and knifings were reported. The Virginia and North Carolina Continentals, arriving at long last, were given to looking down their noses and asking why South Carolina couldn't boil her own kettle?

All in all, Mr. Proveaux felt that the time had come for Antoinette to join the balance of the family in safety. Desire was to accompany her. The house on King Street would be closed, boarded up like the rest.

Desire, descending from a nap, found Pansy and the other servants bustling about at a great rate. When Antoinette appeared with an extra big basket of flowers Desire raised slim, questioning brows.

"Well, honey, I reckon our last evenin' in Charleston will be one to remember," Antoinette gaily announced. "Roger vows that tonight I shall meet my fate."

"That Yankee friend of his?"

Antoinette bent studiously above the flower basket. "Roger's groom said he would bring him to dinner tonight." She giggled like a small girl. "And what shall I wear to dazzle this cold countryman of yours? The blue chintz or my yellow dimity?"

"The dimity, by all means." Desire felt years older. What would this stray Northerner make of her? Lord's mercy, during the past week she had grown simply enormous and got taken with strange breathless spells when she least expected them.

Antoinette, however, declared that she looked lovelier each day. "I know our Charleston boys. If you ain't married short of six months, honey, I'm a perfect ninny. Besides, Grandmère vows war makes for marriage and babies. Pansy, you take these flowers. Mrs. St. Clair and I must pretty up."

Back in her own room, Desire felt so happy she began softly to sing. This leaving for the country would remove the last faint chance that anyone from Newport might happen in town. The appearance of General Lee and his staff had caused her some uneasy moments.

If one officer came South from New England, more might follow —especially since Lord Howe had given up and had evacuated Boston. If, as 'Toinette so confidently predicted, she married well, Desire Harmony might yet live out a life of peaceful happiness—with John's child to worship and worry over.

She felt she *would* marry well. At Mrs. Norton's and on the stage, she had learned a lot about pleasing men. Listening with half an ear to the chatter of servants downstairs, she began to redress her hair.

How naïve, how beautifully impractical would have been the life she and John had contemplated! Of course, his fierce old father would have disinherited John on the spot.

Briskly, Desire brushed and combed her dark red hair. Curious, the only hair which had ever approximated her own in color was Nathaniel Coffin's. Again she wondered where he might be at this moment. Could a girl ever get to know what was going on in the back of his mind?

Sometimes it seemed as if Nat were laughing at her, or was it at himself? Imagine examining life as if it were some strange insect pinned under a reading glass! For all Nat's easy ways, she guessed he must be a rock-ribbed conservative at heart.

It was growing so dark, Desire meditated ringing for a candle. Down in the kitchen Pansy was singing to the accompaniment of the curious musical instrument which Linden had fashioned out of three violin strings stretched over half of a dried gourd.

How very secure and comfortable this was after the sordid turmoil of life with Brian Montaigne.

Heavenly days! Already horses were in front of the house and Roger's voice was calling for a groom.

Oh, but it would be fine to talk with someone from New England—from home.

She arranged and re-arranged one of Antoinette's best Cashmere shawls with studied attention. Tonight it wouldn't do for the baby to show any more than was inevitable. She moistened her fingertips and, by the fading light, smoothed her long, gently-arching brows. Her dark blue gown went well with her hair, her shoes were dainty and her ankles cased in silk.

"It's been a pretty task to get you here," declared Roger's voice, high-pitched and nervous as ever. "Hope Linden ain't forgotten how to mix a bombo Martinico."

Already 'Toinette was hurrying downstairs gurgling hospitality and cordial greetings.

Desire arrived on the top landing in time to witness 'Toinette's curtsey, a thing of fluid perfection. Roger's buttons flashed in the candle light as he brought forward the guest.

The stranger, Desire perceived, wore an unfamiliar uniform of grass green turned up in white and his epaulet was silver instead of gold. La! This fellow countryman cut a fine, sturdy figure. He looked red haired, too.

Suddenly, a deep, well-remembered voice declared, "Your humble servant, Mistress Proveaux. This moment has long been anticipated."

Luckily, not one of the three persons below cast a glance upstairs; to save her life, Desire could not have stirred.

Roger said, "Well, honeybunch, have you food enough for a pair of hungry wolves like Mr. Coffin and me?"

"The bombo is quite ready, Roger. I trust Mr. Coffin favors bombo?"

"He does," chuckled Roger. "His bibulous education has made great strides since he came among us. Rascal's got the head of a marble statue, too. Haven't sent him under the table yet."

He turned to Antoinette. "And where are you hiding the ever-charming Mrs. St. Clair? Nat, here, is all of a tizzy to make her acquaintance."

Jerkily Desire's hand went up to stifle a gasp that almost escaped when Nat said, "Mrs. St. Clair? *Mirabile dictu,* the name is very very familiar. I wonder—"

On legs which seemed to have no knees at all Desire groped back to her room and stood there staring blankly into space. How foolish it had been to hope. Sooner or later someone would—must—appear, but why— If he sees me like this—he'll think— Oh, what was it I told him in Providence? John was from Maine. Told Proveauxs he was British. Stupid little liar. He mightn't tell them about Mrs. Norton's—but, but Nat would know— Dear God, if Charleston ever learns that the Proveauxs, Roger—'Toinette—Mr. Proveaux, had been entertaining a common whore.

What a hideous, tangled web her life had become all in a few instants. Ten minutes ago—dreams— Now there never could be a plantation great house for Desire Harmony.

Every time Nat's deep laugh rang out downstairs, it did dreadful things to her heart. Why had Chance betrayed her so? Wait! Suppose —suppose she let Nat think the baby— Why not? Nat had been ready for marriage and she respected him more than anyone alive. He was very fond of her, too fond, maybe. Don't be a fool. Nat will stand by you if he thinks the child is his. But it is really John's.

She could hear 'Toinette calling from the foot of the stairs, "Dee, honey, Roger and his guest are here!"

Just as she used to before going on the stage, she drew a deep breath and commanded her voice to steadiness. "Yes, dear, I'll come down in a moment."

Catching up a hooded cloak, she descended the back stairs so fast she scared Pansy into spasms. As she darted for the servants' entrance, Marigold called something, but she kept on through the vegetable garden until she reached a deserted back street.

If she hurried and didn't fall, she might be able to catch the last ferry across the Cooper River.

16

Dawn, June 28, 1776

Lieutenant Nathaniel Coffin, temporary aide to gouty, doughty Colonel Moultrie, could not sleep. Hot and uncomfortable, he lay listening to clouds of mosquitoes exploring the netting about his head.

How perfectly mistress of the situation Antoinette Proveaux had remained when her house guest had fallen ill with such disastrous inopportunity. If, as Roger had implied, Mrs. St. Clair was pregnant, such a seizure could not be wholly unexpected. Mrs. St. Clair? How curious that, within six months, he should have heard of two Mrs. St. Clairs and both of them widowed.

It was lucky that Roger had immediately excused himself to go fetch a doctor. That had afforded Miss Proveaux and him a chance to talk, even if she was bravely fighting her alarm—or some similar emotion. It must have been exasperating to have seen her carefully planned dinner go awry.

Lying in the hot gloom of the tent he could visualize ever so clearly her warm, petite loveliness. It was sheer bad luck that, for these several weeks, he had allowed matters of no great consequence to delay his going to the Proveauxs'.

He hoped Roger would invite him again. If he didn't he—well, he would make bold to call. He couldn't reason it out, he was aware only that Mistress Proveaux's warmth, her Gallic tact and grace filled a long existing gap in his scheme of things.

None of the few girls he had so far attempted to understand had lent him such a sense of rest, of companionship, of feline comfort.

All in an hour's talk, Antoinette Proveaux had managed to untie many mental knots, to soothe doubts unvoiced and unsuspected.

All at once he became convinced that, as soon as this silly, blundering siege was over, he would beg Antoinette Proveaux to share his perplexities, his fortunes. Instinctively, he guessed that the Family would welcome this warm and tender girl. Though run into a different mould, this child of the Huguenots reflected familiar standards of breeding and intelligence.

Tonight the mosquitoes seemed more intolerable than ever. At sundown great clouds of them arose from the marshes steaming back of Sullivan's Island, relieved chiggers and flies in making life miserable for the garrison.

Nat groped for a canteen and took a big swig from it. He wasn't especially tired yet he felt a curious dis-ease. Why? As near as he could judge, he hadn't a fever. Maybe it was sunburn? Yesterday, the heat had become so intolerable that Colonel Moultrie, ever considerate, had ordered all sentries into the shade nearest their posts.

Sweating profusely, the Nantucketer settled back on his blanket, irritably pushed a palm stem from under his ribs.

Was Charlie MacIntosh finding it quite as hot in Fort Johnson across the harbor? Or quarrelsome Tom Beale, sleeping beside those futile cannon mounted along Charleston's East Bay?

Both of them must be better off than the luckless troops encamped on the eastern tip of Sullivan's Island. Imagine sending seven hundred and eighty militiamen to stand off two thousand British regulars! Sheer criminal stupidity, that was what it was.

Presently he dozed. When he roused once more a gray dawning was breaking. Thank God, an easterly wind was blowing away the mosquitoes.

"Five o'clock, an' a-a-all's well!" A sentry's sleepy call floated down from the parapet. The cry reminded Nat of the Siege. Imagine the Siege being over and Washington's Army in possession of starved, smallpox-ridden Boston.

What was happening to Tim Bennett these days? Had he found his ship in Hispaniola, which the French called Saint-Domingue?

An unusual type Timothy Bennett, with his Quaker rearing forever at odds with a turbulent and dominant nature. He was nobody's fool, was Tim, even if his logic was weak. His argument concerning his lunar enlistment had been naïve to a degree. Now restrained, now impetuous. Nat would have given a lot to foresee which side of the Rhode Islander's nature would win.

R-r-r-tap—tap—r—r—r! He and his tentmate, a humorous Irish surgeon from Beaufort, sat up together. The doctor's dull eyes batted sleepily.

"Faith, Nat," he yawned, "and what has got into that idjit of a drummer bhoy?"

"Something serious must be wrong. That's long roll," Nat was already pulling on his breeches. Faintly, the cries of startled ducks and sandpipers penetrated the alarm. Like a gigantic rattlesnake, the drum kept up its dry, terrifying uproar. Pretty soon, a second drummer set his sticks to work.

Half or wholly naked men came stumbling out of the tents yelling to know what was wrong. Nat saw Colonel Moultrie waddle by, his shirt tail fluttering as he climbed a bank of gray-white sand marking the unfinished west wall.

The Colonel hadn't waited to find his wig so the gray bristles of his natural hair stood up on his scalp like quills on a hedgehog.

Nat Coffin, assigned as aide, plowed along after Moultrie and tried to buckle his sword belt as he ran. When he came up, the commandant of Fort Sullivan had halted. Choking for breath, he peered past the dew-dotted breach of a big twenty-eight pounder, and at once his heavy jaw shut with a click.

"My God," he groaned softly. "So many. So many!"

Among other members of the staff, Nat ran to a neighboring embrasure. He was struck silent by what he saw.

'Way over on the other side of the dim gray harbor the British men-o'-war were making sail. Some of them were hauling up courses, others were shaking out topsails, gallants and royals.

Rr-rr-rr-r-r! The myrtle woods and the dunes behind the fort resounded to the spiteful rattling of the drums. In the murky half-light, all faces appeared gray and sickly.

Colonel Moultrie remained quite a while studying the enemy through a spy glass. When the dawn brightened a little, the garrison could see a long line of small boats pulling away from the anchored transports. Like a procession of titanic water beetles they began crawling in the direction of Long Island.

Moultrie turned a worried face to Isaac Motte, his second-in-command. "Well, Ike, I reckon Admiral Parker has shook the cracked ice out of his lap at last. Hadn't you better dispatch a runner to warn Thomson, case he don't know? For God's sake, somebody make those fools quit drumming! Feller can't hear himself think."

Andrew Dellient, the adjutant, ran up. "Shall we fall in the men, sir?"

Moultrie hesitated, cast a glance at the distant sails and shook his head.

"Tell the boys to cook themselves a bite of breakfast first. With no more wind than this, the British won't get in range inside an hour."

Absently buttoning up the tunic his orderly had brought him, William Moultrie paced the gun platform.

Still little more than outlines, the men-of-war slowly began to seek pre-arranged positions.

"What in hell is she up to?" Moultrie inquired, pointing to a little sloop bowling along well in advance of her consorts.

"It's a bomb ship, sir. H. M. S. *Thunder.*"

"Well, well! She can thunder all she pleases so long as she don't chuck any thunderbolts."

Ample stomach riding comfortably under his shirt, Colonel Moultrie descended a ladder and stumped off towards his quarters, bawling, "Hump yourselves there in the kitchen, we may not eat again in a good while."

Because the tide was still ebbing from Charleston Harbor and the east wind was by no means strong, the enemy men-o'-war—nine in number—made but slow progress. There was plenty of time for gun captains to draw a supply of powder. The magazine lay in an isolated position in the otherwise incomplete north salient but at quite some distance from those batteries covering the channel.

Laughing just a little too readily, gun crews largely composed of ex-privateersmen lounged beside their pieces and speculated on the enemy's intentions, or joshed rifle companies forming up in the sandy square below the parapet.

Quite a few men began falling out of ranks and running back to the latrines. The gunners laughed.

"Say, kinder looks like the foot soljers have taken a dose o' British salts this morning."

When a big sergeant of the second regiment fell out and started to retire, the company next his raised a derisive cheer.

"Heyo, Geo'gia! We-uns didn't reckon a red-hot fighter like you would be took with the runnin' complaint so early."

The big fellow kept right on his way. "You c'n kiss my butt. *Mah* kind o' complaint gits me back in plenty o' time fer the shootin'! Only Ah ain't goin' let no no-count Redcoats spoil my mawnin's mawnin'."

"Land must be mighty rich where you live, Jasper."

The sergeant stopped, faced his tormentors. "Just cause Ah wuz fool 'nough to 'list with a bunch o' Carolina windbags don't mean Ah'm goin' t' take any more sass."

"Go to hell," a voice invited. "Yer just a big mouth from a half-arse joke of a Province."

The Georgian glowered and rolled up his sleeves. "First man

speaks 'gin Geo'gia Ah'll sholy brek his head! Come on out who said that."

A tough-looking gunner swaggered down from the gun platform. "*I* say Georgia don't amount to a pinch o' cow flops! Where were the Georgia delegates when the Constitutional Convention met?"

"Sic him, McDaniel!"

"Hand it to him, Jasper!"

The two squared off. Before they could come to blows, Lieutenant Shubrick ran out and ordered them to separate. Muttering, the Georgian continued on towards the latrines.

Even at this late hour, labor gangs hurried up, set desperately to work in an attempt to strengthen the fort's western wall. Drummer boys, round-eyed and white at the imminence of battle, realized what threatened because very few guns, only six of light caliber, had been mounted along that curtain.

The British had only to navigate a man-of-war or two behind the tip of Sullivan's Island. From that point, they could pour broadsides into the unprotected backs of gun crews manning the south wall. Even a desultory fire would render the fort untenable.

"God help us if the British get any vessels past Sumter Shoals." Roger Proveaux, arriving with a handful of reinforcements, epitomized the general concern. He looked very spick-and-span by contrast with the earth-stained garrison.

The lines of his sensitive, almost femininely fine features were drawn taut.

The sun, though barely above the horizon, was already hot. If this easterly breeze failed, it would be a stinker today. The gun crews—eight men to a piece—waited, looked out over the coffee-hued waters. Everybody anticipated that the chief burden of defense would fall upon the twenty guns defending the southern wall and salients.

The men quieted as Colonel Moultrie and his staff halted below a short flagstaff which had been hurriedly stepped at the apex of the southeastern bastion.

"Been pondering what sort of an ensign we would show," Captain Everleigh told Nat. "Reckon this will be it."

The flag that climbed into the morning sky had a light blue field and bore the word "Liberty" emblazoned in white parallel to its lower edge. In the canton corner some fair hand had embroidered a slim silver crescent.

Colonel Moultrie was smiling, delighted with the device, since his family's coat-of-arms showed three crescents argent on a field of azure.

"Come on, boys, let's have a cheer for our ensign," he called, "and let's keep it flying!"

The contrast to Charles Lee's fulsome oratory was inescapable. Here was no bombast, just a plain, honest officer asking his men to stand fast.

Hats swung off by the hundreds and a great shout went up. The garrison's reaction was spontaneous as a small boy's grin. One, two, three cheers for the blue flag went winging over towards the enemy. In reply, the men-o'-war broke out white ensigns at nearly all mastheads.

Over at little Fort Johnson across the harbor another blue flag was showing. Another floated above the *Prosper* brigantine. This, the only American war vessel, lay off East Bay to make a pretense of barring the entrance to the Ashley River.

His heavy face already bright with sweat, Colonel William Moultrie moved along the gun platform inspecting cartridges, roundshot and, most carefully of all, the quills of fine French powder with which the cannon would be primed.

Here and there, he spoke to a brawny, half-naked gunner—even slapped one on the shoulder. He ended by summoning all officers.

In a curiously detached way, Nat noticed that Colonel Moultrie had a splash of boiled egg on his chin—that Lieutenant-Colonel Motte kept working with the tip of his tongue to dislodge a shred of bacon from between his teeth.

"Well, gentlemen," began the commandant, "I reckon I don't have to tell you what we'll be in for inside a few minutes. Being as we have only twenty guns which will bear on the enemy, General Lee figures we can't hold out. It is my firm intention to prove General

Lee in error. We'll *have* to prove him so. We local men know that if Admiral Parker gets by us he will be anchoring off Charleston before dark."

A tense voice inquired, "Was that powder we forwarded to Thomson ever replaced?"

Colonel Moultrie shook his big head. "That's where the boot pinches. Gentlemen, we haven't much above ten thousand pounds of gunpowder in this fort," he collected the eyes of the battery commanders, "so you fellers can't afford any fancy fire-works.

"Remember this. No matter how fast the British shoot, you *must* conserve your fire. The enemy will fire fast as they can; they always try to smother an enemy with superior fire. We'd try it ourselves, I guess, were it possible."

He lowered his voice and emphasized each word. "Re-lay your piece after each shot and don't touch her off 'til you're mighty certain some splinters are going to fly. That will be all."

The battery commanders saluted and ran back to their crews.

In the hot and airless square below, the infantry cursed their inactivity, chewed grass stems and watched heat waves rise in front of their disorderly rows of tents.

Out on the harbor a cannon roared and something passed with an eerie whistling screech. There followed a deafening explosion among the myrtles behind the fort. Great clouds of sand shot high into the air, then leaves, twigs and bits of branches and sand began to fall inside Fort Sullivan.

17

THE FIRST LINE

H. M. S. *Thunder* lay about a mile and a quarter off shore and, lest she swing with the flooding tide, her crew anchored her bow and stern.

"Great day in the morning! Will you look at 'em come?" an awed voice asked amid the strained stillness ruling Fort Sullivan.

Slowly advancing under head sails came the *Active,* frigate, twenty-eight guns. H. M. S. *Experiment* loomed near with her triple tier of cannon run out and ready. The great line-of-the-battleship would have made two of the *Active* cruising a few cable lengths ahead of her. In her wake loomed the *Bristol,* Admiral Parker's ship-of-the-line. From her foremast was the Admiral's broad pennant. Next in the column sailed another 28-gun frigate, the *Solebay.*

"Let's see what broadside we kin expect." An ex-privateersman with dark blue powder burns peppering his cheek began counting. "*Active* and *Solebay* are twenty-eights so they be fifty-six guns in them alone. The liners will mount fifty apiece—"

He whistled, then spat. "Say, boys, this business ain't going to be all beer and skittles. We mount twenty guns 'gainst the Britainers' hundred and fifty-six. And that's *only their first line of ships!*"

"Ah shut up, you goddam croaker!" snarled a gun captain nervously rearranging slow matches on a tub of sand. Couldn't the fool realize that his companions were already green about the gills and gulping like so many stranded catfish?

Those men-of-war out there made an unforgettable sight with their sleek hulls painted brown or blue or dark green. Their rigging, decks and spars glistened with care. The yellow-white reflections of their canvas were visible on the harbor water.

Nat began to yawn as he always did when deeply excited. Captain Huger, stripped to his shirt sleeves and wearing a brace of pistols stuck into a fine English sword belt, began to laugh.

"I say, Misto' Coffin, you sho'ly do select the damnedest time to act bored!"

"Our English friends are being over-deliberate." Nat smiled. "They came on faster than this at Breed's Hill."

Deep within him, the Nantucketer was becoming aware of an inexplicable sense of apprehension such as he had not felt at Breed's Hill or at Fort Montague.

Until half-past ten, the bombship continued an unsupported bombardment. Her mortars sent shell after shell looping up, up into the air. Everyone could trace the course of these projectiles by the comet's tails of white smoke that trailed after them.

Gradually the *Thunder's* marksmanship improved until a shell fell among the deserted tents inside the square. The nearest militia scattered but returned sheepishly because the projectile, having plunged deep into the soft sand, exploded without causing the least damage.

Hardly had the infantry recovered than, to their horror, a bomb-shell landed squarely on the roof of the powder magazine! In thunderstruck helplessness, the whole garrison watched that dull iron globe hiss and fizz. The infantry wavered, uncertain of which way to run. The gunners sprang to fancied shelter between the dull yellow gun carriages.

It was only when the projectile ceased to give off smoke and had patently failed to explode, that Roger Proveaux felt some invisible giant's hand let go his windpipe.

Colonel Moultrie, puffing on a short-stemmed pipe, quickened his pace along the gun platform as much as his gouty leg would permit.

To the crew of a battery of twenty-eight pounders mounted near the center of the south curtain, he drawled, "That first liner might be in range. Suppose we show the Redcoats our shot is livelier than theirs?"

Action at last! A ragged cry of satisfaction rippled the length of the wall facing the channel. Promptly the cannon were run forward into their embrasures. Solid wooden carriage wheels set up a dull thunder and training tackles whined like a pack of hungry hounds. A row of crimson-banded muzzles peered out over the harbor.

"Stand clear!" the Number One Gun's captain ordered, then adjusted the elevation of his piece by using a mallet to loosen one of the hardwood wedges by means of which the gun's muzzle was depressed or elevated.

The battery captain called, "Round shot! Range about two thousand yards. Battery, fire!" The gun crews promptly leaped clear.

Fascinated, for the first time Roger Proveaux watched a shot

fired in anger. Once the gun captain pressed his smouldering lin-
stock to the touch-hole a small jet of smoke spurted straight up
from the breech of a long twenty-six. A great crashing report followed and madly the steel tube recoiled against a stout cable threaded
through its thimble—a ring forged into the breech of the gun itself.

The whole platform trembled as an immense mushroom of choking, silver-gray smoke smothered the Number One's embrasure.
From his post on top of a merlon, Captain John Blake shouted
through cupped hands:

"Number One Gun—over by fifty yards! Decrease elevation."

"Shucks!" the hot and excited infantry bellowed. "You powder
monkeys couldn't hit a flight of barns!"

Bo-oo-omm!

"Number Two Gun—short one hundred!"

Even as the third cannon went off, the Number Two Gun was
being trundled back by its crew, heaving in unison on the trail
tackles. Promptly, a sponger drove a dripping mass of sodden wool
and spun yarn far down the still-smoking throat of the piece.

This crew must have been extra-well schooled, Nat Coffin decided. They were taking no chances of leaving a spark in the bore
which would blow off the hands of the gunner who would presently ram home a fresh charge.

Roger was by now cursing the day he had joined the infantry—
even the select First South Carolina. The artillery, it seemed, would
earn a majority of the laurels today.

Monotonously, Captain Blake's voice rose above the rasped commands of the gun captains. "Number Three—a bully hit forrard!
Try a round of chain shot at her headsails."

Moultrie came hurrying up, the members of his staff trailing after
him. "Not so fast! Damn it, Blake. Not so fast!"

"We have hit the *Experiment* twice, sir!" Captain Blake's eyes
shone white amid the gloomy billows of burnt powder smoke that
were rolling back over the fort.

"Twice! You must hull her *every* time!" Moultrie roared. "We've
got no powder to throw away. When the Admiral's ship comes up,

I want everybody to concentrate on her."

To Nat, this command raised lively memories of Breed's Hill, of Colonel Prescott shouting, "Shoot at the pretty uniforms! Kill the officers! Sight at the gold lace!"

Except for the *Thunder,* the British had so far not fired a single shot in reply. But now, the *Friendship* frigate shortened sail, dropped an anchor and, rounding to, let go with her starboard broadside at four hundred yards.

It seemed to Roger Proveaux as if the air was being sucked up out of the fort by the passage of some invisible force. The next thing he knew, a series of dreadful gurgling screams beat down from the gun platform.

Toes curling inside his shoes, he felt a brief but almost overpowering urge to make water. All about him militiamen were crouching, covering their ears and crying out.

"My God! The woods!"

In the magnolia and palmetto wood behind Fort Sullivan, a thousand axemen seemed simultaneously to have set to work. Big boughs, bushes, whole tree tops were spinning up, up into the sky.

"Say, Colonel, what'll happen when they gits the range?" quavered a little drummer on runner duty.

"We won't have time to get scared, I reckon," came the imperturbable response.

Keeping pace with Colonel Moultrie's halting progress along the parapet, Nat Coffin realized that the easterly wind was picking up, bringing the big ships of the first line into closer range.

The *Active* had a boat out and was about to drop a sheet anchor from it. This, he immediately perceived, was intended to keep the man-o'-war broadside on to the fort.

H. M. S. *Bristol,* looking mountain-tall, took up a position a cable's length astern the *Active.*

Pipes shrilled, yards creaked about as the great ship's anchors went plunging down to the mud on the harbor's bottom amid a wild flurry of spray. Then the flagship's topmen moved out her yards and, in no great hurry, began furling her canvas.

"God damn it, why don't they come in musket shot?" raged Jasper, the big Georgia sergeant. "What the devil we heah for?"

"You'll get your turn when Parker calls away his boats and tries to take us by storm," Colonel Moultrie grimly reassured him. "We'll all of us get a belly-full of fighting today."

Colonel Moultrie thought it wise to permit his powder-streaked gunners to rig sweat rags about their heads, to pull off shirts and to otherwise catch their breath.

By eleven of the morning, *Active, Bristol, Experiment* and *Solebay* had taken positions all about four hundred yards off shore. Further out, *Friendship* and *Thunder* kept up their nearly futile cannonade of the south wall.

"Look at the Admiral's ship," the cry arose. A string of signal flags, pretty and varied as butterflies, was climbing into the *Bristol's* rigging. Almost at once *Friendship* and *Thunder* ceased firing.

18

BROADSIDES

IN THE uneasy lull which ensued, everybody studied the enemy. How bright those red-painted gunports and muzzles looked. They were as nearly eye-catching as the continued flash of steel on the decks and the red coats of marines manning the fighting tops.

Now that the sun was climbing higher, the wind died away until reflections of the men-of-war grew momentarily more perfect. On its staff, the fort's blue flag dangled almost motionless.

Nat bit his lip. His premonition had crystallized into a conviction that when the enemy fired their first united broadside he would be killed. But Captain Oliphant and Lieutenant Lessessue never guessed it when he said:

"Looks like it might be wise to get behind a merlon."

Where their shirts had previously protected them, the American gunners were beginning to turn red with sunburn. Their ribs could be seen rising and falling quickly.

Mopping heavy red jowls, Colonel Moultrie turned to Nat. "Mr. Coffin, pray go below and cause the infantry officers to appoint relief gun crews. In this heat our gunners cannot work incessantly. Practiced men are to be preferred, of course."

The Nantucketer had barely reached a set of steps descending to the courtyard than such a hurricane of sound stunned his ears that he could only stand still, clutching the pitchy hand rail.

Successive concussions slapped his face so hard he could neither focus his eyes nor collect his thoughts. He was aware, however, that the whole seaward curtain of Fort Sullivan was rocking as if an earthquake had commenced. Over the hissing scream of cannonballs he could hear the fort's palmetto timbers creak and groan.

Dazed, he watched several gunners lose their balance and fall off the firing platform as the uproar reached a crescendo. A series of sharp shocks loosened his hold, sent him tumbling down in the courtyard on his hands and knees.

O-o-o-we-e-e! howled a ricocheting cannonball. Men were screaming shrilly, insistently. There were yells, shouts, terror-stricken howls.

The dull thunder of cannonballs striking the south curtain continued. Shots, aimed too low, kicked from the beach a spindrift of sand which fell in a fine rain on guns, men and timbers alike.

A wild-eyed infantry captain shaking his head like a swimmer freeing his ears of water, swayed over to Nat.

"Lee was right, by Jesus!" he gasped. "This whole damn' thing will be about our ears."

Grinning because he had survived the first broadside, Nat hauled himself erect, brushed sand from his tunic. He'd better try to set an example. He was supposed to be a veteran—and a Massachusetter!

Quite a few men were limping about, nursing hurts caused by the pieces of timber which were still raining down.

Yonder a shell had exploded in the courtyard. The head and chest of a man lay across a couple of bent muskets. Near by was a shattered cartouche box and what vaguely resembled an arm. Ugh! Tendons trailing from it resembled bloody strings.

There was no perceptible slackening of the enemy's fire.

What was it Colonel Moultrie wanted? Oh, yes. Relief gun crews. Gradually becoming accustomed to the tumult, Nat made his way to Captain Horry's company and repeated the order, but couldn't make himself heard. He succeeded at last by cupping his hands directly over Captain Horry's ear. The Carolinian nodded and went among his men.

Though he felt all shuddery inside, Nat winked at Roger Proveaux as he moved on to the next unit. As he ran by on the same errand as himself, young Proveaux was ghastly pale and his eyes looked great with excitement—very like Antoinette's.

The young Carolinian began moving among the men of a badly disorganized company, patting one man on the shoulder, pulling another by the wrist. He would make a good officer some day.

"Get up! They ain't harmed us hardly at all!" he kept shouting. "Get up and see for yourselves, you bloody cowards."

Amazingly enough, this was true. Though ragged holes showed here and there, the south wall seemed as solid as ever.

Hysterically fast at first, then with deliberation, various batteries commenced to return the enemy fire. To Nat whole eternities elapsed between each detonation.

Nat was reporting back to the Colonel when a blast of British grape-shot penetrated an embrasure. It reduced an entire crew to mangled pulp, and filled the hot air with the cloying, musty odor of blood. In rivulets, gore leaked through the gun platform onto infantry crouched under the walls.

Once the American gunners got over that initial shock, they settled down and at almost every shot splinters could be seen flying aboard the smoke-veiled men-of-war. One by one yards were being taken down by charges of bar or chain-shot. In festoons severed lines dangled from the flagship's maintop.

"Hanged if I can understand why we don't suffer more from splinters," Lieutenant-Colonel Motte kept repeating.

"It's the wood we've used, sir," explained a lieutenant of engineers.

"Palmetto is like elm, it don't fracture readily."

"Thank God for that! If only the powder holds out—"

Even at the end of an hour, the British cannonade had diminished not a whit.

By shielding his eyes from flying sand, Nat was able to get a good look at the enemy. It was discouraging to discern the enemy ships lying as before, bow to stern. Periodically, gigantic smoke rings spurted from their gunports.

An ex-privateersman bit off the end of a priming quill, and tilted the French powder from it into the touch-hole of his piece.

"Watch third gun port aft on flagship," he called. He blew on his slow match and once the rest of the crew had scrambled out of reach of the recoil he touched off his long twenty-six.

A section of the man-of-war's bulwarks disintegrated into flame and smoke. Splinters flew high before falling with loud splashes into the harbor.

Gradually the deliberate, individually-aimed fire from the fort commenced to take effect. Aboard H. M. S. *Experiment* a topmast gave way suddenly and spilled a tangle of rigging, yards and men into the water.

19

THE SECOND LINE

As IF exasperated by the refusal of this ramshackle fort on Sullivan's Island to crumble, Admiral Parker ordered up his second line of battle.

Very slowly the *Acteon, Sphynx* and *Syren*—all frigates—crawled into range. They anchored further out and fired between intervals left by the vessels forming the first line. Soon they added their not inconsiderable weight of metal to the iron hailstorm hammering at Fort Sullivan.

When he saw this, Colonel Moultrie sucked hard on his empty

pipe, made a small dredging noise.

"Never mind them, Motte. Let us pound the big ships. 'Tend to the Commodore. We'll need some more powder soon, I take it?"

"Yes, sir, another hour of this will see us scraping the magazine."

"Then you had better send a messenger to requisition some from General Lee's collection at Point Pleasant."

Motte replied, looking gloomy, "It's as you say, Will, but I'll wager ten to one we can't wring a pound of gunpowder out of old Boiling Water. Mr. Coffin, be good enough to come with me.

"Reckon I will have to make out a formal requisition," he added, "or His High-and-Mightiness won't give you any heed."

In handing Nat the requisition, he added, "Whatever you do, don't use that crazy plank and barrel bridge old Boiling Water has rigged up. It ain't fit for use. You will find a picket boat in the Cove."

The pink tip of Motte's tongue appeared and wetted sun-cracked lips. Said he quietly, "You must reach General Lee in a hurry. Way they are shooting, our batteries will be out of powder by three o'clock.

"If you can't get any powder out of Lee, come back anyhow."

20

THE MANEUVERS OF A MAJOR-GENERAL

To DEFEND that narrow ford which divided Sullivan's from Long Island, Colonel William Thomson had laid out the simplest imaginable system of breastworks—merely a pair of giant *flèches* with their points aimed at the soon-to-be-disputed crossing.

The ex-Pennsylvanian's greatest concern was over his lack of artillery. Charles Lee had only sent him an eighteen pounder and a miserable little six pounder with a range so limited it might as well not have been there for all its usefulness.

Why in blazes, Thomson wanted to know, wouldn't the Continental General stop trying to fight this war as if it were taking place on the plains of Belgium? Why keep whole batteries to defend headquarters?

Sergeant Alistair Bryson and his men had got so used to the sounds of battle from the opposite end of the Island that they were able to recognize undertones in the cannonading. There was the bass grumble of a big gun; the staccato crash of an exploding bomb; the nerve-rasping scratch of a ricochet; the juvenile bark of the lighter field pieces. Anxious lest their own retreat be blocked, the Third Regiment and its supporting troops watched lazy pillars of distant gray smoke climb into the brazen heavens.

The Scot rolled over on his back and looked about. In a row of rifle pits to his right lay some two hundred men of the North Carolina line. They wore dark blue uniform coats over an amazing assortment of breeches, stockings and shoes.

Occupying a greater part of the line of defense was the Third South Carolina Regiment of Infantry, mostly from the up-country. No fancy regimentals here. The greater part of the men wore their own clothes and had peeled off most of those.

To the left of the Wateree Company, the Raccoon Company of riflemen had been posted. They wore buckskins and must be very sorry for it, now that the sun was climbing so high. Most of them had already drained their water bottles and were panting like hounds just in from a hard chase.

There was no cover to speak of—not even for the officers. Just a few parched and scarred oleanders and an occasional palmetto with its cabbage-like top.

An oily-looking tide was going out, exposing wide expanses of sedgy flats and attracting hundreds of shore birds.

The flotilla drew nearer, rowing slowly down a channel that wavered through a succession of mud flats.

In all his life Alistair Bryson had never experienced such blinding, intolerable heat. It distorted everything in sight, drew shimmering streamers from the dunes. Fervently, he blessed his ancestors: a kilt admitted air where breeches and trousers would not.

At Lynch's Pasture the armorer sergeants had issued him a short

Tower musket of a sort designed for His Britannic Majesty's light infantry. He deemed it a fairly handy piece. Anyway it had cost him not a groat. He became impatient for the leading longboats and gigs to come into range. When they did, he would learn how this musket shot. He needed to; he was no more than a passable marksman.

Out to sea an enemy schooner, the *Lady William,* cruised slowly back and forth. Every now and then her gunners would fire a shot which invariably went high and lost itself harmlessly among some dunes beyond the American position.

Conversation revived now that the flotilla was really drawing near. In those white-painted boats moved brilliant patterns of color: blue and white of seamen's jerseys, black sailor hats, huddles of scarlet-clad marines and vari-colored revers and cuffs of infantry.

Apparently it was the flotilla's mission to pass by the ford and then to effect a landing in the rear of the American position.

"Look at 'em come!" A sudden startled shout arose from a new direction. "Faces as red as their bloody coats."

Alistair rolled over on the blistering sand and felt his heart flare like a frightened hawk. On Long Island a rank of black shakos seemed to be sprouting from the crest of a gray-white dune. Next, a row of faces came into view, then a blinding flash of scarlet and white cross-belts. Well out in front of the ranks marched a scattering of officers. They were easily recognized by the gold lace on their tunics and the bright smears of light marking the crescent-shaped gorgets which protected their throats.

"Hum. Those yellow facings mean they'll be either the 57th or the 15th," someone in the Raccoon Company announced.

The regulars were trying to keep their ranks dressed but the yielding sand made that next to impossible. Fifers and little drummer boys trudged along on the flanks of the column playing "Strike, Britons, Home!" for all they were worth.

In successive waves more, and still more, scarlet coats appeared on the skyline and started down the long slope toward the ford.

"Christ A'mighty!" cried Alistair's right-hand companion. "Is there no end to them?"

"Dinna' sweer," Alistair heard himself growling. "We stand before God's awfu' throne."

Company on company, regiment on regiment, Sir Henry Clinton's fine troops began to deploy over a wide, slate-gray beach at the western-most tip of Long Island. His army lent the impression that vast scarlet pools were being filled. Like metal reeds, weapons flashed and wavered in the hot white sunlight.

"Damn' tide is still going out," someone announced irrelevantly.

"Reckon we are in for it."

Over to the right, Colonel Thomson's eighteen-pound field piece, goaded at last into replying to the cannonading of the *Lady William*, began to bang away. The little schooner had edged in shore as close as she dared in the shallowing water, and lay with a battery of four guns bearing on the American position. The range, however, was so great that her practice was poor.

The lone field piece accomplished nothing, either. Its shots all fell short, merely raised diamond-like jets of spray.

A Spanish-looking officer came running up, his shirt open clean down to his belt.

"Here they come. Look to your priming."

To the right of Alistair's company fifty riflemen from the Raccoon Company began to fiddle with their sights, and to place bets.

Colonel Dan Horry, reading their impatience, bawled, "Hey, you riflers! Don't you go loosing off without orders. Let the Redcoats come on 'til the smoothbores can range 'em!"

As the enemy flotilla rowed steadily closer more details became visible to the Wateree Company. Now they could distinguish the blue and gold tunic of some naval officer, the brief flash of naked backs swinging over the oar handles.

An unfamiliar exhilaration gripped Alistair Bryson. Out there were the Usurper's scarlet-clad kerls! Feyther had faced similar. 'Twas Redcoats like those out there who butchered Uncle Jamie, wounded as he was, and who had hanged Cousin Donald to a tree in the awful aftermath of Culloden. Ah! the enemy would soon be forced to pass in easy range because a slimy bank of mud forced them away from the opposite shore.

Impatiently, Lewis Campbell blew away great drops of sweat that formed on the tip of his nose. He'd tilted his bonnet way forward to shade his eyes. Heat rose in steady streamers from his twin brother's musket barrel.

Abruptly a rifleman got to his knees. "Ah, the hell with waiting!" He took quick aim at the leading small boat and fired. The flat, dry report of his rifle rang loud over the mirror-like channel. A scant hundred yards away an oarsman in a red and white jersey dropped his oar and sagged sidewise. One limp arm dangled over the thwart and an oar went drifting astern. The other rowers flinched, their oars began wavering like the legs of a crippled daddy-long-legs. Startled shouts began to sound in the flotilla.

Furiously Alistair called at the rifleman, "Dinna' shoot so soon! Gi' us a chance to show what we can do."

The insubordinate only squirted tobacco juice at him as he whipped up his powder horn and prepared to reload.

More rifles began to crack as the Raccoon Company's scant discipline went by the board.

For a brief interval the riflemen had a dandy time of it. Fringes flying, they twirled hickory ramrods over their heads and spat half-ounce balls into the bore.

Almost weeping with disappointment, Jamie Campbell shouldered his musket and fired. His Brown Bess boomed mightily, but its ball only raised a miniature geyser yards short of the mark.

Too late, Colonel Horry ran up and began berating the riflemen, knocking up their rifle barrels. "Stop it, you insubordinate slab-sided sons of squaws! I'll see your shoulders smoke for this sure's my name is Horry!"

But there was no restraining these leathery frontiersmen. Confusion spread in the British flotilla. A squad of grenadiers in the nearer boats opened fire, but their smoothbore muskets were no more effective than Jamie Campbell's.

Once the leading boat had been so punished as to start backing away, the riflemen diverted their attention to her successor. In quick succession they picked off half a dozen figures in white and scarlet. A towering corporal clutched at his chest and fell overboard. He sank like a stone.

"E-e-e-yah! E-e-e-yah!" the riflemen began screeching like so many panthers. A great breathless clamor began to rise from the Carolina regulars posted in the *flèches*.

An officer came panting up to Captain Chesnut and yelled something. Immediately, the Wateree Company and a detachment of North Carolinians were ordered out of the little pits they had dug and sent at the double to reinforce Thomson's main body.

Sand filled Alistair's shoes and the claymore dragged hard at his baldric, but he got his men over in a hurry and posted in a shallow hollow above the main position.

When he got time to glance at the enemy, his heart gave a great jump, like a shot deer. All the British regiments on the opposite bank were on the move! Alistair felt his stomach withering. Spies had reported that Clinton had landed above two thousand regulars, while here Colonel Thomson had eight hundred men all told.

The enemy's field music, drummers and fifers, had massed themselves and, in the best approved style began to play the King's regiments into action.

While there was yet time, the Wateree Company looked back to their former position. The flotilla now was tangled up for fair. Oars, caps and other equipment littered the channel. Too cruelly punished by the Raccoon Company's marksmanship, they were scrambling to get out of range. Wounded men clung to their boats and struggled to climb back aboard.

The little six-pounder commenced to hurl shot in the general direction of Long Island, but its only victims were minnows scurrying about the shallows.

The Wateree Company was only faintly aware of an intensification in the bombardment of Fort Sullivan for now the first ranks of the enemy had reached the water's edge. The officers waded right out, yelling encouragement and waving their swords.

Ankle-deep, the big grenadiers began to advance more and more gingerly. Then the water grew deeper, the officers felt out footing with their swords. The men caught up their cartouche boxes to keep them clear of the surface.

Captain Chesnut said in conversational tones, "Get set, boys; another twenty yards and they'll be in easy range."

All along the hollow the up-country men were getting ready. Old hands stuck their ramrods into the ground, put bullets into their cheeks and tucked paper wads into their belts. There were so many red, white and yellow facings in the water now that soon even a poor shot could not miss.

Up to their armpits in the coffee-colored tide, the foremost officers halted and began to curse. Alistair could hear them calling to know whether this was the correct spot. Gradually the whole British advance halted, patently unable to advance.

A large man in a major's uniform turned and splashed back yelling, "Tide's dead low, sir—and it's too deep."

A group of particularly resplendent officers appeared and hurried down to the water's edge.

"That must be their General," Alistair deduced.

"Yep, that's Clinton, sure enough," Captain Chesnut nodded.

Arriving at the ford, Sir Henry removed a watch and a packet of papers from his pocket and passed them to an aide. Sword in hand, he then started wading past his half-submerged troops. Those regiments still on dry land shifted in their ranks to see what would happen.

Steadily, and quite ignoring the popping of the six-pounder, Sir Henry Clinton advanced into the slack, tan-colored tide. Water, rising to his chest, stirred the elegant white lace of his jabot. The British Commander kept on until only his gold-trimmed tricorne and white wig remained above water.

"Yon's a rare brave mon," muttered Jamie Campbell. "A rifler could hit him, there's nae doot."

From the American side of the ford rose a mighty yell of derision. Wasn't every day you watched a general get his arse wet!

Grimly, Sir Henry Clinton turned and made his way back to shore. When his troops followed suit, the American force fired a triumphant volley which accomplished nothing because the range was too great; it made them feel better, though, and shots kept crackling all up and down the dunes.

"Ye'd have believed," Lewis Campbell remarked, "that wi' a whole week on his hands, Sir Henry would have made sure how deep yon ford might be."

Alistair started to reply when, off to the right, a report sounded. A bullet sang by, severed the hawk's feather in his bonnet. Over a distant dune hung a puff of smoke.

Jamie Campbell turned about shouting, "Take care up there, yer shootin' short, ye blithering moon-calves!"

Alistair Bryson only licked his lips. He had caught just a glimpse of a Ferguson tartan. The treacherous dog!

Come sundown he'd go see whether there was not serving in the Third Company a dark-complected man whose brows met above his nose. He'd be warty and with a lean, mean jaw. If so, Feyther would see a Ferguson dirk thrown onto his table.

"Well, there's an end to the Lobster-backs," someone was calling.

"Like hell," corrected Colonel Thomson. "Most likely Clinton will embark and try to land between us and Moultrie. He hasn't come all this way to stop now."

21

GUNPOWDER

LIEUTENANT NATHANIEL COFFIN, Continental Marines, found it was somewhat cooler out on the water. He was very glad of that. So were the four negro rowers and a courier of Colonel Thomson's.

So far Thomson was making out real well, explained the North Carolinian. Only question now was whether Sir Henry Clinton would attempt to land his unhurt army at some point between Thomson and the fort. The possibility was a real cause for concern. If the British could march across narrow Sullivan's Island, both American positions must inevitably be lost.

Nat nodded heavily. He had learned enough of tactics to understand that this must be the enemy's next step. It was discouraging, too, to hear fire from the fort dwindle like an old candle.

Not so the fire from the fleet. Admiral Parker's ships were doggedly sustaining a furious cannonade. Only crews superbly trained could have maintained so heavy a rate of fire for so long.

Every fisherman's shanty on the western end of Sullivan's Island had been blown to planking.

From the water, one got a much clearer impression of the ships. His body swaying to each oar stroke, Nat judged that some *démarche* impended. Brightly colored signal flags were flying in H. M. S. *Bristol's* battered rigging and frigates, forming the second line of battle, were sending gigs over to the flagship. She had been absorbing punishment. Now that the fort's fire had dwindled to a single shot fired at minute intervals, one could watch the effect of each roundshot.

That last ball had shattered the gilded "admiral's walk" built across the *Bristol's* stern. It made a noise like someone breaking up a chest with an axe.

Because an occasional stray cannonball came skipping over the harbor's mirrored surface, the black oarsmen required little urging. They made the gig fairly fly across the cove separating Sullivan's Island from Lee's headquarters on Haddrell's Point. Their course lay parallel to a useless footbridge of rum casks and planks.

"The firin' sounds mighty weak from the fo't," Thomson's courier presently observed. "Sounds like they was done fo'."

"They will be if we don't get some powder in a hurry. The enemy could walk right in now, if they only knew it."

Because of the heat, Nat held his tunic open, was surprised to notice its white lapels flecked and smudged by burnt powder grains. Must have dirtied them when he had helped to train a long eighteen after its captain had collapsed with sunstroke.

Thomson's courier, a lantern-jawed ensign, viewed the elaborate entrenchments on Haddrell's Point with disgust.

"Wish you'd tell me why old Boiling Water feels justified in hoggin' so much powder and all the best engineer officers. We-all could use some of both down by the fo'd."

A sentry, one of Muehlenberg's well-dressed Virginia regulars, challenged, demanding the parole.

" 'Hancock'!" Thomson's courier bellowed. "Mah Gawd, man, we are in a great hurry."

The sentry kept his musket ready. The fool, as if the boat could possibly contain enemies. "Steady there, that was the watchword. Give the parole."

" 'Virginia,' " Nat supplied. "For God's sake, man, drop this foolishness! Where will we find General Lee?"

Nat ran past regiment on regiment of sturdy Continental troops drawn up in precise ranks. Completely useless, they were moodily watching the unequal engagement continue on Sullivan's.

They found the Commander-in-Chief crouched on an observation platform built into a tree. Hatchet features working, Charles Lee was studying the fort through a pocket telescope. When the messengers were announced, he delayed a good quarter of an hour ere he descended a ladder held by two staff officers.

If Nat Coffin had ever beheld an ill-tempered and hostile countenance, it was the Major-General's.

His uniform, as he liked to keep it in the field, was a mass of wrinkles, spots and splashed food. His wig, Nat decided, looked as if it had been hauled backwards through a blackberry patch. Ignoring the salutes of his aides, he came stamping loose-jointedly along.

"Well?" rasped the gangling figure. "Does our high and mighty backwoods strategist at last admit that a veteran of a dozen European wars might know something of siege warfare?"

"I have no information on that point, sir," stated Lieutenant Nathaniel Coffin.

"Come, come! Moultrie is about to get smoked out. May as well admit it."

"Not yet, sir."

Lee's pale brown eyes narrowed and he snapped fingers that might have been cleaner. "Oh, plague take that stubborn Provincial fool." He turned to the courier, "Well, what do you want?"

The North Carolinian saluted, began earnestly, "Colonel Thomson, suh, sho'ly needs reinforcements. He asks please will you land a strong body of troops half way down Sullivan 'twixt the fo't and the fo'd?"

"Really?" Lee affected great astonishment. "And where does your estimable Colonel think I am going to find such troops? Out of a cocked hat?"

With three thousand men standing idly under arms, Nat deemed the question utterly absurd.

Lee glared at the resentful courier, then spun about, facing his brightly-uniformed aides. "Now you are gentlemen of intelligence—"

A South Carolina major opened his mouth but, before he could utter a syllable, Lee roared, "I'll thank you to hold your peace! Things are going badly enough already. Moultrie's pig-headedness will soon lose me all his garrison and Thomson's force, also. No. I will not doom another man to destruction on the Island. My reputation will suffer enough through this day's work."

Nat seized his opportunity. "But, sir, Colonel Moultrie is not requesting a single man. He only asks that this requisition be honored, and at once." He offered the paper Motte had made out.

Using a bluish forefinger nail, Charles Lee ripped open the requisition. "Only a thousand pounds of powder?" he sneered. "Here's a modest request, stab me if it's not! Gentlemen, dear generous Colonel Moultrie wishes to present the enemy with an additional thousand pounds of our gunpowder!"

He glared at Nat. "Present my compliments to your rustic strategist and inform him I will not risk another private or a single gill of powder in the defense of Sullivan's Island! That's flat.

"You may also give him this order. So soon as his powder is exhausted—" Lee was fairly shouting in order that everyone might hear and bear witness, "—he must spike and over-set all cannon remaining in serviceable condition. We hold a few boats here and I will undertake to bring off as many of his garrison as is possible."

The grumbling boom of successive broadsides from the fleet made the hot air shake.

Tarnished braid flashed on Lee's cuff as he snatched at his pocket telescope.

A growing murmur of dismayed astonishment arose from the staff.

Propelled by just a breath of breeze, all three frigates composing the second line had upped anchor and were setting sail with the obvious intention of rounding the western tip of Sullivan's.

What impended was unmistakable. The *Syren, Acteon* and *Sphynx* were circling around towards the little, low-lying fort's quite undefended rear. From that point the frigates could, and undoubtedly would, shatter Moultrie's batteries. At the same time, the garrison's retreat to Haddrell's Point would be cut off.

Pompous and arrogant though he was, the adventurer Lee had been entirely justified in his fears. There could be no doubt now that the fort must fall, and in very short order.

Charles Lee clicked shut his spyglass lens cover. Grinning like a satyr he asked, "Gentlemen, you shall observe what follows when riflemen and merchants play at strategy. Ha! Ha! Ha! President Rutledge wouldn't listen to me and I owned a lieutenant's commission at the age of twelve! He spurned the advice of one who has campaigned with Frederick the Great. I fear our stubborn friend Moultrie deserves all he will suffer in that comic fort."

Nothing was to be gained from waiting, so Nat unobtrusively returned to his boat. Bitterly he dreaded the necessity of breaking the news of Lee's refusal to send powder.

As he ran down to the shore, the Nantucketer kept one eye on the three frigates. So light was the wind it seemed as if these men-of-war were being drawn along by invisible cables rather than by the pressure of air on their canvas.

"Wait! Wait!" A captain wearing the regimentals of the First Carolina Line came pelting up. "Plague take that damned turncoat Englishman." He jerked his head towards Lee's headquarters. "How is Colonel Moultrie holding out?"

"Well enough, except for powder. He had only one gun out of action when I left."

"*Only one*—why that's impossible!"

"The palmetto timbers give rather than break under a round-shot." Nat turned to the boat crew. "Shove off—"

The dark-faced Carolinian came to the water's edge. "On your word of honor—Moultrie's damage is no greater?"

Nat's color rose above his sweaty white collar. "On my sacred word."

A few yards up the shore were a pair of long, slim pilot boats. Their negro crews lazed on the beach.

Nat heard the officer bark, "You'll row me to Charleston inside thirty minutes or I'll see every inch of skin is flogged off your backs!"

Jumping aboard, he took the tiller himself and the last Nat saw of that Carolina Captain he was alternately calling the stroke and demanding more speed.

22

The Georgian

A TWELVE pound shot from H. M. S. *Experiment* came screaming through an embrasure, shattered the muzzle of a cannon and showered its crew with deadly, jagged iron fragments. Two of Sergeant McDaniel's crew simply disintegrated into mangled lumps of meat. The balance of the stricken crew either fell heavily or rolled crazily about. Bubbling groans, whimpering noises filled intervals in the cannonading. Infantrymen ran to lift the wounded onto stretchers improvised of coats which had been buttoned and turned inside out. Poles had been thrust through the coat sleeves.

A hand that was blue with tattooing landed with a dull thump by the feet of a tall sergeant handling an adjoining piece. His grimy features froze in horror at the slowly relaxing fingers; at the blood slowly crawling over the gritty boards of the gun platform.

"What ails you?" grunted a half-naked gun captain. "A hero from Georgia shouldn't fear a little hot iron."

William Jasper made no reply.

"I never yet seen a Georgian with enough sand to stand up to a fieldmouse."

Slowly the big sergeant looked about. "Whoever said that is a damn' liar!"

"Words is cheap," growled the Number Four of his own gun crew.

Just then the *Bristol* fired such a vicious salvo that the whole curtain trembled under its impact. Squinting over the breech of his piece Sergeant Jasper thought, "Ah'll show these South Carolina bastards! By Christ, Ah'll show 'em! How do they get to fancy South Carolina is God's gift to America?"

Colonel Moultrie, looking years older now, came along to inspect the damage. Somebody called, "Hey, Colonel, what the hell has happened to our banner?"

"That last volley carried it off, I reckon," Colonel Moultrie snapped. Seemed to him like an evil omen to see the Moultries' silver and blue brought down.

"It ain't carried away," a gunner corrected. "It's just the staff is broke. I kin see our flag layin' on the beach."

Jasper sensed a God-given opportunity to shut these fellers up once and for all. He saluted mighty brisk.

"Colonel, suh, we ought to have a flag to fight under."

"True, but we haven't another."

"Then, suh, Ah reckon Ah had better fetch that one up."

As the Colonel shook his head, another salvo from the enemy rattled against the palmetto logs, sent sand skimming high into the air.

"Don't be a fool. Cannonballs are thicker down there than flies 'round a backhouse."

Jasper, however, was already vaulting over the mess about the ruined gun. He crawled out of the embrasure muttering, "Called me yaller, just 'cause Ah comes from Geo'gia! Ah'm gonna show 'em."

A queer buzzing began in his ears when he realized that one of the liners was sure 'nough fixing to fire. Scrambling down a series of splintered logs he was aware, in a frozen sort of way, that those gun muzzles were beginning to protrude through the ports.

Whew! They'd let fly in a minute. He was a great fool to have let them Charleston fellers sass him into tryin' such a fool trick as this. To keep from worrying too much he tried to count the number of cannonballs stuck between the logs. Six, eight, fourteen, not counting chunks of broken bombshell.

Ha! He saw the blue flag lying down there amid a tangle of broken timbers. The staff had sho' 'nuff been clipped a mean lick—was splintered half its length. Just as he reached the beach, the liner let go her broadside. He could see the water grow all rough under the concussion. Just above his head a roundshot plucked a log out of the southeast bastion, sent it spinning off into the air as if it had been a toothpick.

He felt his bowels pucker. Once he'd come across a nest of young jay-birds too young to fly. All naked and helpless they'd lain there waiting for him to do something to them. He guessed he knew how they had felt.

Zoo-e-e! Tchunk! A cannonball sailed right past his waist, another, falling short, drove a shower of salty sand into his mouth, nose and eyes.

Glory be! A charge of grapeshot, whirring like a covey of gigantic quail, roared overhead. That he had hold of the flag was a surprise. He rumpled it up under one arm, any way it would go.

Shucks! That stitching around the word "Liberty" was no great shakes. If this was a sample of Carolina sewing, he was right glad he came from Geo'gia.

Spurred by the knowledge that another broadside would soon be ready, he scrambled up the log wall as fast as he could and got inside just as the *Bristol* let go.

Safe! It was a crazy thing they'd stung him into attempting. But he'd done it. The Georgian took the flag from under his arm, shook it at them.

"Here's your banner, you goddam Carolina swamp rabbits!"

They were yelling—cheering him, maybe, but he paid no attention. He saw a sponge staff belonging to a shattered gun lying idle. It gave him an idea. Somehow he got the flag spread out and his fingers had never felt clumsier than when he tried to tie it to the sponge staff. It handed him a big laugh to see how the Carolinians were gawping.

He'd mount it up where even the enemy could see that he had brought the banner up. This, he reckoned, would quiet all loose talk about Geo'gia sand.

When he climbed up and jammed the sponge staff into a crack at the top of a merlon near the southeast salient Colonel Moultrie snatched out his pipe and joined in the cheering.

23

THREE FRIGATES

DISEMBARKING on Sullivan's Island, Nat noticed parties of infantry deserting that epaulment which fronted Haddrell's Point channel. They knew that, by another ten minutes, the three flanking frigates would be in position to rake the entrenchment from end to end. Even the officers saw that a defense was hopeless. Their little nine and twelve pounders would be quite ineffective.

Lord! how slow the fort was firing. *Age quod agis,* my boy. 'Tend to your business.

Dreading his mission, Nat made straight for the south gun platform. He found Moultrie, Motte and the rest there. They were staring tensely to the westward.

Suddenly, like clock-work set in motion, members of the staff began to cheer, to gesticulate and to pound each other on the back. When he reached the top of the ladder-stair, Nat saw the reason for their jubilation. Either an unsuspected current or the freshening east breeze had caused the *Syren* and the *Sphynx* to foul each other. Yards interlaced, both vessels lost headway and began to drift broadside in the direction of Charleston.

Despite all efforts, the two ships were driven closer and closer together. Soon they lost the last trace of steerage-way.

"Watch the third ship," Captain Huger commenced to shout. "Watch the *Acteon!*"

To avoid her entangled consorts, the *Acteon* was bearing away to port, apparently cutting just inside of a very small black buoy. This was one of several which, during the past week, had mysteriously appeared. Her topsails filling under a strong puff, the frigate drove along so smartly that foam curled away from her cut-water.

Suddenly her progress ceased and her fabric gave an enormous creaking groan. Her bow shot high into the air. Simultaneously all her yards swung wildly over to starboard, catapulting a number of topmen far out over the water.

Wild shouts arose from the fort as the man-of-war settled heavily onto a shoal called the "Middle Ground." Gradually the *Acteon's* canvas canted her so far over to starboard that loose objects tumbled across her decks into the starboard scuppers.

Captain Huger, still unstrung over his sergeant's death, began to hug himself, to laugh until his eyes watered. "Oh, those chuckle-headed fools! Came right on, never taking a bearing! Oh—oh, stab me if this isn't rare. They never suspected that we—oh! oh!—would move their damned buoy hundred feet to port. Oh, burn my breeches. Isn't it wonderful? Look at 'em, Coffin, there's the *Acteon* stuck tight as a duck's foot in the mud!"

Meantime the *Sphynx* and the *Syren* had somehow disentangled themselves, but at the cost of a snapped bowsprit for the former. Her headsails were flapping in a grotesque tangle.

Moultrie roused himself, became lavish with his dwindling supply of powder and roared, "Pour it into 'em, lads."

Joyfully, the handful of guns mounted along the west curtain went into action and at once splinters began to fly and yards to fall aboard the frigates. Punished, they veered off too far and so went sliding up on that same bank of blue mud and sand which was already imprisoning the *Acteon*.

Nat felt his breath come again. Lee, he judged, would be furious because this accident had made a joke of his dire predictions. As for Colonel Moultrie, that stolid gentleman looked mightily relieved, but even yet he did not seem to appreciate how deadly had been his danger.

At half-past three, Colonel Moultrie ordered his batteries to cease fire. Just enough powder remained to supply infantry muskets against the hour when, inevitably, Admiral Parker would land his marines and try to take the fort by storm.

The enemy also slowed down. They must have suffered serious casualties because men from other ships were rowed over to the first line. From their firing platforms the Americans could see carpenters hurriedly clearing away a wild tangle of fallen spars.

The main yard of H. M. S. *Bristol* was so shattered it had to be sent down. Men were sent out in small boats to stuff hammocks into great holes gaping along the flagship's waterline. Over these they nailed sheets of lead. Scarcely less in need of attention was the line-of-battleship *Experiment* and the *Solebay* frigate.

So many bodies were lugged to the *Bristol's* rail and dropped into the water that no one could keep accurate count.

"Dum them Britishers," grunted a saturnine fellow with gurry sores all over his hands. "Now I wunt dare taste a crab in a month." His mates roared as if he'd said the cleverest thing.

Helped by a rising tide, the *Syren* and the *Sphynx* floated free of the bar and, unaccountably, abandoned all efforts to deliver their attack from the rear. Sullenly, they tacked back to join the fleet and, resuming their original positions, joined in the ceaseless cannonade of Fort Sullivan.

The *Acteon* remained where she was despite the frantic efforts of her crew to get her off.

After enduring the enemy's fire for so long, the garrison found it hard to stand around, helplessly awaiting the next move. To Nat

Coffin it seemed as if much more than six hours had elapsed since the *Thunder's* first shell had flown, screaming, above the fort. Already the bodies of the first men who had been killed were bloating, turning a deep plum-color.

On a double row of twisted shapes ranged under the gun platform descended dense clouds of flies which would not be driven off.

The blackened, half-naked officers raged to each other. "Imagine that bastard over at Haddrell's keeping his magazine choked with powder!"

"If only I had a few hundred pounds more," Moultrie groaned, "we could drive off those work parties. The three-deckers will sink if a real wind comes up."

Around half after four, a sloop was discerned leaving Charleston with a smaller sailboat in her wake. The lowering sun was raising an easterly breeze, so both vessels skirted the helpless *Acteon* and ran into the cove behind the fort.

His features luminous with sweat, a dark-complexioned officer hurried ashore from the sloop and came running up to the fort.

To Colonel Moultrie, he panted, "With the compliments of President Rutledge, sir."

Saluting, he presented a fold of paper secured with a flying seal.

As Moultrie read, a smile formed, spread over his unshaven face.

"Listen to this!" he yelled at his staff. "Ed Rutledge says, 'I send you five hundred pound of powder. You know our collection is not great. Honor and Victory to you and our worthy countrymen with you. Be cool and do mischief!' "

24

FLIGHT

"To WADBOO, 4 mi," read the bird-stained fingerboard. Mechanically, Desire fanned herself with a soggy handkerchief and hoped her fraying satin slippers would last such a distance. What Wadboo might be like, or who lived there, she had no idea.

Dully, she realized that that grumbling rumble which had commenced in the early morning was persisting. Of course, a terrible battle must be taking place at Fort Sullivan. Terrified fugitives, overtaking her, had brought the wildest reports.

During the first few miles of her flight, she had hurried off the road whenever a carriage or wagon came along; but now she was much too tired for such a precaution. Due to the relentless drag of the baby, her whole back ached and burnt and her breath grew dreadfully short.

All considered, she had made good time during the previous night. And in the morning a farmer's cart had given her a blessedly welcome ride of five miles. Whenever she felt down-hearted, she thought of her usual good luck. It would see her through this, too.

She received minor proofs to strengthen her conviction. Around breakfast time, a group of refugees invited her over to share a mess of beans and boiled eggs. If they thought it strange to find a well-dressed young woman in her condition plodding along all by herself, they made no comment.

In trying to keep her mind off her heavy, aching body and the fact that her ankles were swelling to almost twice their usual slim proportions, Desire thought backwards.

Why, oh why, did Nat have to re-appear just when, and as, he had? Everything might have worked out if she'd found him without the Proveauxs around. Still, maybe she had been wise, and decent, to leave as she had.

Determinedly, Desire refused to speculate on the future. It was like trying to fashion a rope out of sand. Mercifully, it never occurred that she might become stricken on this untraveled road and die in lonely agony.

The sight of a dead horse in the roadside distracted her. Dozens of hideous, red-headed buzzards reluctantly interrupted their feast and flapped away, leaving behind a dreadful reek of carrion. As, pinching her nose, Desire hurried by, dense clouds of blow-flies rose from the bloated carcass.

She walked steadily until a file of dusty militiamen came tramping around a bend in the road. Hollow-eyed and sunburnt, they trudged along under their strange miscellany of weapons, carried blankets rolled over one shoulder.

"Howdy, Ma'am." The leader, a solemn fellow in a rusty black parson's coat, took off his hat. "Air we goin' to reach the battle in time?"

Desire smiled wanly, said, "I really don't know what chances, sir, except that the cannon have been shooting since morning."

A young soldier carrying a fowling piece almost as tall as himself, licked lips cracked by the sun. "Gee, Pa. Ah sho' hopes the British don't quit 'til we git there."

The leader looked down the dusty little road, inquired, "Have you passed any springs, Ma'am?"

Desire said she had drunk from a good one not far back. In the shade of a slash pine she rested, watched the nine sunburnt men slog on toward the distant cannonade.

All at once she knew she couldn't go any further—not for a while at least. The way the child dragged and dragged at her back muscles made her feel as if she must fall onto her face at any instant. Her breasts felt bigger and tenderer than ever.

Ahead lay what seemed like a promising stretch of pine woods. It looked really shady there and if she came across a stream, she wanted to sit down and bathe feet which stung as if scalded.

Sure enough, a small runlet was tracing a bright green ribbon across the brown floor of pine wood. It took her some minutes to catch her breath but once she had untied her garters and stripped off the stained remnants of her stockings, the water felt unbelievably fine on her feet. In fact, that cool trickle about her ankles seemed to soothe her whole body.

She must be really stronger than most girls. Tim, teasing, always claimed she was tough as tripe until she made him hush up. She'd come at least a dozen miles from the ferry since morning and there would be anyhow two more hours of daylight.

Dozing, she heard the voices of a party of horsemen on the road.

After a bit a wild turkey, a deer, or something, rustled the leaves behind her. She felt so comfortable she paid no heed.

'Way off to the southeast those cannon were still thud-thudding away. Oh dear. It must be a fearful battle. She supposed Nat was in it, and Roger and Cousin Barnard Elliott. When she got a little more strength back she would pray that all of them got—

Quite a heavy noise from behind made her turn her head. At what she saw her fingers flew wide apart and remained fixed in the rigidity of terror. Not six feet away and steadily regarding her from the heart of the myrtle was a fierce black face. One of this negro's cheeks was puckered by a deep brand.

To make matters worse, though the black opposite didn't move, sounds of movement came from deeper in the myrtle.

All at once the apparition's ferocious expression faded. Pointed teeth became displayed in an anxious smile.

"Please, Maum, please doan' raise no rookus."

"You come out of there!" It wasn't hard for Desire to inject indignation into her tone. "The idea your going about scaring people like that!"

"Yas'm." A strapping young negro in tattered denims came out to stand uncertainly on the other side of the rivulet.

"Who is that with you?" Desire demanded, feeling the goose-pimples subside on her arms.

"It's Eve, Maum," he explained. A broad-faced wench appeared, hovered just back of his shoulder. The pair must have been into a lot of briars if one went by the plentiful scratches showing on their sable skins.

She learned that the pair were Barbados-trained and had suffered bestial cruelties at the hands of a Charleston dealer named Ratsch. Cocoa, the man, exhibited heavy welts on arms and shoulders. It was while the slave trader's gangs were being driven to safety in the interior that an opportunity for escape had presented itself.

They had stayed in the woods ever since; everybody knew that these days a runaway slave stood an excellent chance of being shot on sight. Cocoa declared that if Misto Ratsch cotched them, they'd most sho'ly git flogged to death.

Desire, her jangled nerves calming, sat with her feet still in the water.

"What do you want of me?" she asked with an amused smile. "Surely you must have seen that I can give you neither food, clothes, nor money."

The branded negro dropped on his knees as he held out hands joined in supplication. "In de Lawd's name please tek mercy on us, Maum. Tek us for yo' people."

"But how—"

Cocoa's eyes rolled. "If you decla'hs, Maum, Eve and me is yo' propetty, den can't no sodjuhs er patrollers shoot us—tek us up—" He gazed fearfully at the road. "Sway to Gawd, Cocoa an' Eve he'p you plenty. Eve, her puntop cook, fitten belong to quality."

"But I have no money. No home—any more."

" 'At all right, Maum," Cocoa cried eagerly. "Us tek care ob you."

Small John shifted heavily. She could do with some assistance, Desire judged. Anyhow she felt mighty sorry for these poor, scared creatures. "Won't that brand be recognized? I suppose I could be put in prison for slave stealing."

" 'At Barbado brand, Maum," Cocoa hurriedly explained. "Doan' no one know it 'round heah."

"I take it you and Eve were house servants?"

"Yes, Maum, we wuz 'til Sir Joseph done game us 'way."

Although she hadn't even the semblance of a plan of action, Desire had learned enough of Southern ways to appreciate that a woman possessing a pair of slaves thereby commanded courtesy and attention —no matter what her state.

So she must once more play a part. The Fates, it seemed, had decreed for her the life of an actress.

"Cocoa, I have decided to take you both on." Skillfully, she mimicked 'Toinette's intonations. "While I rest, you go down the road and find what Wadboo is. Eve, fetch my stockings off that bush."

At the way both negroes jumped into obedience, she almost chuckled out loud.

As quickly as her fatigued condition permitted, she must evolve a plausible explanation for her situation. She'd better! In some counties, slave stealing was punishable by whipping, hanging even.

Wadboo consisted of a plantation house which had recently been burned. Some troops camped there had credited Cocoa's tale enough to give him some fat-back, hominy grits and bread. The idea dawned on Desire that her new acquisition must also be something of an actor. Possibilities in that direction? Maybe, but she was too exhausted to think of it now.

At sundown the cannon were rumbling away in the direction of Charleston. Was the town falling? Powder was so short that she expected so. When with dark the firing gradually faded, she guessed the British were in possession.

Desire, with food in her stomach, felt almost chipper. Here was luck again. Oh, it never would break after this. Singing softly and smiling at Eve, Cocoa broke boughs with which to build a shelter over her pine-tip bed. Eve was smiling too, as she gently plaited her new mistress's dusty tresses.

Even at sundown stragglers from militia companies kept limping by. Quite a few of these, so Cocoa said, were riflemen. Because buckskin men must be sure 'nuff strangers in these parts, he wasn't so afraid to address them.

"Evenin', folks, reckon you could stretch yore provender a speck?" Desire gasped, Eve squealed and Cocoa jumped. None of them had had the least warning of this buckskin's approach.

"Sorry, Ma'am," said he simply, "I didn't mean for to startle you."

He pulled off a cap of bobcat fur. "I will fix you a real lean-to, Ma'am, to pay for any vittles I eat."

There was something forcefully reminiscent about that outline, half-seen among the trees.

Desire's heart gave a queer little flip as she called aloud, "Well, Mr. Higsby, do you still seek a good fight?"

Sam Higsby jumped as if an arrow had stuck in the tree beside him. Cap still in hand, he bounded forward.

"Why, Miss Desire! What in Gawd's name—? Tim an' me hunted everywhere."

When, out of sheer relief, she kissed him, Higsby reckoned he was in luck at last.

Long after Eve and Cocoa had gone off to sleep under the pines, Desire and the Pennsylvanian talked, watched the stars wheel slowly by above the tree tops.

25

THE DIRK

THE belated arrival on Long Island of Colonel Muehlenberg with seven hundred Continentals evoked gales of ribald derision among the troops already in position. From Colonel Thomson down, the fly-bitten, up-country companies were pointedly curious to learn just why these Virginians and North Carolinian gentlemen had dropped in.

Was there to be a wedding? Or did they think a brothel was handy? Perhaps these gentlemen in pretty regimentals fancied somebody had been shooting wild fowl and wanted a share of the bag? No, of course not. It was plain they had come expecting to witness a pyrotechnical exhibition. Too bad they were a trifle late; the fireworks were all over.

Furious after their futile march the length of Sullivan's, the Continentals gave hot retorts. A big captain bellowed angrily, "If you damn' hay-shakers and squaw-chasers weren't scared stiff why'd you send a dozen couriers for reinforcements?"

Before the new arrivals had pitched a camp of sorts among the dunes, some savage minor riots took place.

Sergeant Alistair Bryson saw that his men got their share of the meager rations brought along by the Continentals, but he was still boiling mad. Despite all Feyther's warnings, somehow he hadn't believed that even a Ferguson would attempt the murder of a fellow soldier under cover of battle.

Losh! That sneaking kerl had tried to shoot him down, never granting him a chance to defend himself. He had only the good Lord to thank that, right now, he was not sprawled on the sand with a cake of bloodied sand at his mouth.

He would kill the Ferguson. He must. Alive, such an enemy would constitute a perpetual menace. But why should this utter stranger want to kill him? Not even Feyther knew why the feud with the Fergusons had begun, or how. Probably 'twas some bicker over a strayed sheep had started it all.

"Ne'er grant a Ferguson the first blow," Feyther had warned. He had been entirely right, it appeared. Tonight when the moon rose he would reconnoiter the other up-country companies for a gleam of the hated tartan.

First thing he would scan those two companies which had been raised along the Yadkin. If he found the Ferguson, he would call him out. No sneaking, bushwhacking for a Bryson.

Heigh-ho. He was tired. A man couldna' be up at four and feel so braw after supper.

"What would yon sonsie Proveaux girl make of a Highland feud?" he wondered. "Wi' so large a country as this there seems sma' point slaying a fellow man over an ancient quarrel. 'Tis wasteful wi' the population so sma' and scattered."

The Ferguson must die, all the same. It was not safe to leave such a viper free.

Alistair's kilt which, during the day, had been a blessing, now proved a torture. In multitudes, mosquitoes feasted on his bare knees and, worse still, rose under his tartan and went to work. Though Jamie Campbell rubbed himself with a strange compound which stank worse than fifty polecats, there was no escaping the pests.

Because he wanted to remain undisturbed by the gabble about the camp fire, he sought, a resting place in a dense thicket of myrtles. There, in desperation, he shoveled sand over his tortured legs and folded a blanket beneath his head.

How very bonnie was the Proveaux lass! His breath had quite failed when, two days ago, she appeared so slim and elegant in the camp. Mistress Antoinette reminded him most of a cedar waxwing.

Softly dark, with flashes of bright color.

But Mistress Proveaux was practical, too, for a' her modish manner. When he had asked her what the cakes had cost, she had known to a farthing. Antoinette, a fair name indeed. Like the sound of a brook falling down a rocky slope. In sighing, Alistair blew a mosquito from the tip of his nose.

"—And why shouldn't I know?" she had demanded, ever so demure. "Papa built his fortune by knowing prices. La, Sergeant Bryson, an you but read history, you will learn that the French and the Scots are greatly sympathetic and not only in the matter of monies."

Twisting fingers into his long dark hair, Alistair stared unwinkingly at the myriad glowing stars. Had she—could Mistress Proveaux have been—?

Suppose—at his own audacity he drew a deep breath—suppose Mistress Proveaux's money and learning could be combined with his sound understanding of ground, timber and cattle? Why the rich soil o' the Wateree could be made to yield harvests bountiful beyond belief. Slaves—that was his greatest need—stout blackamoors to dig up the larger stones, to grub the fields and to burn stumps which resisted the plow.

Losh, but it was fine to lie here building castles under the stars. What would Jean make o' a sister-in-law who wore earbobs, tortoise-shell combs and silken stockings? Could Mither take to a lowland daughter-in-law? And Feyther?

Once yon Ferguson was attended to, Feyther could have little to say.

Antoinette Proveaux. He was trying to picture her, small, dark and smiling, among the constellations, when they were blotted out by a figure launching itself through the myrtles.

All he had time to do was to try to fend off the apparition with his leg. His brogan's hob-nailed heel struck the pouncing figure full in the sternum, extracting a whistling grunt. As they rolled over and over on the sandgrass Alistair tried to reach his claymore, but couldn't.

Momentarily underneath, he saw the flash of the attacker's long-bladed weapon—a Highland dirk. His left hand lunged upwards, gripped a bearded throat. But the Ferguson twisted out of his grip. A breath, indescribably foul, beat in his face when he made a desperate sidewise lunge that sent the two of them to rolling about again.

Where was that dirk? His eyes were so full of sand he could hardly see. Why didn't he feel the searing sting of the blade in his side? in his back? worse still, in his belly?

Earth and sky changed places and he saw the dirk before his eyes. Proximity of that razor edge taught him things he hadn't known about fear. The throat of that pig last fall—how furiously it had gushed.

His enemy struck, but the sand gave way and this black-bearded Ferguson swayed like a drunkard. Spitting sand from his mouth, Alistair got off the ground and grabbed at his stocking.

Blazes! His dirk was gone! Now the Ferguson, his eyes dark smears in the pallor of his star-lighted face, had recovered, was gathering himself—a dark blur against the whiteness of the dune. In his hand the dirk glinted.

Alistair wouldn't have been so worried if he'd a coat to whip off and swathe about his left arm. With it he could ward off the Ferguson's first stab, then grapple.

A flood of hot shame heated Alistair Bryson's soul. Imagine his getting caught napping again! The other, a thick-set fellow with powerful bare knees and long arms, continued to circle, circle—panting loudly into his ragged beard. This clansman was older and wore a fringed buckskin shirt; an absurd contrast to the kilt and sporran swaying below his hips.

Twice he feinted, as if testing Alistair's speed.

A wrong move now, Alistair realized, and he would die. No house of his own—no cow—not even the possibility of Antoinette Proveaux.

Circle—keep moving. Too bad about that dirk—must tie his garter tighter after this. How white the Ferguson's eyes looked.

On the other's features he saw little save a glimmer of teeth in the depths of a wild black beard. Why didn't he come on? Suddenly it came to Alistair that his kick must have hurt his enemy more than he had imagined. He sprang in and as the Ferguson's blade licked out to meet him, he spun sidewise. The point snarled through the fabric of his shirt, grazed his ribs.

At the same moment the loose footing betrayed him and he went down on one knee, his fingers writhing through the cold sand.

The bearded man emitted a whistling gasp of triumph and, turning, aimed a powerful thrust. Alistair shrank lower, then flung a handful of sand full into that contorted face above him. Coughing, the Ferguson threw his head back.

Alistair leaped up and slapped the dirk free. The other gave ground, panting curses, digging at his eyes with both hands. He cleared one eye in time to see Alistair snatch up the dirk.

For all his excitement, Alistair recalled Feyther's oft-repeated instructions and aimed his point not 'way over at his enemy's left side, but almost straight for the center of that leather shirt.

The dirk was almost jarred from his grasp, but suddenly it slipped on in almost without effort.

He felt his hand drenched with a sticky heat—and couldn't keep hold. Arching violently forward, the Ferguson began coughing hard, harder—a stain appeared, spread rapidly down his buckskin shirt. All at once the bearded man's knees yielded like a couple of well-oiled hinges as, fighting for breath, he toppled forward onto all fours.

He continued to cough. Hard, racking coughs. Breathless, Alistair watched the shaggy head droop, spatter the sand. He heard a sound like thick soup being poured onto a plate. The other stopped coughing and sank gently, almost gracefully, flat on the ground.

Eyes freed of sand at last, Alistair grimly watched the Ferguson's fingers cease twitching, saw his bare feet stop digging into the trampled sand.

From under the fallen clansman's body appeared a little rivulet. Quickly it filled a footprint, another.

Alistair's breath came less wildly. Aware that his hand and forearm were bloody, he knelt and, suppressing a little shiver, wiped them on the Ferguson's kilt. When carelessly he flung the hated tartan aside, he exposed lean, hairy thighs to the starlight.

He saw the dirk's brass tang winking a wicked golden eye and had to plant a foot on the dead man's breast before he could get it free. Down by the ford he scrubbed its dimmed blade.

So much for this one. But had he left kin, children up on the Yadkin? No peace for Alistair Bryson until he made sure. Five, ten years from now a rifle might crack from a thicket—as it had today from among the sandgrass.

Foolish, this feuding, wasteful too.

For all that, Feyther would be well pleased to see this dirk.

26

THE EBB TIDE

AT SUNDOWN there was no doubt that even so stubborn a fighter as Admiral Peter Parker had had enough. Officers, training spy-glasses on the *Bristol* and the *Experiment,* declared both liners to be barely afloat. Why, the flagship, alone, had suffered along her waterline nearly seventy hits. Had any kind of a sea been running, both liners would undoubtedly have filled and sunk.

Observers described dozens of little scarlet rivulets dripping from the shattered bulwarks and streaking the yellow stripes along the liner's side. Most of the *Experiment's* yards had fallen and her topmasts canted drunkenly, supporting a hurrah's nest of tangled rigging and sails. On the sea floated splintered sections of bulwark, spars, corpses and stove-in boats.

Thanks to an enforced deliberation, the gunners in Fort Sullivan had, all afternoon, fired each piece as if it were a rifle. It afforded the garrison a poignant object-lesson; they, and the rest of America, learned that a single shot, well aimed, did more damage than twenty hit-or-miss.

Nat determined to enter this discovery in his "Observations." Um. Had he not arrived previously at such a conclusion? When? At Breed's Hill, of course. There, also, the Provincials had sighted carefully and fired slowly. Maybe it was lucky that the Colonies were so dangerously destitute of powder?

At precisely nine o'clock Admiral Parker's ships sullenly fired their last shot and, by the dim and uncertain light of battle lanterns, prepared to return to their anchorage.

Standing on a merlon, Nat Coffin enjoyed the evening's cool and, with his foot, prodded a roundshot embedded in the woodwork. Below the gun platforms the infantry were commencing to light cook fires. Thoughts of Antoinette Proveaux returned.

Laus Deo! He had come through all this long battle without so much as a splinter scratch. A fig for future presentiments! Merely the nervous reaction of an imaginative mind. Tomorrow, he guessed Colonel Moultrie would grant him leave to go over to Charleston.

The Colonel was feeling all set up tonight. Chortling, he was offering drinks to any officer who wanted one.

Then Nat remembered that Antoinette had gone to join her mother. Maybe it was just as well. No use rushing matters. A talk with Roger should be helpful. Good steady lad, Roger. Steady in the pinches for all his Gallic sensibilities.

Now that the cannon were silent, Nat's ear drums throbbed amid the comparative stillness.

Of his morbid doubt that morning he felt ever so much ashamed. Imagine crediting anything so utterly illogical!

From the direction of the hospital tents came such terrifying screams he deduced another poor wretch was undergoing an amputation.

They got rough treatment in there. Four burly privates to hold you down, a leather gag was jammed into your mouth, then three slashes to the bone with cold steel—it was warmed if you were an officer—then the saw.

And still men went on fighting!

Roger Proveaux passed just below him. From where he sat, Nat could see that the Carolinian's shirt was a grimy mess of tatters and that his white nankeen breeches bore grim splashes. He'd see Roger at mess. Right now it was wonderfully quiet on the merlon.

Antoinette! Never had he felt so burning an impatience, so consuming a hunger for any girl. Could this craving for tenderness be born of the death all about? An urge to replace wasted lives?

Colonel Moultrie appeared limping along, dragging his gouty leg. Said he, "Well, now, Mr. Coffin, what do you think of the way us fellers can fight?"

"There can never be a more spirited defense fought by braver men, sir."

"Thank you. I was wondering what a Yankee might say." He winked. "You know you are right fortunate, Mr. Coffin?"

"And why, sir?"

" 'Tain't many of us are privileged to see *both* the British Army and Navy take a lacing. By God, didn't we surprise our seagoin' friends today? This should sting the King's Ministers worse than Breed's Hill."

The Colonel wore a bandage about his arm where a shell fragment had grazed him, so he carried his tunic draped over one shoulder. As he paused, watching the enemy, a clay pipe clamped between his powerful jaws, William Moultrie more resembled a merchant than a successful field officer.

"Yessir." The Colonel smiled, blowing a big cloud of smoke over the merlon. "I reckon plenty of people won't credit that we beat the tripes out of Peter Parker with twenty guns against two hundred and seventy."

Nat nodded respectfully but, as Colonel Moultrie limped away, he couldn't help wondering what might have happened had the *Syren, Sphynx* and *Acteon* not gone aground? Suppose Clinton had been able to get across? What would have followed had the King's principal officers not stooped to petty jealousies? Someone certainly had lied about the depth of that crossing from Long Island.

A cooling breeze stirred the Nantucketer's hair, strengthened his return to normal thinking.

It had grown so dark he could barely discern the receding outlines of the line-of-battleships. Off to starboard, he could hear oars threshing the water as the squadron's boats labored to pull the *Acteon* off Sumter Shoal.

Chide himself as he would, he was, nevertheless, mighty relieved to have come through this affair with a whole skin—more surprised than after Breed's Hill. Maybe in the other battles events had succeeded each other too quickly and he'd not been given time to get scared—on June seventeenth of last year there had been no tense, all-day existence in the shadow of death.

If they would submit to discipline, these Carolinians would make fine soldiers—Nat was sure of it. Hadn't the garrison been able to laugh even when they were sweating with fear? Hadn't they stayed when the powder ran low?

The receding tide was leaving a lot of half-naked bodies on the beach. They were corpses from the ships. Many of them lacked limbs, heads. Already dozens of great blue crabs were busy with them.

Everybody now was making much of Sergeant William Jasper—putting all kinds of heroic words into his mouth. Perhaps it was just as well that what he had really said, when he got back, wasn't repeated. He certainly had told the South Carolina men what he thought of them in a series of well-chosen four-letter words.

They were doing the same thing about Sergeant McDaniel. He hadn't gasped, "Fight on, my brave boys; don't let Liberty expire with me today,"—or anything else.

Suddenly he became aware of the smells of boiling ham and frying onions. A gnawing began in his stomach.

He guessed he'd go below and stop in at Roger Proveaux's tent for a swig of straight Barbados. He needed a drink, had earned it, maybe.

On nearing the steps down to the courtyard, he heard the Sergeant of the Guard barking:

"Fall in smartly. You fellers been sittin' 'round on your fat butts all day. Make sure your priming's right."

Half way down the ladder steps, Nat Coffin paused, aware of a magnificent greenish star glowing above the roofs of Charleston. It must be a planet. If he weren't so tired, he could recall its name. Jupiter? Saturn? Or was it Venus? No, Venus was blue—

From among the guard detail sounded a frightened curse. "Take your finger off that trigger, you fool! Don't you know—"

The musket exploded in Nat Coffin's face, and as he fell the greenish star paled, went out forever.

BOOK III

☆ ☆ ☆

LETTER-OF-MARQUE

PART I—SAINT-DOMINGUE

I

MADEMOISELLE DULAC

APPREHENSIVELY, the four body slaves of Mlle. Jeannette Marie Angélique Joséphine Dulac watched their mistress test the water with a rosy big toe. Her deep bath tub of black and yellow marble stood in magnificent isolation in the center of the room. Beneath yellow turbans soft brown eyes rolled anxiously and yellowish fingers closed nervously over full, lilac-tinted skirts.

Even Irène, *cocote* to Jeannette Dulac, held her breath. As yet, none might predict Mademoiselle's temper. Were this water but a shade too hot or a trifle too cold, an explosion would inevitably ensue. An audible sigh of relief arose when Mademoiselle settled her small pink figure in the tub and languidly lay back. Her head looked enormous in the bright green cloth with which Irène had secured hair of lustrous light brown.

This was better, thought Jeannette Dulac, lazily flexing her toes. June in Saint-Domingue was always intolerably hot and today she had slept badly. She wished breakfast did not come during the heat of the day. Suddenly, a frown disturbed the alignment of Jeannette Dulac's slender brows. "Coralie, come here!"

Lip caught between teeth, a mulatto maid fearfully approached the yellow marble tub.

"Hold out your hand, imbecile!"

The slave winced, stifled a little cry, when Mlle. Jeannette cracked her fingers with a long-handled bath brush. ⋅

"Yesterday, I distinctly told you that I required my bath violet-scented on Wednesday. This reeks of hyacinths!"

Irène, privileged as always, hurried forward. "But, darling girl, you forget. There can be no more violet until the ship from Bordeaux makes port. Not a drop of violet scent exists in all Cap François."

In the tub, Mlle. Jeannette's narrow shoulders rose. "Of course, how stupid of me to forget. Berthe, you may wash my feet now."

While Coralie, very glad to have gotten off so easily, covertly sucked swelling fingers, another slave girl soaped her mistress's arms. She was glad she didn't have to wait on that little she-devil, Mlle. Jeannette's fourteen-year-old sister Diane.

From down the hall rang Mlle. Diane's shrill curses. They made the whole wing resound.

"Worms! Sows! Black gutter bitches!" One could hear the agitation among her tiring women. "Are you trying to tear the hair out of my head?"

"One perceives, dear Irène, that my adorable little sister is today more charming than ever."

Mlle. Jeannette stood up, a slight, almost fragile figure equipped with long slim arms and legs. Like most French women of the day her hips were a trifle wide to have permitted truly classic proportions. Her bust, too, was somewhat fuller than one would have expected of her stature and build. Yet it was in her breasts that Jeannette Dulac found the most satisfaction. Ever so many people had maintained there was not a prettier bosom in all Cap François—not to mention Port-au-Prince, Fort Dauphin or Marmalade.

Once she had stepped out of the tub and had been gently dried, one of the smiling, barefooted maids released the loose turban securing her abundance of brown hair.

"My darling looks especially ravishing today," declared Irène, head tilted to one side and palms joined beside her cheek.

Irène should know, Jeannette thought. On the day of her birth, this pale mulattress had been bought for her. As *cocote,* Irène had, these eighteen years, been her closest companion, her inseparable playmate. Often the mulattress shared her bed, shared her food when she ate in her room. It was into Irène's ear that she poured her heartaches, her worries, her ambitions.

Few Créoles could boast so discreet, so well-informed, so pretty, so intelligent a *cocote* as Irène. That snip of a Mélanie Clement put on airs over her Virginie, but everybody in Cap François was aware that, for a few sous, Virginie would blab just what Mélanie had done after M. de Cockburn's fête—and with whom.

As for Marie Desdunes's Sophie! She had initiated and abetted her young mistress into the most depraved of pleasures. Of course, Jeannette didn't deceive herself into imagining that Irène was a beige-tinted angel. She had had her moments at the mulattoes' ball with a tall, ginger-colored lackey in the employ of M. de Vaivre, Intendant of the Colony. Mélanie Clement's *cocote* had told her all about it with such a wealth of detail that she couldn't have been lying.

When Jeannette Dulac cried, "Mirrors!" three maids scurried to bring hand mirrors of various sizes. The other stood ready to adjust a tall, movable pier glass.

Irène slipped onto Mlle. Dulac's feet dainty wooden sabots which, garnished with bows of enameled leather, set up a soft clicking on the red tile floor when she walked across to the mirror. The maids powdered her from chin to foot. The soft talc felt indescribably pleasant on her skin.

Suddenly Mlle. Jeannette wrinkled her nostrils. "One of you smells like a pig pen," she shouted. "It is you, Clio! Go, you wretched girl, tell the *huissier* to deal you a dozen with the strap. But wait." She checked herself, sighing. "No, Irène, I won't have Clio punished. I am too happy. I will not." She waved her hand at the cowering negress. "Go away, you offend me."

As the slave girl began slinking away, a scurry of bare feet sounded in the corridor. Through the door, left open for the sake of coolness, Jeannette saw one of her sister's body servants being dragged along with her blouse hanging in shreds from her shoulders.

Diane Dulac had wrapped her fingers in the luckless girl's hair and was belaboring her with the same kind of long-handled bath brush that Jeannette had been using. That she was completely nude seemed to be of no account.

"Sow! Stupid imbecile! I'll teach you to singe my hair!" Presently Diane gave the girl a kick, flung the bath brush after her and paused, panting at the door of the bathroom.

Perhaps half a head shorter than Jeannette, Diane was even more petite. Her glossy blue-black hair and lashes and her small red mouth held an irresistible attraction for most men.

"I don't see why Papa gives you every intelligent slave in this miserable place!" she snapped. "You must lend me Coralie. Not one of my creatures is fit to coiffe a mulatto."

"I will not," came Jeannette's prompt reply. "I will not have my servants scratched and bitten by you. Poor Léonie is still black and blue from last week."

Diane glowered, declared solemnly, "You always were a selfish pig and someday I'll make you pay for it. See if I don't." Angrily she turned and pattered back to her dressing room.

Jeannette realized her own maids were smiling. These creatures knew how well off they were. Marie Desdunes, whenever she got ill-tempered or bored, would make her maids strip and bend over to suffer a sometimes cruel beating.

A glance in the mirror confirmed Irène's opinion. Despite her poor sleeping, she was looking very well today. Seating herself, she allowed Coralie to slip white silk stockings onto her legs. Expertly, the maid smoothed them then gartered them with lengths of yellow ribbon.

"What shoes today?" Jeannette demanded of her *cocote*.

"The turquoise slippers, darling. Yes, decidedly, the turquoise slippers. He noticed them the other day."

A flush appeared at Jeannette's throat, crept up towards bright brown eyes that were set very far apart. *"Ma foi!* And how did you know M. Bennett was coming today?"

"Oh, a lovebird told me; or was it a cute little boy with wings?"

"Bah! Bird nothing! It is just backstairs gossip."

It was amazing how quickly Irène learned what was going on, not only in this house but in all the elegant quarter of Cap François. She even suspected that this narrow-faced quadroon understood the true state of the Colony better than the Governor-General and the Intendant combined.

Nude body more statuesque than ever under its coat of powder, Jeannette sat very still while Irène applied a faint blue shading above her eyes. Next, the mulattress put a tiny touch of vermilion at her eye corners, then brightened her lips so skillfully that few could have suspected an improvement on Nature.

"*Voilà*, my sweet little pigeon. This afternoon your American will open those fine eyes of his wider than ever."

In conclusion of this phase of the toilette the *cocote* passed the tip of a goose feather very lightly over a rouge pot. Delicately she brightened her mistress's small and well-proportioned nipples. Extra thin muslin blouses were all the mode today; why permit so vain a creature as Suzanne de Flaville to enjoy an unfair advantage?

In Jeannette Dulac's dressing room the air beating through her jalousies was nearly suffocating. Perspiration began to break through her powder as Irène laid out her usual costume—a single skirt, a belt and a muslin blouse. State occasions excepted, a Créole *à la mode* wore no underwear and affected none of the corsets and other paraphernalia with which the snobbish European women swathed themselves.

Poor creatures, they soon found they must adopt the Créole costume or suffer the tortures of the damned. It was quite a pleasure to watch haughty, France-born dames surrender piece after piece until they were as nearly naked as any native-born girl.

"You have chosen well," Jeannette told the *cocote*. The selection of her canary-yellow skirt and a nearly transparent blouse of turquoise muslin were a happy combination. The neck of the blouse was cut low enough to almost completely expose the *val* between her busts. If a careless motion exposed one or both of her breasts, she would think nothing of it. In Cap François one did not become aroused over such a costume. Custom and the climate had rendered it both modish and sensible.

"Now, my angel," she said to Irène, "shut the door and give me today's gossip." Dressed, Jeannette sauntered over to a chaise longue and settled her frail body upon it. She was feeling wider awake now, which was well.

At one o'clock breakfast would be served. Half an hour must pass before she could again see this gravely-handsome young New Englander who was doing such serious business with Uncle Claude Prenet.

Timothée—what an ugly name! Teem? No, the "i" was short. Tim. Had M. Bennett a great deal of money? She hoped so. It was high time she was married. Every last one of her convent friends either had children or had perished in bearing them. Why, Marguerite Flaville had a son of four, and she was just turned eighteen. Maybe it was the having to wait that rendered Diane so reckless, so cruel.

For reasons best known to himself, Papa had long ago sworn that neither of his daughters nor his sons should marry a native of Saint-Domingue. Above all, he wanted a title for his daughters. For his sons, a commission in the Garde du Corps.

Poor, poor Papa. This condemned drought had begun in September, 1775, last year; now it was June and not so much as a hatful of rain had fallen.

Abruptly she asked of Irène, "How go things?"

"From bad to worse, *ma mie.*" The *cocote* sighed. "On the estates of M. Desdunes over a hundred slaves are dead and more are dying of starvation. The sugar planters on the Cul de Sac can no longer bury their dead.

"The good God's heaviest curse on England! Why should they stop our American supplies? Why do these Americans not beat the British vessels of war aside? It is dreadful to see the poor blacks gnawing at the roots of plants, eating palm wood."

"Yes, I suppose so," Jeannette sighed. She sat up a little, raised her brows. "Enough of such gloomy business. How progresses the affair of Suzanne Flaville and the Chevalier de Maurepas?"

The *cocote's* eyes glistened. She came closer. "Oh, I have been bursting to tell you. But what they do is incredible. So stupid, so transparent. Yesterday they met at the house of her cousin. The Chevalier was in the summer house."

Irène giggled. "*Ma foi!* They made love in there for *two hours!* One would not have credited a gentleman of his age with such endurance. Phèdre, who was on guard, watched what went on. Oh, la! la! she was most intrigued."

Jeannette smiled a quiet, satisfied smile. Ever since Suzanne had kept the best coiffeur in town a prisoner in her house the night before the reception for the new Governor-General, she hadn't forgiven her. Imagine such selfishness! No one else could arrange a headdress with little ships sailing all over it.

At the ball for the Comte de Ennery, half the ladies of Cap François would cheerfully have tasted the blood of Suzanne Flaville. Preferably, they would have bathed in it.

When a trickle of perspiration began to creep down her neck, Jeannette clapped loudly and ordered Coralie to send a deaf-mute boy. Grinning and making gagging noises, an ugly little negro presently appeared. He took his post beside her chaise longue and set to work with a huge fan of woven fibers.

Though Sphynxe had cost all of two months' allowance, he was well worth the investment, Jeannette felt. In Cap François a lady of fashion was not wise to have about her too many ears that heard or too many tongues that could talk.

Once the boy had set a current of air moving about the head of her chaise longue, Jeannette Dulac beckoned closer her *cocote*.

"And now tell me about M. Bennett. What has he been doing? Whom does he see?"

"One hears that M. Flaville has at last paid M. Bennett for the little vessel he bought."

"You mean the *Hope?*"

"Yes, my sweetheart, all in Spanish gold, too."

"Enough of that," Jeannette cut in impatiently. She hesitated, looked at the floor. "Has he—does he often visit the Rue des Dames?"

The mulattress smiled, toyed with an acacia blossom. "For a wonder he does not. This strange individual is wholly intent on the outfitting of his vessel, save that—" Provokingly she left the sentence incomplete.

"Save what, you fool? Don't you dare to irritate me."

"—Save that he is interested, greatly interested, in *you,* my dearest little pigeon."

Jeannette sat up, wide-set eyes bright. "Oh, Irène, I hope so, I do hope so! M. Bennett is so *vif,* so energetic, so serious. This *sacré* climate has not yet boiled away the juices of his youth."

Jeannette thought back to the first time she had ever beheld Timothée Bennett. She had been to confession and was on her way home when she came upon Uncle Claude Prenet waving his arms and talking to a sunburnt young man. He had seemed not at all impressed by Uncle Claude's arguments that freight and assurance prices were soaring, that iron chain and manacles had risen a third in cost.

"A price is a price, Mounseer Prenet," the young American was saying, "and I happen to know that assurances haven't risen a speck. And another thing. I want my eighteen pounders ready on the first of June."

The American hadn't looked particularly fierce, he was even grinning as if he had caught Uncle Claude in a practical joke.

Of course, when she stopped, Uncle Claude had had to present the stranger. La! La! How the New Englander's nice gray eyes had widened when she curtseyed and her blouse had fluttered.

Because Uncle Claude told Papa the business would not suffer, M. Bennett had been bidden to dine and had made a vast impression on Papa.

M. Bennett was most amusing, too, when he had a third glass of champagne and forgot that he had responsibilities. He must have had tragedy in his life. Sometimes when he was talking to no one, it was to be read in his expression.

"You think of the young American," Irène announced in one of her uncanny prescient flashes. "You recall your promenade of last week. Tonight you will show him the purple and white passion flowers flowing over the garden wall."

Jeannette snatched up a book, threw it with all her force at the *cocote.* *"Tais-toi!"* It was inexpressibly annoying, frightening almost, to have one's mind read like this.

The deaf mute kept on fanning as if nothing had happened. Irène dodged, managed to smile.

"La, so you *are* in love at last."

Downstairs commenced sudden activity.

"Mercy, there is Papa! Quickly, Irène, quickly!" It surprised her that her heart should begin pounding so. "Powder, you stupid idiot, powder. M. Bennett is here! Quick, my jewels."

"Softly, softly," Irène urged. "First a yellow ribbon for your hair. Then, your gold and sapphire earbobs and the necklace to match. A blue and yellow flower at your breast, perhaps?"

"No, stupid! Papa would be furious. Am I to ape the prostitutes of the Place Clugny?" She recognized her father's deep voice and that of Uncle Claude, but not M. Bennett's.

Presently, she heard Papa's heavy tread climbing the stone stair-case. Then came a sound of running feet and Diane's ecstatic, "Oh dear, darling Papa, what a dreadfully hot day. I hope you are not all tired out. Let me bathe your eyes—"

"A migraine on Diane!" snapped Jeannette. "The brat is always cooing and gurgling over Papa; last week she wheedled ten livres out of him."

"Have patience, little dove," urged the *cocote*. "Monsieur begins to understand Mademoiselle."

"Now may the Seven Devils fly away with your solicitude," boomed Anatole Dulac. "Today I have not a louis to spare." The ponderous tread paused. "Another thing, Mademoiselle; greater dis-cretion becomes necessary on your part. Whispers have reached me. If I imagined there could be one shred of truth in certain rumors con-cerning you and a certain lackey—"

Dulac left the sentence unfinished, but his manner must have been forbidding because Diane ran, sobbing, back to her room.

As her father's vast bulk entered the door, Jeannette Dulac arose, made him a swift and very graceful curtsey. Poor Papa's white linen clothes were wringing wet with perspiration, and his utterly hairless head shone like an ivory ball. With an enormous handkerchief he was mopping the rolls of fat rippling down to his stomach. Neverthe-less, he smiled at his daughter and cast Irène a look which sent her curtseying and backing out of the dressing room.

With a grunt, he dropped into a chair so heavily that it creaked and crackled. His keen little blue eyes considered her with unwonted gravity. She could tell he was not angry, just thinking hard.

"My little cabbage," said he at last, "a word concerning this M. Bennett."

"Yes, Papa." Jeannette stood dutifully erect and kept her eyes on the floor.

"I note you find an interest in him?"

"He is not unattractive to me," Jeannette admitted with a caution born of long experience.

"That is well. I wish you to be pleasant to him. This American is a sound type, unexciting perhaps, yet his father made a fortune." Anatole Dulac sighed. *"Mon Dieu,* one could wish this Colony could boast young men of his cut. Bah! How many of your friends have a mind for more than taffia, écarté and mulattresses. You will cultivate him."

"Oh, ho!" thought Jeannette. "Timothée must be rich and Papa has just learned of it. This *sacré* drought must have cost Papa many thousands of livres."

The fat man sat gasping. Sweat, dripping from his enormous legs, made dark spots on the tile floor. Ceaselessly he kept mopping his rather flat head and bull neck. Quiet amusement entered his glance.

"You fancy he is rich, do you not? Well, you are wrong. He is not." Momentarily, his expression became strangely somber. Thoughtfully he glanced at bright sunlight beating on the jalousies. "If M. Bennett can settle a reasonable sum on you, I—well, you could do worse, my little cabbage. Much worse."

Jeannette could not have been more completely thunderstruck. What had come over Papa? Perhaps he had taken a fever? But his little China-blue eyes looked clear, even though they were, as always, a trifle yellowish.

2

CAP FRANÇOIS

SOMETHING wholly unforeseen must have occurred, Timothy Bennett concluded, else why should Messrs. Prenet and Dulac have sent for him posthaste and in the middle of a June day. What the devil could be wrong now?

Irritably, he ran over a string of possibilities. So many obstacles had arisen it was a shining wonder that any more remained.

On deck he flinched at a withering heat which was melting the tar between the deck planks. Like red-hot arrows, heat waves penetrated his white duck coat and trousers.

He wished to God he had had sense enough to follow the sloppy Créole custom of discarding a cravat and leaving his shirt open clear down to his belt. But somehow he couldn't. It would set a bad example for the men.

While waiting for his boat's crew to pull up under a ladder slung over the *Narragansett's* waist, Tim studied the shore line. Whoever had laid out Cap François had been a prime fool.

This thriving port of nearly thirty thousand souls—black, brown and white—lay jammed tight against the base of a semi-circle of high, rugged hills which effectively cut off all the prevailing southerly breezes. Red roofs, gold-tipped Cathedral towers, white walls, brown walls, blue walls and gray-white fortifications, all shimmered dizzily under the noonday sun.

Thanks to an unprecedented drought, luxuriant foliage which normally would have showed emerald and sapphire tints had been dried to a pale brown. A shimmering blue haze obscured landmarks further inland than the barracks on the extreme side of town. Crimanently! The towers of the Church of Notre Dame wavered as if an earthquake were in progress.

Dripping from the water that a cabin boy had just poured over him, Captain Freebody emerged from under a spare sail slung over the main boom.

"Mr. Bennett," said he, "it's mighty important you get honored our permit to arm. Two more men are down with sunstroke, and three died last week, ye'll recall." His thin ribs were working like bellows. "Half the time I feel giddy as a goat myself."

"I'll do all I can, Freebody," Tim assured him. "You can count on it. Keep the decks wet and the crew under the awnings 'til four o'clock. We mustn't lose any more men from home."

How to round out the crew was growing to be a serious problem now that more and more would-be privateers were dropping anchors in Saint-Domingue. Most of these late-comers could, and would, pay fancier wages than Bennett & Son. With a stubborn affection, Tim had clung to the name.

Freebody said, "Soon's the sun lowers I'll go ashore. See if I can't pick up a few hands." He jerked his head at a massive ship-of-the-line which had made port the night before. "She may have brought some new blood."

La Dédaigneuse was of the first rating and therefore huge. Mounting a hundred guns, her crew would number around nine hundred and fifty men. She lay off a battery at the near end of the harbor, her enormous gold and white ensign barely astir. When it came to gilding and scroll-work, the great vessel certainly was a creation of rare beauty.

It was infinitely discouraging to view the *Narragansett's* completed gunports, the ammunition racks all ready to receive round-shot. Frames built along the bulwarks and at the base of the main mast to receive small arms also were complete—and empty.

Not a quarter of a mile distant lay the brig's war-like stores. How long would cannon, pikes, cutlasses, boarding pistols, muskets and varying kinds of shot remain idle in the warehouses of Messrs. Pliarne, Prenet et Cie?

Most of all, Tim yearned to see mounted the *Narragansett's* four 9-pound and four 18-pound cannon. They were beautiful, brand-new pieces, much superior to any a late-comer might hope to purchase.

How utterly exasperating it was to meet with still another complication.

He had been smart about getting in on the ground floor—maybe too smart. It was he who must first learn the ways of French officialdom, who had to overcome initial objections, had to bluster here and bribe there.

Since the middle of May, he, Prenet and Dulac—the Norman's silent partner—had waged a continuous struggle with an incredible array of functionaries. By comparison with the intricate structure evolved by Louis XVI's Minister of Marine, British Colonial governments were dead simple.

"Boat ready, sir." Below, the coxswain touched his straw hat.

Tim seated himself in the gig's stern sheets but bounced right up. The wooden seat was so unbearably hot that he remained standing while four seamen pulled slowly through a colorful tangle of shipping.

Certainly the harbor Cap François could never have seen busier times. Besides the great *Dédaigneuse,* a pair of frigates, the *Cerf* and the *Surveillant,* a Spanish man-of-war and a Dutch sloop swung to their anchors. Of course, there was a great swarm of French merchantmen, slavers and vessels plying the inter-island trade.

No less than six would-be American privateers lay in the roadstead waiting to take on their armaments. He recognized two of these. Nicholas Brown's fast-looking *Industry* and Abed Thaxter's big, ship-rigged *Retaliation.* The other vessels hailed from Connecticut, Massachusetts and New Hampshire.

Tim suffered a twinge on passing the *Hope.* There she lay to M. Flaville's wharf and flying a French flag. To part with one of Pa's vessels had come hard, but he'd had no choice in the matter if he wanted properly to convert and to pay for the *Narragansett.* He had done this with a minute thoroughness. Even Loammi Freebody admitted that the brig's transformation had been carried out with a careful economy worthy of Asa Bennett himself.

The *Narragansett's* decks had been so stoutly reinforced that no one need worry whether her larger cannon—weighing twenty-three hundred pounds each—would go crashing through into the hold some stormy day.

Sails and rigging had been scrupulously overhauled and all the yards severely tested. If ever his brig need run for her life, Tim intended to feel no fear over the soundness of the *Narragansett's* top-hamper.

The overhaul, of course, had proved expensive far beyond any calculation. For instance, the brig had required careening to remove the rich variety of marine life with which the tropics had decked her bottom.

Another expensive item had been the construction of quarters to accommodate an enlarged crew. From a normal complement of around twenty hands, the *Narragansett* would now go to sea carrying nearly one hundred officers and men. One had to figure on at least three prize crews.

So it had been good-bye to the *Hope*. That night he and Pa and Desire Harmony had watched the little brig lose herself amid the darkness of the West Passage was part of another existence.

What could have happened to Desire Harmony? In his most recent letter, Captain John Lawton declared that no trace of his sister had been uncovered despite diligent searching. Of Lucy Percival, Lawton merely stated that she was well and occupying herself with the relief of poor and distressed persons in the town.

The privateer and letter-of-marque's commissions, the innkeeper wrote, should long since have been ready. Everybody was furious over the delay. Privately, Tim wondered whether the Congress had not reverted to its original stand against privateering. Was the pro-Navy party forcing an indefinite delay? Suppose no privateers or letters-of-marque were ever to be granted?

The instant the letter-of-marque's gig drew in beside the foot of a flight of slippery, greasy-looking steps at the end of the Rue Saint Jean, a noisy swarm of hawkers, pimps, beggars and urchins came charging down.

After his first day ashore in Saint-Domingue, Tim had adopted the use of a native implement, a coco-macaque, which was a species of heavy cane. Flourishing the stick about his head, the Rhode Islander drove before him a dreadfully eager and persistent throng of ragged blacks and mulattoes. He didn't like the looks of these negroes. They didn't in the least resemble the comparatively easy-going and good-natured blacks he had met in the Bahamas.

Before they would grant him a passage, he had to hit quite a few of them. These screamed, shook their fists at him and hung back scowling.

When first he had landed at Cap François he had been amazed to find so many cripples, so many mutilated persons in any one place. Why, it seemed as if every fifth black, or part-black, lacked a finger, a hand, a foot or an ear.

He soon learned that legal mutilation punished even the most trivial offenses, that death was the penalty for well over two hundred crimes. Practically every negro displayed one or two brand marks on back, shoulder or face.

His progress was almost checked and things were growing uncomfortable when two privates of the *maréchaussée,* or horse police, rode up and began indiscriminately to use riding crops on the crowd. The two *maréchaussées,* both mulattoes, spurred their stallions back and forth over the quay. Slashing and cutting at the hawkers, they exhibited no more emotion than a grocer killing flies in his shop.

Cursing, screaming, the ragged throng ran off, took shelter outside the stone balusters of the water steps, or sought refuge among the guns of a battery covering the waterfront. Howling, four or five mendicants staggered off nursing dripping heads.

Already drenched by torrents of acid perspiration, Tim turned right, heading towards the arsenal and the Parc d'Artillerie.

For several reasons Anatole Dulac had built his mansion on the Rue Picolet at the extreme right of the town. It was well away from the noise, smells and bad water at the center of Cap François. For all his casual, slack appearance M. Dulac was long on foresight, very like M. Prenet in this respect.

Um. Why had the Dulac residence been built with such an obvious eye to defense? Most of the many luxurious homes in the capital had not been.

"Allo! John-ee!" "Hey, you come wiz me, John-e-e?" "Ver' cheap, ver' washed, almost white. Onlee two louis!"

From under an arcade a bevy of mulatto prostitutes bore down on him, leering, giggling, swinging their hips.

"*Non, non!*" Desperately Tim exercised his pitiable knowledge of French. Some of these trollops were not unattractive, and a good many were dressed with an astonishing degree of taste and elegance.

To begin with, Tim had deemed the jewels flashing in their turbans and on their arms to be false. But such was not the case. Prenet and his associates swore that most of the stones were real!

Nearly all of these females wore turbans of a peculiar shape. They fitted tight about the wearer's forehead, then, rising to a height of six or eight inches, suddenly belled out with a top-heavy effect. Invariably such headdresses were of brilliant colors and made of batiste, madras or calico.

Many of these seemingly numberless street walkers swung elaborate purses, or poised parasols edged with dingy lace. Even when they talked they never removed the little sticks of sweet wood which they forever carried in their mouths.

"*Va-t'en!*" Tim kept crying. "Go away, you blasted baggages. Leave me be!"

From previous experience a few of them recognized him as a hopeless prospect and turned aside with a shrug and a smile. But others kept trying to take his arm until at last his temper gave way and he slapped a couple.

It made him shiver to hear their pathetic squeaks. Imagine Tim Bennett striking a woman! A far cry from Conanicut, all this.

At length even the most persistent gave up, left him free to hurry along in the scorching shade of a double row of royal palms lining the Cour le Brasseur.

Beyond the Parc d'Artillerie the streets were utterly deserted save for the buzzards and curs disputing choice items of garbage with a pack of hideous, starved-looking beggars.

There was, he decided, but one redeeming feature to this wretched excursion. He might get another glimpse of Mistress Jeannette Dulac. He couldn't explain to himself why he had been so thoroughly fascinated by her. Maybe it was because this dainty Créole held for him the very essence of mystery. She was so completely dissimilar to any girl he had ever met. Every word, thought and deed presented a continual, and usually pleasing, surprise.

The time he had first met Dulac's daughter there on the street, he had felt nearly-forgotten flames begin to rise. Never had Lucy kindled so consuming an emotion.

Jeannette Dulac certainly was fashioned along lines calculated to heat a man's vitals. Those wide-set, sloe-lidded eyes, that tapering neck, those fragile shoulders and softly-rounded breasts set the blood surging to his temples every time he saw her.

He wouldn't have believed that feet could be so narrow and long, that fingers could be so infinitely graceful. Why, Jeannette Dulac could do things with her fan that held him, fascinated, for minutes on end; her manipulations were as graceful as the idle wheeling of a seagull.

Then, too, she favored a perfume which made Lucy Percival's scent seem as crude as hers had made Joe Child's French cologne.

At night when Anatole Dulac's daughter wore diamonds in her ears and a great glittering necklace of the same stones, she presented a picture to be remembered. She was clever, too, in her small talk; could reel off whole scenes from the plays of Racine, Molière and Corneille.

Nor was Jeannette in the least ignorant concerning politics, or her father's business affairs. It appeared that she kept his letter book in order.

Lord, wouldn't a girl like her dazzle the folks around Newport? The Percivals would turn green in envy if he were to bring her home.

Suppose he did well in privateering? Why not construct on Spring Street a copy of one of these handsome houses built in the architecture of Versailles?

As he stalked along feeling the heat eat through the soles of his shoes, an idea took form, grew. Down here he was learning a lot. Take what John Petty had said, for instance. Because a thing was beautiful didn't necessarily mean it must be wicked.

Come to think of it, Jeannette's eagerness to please approached that of Adelina. There Petty had been wrong. A white man shouldn't marry color. Nor was there any necessity of his doing so—not when there were submissive, intelligent girls like Jeannette Dulac in the world. Yes, sir, the way these French women got busy when the head of the house so much as raised an eyebrow was something to admire.

Before he knew it, Tim was ringing the bell-pull before an elaborate iron grille guarding the entrance to M. Dulac's handsome stone residence. In America such a mansion would have constituted a sure-enough show place, yet such was the incredible wealth of this Colony that this structure's elegance was only average.

An old, barefooted porter in a seersucker uniform ran out the instant the bell clanged and, bowing very low, conducted the caller into the shade of an awning. This, descending from the house itself, sheltered a visitor from gateway to front door.

If the butler on duty was inclined to be slack, Tim guessed it was because, unlike a French shipowner, he refused to bother with an escort of half a dozen sailors.

He was invited to wait in a stuffy little antechamber. At first he had resented such a delay but soon he had learned that it was only a part of a long-established routine. Nobody, who was anybody, would dream of receiving a visitor in under twenty minutes.

Crimanently! but he was glad of a chance to cool off. An awning outside cut off the sunlight, and a tiny fountain playing musically in the center of the waiting room at least suggested coolness.

Not very far away he could hear some colored girl singing in the local dialect:

> "Si to rencontre la belle
> To va fair zie doux ba li.
> Pis to trouve li si belle,
> Hé! bin, to n'a qu'a prend li.

> Taille à li semble gaulette,
> Visage li semble moineau.
> Avio pendant d'oreilles d'o . . ."

Just as the song ended a small object fluttered in through the door
and shod feet raced lightly away. By means of a ribbon, a card had
been attached to a tiny nosegay of orange blossoms.

Picking it up he read:

Brave Américain:
    For your happiness, it is imperative that you come to the shop of
Caumartin, the chocolate maker, at seven tonight.   D.

"D?" Who? Oh! That must be Diane, Jeannette's pretty young
sister. What could she be wanting with him? He was still puzzling
when a shiny black lackey announced that M. Prenet and M. Dulac
requested the pleasure of his attendance in the library.

3

THE BRIBE

UNDOUBTEDLY the arrival of more, and still more, American vessels
was pleasing to Claude Prenet. It showed that his hard work in
Philadelphia and Newport, that François Pliarne's efforts in Massachusetts, had not gone for nothing. The Norman's blue eyes were
sparkling, and he waved his wine glass with energy when a shoeless
black lackey flung back a pair of folding doors and announced, "M.
Bennett!"

Both M. Prenet and M. Dulac arose and bowed with decorum.
Through a humid semi-darkness, Dulac's enormous frame waddled
forward.

"Welcome, Monsieur," he boomed in good, but heavily-accented,
English. "One laments the necessity of bringing you ashore at such
a barbaric hour, but," he shrugged, "it becomes necessary for the
three of us to take immediate action. It is heard that the King's Lieu-

tenant, the Chevalier de Labouisse, is, in three days, leaving for Cap Jacmel."

"And the cause?" Tim inquired anxiously.

A slave in a yellow uniform brought in tall glasses of cool claret punch. All three men drank eagerly. Tim deemed this a more sensible concoction for these latitudes than the fiery stingarees and bombos popular in New Providence.

"But, what has the King's Lieutenant—?" Tim began.

"My friend and brother-in-law anticipates," Prenet put in.

"Your pardon, M. Bennett, I was merely attempting to cover the ground quickly." Dulac indicated a wide settee of superbly woven rattan. "Breakfast will soon be served. Pray render yourself comfortable."

It must have been easily fifteen degrees cooler here than on the street. Tim seated himself and, sighing, unbuttoned his white linen coat. Even this library office was typical of the country. Its latticed but unglazed windows were enormous, and in various pots and jars grew a profusion of tropical flowers. These, arranged against walls of pale blue, created bright splashes of color among the business-like furniture.

"In brief—" Prenet began, then gave Tim a wry smile, "—in North America, one learns to be brief—we enter a very dangerous, one might say, phase in our negotiations with the M. de Ennery, His Majesty's Governor-General.

"If the Chevalier de Labouisse, who is a member of the Superior Council here, cannot be won over, we shall not receive permission to export munitions." He spread his hands, said grimly, "I must confess that M. Achard de Bonvouloir, our agent in Paris, misled my partner and me on this point. We understood that this permission had already been granted."

A cold sensation filled Tim's being. No permission! Great God! He *had* to have his cannons, his munitions.

M. Prenet spoke slowly, methodically joined fingertip after fingertip under his chin. "Failure to receive the necessary *permis* of course means the ruin of us all."

For all the Norman's thinness, he, too, must be feeling the terrible heat. His opened shirt was dark with perspiration and great clear drops stood out on the bony frame of his chest.

Dulac gulped a tall glass of punch, solemnly wiped his lips on a blue bandanna. "Matters stand thus," he explained. "We have reason to believe that the King's Lieutenant is open to—er—persuasion. All of the Intendant's party are with us."

"Just what is this Intendant?" Tim wanted to know.

"It is the policy of our amiable government to set over each Colony two men of a nearly equal position. To repose too much responsibility and power in one pair of hands is often to invite trouble, no? As it is, M. le Gouverneur-Générale administers the courts, the naval depots, the military and the police; M. l'Intendant, all matters of finance, commerce and the customs service.

"Now on the Superior Council, we lack one vote of a majority. M. de Vaivre, the Intendant, favors close relations with your revolted colonies. M. le Gouverneur does not. *Voilà tout.*"

"I see." Tim nodded. "And this man, de Labouisse, represents the deciding vote?"

"Precisely so," the Frenchmen said together.

"What is he like?"

"Hector de Labouisse leads a life far from the exemplary, but that is of no concern to you. His good-will is invaluable, essential."

"Well, what do you want me to do? Where's the hitch?"

"M. le Gouverneur fears we may attempt to corrupt his lieutenant." Dulac smiled. "Which would be indeed gilding the lily!"

"Oh, Lord," Tim groaned, "another bribe! I thought we'd bought everybody from the Intendant's groom to the Attorney-General. You fellows will have to find the money. When I sail, I'll have just one week's pay aboard."

Prenet said smoothly, "There is no call to disquiet yourself, my friend. The bribe money has already been found. There are diplomatic reasons why *you* must present it. One does not anticipate the least difficulty," he added hurriedly.

"Now there remains one other matter which only you can arrange.

You must promise M. de Labouisse that you will direct not less than two prizes, taken by you, into Savannah in the Colony of Georgia."

"Savannah?" Tim started to object at this dictation but recalled Pa's advice about holding his tongue.

"You have good reason to wonder. Briefly, the worthy Chevalier has friends in Savannah who would like to buy fast English vessels." M. Prenet irritably blotted still another row of drops from his brows. "They fear to make purchases further north because there the British blockade is very strong."

Dulac leaned forward eagerly, more strongly than ever lending the impression of a great egg which, mysteriously, had grown a head.

"*Mon cher* Bennett, de Labouisse or no de Labouisse, you would not be ill-advised to send your prizes alternately into Northern and Southern ports." He winked ponderously. "Prizes sold in the North will gain you more money, but what business you do in the South will bring you more certain returns."

Tim deliberated just long enough to make the others think he wasn't giving in too quickly.

"All right," he said. "When shall I go see the King's Lieutenant?"

"You must make the journey to Les Délices tomorrow," Prenet announced. "Limonade is not far and we shall arrange that you depart in a style suitable to the gravity of your errand."

Fat cheeks wabbling, Anatole Dulac got up and crossed the room to stand sipping water from a porous stone jar.

"A word of caution, *mon ami.* New England prejudices are best left behind. It is wise to remind yourself that we in Saint-Domingue exist as a tiny white island in a black and savage ocean."

Jeannette's father fetched a deep sigh. "Once you see plantation life on the Plain du Nord, you will not conceive a pretty opinion of us Créoles."

Prenet came over too. "Never forget that without this *permis* you are even more hopelessly ruined than we. It is necessary, therefore, for you to favor his every whim."

"You'll have no call to fret on that score," the Rhode Islander assured them grimly.

What lay back of these elaborate warnings? Some of the new hands mentioned bestial, incredible happenings on estates lying back from the sea, but nobody had credited them.

"What about clothes?" Tim demanded. "I only have the rough things I brought down from the North."

"Leave that to me and to Jeannette," Dulac reassured. "She will see that you will command the admiration of Hector de Labouisse."

A lackey knocked, announced breakfast. Familiar by now with the amazing formality attending even the simplest of meals, Tim writhed inwardly. When the dining room's mahogany double doors were thrown back, Tim counted no less than eight barefooted footmen at the far end of the room solemnly ranged in a double rank.

To observe etiquette, no less than three servants handled each dish, even though it contained nothing more important than a mango or a slice of the infamously tough beef native to the island.

Approaching his place, Tim stole a quick look at Jeannette and felt much of his weariness evaporate at the warm smile she flashed in return. Crimanently! Dulac's elder daughter looked lovely today. Her gold and turquoise jewelry was infinitely fetching.

Jeannette's initial elation was spoiled when she noticed the shameless ogling, even sheep's-eyes, Diane was casting in the visitor's direction.

La! She was out-doing the girls of the Place de Clugny and had dressed herself in a flame-colored skirt and a white blouse which made a spider's web look thick by comparison.

Someday, Jeannette foresaw, she and her dear little sister would have serious trouble.

By half-past six of the afternoon Tim had settled with M. Dulac and Claude Prenet what he hoped would prove the final details.

Once a *permis* was secured, the *Narragansett* would be laid alongside M. Dulac's wharf. His was one of the few private yards equipped with a crane powerful enough to handle heavy cannon. It was no coincidence that Dulac's wharf adjoined the busy warehouses of Messrs. Pliarne, Prenet et Cie.

594 STARS ON THE SEA

As he set off down the Rue Picolet, Tim realized that the atmosphere had grown perceptibly cooler. At this less brazen hour the harbor fairly swarmed with activity. Bumboats sailed about hawking turtles, fruits, basket-work, Congo work, pets, rum and a hundred other commodities.

Detachments of the French King's troops in uniforms of white turned back in green, were strolling the streets arm in arm with marines and bandy-legged Breton sailors.

Everywhere Tim met black women swaying along under great baskets of fruit and other supplies. Stark naked negro children played cruel games in the gutters and peddlers yelled incessantly.

Now what the devil could Diane be wanting of him? From the little he had seen of her, she appeared to be a strange creature. For all she was only fourteen, she acted as if she had already lived several lifetimes on earth. There was no denying that she was attractive. Her eyes were simply huge and her mouth, had it not been so small, a thing of rare beauty. More than once he had found her smiling at him from under heavy-looking eyelids.

She seemed always to resent the fact that she had been off on a visit when first he had visited the Dulacs. So she wanted a rendezvous— about something concerning his happiness? It might prove amusing to learn what was on her mind. Probably some tattle-tale about Jeannette. That Diane was fearfully jealous of her elder sister, anybody could tell with half an eye.

To be polite he would hear her out, then buy her a box of bon-bons and ship her home in short order.

Meanwhile he had just time for an interview with the man he intended to ship as surgeon. In fact, it was the man he had to ship, or put to sea without a medico. These other privateers had snapped up every available surgeon.

Yes, even a drunken Irish surgeon would be better than no doctor at all.

Why should a man of Alexander Boyd's obvious intelligence elect to drink himself into the grave? Yet that seemed to be his end and aim in life. He found the surgeon just about where he had expected—

in the courtyard of a third-rate tavern kept by a free mulatto.

Fortunately, Dr. Boyd had not yet become too drunk to talk intelligently.

"I've been mullin' over what yez said the other night, Mr. Bennett. Maybe you're right. Maybe I am a loony to ruin me health over a sad matter that is finished and done with." He cocked a blood-shot eye at Tim. "Ye'll never guess my main reason for signing on?"

"I only know, Doctor, that I'm glad you intend to."

The drunkard waved a loose hand, indicated a seat. "It's because ye've niver inquired why I'm here rotting me gut with cheap rum."

"To tell you the truth, I'd never believe you capable of committing a particularly dreadful offense."

Dr. Boyd stared, his bruised-looking jaw sagging. "And wouldn't ye now? I wish there had been more o' the jury who'd agreed with you," the Irishman said. "Tell you all about it someday. When do you plan on sailing?"

"Next week," Tim said firmly, though he hadn't the vaguest notion as to when the Narragansett's commission would turn up.

"In that case, d'you think I'd best begin sobering up?" Dr. Boyd held up a short-fingered hand. Its fingers quivered and jerked spasmodically. "How'd you like to have a paw like that cut you open?"

Tim lost his easy manner. "Not much. By the bye, I'm giving you fair warning. There's to be no drinking while the brig's at sea."

"What! No drinking?"

"No drinking," Tim repeated. "Before you pull up sticks here you had better come aboard and read the Articles we sail under."

The Irishman rubbed his chin. Because he hadn't shaved in three days, he made a slight scraping noise.

"Ye'll have a medicine chest aboard, Mr. Bennett?"

"Of course; that's the owner's responsibility. But you'll be required to bring your own instruments."

"Me own instruments!" The drunkard threw back his shaggy black head and laughed harshly. "Man dear, the lot o' them went for rum a year ago."

Another unforeseen expense. Tim drew a deep breath. "Well, as soon as you have signed the Articles, I'll advance you the price of a set. However, a ship's doctor is supposed to furnish his own instruments."

"Sure and I know that. A drink?"

A burst of laughter from the tavern attracted his attention to a group of mulattoes. Both men and women were unusually handsome and wore their clothes with better taste than many a white.

Why were the mulattoes of Saint-Domingue so badly treated? Some of them were fabulously rich, having inherited from white fathers who had themselves provided no legitimate heirs.

The life of an *affranchi* must be hell, Tim judged. The law barred mulattoes from the practice of any profession. Neither could they hold any official position, civil or military. Their personal rights were practically non-existent—legally, they were only a step above the black slaves.

Hated by the blacks and despised by the whites, the "gentlemen of color," as they called themselves, gathered on their splendid estates and muttered.

"What do you make of them, Doctor?"

"They suffer, poor devils," grunted Dr. Boyd. "Did yez know a lot o' them had been educated in France?"

He lolled forward on his bench. "Tell yez something else, Mr. Bennett. If I owned so much as a square foot o' Saint-Domingue, I'd sell it. It'd be like owning a square foot o' the lid o' hell."

Boyd drained a terrific gulp of rum and water. "Now 'tis a strange thing I've noticed here. Yer white man changes fast in these parts. I've watched 'em, these very government employees who flatter themselves they're shaping the blacks to suit their pattern. Mr. Bennett," said he hoarsely, " 'tis more often the other way around!"

"Surely, you exaggerate."

"I do not! Look at yer average Créolian. He's just like a blacka-moor. He's vain, he's arrogant, he's cruel, he's vicious. Only differ-ence betwixt him and his slave is that the white can look forward and so save against the rainy day. Och! 'Tis a rare philosopher has been lost in Alec Boyd!"

"You'll come out to the *Narragansett* then, early day after tomorrow?"

"Aye, Mr. Bennett, ye may depend upon it. And now get along, Mr. Bennett, so's I can settle down to steady drinking. If I'm to bid dear old Bacchus a long farewell, I prefer to do it in style."

Tim found the shop of Caumartin, the chocolate maker, all but deserted. The proprietor proved to be a free negro with an engaging smile and alert eyes.

"Mlle. Dulac? But yes, certainly, Monsieur," the negro gurgled. "Mademoiselle has instructed your miserable servant to conduct Monsieur to her immediately."

Tim was surprised and a little amused, but he followed the pitiably obsequious proprietor through the shop and into a small garden enclosed by high walls crowned with broken glass. At the far end of the garden the white dome of a small pergola showed above a dense draping of vines.

Now that the sun was below the high hills, the town was growing cool, the first sheen of dew was forming on the leaves.

Caumartin halted, bowed deep in the direction of the pergola. "Monsieur will find Mademoiselle in there."

Tim was abruptly reminded of some of Desire Harmony's giddy notions. His sister was always pretending to be this famous historical personage or that. Well, out of consideration for Jeannette, he would humor Diane, find out what was on her mind. Followed by fragrant odors of chocolate and vanilla, he set straight his cravat and strode up to the pergola.

It was much darker inside, but he could see a grass rug, a settee and a couple of wicker chairs.

"Ah, *mon héro!*" Two arms went about Tim's neck and warm, fragrant lips became glued to his. He was much too taken aback to move. The girl clung to him, her hands busy in his hair.

"I knew you would not disappoint poor Diane. Of course, Jeannette lied. It has been *me* you have sighed for all this time!"

God above! The child wore next to nothing above her waist. Quiv-

ering like a strained hawser, she pressed herself against his chest.
An infinitely provocative perfume eddied about his head.

"Ah, Teem, I love you so dearly," she whispered. "I *must* have
you. I will have you! My whole body craves your caress."

"But—but, Mistress Diane," he blurted, "I— My stars and crown,
I don't want to marry!"

"Marry? Bah! Who said anything about it?" Her tiny hands fon-
dled his ears, stroked his hair. *Dieu,* but he was firm and smelled of
the sea, not of some coiffeur's lotion.

What a conquest! A tame American all her own. Oh, la! la! She
would set a new fashion. He was even more desirable than that young
English milor' who had come to the British Consulate.

"Sit on the settee," she pleaded in low, tremulous tones. "Swear
to me that Jeannette has lied, that you never asked her to marry you!"

Tim floundered. Crimanently! Could Jeannette have said such a
thing? Futilely, he attempted to disengage this figure clinging so
passionately to him. Good Lord! Diane's clothes were so scanty it was
just as if she wore nothing at all.

That her perfume was beginning to take effect he realized. Why
wasn't he trying to push her away any more? Her lips were avid—
kissing his eyes, his chin, his throat—her fingers kept kneading at the
small of his back.

"But Diane," he gasped. "This can't— You're too young. You're
only a child!"

"A child?" she murmured, her small nose nuzzling under his chin.
"Bon Dieu! I knew my first lover at twelve and since then—I have
had others—many of them."

To the ultimate depths of his being, Tim was horrified. How could
any girl talk like this? Worst of all was the realization that she
probably wasn't lying. How truly Adelina had spoken.

Diane's waist had slipped down from narrow shoulders; in this
half-light she seemed all at once not so child-like.

"Why do you lie to me, Diane?" He felt his voice thicken. "You
must be more than fourteen. Tell me so—I—I—need to think—"

For the first time in many months the barriers of his self-restraint began to crack.

Diane's softness surged against his chest, her lips became voraciously tender.

"Entertain no fears, *mon amant,*" she breathed, "I will give you no heirs. My *cocote* knows ways."

Tim was unspeakably repelled. "Don't say such awful things."

"One must remain practical," her voice came to him through the twilight, "even during *une affaire.*"

She stood an arm's length away, great eyes burning, blouse slipped nearly to her hips.

"Teem! *mon adoré.*"

He couldn't hold back any longer; Nature was too strong. He had started to catch her to him when Diane was knocked reeling to one side. A squalling fury pounced on her.

"Miserable imp from hell! Child of the Devil! How dare you! How dare you interfere in my affairs?" Jeannette Dulac was not acting; she was fairly sobbing with outrage. "Why must you try to spoil my friendships? Is it not enough that you sleep with every pair of breeches that arouses your fancy?"

Jeannette had pinioned her sister by the hair and, holding her down on the settee, dealt her a series of stinging slaps.

Kicking, panting and weeping, Diane fought back. "Let me go, you fiend! Let me go, you miserable icicle!"

As they struggled about on the settee, legs waving on high, Tim started to intervene but another of Pa's adages restrained him. He could almost hear the old man saying, "A man gets slim thanks for interfering in another's family affairs."

Because she was heavier, Jeannette succeeded in throwing her slighter sister down. Instantly she pulled up Diane's skirts and began to spank her with a slipper wrenched from her own foot.

Every time the leather struck her bare flesh, Diane wriggled, emitted a furious wail.

Diane soon got free and darted across the pergola, hissing like a scalded cat as she rubbed her martyred buttocks.

"I'll kill you for this! I'll poison you!"

Tim thought she sounded as if she meant it.

"You will not! You are too stupid," Jeannette panted, pushing hair from her eyes. "Else how would I know you were here? Oh, you silly, shameless little baggage. The next time you attempt to interfere with my affairs, I'll scratch your cheeks to ribbons. Now get out!"

"We shall see." Diane gave her sister a look dripping with venom, then managed a tearful smile at Tim as she hurried by.

Once the gate at the far end of the garden had slammed shut, Jeannette ran to Tim, bursting into a wild flood of tears.

"Oh, Teem, Teem, what can you think of us here in Saint-Domingue?"

He led the weeping girl to a chair and, kneeling beside her, tried to restrain the spasmodic heaving of her shoulders.

"Please—please don't, Jeannette," he pleaded. "It makes me feel so wretched. I think I understand—"

Her sobs diminished, but she clung to him tighter than ever. "Oh, Teem, please take me from this dreadful island. Save me! Take me away before I become like Diane—and all the rest."

4

LES DÉLICES

THE smoothness and perfection of the roads in this Colony were to Tim Bennett never-ending sources of astonishment. Their condition was due, he discovered, to the ancient law of *corvée*. Every property owner was required to send his slaves to perform a given number of work days that the highways might be kept in order.

A buff-complexioned postilion, astride the near horse of a team pulling the curricle, turned and with his whip pointed to a long slope ahead.

"Voilà, Monsieur. Yonder lies the domain of the Chevalier de Labouisse."

Through whirling clouds of dust raised by six *maréchaussées* forming his escort, Tim made out an imposing stone structure situated
half way up a steep hillside. Clustered below the mansion house were
a sugar factory, distillery, overseers' quarters, slave barracks, stables
and barns enough to make a miniature village.

He glimpsed a long driveway lined with royal palms. What had
once been elaborate formal gardens swept off to either side. Now
these gardens were brown as a winter pasture in Rhode Island.

Here, as elsewhere, evidences of a terrific drought were inescapable. Emaciated blacks, retaining barely enough strength to raise skinny
hands, had occupied the ditches all the way out from Cap François.

When one of these scarecrows, stronger or more determined than
his fellows, had crawled out to the tar road, a Dulac lackey—no less
than six had been sent along—spurred ahead, and with a cudgel
knocked the wretch senseless into the roadside.

Among other grim recollections Tim recalled the sight of a human
leg dangling from a post set up at a crossroad.

"It is part of a slave who has, for the third time, run away," explained a sergeant in command of the *maréchaussée.* Occasionally he
would rein in to ride beside the curricle.

"The first time a slave runs away, he earns a whipping and loses
one of his ears. On the next occasion, the fugitive is generally ham-
strung. For a third offense, he is cut into four pieces. His head is
mounted before the nearest police station and his limbs are dispatched
to the four corners of his parish."

The phenomenon of buzzards squabbling over bodies, the sight
of skeletons lying white and grisly in the parched fields swiftly became
so commonplace as to attract no attention.

This then, was what happened when New England fish, cornmeal
and salt meat were kept from the open sea.

Adding to a general impression of desolation were the large number
of factories which, ruined during the great earthquake of 1770, had
not yet been reconstructed.

Only on the hilltops or near the source of some spring was there any greenery. Correspondingly, the coffee planters had fared better than the growers of citrus fruits, cane and pimentoes.

The cavalcade, numbering nearly twenty riders in all, clattered past a gang of chained black brutes toiling to build a culvert.

Thank God, this dreadful journey was at an end. Using a lace-trimmed handkerchief, Tim flicked layers of white dust from the splendid coat of burnt-orange colored satin with which Jeannette had equipped him. Tim guessed the garment must belong to one or the other of the Dulac sons who were finishing their education in France.

Tim felt at once ridiculous yet pleased with his silk stockings, white breeches and gaudy green silk waistcoat. Hardest of all to stomach were pumps boasting high red heels and large paste buckles. The Dulacs had been hard put to find pumps large enough. Genuine diamonds flashed on the bosom of his shirt and it was only because he had flatly refused, that he was not wearing a dozen finger rings instead of only two.

"You must credit me," old Dulac had puffed. "I know what I am about. This is the only way properly to impress de Labouisse. We must overlook not the smallest detail. We *must* have the *permis*, and promptly!"

That the drought had put Dulac in a very bad way financially, Tim gathered from an increasing number of sources. The Créole needed ready money to finance his share of the armament importations. Maybe that accounted for the warmth of his hospitality, for Jeannette's eagerness to please?

As the cavalcade turned in off the main road, a bell commenced to clang and clatter. Up at the great mansion house, servants could be seen running in all directions.

The sergeant ordered his men to dismount. The *maréchaussées* dusted themselves and wiped off the blue and silver housings of their saddles, then straightened bows tying their powdered hair. They were mulattoes, nearly all of them—required to serve for two years without pay.

It was late afternoon and growing cooler. Prenet had insisted that their arrival should be made at this time.

Presently the cavalcade remounted, proceeded at a leisurely pace up the hill. Passing a pair of fountains that were without water, the curricle rolled into a paved court. Standing in it were a dozen uniformed servants.

Never in his life had Tim seen more sullen, savage expressions than decked their faces. The sergeant must have noticed it too, for he rode over and addressed one of the grooms in the local *patois*. Tim, of course, could understand no part of it.

The sergeant tramped back wearing a solemn expression. In a stage whisper he said, "I fear you have come in an evil hour, Monsieur. Yesterday, there was a case of poisoning on the domain. I fear Monsieur will find the Chevalier in an evil temper. 'Tis the devil's own luck."

Tim felt his hopes wither; if there was one fear which tormented the white Créoles out of all reason, it was a lively dread of being poisoned. Few of them were able to forget the famous plot of 1755 when a black named Macandal had barely failed in poisoning the whole white population of Cap François. Most Créoles made their slaves sample everything they ate.

Stiffly, Tim descended from the two-wheeled curricle and followed a white major-domo in an elaborate blue and gold livery into a spacious antechamber.

The Rhode Islander was not kept waiting long, and to his surprise, the Chevalier de Labouisse gave him a warm welcome.

"My dear M. Bennett," he cried in tolerably good English, "one is delighted to receive you, positively overwhelmed with pleasure. You could not have called at a moment more thoroughly opportune. It rounds out my party most happily. You must spend the night. You will enjoy making the acquaintance of my good neighbor, M. de Cockburn, and of the Chevalier de Cohars who commands our ship-of-the-line now lying at Cap François."

He beamed, shouted a torrent of orders at the swarm of servants.

"Yes, yes! To perfection, your presence balances my party. At nine-pins we shall play two to a side. And what do you make of Les Délices?"

"I— Well, sir, I'd call it mighty handsome."

The Chevalier de Labouisse lived in certainly the most magnificent building Tim had ever entered. Exquisite paintings and superbly-worked tapestries decked the walls. Crystal sconces, girandoles and chandeliers sparkled in all directions. The floors of tessellated stone had been polished to a mirror smoothness.

Opposite the front door an imposing stone staircase wound upwards, protected by an ornate balustrade of marble filigree work. Velvet and damask hangings glowed about tall French windows. Magnificent furniture filled a bewildering succession of apartments. An impression of unreality suddenly seized Tim. Maybe he was suffering from a touch of sun?

Crimanently! If the folks back in Newport could see him in these macaroni fol-de-rols, in silk stockings with red clocks on them, in high-heeled pumps and sporting diamond and ruby finger rings! He'd like to see the faces of the Second Company if they ever caught him like this.

Suddenly, he couldn't keep from grinning. It seemed a fellow had to do some mighty queer things in making a living, nowadays.

If Les Délices was unusual, its owner was no less so. The Chevalier de Labouisse must be nearing sixty. Those deep lines about his restless eyes and sloping forehead left no doubt of that. And most of his teeth were false. In his coat of glaring yellow, the Créole's complexion looked as sallow as that of a mulatto.

Paint had been applied to the Chevalier's cheeks and to his brows as well as to his lips.

By now, Tim had learned that in Saint-Domingue a fellow couldn't get down to brass tacks right away. All this waiting and formality was a silly waste of time, but you had to put up with it. He judged it might be smart to butter up the King's Lieutenant a bit before he got 'round to talking about the *permis*.

In a sitting room two other gentlemen were throwing dice over a little green table. Watching them stood three white women clad in scandalously scanty fashion.

The host's high heels clicked briskly over the parquet floor. "De Cockburn," he called, "I present to you M. Bennett. He represents a new species. He is an American, one of those rebellious, indigestible rascals who are giving our dear English cousins such bellyaches."

De Cockburn, a huge, bloated individual with pimples standing out all over his face and neck, languidly lifted a lorgnette, surveyed Tim from head to foot.

"How do you do?" he lisped. "Can you play ninepins? Good. You will be privileged to witness a new form of the game I have invented for the benefit of my friend de Labouisse."

The host bowed to his other guest. "The Chevalier de Cohars."

"An American, eh?" In a blue and white naval uniform, the Chevalier seemed like a lean and vicious greyhound among overfed lap dogs. "Then you must be one of those beastly anti-Royalists?"

Feeling like a fish out of water, Tim reddened. "We don't have any party except the liberty party. In America we're not anti-Royalist, unless the King ignores our rights."

"Since when do subjects question the Divine Right?"

"Since the Stamp Act," Tim replied sturdily.

De Cohars turned a hawk-like face. "There are no nobles among your sort, I take it?"

"No. Although Lord Stirling and a few others stayed with us, most noblemen in America went over to the King's party."

"I see." The captain of *la Dédaigneuse* picked up the dice box, rattled it impatiently. "Come, Monsieur, your point is six."

De Labouisse murmured, "You must pay no attention to de Cohars. He is in a foul mood. The smallpox has broken out on the poor devil's ship. Come, you must meet my *petites amies.*"

The three girls had been appraising Tim with obvious approbation. They hung in the background, but when the host nodded, a pretty blonde with faintly protuberant eyes came gliding across the floor. She had a pair of dimples that were fascinating to watch.

"This is Adrienne," de Labouisse said carelessly. "She's a good wench, in a bed or out of it. Come along. Our friends wish to finish their game."

A trifle hesitantly the King's Lieutenant approached the gaming board. Tim guessed he wasn't any too sure of where he stood with the wolfish nobleman called de Cohars.

"Watch out, de Cohars," he said just a trifle too heartily, "de Cockburn is the biggest gambler on Saint-Domingue."

"Bah!" snarled the Captain of *la Dédaigneuse*. "You Créole savages call a mere thousand livres a throw, gambling? At Versailles my lackeys risk as much.

"Come here, Héloïse," he barked at one of the girls. "Kiss every card in the deck. My luck continues incredibly bad."

It astonished Tim that the whole group should so complacently tolerate this nobleman's patent contempt. Why, de Cockburn and de Labouisse were actually smirking!

As the host led Tim and the blonde girl onto a terrace, Tim's blood was congealed by a series of piercing screams. They appeared to emanate from a group of white-washed buildings at some little distance from the house.

"Good God, sir," Tim burst out, "somebody is being killed!"

"Not killed," twittered Labouisse. "Hurt, perhaps, but not killed."

The girl Adrienne slipped a heavily powdered arm through Timothy's. "There was an unfortunate occurrence yesterday. A mass poisoning. Today come the punishments."

"Poison?"

"Yes," sighed the King's Lieutenant, tendering a tortoise-shell snuff box. "These blacks of mine are so lazy. They are fearful that I will grow coffee in addition to sugar."

"But what has that to do with the poisoning?"

"They murder one another so that I will be forced to purchase more slaves. By using my profit in that fashion, I will be rendered unable to expand and so, possibly, require more work of them."

De Labouisse frowned. "On this occasion, one has had to be a trifle severe. This plot has so far cost me a dozen valuable slaves. I will show you."

There was nothing for Tim to do but follow his host's gorgeous figure down a path lined with lemon trees. Brilliants, garnishing his heels, flashed as he led the way, sniffing now and then a yellow rose. The girl Adrienne sidled along beside Tim. She rolled her eyes at him.

"You like me, Monsieur?"

"Why, yes, Ma'am; you certainly are pretty."

The girl's painted features relaxed and she patted his hand. "Bon! Then Adrienne will be your *amie* while you visit. Money? I don't care about money. How Héloïse can put up with an old boar like that de Cockburn, I will never understand. *Pfui!* His breath is enough to sicken a mule. And as for the Chevalier, one cannot know for sure, but I think he is *un vrai vicieux.*"

"But, but—" Tim stammered. "What will—?"

"Hector de Labouisse? Oh la! la! That is why we are at Les Délices. Madeleine, Héloïse and I entertain his friends. Hector will have nothing but of the purest black."

Never had Tim felt more utterly at a loss. Crimanently! What to think? What to say?

De Labouisse slowed his walk as they neared the out-buildings. On all sides slaves were falling onto their knees and as their owner approached, they sullenly bared their heads. They did not dare raise their eyes.

"Here we are," the host announced. "This is the hospital. You must see what damage the miscreants have caused."

In a dark, stifling-hot room some fifteen or eighteen negroes of varying age and sex lay quite naked on pallets of dried sugar cane tops. At first glance Tim knew that eight or nine of the victims were quite dead. Others, lying in dreadfully contorted positions, were barely able to keep their skinny breasts in motion. Another group writhed endlessly, whimpered in some Congo dialect.

"This, M. Bennett, is the result of a little ground bamboo added to a bowl of *tassau* and rice."

Here was a sight he could never forget, Tim thought.

"See how the poor creatures suffer," de Labouisse invited. But to the Rhode Islander there was little of genuine pity in his tone.

"In Heaven's name, Hector." The girl Adrienne was pinching her nose and backing towards the entrance. "Before we stifle, let us return to the house."

"Not so fast, my pretty crane, not so fast," de Labouisse objected smoothly. "Since slaves are held in North America, it may be well for M. Bennett to observe, to remember methods which may prove useful in his country as well."

His painted features animated, de Labouisse took Tim's arm, talked with a confidential air. "At the investigation I learned that one 'village' had managed to poison the other."

"Village?"

"We subdivide the Quarters into what are called 'villages.'"

Steadily, the King's Lieutenant advanced towards that small square structure from which continued screams arose.

"I forced the guilty villagers to cast lots," de Labouisse continued. "Every fifth person is made to pay for this dreadful crime."

"But," Tim protested, "how can you do that? Innocent folks would have to suffer for something they hadn't done!"

"Undoubtedly!" sighed the Créole. "But what can one do? These rogues are such master liars it would be impossible to arrive at the true criminal, even had one the energy to devote to such a task.

"As for me, I divided such malefactors into three groups. One is condemned to suffer branding and the loss of both ears. This has already been attended to. The second, to severe flogging. That is what is going on now."

De Labouisse spoke precisely, like an academician. "Lastly—*peste!* I shall not spoil the surprise. It would infuriate de Cockburn who is the author of this amusement."

De Labouisse drew near a small square structure. Whitewashed, it shone dazzling white. From inside sounded a sibilant hissing sound. Outside crouched two heavily chained negroes, a man and a woman. Their skin was gray with the peculiar hue of a thoroughly terrified black. A pair of mulatto guards saluted with their musketoons as the King's Lieutenant and his guest approached.

The skin on the back of Tim's hands tingled and his mouth went dry when he saw a series of bright scarlet rivulets crawling across the dusty stone threshold and dripping onto the ground.

"Mounseer, I—I really don't—think I'd—"

De Labouisse frowned, but relaxed instantly. "My dear fellow, you really must see how thoroughly we administer justice. Think of those poor, innocent creatures we saw suffering below."

To his surprise, Mlle. Adrienne made no effort to hang back. "One cannot afford pity for these animals," she said, calmly fanning away a nimbus of flies. "The wolf, the tiger and the negro understand no law save that of fear."

A musty, sickish-sweet odor beat in Tim's face when a beetle-browed individual in spotted white hastily opened the door wider. Tim could see a limp, stark-naked figure dangling by its hands from an iron eye-bolt let into a stout beam. Shoulders, back and loins had degenerated into a sticky, purple-red pulp. The punished slave's head lolled loosely forward and Tim thought him unconscious.

A burly mulatto executioner put down his whip, looked anxiously at his master.

De Labouisse sniffed a pinch of snuff, flicked the grains from his neck-cloth, and said carelessly, "That black brute is shamming."

"Yes, *mo' maître.*" The executioner plunged a ladle into a pot steaming in a far corner. *"V'là."*

Hot oil, splashed over the black's lacerated back, tore from him screams that turned Tim pale.

The Rhode Islander was hard-put not to drive his fist at this sardonic, painted creature beside him. He guessed he knew now what Adelina had meant.

"I don't fancy this sort of thing," he choked. "Shall we go on—"

"Of course, of course!" agreed the King's Lieutenant. "My dear fellow, justice must be administered so you must forgive my offending your sensibilities like this. Punishment, you see, must be inflicted in terms these barbaric creatures can comprehend."

De Labouisse plucked a sprig of orange blossoms, sniffed it, then tucked it carelessly into Adrienne's carefully curled hair.

"You are fond of dogs, perhaps?"

"Yes." Tim felt infinitely relieved. "I had a dog of my own; called him Snapper."

"Then you must see my pets." All of a sudden he shot his guest a searching glance. "By the bye, what occasioned this delightfully un-expected visit?"

"Why, sir, I wish to place a letter-of-marque in commission," Tim explained. "And I want your advice, if you'll be so kind, as to the best disposal of such prizes I may take."

He did a very creditable job. Soon de Labouisse was suggesting his agent in Savannah. As they descended a walk edged with lime trees, the King's Lieutenant showed yellow teeth in a shrewd smile.

"All very well, my friend, but how are you to get your vessel to sea? There is the matter of a *permis,* is there not?"

"Of course, perhaps we can speak of that later? I—er—understand there may be some extra fees for—er—special stamps. I have money to cover such expenses—with me."

Adrienne caught up with them after having paused to pluck a nosegay. "We must be near the kennels."

From beyond a hedge of acacias arose a great snarling and yelping.

"Feeding time," de Labouisse explained. "My pets are not usually so noisy."

Once the three had entered a courtyard, Tim saw a row of stout iron cages ranged under a shed. In them prowled a dozen or more of the largest, most savage-looking dogs imaginable.

"My bloodhounds," sighed de Labouisse. "Pure Cuban stock. Are they not handsome brutes?"

These shaggy monsters did not at all resemble the mournful, long-eared animals bearing the same name in America. These, Tim saw, were more like wolfhounds; rough-haired, short-eared and tremen-dously powerful.

"Mon Dieu, Hector!" The girl emitted a little squeak of surprise. "What is that affair?" She was watching the approach of a device trundled along by a pair of blue-jawed white keepers.

"That? Only the feeding machine, my dear."

What Adrienne had referred to was a human figure made of wicker work and painted a dull black. This crude effigy wore a kilt of slave cloth and boasted a woolly wig.

"Now, watch," invited Tim's host.

Once the effigy was close to the first cage, one of the keepers cast loose a little hook. Immediately, the black manikin's stomach gave way, spilt into the cage a mass of blood, bones, meat. Snarling, the great animals fell upon it with a dreadful ferocity.

"Ingenious, is it not?" demanded de Labouisse with pride. "Teaches these, my most faithful friends, to regard a black man as a potential source of nourishment."

He turned to the nearer keeper. "Jules, send me a black. Pray observe this."

To Tim's astonishment, the King's Lieutenant boldly thrust a lace-trimmed sleeve among the imprisoned hounds. With every evidence of affection the huge brown, black and white brutes licked his fingers, whined, wagged their close-cut tails.

The instant Jules re-entered the courtyard in company with a frightened-looking colored man, the effect on the bloodhounds was instantaneous. Hackles flaring, they hurled themselves frenziedly at the bars, yammered, scratched at the wooden frames.

De Labouisse thrust a stick into his slave's hand. "Beat those dogs, see that you beat them hard!"

"But, *Maître,* I—I'm afraid to—"

"Do as you are told! You can believe, M. Bennett, that not many of my slaves attempt to desert Les Délices?"

<h1 style="text-align:center">5</h1>

M. DE COCKBURN'S NINEPINS

FOLLOWING a refreshment of champagne and iced cakes, the Chevalier de Labouisse appeared smiling, rubbing his hands. He went immediately to de Cockburn.

"I am convinced, my dear Joseph, that you will find nothing to criticize. The turf could not be more level. I have examined it myself."

"Eh? What is this game?" The Chevalier de Cohars, a trifle exhilarated by the champagne, had relaxed his forbidding manner. He sat on a flag-stoned terrace with Madeleine, a pretty brunette, perched on his lap.

De Labouisse used his most silken manners, almost fawned on this acid gentleman wearing the scarlet stockings and breeches of a French Naval Captain.

"Yes, *mon ami,* a game of bowls *à la* Saint-Domingue. I fear we must hurry before it gets dark. Everything is in readiness."

Adrienne, an arm about Tim's waist, said, "I hope M. de Cockburn's game will prove amusing." She fetched a deep sigh. "You can have no idea how intolerably boring life becomes on an inland estate. *Ma foi!* Until today, Madeleine, Héloïse and I have not seen another white face in two weeks. Say what you will, the life of a Créole's mistress is not all honey and silk."

The girl looked sadly out over the vast, sun-blasted Plain du Nord.

"For all my five thousand livres of salary, for all the presents Hector showers on me and the other girls, many and many a time I have prayed to go back to Bordeaux."

"I guess everybody gets homesick after a while," Tim sympathized. He was really sorry for this pretty, painted young woman. "Right now I'd give a pretty to draw a breath of cold New England air." He wanted to get the sour reek of fermenting sugar cane out of his nostrils, to smell instead the salted wind beating in from the marshes on Beavertail Point.

Right now he must mind his P's and Q's, fall in with whatever de Labouisse suggested. After what he'd seen in that whipping house, he guessed he could put up with 'most anything.

Lining the far end of a formal garden a crowd of at least three hundred slaves were waiting under the eye of guards in ill-fitting seersucker uniforms. A majority of these carried blunderbusses in addition to pistols and whips.

Forming a separate group, the house slaves, infinitely better dressed and fed, were assembled along a stone wall. They eyed the congregated field hands with open contempt.

What looked like an old sail was spread over a plot at the end of a long alley of lawn which, miraculously, had been kept smooth and green. At no point did this canvas rise higher than a foot and a half above the earth.

At the opposite end of the alley some chairs had been placed beneath a scarlet canopy. A table laden with pipes, cigars, fruits and various liquors lent a tournament atmosphere.

Tim noted that parallel white lines indicated what looked like a ninepin ground. Save that the alley had a gentle downward slope towards the canvas, the arrangements differed not at all from the regular game.

"Do you play?" demanded de Labouisse.

Tim nodded. "After a fashion. We used to have a pitch at college."

"Capital! Then you and I will form one side, de Cockburn and the Chevalier, the other." So saying he opened a chest, brought out of it what was undoubtedly a ten pound roundshot.

"Eh?" De Cohars stared. "What's this?"

"An improvement, *mon cher ami*. You will agree presently," smiled the King's Lieutenant stripping off his coat. When the others did the same, Tim followed suit.

"Your side must win," Adrienne whispered. "It would make the other girls furious to lose. We have already put up ten livres apiece."

From the sable throng rose a low, inexpressibly dolorous undertone. The guards straightened, peered this way and that. Tim rubbed his eyes; he was almost sure that something beneath had moved the old sail.

"Eight or ten pound ball?"

"I imagine I might do better with an eight," Tim answered. "You had best lead off, too."

"Good," smiled de Labouisse. "Very well, Jules!"

The overseer beckoned forward a mulatto guard and, bending, they each grabbed a corner of the tarpaulin and pulled it back. From the slaves rose a deep groan.

Arranged at the end of the long slope and in the conventional "V" pattern of ninepins, the heads of nine living negroes were exposed. Buried up to their chins and with turf tamped tight about their necks, they could only roll their eyes. Gags stopped their mouths.

"The poisoners I condemned to death," explained M. de Labouisse. "You bowl first, de Cockburn, this is your invention. By the bye, you are sure their heads will—?"

"—Like so many egg shells," grunted de Cockburn handling his roundshot.

A next to impossible situation for Tim was relieved when the Chevalier de Cohars gave one amazed glance at the spectacle, turned on his heel and stalked back to the tent saying in frigid accents:

"His Majesty's Naval officers do not make a sport of executing felons. Really, after a few years, you Créoles become too much like your property."

Tim cast the Captain of *la Dédaigneuse* a bleak smile.

De Cohars said, "You look as disgusted as I feel, Monsieur. Let us leave these gentlemen to their—er—sport. I feel a sudden need of champagne."

"Let them go, Hector," snapped de Cockburn quite unruffled. "Takes a real Saint-Dominguais to play this game."

Long before they regained the house, a low and ominous wailing arose among the assemblage.

When Tim got back to Les Délices, he had to run for the lavatory.

6

Night-Blooming Cereus

Had anyone suggested to the Chevalier Keroulas de Cohars that he might one day invite a common merchant into his coach, that erect individual would simply have stared in resentment. Yet here he was entering Cap François after a most instructive and almost enjoyable journey.

The hard, analytical eyes of the Captain of *la Dédaigneuse* narrowed.

"There is a quality about you Americans, M. Bennett, which intrigues me. I will confess it now, quite frankly. You Yankees, unlike the lower classes of England, do not bow and scrape to your betters; yet this temerity lacks any quality of intentional rudeness."

"Well, I guess that's true, Chevalier," Tim chuckled comfortably. "Most of us Yankees figure we don't have any betters—or, to put it differently, we figure we're no better and no worse than our neighbors. Now take you. I didn't like you at all to start with."

The Chevalier started. Color poured into the Frenchman's leanly sensitive features. He broke into a rasping laugh. *Nom de Dieu!* It was something novel to hear a common merchant daring to disapprove of a Knight of St. Louis. *Heu!* That a bourgeois felt qualified to judge a nobleman whose family enjoyed the privileges of the Louvre.

Peste! One simply could not get angry with this clear-eyed young fellow. He was so completely ignorant of intentional offense.

"So you—er—disapproved of me at first?" he demanded as his coach rumbled across the Place de Clugny with Tim's party of *maréchaussées* clearing a passage.

The Rhode Islander shrugged, and his deeply-tanned face broke into a grin. "I took you for a stuck-up macaroni. Guess you must have thought me pretty queer, too, in these fancy clothes. They ain't mine," he added.

The Chevalier's eyes twinkled. "Indeed? One never would have suspected it. Tell me—when did you—er—revise your opinion?"

"Why, 'twas when you wouldn't fall in with that game of bowls. And I want to thank you, too, for your helping me land that permit to arm."

The Chevalier waved a long-fingered hand decorated with many diamonds and pearls.

"It was nothing. It pleased me to threaten de Labouisse. Though he imagines to the contrary, the Minister of Marines shall hear of these savageries." De Cohars' carefully rouged cheek stiffened. "The Saint-Dominguais are utter pigs; callous barbarians!"

"But surely this de Cockburn and—er—our late host are exceptions?"

"Unfortunately, those specimens are not," snapped the Chevalier, sniffing at an orange as the vehicle rolled through a very smelly little street. "From its roots to its top this Colony reeks of decadence! Until one was ordered here, one had imagined Versailles to be the very nadir of debauchery and corruption. Thank God, one is ordered back to Toulon within the month. Faugh! What a magnificent concentration of stinks is this Cap François."

The naval officer reached into the pocket of his Prussian-blue tunic and produced a crystal flask of cognac. He took a sip, made no effort to offer any to his companion.

"My coachman will halt first *chez* Dulac," the Chevalier announced.

"Don't go out of your way—"

"But it is no trouble. It was good of you to bear me company on this infernal trip."

From a handbag, de Cohars produced a mirror and, as best he might despite the lurching of the coach, applied a tiny, star-shaped beauty patch at the point of his jaw.

At Tim's frank amazement, the Frenchman smiled. "One feels inspired to stop in the Rue de Rohan before returning to one's ship. They have there a red-haired Spanish girl who is—to put it simply—but ravishing!"

The combined escorts served to create quite an imposing little procession. As de Cohars' coach, blazoned with his coat-of-arms, rattled up the Rue Penthièvre, sailors from the ships saluted, horse police drew sabers, and beggars, hideous with disease, ran out to fawn in the dust. When de Cohars carelessly flung a handful of silver from the window, the crowd fought like starving dogs.

Once the coach came to a halt before the home of Anatole Dulac, Tim offered a broad, well-calloused hand. "Much obliged, Captain. If you ever find time, I'd enjoy seeing you aboard my craft. She's small, but she's fast and I've rigged some new-fangled tackles to her guns. Might interest a naval man."

De Cohars managed a smile, but he was no longer amused. Even a naïve fellow like this should know better than to offer such an invitation. Fancy a captain commanding a Royal ship-of-the-line visiting an upstart privateer which even now was little better than a pirate!

"One fears he will be too—" de Cohars was beginning when suddenly his steely eyes widened.

Standing just inside the gate and obviously astonished at the long line of trampling horsemen, at the coat of arms glowing on the doors of the coach, was Mlle. Jeannette Dulac.

"*Ma foi!*" exclaimed de Cohars. "And who is this? But she is lovely! Graceful as a gazelle! Quick. You may present her to me."

Tim hesitated. Back home, ladies weren't commanded to meet gentlemen. Said he, "You wait here and I'll go and see if maybe she wants to meet you." Fortunately, he turned and so lost de Cohars' furious expression.

To his astonishment he found Jeannette visibly trembling, pale. "Hello," he greeted. "My friend here—"

"But, but how in the world?" she fluttered. "The Chevalier de Cohars is allied to the de Rohans—his is one of the first families of France! What is the Chevalier doing here?"

"Why, he just gave me a lift back in town," Tim explained. "Do you want to meet him? He's a nice fellow when you get to understand him."

"I, a little bourgeoise, meet the Chevalier de Cohars?" babbled Jeannette, going pink and white by turns. "Oh dear, I—I'm not dressed—"

"—There is no need, Mademoiselle, I will present myself." De Cohars had descended from his coach and, making a splendid figure in his blue and scarlet, came stalking up the footpath. Eyes riveted on the young Créole's features, he made her such a profound bow that his gold-laced hat brushed the paving.

"Oh, oh, Monsieur," Jeannette sighed. "Your Excellency does a poor girl too great an honor." She made a graceful curtsey so deep her little chip hat almost brushed de Cohars' knees.

Tim was puzzled over all this to-do. Why, Mistress Dulac was acting awed and scared as any school girl before an elder.

"Say, Mounseer, I don't know about you, but I'm just a mite thirsty. Mistress Jeannette, think you can find us something that will wash the dust out of our throats?"

Jeannette turned horror-stricken on him. "The Seigneur de Cohars would not deign enter so ordinary—"

"Ah, but you are very mistaken," de Cohars smiled. "I shall be very grateful for a glass of claret."

To Tim, the ensuing half hour was a revelation. He couldn't get over the way the servants groveled, how Anatole Dulac stammered and nearly turned himself inside out in welcoming the naval officer. Diane was fairly beside herself with excitement. As for Jeannette, she quickly found an excuse to disappear.

Presently she returned, wearing her most magnificent necklace of rubies, diamonds and gold, with earbobs to match.

She had changed to a skirt of gold-colored taffeta and a blouse of a dark cherry red. Its shade reminded Tim of Desire Harmony's mouth.

Affably enough, the Chevalier de Cohars lingered, sipped some wine and made polite conversation with Dulac and Tim. He remained quite oblivious of the brazen way Diane undulated all over the salon and kept crossing so that the light would beat through her shirtwaist.

It was on Jeannette, dark and demure in a far corner, that Keroulas de Cohars kept his attention. He announced at length his regret at leaving so agreeable a spot, but there remained the deplorable necessity of making *la Dédaigneuse* ready for sea.

"For one's sins," laughed the Chevalier, "one must sail our excellent Governor around to Port-au-Prince."

Crestfallen, but still bowing and scraping, Anatole Dulac escorted his visitor all the way out to his carriage. The girls curtseyed again and again on the threshold.

Jeannette heaved a little sigh. *"Bon Dieu,* what an honor! Teem, how *did* you manage it? The Chevalier de Cohars is reputedly the most distant, most inaccessible and distinguished nobleman in Saint-Domingue today."

"He seems like a nice enough feller," the Rhode Islander admitted, "but why get so foamed up over him?"

"Why, the de Cohars' are of the very ancient noblesse! Their line descends from the reign of Saint-Louis."

Tim began looking serious. "Well, now, that may be so; but is that any reason to, well, like him?"

"Like?" Jeannette's laugh tinkled. "That old hawk? But no. I do not admire him personally, but he is a great Seigneur. Oh, la, la, Teem, you could never understand! The Seigneurs are not like us bourgeois."

Tim wanted to point out that de Cohars belched, joked and cursed like everybody else, but didn't.

"I do believe you are just a little jealous."

Color welled painfully above Tim's stock. "Why, no, Mistress Jeannette, I ain't jealous; but hang it, you and your folks made such an almighty fuss over that painted macaroni."

Jeannette laughed, brushed his cheek with her fan. "But of course you are! Never mind. Everybody we know will hear of the Chevalier's call and they will be green with jealousy because, until today, he has never entered a Créole home in Cap François. This will help Papa's affairs a great deal."

When Anatole Dulac learned of Tim's complete success with the King's Lieutenant, he sent a slave running to fetch Claude Prenet and dinner that evening approached banquet proportions: sea food, ortolans, guinea fowl and a host of native vegetables, salads and desserts.

Even Diane forgot to sulk.

M. Prenet raised his glass. "*Mes amis,* a toast for the beautiful little *Narragansett!* May her first cruise prove all that we hope!"

"Don't leave out the subsequent ones," called Dulac, his huge stomach indented by the table's edge.

Jeannette added quite gravely, "—And may *le Bon Dieu* guard and watch over her master."

Diane said nothing, merely looked into her wine glass.

Tim, having remembered a lot concerning Desire Harmony, concluded that yonder sat a young woman who would bear watching. Crimanently! A girl might forgive almost anything save the supreme indignity of having her bare bottom paddled before a man she had been seeking to enthrall.

The increasing cool added to the party's gaiety and the bare feet of the lackeys repeatedly slapped away in quest of champagne.

At length Claude Prenet abandoned his taciturnity and sang a Norman ballad concerning a knight called Tristan, and Yseult, his fair lady.

Tim couldn't understand a word, but applauded like anything. This champagne sure made a fellow feel fine as silk. Dulac waved a hairy hand at his elder daughter.

"*Ma chère,* will you not oblige us with one of your Créole chansonettes?"

"*Meow!*" was Diane's audible comment when Jeannette left her seat and posed at the far end of the room, looking incredibly petite and fragile.

> "Quand cher zami moin va rivé
> Mon va fair li tout plein caresse
> Ah! Plaisir la nous va gouté
> C'est plaisir qui douré sans cesse
> Mais toujous tard
> Mais toujous tard
> Cher zami moin pas vlé rivé.
> Cher zami moin pas vlé rivé."

Anatole Dulac's daughter sang for Tim only, her limpid dark eyes yearning, her white throat quivering to the high notes.

Tim realized now that what she reminded him of was one of those little china figures from Europe. Rich Captain Maudesley kept a whole what-not full of them.

When she had done Dulac heaved himself to his feet, winked elaborately at his brother-in-law. "Claude, we must consider the armaments for the *Young Cromwell*. Diane, I will need you to copy the orders."

"Such a lovely moonlight night," she complained, "and I am made to work while Jeannette is free."

"*Tais-toi!*" thundered her father and Diane subsided.

In the garden all was dewy moonlight, and sweet odors from the chocolate factories further in town vied with the scents of the flowers. A little Temple of Love at the far end shone white as chalk. Before they had advanced half-a-dozen steps down a rose-arbored walk, Tim knew that he would ask Jeannette Dulac to marry him. He felt positive, too, that this exquisite girl would accept him.

They halted by a wall which, purposely, had been left unfinished in order to simulate ruins. Two broken Ionic columns heightened the effect. Over this wall poured a cascade of flat, snaky-looking night-blooming cereus. Tonight the cactus glowed with a profusion of luminous white blossoms. Every instant more buds were slowly opening.

As easily as a young new moon entering a cloud, Jeannette Dulac slipped into his arms. She was trembling, yet restrained as she murmured, "It is well I have waited so long—"

Cradling her in his arms, Tim was frightened at the very lightness of her. "Jeannette, I wish I could make some fine speeches, tell you how fine, how pretty you are, but—I guess my jib is cut different. I feel it though. Honestly."

"I know, my heart, I know. I love you for that very lack of pretty phrases."

He held her with the moonlight silvering her half-closed eyes, her slim arms and glistening breast.

"Ah, *mon brave,* you are as strong and enduring as that wall," she whispered, pressing a cool fragrant cheek to his. "Perhaps I am like the cereus, grown to soften its harsh outlines."

"Oh, Teem, Teem, I will try so very hard to make you a fine wife." She clung fiercely to him. "I will know how to please you. What you wish shall be my law. Ah, *mon cœur,* I shall give you many, many children."

Tim all but laughed at the idea of this fragile little thing raising a great brood of children.

Eyelashes brushing his chin, she murmured, "Now you think nice things of me, but I may do many wrong things, Teem, out of my love for you. And you, my great bear, will annoy me sometimes with your directness, with your lack of subtlety. But always I shall love you, and only you."

Not knowing what to say, Tim kept quiet.

Her great eyes became like dark mirrors raised to his. "Teem, though I know I risk everything, I will not attempt a deception. Teem, you will not be the first. There has been one—no, two others." She sounded so very frightened he hastened to whisper:

"It don't matter, dearest. When folks live in a place like this, they can't act like New Englanders. It ain't nature. It's a wonder—"

Tiny fingertips flew up to seal his lips. "That is what I hoped to hear, Teem. Promise to take me from Cap François!"

"Of course. This is no place for you—or for me. When I have finished with privateering, we will build a house in Newport." His voice rushed on, a-brim with eagerness. "If you wish, we will bring an architect over from France. You will be happy there."

As the moon rose, they said a great deal, little of which made sense. But they enjoyed it.

Eventually Tim got up, took a short turn down to the arbor walk. "I don't know how your people do these things, Jeannette, but I'm wondering what your Pa—er, father—will say? I suppose he has to be talked to. That right?"

She stirred, said without opening her eyes, "There is always the marriage contract to be arranged, but I think you have nothing to fear from Papa. He likes you—so very much. Indeed, I sometimes wonder why."

"Eh?"

She laughed, kissed him lingeringly. "Being what and who he is, of course.

"Perhaps, yes—I think you'd better talk to Papa tonight. He could not be in a more propitious humor."

7
PRICES

STEADILY Anatole Dulac considered this bronzed young man in sea serge and white duck standing very straight at the far end of his library table. The Créole's pudgy fingers kneaded his second chin a moment ere he raised a jet eyebrow.

"*En bref,* M. Bennett, you would make an alliance with Jeannette?"

"Yes, sir, I hear it's customary in these parts to speak to the girl's father; to, well—er—sort of talk matters over."

"But, yes," Dulac smiled. "It is also that the head of your family must be in agreement with me. You see, I must be assured that he also approves this projected alliance."

"Since my father died, I have been head of our family." Our family! Dear God! Zeke was dead and Desire Harmony vanished into the blue. Well, with Jeannette's love and help, he would build a fine, strong, new generation.

"Ah! Then there is no need for disquiet on that score. Tell me, M. Bennett, what have you in—er—a material way to offer my daughter?"

"Little more than myself," Tim admitted slowly.

"Then it is not possible for you or your family to make a settlement on my daughter? That is the French custom, you know."

"None at present, sir."

Dulac made a soft clucking sound in his throat and the lamp wrought a big yellow high-light on his glistening bald head.

"I had imagined so, yet I believe, Timothée, you have a real future, also this new country of America. Claude agrees with me."

The fat man surged forward in his chair, poured himself a stiff nip of cognac, then settled back, slowly revolving the glass on a level with his eyes.

"You have seen Saint-Domingue," he continued. "You need no one to demonstrate how, daily, we slide deeper into the morass of dissipation, luxury and viciousness. You have moved among us Colonials —'beastly Créoles' even the French call us."

It was a shock to hear a man of Dulac's connections make such a confession. "Why, I wouldn't say that, sir," he protested. "Cap François is a mighty fine place; a smart man could grow rich trading—if foreigners were allowed to get at the real profits."

"That will never become possible. Only French subjects are allowed to supply more than necessities." Some of the heaviness left Anatole Dulac's features. He seemed to be pleading when he continued:

"My first concern is for the ultimate good and advancement of my family. I have hoped that, before I die, at least one of my children might become one of the *petite noblesse."*

He sighed, made a wide gesture. "But that will never be. Consider my children: Albert and Hercule live in France, throwing away my hard-earned money in the vain hope of gaining advancement at the Court.

"Then there is Diane. She is but fourteen, yet already her name is become a scandal as far as Marmalade and Fort Dauphin." Dulac's heavy head sank until its three chins rested on his chest. "Jeannette remains my one hope to make a fresh start for the Dulacs. She is a good girl, Timothée, obedient, intelligent and affectionate.

"I had dreamed of a title for her, but no longer. In France, we Créoles are despised for everything except our wealth—though many of us come of older blood than the mockers themselves."

Tim relaxed, looking with new understanding on that great, shapeless figure overflowing a rattan chair.

"No, Timothée," came Dulac's deep voice. "It is because I have lost faith in Saint-Domingue, in France herself, that a marriage between you is not impossible."

"Do you mean it, sir? Do you really mean that?"

"Of course," Dulac snapped. "I was about to say that I notice in you Yankees a readiness, nay, an eagerness to learn. Unlike the English you are, as a race, neither hide-bound nor intractable. Yet to a certain degree, you have inherited their virtues of dispassionate action, mercantile honesty and physical energy."

Dulac selected a cigar and lit it before he said, "Should this marriage be arranged, it must be with two understandings. First, you will carry Jeannette far away from this tropical stew of an island and you will never bring her back. I wish to have her children grow up strong, clean-minded and unafraid—in the fashion of my grandparents back in Artois.

"*Mon Dieu,* it was something to see you, a mere merchant, so at ease with the Chevalier de Cohars today. Yes, I can tell you it gives one to think."

Jeannette's father fell silent, whereupon the tree frogs, trilling songs in the garden beyond the awnings, sounded very loud. Further away plaintive negro voices were singing:

> "Simbi en Deux Eaux
> M'we jé p'ou
> F'e p'moin
> Fi-á. Lembe."

"—And that other provision," Tim reminded, sucking at his pipe.

The Frenchman's little blue eyes swung up to meet his. "A settlement on Jeannette of twenty thousand livres. To be paid on signature of the marriage contract."

Twenty thousand livres! Why, that was practically twenty thousand pounds, one hundred thousand Spanish dollars! Tim was badly jolted.

Dulac saw it, said easily, "In your fine new letter-of-marque, you should not find too much trouble winning such a sum. *Mon Dieu,* in the last war, the little *Fleau* of St. Malo made two prizes worth above one hundred thousand livres apiece."

He bent forward. "Every day unguarded vessels of the English pass on their way to and from Jamaica through the Windward Passage. Ha! Ha! You will find that sum and more in a fortnight's cruise, provided you are prudent—and lucky."

He shrugged. "I am a fool, I know. I should demand a settlement of sixty thousand livres. God knows I need it." He nodded at a tall pile of documents. "Bills, demands for payment, threats of action—

all of them. This accursed drought is ruining me.

"Timothée—" he looked hard at the Rhode Islander—"I cannot settle a *dot* upon my child, I confess it with shame. Indeed, I am in desperate need of that twenty thousand livres."

"I'm sorry, sir," Tim murmured, but his thoughts were far away. It would be something, in a few days now, to take the sea against the British, to carry his first cargo on the high seas.

Dazzling visions of prizes taken flashed across his imagination. Crimanently! He'd make the British pay dearly for the nightmare they had caused on Conanicut. But for the British he'd never have lost Lucy. Lucy! How inflexible she could be, for all her gentle, soft-spoken ways.

He roused himself. "I will do my best, sir, you may rely on that. In the meantime, is it too late to discuss the cargo I am to load?"

Dulac broke into a cackling laugh. "There is a proper son-in-law! Chance what will, he never forgets business! Come, my boy, into the office. I know of excellent pimento and some muscovado sugar that can be come across at distress prices.

"For you I can procure all the taffia—or rum as you call it—you want, and manufactured by the best distillers in the West Indies. Ah, you do an old man's soul much good. If only Hercule or Albert would exhibit a trace of interest in these matters."

8

The Private-armed Brig Narragansett

To SEE the brig's batteries finally mounted was a great satisfaction to everyone from Tim Bennett down to Phil Hull. The *Narragansett's* hands could not leave off admiring her eight guns: four each of long eighteens and sturdy nine pounders.

The cannon looked quite gay, painted as they were, gray with a jaunty scarlet band about their muzzles and boasting a gold stripe around their pomelions.

"French nonsense," snapped Captain Loammi Freebody. "And will you look? Them idjits have painted a big red "N" on all the gun tackle blocks!" But he was pleased all the same.

Certainly Messrs. Pliarne, Prenet and Dulac had made a thorough job of marking. All the ammunition chests had had the letter-of-marque's name painted on them, and an "N" was burned into each of the powder ladles, muskets, blunderbusses and musketoons.

In an unprecedented burst of generosity, the outfitters presented Tim with four fine swivels, peculiarly deadly weapons which could be mounted on the bulwarks and trained fore and aft. Enemy boarders, attempting to cross the rail, would wither under a shower of lead.

Preoccupied and busy with a familiar round of inventories and inspections, Tim had worked from the first ray of light. Stripped to a cotton jersey and linen breeches, he went up to the quarterdeck.

"Well, Captain, how did the recruiting party make out last night?"

Freebody shrugged. "Well, sir, Mr. Crabtree secured our complement. Mostly in free blacks, though."

Tim nodded. "That's all right. I notice the pure blacks take to discipline better than mulattoes or low-class French. But I don't like it much."

"Well, Mr. Bennett, beggars can't be choosers, they say. Americans and English nowadays are skurce around the French Islands as snowballs in hell."

The brig's company now numbered ninety hands. Little more than half of them hailed from the American colonies. Around ten gunners' mates and gun captains were ex-British men-of-war's men.

Now, more than ever, he and Freebody lamented the untimely death of Captain Griffin and nearly half the crew of the *Narragansett*. They had perished in agony after eating some tainted dried beef imported from Hispaniola, the Spanish end of the island, when the drought had got very bad.

Descending to his cabin, Tim, with considerable satisfaction, viewed a simple uniform tunic he had had made ashore. It was blue and sported silver buttons along the edges of a white plastron. White cross-belts supported his sword on one side and a pistol holster on the other.

In his position of officer over the letter-of-marque's handful of marines, he judged it gave him a smarter appearance. His men too would be put into uniform—of sorts—because, aboard the *Alfred,* marines wearing uniforms had always handled themselves better than those who went about in civilian clothes.

A boat bumped alongside and presently Phil Hull announced the arrival of Dr. Boyd.

"Well, Doctor, and how do you feel?" he demanded when that red-faced individual appeared below.

Dr. Boyd made a comical face. "Faith and I feel drier than a last year's bone on a hilltop. Still, I've been off the stuff three whole days now, and I'm grateful to you, Mr. Bennett, for wanting me."

Already a good deal of the puffiness had disappeared from about the little Irishman's eyes and that white matter which usually had gathered in their corners was quite gone.

"Well, then, here's a copy of the Articles. Pray read it with care."

ARTICLES OF AGREEMENT made and concluded upon this 14th day of June in the year of our Lord, 1776. BETWEEN the Owners, Captain, Officers, Seamen and others belonging to the private Brig of War called the *Narragansett,* commanded by Loammi Freebody.
—that is to say—

Article 1st. The owner is to fit out and provide with provision, etc. (for the cruise) the said brig at his own expense.

2nd. All prizes taken by said Brig shall be sent alternatively to the Colony of Georgia and to the Port of Philadelphia unless urgent necessity shall oblige them to make some other port.

3rd. The owner is to provide a medicine chest and instruments for the Doctor which is to be paid out of the first prize before a division be made.

4th. All prizes taken after the condemnation and other necessary charges are paid shall be divided into two equal parts or moities. One moitie for the use and benefit of the owner, the other moitie or half part for the use and benefit of the Captain, Officers, Seamen and others belonging to *sd* Brig.

5th. The moitie or half part belonging to the Captain and Company of the Brig shall be divided into so many shares or parts as the share of the said Captain, Off. seamen & others shall amount to with the addition of deserving shares and shall be divided as here after mentioned.

6th. The Captain shall have 8 of such shares.

7th. The First Lieutenant shall have six shares and the master shall have four shares.

8th. The Second Lieutenant shall have four shares, first prize master & Captain's Clerk and purser shall have 3 shares each.

9th. Second & 3rd prize masters 2½.

10th. Master's mate, Doctor, Carpenter, Boatswain, gunner and armorer 2 each.

11th. Doctor's mate, gunner's mate, boatswain's mate 1½ shares each.

12th. Cook 1¼ share.

13th. Seamen and others on board 1 share except boys who shall be rewarded as the Committee hereinafter mentions shall think proper to allow them.

14th. The man who first discovers a sail if she prove a prize shall have a half share over and above his share or shares of the said prize to be taken out of the *deserving shares.*

15th. The man who first boards a vessel in engagement (if she is taken) shall have ½ share over & above.

16th. Remainder of deserving shares to be divided betwixt the most deserving of the Company.

17th. Whoever shall die on the cruize his heirs, executors, administers shall be entitled to his shares of all prizes taken before his death, or if he be killed in engagement they shall have his share or shares of any prize taken in consequence of such engag't.

18th. The owner shall advance 16 shillings sterling to each man before sailing which shall be repaid him out of the 1st prize.

19th. Whoever shall lose a limb shall be paid 100 dollars—one-half by the owner, ½ by the Capt., Off., etc.

20th. Whoever shall be maimed or disabled as aforesaid shall be allowed a recompense and the Owner, Capt. & Off. shall judge competent.

21st. Whoever shall breed mutiny or disturbance on board to the detriment of the cruize shall forfeit his shares to the Company.

22nd. Same for second offense of stealing.

23rd. No drinking or gaming aboard.

24th. Capt., 1st Lieut. & Master shall form committee to divide *deserving shares* and the shares of the boys.

25th. These articles shall be and remain in force during the cruize which shall continue three months from departing the Cap François and no longer except by consent of all parties and the cruize shall be broke up on the brig's return to Pennsylvania.

26th. The Captain & Officers and others shall be subject to the Regulations and Resolves of Congress (Continental & copy instructions delivered the Captain with his Commission).

27th. And for the true performance of the above Articles of Agreement the said parties do bind themselves to each other and to these presents have subscribed their names respectively:

At length the Irishman set down the paper and for a long while looked out of the porthole at a French frigate which, raising its topsails, was setting out to sea scudding past a trio of slavers coming in from Africa.

"I'm hoping you'll sign on," Tim said. "I hate putting to sea without a saw-bones aboard."

"That's very decent o' yez, Mr. Bennett. And—I, well—I will do my best to abide by these Articles."

From the tail of his coat the doctor pulled a length of sugar cane. This he began sucking earnestly. "If ye've no objection, I'm having a supply o' cane sent aboard. 'Twill help to discourage the rat which keeps on gnawing in my stomach." The Doctor hesitated.

"I'd better tell ye why I've been hitting the bottle. Five years ago, in London, I was working over a bit of a vaccine which I hoped would reduce the ravages o' the smallpox."

The little man's round eyes batted rapidly. "Something went wrong. The poor divil o' a trollop I had hired to take my vaccination died."

Dr. Boyd's hands opened and shut nervously. "Faith, and the Court was lenient—only sentenced me four to five years' hard labor in Dartmoor. As an afterthought, His Worship forbade me ever to practice in any part o' the United Kingdom."

"You have nothing to be ashamed of, I'd say," was Tim's opinion. "This cruise may mean a new beginning. I honestly hope so. Now you'd best get to your berth and make sure the medicine chest is complete."

"Yes, Mr. Bennett." The little Irishman's bright blue eyes were full as he turned away. "I shan't forget this confidence."

By the morning of June 18, 1776, nine Yankee privateers lay among the other shipping crowding the harbor of Cap François. And from M. Dulac's wharf a succession of barges kept sailing out to one or another of them.

Nearest to the *Narragansett* lay a newcomer, the *Gamecock*. This trim little schooner had saluted the town less than an hour earlier. Even as Tim appeared on deck, a boat put off from the *Gamecock* and began pulling over.

In her stern sheets sat a bony, long-jawed individual with "Yankee" written all over him.

"*Narragansett,* ahoy!" he hailed through cupped hands. "The owner aboard?"

Tim caught up a leather speaking trumpet. "Yes, come aboard and give us the news."

Said Freebody suddenly, "I know him, that there's Charley Pierce out o' Providence. We was on the *Gaspée* raid together and got near enough hell that night to smell the smoke."

The other began waving his hat. "Got better than news, Mr. Bennett. I've a signed and sealed copy of your commission. Captain Lawton sent another by *The Three Brothers.* I take it she ain't arrived yet."

"Come aboard, Captain, and for God's sake hurry!" Tim felt ready to jig, to beat Freebody, Boyd, anyone on the back.

The news spread through the letter-of-marque like wildfire. Even the watch off duty tumbled out of the forecastle, rubbing their eyes and demanding what in blazes was wrong.

"Howdy, Loammi, still layin' to an' takin' it easy?" Grinning, the *Gamecock's* master passed over a scroll of paper done up in a waterproof wrapper. "Wal, there she be."

There, at long last, lay his commission! Tim could hardly believe it. On Roxbury Heights was where this moment had had its inception.

Chuckling, he turned to Captain Freebody. "You'd better pipe all hands on deck." A moment later the boatswain's pipe began an insistent shrilling and peeping.

Captain Pierce looked on with grim approbation while the crew, black, white, French, English and Yankee, gathered at the break of the quarterdeck.

"All hands," Freebody called, "pipe down and listen hard. Mr. Bennett is goin' to read out the terms o' commission."

"THE DELEGATES OF THE UNITED COLONIES, Massachusetts Bay, Rhode Island, Connecticut, New York, New Jersey, Counties of Kent & Sussex on the Delaware, Maryland, Virginia, North Carolina, South Carolina, to all unto these Presents shall come send Greeting. Know ye:

That we have granted and by the Presents do grant License and authority to Timothy Bennett owner, Letter-of-Marque *Narragansett,* and to Capt. Loammi Freebody, Mariner, commander of the Brig called the *Narragansett* of the burthen of one hundred and fifty tons or thereabouts belonging to Timothy Bennett of the Province of Rhode Island mounting eight carriage Guns and navigated by ninety Men, to fit out and set forth the said Brig in a Warlike manner, and by and with the said Brig and the crew thereof by force of Arms, to ATTACK, SUBDUE and TAKE all Ships and other vessels whatsoever carrying soldiers, Arms, gunpowder ammunition, provisions or any other contraband Goods to any of the British Armies or ships of War employed against the United Colonies and also to ATTACK, SEIZE and TAKE all vessels belonging to the inhabitants of Great Britain or to any subj. or subjs. thereof with their tack'll apparel, Furniture and ladings on the High Seas or between high & low water mark. (The ships or vessels belonging to any Inhabitant or inhabitants of Bermuda and such ships and such other ships or vessels bringing Persons with intent to settle and reside in the United Colonies or bringing Arms ammunition or war-like stores to said Colonies for the use thereof, which said ships or vessels you shall suffer to pass unmolested, the Commanders thereof permitting a peaceable search and giving satisfactory information on the contents of the ladings and Destination of the voyagers, only excepted.)

* * * * * * * * * *

And we will and require all our Officers whatsoever in the Service of the United Colonies to give Succor and Assistance to said Timothy Bennett in the premises. This Comm. shall continue in force until Congress shall issue orders to the contrary. Dated Philadelphia ye 7th day of April, 1776.

By the Congress,
John Hancock, Pres."

Attest: Stephen Hopkins

9

FAREWELLS

BECAUSE of the necessity of securing properly stamped clearance papers and of taking aboard such last minute supplies as sea turtles, fruits, fowl and a long boat's load of pigs, Tim did not set out for shore until almost nine of the evening.

As Tim's gig threshed by under the stern of the great, glowing *la Dédaigneuse,* voices and music floated down. Dozens of lanterns glowed high overhead, and through the open gun ports Tim, Loammi Freebody and the men from the *Narragansett* could see hairy members of the battleship's crew sprawling in their hammocks, gaming or repairing some item of equipment.

For all the ornate gilding and carved stern galleries, from the liner came fetid odors of stale sweat, rank tobacco and bilge water. Crimanently! She surely made the *Narragansett* seem like mighty small potatoes by comparison.

Still, it meant everything to know that, by this time tomorrow, he would be far out to sea. He had, of course, notified Prenet and Dulac the minute he'd finished reading out his commission.

How would Jeannette act tonight? He hoped she wouldn't cry and get all upset. That was one thing about the home folks. They seldom let on how badly they felt.

In the Dulac home Claude Prenet, the harbor master, the chief shipwright and all the principal merchants who had helped outfit the letter-of-marque were congregated around a huge bowl of champagne punch.

"Ah, le voilà!" Dulac called. "Congratulations, my boy!"

The whole company crowded about, clapping the two Americans on the shoulders, wringing their hands and clinking glasses.

Gradually Freebody's brown nut of a face relaxed, even though he wouldn't touch a drop of anything stronger than beer.

"Long success to the *Narragansett!*" shouted the harbor master.

"Down with the Lobster-backs!" countered Freebody, and the whole house rang to the cheer that followed. It was certain that these French and Créoles nursed a deep fear and hatred of the Royal Navy. Characteristically, it never occurred to Tim that these foreigners were honestly fond of his cheerful, plain and above-board ways, that they might be genuinely hopeful for his success.

A grizzled old Breton who had supplied most of the carpenters came over presently and under his breath said:

"A word of warning, Mr. Bennett. Only today I have received private intelligence from Jamaica. My agent there warns that the English Admiral has learned of our activities. This admiral is dispatching from Port Royal a small squadron of cruisers and a heavy frigate."

Tim listened hard over the babble of voices, wished Loammi Freebody could hear this. He found that, more and more, he was forced to rely on the old privateersman's experience. Well, he intended to learn, to become more than a sort of glorified supercargo on his own ship.

"That's worth knowing. Where are they?"

"Between Cap de la Pristelle, Cuba and Great Inagua." The Breton winked. "In putting to sea one would be astute to avoid the Windward Channel."

Tim nodded his thanks, then asked, "There are English agents here in town?"

"This port teems with them," the Breton assured him. "Your compatriots will be wise to keep a close mouth. A careless word and they will find themselves prisoners."

Toast followed toast. After Tim had drunk to the health of His Most Christian Majesty, Louis XVI, M. Prenet raised his glass and signaled for silence.

"Gentlemen," he called, "I give you a toast to a nation yet unborn, but one which I am certain will soon see the light of day. Friends and neighbors, I give you the United Colonies of America!"

"Hurray!" Freebody yelled. "That's more like it!"

After a bit, Tim could no longer delay. He simply had to find Jeannette.

She was awaiting him on a vine-hung balcony which circled the whole second floor. Never had she seemed so exquisitely fragile and lovely as when she floated towards him through the starlight with the fireflies dancing all about and a mocking bird warbling in an acacia and camellia grove below. Over the tops of the palms, they got a clear view of the harbor, and of the myriad lights glancing off its glassy surface.

"Oh, my heart, return to me soon!" Jeannette breathed at the end of an exquisitely tender hour. "Not only for my sake, but for poor Papa's, too." She was looking at him very steadily from wide-set dark eyes. "If you are not successful, he will meet with terrible difficulties to pay his debts."

"I'll head for Cap François the first instant it's feasible," he promised, lips brushing her delicately scented forehead. "I'll come back soon—soon!"

Just before he left, her composure cracked and she clung to him, sobbing, "Oh, Teem, Teem, you will be very careful? You will not expose yourself? Last year one of Papa's sloops fought some *boucaniers* off Cuba. I have seen what splinters and cannonballs can do." She shivered.

"One last thing," she cautioned. "Be careful of what you write to me. Diane has conceived for us such a violent hatred I would put nothing past her. Yesterday, she attended a reception at the English Consulate. Anything you have to say of your heart would best be written in lemon juice."

Tim nodded then produced a little comb of delicately fashioned ivory. "One of my men made this," he said. "It's carved from a walrus's tooth. Though it doesn't match up with your gold and tortoise-shell combs, I'll warrant there ain't too many of these around Cap François."

"Oh, it is beautiful, beautiful!" cried Jeannette running over to the starlight. "See, there are little dolphins frolicking along the top, and a mermaid! I had never imagined a North American would have such skill."

Placing her hands on his shoulders, she peered into his eyes and came slowly forward until their lips met. "All my love goes with you, *mon adoré.*"

10

OFF TURKS' ISLAND

BRACING himself against the slow, steady roll of the *Narragansett,* Timothy Bennett watched Loammi Freebody make an entry in the brig's log book:

> June 27, 1776. This day fine. Moderate breeze from N-NW. Position: Longitude 70° 4 min west. Latitude 22° 7 min north. Course: W by S. Remarks: 9:15 a.m.: Overtook & made Prize of the *Swallow,* schooner, 90 tons, Arthur Watson, Master. Out of Lisbon for Montego Bay, Jamaica. Raised his topsails at dawn. Gave immediate chace. Prize proved very slow. When I fired a gun he came into wind. Haul'd down his Colours at 7:30 a.m. Ten men to secure the Prize. Schooner's lading was found to consist in the Main of Sheffield goods, calicoes, canvas, chinaware, music Boxes, Harnesses, & sev'ral tuns of Oporto Wine. Ship & cargo are Assur'd in the am't of £6500 sterling. Vessel seems well Found. Should fetch a handsome price. Discovering share to Phillip Hull, ordinary seaman, who first spied prize. Owner hath ordered prize master to make for Savannah in the Colony of Georgia.

"Not a bad start, Mr. Bennett, not at all bad," Captain Freebody grunted, carefully sanding his entry. "Could wish the some o' the hands showed more keenness, though."

Three days later, Captain Freebody made another entry in the *Narragansett's* log book:

> June 30, 1776
> 2:45 p.m.
> Have just rais'd topsails of a large Brig.
> Have hoisted Spanish colours and am giving chace. Stranger brig refuses to show colours but hath shap'd a course for Gt. Inagua.

4:05 p.m.
Hull of the Chace now above the horizon. Am closing in fast. Crew
restive over large size of Stranger.

5:50 p.m.
Chace is abandoning Boats & cutting away Anchors in effort to better
Speed. Continue to overhaul. Hope to Close with Brig before Dark-
ness prevents.

Having completed this entry, Captain Freebody stumped back on
deck. With all sails set, the *Narragansett* was fairly hissing over a
bright blue sea with her topsails turning gold in the late afternoon
sunlight. By God, this was just like the good old days of '61 and '62!

Freebody found his owner pacing steadily back and forth at the
break of the quarterdeck and studying the set of the straining canvas.
Below, powder monkeys were sanding the deck, stowing loose gear
and otherwise preparing for action.

Long since, tompions had been withdrawn from the *Narragansett's*
cannon; roundshot clinked and flashed in all the racks; slow matches,
lying on tubs of sand, gave off small blue tendrils of smoke.

Right now the crew, in order to reduce the havoc of flying splinters,
was busily lashing hammocks filled with bedding along the tops of
the bulwarks. Others were rigging fine chains to supplement vital
halyards, braces and stays.

It was a glorious afternoon with a bright blue sky sketching glowing colors in the sea. Quantities of silvery flying fishes kept springing
from the wave crests and skittering along parallel to the free-running
letter-of-marque.

If nothing happened, Mr. Bennett would make a good privateersman before long, Loammi Freebody reflected. Under stress, he was
calm and foresighted; just like his Pa. He was a born fighter, but he
might meet up with trouble if he didn't slow down a mite in his
judgments.

Arranged in regularly repeated patterns along the deck, the gun
crews were waiting. They weren't by any means as calm as they
might be—especially the foreigners. These would crane their necks
over the bulwarks and peer through the gunports awhile. Then

they'd draw aside and talk excitedly, wave their hands.

From its rack beside the binnacle, Loammi Freebody took a heavy, old-fashioned brass spy-glass and trained it on the chase. Hum! A fine, strong vessel. Why should she run? A ruse? Or was she really unarmed?

"Well, Captain, and what is she?"

"Might be one of His Majesty's transports," Freebody suggested. "Or maybe another private-armed vessel."

"What makes you think so?" Tim was trying to subdue a fierce excitement.

"The chase is better painted than the average merchantmen."

"Any guns?"

"She shows ports for a broadside of six cannon," the sea captain announced, eye glued to spy-glass. "But, being as the lids ain't raised, there's no tellin' whether she's armed or not."

"How soon do you judge we will be in range?"

"Ten, maybe fifteen minutes if this slant o' wind don't fail us," Freebody predicted. He straightened, his lanky figure yielding easily to the brig's motion. "Mr. Bennett, I opine we had better show our true colors. That there Spanish ensign ain't foolin' a soul."

It lent Tim a rare thrill to watch the red and yellow ensign of Spain come flapping down, to see his rattlesnake flag replace it at the *Narragansett's* signal gaff.

Curiously, as he stood there absently looking at the checker work wrought by the rigging's shadows on the white deck, he remembered what Lieutenant Jones had said about failing to see why a venomous serpent should represent an honest people fighting to be free.

The *Alfred's* lieutenant had been quite right. This yellow banner was not a particularly inspiring emblem. With amusement, Tim noted that whoever had painted the motto, "Don't Tread on Me," had spelled the word "tread" without an "a."

"Mr. Bennett, sir," a voice hailed from the deck. The boatswain shuffled forward, cap in hand. Respectfully enough, he knuckled his forelock.

"Mr. Bennett, a lot of us don't like the look of the chase. She's mighty tall and might prove too tough to handle. Hadn't you better sheer off a bit? Feel her out at long range?"

"No! Get back to your post," Tim ordered in the voice he'd used at the Siege. "Leave it again and I'll—"

"—Talk easy, sir," Freebody begged. "Remember these ain't no men-o'-war's men."

"—Dock you your share," Tim concluded lamely. He was angry, though, at the impudence of the fellow.

Freebody was quick to capitalize on the boatswain's sullen retreat. "Number One gun, port battery prepare to fire."

The crew shuffled to their posts, the gunport of the port bow chaser was raised and the piece, a long eighteen, was run out.

"Fire!"

The letter-of-marque shuddered as a great cloud of gray-white smoke went whipping off to leeward. A cable's length ahead of the fleeing brig rose a silvery jet of water. Simultaneously, a British jack climbed to the stranger's signal halyard.

A low cry arose from the *Narragansett's* gun crews when the chase yawed a little and let fly with a pair of cannons. Her shot screamed by, punching harmless holes in the fore-topsail.

"Very light," Freebody snapped. "Reg'lar bean shooters. Let's hope he ain't bein' 'cute and is drawin' us in close for a real broadside."

Encouraged, the *Narragansett's* crew reloaded, and this time an eighteen pound shot hit the stranger amidships. Everybody yelled like mad to see a cloud of yellow splinters go a-flying. Stung, the chase let fly again. A six pound ball struck the taffrail, made a loud crackling noise.

To Tim, it seemed as if someone had dealt him a hard whack across the forehead. Half stunned, he reeled, clapping a hand to his forehead. Blood began pouring in torrents down his face. The hot sticky stuff filled, blinded his right eye and clouded his left.

A steadying arm went about his waist and he heard Freebody's staccato voice saying, "Hold hard. 'Tain't nought but a splinter graze."

Tim, steadying himself on a back stay, could hear the port broadside let go with a thunderous report. Using the heel of one hand, he cleared an eye and, with a great lifting sensation, watched the brown and blue painted chase come into the wind.

Jerkily, her ensign sank out of sight behind the bulwarks.

II

H. M. S. GROWLER

THE brig proved to be H. M. S. *Growler*, supply vessel, out of Cork for His Majesty's Dock Yard at Port Royal. The minute he set foot to her deck, Tim understood the brig's feeble defense. She was practically unarmed since her armament consisted of four puny six pounders, little larger than signal guns.

Long and loud, the supply vessel's beefy, red-faced captain cursed and raged at an Admiralty which had sworn that no armed American vessel cruised the sea. Sputtering, he stamped about, called the New Englanders pirates and swore he'd live to see his captors swing from Execution Dock. He even shook a fist at the rattlesnake flag displayed above his Union Jack.

Though his temper nearly boiled over, Tim remained polite and equably ordered his prize crew to secure the Englishmen seamen and twenty-five crestfallen private soldiers, replacements for His Majesty's 50th Infantry which, it was learned, formed a portion of the Jamaica garrison.

Not since that November night on which he had met Lucy in the Congress Tavern had Timothy Bennett's heart been lifted so high. It didn't seem real, somehow, to find himself on the quarterdeck of a fat prize taken by his own letter-of-marque! Yet there rocked the *Narragansett*, less than two hundred yards away, with her topsails backed and her cannon run out. Captain Freebody was taking no chances.

The *Growler*, 120 tons, proved to be a brand-new vessel. When an army quarter-master sullenly surrendered bills of lading and the cargo manifest, Dr. Boyd scanned them, uttered a piercing whistle.

"Faith, Mr. Bennett, ye must indeed be Fortune's favorite! If their Lordships of the Admiralty had studied to please ye, the rascals couldn't have selected better. Holy Mary! Will yez listen to this?"

Running a stubby finger down the manifest, he read aloud:

> "2,500 pair leggings
> 2,500 pair shoes
> 900 stands of Muskets, King's Arm
> 110 tents, canvas
> 4800 cartouche Boxes, leather
> 1500 Bayonets
> 15 barrels of 3F gunpowder
> 4 pieces field ordnance."

Nor was that all. From the *Narragansett's* prize officers burst delighted cries, chuckles of satisfaction, as they paused, pistol in hand, to learn the nature of the cargo.

A sheaf of lists described ample supplies of saddlery, uniform coats, great-coats, chests of medicine and musical instruments; in short, everything useful to a force on active duty.

When Tim thought of the Continental Army's crying need for such supplies, the golden splinters sparkled in his eyes.

"At a rough guess, Doctor, how much do you think such a cargo will fetch?" He was forgetting the ache of his bandaged head, the burning of the three-inch gash across his forehead.

Dr. Boyd couldn't guess, but Silas Turner, the prize master appointed by Freebody, turned leathery features lit by the deepening sunset. "Mr. Bennett, if this here cargo dunt fetch nigh fifty thousand pounds sterling, I'll eat my wig!"

"Fifty thousand!" The whole cabin spun and swayed about Tim's head. Wait 'til Newport heard of this! "And what about the brig herself?"

Mr. Turner scratched the grizzled stubble on his jaw, deliberated, his body rocking to the ship's motion. "Provided she proves a handy sailor, this craft will bring around ten thousand—mebbe a mite more.

Her spars and cordage look spandy-new to me."

A hulking marine stepped up and whispered into Tim's ear. "That there Army feller just now acted like a cat round a dairy house. Figger he's hiding somethin', sir. Better take a look at his cabin."

When Tim ordered a pair of marines to conduct a search, they found at the bottom of a sea chest, a smaller chest which was elaborately bound with iron and secured with twin padlocks. When the privateersmen hefted it, it proved to be enormously heavy.

Tim turned to the quartermaster. He was standing between a brace of marines carrying cocked blunderbusses.

"The keys, please."

"You can go to hell, you damned picaroons," snarled the officer, turning as red as his coat. "I suppose you bloody pirates can force it open, but I give you fair warning, that chest contains Crown property. You touch it at your peril."

"Wal, now," drawled Silas Turner, looming tall above the indignant Englishman. "Naow, don't you git all foamed up and b'ilin', Mister. The *Narragansett* is a duly commissioned letter-of-marque. 'Twun't change matters to act childish. That there's a real pretty chest. 'Twould be a sin and shame to spoil its looks."

His hand shot out and, pinning the scarlet-coated figure to the cabin wall, he searched until he found a pair of keys tucked into the fellow's waistband.

As Tim prepared to open the padlock, Turner said to the marines, "Naow, yew fellers escort this gentleman to the fo'c's'le. By the look o' him, he's liable to come down with the strangary."

The marines obeyed, but they went with an obvious reluctance.

"Why send them away?" Tim queried curiously.

"I bin 'round privateersmen before," Turner grunted. "Ain't none o' 'em I'd trust out o' sight wi' a red-hot penny. Give some o' these lads we've shipped an eyeful o' gold, an' you may well find your vessels piled up on a reef so's to end the cruise and bring about division of the shares."

Dr. Boyd stared. "Not really!"

"Aye. The hands don't like risking their necks at any time, least of all when they stand to collect a rich share."

Lantern light revealed in the chest a great number of paper-covered cylinders arranged in tight orderly rows. Lying on top of them were two small canvas sacks. When Tim hefted one of these, an electric shock shot up his arm. Hurriedly, he jerked a pucker string. Into his palm clinked a flood of heavy, golden-red sovereigns!

With Great Inagua a low-lying black smear on the western horizon, the two vessels cruised on parallel courses all night in order that certain choice items of plunder and the iron-bound chest might be transferred to the *Narragansett*.

Just as dawn was sketching lovely turquoise and crimson patterns across the sky, the *Growler* dipped her colors in salute, swung her yards about and departed on her way to Philadelphia.

Locked securely in the transom of Timothy Bennett's cabin was the contents of the quarter-master's chest—nearly £22,000 that would never serve as pay for His Majesty's armed forces in Jamaica.

Nothing was pleasanter for Tim than to heed Loammi Freebody's earnest advice that the *Narragansett* return with all speed to Cap François. Recalling what Mr. Turner had said about privateersmen and their ways, Tim judged it would be wise to remove temptation at the first possible instant.

Yes, it would be only sensible to deposit the specie in escrow in some bank. Under such conditions, none of the hands would want to quit until the contracted cruise was at an end.

There also existed the necessity of replacing the prize crews sent aboard the *Swallow* and the *Growler*. Too bad he'd had to lose his New Englanders and two of his most dependable officers.

That was the hell of it. One couldn't entrust to less efficient men the responsibility of fetching the prizes safe into port. What with that press of private-armed ships equipping themselves at Cap François, it would be the very devil to find even half-trustworthy men.

Perhaps Dulac or Prenet could find him some dependable Breton and Norman seamen off the ships that were continually making port. When it came to Frenchmen, there was a lot even Freebody didn't know.

THE CHEVALIER DE COHARS

THAT he was not the first successful private-armed vessel to put in at Cap François, Tim Bennett was not long in appreciating. During the *Narragansett's* absence the number of American vessels in Cap François harbor had more than doubled.

Yonder lay a big ship-rigged privateer. She flew the pine tree flag of Massachusetts and had two stubby British merchantmen lying alongside. Further away was a brigantine flying a blue beaver on a white field for an ensign. Some few rattlesnake flags fluttered at various mastheads and these fired salutes when the *Narragansett* came rolling in past a line of slow-flying gray pelicans and showing the captured British jacks below her yellow ensign.

Once the *Narragansett* had saluted the port with seven guns, she tacked to her old anchorage and made a brave showing in the smart way her crew handled her.

"We will put in just long enough to attend to our business and to recruit the crew," Tim had told Freebody. "There will be no shore leave."

There was loud grumbling over this, but the letter-of-marque's marines were posted in the gangways and at bow and stern as soon as the canvas had been snugged down.

"You'll be calling over to Mounseer Dulac's, I take it?" Freebody suggested when Tim ordered the gig overboard.

"Aye, and when I come back, it will be to show my future wife over the ship."

"*Wife?*" The sea captain's blood-shot gray eyes narrowed. "Mr.

Bennett, you're not thinkin' o' marryin' with that Frenchie, are ye?"

Tim glared, "That will do, Captain. I'll tolerate no criticism of Mistress Dulac. You may expect us aboard in two hours. Once it gets cooler, have the ship dressed and issue a double tot of rum.

"Plague take it, man," he thumped his captain between the shoulder-blades. "We've done well! I'll wager no other private-armed vessel has done any better. Come, wipe that sour look off your face—at best it's no thing of beauty."

Loammi Freebody managed a mechanical grin and said, "Aye, aye, sir." But his jaw remained set at an angle of uncompromising disapproval.

Gloomily, he went below. For nigh on fifty years Loammi Freebody had believed, like every honest Englishman, that the French were a mighty funny race. They'd strange ideas about the use of feet in a free-for-all. Some of their notions about the way to make love didn't set so well, either.

That splinter gash was still a sight too tender to admit wearing a hat, but Boyd could apply a fresh bandage, Tim decided as he shaved in his cabin.

Now he was pleased he'd never let Jeannette see his blue and white uniform. Wouldn't she be pleased! She had always set quite a store by a smart uniform.

Crimanently! He'd even wear that slender sword he'd selected from the plunder of the H. M. S. *Growler*. Was he silly? Would it look as if he were play-acting? Hurriedly he reminded himself that he was officer over the *Narragansett's* marines, even though they were private-armed and equipped.

Tomorrow morning he would send the pay chest ashore and set about some serious recruiting. But this afternoon—

Lord! His heart lifted. He'd done it, by God, *he'd done it!* Now they could become properly, publicly affianced! He ached to feel Jeannette in his arms again, to sense her unearthly fragility. He was eager to feel her respond to his touch like some delicate musical instrument.

Anatole Dulac, too, would undoubtedly be relieved to have the settlement money so early, and all in un-clipped, un-sweated English gold.

Tim sat very erect in the stern sheets of his gig as she skimmed by *la Dédaigneuse*. The liner, he noticed, was again making ready for sea. Her topmen were busy bending on sails and a series of barges were rowing out detachments of troops homeward-bound after the expiration of their tour of garrison duty.

They sounded mightily pleased to be going, did those big-mustached fellows in their white uniforms and red revers.

"They are from the Soissonais regiment," explained a French member of the gig's crew.

Presently, Tim's boat pulled in beside a series of water steps near the end of the Rue des Brasseurs.

Despite Loammi Freebody's insular misgivings, Tim felt it intelligent to make a clean break with the past. Jeannette was ideally suited to this philosophy. There was nothing about her to remind him of the disease and death of the Siege, the dreadful mistake about the lunar enlistment, Conanicut, or Lucy's faint-hearted betrayal.

Now he stood at the brink of a new and prosperous career. Good thing he hadn't heeded Petty's arguments for a passive, sensuous happiness.

He had been lucky, of course, but no more so than many another. And his luck would continue. Yes, in finding a girl for whom he could fight, who would make him a charming, amusing and intelligent wife, he had turned the corner of his life.

"Jeannette!" he murmured. "Only a moment more—only a few moments more."

The hot cobbles under his patent leather pumps ceased to burn. He felt like singing something, anything. But for his sword and uniform and dignity as owner of the *Narragansett,* he would have broken into a run, he was so impatient. When he got to the Dulacs' he'd snatch Jeannette into his arms and whirl her around. Soon as he had time, he'd buy presents for the whole family—even for silly little Diane.

Never had there been such a grand and beautiful a town as Cap François, nor such pleasant, elegant people. He beamed so broadly that people turned to stare after this tall young man with the swinging sword and bandaged head.

Fifty yards more and he'd be before old Dulac's gate.

A small group of people had collected there. They seemed to be watching a platoon of the Soissonais regiment tramp down to the landing.

All at once the gate swung open and Jeannette appeared in the midst of the group.

"Darling!" Tim called. "I—"

He broke off because just behind Jeannette strode the Chevalier de Cohars, looking mighty pleased and at ease. Old Dulac was waddling after them, his huge stomach undulating like a bowl of suet in motion.

When Jeannette saw the compact figure in blue and white drawing near, she stared round-eyed an instant, then went deadly white.

"Oh, *Mon Dieu!*" Catching up her skirt, she ran back into the house. The Chevalier de Cohars swung sharply about, stepped sidewise to block the gate.

Some inner instinct conveyed a message to Tim which set an icy gale to blowing through his soul.

De Cohars' bleak mouth drew itself into forbidding, arrogant lines. He bowed stiffly. "One is positive, Monsieur," said he in clipped English, "that you will forbear to embarrass Mlle. Dulac with your presence."

"She—doesn't want to see—me?"

"One is certain of that," stated the nobleman coldly. "Mademoiselle Dulac is now under my protection. We sail for France tonight."

Stiffly, the Captain of *la Dédaigneuse* turned away and joined a group of officers waiting beneath some palms.

"Good day, M'sieur Bennett," Dulac waddled forward, a mechanical smile on his shiny features. "I regret that your unexpected return has caused such a *contretemps*. You have my sympathy. This intelligence could have been more tactfully presented."

"But—but—you—she promised—"

Dulac's black brows met. "Nothing was promised by either of us until the settlement was made. You will recall that?"

"Yes, but I—I understood she was to wait." The words escaped without Tim's volition.

The Créole shrugged, spread his hands. "Privateering is a risky profession and one must always be practical. After you sailed the Chevalier de Cohars deigned to consider my daughter with marked approval."

Dulac's gaze wandered down to the battery and lingered there as he said, "As a result the Chevalier was kind enough to settle all my outstanding obligations. Further, he is investing in some sugar lands I propose to cultivate this autumn."

He gave Tim a steady look. "What else could I do? Was there any assurance that either you or the *Narragansett* would ever return? No!"

"But de Cohars *can't* marry Jeannette," Tim choked. "His wife is living, he—he told me so himself!"

The Créole's enormous shoulders rose a fraction of an inch. "You foreigners cannot comprehend such matters. Consider that Mme. de Cohars lives in very poor health. To me, the Chevalier has indicated that when Mme. de Cohars goes to her heavenly reward, my Jeannette will become her successor."

"And in the meantime?" Tim rasped.

Dulac's smile was bland. "She will do her best to make him happy. *En fin,* the end justifies the means, does it not? For Jeannette, this is an undreamed-of opportunity. She made the decision of her own free will."

"That's a lie!" Tim shouldered aside the Créole and, charging into the house, found Jeannette mechanically superintending the cording up of various chests and hampers.

"Jeannette, are you really willing—"

Said she, avoiding his eyes, "In France it means everything for a bourgeoise to become one of the nobility."

"But Great God above, de Cohars is not marrying you. He can't!"

"I shall have fifteen thousand livres a year," came the equable reply, "and Keroulas is much older than I. If I am so stupid I cannot charm him into marrying me, then I do not deserve to pass into the nobility. Soon Keroulas will be a marquis—his uncle is a dying man—and I shall become Madame la Marquise de Cohars."

Had not Tim been fortified by that overwhelming disillusionment of the year before, he could never have retained his air of frozen calm.

Said he jerkily, "Permit me, Mistress Jeannette, to wish you the happiness you deserve!"

Turning on his heel, the Rhode Islander stalked blindly back into the blazing sunlight.

An hour later, the *Narragansett* broke out her anchors and steered for the open sea.

"We will recruit the new hands at Môle Saint-Nicholas," was all he would say to Loammi Freebody.

13

PRIVATEERSMEN

TIMOTHY BENNETT was surprised at his ability to close a mental door on the whole matter of Jeannette Dulac. Maybe Lucy Percival had taught him how to do that. Fortunately, there was plenty to occupy him once the *Narragansett* was at sea. The gun crews needed an amazing amount of drill and, under Loammi Freebody's irascible tutelage, he was mastering the fundamentals of navigation.

One thing gave him concern. Ever since that brush with H. M. S. *Growler,* the crew kept looking at him as if he were something unusual. Whenever he addressed the petty officers, they seemed markedly reserved, suspicious of him.

On mulling over this impression, he set it down to a lack of confidence in his judgment, or did they lack confidence in their own abilities? Naturally, a crew composed of two races and three nationalities would find it hard to develop into a smoothly operating unit, yet they were no different from most privateer crews.

He frequently encouraged Carradine, the gunner, and Hawley, the boatswain, by reminding them that, in the old French war, Loammi Freebody had been a successful captain and had always brought his command home safe and comparatively undamaged.

Captain Freebody had wanted to touch at Môle Saint-Nicholas for the needed seamen but he had forgot all about that when the look-outs sighted the topsails of a British frigate crawling along the horizon to leeward.

Tim figured it would be smart to shape a course for Savannah through Crooked Island Passage. First, he would sell his cargo of Island goods; second, the failure or success of the *Swallow* in reaching safety would become known; and, most important, the needed hands would be Americans.

He was blest if he enjoyed cruising with such a polyglot crew. Right now, New Englanders formed a little more than half of the complement. Due to his efforts, a good proportion were ex-privateersmen. They were an irresponsible lot and given to tall talk. Carradine, the gunner, a burly rascal, especially set himself up as the ideal privateersman.

"Seems a mite big for his britches," Freebody once growled when the fellow displayed a disinclination for prompt obedience. He minded Freebody well enough on the whole, however.

The *Narragansett* was clipping along under a fine brisk south-easter, her canvas full and the water flying from her bows in a sparkling white smother when Tim was roused by a long-drawn hail of, "Sail ho!"

"Where away?" Freebody demanded through his speaking trumpet.

"Six points off port bow, sir," replied the look-out.

"Masthead, there! How does she sail?"

"Can't tell, sir," came the reply over the whining of tackles and the rhythmic creaking of the freshly painted yellow yards. "She's hull down. Deck! Deck! I spy another sail!" the look-out shouted.

"Where away?"

"Four points off our port bow, sir."

Men came tumbling up from below, crowded the rigging and lined the bulwarks. A prize? Probably a couple of sluggish merchantmen. More fat pickings. Everybody envied the look-out. He would get two deserving shares for this day's work if the yonder vessels proved fair prizes.

At the end of twenty minutes even those on deck could make out a pair of tiny white specks 'way off to port.

When for a third time the look-out called, "Sail ho!" over the *hush-hushing* of the seas alongside, all hands began to look serious.

Captain Freebody merely ordered the Quartermaster to hold the brig on her course.

"Where you going?" Tim queried.

"To the main-top, Mr. Bennett. Figger it's time I take a look my own self."

When he realized that his owner intended to follow him aloft, Loammi Freebody's wrinkled-seamed brown face tightened. He hoped to hell his owner wasn't going to interfere because he'd be flogged and keel-hauled if he enjoyed privateering subject to somebody else's say-so.

Tim found it quite a job to gain the main-top with the brig rolling and bucking under a smart breeze like this. By the time he reached the main-top, Freebody already had a short spy-glass trained on the three sails. From this elevation, Tim found he could see the strange vessels more clearly.

Soon it became unmistakable that two small vessels were being chased by a large, black-painted schooner.

Freebody turned, wiped wind-started water from his eyes. "Mr. Bennett, it's my judgment we had best put about and steer clear."

"And why, pray? It appears to me that, one way or another, we may take a prize."

His gaunt figure raking across the sky, Freebody set his jaw to an obstinate angle. "Can't say for sure, Mr. Bennett, but I don't like the look of it. That schooner looks turrible spick-and-span."

"And what of that? She looks no heavier than us."

"Mr. Bennett, that's as may be." He looked desperately uneasy as again he leveled the spy-glass.

Tim said, studying the fleeing vessels, "Those look like the kind of snows we build 'round home." Hair, whipping about his forehead, stung the red scar. "They're being chased, Captain. The schooner acts like a picaroon. If she is, I don't intend to stand by and watch them taken."

Freebody said after a long pause, "Mr. Bennett, yonder schooner don't look like a picaroon to me. Too clean. Buccaneers and such are dirty as pig pens." He closed the spy-glass with a decisive click. "It is my bounden opinion, sir, that yonder cruises a British bulldog—a reg'lar cruiser o' the Royal Navy."

He braced himself against the guard rail of the top. "Mr. Bennett, there ain't but one thing to do and that's to come about, and do it all-fired quick. That schooner's coming up hand-over-fist!"

Timothy Bennett shook his head. "We will not run away, Captain Freebody. Why do we mount eight carriage guns? What have we been drilling gun crews for? Eternal blazes, man, we are at war with England! It's my conception of duty that we should help those snows escape."

Captain Freebody's expression hardened. "All along I been a-feared somethin' like this would happen. Mr. Bennett, I don't know where you get the idea this here brig is out to fight men-o'-war. She ain't. Any privateersman will tell you there's nothing to be gained from a bulldog but hard knocks and an empty hold—*if* you manage to take her."

"But those snows—they're our countrymen."

"If they were afraid to take their chance, they'd no business to leave port," came the grim retort.

"I'm mighty disappointed in you, Captain Freebody," Tim said stiffly. "I'd always counted you a true American."

The other's bony features reddened and he peered anxiously at the distant schooner which was rushing over the bright blue sea with a silvery scroll streaming away from her bow.

"And so I am, Mr. Bennett! This is no time for you to question that. Right now, I've forgotten more about privateering and privateersmen than you'll ever know. Them there snows will have to look for themselves."

He turned in desperate entreaty. "Please order the brig about, even now we can just about make it."

"We'll stay and fight—"

"Fer God's sake look! The Britisher has the weather gauge of us. If he proves too heavy for us, we can't run; he'll drive us onto Great Inagua before sundown!"

Strong in Tim's memory was that night the *Patience* came home. He still could see Polypus Hammond, his hurt ear and the ragged remnants of his crew. Said he evenly, "Somebody's got to teach people in these parts some respect for our flag. Keep the brig on her course!"

Captain Freebody started a hot retort but instead swung over the main top and started below. Tim descended by the opposite shrouds and as soon as they reached the quarterdeck, he snapped, "You may clear for action, Captain."

"I ain't never questioned an order of yours before, so credit me this time," Freebody pleaded in an undertone. "The hands won't stand for this. For God's sake order the ship about!"

All along the bulwarks, the crew, in evident uneasiness, were watching the fleeing merchantmen come rushing straight towards the *Narragansett* in a panic-stricken search for protection. One of them was flying a blue and white flag; the other, a yellow flag. As yet, the brown-and-yellow-painted schooner was showing no colors whatsoever.

"That's a bulldog!" yelled one of the men. "The *Niobe,* I seen her in St. Kitts last winter."

"Will you clear for action, Captain?" Tim rasped. "Or must I dismiss you?"

This was his owner talking. Habit won. "Aye, aye, sir," Freebody grunted, face like a rock. "But on your head be it!"

"Oh, don't be such a damned gloom. That fellow's no bigger than we are—if as big—and I'll wager he can't come near matching our weight of metal."

Tim sped below.

He didn't pull on his uniform tunic, just buckled on a heavy cutlass and jammed a brace of boarding pistols into his belt. He was pounding up the after companion when the brig faltered, as if she were changing her course.

Rage welled hot into Tim's head when he saw a knot of men gesticulating, shoving and pulling at the wheel. He was among them in a flash, cuffing them aside.

"Get off this quarterdeck, you bloody mothers' mistakes!"

Before his blazing eyes they scattered and Tim himself spun the wheel until the *Narragansett* heeled over on her original course. He posted Dr. Boyd, pistol in hand, to see that the gray-faced quartermaster made no change.

Though the bosun's pipe kept shrilling, calling the men to quarters, they only milled excitedly about the deck. By the foot of the quarterdeck ladders a small crowd was gathering, shaking their fists, yelling:

"We'll not fight a bulldog." "She'll blow us to blazes!"

" 'Tain't right. 'Tain't in the Articles."

"Get to quarters, damn you!" Tim snatched out his cutlass. "Get the ship back on her course. Sparks! Carradine! Johnson! Get your matches going."

What in God's name ailed these fellows? He couldn't understand it. Why should the very mention of a regular war-vessel scare them into spasms? Why, the *Niobe* was obviously smaller.

Mr. Bennett never had seemed so tall, so fierce, young Phil Hull thought, as he, along with a handful of the steadier men, dashed for his post. French, Créole, Cockney voices bellowed protests, threats. Men in striped jerseys ran aimlessly about.

Only two gun crews made any pretense of obeying orders. Freebody bawled orders which nobody heeded. The strange schooner was closing in fast.

"Raise our flag!" Tim ordered in the frantic hope that the gesture might inspire discipline. Hardly had the rattlesnake flag straightened out to the freshening southerly breeze than the schooner fired a gun. White ensigns were broken out from her mastheads.

Sullenly, purposefully, the *Narragansett's* crew came running aft with Carradine, the gunner, out in front.

"Now, Mr. Bennett," Freebody invited acidly, "suppose you handle this?"

Leveling a boarding pistol, Tim shouted, "First man puts foot to this quarterdeck, I'll see hanged for a mutineer." Savagely, he pleaded with them. "See that nearest vessel? She's showing Rhode Island colors. The other's from Massachusetts. We ain't going to stand by and let an enemy smaller than us make prizes of them under our noses!"

"To blazes with 'em," roared Carradine. "We can't fight a King's cruiser. She'll shoot us to bits." He climbed half way up the quarterdeck ladder, spoke threateningly. "You order this vessel about right away, Mr. Bennett, or there'll be trouble."

Shame, biting disappointment raged in Tim's soul. He called his privateersmen cowards, traitors, self-seeking vagabonds; he implored them to stand to their guns, even promised lavish extra shares.

Dipping their colors in gratitude, the two snows went racing by. The cruiser was now less than a mile distant and charging up with guns run out.

"Use your eyes!" Freebody begged. "These fellows won't fight. Why should they risk getting killed? They'll be captured, aye, and turned loose unharmed at the first port. They know that. Don't be a fool!"

Suddenly, he turned, barked an order which set the brig's wheel flying over. At the same time, he snatched away Dr. Boyd's pistol. In a frantic hurry the crew ran to man the stays. Momentarily, the *Narragansett* hung in the wind's eye, yards rattling and canvas flapping.

"You yellow bastard!" Tim swung his pistol on Freebody, but a belaying pin, whizzing up from the main deck, knocked the weapon out of his hands, sent it overboard.

Tim realized it was no use. There was nothing to do but run.

"You ain't got the sense of a bedbug," snarled Carradine, helping to grind down the wheel.

Having turned in her tracks, the *Narragansett* commenced to gather headway and started after the snows. Numbly, Tim watched the topmen lie out on the yards, setting every inch of canvas that might draw. The masts groaned, stays creaked and the main boom bent under pressure of the wind.

What Tim couldn't get over was the fact that it was the New Englanders in the crew who were largely responsible for this shameful exhibition. It was they who had forced the letter-of-marque to decline battle.

At half a mile's range the cruiser opened fire and her first shot raised a terrific geyser of water not twenty yards short of the *Narragansett's* stern. Spray fell over the quarterdeck. Solemnly, Dr. Boyd spat in return.

Tim snatched up a leather speaking trumpet. "We can't get away without a fight. Get to your stations, you seamen. Look! The schooner carries only four guns to her broadside. We can lick her if you'll half try."

"No! No! Haul down the flag! Come into the wind," yelled terrified voices.

The deck was crowded with figures running aimlessly about, like hens threatened by a hawk. The few men who did try to man the *Narragansett's* guns were chased away, showered with curses and belaying pins.

The schooner's second shot plowed into the back of an ultramarine roller. Weeping with fury, Tim ran to the one cannon which had been loaded and run out. Rammer, sponger and ladle lay abandoned across its trail but the gunport lid was up and the recoil breeching was adjusted.

Phil Hull appeared, a cartridge under each arm.

"Find me a lighted match," Tim yelled. "We'll show these yel—"

He got no further, for high over head sounded a thunderous crack.

Boyd screamed and like a felled pine the main gaff came whirring down as a shot from the cruiser smashed its jaws to smithereens. Instantly a vast smother of flapping sailcloth blinded the quartermaster, choked the quarterdeck as the main topsail yard broke. Gradually the letter-of-marque lost way, began to roll.

"We'll fire one gun anyhow," Tim panted, and from his belt pulled the remaining pistol. He fired it full at the touch-hole of the long eighteen.

The cannon recoiled like a scared horse and, a quarter of a mile distant, a little jet of spray marked the *Narragansett's* single pathetic gesture of defiance.

To see a British jack flying above his brig's rattlesnake flag sent a bitter taste into Tim's mouth. It seemed somehow unbelievable that the thought, worry and planning of these last weeks should so abruptly have come to nothing. And for no sound reason either; that was what hurt.

There had been no earthly reason why the *Narragansett,* shorthanded or not, shouldn't have been able to whip this paltry little cruiser.

To the depths of his soul, Tim Bennett felt sickened, utterly discouraged, and wholly disillusioned. Was there nothing true or dependable in all this world? Three times he'd put forth all his faith —in Lucy, in Jeannette and in the *Narragansett.* Which had failed him, hurt him the most deeply was a question.

He judged he would never be able to understand why the very sight of a Royal cruiser was enough to shake the courage of his men. Freebody had been right, all right about this crew. Where lay an explanation for privateersmen's refusal to fight except for cash on the line?

The sun was sinking as, plunged in gloom, he watched a squad of barefooted seamen lug from his cabin that small, ironbound chest. They lowered it carefully into the *Niobe's* longboat.

What an utter fool he'd been to let his emotions run away with him back in Cap François. There went over ten thousand pounds!

He might at least have waited long enough to send the precious specie ashore.

A British prize crew, contemptuous of so spineless an exhibition, shackled the letter-of-marque's men hand and foot and, jeering, herded them down a ladder into the forehold. A pink-cheeked and arrogant young sub-lieutenant loftily condescended to accept the paroles of Tim, Dr. Boyd and Captain Freebody.

Dr. Boyd, alone, seemed to comprehend the measure of Tim's grief and bewilderment. Twice, thrice the little man patted his shoulder. "Ye've heard where they're sending us?"

"It can be to hell, for all I care," Tim growled. Every time he saw that neat brown and yellow schooner riding the waves but a few hundred yards to windward, he wanted to burst into a string of curses. She must be lighter than the *Narragansett* by twenty tons.

"'Tis into New Providence for condemnation proceedings," Dr. Boyd informed him. "Most likely they'll turn the crew onto the beach as usual and hold us for exchange. Though what they'd swap for me would be the divil of a poor soul!"

To New Providence once more?

There might have been far worse destinations. Fever-ridden Port Royal, for instance. Fervently, Tim hoped the new Governor of the Bahamas would recognize the validity of his letter-of-marque's commission. It would be no fun at all to be hanged for a pirate.

PART II—KENTUCKY: 1777

I

ROCKCASTLE CREEK

MIKE STONER's moccasins had sketched a series of black prints on the newly fallen snow. Desire Harmony could see them winding down among the beech trees on the far side of the ravine. There were other tracks among the bare sumac and blackberry bushes. Those of several rabbits, of a squirrel and, of course, plenty of pug marks left by Snapper, second of that name.

This Snapper didn't much resemble Tim's pet; would have made two of her brother's pup, in fact. But Sam Higsby had been pleased as Punch when she had suggested the name.

"That's a mighty fine term fer a bear dog," he'd chuckled, fondling the great hound's pointed skull between his knees. "You should have seen him nippin' at that big 'she' down to Crab Orchard bottom last November. Handiest dog I ever see."

Because she couldn't see through the cabin's window of oiled deer's bladder, Desire Harmony Higsby sought the door. Two brown figures could be clearly seen against the snow. Sam and Stoner, the big Pennsylvania Dutchman, were talking beside the carcass of a fresh-killed buck Sam had been flaying.

Sam, she saw, was bloodied, stripped to his doeskin undershirt while Stoner was weighted down with traveling gear. A long rifle rested in the crook of his arm and he'd a dead rabbit slung to his belt.

She couldn't hear what they were saying because they conversed in the characteristically soft undertones of the frontier. Unless a timber beast got drunk, he would never raise his voice in the woods, or shout, or really laugh out loud.

Desire knew enough not to call from the doorway. A slender

but sturdy figure in gray-brown linsey-woolsey, she crossed a cleared space in front of the fine long cabin Sam and Mike Stoner had put up last autumn. She wished she could wear moccasins, but she couldn't—she had worn heels too long. Her leg muscles ached every time she tried it.

"You will stay to supper, Mr. Stoner?" she invited. She hoped he would accept. It was something to get news, no matter how stale and it was six weeks since she'd seen a new white face. Skanawati, the Catawba trapper who worked the valleys to the south, would stop by every week or so and sit picking his vermin before the fire a while, but he could talk only a little English and seemed shy of her.

Stoner clawed off a squirrel fur cap. The hair was worn off it on the sides and it was yellowed with grease above the ears.

"Ach, Mrs. Higsby, dot vould I admire," he rumbled from the depths of a shaggy yellow beard, "but I vant I should reach Flat Lick by der moonrise."

What had caused the Dutchman to come so far out of his way —all of fifteen miles off the Warrior's Path? A small stab of anxiety stung Desire's heart.

"Is—there isn't any Indian trouble?"

"Nein!" The giant grinned, unslinging his war bag. "All has been still since dot Chief Pluggy got beat so bad at McClelland's Station der end of December." He smiled, teeth gleaming in the depths of his beard. "Und der leetle girl, she iss vell?"

"Oh, yes, thriving. She grows so fast I venture she will match you for size in a short time," Desire laughed, settling a plaid shawl tighter about her shoulders.

"I pring her somedings ven from der settlements I come back," the giant promised. Gott! What a beautiful woman! Her eyes and those shadows under them. She was too pretty for the frontier, even if she was strong and willing.

"Really you must stay, Mr. Stoner. We are just about to have a bowl of sagamite. Eve has made a fresh batch of pone today, too."

Stoner shook his head so strongly that long yellow strands of hair mingling with the fringes at his shoulder swayed.

Prettily, Desire passed an arm through Stoner's, led him indoors. "Well, you must at least take along some of Eve's buckwheat souens. She made some this morning."

Sam whistled Snapper in, lest he take to feasting on the deer's head. He slapped the giant between his shoulders. "I'll give you that buck's tongue if you want it."

Stoner was both flattered and pleased. Along the frontier few greater delicacies than a deer's tongue were available. Even smoked, a tongue had lots more flavor than other unsalted meats.

As the three of them stamped into the gloom of the cabin, Stoner looked about and, seeing Sam's spare moccasins drying before the chimney piece, stroked his head in satisfaction.

"*Mein Gott,* Mrs. Higsby, already a home you haff made of it."

"It's prettier than an Indian lodge, anyhow," Desire smiled. She was very pleased that yesterday Sam had finished building a rough wooden barrier which, head-high, divided the cabin two-thirds and one-third. It wasn't nice to have Eve always under foot and looking on. Now she did her cooking and sleeping at the far end.

"Please, Mr. Stoner, you are very sure there are no Indian signs?"

"Not vun," Stoner reassured her so earnestly that she believed him. "It vass aboudt somedings else I vass talking to Sam."

"Really?"

"Very soon ve in dis country a government must haff." His big dark head inclined gravely. "Me, Wide Mouth—Colonel Boone, I mean—und some odders t'ink Sam maybe should represent der district in der Virginia Congress."

In the act of smoothing the beaver blanket over Joanna's crib, Desire hesitated. "We—a part of Virginia?" she said. "Why, I thought Kentucky was going to be a separate State."

Sam, reaching up to the shelf over a rough sideboard, said, "All in good time we will be. You cain't raise a oak over-night. Virginny is in a fix to help us better than Caroliny or Pennsylvany." He lowered a big gray-stone jug that gurgled. "I always claimed 'tain't no harm to use a little help when it's needed."

No Indian trouble! Desire was so immeasurably relieved she felt like singing. Ever since Stoner's arrival she'd been wondering whether they'd have to pack their things and "fort-up" at Flat Lick.

She ran over and slipped an arm about her husband's narrow waist. "Sam, I do protest Mr. Stoner is quite right. You *should* run for office."

It was so obvious that Sam was the man for the position. He got along well with everybody along the frontier—with the settlers, the land company agents, the surveyors, the bullies, the faint-hearts, the young and the old; any stray Catawba, Cherokee or Creek who came hunting through the country generally made a bee line for the cabin of Tskili, the Black Racer Snake, otherwise Sam Higsby.

Sam, Desire sensed, was settling down into a natural-born leader for those men and women who, during the past year, had come toiling up through the Cumberland Gap, following the tortuous Wilderness Road to the brand-new outposts of Harrodsburg and Boonesborough.

She was discovering in Sam an unsuspected caution and common-sense. For all his ferocious talk, he hadn't taken her and the baby to live and to tremble 'way out on the exposed fringes of the new settlements.

Of course, if the Indians really rose, they were only a little better off here on Rockcastle Creek. The only thing that really bothered her was that Sam had made it plain he didn't intend to homestead. There was nothing of the farmer in him.

So long as game remained plentiful here in the foothills of the Cumberlands they would remain. He figured that if prices stayed anywhere near right—and they should, now that the United Colonies had become the free and independent United States—he'd make all the money they'd any use for. When the game got scarce, they could always pack up and move on.

Stoner moved over to finger a pile of pelts. A whole row of baled skins were ranged along the north wall of the cabin. "Dot is vun prime marten. You haff done vell."

"Can't complain," Sam admitted, his red-brown features relaxing.

From the stone jug he splashed some whiskey into a pair of cow-horn cups.

"How!" said the Pennsylvanian, and he and Stoner swallowed their drinks in a single gulp.

"Sehr gut," Stoner sighed and, wiping his mouth on the back of his hand, inquired, "vot iss?"

"A iron trap," Sam explained not without pride. "Bought me half a dozen last trip—Boone was braggin' about his."

"Ja?"

"Such traps hold the game better. 'Sides, a feller can move a iron trap 'round where he cain't fix a twitch-up or a dead-fall."

"How much?"

"Cost me two bucks the trap."

"Ja? Vot does a buckskin bring in Virginia?"

"Just about one Spanish dollar apiece," answered Sam. "A doe, right now, brings only forty to sixty cents. Now that there cuttoe knife—" he pointed to a heavy-bladed cleaver—"cost me three buckskins, but she's a mighty handy article when you go to cutting up a carcass."

When the giant Pennsylvania German lumbered over to bend curiously above Joanna's basket of hickory splints, she awoke, balled tiny fists and began screaming.

Sam roared, then gravely informed the squalling infant, "Mike sure ain't no ravin' beauty, but jest you wait, honeybird, 'til you spy a Shawnee in his feathers and war paint. Mike will look real handsome, then."

Desire emerged from behind the screen carrying some johnny-cakes and buckwheat souens wrapped in a cone of birch bark. Her face glowed from the heat of the cooking fire and under her loose-fitting dress, her breasts, heavy with milk, rode easily.

"How are the settlers coming in?"

"Fast enough, Ma'am," Stoner replied, running fingers through his greasy yellow hair. "Dot Dick Henderson, Colonel John Williams und fellows in der Transylvanian Company vould haff efferybody believe iss paradise in Kentucky."

"They ain't far wrong," Higsby said offering a bladder of smoking tobacco. "There's fine rich country 'round Boonesborough."

"*Ja?* But suppose Mkahday-wah-may-quah und his Shawnees say, 'Go avay, dis iss our hunting land'?"

Desire, who had picked up the baby and was quieting its terrified howls, called over the clamor, "What's that about the Transylvania Company?"

Sam picked up the stone jug, eyed it an instant, but reluctantly put it back on the shelf. Wouldn't do for a feller to get to hankerin' for that red liquor too much.

He turned to his wife and said, "Well, honey, it's this way: Back in the spring of 1775 Dick Henderson, Nat Hart and Dan'l Boone rigged a treaty with the Cherokees. They dickered fer, and bought, the hull east end o' Kentucky fer to divide up into land holdin's fer settlers.

"By that there treaty o' Sycamore Shoals, Ataculla-culla and Oconestota of the Cherokee Nation deeded this land over to the Company. Henderson and the others paid fer it, fair and square, and them Cherokees made a big pow-wow and said, 'All right, Mister, now the land's yourn.'"

With his fingers Mike Stoner crammed a buckwheat souen into his whisker-framed mouth, then dipped into a bowl of maple sugar to top it off.

"*Ja,* Mrs. Higsby," he winked laboriously. "Dere iss vun t'ing Sam don't tell you. Dot Mr. Henderson didn't make no treaty mit der Shawnees."

"Why, do they claim the land, too?" Desire demanded.

"*Nein,* not any more. Dot vass fixed up after der battle at Point Pleasant. You remember dot battle, Sam?"

"Ain't likely I'd forget. Came mighty near to growing bald."

"Then why do the Shawnees object to settlers?" Desire persisted.

"Der Shawnees live across der Ohio. Dey know der settlers vill scare avay der game. Injuns don't like vite settlements so close."

Desire's eyes grew quite round and the shadows beneath them

seemed to deepen. "Mercy! You don't mean there's going to be more —more trouble?"

The ranger waved away the suggestion, and he laughed easily. *"Nein, nein,* not this year. You keep right on raising babies, Mrs. Higsby. For vy vould hostiles come so far south?"

"Well, I'm mighty pleased to hear that," Desire declared. All fall long she had lived in an agony of dread. Sam had been nervous as a cat, too.

Gently, she slipped the tip of her little finger into Joanna's mouth. She knew the baby must be hungry but somehow she couldn't bring herself to nurse the infant in the presence of a stranger, though other women along the frontier thought nothing of it at all.

Stoner pulled on his fur cap, hauled his haversack and war bag into position and resettled his war hatchet in its beaded sling.

"Next month maybe I come oudt, Sam, und ve go after bison. Last fall I found a lick down on der Rolling Fork. Bisons, dey vass thick like turds 'round a barn."

"A new lick?"

"Ja. I saw plenty of dem t'ings." Stoner's shaggy head inclined towards a huge fossil vertebra doing duty as a stool.

There were a lot of such bones 'round about this country, especially in the marshy places and canebrakes. Most people claimed they were elephant bones, but somebody had told Desire they weren't exactly that. They were mammoth and mastodon bones. Beasts of a species that had died off thousands and thousands of years ago. Sam had promised to take her to see a whole gulley full of such giant bones. Just as soon as the next baby was born.

In one corner she kept the end of a fossil tusk she had traded from an Indian for a half-dozen nails. The Indian had pretty near spoiled it, though, with his crude scratching.

"Ach, I nearly forgot! Colonel Boone say vhen he comes by he vants a talk mit you. He likes you, Sam, und he knows you to var haff been. Ho! Ho! Maybe he vants to make you captain, or maybe a general! Ho! Ho! Ho!" The giant's booming laughter again sent the baby off into fits of squalling.

Desire said in perfect gravity, "Really, Mr. Stoner, I don't see why Sam shouldn't be made at least a major. He can read and write, and that's more than most men along this frontier can say."

She kept her gaze fixed hard on Stoner; let him dare to laugh!

"*Ja,* a major anyhow. Vun t'ing, Sam. Chust vatch dese land yobbers don't skin you out of your land title."

The huge man poked the baby in her ribs, jerked a nod to Desire and, followed by Sam, swung out into the sunset.

The whole ravine now was a-glow with the thin, cold light of a winter sun. Chickadees which had been feeding about the door went fluttering off and Snapper ran over to nose hopefully at the half-skinned buck.

Desire said goodbye, then disappeared behind the barrier, aware that the men probably wanted to crack a couple of coarse jokes.

"Eve," she said, her breath vapor circling upwards, "make sure there's plenty of hot water. Joanna hasn't had a bath in two days. It seems warm enough this evening to give her one."

"Yas'm, Mist'ess Higsby," the negress replied and threw some firewood under a big iron kettle which, standing on its own three legs, filled one whole corner of the cook place.

Eve was beaming. Of course, she had listened to every word uttered beyond the barrier. Lawd's mercy! but she was powerful glad to hear there weren't no Injuns sneaking about these woods. The smell of them stinking, greasy devils was awful.

White folks, even clean ones, smelled queer, too, but all the Injuns she'd ever seen was alive with varmints and hadn't no use for wummen folks. What in the world had ailed Cocoa? He surely had knowed how mighty poor the Injuns fed, yet he'd runned off and joined them.

Of course he'd still be a slave among them Injuns, but they would let him carry weepons and fight. She guessed he'd got the idee from hearing a parcel of long-hunter talk about a nigger warrior named Pompey who lived among the Shawnee people up north. Why, the savages held this Pompey 'most like a war chief among them.

Only trouble wth Cocoa was he came from Senegambia and, like most Senegalese, was a fighter at heart. Still, he needn't have gone traipsing off with her best earbobs and red cloth petticoat.

Laws, Misto' Higsby sho'ly had been boiling mad when he'd learned about the worthless nigger having run off. Eve guessed Mr. Sam would have brought back the runaway if a war party of strange Indians from the west part of the country hadn't taken Cocoa first. He'd cussed so terrible Mist'ess Higsby had covered her ears and run into the cabin.

Yessiree. Misto' Higsby had been so mighty put out that he had had to kill two of that war party before he felt any better. But he never did get a shot at that triflin' Cocoa. Secretly, Eve rejoiced. Maybe Cocoa would come back for her in the spring?

Lawd's mercy! Milkin' time already. Hurriedly, she crossed to a hutch door Misto' Higsby had let into the back of the cabin to connect it with the cow shed.

It wasn't a real door because, as a frontiersman, he was dead against such things. It was only three feet by two an' was protected by a stout sliding panel. Of course, a body had to stoop to get through such a door, and anyone entering in a stooping position was practically helpless.

The cow sounded restless; probably she wanted water. Eve hurried to prop open the hutch. Mist'ess Higsby set a great store by Molly; she was the only milk cow within a hundred miles.

2

THE WAR BAG

DESIRE HARMONY HIGSBY relaxed comfortably into the deerskin armchair Sam had rigged for her. She guessed she would never cease to marvel at her husband's skill with knife and hatchet. Why, with just those two implements he could approximate the products of a joiner or a carpenter.

He'd even made her a rough sideboard to hold her pitiful store of pewter plates—there would be plenty of them, sometime—and their bed was the envy of everyone who saw it. Instead of slats or fir boughs, she and Sam rested on buffalo hides laced to a frame. Four buffalo calf skins served as a mattress and in winter they certainly kept the bed wonderfully warm—even if they did smell a little gamy.

Smiling, she undid the laces at the front of her dress and gave breast to the infant. Joanna gurgled and, clamping her lips down on the nipple, puffed like a little seal.

Out back of the cow shed, Sam and Mike Stoner were laughing like anything—the liquor must be going to work. That was good. Sam loved a good laugh.

Joanna was growing quite a bit of hair now, yellow-gold like John's. Soon there would be enough to support a ribbon. It had been a terrific surprise when Joanna had turned out to be Joanna and not John. She would have sworn the infant would be a boy.

Settling deeper in her chair, Desire Harmony Higsby let her thoughts ramble backwards to that August day on the Watauga when Joanna had been born. Mercy, how hot it had been! If it hadn't been for Sam she guessed she would have gone out of her mind, what with fear, pain and shame.

Right now, staring down at that small pink head in the bend of her arm, she knew she'd try all her life to prove how eternally grateful she was. Never once had Sam inquired into her life subsequent to the raid on Conanicut. Of course, he must have wondered, but he expressed no curiosity as to who, or what, Joanna's father might have been. Soberly, he had accepted her pregnancy as an accomplished fact.

Because of this she was glad that, late next summer, she would bear a child of Sam's own. This baby would serve to weld them inseparably.

Every day now she was surer that coming out here had been the right thing to do. The frontiers were Sam's homeland and now that her own world had become a forbidden paradise, the West must be her home also.

They would get ahead. Sam's energy, courage and deep-seated sense of loyalty, reinforced by her New England practicality, her ambitions for the children, and her urge to restore the Bennett strain to respected security, should take them far. This question of running for office might prove the entering wedge.

They were getting along much better than she had ever dreamed possible. True, every time he went down to the settlements, Sam would get more or less drunk; but so did noble lords over in England, the rich planters of Virginia.

Again, Sam's temper was of a fierce, savage, flaring kind which, fortunately, was difficult to arouse. She would never forget that day he'd beaten the daylights out of a couple of Land Company men who had presumed to pass a light remark about her.

Yes, Sam should go far if she could wean him away from his wild way of life, could make him see that trapping was a hazardous occupation with no future. Maybe she could get him into the factoring business?

Her thoughts ran on and on to the accompaniment of Molly's milk drumming steadily into Eve's wooden bucket. *D-r-r-r! Dr-r-r-r!* Milking had a soothing rhythm.

Even now, after nearly eight months of marriage, she was surprised how little she knew about some things concerning Sam Higsby. All she knew was that he'd been born in York County, Pennsylvania; and that he had roamed the woods since his early teens.

The baby was feeding less greedily now, kneading at the breast with tiny rosy fists.

She had been mightily relieved to hear that Tim was recovered of his wound, that he aimed to fit out the *Narragansett* as a privateer. He would succeed, one way or another. He was stubborn stuff, was Tim.

How strange that Nat Coffin should also have sailed on the expedition against the Bahamas. Yet was it? Even back in Providence, Nat had spoken of joining the Marine Corps. She wished it were possible to learn what had become of him. Probably she would never learn, except by accident. Certainly she wouldn't dare make inquiry.

It was something, though, to know that all of Admiral Parker's great ships and Sir Henry Clinton's fine regiments had not been able to capture Fort Sullivan, let alone Charleston.

She forced away the baby's lips, dried the breast and shifted Joanna to the other. If Joanna grew to look like John, she would make a remarkably handsome girl. John's features had been so regular, his brows so straight, his skin so thin and smooth.

It would be interesting to learn what the Honourable Sir Joseph St. Clair, this child's paternal grandfather, would say were he able to behold his grandchild peacefully nursing in the midst of a howling wilderness. A far cry this from the roar and bustle of London!

Well, Joanna would never learn that she was not Sam Higsby's own daughter. No one in these parts could know that she wasn't.

The baby emitted a satisfied sigh, her mouth fell away from the nipple. Joanna slept soundly. Desire was annoyed with herself. She shouldn't have fed the baby before her bath. Now it would have to come later, but that would be all right because Sam liked to watch the pink little thing gurgling, wriggling on a beaver-skin comfort.

She heard Eve crawl back through the hutch; so, restoring the baby to her cradle, Desire set about preparing the evening meal. She would have given a year off her life to have sat down tonight to beef instead of venison, to taste some vegetable other than frozen turnip, to swallow real, instead of raspberry-leaf, tea.

Snapper lay in front of the fire toasting his toes. When she spoke to him, the hound commenced to flog the floor with his heavy tail. At last he got up, stretched his legs and bowing in his back, emitted a small luxurious yelp. At the end of the operation, he came clicking over to her, one ear hopefully cocked.

"Go find Master," Desire told him. "Tell him supper will be ready mighty soon."

When she opened the door, Snapper rushed about in furious circles. Desire knew that he wanted to bark, but he only whined softly; Sam had trained him too well. Sam, she saw, was back skinning the buck. He had slung it from a fork in a big beech tree.

She turned and bent above the pots and pans. She was lucky, Desire realized. Blessed few females along the frontier could boast of a negro slave woman, of a cow and of a husband so handy in the woods.

By the light of a wick floating in an earthenware bowl of bear's oil, Higsby's face screwed itself into a frown of concentration and he continued working over his second gun. This was a big bear gun, far too heavy to carry about much; but where it hit the fur didn't grow any longer. He had been having trouble with its lock.

"Desire," said he over his shoulder, "trot out the lead kettle, will you? Cast me a few balls for Bella."

"Why, Sam, you're not going off again?" Desire exclaimed. "You've just run your trap lines!"

"Yup. Reckon I'll make a cast down South Fork way. What with all this snow, ought to find a passel of deer yarded up." He winked. "And from the lay o' the land I figger there just might be some beaver dams—but don't tell nobody I said so."

"But, Sam, South Fork is quite a way off." She cast him a quick, uncertain look.

"Ain't nothin' to be fearful of, honey; honest there ain't." He smiled, pushing the jet hair back from his eyes. "Too cold. All the Injuns, exceptin' trappers, is holed-up in their lodges.

"Mike told me Blackfish, the Shawnee war chief, has been listening a heap to Hanging Maw—he was the Cherokee got slapped down so hard last fall when he kidnaped them kids near Boonesborough."

He bent further over the gun lock, working with the point of his knife. "Nope, there ain't no Indians south o' the Ohio. You and Eve kin keep house two or three days 'thout no cause to fret. You'll tend the inner trap line?"

"Oh, yes, Sam, I can do that easily," Desire promised. Fetching out a small cast-iron kettle, she stirred a bed of hickory coals until they began to crackle and snap, then she set the little pot among them and dropped in the end of a lead bar. Using a turkey wing, she fanned the coals until they glowed white near the pot.

She would have got a bullet mould out of Sam's war bag without being told, but this bag was about the only belonging he kept strictly to himself. Desire could understand why he did this. No woodsman wanted anybody else messing with his kit. In the wilderness it was impossible to replace a lost screw, or a spoiled implement. Besides, a trapper had continually to know the exact state of his replacements. The scarcity or plenty of such essential supplies governed his most important decisions.

She really wasn't curious to go poking about in the war bag—most of such things were indescribably messy—but when she'd nothing on her mind, she sometimes tried to guess what he kept in it. Essentially fair-minded, she never yet had gone nosing about when he was away.

It must contain a minor museum of odds and ends, she judged, because it was so heavy. She did know, though, that he kept his scalps in there, and some souvenirs of the Siege of Boston. From the start, Sam was strangely loath to discuss the Siege or anything to do with it. To him, service in General Washington's Army must have been a great disappointment. He felt he hadn't done anything there fit to brag about.

Come to think of it, his attitude was reminiscent of Tim's. Looking back, she guessed poor Tim hadn't much reason to remember the Siege with any great joy.

Tonight, with a southwest wind sighing about the cabin, it was singularly peaceful in here. The baby, bathed, lay plunged in dreamless slumber. On a pallet beyond the partition, Eve snored lustily or mumbled in her native tongue.

Eve was a good wench, Higsby was thinking, but he sure would like to lay hands on that goddam worthless Cocoa. The idea of the black bastard's running off to the Indians for no call at all. From the first, he had counted on Cocoa to mind the cabin while he was away. Already he had taught the black to dress and flesh a pelt, tedious labor which he would have gladly spared himself.

By God, if he ever found him, the Leman's barleycorn would teach that nigger to run off.

Maybe, if the trapping continued good and he found someone to freight the pelts to market, he would clear enough to afford another nigger—*not* one of the fighting kind. 'Course he'd no real call to complain. Eve and Cocoa hadn't cost either him or Desire a copper penny.

Higsby was mightily thankful Eve hadn't run off, too. He didn't aim to let so pretty a wife as his grow leathery-faced and crooked-backed from bending over too many fires or from washing too many clothes. He didn't want to see Desire Harmony's fine skin grow tanned-looking, like a squaw's.

Desire Harmony was a real pretty name. Fit for the prettiest gal he would ever rest eyes on. Sure had to admire her independent ways. She wasn't like other girls, no sir. Different from the rest of them as a cross fox was from a common red. He reckoned he would always recall the cool way she'd stood up to men folks, to her own Pa, even.

Desire? She was right well named at that. Them shadows beneath her eyes weren't there for nothing. He looked pridefully across the cabin. Her hair was red-brown, the color of a prime beaver pelt; and it was every bit as soft.

Everything would be finer than fine if the next baby turned out to be a buck. Along the border, a family of boys came in mighty handy. He'd name him for Desire's Pa—Asa. It would tickle Desire, and, well—he himself certainly held the old man's memory in high respect. That old Quaker was truly the Godliest and humanest man he'd ever come across.

Maybe little Asa would grow up to be a smart scout? Maybe get high up in the Army? The Thirteen Fires, as the Indians called the new nation on the seaboard, would surely stand in need of an army for a right long while.

Higsby could look ahead and see the shape of what was to come. Sure as shootin', there would be more and more settlers and movers

going West, crowding the Injuns until the Injuns fought back. Not
that you could blame the tribes so much.

Narrowing his eyes, Higsby gave over day-dreaming and prepared
to set a pin securing the bear gun's hammer. Hell's roaring bells!
Half the pin cap came away under even the very gentle pressure
he exerted. Yep, that screw was too worn to be of any more use. It
had better be replaced, yet he didn't want to put the gun down because he had the hammer nicely adjusted.

He said to his wife, busily stirring the melting lead, "Reach into
my war bag for a spare lock-pin—there's three of 'em—in that leather
pocket furthest to the right. I want the longest screw."

"But, Sam, I couldn't find it. That war bag is a mess. Besides I
don't like to go poking—"

"Needn't worry." He grinned at her, dark eyes a-twinkle. "Them
skelps are done up separate."

"Oh, all right." The bullet lead was beginning to break into
silvery little bubbles, so she added, "Lead's ready. Shall I get out a
mould at the same time?"

"Yep, but fetch me the screw first."

Desire, crossing to where the war bag hung from a peg driven
into the log wall, eyed it curiously. It was a fine new one, of well-
oiled elk hide and with long fringes that were hardly torn at all.
Some squaw must have spent a lot of time to decorate it so handsomely with red and green quill work.

Standing on tiptoes she began to fumble about.

"Better unhook it. You'll rip the edges, else," her husband told
her.

When Desire set it on the elephant-bone stool, the bag made a
small clinking noise. Heavens! There must be even more in it than
she had imagined. She recognized a whole spare gun lock, a prouvette, two bags of flints, some small pigs of lead, a bladder of pemmican and two or three bullet moulds, then some odds and ends of
rifle parts.

Her hand encountered a cold, flat metal plate. Pulling it out she
held a polished pewter ornament to the firelight. *"Per Terram, Per*

Mare," she read on a scroll winding about an anchor. The King's cipher was on it, too.

"What in the world is this pewter plate for?"

Higsby looked up sharply. "Nothin' much. Came off the cap of one of them Britainers, night o' the raid on Peaceful Haven."

Per Terram, Per Mare. That was the motto of the Royal Regiment of Marine Light Infantry, she recalled.

"Oh!" Desire said in a small voice. It was their first mention of that dreadful night.

Hurriedly, she fumbled deeper, hunting the inner pocket containing the screws. Her fingers encountered something smooth, something heavily carved. In spite of her first instinct, she drew out the hilt and guard of an officer's sword. The grip was gold mounted and protected by an ivory guard carved in the shape of a mermaid.

"Where did you find this?" she asked, stepping over to the fire.

"Shucks!" he drawled amiably. "Ain't nothin' in Nature like a woman for curiosity, is there?"

"But, Sam, it's lovely, where did you find it?" She turned it over and over, wondering why it should look faintly familiar.

Higsby grinned, set down the bear gun and began to stuff a red clay pipe he'd traded from Skanawati.

"Ma'am, that there hilt is a token o' the prettiest shot *I* ever made in my life. Near bragged on it a hundred times, but I didn't, 'cause it happened the same night I collected that there hat badge."

Slowly, Desire's eyes sought the guard, remained fixed on it. "You mean the night of the raid?"

"Yep! 'Twas after I'd killed three Britainers up near the barn and I was a-driftin' along after the enemy aimin' to pick off stragglers when, all of a sudden, out of the snow and dark comes one of their officers. He was runnin' hell-fer-leather; easy though, just like a deer. You ought to have seen him travel!

"Show you what a hard mark he made—'twas snowin', a brisk breeze was blowin'. I got fixed to drop him comin' on but, sez I, 'Sam, you've already bagged three. Let's be sportin' about this.'"

As Desire Harmony stood staring at the hilt, Sam's voice moved further and further into the distance. When she saw the name Jno. St. Clair, engraved in a fine script, a cold, killing wind began to roar through her.

As faint and distinct as the tapping of a distant woodpecker, Sam's voice continued. "Yep, I always been mighty proud o' that shot. Sighted center, betwixt his shoulders. Figger it out fer yerself. He was a good sixty yards off and runnin'. I'd have told you 'bout it before, only I didn't want to remind— My God, honey— you ailin'?"

Outlined before the orange glow of the fireplace, his wife's figure stood, a rigid silhouette. When he drew near, he could see that she had turned a ghastly white. Not even when Joanna was being born had her face become so completely drained of color.

"You, you—!" The words struggled through lips twisting like those of a soldier suffering amputation. She held up a rigid, fending hand. "Get back!"

"But, honey, what's the matter. Do you feel sick?"

Through Desire's mind was cascading a white-hot stream of thought. In this same cabin stood the man who had blasted her life's happiness, who had cruelly, in a spirit of sport, robbed her of the only wholly fine force she had ever known.

Because of Sam Higsby she had had to cower, trembling, shivering, in Martin's woodshed. Because he had robbed John of life, she had had to go tramping, hungrily, hopelessly, the streets of Providence. She had had to suffer Mrs. Norton's beating, had had to offer herself to strangers.

Because of this ignorant barbarian in buckskins she had been condemned to the tawdry disappointments of life with Brian Montaigne. Because of that shot she had lost Nat; she had had to flee, like a leper, from the decent home of the Proveaux.

Crescendo, a sense of outrage clamored at her. She began to tremble.

"Desire—" Sam tried to take her by the elbow. "You look like you're seein'—"

Her fist took him viciously on the side of the jaw. He was so surprised he could only stand staring, puzzled, with one hand clapped to his bruised cheek. With the speed of a snake she lashed out at him with the sword hilt.

"Murderer!" Her voice was shrill, unearthly. "Don't touch me! Keep thy bloody paws off me!"

Higsby fell back a couple of steps, drew himself up, his cheek bones jutting like cliffs. "You gone crazy? Listen, woman, this ain't funny. I ain't done nothin' to—"

"—Haven't done anything?" she panted. "Oh, thee's a filthy savage! Thee's a stinking butcher! And it was *thee all the time!*" Teeth bared, eyes a-glow with hatred, she shook the mermaid-guarded hilt before his eyes. *"Thee* killed *him!* I loathe thee. Go away—"

"Shut your trap!" Sam snapped. He was beginning to get mad. No female woman dare address him like this. "I don't know what ails you, but you're layin' terms on me—"

"Oh, I wish I could kill thee as thee killed John St. Clair!"

"Jesus Christ!" The oath escaped Sam amid a whistling gasp of surprise. In a flash he saw it. That officer on the road must have been the whippersnapper the neighbors had spied leaving the barn with Desire.

He felt the hot blood seethe up to the roots of his hair. So it was that damned Britainer's whelp he was expected to bring up. Like hell he would! Knowing who the brat's father was made all the difference.

He gathered himself, the muscles on his neck growing thick. So she still loved that macaroni feller, not plain Sam Higsby? "You needn't rail at me fer a savage," he snarled. "Fine sort o' gentleman who'd ravish a sixteen-year-old gal!"

"Silence! Thee is not fit to mention John's name." She was looking about as if seeking some weapon.

"Ain't I?" Higsby roared so loud that Eve began to whimper beyond the barrier. "By the livin' God, I wish'd I'd put my foot on that Britainer's dirty neck and skelped him!"

"It's a wonder thee didn't. Thee is lower than the Indians. Kill! Kill! That's all thee thinks of. Stay away from me," she panted.

"Don't thee dare ever to touch me again!"

To think she had lain in this man's arms, that she had made love with John's murderer was maddening.

Joanna woke with a startled yelp and began to whimper. Neither of them paid any attention.

"Sit down, else I'll cuff you down!" he snapped.

Desire was the last person to heed such a command. With a furious sob, she hurled the hilt full in his face. The stump of the blade dug into his chin. As a trickle of blood spurted from it, his hand shot out, gripped her arm. Twice, three times, his open hand dealt her slaps that exploded a series of brilliant purple-green lights in her eyeballs. Next he shook her until she was quite breathless, then sent her spinning across the cabin.

Undaunted, she glared up at him. "Hate—thee to—end of my days!" she choked. Her eyes were swimming, her head roaring inside. "Would to God I could tear thy child out of me!"

"By Jesus, I wish you could!" He towered, menacingly black, above her, his breath showing in silvery puffs. "Then my seed wouldn't be asked to grow up along of any Britainer's bastard!"

" 'Bastard!' Oh, you—"

By the distorting play of the flames, they glowered at each other in a white fury.

"Open that trollop's mouth of yours again and I'll ram my fist through it."

Devils looked out of Higsby's jet eyes. So she still loved the Britainer? He couldn't get over it. "You got no right to call me out o' turn, you poor, dirty female critter. I've used you too kind fer yer own understandin'."

He flung about, walking on the balls of his feet like an angry dog. "Eve!"

"Y-yassuh?"

"Get me some food! Pemmican, smoked fish, meal and souens."

Sprawled on the bed and rubbing aching jaws, Desire Harmony could hear his moccasins stalking about. He kept muttering. Once she opened her eyes and met a deadly look.

At the end of ten minutes, he had collected his familiar kit, war bag and all. He poked her with the handle of his war hatchet, spoke in a deep, quivering and unfamiliar tone.

"Attend what I say." He spoke as to an Indian who couldn't speak much English. "We both been pretty hot. Mayhap I'll fergive you—mayhap I won't. I'm goin' down to Rollin' Fork. If I figger I kin fergit about this, I'll be back in two days by sun-down. If I cain't, you won't see me ever again."

With that he walked out and slammed the door.

Snapper whined and tried to follow, but Eve grabbed him by the neck. Long before anybody, Snapper could tell if a bear or any other hostile creature was about.

3

SKANAWATI

FOR a day and a half Desire moved about very quietly, as if she were acting in her sleep. Gradually the swelling of her cheeks subsided, but a faint discoloration marked one of them. Those shadows under her eyes had deepened, but she was still the prettiest girl Eve had ever laid eyes on.

Eve felt mighty oneasy. 'Tweren't like Mist'ess Higsby not to be singing at the baby or to herself. Old times she would walk up and down in front of the cradle, talking all sorts of grand talk, play-acting. 'Twas silly because Joanna couldn't understand a word.

Lawd's mercy, it did sho'ly cut Eve's heart to see Mist'ess dragging about like this. She just couldn't make head or tail out of what happened. What could have vexed a true-loving couple like they had always been?

All Eve recalled was waking up to hear the white folks calling each other the most terrible names. Lawd's mercy! Misto' Higsby had been razor-mad, almost.

She wouldn't forget in a hurry the look on his face when he'd stormed out of the cabin with blood dripping from his chin, with his war bag filled and his littler rifle a-swinging to his shoulder. My, my, he sho' had handed Mist'ess a couple of mean clips.

What worried the slave most of all was that, early next morning, Snapper got out and, right away, ran off following his master's trail. She sho' hated to see that hound go high-tailing down the ravine. Yessuh, Snapper could scent a Injun or a catamount half the length of Kentucky.

When noon rolled around, she gently approached the brooding girl. "Please, Mist'ess, better eat a l'il somethin'. You cain't feed dat baby on sighs. Ah done fixed you a elegant dinner."

"I'm not hungry, Eve," Desire replied with a wan smile.

"Doan' grieve so, l'il buhd," Eve pleaded; she was really devoted to her mistress. "He gwine come back. De men folks gits fractious sometimes, but dey ginerally gits over it when dey dander dies down an' dey craves a mess o' home cookin'."

"I—I hope you're right, Eve."

Desire accepted the wooden bowl of mush and milk with bits of fried pork stirred into it.

"You are right. I suppose I should eat." She brightened. "Let's hope Mr. Higsby will bring home a turkey."

When she had finished eating, Desire felt much better and drew a series of deep breaths before she set about putting the cabin to rights. She swept out thoroughly with a birch broom, cleaned the bear oil lamp, put fresh oil on the deer-bladder windowpane and tidied up generally. It lent her a sense of self-confidence. In conclusion, she picked a few sprigs of holly and stuck them over the pegs on which Sam's Leman rifle usually rested.

She didn't touch the bear gun, but left it lying across a side table just the way Sam had set it down, with its lock still unassembled.

How could she have acted such a perfect fool? Her only possible excuse was that where John St. Clair and his memory were concerned, she was not quite rational. All her life she would try, ever so hard, to make Sam forget that the night of February tenth, 1777, had ever been.

Of course, Sam hadn't minced words, either, once he got mad; but for her it would be simple to erase those searing terms from her memory.

Sam, Desire calculated, would probably make a cast through the Rolling Fork country. He had been planning to hunt that way anyway. Yes, she hoped he would "hoppus" home a turkey or maybe a haunch of bison. She certainly was getting tired of venison, venison and more venison.

For supper tonight she intended to serve his favorite meal: corn meal mush fried in pork fat with plenty of dried huckleberries in it. Also she'd have Eve fry up the liver of that deer he had killed on the day of their quarrel.

As she sped about, she smiled to herself. How lucky that she would have ready at this time a small surprise. At odd moments she had been working Sam's initials onto a pair of brand-new moccasins. The ones he was wearing were pretty well through. The new ones were made of smoked elk skin by a woman of the Creek Nation. Elegantly stitched, they were soft on the foot, yet tough and moisture-proof.

Why not lay them out on the table where Sam could see them when he first came in?

What in the world could she say to Sam? She must make him understand, must make him believe that her outburst was only the last gasp of a life that was dead and gone. Of course this new life was all that really mattered. In silence, she rehearsed several speeches, but could not decide on any one.

Before a bit of mirror, Desire rebraided her hair, wound it into a gleaming casque about her head. Humming, she stitched her Cashmere shawl in place. Joanna she dressed in the little Indian dress of doeskin Sam had fetched back from Harrodsburg. Though the garment was still a trifle large, Sam might be pleased to see the child wearing it.

For all he had said about Joanna, he was really fond of her.

Abruptly, her fingers faltered, began to fumble. Suppose—suppose Sam *didn't come back?*

"It is quite possible he will not," a small, deadly voice insisted. "Sam is fierce and full-blooded, he dislikes civilization and responsibility. He will make this an excuse to break away."

Suppose Sam didn't return? The possibility made her feel all hollow and quivering. She supposed she and Eve could find their way to the Wilderness Road—it lay only fifteen miles to the eastward and Sam had blazed a trail extra clear, just in case— The people at Flat Lick would take them in for a while.

The baby emitted a moist gurgle and jerkily flourished a tiny gourd rattle which Skanawati had brought her one day last fall. Desire liked Skanawati better than most of the Indian trappers who chanced by. It was probably because the Catawba didn't go in so heavily for bear grease and had the delicacy not to pick his lice in her presence.

All through the afternoon she kept an ear cocked for Snapper. His joyful whines were usually her first warning of a return from an expedition.

Once she heard a rustling. Her heart soared at the prolonged sound, but it was only a squirrel. Another time she saw a curious doe on the edge of the clearing. The creature flared its tail and bounded out of sight in an instant.

Since it was going on towards four of the afternoon, she judged Sam would be along pretty soon.

"Fetch a noggin of water from the spring. I expect Mr. Higsby would like a drink of liquor when he gets home," she told Eve, then removed the stone jug from its hiding place under their bed.

"Yassum, Ah sho' will," beamed Eve. "An' axe him please, Mist'ess, cut me some fiahwood. Us is runnin' powerful low."

To occupy the time, Desire tallied once more a pile of furs waiting to be baled. Ten red foxes, six lynx, six martens, eleven beaver, a fisher and a dozen raccoons gave off a pleasingly exciting odor. My, but she did love to feel a beaver skin. The fur was so incredibly soft and fine; the marten and the fisher skins, too.

All at once the cow began to snuffle, to toss her head. Desire heard her horn scraping the wall. Heavens! That meant only one thing. Her heart began to pound. The cow had heard Sam's footsteps.

Hurriedly she put away the account book, smoothed the fur rug over Joanna and, straightening her blouse, ran to the door and eased back the heavy panels.

Not Sam but two Indians were descending the ravine! A single glance disclosed two all-important facts: the foremost savage was carrying his gun with its stock held 'way forward; neither Indian was wearing black or red paint so they were not members of a war party.

Dark and silent against the snow, the two braves came drifting down between the gray trunks of the beeches, their heads turning restlessly this way and that.

When she saw a blue turtle painted on the front of the leader's filthy hunting shirt, Desire recognized Skanawati. In her relief she almost sobbed. The other was a strange Indian whose head was clean-shaven except for a coarse crest. He didn't look like a Catawba to Desire but he, too, was of the turtle clan.

Had the caller been any other than Skanawati, Desire would have been terribly frightened; but here he was making the peace sign and holding up a pair of rabbits. In silence he dropped them onto the bare ground before the front door.

Desire smiled a "thank you." She knew what procedure to follow because Sam had told her again and again. One must invite a friendly Indian into the cabin; give him food and a present if possible; ask no questions; a woman should never address a warrior first.

Today Skanawati seemed more dressed-up than she had ever seen him. His headdress was composed of scarlet-dyed hickory splints joined to form a sort of crown which rested on his denuded scalp. A clump of brilliant scarlet feathers, spurting from this headpiece, concealed in their midst a silver tube so arranged that a single eagle's feather, let into it, was left free to revolve.

For weapons, the Catawba carried the usual old French musket, a knife and a war hatchet. But his companion had no more than a bow and a quiver of arrows.

To Desire, Skanawati's present color scheme was deplorable. A design executed in a bilious yellow on a yellowish green ground swept down to either side of his hairless brows to end in dizzying spirals over each cheek. His nose, which was both large and prominent, had been tastefully colored the brightest imaginable of blues.

The second Indian, a Shawnee, whose name proved to be Uguku, or Hooting Owl, was shorter than his Catawba friend, and lacked a right eye. Certainly he was no dandy. The blue and orange paint applied in chevrons across his forehead and down his cheeks was smeared and dull and a weather-beaten heron's feather, laced into his scalp-lock, drooped like the tail of a whipped puppy.

Driving a furrow across this warrior's cheek ran a terrible scar. Desire guessed a war hatchet must have done it. His only attempt at originality was a necklace composed of four red fox tails interspaced with strands of white hair from a buck's tail. He was younger than Skanawati and much darker complexioned.

Into a slot cut through the distended lobe of the Shawnee's left ear was thrust the skin of a red-headed woodpecker and from the septum of his nose dangled a little silver crescent.

Unslinging a mantle of lynx fur, Skanawati followed Desire indoors while his companion stripped off a covering of mangy-looking wolf skins.

The instant the baby saw those painted and bedizened figures, she raised terrified wails. Hooting Owl regarded the infant with obvious disapproval. Skanawati kept his attention on the stone jug Desire had laid out in expectation of Sam.

Desire forced a smile and waved to the fireplace. Oh damn! Why did that jug have to be standing in plain sight? Now, if she didn't offer them liquor, the visitors would feel affronted. If she did—well, even Sam admitted an Indian with a few too many drinks in him was a devil and mighty hard to control.

Joanna was still screaming so she guessed she'd better put the baby beyond the barrier. She found Eve trembling like a horse which has scented a bear.

"Don't be silly," Desire warned sharply. "It's only Mr. Higsby's friend, Skanawati." She placed the infant on a little rack beside the cook-place. "Eve, you bring some food, quick as you can!"

"Ain' dey hurt us?"

"No, you idiot."

"Lawd! Lawd! If only Misto' Higsby was heah!"

"Well, he will be soon. Now hush your fuss and get busy."

What a nuisance. These two savages would probably eat up all Sam's fine supper. Still, it would sort of make her reunion with Sam a bit easier. Maybe it was lucky, after all, that these Indians had stopped by.

When she went out front again, there was a smell of whiskey in the air; Hooting Owl was covertly licking his lips. The Indians had spread their mantles on the floor and were squatting on them, cross-legged. They sat impassive, expressionless. Only their flat black eyes looked alive. Hooting Owl had set his moccasins to dry at the fire and they were filling the cabin with the rancid smell of stale grease.

"Where my brother, Tskili?" demanded Skanawati at length. He gave Higsby's Cherokee name.

"He went down the ravine a little while ago. He will be here soon to welcome his brothers."

Skanawati blinked. He admired Tskili's squaw for being able to lie so well. All of Tskili's footprints had been made nearly forty-eight hours back. Why should the squaw have lied? No matter. Maybe she would give him bread made of sunflower seeds.

He rubbed his belly. The liquor burned fine. He felt a little guilty about having stolen that drink, but surely an old friend like Tskili would not deny his brothers refreshment. What about another little drink?

Copper bracelets gleamed as he pointed to the stone jug.

Desire hesitated, but gave in. It didn't seem advisable to irritate

the Indians when they were so obviously friendly. Besides, Skanawati was dependable. The Indians set the jug to their lips and swallowed several deep gulps.

Hooting Owl fixed on her his one eye. Framed in alternate circles of brilliant blue and yellow, it looked singularly baleful.

"E—e—" he belched, then deliberately studied the baled pelts along
the opposite wall. The woodpecker skin in his ear flashed in the
late sunlight as he turned to address Skanawati. They exchanged
several guttural sentences, but Desire could understand not a word
of what was said.

4

THE STONE JUG

DESIRE HARMONY HIGSBY cast anxious eyes at the barrier. What in
the world could be delaying Eve? If food could be gotten into these
smelly creatures promptly enough, they might not want more to
drink.

Whew! The fire, blazing up, had warmed the visitors enough to
start them perspiring, and now the whole cabin reeked with their
sour, feral odor. Their body-smell was rather musky, like that of
freshly dressed fox or mink pelt.

What a nuisance! As soon as they had gone, she would have to
pour scalding water on the floor of hard-packed clay in order to
kill the lice which were undoubtedly dropping from their fur
mantles.

From the kitchen came a sudden clatter and a splash. Eve ran out
whimpering, "Lawd's mercy, Mist'ess. De ole lug-pole done buhnt
through an' drap all de vittles in de fiah!"

"Never mind," Desire told her hurriedly. "Slice some smoked
tongue, dish up a mess of pemmican and fetch some corn bread,
and," she added urgently, *"be quick about it!"*

Suddenly, Skanawati got up and, his single feather revolving gently, stalked silently out of doors. While the cow snuffled and fussed, he made a methodic circle about the cabin, then climbed the ridge above it and stood quite a while listening intently.

When the Catawba descended, he was breathing quicker and his faintly oblique eyes were more restless than ever. Under the greasy hunting shirt his ribs worked like bellows.

Next time the Indians asked for a drink, Desire figured she had better drop the jug and break it. Sam would be hopping mad, but there was no help for it. She didn't like the look of this Hooting Owl at all. He acted a sight too bold.

"Rum," grunted the one-eyed warrior pointing to the stone jug.

"Surely," Desire smiled, and, in lifting the jug let it slip through her palms. Unluckily, it only glanced off the wooden bench and rolled, splashing its contents across the floor.

Hooting Owl snarled like a scalded cat and grabbed it up before more than a cupful of whiskey had escaped.

"*Kehella!*" The chevrons on his forehead flashed as he tilted his head and let the whiskey gurgle freely down his throat until Skanawati snatched it away for his share.

Desire's heart began to pound. Oh dear, what should she do?

Swaying slightly, Hooting Owl, giggling to himself, eased the war hatchet over his right hip; legging fringes rustling softly, he went over to poke and probe among the loose pelts.

The question arose in Desire's mind, should she be harsh with the visitors, put up an angry front and threaten? Or should she play for time and humor them? In any case, soon as Sam came in they would surely be made sorry they'd ever abused Tskili's hospitality.

Certainly it wouldn't be long now before Snapper came bounding down into the ravine.

My! Those Indians certainly were getting drunk in a hurry. Why did Skanawati keep looking at her and grinning so foolishly? Did he want something?

The Catawba, amused to feel the ground sway so pleasantly, was thinking: Tskili is a fool to hunt so far from his lodge. Here are furs worth five big barrels of rum. All good furs because Tskili is a skilled trapper. If something happens to this lodge, can Tskili tell who to blame?

Skanawati pulled himself up sharp.

"Ke-we!" It was bad even to think along these lines. The white man had a very bad way of not forgetting such things.

Hitching up his belt, the Catawba shuffled over to one end of the barrier and considered Eve with inward approval. By experience, he knew the black woman could cook very well, and she looked as if she could stand travel under pressure. Three Tall Feathers, his brother, had a black slave and was always boasting over it.

"Go 'way, Misto' Injun," Eve quavered. "Ah's gittin' yo' vittles fastes' Ah kin." She was simply terrified at the blank stare Skanawati gave her.

Mercifully, the baby was sound asleep because, fringes a-sway, the Catawba stalked over and regarded her, his painted features set in speculative lines.

Trapping this winter had been none too good along the Clinch; too much ice and sleet. Skanawati had other doubts on his mind. Hooting Owl was positive that the English King would soon put out The Thirteen Fires. Did he not rule the seas?

In Detroit lived the great Colonel Hamilton and he had sent word that, with the coming of spring, a great attack on the Kentucky settlements would be delivered. Already the Shawnees were making war medicine, and the great Colonel was paying ten dollars for American scalps, without regard to age or sex, and no questions asked.

"No," Skanawati reminded himself, "Tskili is my brother." Though expected back, the ranger must still be a long way off because when he went to the ridge top he hadn't heard any jays calling or any squirrels scolding.

Trembling and round-eyed, Eve brought in wooden platters heaped high, but Hooting Owl brushed his portion contemptuously aside and went on fingering a prime beaver pelt. The Shawnee was hot now, and bright beads of sweat kept breaking through the paint on his forehead.

To Desire, that red empty eye socket was utterly repellent.

"*Koco ktel-lunsi?*" he mumbled as she went by.

Of course she couldn't understand and unwisely shook her head. The sunset caught her braids.

Wagh! What a rare red color! Hooting Owl felt moved to touch it, but Desire was too quick.

"Tell him to keep his hands to himself," she told Skanawati, but the Catawba was too busy finishing the stone jug to bother.

Desire put her head behind the barrier, whispered urgently, "Take Joanna. Make for the Wilderness Road. Run as fast as you can. Quick!"

The negress went gray with fright but jerked a nod and began pulling on a shawl. With this responsibility off her mind, Desire turned, surprised to feel less frightened. From somewhere she had gained an ample supply of self-confidence. She could handle these befuddled brutes. Hadn't she been in tight corners before? Her luck was good, too.

Of course, Sam would appear now any instant. My! Wouldn't he be mad over the way these smelly savages had made bold with his liquor! Almost impersonally, Desire watched the shaggy, painted figures sway about, inspecting the cabin's least important furnishings.

With alcohol fumes rising in his brain, Skanawati began to speculate again. He was feeling mighty strong, brave and wise—important, too. Why not take prisoner Tskili's woman and the black slave? Why not load them with the choicest furs, set fire to the cabin and leave Cherokee sign about? Hooting Owl had some Cherokee arrows in his quiver.

Belching, he draped an arm over Hooting Owl's shoulder and made the suggestion. Tskili, he pointed out, must be far away, the cow was so still. To ambush him in his camp should be easy: the country was still at peace. Ten dollars from Colonel Hamilton. Maybe twenty.

Desire pretended not to notice anything, merely picked up the food Hooting Owl had spilled. When she heard the slow scrape of the hutch door closing, a deep sigh escaped her. A good thing Eve wasn't fat and had plenty of incentive to put distance between her and the cabin.

The sunset beat hard at bladder window-panes, dyed them a blinding crimson. Indeed, the whole interior of the cabin glowed with an angry light which brightened the paint on the savages and the copper tones in their skins; it reddened three copper rings set one above the other in Skanawati's ear.

They were up to mischief of some kind, that was plain as day. But what? Should she go on humoring them? Maybe she could load the bear gun? But there it lay with its lock taken apart.

What about Skanawati's antique musket? If worse came to worst, she could grab it up and have nothing to fear because Hooting Owl carried no musket, only a short bow and some arrows stuffed into a quiver of spotted wildcat skin.

Skanawati jerked out his skinning knife and slashed through the cords securing a bundle of fisher skins; at the same time, he shot her a truculent glance, as if daring her to protest. She didn't. Sam could have told her this was an error of the worst sort. To give in to an Indian never placated him, only made him mad, the more eager to assert his dominance.

Both the redskins were drunk as billy goats, kept belching and a-giggling foolishly. She watched them explore one bale after another, selecting the most valuable furs. They were pretty clumsy about it, and flung the discarded skins in all directions.

How long had they been here? Nearly an hour, Desire estimated. Sam couldn't be much later since he'd said he'd be back by sunset.

What would the gentle Quaker girls of Newport make of a scene like this? What would Antoinette Proveaux do?

The fossil footstool got in Skanawati's way. The Catawba fetched it an angry kick and howled when he stumped his toes. Desire couldn't restrain a burst of hysterical laughter. This big Indian was so utterly child-like.

"Gissa!" Skanawati gave her a vicious slap across the mouth. She had never seen eyes like this Catawba's. They held a clear, merciless, reptilian glitter.

Pressed flat against the cabin's wall, Desire knew now she must make a stand of some sort. Oh, why *didn't* Sam come? She hadn't the least doubt that he would appear, because her luck had never yet failed her. Never! She must cling to that reassuring fact. Hooting Owl scowled at her, then reeled over and looked behind the barrier. When he realized the kitchen end of the cabin was empty a furious bellow burst from him.

Desire thought, "I've got to stop him. That red devil can catch up with Eve in no time. If I can only delay him a little while, it will be dark."

"Look!" she cried. "You have not seen the best skins even yet. In that bundle are some beautiful otter skins. I am sure Tskili would like to present them to his brothers."

Eagerly she tugged the bale into the center of the floor—and got pushed sprawling. When her head banged against the wall her eyes filled with tears of outrage. She thought furiously all the same, tried to foresee what might happen.

From the floor, those Indians looked gigantic, monstrous. She must get to Skanawati's musket. Under its threat, she would drive out both intruders and bar the door. Once she had slammed the window's heavy shutter, the savages couldn't get in for quite some time. Sam would be back long before then.

While pretending to collect the far-scattered skins, she worked closer to the Catawba's musket. Suddenly the woodpecker's skin flashed. Hooting Owl was studying her over the stained and broken fringe along his shoulder. Sensing that the Shawnee had guessed her intention, she flashed across the remaining interval, got the weapon cocked and leveled before either intruder could turn around.

"Raise your hands!" she cried. "Quick, both of you! I'll shoot!"

Hooting Owl's dirty hands started upwards, but Skanawati's did not. With a diabolical chuckle he jerked forward his powder horn, tilted it upside-down. Shook it derisively. It was empty. That was really why Skanawati had come to Rockcastle Creek.

Deliberately, the Catawba let go the powder horn and his hand wavered towards his war hatchet, then sought the knife in its fringed sheath. His painted face like that of a clown from hell, he took an uncertain step forward.

"You not tell Tskili!" he said thickly.

"Get back! I—I'll shoot. It's loaded! I know it is!"

Hooting Owl, too, began sidling forward. Wave on wave of horror-stricken terror beat on Desire's intelligence.

"Sam! Sam!" She screamed the name again and again, then in desperation, squeezed the trigger. Only a squalling cry from one of the Indians resulted.

"Oh-h, don't!" she wailed. "Don't hurt me. You— I— Tskili is your brother—"

Nothing would happen, she kept telling herself, nothing serious anyway. She was lucky—always lucky.

A hand, tipped with writhing fingers, came shooting towards her. Sick with fear, she tried to strike it aside with the musket barrel. The odor of whiskey was stupefying. The world became a pattern of garish colors, yellow-green, blue-orange. The woodpecker skin.

She felt herself jerked forward and the gun went clattering to the floor. A foot tripped her and she fell flat.

Her face pressed against a loose fox fur, she screamed in a piercing voice, "Help! Help! Sam!"

What were they going to do to her? *What?* A thousand horrible tales of the frontier flashed across her mind.

Hooting Owl, laughing horribly, went staggering over to the fire on uncertain legs while Skanawati held her pinioned by a knee on the small of her back.

"Sam! Help—they—"

A bare ankle appeared before her glaring eyes, and, instinctively, she bit it as hard as she could. A hoarse scream of pain filled the cabin just before something dealt her a stunning blow. By a narrow margin she failed completely to lose consciousness.

. Her senses began swimming. She must not be afraid. Sam was here! At last! At last! She listened for a rifle shot.

Another blow on the head failed to land squarely.

"John," she gurgled. "Help me, John, darling!"

A foot descended, crushed her neck against the gritty clay of the floor. Fingers knitted themselves into her hair, then a pang of unbelievable anguish shot through her head. Spasmodically, her body jerked, twisted.

From far away, she sensed that something was giving, tearing. Cascades of blinding, outrageous pains descended, assaulted her failing consciousness. All the fires in the world began beating upon her head. As suddenly, they went out, leaving it deadly cold.

A sensation of drifting became more pronounced. Desire Harmony felt herself whirled away, thousands on thousands of miles. She smiled because she could see John St. Clair awaiting her.

PART III—STARS ON THE SEA

I

THE SEMPSTRESS

THE EVENING breeze conveyed a balm redolent not only of mid-June but of flowering fruit trees, of wide, sun-warmed meadows bursting into full bloom. At seven o'clock, it was still daylight and bright enough to admire the remarkable cleanliness of the broad tree-lined streets of Philadelphia.

To Lucy Percival, the many squares and scrupulous neatness of this city were a continual source of envy. The muddy, cramped alleys and narrow streets of Newport suffered even by the most charitable of comparisons.

Walking along Seventh Street in the direction of the Market, she and Martha Bradley could glimpse against the early sunset the twin towers of the great Bettering House.

A shower that afternoon had cleaned the brick footpaths, and rows of red brick houses glistened like urchins with freshly washed faces. Here and there eaves still dripped onto flower beds and silvery puddles gleamed in the streets.

Mechanically, both girls turned down Second Street, still crowded with farmers homeward bound, with the forage carts of various military units and cavalcades of postriders, messengers and travelers. Their dust hung low, veiled the distance with a golden haze.

"It's a wonder you keep calling at that inn," Martha sniffed with one eye on a fine bonnet riding by in a sedan chair. "Blest if I'd flatter any man with such devotion."

Lucy eyed the plain, dark-haired girl at her side with some impatience. Why would Martha remain so tactless? Hadn't she explained time and again that she was obligated to await Mr. Bennett's arrival? As for flattery! Poor Tim had never had so much as a taste of it—from her at least.

Martha said, drawing aside to permit the passage of a negro porter, "Mama thinks you a ninny not at least to consider Lieutenant Andrew Allen. La! Lucy, you really ought. He's rich and well-born and cuts a brave figure. He ain't an officer of the First Troop for nothing."

Martha sighed, swung her bonnet by its ribbon ties. "I declare, Lucy, half the girls in Philadelphia would lose a finger for this opportunity you—"

"—In pity's name, Martha, talk of something else!"

"—Or do you really like Mr. Allen?" The shorter girl shot her companion a baffled look. Somehow, she never yet had learned to understand Lucy as she did other girls, and here Lucy had been working, sewing for Pa going on three whole months—had boarded with them six weeks.

Sweet and unaffected as was this Yankee girl, there were things you never could pry out of her, until she was quite ready to talk. For instance, she had just appeared at Pa's tailor shop one day, cool as you please, and said she wanted work and knew that Pa needed a sempstress because he had been awarded a whopping big contract to make uniforms for Shee's Legion. She had fooled everybody because, despite her lady-like ways and speech, she could sew faster and better than any of the tired old creatures who'd been in Pa's employ for years.

On entering Walnut Street they could see the Delaware shining in the distance and Lucy gave a small cry.

"Look! There's a frigate out there. It must be the *Effingham* fitted out at last." She thrust an arm through her companion's. "Come, Martha, let's go admire her."

Quite a crowd had collected on Mr. Parrock's wharf at the foot of Race Street. With considerable pride they viewed the United States frigate *Effingham,* 36 guns, and the *Washington,* 32 guns. About a quarter of a mile up stream a whole flotilla of row galleys lay under the protecting guns of the *Sachem,* brig of war.

Dressed with strings of vari-colored flags, the new vessel was swinging slowly to a change in the tide.

"Oh, she's beautiful, beautiful!" Lucy sighed. "And I warrant she will prove fast as a scared cat."

"Oh gammon! How do you know?" Martha demanded in open suspicion. "You're only a girl and girls don't know anything about ships. I think men talk a lot of nonsense over them."

It is sometimes hard to be patient with Martha, Lucy reflected. She suffered such ridiculous outbursts of jealousy. Poor girl! She didn't like anyone's having, or knowing, more than she. What a pity the pox had marred one of her cheeks. The disfigurement wasn't nearly as bad as Martha deemed it, and her soft, violet-hued eyes were really very lovely.

Said she simply, "Of course, I can't be sure, dear, but Papa and his friends have been building ships ever since I can remember. Ours is a great port. We Newporters sort of grow up with a feeling for a vessel in our bones."

The other flushed, looked down to the shipping-dotted stream. "Of course, forgive me. I guess I'm fidgety this evening." Poor Martha blundered on. "Ma said you got a letter today. Was it from Mr. Bennett?"

Slowly Lucy shook her pale head, and her lips tightened a little. "Not yet. It was just a note from a school friend back home."

"From Newport? I thought the King's troops had captured it."

"They did, last December. Susan writes they are draining the countryside of supplies. It is believed Sir Henry Clinton intends to hold Newport no matter what the cost."

"Did she write anything about your—about your people?"

Oh bother Martha and her inquisitiveness! Lucy's blue eyes sought the stately white steeple of Christ Church. The gilt cross on its apex was glowing blindingly bright in the sun.

"Why, yes," she said softly. "Papa has turned Loyalist. The British threatened to burn him out if he didn't. It was the only thing to do." Yes, Papa would take that way out.

Martha slipped a hand under the taller girl's elbow. "Will you ever go home?"

"No!"

"Why? Don't you reckon they will forgive you for running off?"

"Papa might," Lucy replied, her eyes on a barge pulling out to the new man-of-war, "but I am sure Mama never will. She can forgive anything except disobedience—I understand her now." Lucy's fingers tightened on the strings of the plain little pocket she carried. "We didn't get on for a whole year before—before I left home."

This was no less than the truth. Try as she might, she had not yet been able wholly to forgive her parents their lie about Tim's following her to Plymouth. Neither they, nor any parents, had the right to disrupt the lives of grown people—even those of their own children—like that.

But for that deliberate lie, she and Tim might well be married right now. Instead, Tim was risking his life privateering on the high seas, and she was glad to ply her needle for eight shillings a week—and board.

She only got so much because wrinkled, rheumatic Mr. Bradley was making such a good thing of this war. The old tailor had never been as busy. Imagine little Mr. J. Withington Bradley as the proprietor of a loft full of girls and women cutting and stitching in his interest!

She had been in luck, also, to have so readily made friends with Martha. Mrs. Bradley had suggested that Lucy board with them, for all that Martha could boast of six sisters and four brothers.

As they resumed the familiar route up Second Street towards the City Tavern, Lucy remembered how very different Philadelphia had seemed on that dismal March day—the twelfth if she remembered correctly—when a muddy stage had deposited her, scared and shivering, before the Tavern's door.

Martha now anticipated the familiar preparations. At the corner of Front Street Lucy would stop, smooth her hair and, resetting her shawl, ask her to wait. Stately as you please, Mistress Percival would then enter the Tavern's gleaming brass and oak door. Generally, she reappeared right away, but if she heard any news she felt was significant, she lingered.

Mr. Smith was always extra polite, and for all she never spent any money, he usually led her into his private counting room. Once she had come out bubbling with excitement. By chance she'd learned that, nearly a year back, a fat prize taken by Mr. Bennett's letter-of-marque had made port and had been duly condemned by a Court of Admiralty.

Nor was this *Growler* the *Narragansett's* only prize, she found out somewhat later. A sailor who had been serving aboard a Connecticut vessel in Cap François Harbor told of the *Narragansett* making port flying the colors of *two* captured British vessels. Tim must be sweeping the seas, piling up riches.

Lucy was glad. After so many disappointments, a measure of success must mean much to Timothy Bennett.

At night when she and Martha lay waiting to go to sleep, she sometimes spoke of him, of what a fine soldier he was, of how clean-minded and how earnest he was. Martha laughed sometimes when she declared Tim the handsomest man alive.

Most of all, she liked to tell about the time they had met up in Roxbury during the Siege of Boston. Only once did she ever mention that dreadful, terrible night during which Tim's family had been broken, scattered and ruined.

Yes, it was pleasanter to describe how a water-spotted and well-thumbed letter posted from the Bahama Islands—wherever they were—had reached her, via Philadelphia and New York. Brief as it was, it had served to rouse her from the miserable despair in which she had been existing for almost a year.

At a clatter of hoofs rounding a corner, Martha Bradley raised her eyes and her hopes. A detail of cavalry from the First Troop came trotting into sight, sabres clattering, carbines riding snug across their shoulders. They made quite a picture in dark brown uniforms faced with white, in polished, high-topped boots and jaunty black leather helmets sporting a buck's tail. Yes, they were mighty smartly turned out—right down to the brown and white housings covering their saddles.

At their head rode young Lieutenant Andrew Allen, his smooth features gilded by long hours in the saddle.

" 'Pon my word!" he ejaculated, and promptly reined in.

At the very elegant salute he gave Lucy and her, Martha's heart soared. From the sidewalk Lucy swept him so demure a curtsey that an old Quaker nearly got ridden down what with watching her.

Martha didn't deceive herself. Mr. Allen would never have halted on account of a tailor's daughter. Oh, why couldn't Lucy forget this Bennett fellow? She'd be wise to. Maybe she would.

As, perfectly at home in his saddle, Lieutenant Allen halted and soothed his mount with one white-gauntleted hand, Lucy couldn't help thinking him a very gallant gentleman.

Why, oh why hadn't Tim appeared on the day he'd set—on March eighteenth? She had been disappointed, of course, when he hadn't appeared, but any daughter of Isaac Percival knew how very unpredictable were the ways of ships and winds. Not until a month had gone by had she permitted even a little doubt to raise its head.

"Your humble servant, Mistress Percival. 'Evening, Mistress Bradley," Andrew called, eyes bright beneath the visor of his helmet. He hardly gave Martha a look but bent eagerly forward in his saddle. "Pray forgive my not dismounting; haven't time. Mistress Percival, may I give myself the pleasure of calling tomorrow evening? There's to be a *feu de joie* fired on the Common in honor of this new flag the Congress is adopting."

Lucy hesitated, then felt Martha squeeze her arm and heard her whisper fiercely, "Accept, you ninny, or I'll never speak to you again!"

"Why, yes, sir, I do protest I would be charmed."

A great grin burst through gravity carefully maintained until now. "Capital! I'll be forever in your debt," he almost shouted. "Sorry—must go—will call at seven—"

So saying, young Lieutenant Allen spun his big bay charger about, touched it with bright spurs and went clip-clopping down the street after his men.

Once the City Tavern's swing-board materialized beyond a cluster of wisteria, Martha turned aside and, without being told, began to inspect the contents of a book seller's window. Within was a volume by Defoe and any number of copies of Tom Paine's "Commonsense" and quite a few books in French and Latin.

As always, Lucy's wrists began to throb once she crossed the well-worn soapstone threshold of the Tavern. Mrs. Smith, a buxom, red-faced woman in a blue mob cap, saw her coming and got down from the accountant's stool on which she kept the cash box—and an alert eye on all that happened.

"Evening, Mistress Percival," she greeted. "Still no real news, though Jeremy says a pair of prizes and a vessel from the Indies have made port."

The innkeeper's wife cocked a beady eye on the slim girl standing before the pulpit-like cashier's box. "Did you hear that the *Speedwell,* one of our own privateersmen, has took no less than six Britishers in the Florida Channel? One o' them two prizes lying off Mr. West's wharf is his."

"Why, no!"

"Well, they're fine big ships, both of 'em," Mrs. Smith puffed, licking an ink spot from the back of her hand. "One was loaded to the gunnels with slaves.

"Joe declares Captain Rob Ashton, her master, stands to make close on three hundred thousand Spanish dollars. The other might be one o' your friend's prizes."

"That would be mighty pleasing." Lucy smiled, letting her eyes range through the door into the taproom. Quite a group of Naval officers in decorative blue tunics and red waistcoats were playing "Spoil Five." They didn't look too smartly turned out, though; nothing like the officers of the Royal Navy.

Lucy lingered a full moment, studying the rest of the rugged, weather-beaten features within. A majority of the patrons looked far from soldierly. Yonder a pair of contractors were arguing with, and trying to get an army quartermaster drunk enough to sign an order. Merchants, professional men, members of the Congress formed the bulk of the patronage.

As she went out-doors again, Lucy thought, "Maybe one *is* a prize of Tim's! He must have taken several vessels since the *Growler*."

When she suggested the possibility to Martha, the girl cast her a compassionate look.

"Really, Lucy dear, you must be blind as a mole. This Mr. Bennett has forgotten all about you." She directed her companion a spiteful look. "Very likely he has had intelligence of your father's near ruin."

"Oh, no, Martha," Lucy burst out. "I'll thank you not to say such things. Mr. Bennett said he would look for me here. He will come to the City Tavern—"

"When? It's three months now."

"Sometime. I am very sure of it."

Once more the bitterness against her parents returned, chilled her heart. How *could* they have taken so much on themselves? She often wished she knew exactly what had passed between Tim Bennett and Mama that time he had come in search of her after recovering from his hurts.

"Tim will come," she thought, "he must!"

But a faint and mordant doubt persisted. The sea had such an unfathomable power of making men forget women. Women resented the way the ships took their menfolk away; sometimes changed their whole characters; sometimes returned them as broken, dejected wrecks; sometimes never returned them at all.

In silence she walked along, listening not at all to Martha's steady flow of conversation.

If Tim didn't come back, what was she to do? So long as unctuous little Mr. Bradley kept on getting contracts from the Marine Committee, she guessed she would make out all right. Martha's father was an honest, capable tailor and Captain Farish, Inspector for the Marine Committee, saw to it that he stayed so; that he didn't scamp materials; that the workmanship was sound.

Gloomily, Lucy pictured Tim striding about a quarterdeck, his brown hair flying in the breeze, his wide mouth set in stern lines. Probably he would have adopted a uniform of some kind—he'd always been passionately fond of uniforms. Most likely, Tim Bennett was well on his way towards becoming a millionaire. Oh dear!

Suddenly, she reached a decision. She would not call at the City Tavern any more; self-respect wouldn't allow it. Tomorrow night she would make herself extra agreeable to Lieutenant Andrew Allen. After all, the Allens were one of the very first families of Philadelphia.

2

THE SEAMAN

"ALAS, Mistress Percival, we have none too promising an evening for our *rencontre*," observed Lieutenant Andrew Allen, fixing a rueful eye on the heavens.

"Oh, 'twill do no more than shower." Lucy smiled, collecting her pocket, bonnet and shawl. "June and I have an especial understanding."

Nevertheless a bank of low-flying clouds was rolling up over a peculiar purplish haze which argued a "spell of weather," as folks would have said back in Newport.

"La, sir, those doeskin breeches fit mighty well," Martha giggled when Andrew Allen arose, slipped his sword into its carrier and reached for a black leather helmet with a flaunting buck's tail crest. "They'll be English tailored?"

"Quite right." Allen smiled. "Though I warrant your father could match them with ease."

"Oh, he could, he could," Martha cried flushing and recklessly crumpling her best apron in self-consciousness. "Sometime soon, you must let Pa cut you a set of regimentals. He has all the designs for the First Troop—Captain Morris left them."

Avid of attention, the tailor's daughter babbled on. "Pa is becoming the best-known military tailor in Pennsylvania. Why, he has cut

uniforms for Captain Read of the *Washington* and Captain Barry
of the *Effingham*."

"Barry!" The cavalry officer's long features lit. "There's a real,
fighting sailor for you. Nothing mealy-mouthed or mean about
him. I would to God we'd him in command of the Navy. That old
woman, Esek Hopkins, has near wrecked it."

"Oh, really? How interesting." From the bottom of her heart,
Martha envied Lucy so unconsciously tying about her shoulders a
Lincoln-green cape with a scarlet lining.

"Come, Mistress Percival," begged the figure in brown and white
looming tall in the doorway. "If we are to reach the Common on
time, we must hurry. You will excuse us, Mistress Bradley?" He
made such a gallant bow that color went rushing up to her eyebrows. Spurs gently clinking, he offered his arm to Lucy.

As they descended the white stone doorsteps, Andrew Allen was
deciding that Mistress Percival was looking monstrous pretty tonight. Why? Had she at last given over moping and pining for
that incredible seafaring fellow, for that dull dolt who dared so far
to trespass on her patience?

They strolled along, Lucy putting to him a dozen questions concerning the city's management. Although he wasn't in the least interested, Allen answered her carefully. He even described the principle on which the Bettering House was operated.

Homeless persons and vagrants, Lucy learned, were taken there
and given work to do. For this they were paid, and when they had
earned a certain sum the inmates were liberated, given their earn-
ings and told to leave town. Lucy thought this a vast improvement
on the workhouse system prevalent in the North.

The way this slim young woman hung on his every word, and
the readiness with which she accepted his arm at street crossings,
sent Andrew Allen's hopes soaring to undreamed-of heights.

They made a striking couple. More than one passerby paused,
turned for a second look. Once, Lucy heard a fashionably-dressed
woman in a sedan chair call to the gentleman walking beside her,
"Bertram, who is that fascinating creature walking with Andy

Allen? I don't seem to place her. Not from Germantown, is she?"

"If only this wretched war weren't being fought," Allen sighed, "I vow you would dote on Philadelphia. Peace-times we find ever so much to do. We have a Dancing Assembly here, and then there is the Schuylkill Fishing Company and—"

"A fishing company? Really, Mr. Allen, that doesn't sound like much fun."

"The word, 'Company,' doesn't hold in the commercial sense, Mistress Percival."

"I see," she replied, eyes on the freshly cleaned footpath.

"Do you—er—ride horseback?" he inquired very seriously. "I hope you do."

"Not much." Lucy laughed. "You should see me bumping around Mr. Bowen's pasture on his old black mare."

" 'Pon my word I'd like to," Allen assured her. "Pity you don't ride—"

"Why?"

"You'd look dashed lovely on a certain bay filly I've in mind," Lieutenant Allen confessed. Sword hilt caught in the crook of his arm, he strode easily along beside her.

"Across the river in Gloucester, we do quite a bit of fox hunting. Used to meet at the London Coffee House. We've a wonderful kennel master in Natty. Old fellow's as black as a pocket, but the way he cares for our hounds is a caution."

As they entered one of the many squares which lent to Philadelphia such an air of spaciousness, evening bells commenced sounding from the steeple of Christ Church. Lucy was learning to anticipate their ringing. She loved their rich, mellow notes. Like a benediction, a whole octave of them shed their melody over the city each evening and on holidays.

She was pleased to see that Lieutenant Allen, also, was listening with enjoyment. As a jarring note, a faint clap of thunder rumbled from the direction of the Delaware.

They passed a pair of Quakers, the woman in blue-and-yellow-striped skirt and with a handkerchief at her throat. Her husband wore a mulberry coat, nankeen waistcoat and breeches and stockings of the same color.

They smiled in friendly fashion and sauntered on, towing a small brown dog at the end of a leash.

"Their dress here is very different from the Friends at home," Lucy observed. "In Rhode Island, gray and brown are the only colors permitted.

"Mr. Bennett was a Quaker once," she added irrelevantly.

"I greatly admire the Friends," Allen interrupted hurriedly. "Backbone of our industry."

The last thing in the world he wanted was to let Mistress Percival begin thinking and talking about that confounded Bennett fellow.

They skirted a long market, the sheds of which were mostly closed, and progressed more quickly once they reached Second Street. The wind was stirring restlessly a succession of buttonwoods and elms shading the footwalk. Towering clouds were fast eclipsing a brilliant sunset, plunging the street in gloom.

Everyone began to hurry, even soldiers in faded blue, merchants, bound-boys and negro servants.

Andrew Allen's hopes took a further rise when Mistress Percival started across the upper side of a little square opposite the City Tavern. Usually, she elected to follow the square's lower edge in order to make inquiry.

In spite of himself, the cavalryman had to admire such loyalty. If once a fellow were able to get Lucy Percival to wife, he could surely count on her.

He looked down at Lucy. Her head looked incredibly fine and pale under that jaunty little hat. He wondered how it had come about that a girl of such obvious gentility should be sewing for a living in the employ of J. Withington Bradley—or of any tailor for that matter.

A flash of lightning threw the steeple of St. Peter's Church into relief and drivers commenced whipping up their horses at the peal of thunder that ensued. What a shame that it was, sure enough, going to rain. Now the *feu de joie* would be called off, and he'd have to hire a chair and take Mistress Percival home. Oh, rat the weather!

The darkness deepened rapidly, but, strangely, the scent of flowers in gardens and window boxes grew stronger.

Suddenly, Lucy Percival's stride slowed and her wide-set blue eyes swept up to his. She gave him an uncertain smile.

"Do you mind if we pass through the square, Mr. Allen? We may as well take refuge at the City Tavern. It seems ready to pour."

"Your wish will ever be my law, Mistress Percival." The buck's tail crest of his helmet whipping to a freshening breeze from the river, he handed her across the street and they entered the square.

Usually, the benches here would be crowded, but now they were deserted. Ahead of them the lights of City Tavern were visible through the tossing branches.

"Why hurry?" he asked as they entered a graveled circle in the center of the square. "It will be hot within and the rain may not begin at once. I fancy yonder tramp will not mind our company."

Lucy nodded, followed his look. On one of the benches was huddled a figure in the ragged clothing of a seaman. He must be very poor, he was so thin and the vamp was gaping away from the sole of one of his clumsy, square-toed shoes. Every line of his body suggested overwhelming fatigue.

"Poor, homeless fellow," Lucy murmured. "He looks exhausted."

"He's more likely drunk," Allen drawled, "and he'd better look alive or the watch will take him up."

"He's only asleep," Lucy insisted. "Look, he must be quite penniless." She indicated a battered black felt hat lying beside the sleeper on the greasy wood of the bench.

By a flash of lightning he saw that one of its tricornes had been broken clean away and that another was crudely secured in place with cotton twine.

"Won't you please wake him?" Lucy said. "I'm afraid he'll get drenched, and he looks so poorly it might give him a fever." She fumbled in a pocket of blue dimity and produced a coin. "Here, Mr. Allen. Will you give the poor creature this?"

"You are very charitable," Allen said. "I will match your generosity."

For a fact, the seaman did look pretty gaunt, and he was sleeping as if the end of the world had come.

Nervously watched by Lucy, Allen advanced through the humid darkness and touched the fellow on the shoulder of a grimy, striped jersey.

"Le' me 'lone, damn you," mumbled the seaman without stirring a muscle. "Can't be m' watch yet."

"Wake up, my man, wake up!" Lieutenant Allen urged, his buttons gilded by a very brilliant play of lightning. "It is about to rain. The lady thinks you had best find shelter. Here is a shilling to buy a bite of supper and a pot of ale."

"Eh?" Heavily, the seaman raised an unkempt head, stared blankly upwards. "Obliged to you," he yawned, "—only tired. Got money—paid off today. Jus' le' me sleep—"

Another very bright flash of lightning lit the whole square, illumined Lucy Percival's staring eyes and stiff, parted lips. The seaman leaped to his feet with Lucy's name on his lips and, rushing forward, sent Andrew Allen reeling to one side.

"Why, damn you!" rasped the cavalry officer. He started to fling himself on the man in tattered petticoat breeches but halted in frozen astonishment. Lucy Percival was clinging to this smelly, shabby figure, pressing her face against the bristles on his cheek.

As she strained to him, she was sobbing, "Tim, Tim, my dearest darling! Oh, what have they done to you?"

As for Timothy Bennett, he could only hold her tight, brushing her pale hair with his fingertips. Warm, delicious impulses were refreshing his weary body. Oh, the sweet naturalness, the fine simplicity of her.

Because Lieutenant Andrew Allen was intelligent and a gentleman to boot, he perceived swiftly enough that his presence was as welcome as that of a two-headed calf.

"Fortunes of war, plague take it!" he consoled himself. "He's a lucky dog."

Neither of them noticed his quiet retreat from the circle in the center of the square.

"Lucy—my own sweet Lucy." Over Tim Bennett's being was drifting a healing aura, a sense of peace all but forgotten.

For the life of him, he couldn't find anything to say, save, "Lucy, my darling!"

Even when the rain commenced, descended in a lashing fury, they clung together. For all Lucy Percival knew or cared, this might have been the brightest, loveliest of evenings. She was aware of only one overwhelming fact: Tim's arms were about her once more.

When had they last kissed? Heavens! How many lifetimes had dragged by since that December day when she and her family had come to call on the Bennetts; that day Desire Harmony had been so spiteful. How little she had dreamed that, when she kissed him good night, so much must happen ere their lips were again to meet.

Unaware of the warm rain pelting his lean shoulders, of the volleying thunder, Tim held Lucy at arm's length, feasting hungry eyes on her uplifted, streaming and radiant features. A puddle gathered, but still they kissed, released long pent-up floods of words.

Quite suddenly, the shower thinned and stopped, but they were drenched clean through and Lucy's hair hung in limp Gorgon's locks. She was the first to recover. Firmly she took his arm.

"Tim, you must get something to eat and drink. You look worn out."

They had to try three taverns before a proprietor would admit such bedraggled, sopping specimens.

3

At the Crooked Billet

Though a majority of its patrons would scarcely have qualified in the stately mansions dominating Prune and Vine Streets, the

Crooked Billet was warm and radiated a hearty hospitality.

Across the room a trio of tipsy troopers from Captain Morrell's Volunteer Green Cavalry were teasing the painted damsels who were pretending to enjoy their company. A fiddle squeaked from beside the fireplace. At the next table, a big privateersman, evidently in from a successful cruise, sat dandling a trollop on either knee and watching a small colored boy dance a curious, loose-jointed dance which set his bare feet to patting the floor as nimbly as a drummer's sticks riffled the head of a drum.

Comically, the gay flowers on Lucy's hat drooped over one ear and a bright green trickle meandered over one cheek and down her neck until the dye had spread into the sodden white muslin of her kerchief.

Over hot buttered rum, Tim studied a girl who might have been the elder sister of the gay, immature Lucy Percival he had known. Her mouth had lost a certain indescribable air of indecision. And in her eyes was a clear, grave expression.

Lucy had thinned out quite a bit. The line of her cheek was no longer convex. Her eyes, though, were the same serene, heart-disturbing blue and her honey-colored hair, wet as it was, was still full of fascinating lights.

As for Lucy Percival, she considered a Timothy Bennett who had developed much as she had anticipated. His jaw was thinner and his mouth a shade more severe. Her heart lifted, as always, to see those golden splinters in his widely-spaced gray eyes.

Right now his eyes were hollowed and his expression lacked the eager optimism of the old Tim. She wondered where he had got that scar across his forehead. During the raid on Peaceful Haven, or in some sea battle? Yes, his neck was thinner, and his hands were all rough and marked by tar, by the traces of old sores and by broken nails.

For all his loss of weight, his shoulders, under the blue and white jersey, looked wider than before. A new, quizzical quirk marked the corners of his mouth. It was as if he had found an answer to a question long asked.

Brazenly, they held hands on top of the table; after all, the other patrons were presenting far franker evidences of affection.

"Tim, darling," she begged at length, "will you tell me a little of what has chanced? My last intelligence of the *Narragansett* was that she was being monstrous successful. Here in town they still talk about the auction following the *Growler's* condemnation. She was the richest prize in many months."

"Was she?" He sighed. That helped matters.

"But tell me how, why, you make port like—like this?"

He shrugged. "I made a mistake, I guess. Realized how big it was today, when I learned about the way the *Randolph* fought the *Yarmouth*. You've heard?"

"Why, no, Tim. What has that got to do with you?"

"A vast deal, my darling," he replied seriously, "a vast deal. Just consider that Nick Biddle in the 32-gun *Randolph* stood up to and fought H. M. S. *Yarmouth,* a line-of-battle-ship mounting 64 guns! And with never a tremor. His crew didn't run, didn't scare worth a thin damn. Crimanently! Biddle's men were swapping broadsides with that liner, bold as you please, when something happened and the *Randolph* blew up."

Lucy's eyelids fluttered and, absently, she poked a damp curl away from her forehead. She was thinking she might catch the very devil of a cold, but she didn't care. Oh, but it was good, *good,* to hear Tim's voice again!

Said she softly, "They were very brave, but I still don't see what the *Randolph* has to do with you and the *Narragansett.*"

"I'll come to that later," he told her, sucking at the lemon peel of his drink. "In brief, what happened was this. After making two easy prizes my crew—"

She watched his brows merge into a single line.

"—wouldn't close with a little British cruiser, not even our tonnage." He frowned. "We were captured after a disgraceful showing."

"Oh, Tim, I am so, so sorry. And to think I've been picturing you grandly sweeping the sea. For a fact," she cast him a timid smile, "I was beginning to fear you were becoming so grand that you might clean forget poor Lucy Percival."

He shook his head so vigorously that drops flew from the end of his long, light brown hair. "No, Lucy, I never did. I would have come here in March as I wrote to you," he made a wry grimace, "only I was inhabiting a prison in New Providence at that time."

"A prisoner? Oh, Tim, was that where you were sick?"

"How did you know I was ill?"

Her low laughter rippled through the low-ceilinged, smoke-veiled room. "How do I know? Look at you! You look ill-fed as a wash-woman's step-child."

Her eyes narrowed, sparkled deliciously. "Oh, Tim, it will be such fun feeding you up, hearing all you have to tell. Please go on."

"You were right. I was stricken in New Providence." Tim relaxed against the wooden backing of his seat for all it was dark with the pomatum and the hair oil left by a thousand customers.

"Yellow-jack broke out in the prison. For a month it cut us down like flies, the jailers, too. Worst of all I remember, was seeing young Phil Hull—remember him?—carried out. He wouldn't leave me when the rest of the crew was turned loose. That was what made me feel so bad."

"What! They didn't imprison the men?"

"They seldom have—so far in this war. They just jail the officers, supercargo and any responsible person. Most of my heroic crew, I expect, have been besieging the Court of the Admiralty here for their shares long since.

"Loammi Freebody, my captain, got a chance to escape. I expect he's commanding somebody's privateer this moment. When he escaped in January he wanted to take me, too, but I was just over the fever and I couldn't go."

Lucy's hand tightened over his, stroked it gently. "There is no need to talk, Tim. Not unless you care to."

"May as well tell you the whole of it," he replied. After gulping the last of his drink, he ordered food.

An hour later, he was feeling much better, stronger, too. Crimanently! He'd never realized how much he really needed Lucy. Come to think of it, he had Nat Coffin to thank for tonight. But for the Nantucketer, he might never have written that impulsive note from the Bahamas. He wondered where Nat was, what he was doing. Probably he'd be 'way up in the Naval Service. Nat was too intelligent to remain long unappreciated.

"You were going to tell me how you got away—" Lucy suggested.

"Of course. A friend of mine, John Petty—he's a merchant in New Providence—did all he could for me. He and his house-keeper saved my life, I guess, when I'd the fever. When I got strong enough, he advanced me money to bribe a jailer. One night I swam out and stowed away aboard the *Three Friends,* a supply ship intended to revictual the British Army in Newport."

Tim sat a little straighter. "Lucy, I find it mighty hard to credit that an enemy army is holding Newport—home. They've got to be driven off. They've *got* to be!"

"Yes, dear, I know. But what happened when you stowed away?"

"This supply ship, a brigantine, was about off Hatteras when over the horizon sails a trig little privateer, Bermuda-built and fast as an arrow.

"The *Speedwell*—that was her name—took us without much trouble. Her captain was a damned likeable cuss, name of Ashton, Robert Ashton. Well, when he heard my story he signed me on as a member of his prize crew.

"It was the very devil of a rough trip in and, being short-handed, we had to stand double watches."

"Oh, you poor dear, no wonder you look worn out."

"I was dead for sleep when we made port late this afternoon. You can see the *Three Friends* lying up river; a dumpy little Bristol-built brig."

He reached over, stroked her cheek. "At first, when I knew the *Three Friends* wasn't going to Newport I felt sick."

"Oh, Tim, you really didn't think I would ignore your letter?"

"I wasn't sure you would ever get it," he said, lighting a pipe. "I figured if you weren't in Newport, I would try to follow you. As soon as we got paid off this afternoon, I came ashore and went to the City Tavern."

Her fingers laced themselves tighter over his. It scared her to think what might have happened had she listened to Martha.

"Mr. Smith wasn't at the Tavern, only a fool clerk at the desk. He told me Mr. Smith would return at eight." He smiled one of his wide boyish smiles. "Well, Lucy, they worked us so hard aboard the prize I thought I'd take a little snooze before I went back to the City Tavern. I hadn't really expected; of course, you'd be there. But still I wanted to know if you had been."

"Oh, Tim, I've called there every night since early in March."

4

THE NEW FLAG

THE passage of three days made a new figure of Timothy Bennett. After securing lodgings at Mr. Harry Epples' inn on Race Street, he'd done little more the first day than to sleep the sleep of the just —and the thoroughly exhausted. In many ways it was the most completely restful sleep he had enjoyed in over two years.

From Mr. J. Withington Bradley, tailor to gentlemen and military officers, he procured a suit of dark green, nankeen breeches and stockings. Hat, pumps and hair ties he secured elsewhere. With his hair trimmed and neatly clubbed, his body scrubbed and his hands somewhat recovered, he felt years younger than the grimy, insect-troubled wreck who had been rowed ashore from the *Three Friends*.

The radiance of this particularly glorious June afternoon matched the warmth in his heart. Crimanently! Soon as he met Lucy they would go interview the rector of the Second Episcopal Church on Pine Street.

Imagine it! In a very few days now, Lucy would be his—the struggle of nearly three years would be at an end.

A printer's apprentice came by, bawling out something and waving a sheaf of newspapers. Tim bought a copy of the "Pennsylvania

Ledger" and paused in the shade of a giant chestnut tree. What he read was not cheering.

Major-General John Burgoyne reputedly was massing a great army in Canada with the obvious intention of carrying fire and sword down the Hudson River Valley and of cutting the rebellious Colonies in two.

In New York, Lord Howe was greeting fleet after fleet of transports bringing still more regulars and mercenaries to augment his already large, compact and well-drilled army.

As for General Washington, the latest dispatches declared him to be retaining but a precarious foothold in New York State, hampered by dissension and broken promises and local jealousies. The victorious army he had led away from Boston had dwindled by desertion and discouragement to a few thousand ill-supplied and weary men. Nor were matters on the sea going any better for the infant nation.

The *Lexington* had been lost, also the *Cabot* and the *Alfred*—serious blows to a tiny navy.

An editorial, employing the old specious arguments Tim had heard back in Newport, advocated the advisability of abandoning all efforts to fight the King on the sea.

Shining like a bright torch on a starlit night was a further report of the little *Randolph's* action with the great, towering *Yarmouth*.

Tim was not greatly surprised. Nicholas Biddle had always been far-and-away the ablest officer in Hopkins' fleet. That he and his men chose to trade broadsides with a ship-of-the-line proved what might be if—aye, *if!*

Thoughtfully, Tim folded away the newspaper, tucked it in his pocket and resumed his progress. Presently, the neat, white-trimmed brick façade of J. Withington Bradley's tailor shop loomed ahead.

Today the shop seemed busier than ever, if that were possible. Nevertheless, Mr. Bradley came rushing to the threshold and began dry-washing his hands at such a furious rate that Tim reckoned word of his standing to collect 150,000 Spanish dollars as his share of the H. M. S. *Growler's* condemnation sale had got abroad.

"A pleasant day, Mr. Bennett. A vastly agreeable afternoon, sir."

If the *Swallow* had got safely into Savannah and been well sold, he might add another twenty-five or thirty thousand to his modest fortune. So far, however, he had been unable to learn a word of her fate.

"Green becomes you, Mr. Bennett," beamed the bent little tailor. "Coat fits to perfection, too, if I may be so bold as to say so. This way, sir, pray step this way. Mistress Percival will be down directly. Billy!" He beckoned a gangling apprentice lad. "Pray announce Mr. Bennett's arrival to Mistress Percival."

Tim, however, held up a restraining hand. "No need, Mr. Bradley. If you've no objection, I'd like to look about."

"Precisely! Precisely! Fear you'll find the work room a trifle warm."

Martha's father thrust some pins into his lapel and led the way to the rear of the property. There a quartet of male apprentices squatted cross-legged on a series of tables and a number of girls and women stitched industriously.

Whenever they dared, the sempstresses stared and flashed smiles at this tall, weather-browned young man. The whole shop, of course, knew all about Lucy's romance. They giggled and whispered—even the oldest and plainest of them.

Stacks of regimentals—brown, green, blue, in fact almost every color except red—lay about in heaps upon the tables. Patterns, irons, shears and boxes of braid crowded other work benches. An odor of damp wool pervaded the whole establishment.

"Where is Mistress Percival?" he asked presently.

"Upstairs, sir; she is one of our skilled workers." Mr. Bradley made a small clucking noise indicating regret. "We shall miss her sorely. Ah, Mr. Bennett, you are a lucky—" he started to say "rascal" but thought better of it, "—gentleman," he concluded lamely. "We have indeed been charmed—and flattered—to have had Miss Percival under our humble roof."

"Both she and I vastly appreciate your kindliness to her, Mr. Bradley; as soon as the prize money is paid, I trust you will permit us to make a more practical expression."

Mr. Bradley raised hands in horror. "Oh, no, sir. I wouldn't dream of accepting such. It has been a privilege to have known you both. You'll mayhap be wanting a uniform soon, sir?" He cocked his head to one side, like a bird considering a promising worm hole.

"Possibly, Mr. Bradley."

"Capital! Capital! We've today received some fine new serges—British made, sir. Captured by the *Speedwell*."

Tim couldn't help smiling. "Yes, I know about that. I helped bring it here."

"God bless my soul! Did you, really?" The tailor led the way up a narrow, creaking staircase. At the head of it, Martha, two of her sisters and Lucy Percival were working. The sisters were busily stitching epaulets to some naval officer's blue tunic, but Lucy and Martha were working over a pile of red, white and blue bunting.

As Tim's head came above the landing, Martha gave a final snip with her scissors, held up a white star. "Five points *are* handsomer, ain't they?"

"Much prettier than six," Lucy agreed.

"But not as pretty as you, my dear," Tim called. He very much wanted to kiss her, but was much too shy of all this audience.

Work fell forgotten to the floor as Martha and her two sisters jumped up to bob their curtseys.

"What's all this?" Tim inquired, one eye on the bunting. "Looks mighty gay."

" 'Tis a commission we received but a few days ago," old Bradley replied carelessly. "Still another flag the Congress has adopted." He sniffed. "Wish to Heaven they'd make up their silly minds. They keep changing so fast it's a bother."

"How many of them are we to make, Pa?" Martha asked.

"Four. Patterson & Jones only got orders for two. Martha—" the old man squinted at the work table—"you sure you got them proportions straight? The feller was fussy on that score."

"Yes, Pa. Here's the drawing the clark brought and here's the flag. You may judge for yourself."

It was Lucy, however, who picked up the flag and carried it across the room to where the sun could beat upon it. In glowing brilliance were revealed thirteen alternate red and white stripes and a graceful circlet of thirteen white stars on a blue field.

"Isn't it lovely?" demanded one of Martha's sisters. "I declare, it's the handsomest banner we have ever made. I do hope those Congressmen won't alter it."

" 'Tis well designed," the tailor declared. "Yes, a fine, elegant composition."

"What's the matter, Tim?" Lucy demanded. "Don't you like it?"

Tim didn't answer. He couldn't take his eyes off that new flag. In his mind he seemed again to see the *Alfred's* icy quarterdeck, seemed to be hearing acid little Lieutenant Jones voicing his objections to fighting under the rattlesnake flag.

He himself had experienced much the same repugnance at hoisting that yellow ensign over the *Narragansett*. This, well, this was a flag a man could come to love and respect. In its serene dignity it was somehow inspiring.

Martha giggled. "The man who brought the order declared the stars are meant to represent a new constellation. See? We're like a new nation in the sky."

But still Tim could say nothing. He could imagine this flag flung boldly against the pure blue of the heavens, its red, white and blue reminiscent of a freedom inherited from, then denied by, the Mother Country.

"Why, Tim, don't you like it?" Lucy repeated.

"Too much to express myself," said he slowly. "How soon will it reach the ships?"

"About as soon as the Marine Committee makes up its mind, I presume," Bradley replied.

He turned briskly to a closet and brought out a garment. "Now this, Mr. Bennett, is a mighty elegant tunic. Warranted pure gold buttons and braid. 'Twas ordered last winter by a rogue of a privateer captain who paid me with his main sheet. He'd have been about your size and inches."

Soberly Tim considered the blue and gold tunic. It was handsome, and no mistake. He said as much.

"Thought you might fancy it, sir. You'll be going to privateering again, soon, I take it? Well, sir, when you've found you a vessel, I'll send this aboard. I'll make you a compliment of it for a wedding gift."

"No, Mr. Bradley, you're much too generous," Tim protested. "Just attend the ceremony and get properly drunk afterwards and I will be as well pleased."

Once Lucy had collected her bonnet and shawl, they descended into the street, very sober and serious, as young people should be when they go to meet the minister who is to marry them.

Now it was all settled. At noon of the twentieth of June, Timothy Bennett and Lucy Percival would be made man and wife. From then on their fortunes, their hopes and disappointments would no longer be met alone.

To Tim it was a sobering realization that soon he would assume those responsibilities his father, his grandfather and his ancestors beyond them had borne so capably. Up 'til now he had never quite appreciated what it would mean to find a wife, and probably children, looking to him for support. If he guessed wrong or made a faulty decision, not he alone would pay for it.

When they continued down Vine Street instead of turning right along Front, Lucy cast Tim a look of inquiry. But he said nothing, only led the way clear out to the end of Mr. Charles West's wharf at the end of the street.

For many minutes, Tim stood quietly regarding the broad river and its busy shipping. Lucy noted that the newly commissioned men-of-war were still where they had been. She saw Tim's look swing towards, and remain on, half a dozen privateers which were anchored off the mouth of Pool's Run.

Smiling, Lucy laid a hand on his arm. "I presume you already have your eye on a vessel, Tim?"

"Yes," he replied gravely, "I have."

"What is she to be?" she demanded. Oh dear, would he go right off to sea? "A schooner, a brig?"

"Neither, darling. She will be a frigate."

Her eyes flew wide open. "Oh, Tim, don't fun me. I am quite serious."

"I am not funning, dearest."

"But, but, you couldn't afford— What *do* you mean?"

Tim drew a deep breath, turned to face her, clear gray eyes intent. "Lucy, when I was sailing up the Delaware in the *Three Friends,* a truth came to me."

"Why, what do you mean?"

"As you know, Lucy dear," said he speaking slowly, deliberately, "I have spent well over a year in foreign parts and I suppose I've seen quite a bit of foreign people and customs. For a while they are mighty interesting, full of surprises and excitement, but after a spell, you begin to understand what a truly rich, beautiful and unspoiled country this is."

He wished he could, in a breath, make her see the supine, heat-blasted islands he had visited, know of the cancerous decadence eating at the vitals of Saint-Domingue, of the bestial, calculated brutality ruling the Spanish islands.

Instead, he said, "It wasn't until I got home that I understood the true strength of this land. If only we can stick together, like the stars on the constellation on that flag, I feel, I *know,* we shall go far as a nation!" His deep voice momentarily died away. "Maybe I'm wrong, Lucy, but I feel America has a future worth fighting for."

They stood in the shade cast by the mainsail of a fishing boat. It was drying, flapping gently in a breeze beating down-stream.

"But, Tim, of course you'll be fighting for this country. You are going to go on privateering, aren't you?"

He glanced away, then placed a hand on her shoulder. "Lucy, would it disappoint you greatly if I did not?"

Utter bewilderment filled the delicate pink and white oval of her features.

"But—but, Tim, how else could you make half so much money

as you won in even the *Narragansett's* short cruise?"

"I can't," he said simply. "It's only that private-armed vessels will never win freedom for this country. I am sure of that now. Until the day I die I will never forget the way those men of mine ran about yelling for surrender."

"Not all Americans are such cowards," Lucy said.

"You are wrong there, my dear," Tim corrected gently. "My men weren't cowards. I'll wager at bottom they were just as brave as the men who manned the *Randolph*. They figured that fighting a man-o'-war just wasn't part of their task—it wasn't the purpose of the cruise they had signed on for."

"But, Tim—couldn't they be made—"

"No, it requires more than a few months to train officers and men to think of serving the United States, instead of lining their pocket-books. If we're to have a Navy, we must have men so trained and so inspired."

"I think I understand," she said very quietly. "You are intending to adopt the Navy?"

"I will try for a commission if they will have me."

"They will," Lucy assured him. "Yonder frigates out there can't sail for lack of officers and men." Then she added, desperately trying to keep her voice steady, "Tim, dear, I am glad, and oh, so proud you feel this way."

Despite the stares of fishermen mending nets alongside, Tim drew her close. "Out of the prize money we should have enough to make out quite comfortably. I know it will be small fun for you—and for me—to be separated months, maybe years, at a time, yet some-one must suffer such a sacrifice if these United States are to survive."

From the serene way her gaze swept up to meet his, he knew that, no matter how long he might cruise abroad, always confidence and great love would be awaiting him at home.

THE END

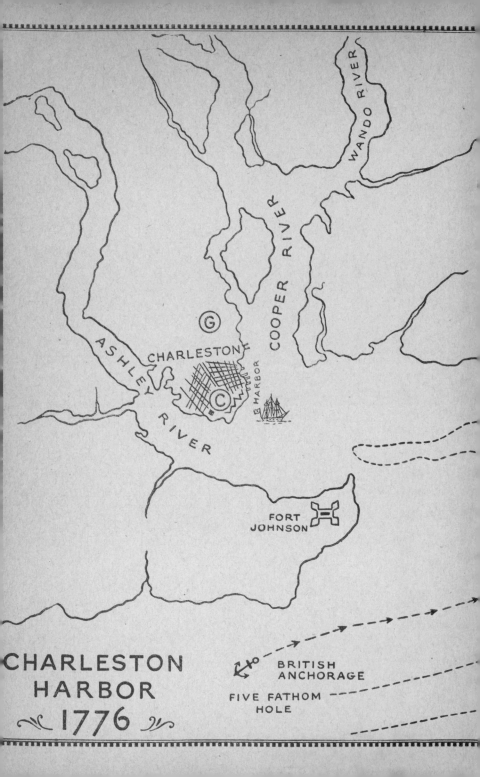

WANDO RIVER

COOPER RIVER

ASHLEY RIVER

(G)

CHARLESTON

(C)

HARBOR

FORT
JOHNSON

CHARLESTON
HARBOR
1776

BRITISH
ANCHORAGE

FIVE FATHOM
HOLE